ILARIO:
THE LION'S EYE

ILARIO:
THE LION'S EYE

The First History

MARY GENTLE

First published in Great Britain in 2006 by Gollancz

An imprint of the Orion Publishing Group
Orion House, 5 Upper St Martin's Lane,
London WC2H 9EA
An Hachette Livre UK Company

This edition published in Great Britain in 2007 by Gollancz

1 3 5 7 9 10 8 6 4 2

A CIP catalogue record for this book is
available from the British Library

ISBN 978 057508 0 416

Printed in Great Britain at
Mackays of Chatham plc, Chatham, Kent

The Orion Publishing Group's policy is to use papers that
are natural, renewable and recyclable products and made
from wood grown in sustainable forests. The logging and
manufacturing processes are expected to conform to the
environmental regulations of the country of origin.

www.orionbooks.co.uk

A legend of Classical times says that, so strong is the eye of the lion, that its sight does not die with its owner. And here, by the lion's eye, we see prefigured the art of the true maker of images: the painter whose vision remains long after he himself is dead.

Leon Battista Alberti, fragment, in the rough drafts of *De Pictura* ('On Painting'); not included in published version AD 1435

Contents

Part One

Under the Penitence

We are so often a disappointment to the parents who abandon us.

A male voice interrupted my thoughts, speaking the language of Carthage. 'Papers, freeman—'

The man broke off as I turned to face him, as people sporadically do.

For a moment he stood staring at me in the flaring naphtha lights of the harbour hall.

'—freewoman?' he speculated.

People shoved past us, shouting at other harbour guards; keen to be free of the docks and away into the city of Carthage beyond. I had yet to become accustomed to the hissing chemical lights in this red and ivory stone hall, bright at what would be midday anywhere else but here. I blinked at the guard.

'Your documents, freeman,' he finished, more definitely.

The clothes decided him, I thought. Doublet and hose make the man.

The guard himself – one of many customs officers – wore a belted robe of undyed wool. It clung to him in a way that I could have used in painting, to show a lean, muscular body beneath. He gave me a smile that was at least embarrassed. His teeth were white, and he had all of them still. I thought him not more than twenty-five: a year or so older than I.

If I could get into Carthage without showing documents of passage, I would not give my true name. But having chosen to come here, I have no further choice about that.

The Carthaginian customs officer examined the grubby, wax-sealed document that I reluctantly handed over. '"Painter", Freeman ... Ilario?'

King Rodrigo Sanguerra had not been angry enough to refuse me travelling papers, now he had freed me, but he left me to fill in my own profession – furious that I would not consent to the one he wanted. But I am done with being the King's Freak. Nor will I be the King's engineer for machines of war.

'My name is Ilario, yes. Painter. Statues; funeral portraits,' I said, and added, 'by the encaustic technique.'

Show me a statue and I'll give the skin the colour of life, the stone draperies the shadows and highlights of bright silks; ask me for a funeral portrait, and I'll paint you a formal icon with every distinguishing symbol of grief. I thought it likely that people in Carthage would want their statues coloured and their bereavements commemorated, as they do elsewhere.

'It's a good trade.' The man nodded absently, running his wide thumb over the seal of King Rodrigo of Taraconensis. 'We get a lot of you people over from Iberia. Not surprising. You shouldn't have any trouble getting Carthaginian citizenship—'

'I'm not here to apply for citizenship.'

He stared at me as if I had taken a live mouse out of my mouth. 'But you're immigrating.'

'I'm not immigrating.'

The Visigoth Lords of Carthage tend to assume that every man and woman would be one of them if they could. Evidently the assumption extends to their bureaucracy.

'I'm *visiting* here. On my way to Rome,' I said, using the Iberian term for that city that the Europeans call 'the Empty Chair', since St Peter's Seat has stood unoccupied these many generations. 'There are new things happening—'

They are putting aside painting the iconic meaning of a thing, and merely painting *the thing itself*: a face, or a piece of countryside, as it would appear to any man's naked eye. Which is appalling, shameful, fascinating.

'—and I intend to apprentice myself under a master painter there. I've come here, first' . . . I pointed . . . 'to paint that.'

This hall is the sole available route between the Foreigners' Dock and Carthage itself. Through the great arched doorway in front of me, the black city stood stark under a black sky, streets outlined by naphtha lamps. Stars blazed in the lower parts of the heavens, as clearly as I have ever seen them above the infertile hills behind Taraco city.

Stars should not be visible at noon!

In the high arch of the sky, there hung that great wing of copper-shadowed blackness that men call the Penitence – and where there should have been the sun, I could see only darkness.

I glanced back towards the Maltese ship from which I'd disembarked. Beyond it and the harbour, on the horizon, the last edge of the sun's light feathered the sea. Green, gold, ochre, and a shimmering unnatural blue that made me itch to blend ultramarine and glair, or gum arabic, and try to reproduce it . . .

And yet it is midday.

Even when the ship first encountered a deeper colour in the waves, I had not truly believed we'd come to the edge of the Darkness that has shrouded Carthage and the African coast around it for time out of mind. Did not believe, shivering in fear and wonder, that no man has seen sunlight on this land in centuries. But it is so.

It alters everything. The unseasonal constellations above; the naphtha

4

light on ships' furled sails at the quayside; the tincture of men's skin. If I had my bronze palette box heated, now, and the colours melted – how I could paint!

'You're a painter.' The man stared, bemused. ' . . . And you've come here where it's *dark.*'

A sudden clear smile lit up his face.

'Have you got a place to stay? I'm Marcomir. My mother runs a rooming-house. She's cheap!'

My mother is a noblewoman of Taraconensis.

And she will attempt to kill me again, if she ever finds me.

Marcomir looked down at me (by a couple of inches), slightly satisfied with himself. I thought there was a puzzled frown not far behind his smile. *This short, slight man* – he is thinking – *this man Ilario, with the soft black hair past his shoulders; is he a woman in disguise, or a man of a particular kind?*

The latter will be more welcome to this Marcomir, I realised.

The brilliance of his dark eyes would be difficult but not impossible to capture in pigments. And the city of Taraco, while only across the tideless sea, beyond the Balearic Islands, seems very far away.

'Yes,' I said, automatically using the deeper tones in my voice.

There'll be trouble, accepting such an invitation, since I'm not what he thinks I am, but that kind of trouble is inevitable with me.

I shouldered my baggage and followed him away from the harbour, into narrow streets between tall and completely windowless houses. And steep! The road was cut into steps, more often than not; we climbed high above the harbour; and it had me – I, who have hunted the high hills inland of Taraco, and habitually joust in day-long tourneys – breathing hard.

'Here.' Marcomir pointed.

I halted outside a heavy iron door set into a granite wall. 'You do know I'm . . . not like most men?'

Marcomir's eyes gleamed bright as his smile when he flashed them at me. 'Was sure of that, soon as I looked at you. You got that look. Wiry. Tough guy. But . . . elegant, you know?'

I know. It's one of the two ways that men look at me.

He used my name without the honorific. 'Come inside, Ilario.'

He hastened me past his mother, Donata, a white-haired elderly woman with the hawk-face that would be Marcomir's too, some day, and I didn't protest the brief introduction. The walls inside the cool house were swathed in baked clay, the light of oil-lamps turning them Samian red, and our shadows moved ink-black on the wall behind Marcomir's wooden-framed truckle bed.

'You ought to know this, at least.' I sighed, having undone the ties of my hose; reaching to strip off doublet and shirt together.

Marcomir's response was lost in the rush of cloth past my ears.

5

I have, occasionally, concealed what I am, under circumstances like these. I have no desire to attempt it again. I wriggled the knit cloth of the hose down my thighs and off my feet, and stood naked, with the faint chill of the room prickling my skin.

'Not what you were expecting?' I said wryly.

The Carthaginian Visigoth sat down on the edge of the bed. 'You're . . . '

His gaze went from my rounded breasts – not quite large enough to dimple the front of an Iberian doublet – down to the phallus already standing up with desire.

Standing no taller than my clenched fist. God was not generous when He made me.

I watched for either a sneer or amusement on this man's face.

'Are you—' Marcomir stood, and stepped close.

He touched a finger to my chin, feeling the soft, ephemeral scatter of hairs which I had let grow for travelling. His wide, capable hands slid down my side, feeling the curve of my hips. The tension of his not touching my penis made me shiver. And – as ever – my penis curved over as my stiffness grew, pointing somewhat downwards.

I searched his expression for something – something – I didn't know what.

He put his hands between my thighs, fingers going up into the wet cleft of my female parts.

'You're a man-woman.' His voice sounded ragged.

An hermaphrodite. Hermaphroditus, the offspring of Hermes and Aphrodite. I didn't bother Marcomir with that.

I said, 'You don't need to have any part of me that you don't like.'

There is little else I *can* say, and it took me all the years between fifteen and twenty to devise that particular remark.

His face altered. I steadied myself. I have been put out onto the street before now. I guessed him not the kind of man who uses violence in an uncontrolled manner. But I can be wrong. There was a knife close to my hand, in my discarded clothes.

The height of him hid the lamp's flame. The close warmth of his body made every hair on my skin stand up.

His frown emerged. 'I thought you were a man like me. Not a ladyboy.'

'Marcomir . . . ' I sighed, reaching for my shirt.

His skin was shadowed ochre- and soot-coloured as he stood with his back to the lamp. Despite the keen sensation of my body, satisfaction is not always worth what one must go through to gain it.

Marcomir sounded uncertain. 'Do you want this? Are you sure?'

'Being a slave,' I said, 'I have not, until recently, been able to take decisions for myself. And now that I can . . . I intend to take every decision I can get!'

He lifted his hand, closing it on my right breast so tightly that a pang of desire shot from there to my groin.

He took my down-curving phallus in his hand.

I could dimly feel that he fingered for balls. There is a lump in the lips of my flesh, there, that sometimes deceives men into thinking I have them. The desire to spend came over me with such force that I barely noticed his investigations.

'Come here!' He urged me at the bed. Not expecting it, I stumbled; fell on my knees on the padded-cloth mattress and wool bedding.

His hands arranged me firmly, belly down on the bed so my breasts couldn't be seen; head to one side, so that we might look at each other in the face. His weight came down on the bed with me as he knelt between my thighs, pushing them together, urging me up onto my knees so that he could get at my buttocks. I felt the position absurd; it still made my heart thump, and my penis become harder.

His hand rubbed flat against my spine, sliding over the breadth of my shoulders. As his palm cupped my hip again, the heat and weight making me shiver, he abruptly took it away. 'I'm rider, not horse. And I don't fuck women.'

I could barely catch my breath. 'Then don't!'

He leaned forward and stroked my wispy stubble. For the first time, I allowed myself to hold his gaze. His pupils were wide and black.

With a rush of relief, I realised, *He wants me.*

Just – not all of me.

Passion fires passion like nothing else. Face-down on the rough wool of his bedding, I spent into it with my male parts before he was fairly in the saddle.

Towards the middle of what I could not keep in mind was the dark afternoon, when he had slept for a short time, Marcomir took me between sleeping and waking as a man takes a woman. I spent as a woman does. He sank asleep again. He won't recall this, later, I thought, as my body shed his seed.

The relaxation of flesh after sexual congress is an infrequent joy for me. I dressed myself, looking down at him stretched out naked and sleeping.

Can it be possible – might I stay all my time in Carthage here?

I didn't dare hope.

Will this man Marcomir be willing to look me in the face when he wakes? Can we do this more than the once?

I have learned, from others unlike this man, that afterwards is always the more dangerous time. I went downstairs. Even if he comes to regret what we did, he is less likely to hit me in front of his mother, I think.

In the warm, fire-lit kitchen, Donata got up from the floor-carpets as I entered. She crossed to the hob, and took the lid off a pot.

'You'll be hungry.' She said it so plainly that either there was no innuendo, or she was used to her son bringing home men for the occupation we had been about. 'Here.'

I seated myself on the cushions beside the hearth. In Taraco, we would be sitting around a wooden table, on wooden benches; here . . . even the house-door had been iron, and not iron-studded oak, I reflected.

Because nothing grows here, under the Penitence. It must all be shipped in. Corn for bread, olive oil for lamps, charcoal for fires, timber for construction. Brought by sail and caravan from Iberia and Egypt, to this great city, so rich . . .

'I can make you meals of an evening, as well as hire you a room.' Donata handed over a full pottery bowl, and sat down as limberly as a woman half her age. I decided there was a glimmer of amusement in her bird-of-prey gaze. Some indulgence of her favoured son?

'I don't know how long I'll stay.' The crushed grain porridge tasted unfamiliar, but was pleasantly filling – *And I haven't eaten since the ship!* I thought.

And since then, I've had . . . physical exercise.

That made me smile. Shovelling up the thick porridge, I scraped the bowl empty within minutes. The old woman Donata gave an amused snort, and went to a capped well in the corner of the room to draw up water.

I realised I was more tired than I thought: the room swayed about me. *My body thinks, because it's dark, I should be asleep.*

I miss the light.

'A drink will be welcome – is the water safe, here?'

'Safe as anything else.' The old woman scooped water from the metal pail with something that flashed silver; I couldn't see what it was. A cup, a ladle?

The walls swooped up. I felt sick and dizzy.

The carpeted floor filled my vision as I floated down among the cushions. I felt the thud of my body falling as if muffled by more than eiderdown. A wave of heat and dizziness mounted up into my head.

In Taraco, the court once thought it amusing to give the King's Freak opium.

And this is how I felt then—!

Marcomir's feet came into my field of view, bare on the dusty floor. He rumbled something to his mother. Not surprise. Not a complaint. My baggage appeared in my field of vision; he must have carried it down from 'my' room.

I wondered muzzily, Will they cut my throat when they've finished going through it?

The last conscious thought I had was *How many strangers have they done this to?* and *How could I fall for it!*

2

'Who's "Rosamunda"?'

I ignored the voice at my ear and fumbled at my face. What I touched was smoother skin than I am used to, unless I use depilatories, or pluck out hairs painfully as the ancient Romans used to. It stung.

'Oi! *Girl!* Shut up about Rosamunda, *whoever* she is!'

My throat felt sore. There were cold, cracked tiles under my hands. I pushed myself up into a sitting position.

The man squatting in front of me said something over his shoulder. I didn't catch it. He stood and walked away, his robe's hem flicking me painfully in the eye. The same style robe as Marcomir's.

I am in Carthage, still? – Or at least in lands of the Carthaginian Empire—?

I heard him say, 'Probably shrieking for her mother. Shut her up if she does it again.'

She?

Nausea rolled through me. My sight focused.

Along the granite wall beside me, men and women sat with heavy leather collars around their necks. Chains ran from the collars to ring-bolts. The stink of old sweat and piss haunted the air. Beyond a grille, a few yards off, men walked up and down. Naphtha lights hissed.

I am in a slaver's hall.

And Marcomir and his Hell-damned mother have shaved me, because I won't sell as a skinny man with no strength for manual labour.

The urge to shut my eyes and shut out the world was strong. I didn't follow it – my opium dreams are detailed, precise, and lengthy, and I had indeed been calling for the mother who bore me: Rosamunda.

Calling for her not to stab me.

My fingers felt fine skin at my jaw-line. The next man along from me dropped his gaze, leaning away. The man on his far side muttered; I heard '—woman built like a *stonemason!*'

Oblivious of their cynical laughter, I blurted, 'I can't be a slave again!'

Once, when I was sixteen, King Rodrigo and his court thought it amusing to hold mock-marriage ceremonies for me, to a woman the first night, and to a man the second night. After that, my bride and my husband got to tell the assembled nobles the particulars of the 'wedding night'.

That gained me two things. Firstly, the friendship and sympathy of Father Felix, a priest of the Green Christ who disapproved of such blasphemies. And secondly, the irrevocable knowledge that when my foster father and foster mother gave me to the King, they gave me soul and body with the legal deed of sale.

I glimpsed, down the hall and outside a stone archway, the identifiable skyline of Carthage.

A sweat of relief soaked my robe.

'Where's my papers?' I staggered up onto my feet. Bare feet on cold tile. 'I have King Rodrigo's writ of manumission; I'm a free—'

A moment of split-second decision.

'—woman; I can prove it! If you try to sell me, I'll appeal to the King-Caliph!'

The man who had shaken me awake put a hand on the whip at his belt. The chiaroscuro of his face gave him one gleaming eye and one empty socket.

He stepped towards me, and the shadows shifted. I saw he did indeed have but the one eye.

'You think the King-Caliph here's going to care about some poxy little Spaniard king over in the border states?' He chuckled. 'You might have been free then. And you might be free in the future. You're not free *now*. So shut up while I get a good price for you – although Christ-Emperor Himself alone knows, I couldn't sell you to a halfway decent whorehouse! Look at you! Damned cart-horse of a woman, you are.'

My hands touched wool. I looked down. I wore a much-darned robe, almost long enough to be women's skirts in Taraconensis; a belt pulled it in to show the shape of my breasts beneath.

The shock felt like cold water.

Not to see my baggage here – *well, Marcomir and his mother are thieves, yes*. Not to have concealing clothing; to know they must have undressed and dressed me again while I lay drugged . . .

And King Rodrigo's papers will have gone in their fire.

'Was anything brought in to be sold with me?' I asked the one-eyed man. He was not particularly tall; I stood on a level with him.

'What?'

'My tools, my equipment.'

He stared at me.

'I'm *literate*.' It was no more than the truth. 'I'm apprenticed to a master painter's workshop—' The truth, stretched. '—and I shouldn't be sold as unskilled labour! You can get four times the price for what I can do.'

He gave a thoughtful nod.

Part of his thought, I knew, would be the realisation that I had not always been free, since I knew so much.

But then, that's not uncommon: even in the kingdoms of Iberia, there's many a general, or chancellor, or powerful merchant, who either began life in a slave's collar, or wore it at some time in their career. They tell me it's different with the Franks in Europe; that even serfdom is gone a millennium, there.

Another reason for going to Rome.

Sell me; I'll be gone within the hour.

One-Eye could likely guess that too. I found I didn't care. That Marcomir and Donata must have a habit of drugging and selling unwary travellers – that didn't rouse my fury like the thought of my pigments and Punic wax, my scapulas and heating-irons, tossed on the trash somewhere, or sold off piecemeal for a tenth their value.

For all that Federico and Valdamerca (I wasn't invited to call them 'foster father' and 'foster mother' to their faces) picked me up as a foundling, I have all the skills of a noble soldier of Taraconensis. I was taught well, so as to be their gift for the King. Taught the arts of embroidery and the harp, and singing, as a woman; taught to joust with the lance, and fight with the sword, as a man.

Marcomir isn't worthy of a sword. A wooden cudgel will do for him, once I'm free.

'There were some old metal boxes and knives in a sack.' One-Eye gave me a shrewd look. 'They dumped them with you. I'm not letting you have anything sharp. Now shut up, before I have to mark you and make you worth even less.'

Abruptly, I found my gaze drawn by something – someone – over his shoulder.

Drawn by stillness, I realised. The man had been standing, an uncounted shadow in the background, for a little time. He stepped forward to the grille as I made eye-contact with him.

'You are literate, you claim?' He spoke directly to me, across One-Eye as the slaver turned around. 'More than merely to write your name?'

'I'm a painter; I can both draw and write.' Possibly I sounded stubborn. 'My name is Ilario. Give me parchment and a pen, and I'll show you how literate I am!'

Once out of the shadow, the newcomer was a large man, with a shaven head and naked broad shoulders. In the naphtha light, his reddish-tan skin shone very smooth. A woven reed and cloth headband kept sweat from running off his shaved skull into his eyes.

I noticed that his hands, crossed at his chest, were too large to be proportionate. *Also his feet*, I thought, as I glanced down at his sandals. The white cloth kilt that wrapped his waist was not wool, but some weave of flax; and not a Carthaginian garment, either.

To be sold to a foreigner . . . who may take me *anywhere* . . .

'She's special, is Ilario.' One-Eye picked my name out of the air without a stumble. 'And not cheap, because of that. Now—'

I folded my arms and stood watching them. Something about the stranger's body made me want to sketch him, to see where those odd proportions of hands and feet would lead me. He carried his head high, almost daintily; I wondered if he had made the same error that Marcomir had, and took me for an effeminate man.

'No more than one hundred,' he said mildly, his large, lustrous eyes turning towards me. His voice was resonant, because of his depth of chest, but I thought he would sing tenor if he sang. Possibly higher.

I was so lost in speculation about where his people might live that I didn't pay attention to the negotiations. A clatter of metal startled me into alertness as a bag landed at my feet.

'Don't *drop* that!' I instantly knew, by the sound; and fell to my knees to yank open the hessian sack.

The pigments had gone, being saleable. Likewise the small sculpted heads, and the acacia and lime-wood boards I'd prepared with size for painting icons. No surprise. As for my battered tools . . .

One-Eye caught me with hands full of rush-stalk *calami* and reeds, spatulas and scrapers; bent close over my bronze box and *cestrum* and *cauterium*-iron, scrutinising them for damage. Before I realised, he had unlocked the chain from the ring-bolt, and put it in the stranger's hand.

'My name is Rekhmire'.' The foreign man spoke to me gravely, in barely-accented Iberian – as, indeed, he had spoken barely-accented Carthaginian to the slave-owner. He had a rounded aspect to his chin and nose that should have made him appear soft, but only added to his gravitas, given how tall and broad he stood. 'I have need of a literate slave, here. I don't need one that will run away. You,' to One-Eye, 'will therefore fix a name-collar around this one's neck, large enough to be visible in public.'

'You—' *can't!*, I bit off.

So much for being sold to a fool and a quick escape.

Rekhmire' said, 'The other alternative is a brand. You would prefer your face not spoiled, I suppose?'

Dumb, I nodded.

I stood dumb as the slave-owner and his handlers took the leather collar off me, and knelt dumbly beside the anvil as one of them deafeningly riveted an engraved iron collar closed beside my ear.

I have not often worn a slave's collar, but I was a royal slave from fifteen to twenty-four; I have no illusions that there is any difference.

'Let me have my sack,' I said as I stood up.

Rekhmire' said, 'You won't need—'

I took the risk of interrupting him.

'What am I, your slave all twelve hours of the day and all twelve hours of the night? I came to Carthage to paint. When I'm not working, I *will* paint.'

He met my gaze, calmly staring down at me. The bones of his brows were pronounced, under the roundness. The set of his mouth was strong. He held an authority all the more effective because he seemed to be at pains to hide it.

Behind me, One-Eye chuckled nervously. 'I should have charged you double for her; she's feisty.'

'Provided she can read and copy, she may be as "feisty" as she wishes.'

I wondered, seeing the gaze that went between them, whether the slave-owner had himself been in a collar once, and likewise this foreign man.

Rekhmire' gave a nod towards the sack of my belongings. I picked them up, careful not to pull against the chain.

I can paint; the rest is a problem to be solved.

With my leash in his hand, he walked towards the exit, and I hurriedly followed, the bronze box in the sack banging against my shin.

'"Ilario". An Iberian name?'

I grunted assent, matching my pace through the hallway to his with a little difficulty, being shorter. 'Where's "Rekhmire'" a name from?'

I did not call him 'master'.

He gave a light sigh.

'Alexandria-in-Exile.' He gazed down at me. 'You would call the city "Constantinople", I expect. I come from all there is now of Egypt, under the reign of Pharaoh-Queen Ti-ameny; I am,' he said, 'a royal book-buyer, for the Library. And when I cannot persuade a man to let me buy his scrolls, I can sometimes persuade him to lease me the right to copy them. Hence what you will be doing, Ilario.'

Constantinople: that great city of the east, that has stood as the last remnant of the Egyptian empire for more than a millennium, while Carthage and the Turks debate with war their old lands around the Nile. That great city, that stands as a bulwark against the Turks, with its Queen, and its bureaucracy that – that—

I stopped as we came out between iron-grille doors into a dark street. The chain yanked my neck painfully, but I only stared at him. 'You're a eunuch!'

Rekhmire' halted, giving a gracious, if cynical, bow. 'And you, too, are something of the sort, and not a woman.'

I ignored that. 'I thought eunuchs were fat! I thought eunuchs all spoke in high voices.'

'They do, if gelded as children. I was an adult man before I applied.'

His tone gave me to understand that more trespass would be rudeness, but still he did not speak as a man does to a slave.

Astonished – appalled – I said, 'You had yourself castrated *deliberately?*'

His narrow, plucked black brows came down. 'And you did not? No . . . No, I am wrong. You are no gelded boy. What are you? Is this—'

He made a gesture that took me in from head to heels.

'—this the reason why you left the Iberian kingdoms?'

The shock of waking as a slave again, and the shuddering kinship I felt for this mutilated man, moved me to speak honestly.

'I left because my mother tried to kill me with a poisoned dagger. And . . . she plans to follow me, and try again. But – yes. It is because of what I am. Everything is because of what I am.'

3

Above the roof-garden of Rekhmire''s hired house, the North African constellations shone clear.

By night, I saw, the correct season's stars shone visible; evidently not shrouded by whatever hides the sun by day. On the western horizon, a tinge of brown and gold marked the last of the unseen sun's setting. Above my head, veils of aurora-light rippled in the black sky: blue and green and gold.

Past sunset now. It gave me a sudden ache. *I haven't seen the sun since we entered Carthaginian waters.*

The Egyptian Rekhmire' rested his head on his hand, and his elbow on the couch, watching me as we ate. 'You are too ready to be a slave to be someone who has been free long. You say your King Rodrigo manumitted you?'

I looked up from the carpet on the tiles, where he had told me to sit.

'On the feast of St Tanitta, this year. For "long service". Truthfully . . . ' It hurt to say it. 'I think he was bored. Pension the freak off – after a decade at court, its tricks are all well-known.'

The small smoked fish were a delicacy not to be found in rooming-houses. I crunched them, bones and all, while my stomach settled from the poppy-drug.

'And besides, some other nobleman had given him a married pair of Frankish dwarfs. Cheaper for the King if I have to support myself. He pensioned some of the others off, too; and half his menagerie.'

Rekhmire' gave me a glance that made me feel a dangerous willingness to confide further in him.

Shock, I thought. And the disorientation of opium.

He said, 'And you are a danger to someone at the court of Taraconensis? Or was your mother acting for private reasons?'

That made me blink. I drank water from a silver bowl, to give myself time to consider – and waited while the house-slave refilled it. There is rank among slaves, as in everything else.

The castrated man Rekhmire' said, 'What *are* you, Ilario?'

'Why don't you just order me to pull my skirts up!'

It is not a tone for a slave to take to his or her master. But this man . . .

'*How could you do it?*' I burst out, before he could speak again. 'How could you be born perfect and ruin it!'

His shaped strong brows went up. '"Perfect"?'

His voice, when not speaking to the Carthaginians inside the complex of rooms below, sounded lighter to my ear. Not like mine – which is too husky for a woman and too feminine for a man – but still different from the normal run of men.

'Manhood is hardly perfect. I find it a relief to be castrati.' He also drank from a silver bowl, I saw. 'Not to be always thinking of women, when I should be thinking of books. Not to be—' Here he gave me a swift smile, almost a grin. '—seeking relief by my own hand, twice or thrice a day, or more. I was a brawler, as a young man. I find myself very serene now.'

He looked not more than a few years past thirty, to my eye. I wondered when he'd gone under the knife. The thought made me shudder.

' . . . And besides, it is often a condition of employment in the Pharaoh's bureaucracy.'

'You needed to cut your balls off so that you can go wandering around, searching for books for Queen Ty-ameny's library.'

He smiled equably. 'It does sound a little ridiculous, when you put it like that.'

There was nothing keeping him from beating me, or putting heated irons to the soles of my feet, except what looked like a certain natural decency. As well as it being prudent to tell him what he wanted to know, I thought I should repay that.

I said, 'All of it comes from this – I'm a freak. A true man-woman. I bleed. Oh, not often; two or three times a year. And I shed seed, though not as much of it as a true man does. I've never got a maid with child. I've not birthed one, either.'

Rekhmire' met my gaze. 'If what I've read is true, you should take care not to. It is either the operation which birthed great Caesar from the womb, or the man-mother dies in childbed.'

My stomach felt as if it had a sudden lump of ice in it. I thought of the feel of Marcomir's seed.

Mouth dry, I added, 'I was a foundling. Until I was thirteen, I thought I would never know my true mother or father. Hardly surprising, is it, to expose a baby such as I was? I was taken in by a family who, although impoverished, nonetheless had a claim to nobility; they trained me to be a suitable present for King Rodrigo, and Queen Cixila, who was alive then. By the time they brought me to court, there was only Rodrigo. He was . . . amiable to me. I was his favourite freak for a time.'

Rekhmire' swung his legs down from the couch. I saw the ever-burning street-lights of Carthage on the Bursa-hill behind him. For a long moment he sat staring at me.

I shifted uncomfortably. 'What?'

The house-slaves re-lit burned-out torches, in the warm evening. His long lashes shaded his eyes, and I thought I saw a smudge of soot-black at the corners, accenting them as the Alexandrine Egyptians do. His shaven head accentuated all his clean-cut facial features.

His lips pressed together in a thin line. 'There is no anger in your voice. That you should be trained like an *animal*—'

'It wasn't so bad. 'Nilda and 'Nalda were good to me – Sunilda and Reinalda, Federico's youngest daughters.' I smiled. 'I think they liked having a baby they could dress up as girl or boy. And Matasuntha was married before I grew old enough to get under her feet. With three dowries to find . . . I can understand why Federico acted as he did.'

'And this Rosamunda, this mother the slaver said you speak of; she is Federico's wife?'

'No,' I said reluctantly. 'Federico's married to Valdamerca, my foster mother.'

Rekhmire' stood, and shook out the folds of his linen kilt. He lifted an eyebrow at me.

I rose to my feet, as much to give myself time to think as to seem polite.

'Federico and Valdamerca raised me. It was Valdamerca who found me on the stone outside the Green Chapel. They acted as my foster parents . . . '

Whether it was the shock of slavery, or opium, or this man's unjudgmental face – or Rosamunda's actions the last time I had stood in her company – I found myself speaking of things I had never intended:

'My mother, the woman who gave birth to me, is called Rosamunda. My father is Videric, her husband.'

'And they are?'

'The Aldra . . . the "Elder"—' I stumbled for the word. 'The "Lord" Videric is King Rodrigo's closest councillor. Chancellor, you might say. And Aldro – "Lady" – Rosamunda is his wife, his hostess; the cynosure of the Court of Ladies. You begin to understand,' I said bitterly, 'why they would expose a baby born a freak?'

He nodded, but I went on:

'It's not just that a hermaphrodite couldn't inherit their estate, any more than a cripple or a feeble-witted heir can. It's the scandal of Aldra Videric having fathered such a thing! Aldro Rosamunda having given birth to it!'

Rekhmire' absently rested his oddly-large hand on my shoulder. 'I see, I think – this Lady Rosamunda has just discovered who Ilario truly is. And to avoid the scandal if it was realised that their unacknowledged child lives at court, the butt of their noble friends' jokes, scorn, contempt . . . '

The Egyptian spoke clinically, evidently familiar with kings' menageries and jesters. I felt my face heat.

' . . . No,' he corrected himself. '*That* can't be right! How long has Aldro Rosamunda known you were her child?'

'I came to court at fifteen. Since then.' I shrugged. 'How many other hermaphrodite children of my age would have been abandoned? It was obvious to her, who I must be.'

Rekhmire''s gaze sharpened. 'And her husband, a powerful man at court; he can easily have traced back your upbringing, found in what part of the country you were abandoned – yes, I see it. But . . . this same danger will have been in existence a long time: ever since you came to court. You are dangerous to Aldro Rosamunda now? Why now?'

'I've *never* been a danger to her! I've never wanted to bring scandal down on her; why would I? She's my mother!'

His hand dropped from my shoulder and he snapped his large fingers. 'You said – the King freed you! They might think you couldn't raise a scandal as a slave, but once freed—'

'*I would never have hurt her.*'

The Egyptian looked down at me. I begrudged him the height that lent him an illicit moral authority.

I said, 'She first came to me when I'd been at court half a year. We've spoken together, I don't know, six or seven times after that? Over the years. I knew what a scandal there'd be if gossip got hold of the story that she'd given birth to a freak. I would never tell that secret. She *knows* I won't say anything.'

'Clearly, not. Or she would not have attempted to kill you.'

I've watched stonemasons work; how with one tap of a hammer, and the correct wedge, they can sheer off a great slab of stone. I felt tears well up in my eyes, and I had to grit my teeth to keep my breathing even.

This Egyptian bureaucrat knows far too much about the right wedges to split people apart.

'She's afraid.' I managed to keep my voice steady, although I heard it croak like a half-grown boy's. 'She's mistaken. Since I couldn't make her understand that, I left Taraco.'

'Kek and Keket!' he muttered, as if it were some oath.

'And,' I added with a shrug, it being so much less painful than other matters, 'I'm hardly likely to be in favour enough with King Rodrigo to gossip with him. He wanted me to go north, to crusade against the Franks around Poitiers, as his siege engineer. A builder of trebuchets is more valuable than a painter of statues. I would have had to leave the court in any case.'

Rekhmire' looked me up and down. For all the wool of the robe covering my chest, I felt as if my breasts were exposed. He brought a finger up and stroked my hair back from my cheek.

'By the Company of the Eight!' he said softly. 'What a mess. And a puzzle. I don't understand it all . . . '

The fear that rushed through me – at having trusted; having told things I should never have told – made me curt. 'You don't need to. All you need to do is let me paint, in the hours when I'm not doing copy-work for you. I'll earn enough money to buy my freedom, and you can buy another slave when you get to the next city you're going to!'

In a tone that robbed the comment of offensiveness, Rekhmire' said, 'You're remarkably attractive, too. I didn't buy you as a bed-slave, but I'm open to amending the contract, if you're willing?'

Evidently slavery is different in Alexandria.

Startled, I embarrassed myself by saying aloud, 'Can you – I mean . . . *Can* you?'

'It may take me a little concentration to begin,' Rekhmire' said – mildly, for a man who must have been asked too many times before. 'But the only thing I can't do is procreate.'

His smile shone; I thought him honestly amused.

'The Sublime Porte's eunuch guards, let's say, would hardly be so popular among his thousand wives if they couldn't adequately entertain them. Believe me more than capable of making this offer to you. But answer me as *you* wish.'

Meeting his gaze, I saw such a lack of coercion that I was not, at first, inclined to believe it.

A slave's word is worth less than the wind that stirs the torch-flames, of course. And this man might be cruel enough to sell me, if rejected; worst of all, sell me to Aldro Rosamunda, if he could get word to Taraconensis.

But I am tired of being the whore I was sometimes made to be, as the King's Freak. And this . . . would be two freaks in sexual congress.

'I'm not willing.'

He gave an acknowledging nod. 'I'll show you some of the scrolls I have here, indoors, that need copying. And tomorrow we must go to one of the Lords-Amir's houses, to copy a parchment he won't let me take out of his library.'

Will this man forget rejection – and scandal – so easily? No. I should not have spoken . . .

At the moment, even this early in the evening, the black sky and the sickness of my body insisted that what I needed more than thought was sleep.

The tall Egyptian bent to pick up the bowl I had been drinking from, and absently placed it with his own on the rim of the roof, where it would be easier for the house-slaves to clear it away.

'I could make a few inquiries,' Rekhmire' said, glancing back. 'I meet a number of people in this city, while I'm buying books; I could tactfully find out if they know of any Iberian noblewomen travelling in this area.'

It may have been the mixture of diffidence and confidence in his bearing, or his subtle interrogation of me – or simply the realisation that an Egyptian civil servant travelling for the Royal Library will visit many places . . .

I blurted out, 'You're not a *spy*, are you?'

Rekhmire' grinned. It made him look unlined and twenty, instead of the thirty I suspected him to be.

'I get a lot of that. No. I'm not a spy. Go and make them find you a bed, Ilario. Amun and Amunet! You're falling asleep on your feet!'

I slept. But sleeping or waking, what stayed in my mind was my mother.

4

The next day, I bettered my acquaintance with Carthage – or at least, the part of it that lies indoors, in the rich closed mansions of the Bursa-hill district.

'That,' the Alexandrine Egyptian's voice said beside me, 'will be your *rough* copy, one assumes?'

I frowned. Naphtha gas-lamps hissed and sputtered in this scriptorium belonging to one of Carthage's 'philosopher-lords', or 'Lords-Amir', as they call themselves. A close stare at my papyrus showed me perfectly adequate lettering, by that harsh light, even if the subject itself was capable of boring the most pedantic scholar. I opened my mouth to protest – and shut it again.

Three separate oak-gall ink drawings adorned the margin. Two were approximations of diagrams in the original manuscript. The third . . .

. . . Was half-a-dozen sketched lines that caused me to lift my head and look at the Lord-Amir's cat, asleep on the window-ledge overlooking the courtyard, one front leg hanging bonelessly down against the inner wall.

My hand has a mind of its own in absent moments.

'You have to admit,' I looked back from the dark window at my doodle, 'it's not bad.'

'It's a *cat*.'

The Egyptian might or might not have been suppressing a smile.

'At least you can recognise it! This is my rough copy,' I agreed hastily, knowing that meant extra work by lamp-light, or naphtha gas-lamps. Nothing by daylight here.

And yet I'll *draw* without complaint, until my eyes feel like sand.

Rekhmire' murmured, 'How far have you got?'

The Carthaginians do their writing at a high desk at which the copyist stands, the manuscript held open in a frame. The tall Egyptian bent his head to read over my shoulder.

'"Hasdrubal lies between life and death, tended by his brother-in-law Hannibal",' I read. 'There's a page of Hasdrubal recovering from his wound after a local tribesman attacks him, then, "Hasdrubal, after much speech, persuades Hannibal to abandon his childhood oath of vengeance on Rome; they sign the Treaty of Seguntum with Scipio" . . . Then it's all diplomacy between Rome and Carthage until Hannibal and Scipio –

different Scipio – lead the Roman-Punic Alliance to wipe out the Persians at the battle of Zama . . . '

I thumbed several pages ahead. History bores me. I'd hoped to be copying something like Hero of Alexandria's *Pneumatics* – which, if it *is* Greek, at least has drawings of his steam-driven aeolipile, and a couple of books on engines of war and ballistics that King Rodrigo had me read in translation in Taraco.

' . . . Aaaand . . . Much later, there's the Visigoths defeating the Carthaginians in Iberia. No Roman help; the Great Alliance is breaking down by then. And the great *re*-invasion of Iberia from Carthage, starting in the year Anno Domini seven hundred and eleven. Are you sure you *want* all this? I've seen a far better history of the Classical era in the royal library at Taraco—'

My hand clenched, splaying the split tip of my quill against the papyrus. *Christus Imperator! Can't I keep my mouth shut?*

The Egyptian Rekhmire' nodded, and made the reply I might have expected from a book-buyer. 'It may be necessary to travel to Taraco, in that case.'

'I will have bought myself free before you do.'

It came out, not speculative, but as a flat statement. *I will not go back to Taraco.*

The cat landed on the sanded wooden floorboards with a soft, plump sound, and strolled over to wind between Rekhmire''s ankles. My hand sketched the hoop of the cat's back as it arched up against the eunuch's shin. The Egyptian's brows lifted.

'Why must cats always approach those who can't endure their presence?' He sniffled, watery-eyed, edging it away with his sandal. 'Go, daughter of Bast.'

I added two small relevant curves.

'"Son of Bast", I think. Master,' I added, with the look that slave-owners commonly identify as 'dumb insolence'.

To my surprise, Rekhmire' gave me a look he might have given any freeman or freewoman.

'Balls aren't everything, Ilario.'

I didn't know whether to laugh or cry. Or for which of us. 'No, indeed . . . '

'Theologically speaking, all Bast's children are daughters, female or male—'

An elderly white-bearded Lord-Amir bustled in at that point, to converse with the Egyptian. I took out my pen knife – sharp enough to shave the hairs from my arm, or slice through a slave-owner's throat – and re-cut the quill's nib.

Forget Rosamunda, this Alexandrine Egyptian, these Carthaginian Lords!, I thought doggedly, with a glance out at the roiling waves of light that edged the Penitence today in green and gold. I came here to paint. Everything else is behind me now: forgotten and gone.

The tophet in Carthage is a place of child-sacrifice.

I walked there to paint, towards the end of the first week or ten days after I entered Rekhmire''s household.

Shake the nightmares out of my head, I thought. Even if what I put in place of them is true horror.

Every man knows rumours of Carthage's 'tophet'. That is not a Carthaginian word. I managed to find the place, after much wandering about the hill of the Bursa and down into the suburbs, by asking for directions to the 'child-garden'.

That made me shudder.

The light . . . remained the light Under the Penitence, and I began to wonder how Carthage's citizens bore it.

I wondered, too, what Messer Tommaso Cassai – nicknamed in Rome 'Mastro Masaccio' – might after all make of an apprentice who offered him not the formal faces of saints and the dead, nor statues with ivory-rose cheeks and brown eyes, but only the mundane landscape of the world. Even if it is the world under Carthage's constant darkness.

Must it not say something about a painter, if they can paint this unique light? He'll *have* to accept me!

The way to the tophet was up a street steep enough to make me regret the wooden easel under my arm, and the metal box of tools with me. I carried also a small iron brazier, to heat the hot coals inside the bronze palette. Unlikely I could paint here unless I could heat my instruments.

The naphtha gas-lamps that lit the street became more widely spaced, and stopped as I reached the crest of the hill. Stepping past the last tall building, I could see, beyond a vast rampart, the great five-fingered harbour below me. The shape of the circular ship-construction docks stood out clearly, outlined by lanterns.

A step or two along the rampart-wall brought me to stunted juniper trees, and I stepped down in among them, onto shed twigs, and into impenetrable blackness. I stopped, for my eyes to adjust.

Low, crabbed junipers. Trees I've seen grow in the desert rock behind Taraco, that thrive without rain. Now Carthage's only surviving trees. For all their small size, junipers grow slow enough that these must have rooted here centuries ago, before the Penitence fell on the city.

My eyes accustomed themselves rapidly to the shadow. Perhaps, I thought wryly, more used to Carthage now than I am.

I picked a way over roots, between gnarled low branches. The empty space that opened ahead of me had the smell of sacrifice on the air. That's recognisable wherever one goes, from prayers to Saint Tanitta in some goat-herds' village in the Taraconian hills, to the spilling of the Bull's blood in the Mass of the Green Christ.

But this will be infants' blood, if the stories speak right.

I was in the tophet before I properly knew it.

Squared-off short pillars of stone jutted up from the earth, and I had to step back sharply from the grave-monuments before I barked my knees.

Allowing the afternoon's starlight to guide me, I put my gear down and used flint and steel to light a torch. Far away, across the tophet, I thought I saw a cave-entrance – an associated sanctuary? – but its torches were too distant to help.

My flickering light spread out, there being little enough wind to make it flare, and let me see the carvings on the truncated oblong pillars.

Not saints' faces, these.

I let my fingers trace the mask-faces on the stone. The up-curved mouths were carved deep enough in the bas-relief that my fingers couldn't find the back of the hole. So, also, the down-turned curves of the hollow eyes. Their expressions were grinning mockery.

All the ages, under the names on the stones, were between birth and three years of age.

I puzzled out the unfamiliar inscriptions: 'here is . . . sacred and dedicated to . . . ' My torch drizzled smoke across the masks' hollowed gazes. I straightened up again.

Rumour spoke of fire: I could smell no smoke or burnt meat. What do they call their god? The one that swallows the children whose bones are buried under these stones . . . ? Travellers' tales speak only of 'Baal' – 'God'.

Rekhmire' would know, he being a man who picks up information like an ant carrying away a leaf. I didn't want to ask him.

The carved god's-heads were as bald as Rekhmire''s. I could see an ironic similarity in their prominent stone ears, too.

I lifted my head and looked at the juniper trees silhouetted against the sky. The tophet moved me to shudder and smile wryly, both.

And now we come to the problem of how we shall paint in the dark.

Even if I can use flint and tinder on my brazier . . .

Carthage's darkness was not homogeneous. I realised that, now – I had thought it a freak of the weather, sailing in. But the Penitence swelled into sooty blackness at times, and at other times shrank up the dome of the sky so that all the horizon quivered and swayed with curtains of light.

Unlike statues or icons in the workshop, to paint here, to attempt a sample of the colours, I needed to wait.

Tommaso Cassai was rumoured to paint the ordinary countryside around the city of Rome. So he might have his own experiences of waiting for weather to clear. If not weather like this.

The wood under the brazier's coals began to take fire from the tinder, glowing red and orange. I scented burning on the air. At this rate it would take a long time for my bronze palette box to warm enough to melt the colours.

Every coin the Egyptian had so far given me, I spent on pigments, wax, willow-twig charcoal (since no man was selling the better-quality vine-twig, under the Penitence), and the materials for size, and different grounds. *So this is not a time to waste them.* If I took out a prepared, properly-sized sheet of parchment and a metal stylus, I might sketch in silver-point – *But colour – the eternal problem is mixing raw pigments to match the colour of reality* . . .

Memory washed over me while I knelt, wondering, in that unnoticed corner of the tophet. There was no connection. Indeed, it felt as if the lack of connection was itself the reason: I have spent a month and more putting this out of my mind, and as soon as I relax—

I had been relaxed in Taraco, if slightly concerned about Rosamunda. I take after my mother more than I do after my father, but – understandably, with a freak offspring – there's little physical resemblance even between she and I. Left to myself, it would have been a long time before I knew Aldro Rosamunda for the woman who bore me.

Five weeks ago to the day, now.

And, as on the very first occasion when she and I spoke at court, it was the Aldra Videric who brought me to her.

As he led me past arches that opened onto fountain-courtyards, sunlight burnt white into the corridor, and cast the shadows of fretwork-cut alabaster back on the flagstones. The fragmentary light picked out the few white hairs in his neatly-trimmed yellow beard, and the blue of his eyes in his sun-burned face as he turned his head to speak to me – Frankish ancestry, somewhere in the bloodline.

'She's upset.' Videric sounded embarrassed. 'She wants to speak to you. I don't know why, Ilario. Be kind to her.'

At the doorway, he held back the linen curtain as if to a lady of King Rodrigo's court, although I was today in men's clothes. He would often joke awkwardly with me about women, or discuss duelling skills. My father, this burly, richly-dressed man; who does not know what to make of his son-daughter – except to know what a scandal it would be if the freak Ilario's parentage were attached to the great Aldra who is King Rodrigo's confidant and long-time First Adviser.

'She's there. Be kind,' Videric repeated.

He turned and walked quickly back down the corridor. The wide blue and white stripes on his linen gown – made with hanging sleeves, as the Franks do, but in light material for our hot weather – billowed up as he walked; I glimpsed his silk hose, and his war-sandals. His hand, where it swung at his side, clenched into a fist.

I entered the room, and let the linen drapes fall closed behind me.

Silver flashed in the air.

The fountains of Taraco are a permanent pleasure, in this arid land that is the first and oldest of the Visigoth sub-kingdoms of Iberia. Warriors coming from the north, after crusade, relax with a welcoming sigh when they see the arcs of water in the sun. The ladies of the court sit in the shade of ferns that grow only in those great stone basins.

Of course, the fountains often smell sour, as I noted this one did; and they take hundreds of servants and slaves to maintain. As King's Freak, I was unlikely ever to be put to cleaning out clogged pipes or pumping water through drains, but that doesn't mean I'm not aware of such things.

'Ilario!' Rosamunda turned her head, looking up from the ripples on the fountain-pool's surface. She smiled – nervously, with a quick stretch of her lips.

'The lord Videric said you wished to see me?' Even in privacy, I do not call her *mother*: it's wise to be discreet. 'Are you well, lady?'

Her eyes flicked back and forwards, under half-lowered lids, and she didn't turn, continuing to look at me over her shoulder.

What has she to tell me? I wondered, suddenly.

The times that we had met before, with the awkwardness of her abandoning me as an infant between us, it seemed to me that she wanted to reach out to me. A year might go by, between such meetings. We had drawn close. Now . . .

'What is it?' I said.

Rosamunda glanced down; I saw her in profile. I suppose her forty-five or so. There is no grey in her black hair, and her brows are clean sweeping lines, without needing to be plucked. I would have painted her portrait, if not that I thought the love between us would show in it for all to see.

'I wanted to tell you . . . ' Her mouth has a perfect fullness to the lower lip. She lifted her dark eyes to me, and I forgot to look at her; could see only the pain in her gaze. 'How it was, when you were born. Your father – Aldra Videric gave me a choice. When he saw you, what you were. I could leave, taking you with me. Or I could . . . give you up, and stay. I had nothing of my own. *Nothing*. How would we have lived? We would have starved!'

Gently, moving forward, I said, 'You hinted as much, before. You don't think I blame you?'

'Don't you?'

I am the taller, and I wanted to kneel down, in that pale alabaster room, and hide my head in her skirts, just as a child would do.

She muttered: I realised she had said, 'I left you where I *knew* you would be found—'

The swirl of green silk, that ran in a sweep from her deep bodice to the wide hem, flew out as she spun around; the golden girdle around her hips clinked as her Aldro's keys-of-the-house jingled.

'Ahh!' she cried out, but not loudly. As if stifled.

Silver flashed in the air.

I acted without thought. It was instinct to step back, and slap her knife out of her hand—

Her knife.

The dagger clattered to the flagstones—

The woman who is my mother stared at me, frozen; translucent flax-linen veil floating across, draping over her mouth. Both her empty hands extended forward, the fingers closing into claws.

The dagger on the tiles was a foot long, the blade triangular, all three edges sharp. Something blackened the steel, and the point itself was all black. Poison.

'What . . . ' I stared.

Her eyes, wide and frantic, stared back at me. The noise of the falling knife echoed in my mind—

Will have echoed down the palace corridors. Far off, I heard a sound of sandals slapping against stone floors. Coming closer?

If Videric is still near . . . He will have heard!

Rosamunda caught her lower lip between her teeth.

My mind replayed her action. The dagger as she had been holding it, point-down, clenched in her hand. Flat against her belly, as she turned. Her quick, panicky movement.

'You tried to stab me.'

My words did not dent the silence.

A voice shouted urgently from the corridor. I heard a clatter of feet. My mother's gaze still locked with mine.

'You *stabbed*—'

Rosamunda whispered, '*Run.*'

'—RUN!'

Jolted out of memory, I stumbled up onto my feet; ducking as something flew past my face.

A man's voice shouted again, in thick Carthaginian Latin; I couldn't understand him. *Did he shout that word? Is it just my memory?*

He ran towards me, from the rock-face where torches shimmered; halted at the edge of the stone pillars, screamed in fury—

I had easel and box scrabbled up under my arm in a second, as his robe flapped white in the darkness and he ran to and fro, not coming within the stones.

He'll be a priest, a priest of Baal; I'll be executed for coming in here, a foreigner!

I kicked the torch over and stamped it out. Sparks stung my ankle above my sandal. I ignored that, and snatched at the brazier; jerked my hand back from burning-hot iron.

'*You!*' The priest's ferocity cut through the pitch-black afternoon.

I sucked at my blistered hand for a moment, caught in indecision – and ran, box and wooden stand clasped to me, abandoning the brazier and the coals.

I can earn another iron brazier – more days copying histories—

The Baal-priest's shouts died down behind me.

By the time I found Rekhmire''s hired house again and staggered in, the skirts of my robe blackened with dirt to the knee, I was in no mood to be spoken to. Only the knowledge of how expensive they would be to replace kept me from dropping my box of instruments and kicking them across the floor.

I placed them, very carefully, at the foot of the mattress that served me as a bed; slammed my fists against the clay-plastered walls of the tiny cubicle room, and swore out loud.

Rekhmire''s voice, amused and blasphemous, came from the doorway. 'I must teach you better gods to appeal to.'

I wiped earthy hands down my woollen gown as I turned and glared at him.

He added, 'You may swear by the Hermopolitan Ogdoad. They permit unbelievers to worship.'

'The which-*what*-how?'

'The Company of Eight.'

I was baptised Christian in the faith of Christ the Emperor; but that doesn't mean enough for me to feel inclined to argue with this lunatic Egyptian pagan. God has never helped me, why should I champion God?

Rekhmire''s smooth, monumental face changed to seriousness. 'I've been awaiting your return. I . . . have heard a rumour, from one of the secretaries of a Lord-Amir whose scrolls I'm paying an exorbitant price for, and I went down to check it at the docks—'

'*What?*' I snapped.

He scratched a hand over his shining head, where a faint fine stubble began to rasp at the end of every other day.

'There is news of an Iberian noblewoman having arrived here. Which means nothing in itself. But this woman is searching—'

'For her—' I stopped, helpless with hope. '—"Daughter"? "Son"?'

'For a young man . . . *And* a young woman.' Rekhmire' rested his broad hand on my shoulder. 'For her twin male and female slaves.'

'*Twins!*'

'You could be dressed as man or woman, now. How *else* could she look for you and not give away what it is she's searching for?'

'*Who*', not '*what*'!

I bit my tongue to keep from yelling it at him.

He had taken me up to the roof garden again, and had the slaves serve wine where we sat in the chilling air. I didn't drink. Anger was too pure in me to muddy it with that.

'*Slaves! Twins!*'

I asked Father Felix, once, whether he thought it was possible to be born with two souls within one body. That might explain me, I thought. I bleed like a woman, I spend seed like a man; is that because there's a male soul *and* a female soul in me?

Father Felix explained gently enough that there could not be.

'God has afflicted you. Either you are a woman, afflicted grievously with the ambitions of a man as well as the curse of Eve, or else you are a man forced for some sin to bear the shameful signs of a woman.' He had shaken his tonsured head, in the shadow of his green robe's hood. 'Not *your* sin, Ilario. What have you done, after all? It's the sin of your unknown father and mother, I would judge.'

Rosamunda's here, I thought, stunned.

Is Aldra Videric? He *must* know what she did—

'She won't find you.' Rekhmire''s voice broke the comparative silence of Carthage in the evening. Men's voices called to each other down in the street below; greased cart-wheels screeched. I heard the yelp of an urban hyena come in from the desert to scavenge.

The Egyptian, my master, looked at me speculatively over the top of a glass goblet made in La Serenissima. 'There's no reason you two should meet. I'll keep you busy enough copying books. You will not be addressed by the name "Ilario". But . . . I'm concerned. If this Iberian noblewoman should happen to speak with the man who sold you to me—'

'You *will* this, you *won't* that!' All common sense left me. I glared at Rekhmire' as if he were not my legal owner. '*I* get no say in the matter?'

'You say she's tried to kill you once already.'

'*Run!*' Rosamunda's voice whispered in my memory.

Her expression, if I could have caught it in pigments, would have made my fortune. Torn between fear for herself and ruin, fear for her daughter-son.

But not so much fear for me that she didn't try to hurt me.

'*Where is she?*' I demanded.

'Ilario . . . ' The Egyptian put his glass down beside him on the green ceramic roof-tiles. Their colour echoed the curtains of light flickering inland, where the desert creeps close to the city.

His glance at me was sharp.

'Ilario, she's travelling alone, with very few servants, but those that she does have are armed soldiers.'

I put a finger between the slave collar and the flesh of my neck, lifting up the iron. 'You can chain me up all day and all night from now on, or you can tell me where she is.'

He shook his head. 'Nun and Naunet and the sun-god's *egg!*, but you're stubborn!'

'If you're a foreigner and you can go around asking questions, I'm a foreigner and so can I! I'll find her!'

The iron felt cold, now the evening fell. I let the collar slip down again. If I missed the sun, I missed the changeable light of the moon fully as much, and that would not be new for several days yet.

Under the stars and aurora-curtain of Carthage's Darkness, I couldn't read Rekhmire''s expression clearly.

'You write a neat hand. You cost me an appropriate sum.' His eyes caught the shifting green and gold light as he glanced at me. 'And, sooner or later, your mother will think to send one of her men around the slavers' halls. If you must hear it . . . She's not with the King-Caliph's court; she came in off the *Christus Viridianus* out of Mallorca, and hired rooms anonymously, overlooking the dockyard—'

I scrambled up, interrupting; gathering my skirts around me. I gave him a sudden queasy look. 'I'm sorry – I'll have to hear it in a moment!'

I saw him glance at the edge of the roof, off which it would have been most natural for a man to void his guts were he ill. His expression altered. Thinking of my woman's modesty in such matters.

He gave a curt nod of dismissal.

I stumbled down the inner stairs, into the house – and on, through the intricately tiled hallway, and out of the slaves' door into the street.

It wasn't difficult – if she was not with King-Caliph Ammianus's Carthaginian nobility up at the palace, even a necessity to travel discreetly wouldn't put Aldro Rosamunda, wife of Aldra Videric, in a poor rooming-house of the kind Donata kept.

There were only two establishments rich enough in that particular district; I watched until I saw a man wearing a mail hauberk and cloth-wrapped steel helm, whose face I recognised even if he was not wearing Videric's livery at the moment . . . *Amalaric? Agustin?* Names tugged at my memory.

I followed the soldier in through the crowded eating-area, catching up an unattended jar and carrying it on my shoulder. With the belt of my robe yanked in tight, and my hair loose about my shoulders . . . nobody notices a woman carrying water.

At the top of the stairs I put down the jar, and called her name past him.

'*Rosamunda!*'

The guard spun around, grabbing at me; I saw, past him, my mother standing in the room's doorway—

I snapped, 'She *wants* to speak to me, you idiot!'

The bearded soldier glared, his hands biting into my shoulders. I could see him register my robe and think *a woman, therefore harmless*, even though I was sure I'd fought him a time or two in the training-halls.

Her voice said, 'I do. I want to speak to . . . Ilario. Amalaric, you may go.'

The grip of his hands loosed. He stood back. There was no sound for a long moment but his war-sandals scraping the stone floor, departing.

The striped cloak she wore with the hood back – she had been on the point of going out, evidently – was blue and white silk: Videric's colours, if not the family livery. The richness of the self-lined fabric made her face look the more ill. There were pinch-lines around her mouth. Her skin was crepe-like; more white than white lead could account for.

I saw nothing but women's gear in the rooms beyond her.

She lifted a gloved hand and beckoned me inside, not taking her eyes off me – flinching as the metal door thumped home into the expensive wood-padded door frame.

'Ilario . . . '

There was a window, a striped stone arch looking down into the rooming-house's inner courtyard. Metal-grille shutters had been flung open, flat back against the wall.

A slave drew water at the well in the courtyard. It looked to be a good fifteen feet below the sill of the arch to the flagstones.

No windows at all in the outer wall, where the narrow streets are. This is Carthage.

I said, 'Why did you try to kill me?'

A perceptible, almost-comic trembling made her jaw quiver. I saw the bone-hinge clench, under her skin, hollowing her cheeks for a moment.

'Yes.' Her voice sounded thin. Harsh. No hesitation in that admission, I saw – seeing, also, the strength of this woman who is my mother. 'Yes, I did do that . . . '

'*Why?*'

'Scandal. Ruin. No one must know. *The King would be forced to send us away.*'

The chill that went through me, I felt mostly in my hands. With my fingers this stiff and cold, I could never paint.

Her gaze dropped to my throat. 'You're a slave. Again.'

She seemed unconcerned. I shrugged that minor hurt off.

'So King Rodrigo would have sent you back to your estates.' I know the Aldra Videric's rich lands. Anger began to break the crust of the chill in me. 'And that – would be a *hardship*.'

Men say the faces of the shocked or fearful turn white. To paint them, green and saffron would need to be subtly suggested. Staring at her, I thought, No wonder we paint icons for sorrow and worship. Men's true faces are too complex.

'There'd be scandal!' Her hand clenched. 'Don't you understand? People would see. People would *know*. My child: the King's Freak! My child: born – what you are. *My* baby, abandoned—'

'You need not have abandoned me,' I said, feeling distant enough that I sounded numbly polite. 'It was your choice.'

'Videric made me!'

I realised only then how badly I had wanted not to hear her say that.

'And yet, you didn't kill me.' I sighed and walked further across the room, staring aimlessly down at the courtyard. The slave had gone. 'Why did you tell me to run?'

'Because you're my child.'

I turned about, facing her. There is no one close enough below the window to hear us; the door is solid enough to block all sound. I looked into her eyes, that are green flecked with ochre, and are the same eyes that look at me out of mirrors.

Speaking hastily, Rosamunda protested, 'I couldn't kill you when you were born. Anyone else *would* have done.'

On the last words, her tone came close to a whine.

I blinked. My fingers were cold enough that I wrapped them in the loose volume of my wool robe. They didn't warm. 'So why are you here now? If you haven't come to kill me.'

'I have to take you home.'

Now that you see the collar, why not buy me? – but, no, that will mean disclosing her presence here. Proof of a foreigner's identity is needed for the legal contract.

The wind from the city sifted in through the window, past me. The flames of the oil-lamps wavered. I needed to see her closely. I stepped forward.

She flinched.

Her chin lifted, almost instantly. You could see how little the flesh blurred there, despite her age; she is still the most beautiful of the Court of Ladies. 'I have to take you back to Taraco! Videric told me to.'

If I could see regret on her face, I'd weep. Seeing only desperation, fury, resentment, panic—

Nothing existed to give me proof. But, looking down at her expression, a wash of horror went through me – a sudden picture, in my mind's eye, of how far down it is off deck and dock, how dark and impenetrable to the eye the sea-water down there is. I stopped breathing, for a moment: felt how lungs burn and burst, when the heavy water closes a man in.

'Why are you still going to kill me?'

Rosamunda looked at me.

With shame, I thought. *Her expression shows shame.*

She can at least feel that.

If I were to go with her . . . some way between here and the Balearic Islands, her soldiers – or she herself – will drown me.

Turning, tugging at the gauntlet-cuffs of her gloves, Rosamunda spoke without looking at me. 'Blame Videric. He says I have to do this. Ilario, he's always thought that *something* would happen.'

Her head lifted from the tiny stitching on the gloves. Her gaze flicked briefly towards me.

'When you came to court as a young . . . ' Her lashes blinked down. 'It was *his* idea I should speak to you. Talk with you. Befriend you. Then, if the need came, I would be – close to you. Close enough to do what was necessary.'

I would be close to you.

This – thing – has been planned since I was fifteen.

My legs felt as if they were the lead weights which fishermen tie to their nets. I couldn't walk out of the room; I could barely stand.

This face, of which I know every line – of which, in all honesty, I have sketches which I have never shown any man. My mother's face. Looking at me with . . . impatience?

Murder. And all she feels is impatient?

My mouth dry, I managed to say calmly, 'Why does my father want to kill me?'

Rosamunda switched her head from side to side, as a horse does, troubled with flies. Her gaze avoided me. 'He's not your father. But you *must* see the power and riches we'll lose, if King Rodrigo sends him away!'

'Not my father.'

Her tumbling sentences stopped. She looked at me with tired, frank eyes. I thought she seemed relieved, if only by her own honesty.

'Ilario . . . Videric is only my husband. He's no relation to you.'

Foundlings are bastards, slaves' children, or both. Since fifteen, I have treasured the idea that I am neither. Now . . .

I moved before I intended it, crossing the room, flinging open the iron door.

I found myself staring at Amalaric's solid, mail-covered back.

The soldier stood facing down the corridor towards the steps, hands clasped before him, sword in its scabbard at his side.

Behind me, Rosamunda said, 'Ilario—'

I wrenched the iron door inwards, slammed it towards the room's wall, and it crashed hard against the metal door-stop.

Amalaric, beginning to turn, flinched. I ducked past him as he startled and grabbed.

'No! No disturbance!' Rosamunda's voice whispered, shrill. 'We can't steal a slave in public!'

Her footsteps; his; all sounded behind me in the corridor. A door opened behind me; I heard another man in war-gear clatter out; didn't spare a look back.

'Ramaz!' she hissed. '*Ilario!*'

I raised my voice as I clattered down the steps, not able to avoid the obvious, ironic, bitter thought. 'Oh, you must feel very much at home here – in this city of *child-killers*!'

'Ilario!'

The rooming-house eatery was a blur, an unfocused gallery of faces; I registered nothing as I strode through and out.

8

The two men and one woman dogged my footsteps, as a group; I deliberately pushed them from my mind. I walked the crowded naphtha-lamp-lit streets, arms huddled about myself, hands tucked into my armpits. The windowless houses rose up in four or five-storey tenements to either side.

Videric . . . He . . . Not my father?

How many lies have I been told?

'Ilario!' Rosamunda's steps speeded up. I felt her try to put her silk cloak around my shoulders.

I shrugged it off into the dirt.

The two soldiers stayed back from me at her gesture. As if escorted, as if I led the way, I strode between the blank dark walls, my mother gasping at my heels:

'You'll come with us – we can go to the docks – I've a ship – I can send a slave, get the luggage sent on—'

I ignored her.

The desire to get away ate up ground. I know neither how far I walked, nor for how long. I did know, shortly, in which direction my feet naturally turned.

It was perhaps a quarter-hour, by the city's horns, before I found myself treading on earth and the discarded twigs of juniper trees.

Rosamunda's sudden voice in the dark startled me. 'Where is this?'

'Don't you know? I'd thought you'd know.'

A glance back showed me the black silhouettes of the soldiers, against the stars.

I said, 'This is the tophet. It's where they kill their children. As sacrifices.'

If the light had been better, I could have seen her reaction. The faint torches over at the sanctuary hardly cast illumination here.

I turned my back on her, walking to the sanctuary entrance. Torches stood in cressets at the mouth of the cave. Without looking back, I went in.

All three of them followed me over the dry, tamped-down earth.

Many footsteps are needed to make earth this rock-hard.

I saw no priests as I entered. I was no longer sure what I expected to find, beyond this cave-mouth I had only glimpsed before. Rows of round-bellied urns stood silent on shelves carved out of the rock wall. Above them were rows of expensive beeswax candles. And at the cave's far end, a great mask was carved: the stone mouth of the bald laughing god Baal. The lip had been cut so that anything placed on it would slide down, into the darkness.

Towards fire?

Staring, I stopped. I didn't look at my mother.

'Videric . . . Lord Videric's not my father.'

I could believe, now. Or in some way begin to.

Her tone was nominally apologetic. 'Perhaps I shouldn't have told you. But you'd find out.'

'If he's not – who *is*?'

Rosamunda walked up beside me, moving cautiously. Not because of the smooth earth, or the jars that must contain the bones of children. The movements of her body spoke both of fear and threat.

I don't doubt she intends to kill me, or have me killed. But I am no child, now; I am a man-woman grown.

'Honorius.'

Her voice was barely a sigh. She stood beside me, staring at the hairless, mocking stone face that stood taller than she.

'His name was Honorius. He was a soldier. Videric . . . gave me the chance to go with him, after you were born. Videric's a good man – he was willing to keep you, bring you up with his name. You would have been Ilario Videric Valdevieso . . . '

She pronounced it mellifluously, almost absent-minded, that binding of patronymic and matronymic that I have so often, so privately, longed to have as mine.

'Until you were born. And that became impossible.'

She made a gesture, as if that movement could explain everything.

Perhaps it could: she pointed at me.

'Honorius was *poor*. I told you: you would have had nothing. *We* would have had nothing!' I saw her glance back – checking that the soldiers were not within hearing distance.

They did not hang back far. Absently, I acknowledged that good practice: for all they knew, this cave had other exits.

I could see none.

'Honorius.' I tried the name. 'My father.'

She shot me a glance. 'He went north, afterwards, to the Crusades.'

'And you exposed your baby, at the wolf's hour, in late winter.'

One of the first things Rosamunda told me, when we secretly met, was the day and hour of my birth. Valdamerca had only ever been able to say that I had been a good size. And cold enough to the touch that she was unsure I was alive.

Rosamunda's voice echoed in the shrine. 'Videric sent soldiers with me. I *couldn't* do anything else!'

A thought briefly crossed my mind: to wonder if the midwife had been paid off richly, or lay buried in some grave scraped in the snow-hardened earth. Nearly twenty-five years, those bones might have lain hidden there.

It numbed me. 'And the man I've privately called "father" . . . Videric has been preparing for – nearly ten years? To kill me?'

To make a second attempt. After my birth.

Rosamunda's voice came quietly. 'I couldn't refuse to speak with you when you came to court. Not once I saw you; not once I knew who you were! You were my child. I *made* him permit me. He's always done what I've asked him, until . . . I thought it would never happen, never be necessary; he'd never say to me that you . . . '

Beneath the numbness, I felt myself flooding with disgust and pity.

Disgust for this long betrayal. But pity because, do what she might for the best, this woman has still found herself caught in the position where she must harm what she loves.

'Blame your *father*!' she spat, shrilly. 'If Honorius hadn't come back, now – you're as like him as a painted image! You and he, you've only once to stand in the same room together, and all's lost! He's visibly your father. And you and he may both point to me as your mother!'

The sense of it only came to me slowly. 'This soldier, this Honorius, he's alive?' Twenty-five years on from my birth. 'And . . . come back from the Crusades?'

'Oh, he's back! *Alive*.' She stepped in front of me, her face pinched and spiteful. 'He has new lands near his damned goat-hut of an ancestral estate. I rode out there with your fa— with Videric. To look. No, Honorius hasn't come to court in Taraco yet, but that's only a matter of time!'

Realisation crept slowly in. It is not merely King Rodrigo manumitting me as a freedman, a freedwoman, that has panicked Lord Videric and Rosamunda, but the *visible* proof of what I am to them—

I caught the movement of her hand.

A signal.

Shock held me still for a heartbeat.

Armoured up, there was little visible difference between the two soldiers. Amalaric, taller, and with scuffs on his sandals and the chape of his scabbard, looked awkwardly at my mother, and then at the other guard.

The man Ramaz, speaking for the first time, said, 'All right then. Come on.'

His glance also touched on Rosamunda.

Videric has told them he wants *her* to do this.

The two men stepped forward. Amalaric's sword flew out of its scabbard with the soft hiss of steel against wood-veneer; Ramaz's followed.

Torches and candles don't light themselves.

The flaring torches in cressets, outside these caves, will be thrown away when they burn down to charcoal stubs. The beeswax candles in holders, on the other hand, above those high shelves of urns – those will be extinguished when the shrine needs to be in darkness, and afterwards re-lit, because they're too expensive to waste.

In Taraconensis, only the bell-end of a candle-snuffer would be made of metal. It would be mounted on a wooden pole. Here, leaning casually up against the wall, a black iron pole had a snuffer welded to one end. A pole long enough to reach the high candle-holders.

Amalaric carried his naked sword stupidly loose in his hand. Because he is only arresting a woman.

'Come on, now—' He reached out with the evident intention of putting his other hand on my shoulder.

They've decided Rosamunda won't do this.

Videric will have told them: *If she won't, you must.*

I caught up the six-foot length of iron pole in a quarterstaff grip; shifted my hands on the shaft; slammed the butt of it forward into Amalaric's stomach, full force.

Mail stops edge and point. Blunt impact, now—

Amalaric dropped to his knees as if I were a priest he knelt before. His mouth opened; his chest not able to get in air.

Two swift changes of hand-grip on the iron staff, the weight of it swinging it around. I held it by a quartered grip and one end. What I hold travels in a short arc – and the free end comes around with correspondingly greater speed.

The iron vibrated through my hands on impact.

Ramaz staggered into my mother, knocking her sideways, his sword-arm either bruised or broken, his sword clattering off among the grave-urns.

Rosamunda stumbled up against the rock shelves, sending a jar rocking. She clung, staring at me.

Folk-wisdom speaks of men's jaws dropping open in shock. The little sudden opening of her mouth, followed by no words, let me see Rosamunda come the closest I have ever seen anyone come.

I am man and woman both: is it *so* easy to forget to remind them I've been trained as a soldier?

Evidently.

I wiped sweaty hair back out of my eyes. 'I'm *not* going to claim you as mother. Or him – Videric – as father—'

The iron candle-snuffer, as I rested it down on the beaten earth of the shrine's floor, became a suddenly-welcome support.

'—as – stepfather. I never was! This is all *unnecessary.*'

The two men knelt, crouching, groaning.

She put her hand up to her complexly-braided hair, as if her fingers touching her veil and pearls reassured her. 'How can we believe that? And now you're a slave again, you'll tell, just to be freed! You'll claim Honorius, to be judged freeborn! You will!'

Amalaric choked and heaved in a gulp of air; Ramaz began to scrabble in an uncoordinated way in the dust among the urns.

Rosamunda is a courtier's wife, Aldra Videric not being best fond of the battlefield. Will she see how easily I can kill these two men?

And how quickly I will have to decide, and act, before they recover?

'Tell them to disarm!'

'You *have* to be silenced!' Her shrill tone echoed through the sanctuary-cave.

I swung the wrought-iron pole, bringing it up into a guard position. In the seconds while they remain stunned, I can kill both of them, provided the brittle iron doesn't shatter. But—

I looked Rosamunda in the face. Wanting to see relief. Belief that this need not happen. The flickering candle-flames illuminated only frustration, and greater fear.

'I'd never harm you!' I shouted. '*You have to believe me!*'

A sudden rush of footsteps thudded on the earth at the cave entrance.

Candle-light caught mail aventails, white surcoats, pointed helms; sword-edges, bearded faces – ten, twelve or more armed men running; pouring into the sanctuary—

'In the name of the Lord-Amir Hanno Anagastes, every man and woman here is under arrest!' a better-dressed soldier called out, curtly.

Past his shoulder, in linen kilt and hooded cloak against the night air, I saw Rekhmire'.

9

'You can't *do* this!' I snarled.

Rekhmire' snorted. 'Of course I can. I own you!'

My grip on the cold iron pole would not loosen.

The soldier Ramaz straightened up, swearing. He shot a glance at Aldro Rosamunda – and at the Carthaginian troops, since her face remained white and stark.

At a nod from the commander, Ramaz left his sword, limped across the cave, and picked up Amalaric with his uninjured hand under the other man's arm. Stronger than he looks.

The Carthaginian guard commander marched up to Rekhmire' and nodded casually in my direction. 'This your ladyboy slave?'

Rosamunda's face coloured a stained red that I could see even by this light. She glared at the Egyptian. '*How could you tell him that?*'

'I have no reason to be afraid of disclosing the description.' Rekhmire''s smile was small but complex. 'It is, merely, a description.'

'Enough of this here, sir.' The commander raised his voice from the respect with which he spoke to Rekhmire', giving orders to his men. 'Back to the house. Keep it tight. You and you – bring the slave!'

Not thinking, not feeling, I let one of the Carthaginian soldiers take the iron candle-snuffer from my hand. He had to unwrap my fingers to do it. He was not harsh.

It was not until I found myself walking Carthage's dark, unidentifiable streets among the squad of soldiers, the Egyptian pacing beside my guards, that I began to grab at one solid thing, an anchor in my shock.

I spoke to Rekhmire', across one guard. 'How could you bring these men? You didn't know where I was!'

His expression remained mild in the starlight. 'I thought that I did.'

'You did?'

Rekhmire' gave me an oddly companionable smile. 'I realised you'd just heard where the Lady Rosamunda was. I thought I had only to call out the Lord-Amir's guards and make my way there. And if not the rooming-houses, then you'd have left there and be on your way to the docks.'

'I wasn't.'

'No.'

The paved steps of the street took me by surprise, catching my sandals against the lips of stone. I was not just disorientated – I realised I hadn't been in this part of the city before. And if not for these soldiers, I would be gone.

'So how?'

'I guessed.' Rekhmire''s voice came out of the shadows. 'By two means. The first being that a Lord-Amir's guards have remarkable powers of interrogation – I think there's no man, woman, nor slave they didn't round up and question at the rooming-house. And, second – I remembered where you had been to paint, and one man recalled overhearing a foreign slave shout "child-killers".'

His tone had a shrug in it.

' . . . It's the kind of slur they remember.'

The soldiers' sandals thudded on stone. Taller walls rose up about us. The basalt and steel doors we passed had naphtha lights above them, painfully brilliant to a dark-adjusted eye.

We are among the rich of the city here.

'Of course,' Rekhmire' murmured, with that mildness that I suspected hid humour, 'I had envisaged myself arriving in time to save you from a dog's death. Instead of which, I arrive too late and find you've saved yourself.'

I ignored his irony. 'I'll never "save myself". She'll come after me again. I know that, now. She won't give up. And I do not – do *not* – want to be forced into killing her. Even in self-defence—'

'Is it that way? Yes, I feared—'

The commander's voice overrode Rekhmire''s: the squad turned and marched down a long tunnel that led through the solid walls of a building, sandals clashing on rock, and emerged into more bright naphtha-light and the inner courtyard of a mansion.

The light confused me. I stumbled with the group, guided here and there by a shove. The house was a blur of naphtha-lit corridors, and deep burgundy paint on plastered walls, and slaves peering around archways as we passed. I saw rich oak furniture. The more-than-life-size statue of a man carved in yellow marble, with his joints outlined in brass or gold . . .

We entered a room, and each man went down on his knees like a wind going over corn, except for Aldro Rosamunda, and Rekhmire'.

An elderly small man in a maroon-and-ivory striped robe entered from a different archway, easing himself across the flagstones with the help of a stick. He gestured as he walked; the soldiers rose; and he sank down into a wooden chair with a grunt of effort and satisfaction.

A few servants entered and stood behind him. The room seemed empty enough, apart from the chair, that it must be an audience chamber or justice hall.

I noted the man to have the features of Visigoth Carthaginians. Pale skin. Blue-grey eyes in a wrinkled face; his hair an equal mixture of yellow and silver.

His beard was clipped short and neat. My hand went automatically to my chin, and the soft down that was beginning to re-grow.

Rekhmire' bowed. 'Lord Anagastes; may the eight-fold gods protect the House of Hanno!'

'One will be quite sufficient,' the Carthaginian Lord-Amir said dryly. 'Well, Freeman Egyptian – this is what you disturb my dinner for?'

Rekhmire' bowed again, with no appearance of undue respect. 'This woman is attempting to kill my slave. I paid good money for Ilario; I see no reason why Carthage would allow a poor man to be robbed of his scribe. I therefore appeal to Carthaginian justice.'

The Lord Hanno Anagastes grumbled something to the effect that no man had ever seen a poor Alexandrine yet, and that he, Rekhmire', might have waited until the morrow, and that local magistrates got no rest.

Their tone was one I have often heard between patron and client in the court of Taraco, when not too much obligation separates the social ranks.

Does this house also have a library in which I would have found myself copying scrolls?

'Lord Rekhmire'!' I called sharply. 'May I speak to you?'

Rekhmire' glanced at Hanno Anagastes, received a nod, and crossed the room to loom close over me. In an undertone, he said, 'Unless you wish to be running from your murderous parent for ever—'

'Why should *Carthage* care if a Lady of Taraconensis wants to kill her—' I broke off. '—her offspring?'

Rekhmire's luminous dark eyes met mine. 'You're a slave. Carthage's justice can be invoked purely because killing another man's property is illegal. And because Lord Hanno Anagastes here is a fellow collector of scrolls. Do you want to spend your life looking for hired murderers at every corner? Because the pot *will* eventually be carried too often to the well!'

Stunned, I could only mutter, 'You're trying to *rescue* me? But – you don't know what—'

'I know more than I did before I questioned your mother's servants,' Rekhmire' remarked, expression bland. 'Trust slaves and soldiers for gossip.'

'But – *wait!*' I protested.

One of the Lord-Amir's servants called out in Carthaginian.

Rekhmire' turned his back on me, crossing the room and bowing in front of Hanno Anagastes again.

The Lord-Amir nodded. 'Command the Iberian noblewoman to come forward.'

She is my mother. Whatever Videric may have tried to force her into, she is my mother.

Videric, who, I think, I must accept is not my father. Because there is truth in her when she speaks of that.

Twelve or fifteen armed men in a room are a powerful inducement. I could see, between their surcoats and mailed shoulders, how very little Rosamunda wanted to come forward. She reluctantly allowed herself to be led by the guard commander into the clear space before the Lord-Amir's chair.

I took a step forward; one of the guards looped his fingers into my iron collar.

Air hissed in my throat as I choked. I could neither move properly, nor speak; the collar allowing the exercise of such control.

Hanno Anagastes demanded, in an exasperated tone, 'Why did your husband not offer Freeman Rekhmire' money for his slave?'

Husband. Oh that will please her! Aldro Rosamunda, from a country where noblewomen handle at least some of their own business affairs.

'My husband's not here.' She flushed. 'Lord-Amir – I had no idea who owned this slave. If I let it go, how would I have found it again? If my men had disarmed Ilario, then I would have been able to find this Rekhmire', and . . . ' She paused. ' . . . ask my husband to pay him money.'

I caught the Carthaginian Amir flick a glance to his guard commander. The commander shook his head.

Hanno Anagastes' thin voice filled the chamber. 'Carthage is a city composed of one hundred thousand people, and four times that many slaves. Skilled as this "Ilario" may be, I find it hard to think you could not have found another who would be as good a scribe. And you are a noblewoman, are you not, at your home in – Zaragoza? Taraco? And therefore not poor.'

Rosamunda flinched. 'My lord . . . '

Rekhmire' spoke up. 'She is Aldro Rosamunda Valdevieso Sandino de Videric. Wife of that Aldra Pirro Videric Galindo who is chief councillor to King Rodrigo Sanguerra of Taraconensis.'

That his poking into my business should have led him to get even their matronymic names correct . . . I twisted against the hand on my collar; could not get air to speak. I saw Rosamunda's tight face. There can be no hiding this – Hanno Anagastes would need only to send word to some diplomat up at the King-Caliph's palace for the same information. *But she doesn't want it said.*

Rosamunda carried her chin up, and her spine straight; she did not look at me. 'Is it not permissible, here, to kill a slave who is treacherous, or otherwise dangerous?'

'I'm neither treacherous nor dangerous!' The guard's sharp yank on the iron collar cut me off. I reached to get both my hands under the metal and release the choking pressure; the soldier next to him grabbed my wrists.

It was as if I hadn't spoken.

I am a slave. If slaves are questioned, it's under torture, because it's taken for granted we'll lie.

Hanno Anagastes frowned at Rosamunda, indicating me with his liver-spotted hand. 'This is just a slave: why should a noble lady desire to kill her?' He peered back at me. 'Or "him", is it?'

Rosamunda went utterly still.

Rekhmire's voice broke the silence. 'My lord, it is both.'

'"Both"?'

'Both male and female. The noble lady Rosamunda knows this. Four-and-twenty years ago, Ilario was born her child.'

'Shut your mouth!' I strained to throw myself forward as much as I could; reach the Egyptian.

The guard commander nodded: three of his men seized me under the arms; the flagstones bruised my feet as I tried to jam my toes into crevices, so as not to be forced bodily from the room.

The wall of the corridor hit my shoulder, hip, thigh; caught the side of my head.

The impact was enough that I slid down to sit on the flagstones among the soldiers' sandals. Half a dozen yards away, murmurous voices came from the justice-room.

'Let me go back in! I have to speak!'

The Carthaginian guard nearest to me drew his foot back; I dodged, and caught the well-practised swipe to the head from his companion.

I sagged against the plaster wall, its intricate geometric patterns blurring in my sight, and put my head in my hands. Pain throbbed. I saw Rosamunda's face in my mind's eye.

What else is the Egyptian saying?

Sick in my stomach, I realised I was feeling a cauterising pleasure in hearing these things said aloud. Or it might only be relief—

How could I keep such secrets? Nine years, ten years; how could I go without saying a word of the truth of it?

No, not relief. Nor pleasure. *I can keep secrets: could do it longer, if she will only trust me!* If my blood-father so closely resembles me that it's a scandal – let him go back to the wars in Castile and Aragon!

I suppose that it lasted no longer than a quarter or third of an hour; it seemed to go on all night. Rekhmire''s soft voice recounting, inaudible. My mother's tones rising in protest.

'There's the signal,' one of the guards said.

'Come on.' The nearer soldier reached down and hauled me up, hand under my arm; his fingers closing briefly over the side of my breast.

I glanced up at his impassive face, caught his hand as he moved it, and pressed it to the front of my robe, at my groin.

His stunned reaction let me walk back into the Lord-Amir's chamber without being held.

I looked forward, over the shoulders of the guards in front of me. Rosamunda's expression gave nothing away; Rekhmire' looked urbane. The Lord-Amir Hanno Anagastes didn't cast a glance in my direction.

'Here's my verdict.' Hanno leaned back in his chair, sparing no glance for me, his tone that of a man who has come to his decision.

'Aldro Rosamunda. You are a woman, and not responsible. It is, therefore, your husband, Lord Videric, who is responsible for this attempted theft and killing. And although it is only a slave, we take the sanctity of property seriously, here in Carthage. Therefore, I will tomorrow petition the King-Caliph to send a diplomatic envoy to the court of your King . . . Rodrigo, is it? To give a formal rebuke, that will bid him keep his noble councillor Videric under better control.'

'*No!*' Rosamunda's voice came softer than a whisper. If I hadn't had an agonised gaze on her, I would not have known that she spoke.

Hanno Anagastes stood up from the justice chair, and laughed at some remark of Rekhmire''s.

The soldiers relaxed, talking with each other as if I were not there.

I wiped my hands down the front of my gown, and realised that I was leaving sweat-marks on the white wool. The subtle difference in colour filled my vision.

A voice said, 'May I speak to you?'

I raised my head and looked at Rosamunda.

10

'Think about it before you do this,' Rekhmire''s voice unexpectedly interrupted.

A glance across the room showed me the Lord-Amir speaking to his guard commander, ignoring the fact that Rekhmire' had left his side. Soldiers still surrounded me. I echoed: '"Think about it"?'

Rosamunda glared up at Rekhmire'. The soldiers might have been furniture for all the attention she paid them. 'What business is this of *yours*?'

He spoke not to her, but to me. 'Ilario – *think*, for once!'

'Why do you speak to a slave that way?' Rosamunda's lips pursed together. She slitted her eyes, looking up at him. 'Fellow-feeling, is it?'

Rekhmire''s voice took on an urbane, slightly higher-pitched quality. The voice he used back at the house – and at home in Constantinople, I guessed, where there was no need to hide his being a eunuch. Where it's a signifier of high status.

'Ilario is an excellent scribe. Perhaps a painter, too – if Ilario ever stops thinking of your scorpion's nest of a family before all else!'

I opened my mouth to protest – and thought: He's *noticed* enough to make judgements about my family?

I hesitated; he spoke again before I could.

'And, yes . . . perhaps.' Rekhmire' sounded embarrassed. 'Fellow-feeling. Friendship.'

I couldn't listen to that. I looked at Rosamunda, small beside him. She made me notice not just the breadth of his shoulders and chest, but his height – the cloak he wore, with the hood pushed back, would have been ankle-length on another man; it fell in one clean line on him, barely to his calves.

All her clothing – the wispy veil pinned to her piled braids, the long gown with hanging sleeves – seemed fussy. No clean lines anywhere.

'What would *you* know?' she snapped at him. 'You're not a real man.'

It hurt, even if I knew she only spoke carelessly aloud what most people think.

Nor am *I* a real man. Nor a real woman either.

Rekhmire' turned to me. 'Think before you do this!'

I looked at him, helplessly searching for a response and not finding one.

'How long did you wait after hearing that she might be in Carthage, before you went chasing off after her?' he demanded.

I scowled.

Rekhmire''s shaped brows came down. 'How long was it after she tried to stab you, that you got on a ship out of Taraco? How long?'

'I don't know.' I shrugged. 'A few hours. Perhaps. There was a ship.'

'Ilario—'

'*She's my mother.*'

I took a breath, to steady myself. It might have occurred to me that I needed to speak as slave does to a master, but with Rekhmire' that thought didn't come.

'It was Videric, he was making her, influencing her – and now I find he's not even my father—'

I broke off. Thinking of Videric, showing me into the room of fountains, claiming Rosamunda wanted to speak to me . . . but he didn't know why. Lying. Lying, and with a perfect imitation of true feeling. Aldra Videric, the politician.

I let myself look at Rosamunda.

Pain broke something in me.

'Why did you never stop him? Why did you *let him* make you do these things? Try to stab me? Expose me when I was born? Are you *that* afraid of him?'

An unwelcome pang of sympathy defused my anger.

'Were you so much afraid of him that you couldn't go with this Honorius – my father?'

She gave a sardonic snort, much more the Aldro Rosamunda of the Taraconian court than the humble petitioner to a Carthaginian Lord-Amir.

'Why would I go with Honorius? He gave me a deformed baby!' She made an apologetic movement with her mouth. 'Ilario, I'm sorry. It was hard enough giving you up. The thought of such a birth happening again . . . And he had *nothing*. One of those ancient family titles that goes back to the Visigoth invasion of Iberia, with a tiny hunting lodge in the hills, and rents from a pair of goat-farms. I couldn't have stayed at court.'

She extended a hand to me, the glove off, her fingers pink and free of calluses.

'*You* would have had nothing.'

'I had Federico and Valdamerca and no "hunting lodge".' The words came out flatly; I could hardly believe I said them. 'I had winters where I went barefoot, because the shoe-money went to Matasuntha – she had to be married before 'Nalda and 'Nilda could. This Honorius – You said "nothing". I thought you meant he was just a soldier, like . . . '

I nodded across the burgundy room at Ramaz, who was wincing every time Amalaric leaned heavily on his shoulder, even if it was the other shoulder from his broken arm.

'A nobleman? That's not "nothing"!'

'A *poor* nobleman. *I couldn't have stayed at court!*' Her breasts rose and fell rapidly, under the laced top of her gown. She glared at me. 'I would have had to go north, to the border, to the Crusade. There would have been nothing for me but mud and Franks screaming down out of the hills and—'

'—no influence.' Rekhmire' cut in. He added, into her silence, 'No influence with a king, albeit through a husband. No playing the game of courtiers. "Nothing."'

Rosamunda's head moved fractionally. A nod of agreement, or a shudder of apprehension; it could be taken for either.

'*You could have told me!*' A few of the soldiers were evidently listening; I could take no notice of that, other than to attempt to speak lower, and I could not tell whether or not I succeeded: 'Told me that Videric's not my father! About this Honorius who could stand beside me and be visibly my father – point to you as my mother—'

I shook my head, feeling hot and cold under my skin at the same time.

'*Videric* could have told me. Or – no, that doesn't matter, does it? If you're my mother, and his wife, it'll be assumed I'm his.'

I blinked.

'Either way . . . I see it. It doesn't matter which way the scandal goes. If I'm said *not* to be his child – then you conceived a bastard by some man, and therefore Videric's been cuckolded, and looks a public fool. Or if Videric *is* thought to be my father, then he fathered a hermaphrodite. And in the public eye, that makes him a monster as well as a fool.'

If I had been chilled, speaking to Rosamunda in the room of the fountains, now I was boiling hot. I felt as if I might dissolve in it. Everything I am, melting away.

'*Why* did you tell me to run? Not because I was yours. Not because you didn't want me dead.' As a blow in combat can crush with numbness, before it hurts, saying these things out loud numbed me. 'Because . . . you wanted me to leave Taraco? No matter what?'

She looked at me with no appearance of shame.

I repeated what I had thought was only spite, on my part. 'Child-killer.'

'Evidently not. Here you are, alive.'

'I thought he forced you. Videric. You said he *made* you do it.'

'I never said I didn't agree with him – that it was necessary.' Her face altered. 'And I was right! See what's happened. If there's a diplomatic rebuke from the King-Caliph, it will all come out! King Rodrigo will know! The envoy . . . He will *say* that I'm your mother. Videric will be sent away from court. I— You have to stop this happening!'

Nine years at court has taught me politics enough. The King-Caliph will send his envoy to slap King Rodrigo's wrist. That in itself wouldn't be enough to put Videric out of favour. But if what comes out in public is the parentage of the recently freed King's Freak . . .

If no man knows, yet, about the adultery of my mother, then Videric will be thought the father of a freak hermaphrodite child – whom he has allowed to grow up as a slave in the King's court. Without a word of acknowledgement.

And sent his wife to kill.

Because Taraco is sometimes no more capable than Carthage of thinking a woman responsible for her own actions.

'Videric may have to put you aside. Divorce you. Disassociate himself—' Dizzyingly, my mind swung around. 'You lied. You *would* have killed me when I was born. Valdamerca found me by pure accident. How could you expect anyone to find a foundling, in the dark and the snow?'

This is obvious, now; how can it not have been obvious before?

'I thought you'd been forced into a position where you had to hurt what you loved.' The boiling liquidity of rage threatened to drown me. 'But that's not true.'

'I was! I did . . . need to see you.' She locked gazes with me. 'I did need to speak to you. You were mine. I couldn't . . . '

'You could.'

'You have to stop this happening, Ilario!'

Rage almost choked me. 'Even if I wanted to, there's nothing I can do!'

Rekhmire', his voice lowered so that the guards should not hear more than they had, said, 'Oh, there is a way.'

I looked at him.

'This is a court case over *property*.' He gently put his too-large hand on my shoulder. 'Tell me that you want it, and I'll free you. Formally. Manumit you here and now. And then it's merely a squabble between two freewomen of Taraconensis, and no business of a Carthaginian magistrate. This all becomes mere hearsay. The Lord-Amir will drop the case, I think, rather than bother King-Caliph Ammianus with a witness who can't be tortured into confessing the necessary truth.'

Rosamunda's face, filled with everything from fury to love, anguish to regret, stared at me.

With a wisp of what I thought of as Rekhmire''s own humour, I said to the Egyptian, 'You had to *tell* me this?'

'You would have thought of it yourself, afterwards, and asked me why I didn't.'

I glanced to one side. The soldiers still talked among themselves. I realised we'd fallen into an Iberian dialect of Visigothic – even Rekhmire'. *This must seem a local squabble, natives; nothing to concern Carthaginians* . . .

The Lord-Amir signalled to one of his slaves, turning away from us.

Through the arches of the mansion, I could glimpse other slaves. There would be couches in another room, where Hanno Anagastes' food waited for him.

A bare second, to decide. To speak.

Rosamunda's voice creaked, 'You must want to be freed . . .'

I looked at her.

'I'm done with protecting you. And with protecting him.' I turned towards Rekhmire'. 'I'll earn the money to pay you for my freedom, like I said. Bit by bit. Don't free me now.'

11

A month or more after Rosamunda left the city, I sat in the tophet, my wooden resting-frame in front of me; hot wax and pigments steaming in the cool air.

She has no real compassion or love, but I am not free of her yet.

It's been less than a season: why would I expect it, in that short time?

The sky above me was a black that defied words, containing, as it seemed to, an orange reflection that did not brighten the dark. The shadows of the junipers held a metallic green like the carapaces of beetles.

The desire for sunlight – for the yellow glow of sunlight on old stone – was a gnawing desire. A craving. I want blue skies, deep and shining, with the band of milk-blue haze at the horizon . . .

Instantaneously with my looking up at the viridian line of the sea, a man's voice remarked, 'The weather changes remarkably little, under the Penitence. I dare say high summer is no hotter than the spring you get in Iberia.'

A priest? A man bringing a sacrifice?

Neither.

'Lord-Amir.' I put my irons down and stood, avoiding kicking over my bronze palette box by a minute margin.

Hanno Anagastes leaned on his stick. 'Your master gave me leave to speak to you. He tells me he allows you to paint.'

The little wizened Carthaginian wore white silk, over layers of robes; the two men behind him were less noticeable in the dark, and maroon livery. He took no notice of his armed guards' presence. He leaned forward, peering at the lime-wood board I had been painting on.

'Not an icon,' he said, at last. 'You paint no face except Lord Baal's, and the picture is not focused on him.'

The wax would cool in my palette box soon, if I didn't add more coals. I squatted down by my brazier, picking up tongs, and replenished it, all the while feeling the Carthaginian's displeasure.

'It's all *background.*' His pepper-and-salt brows dipped down. 'All decoration and no subject!'

Straightening, I spared a glance at the painting. The truncated stone pillars that bore Baal's face were not the focus, no. I would not expect such a man as Hanno Anagastes to notice. The outline of the junipers beyond, and the two-thirds of the flat board that was sky – and from which I had scraped off the wax twice, completely, this morning – might seem background, to an eye not educated to new things.

Tempted to say *How I waste my pigments is my own affair!* I gave him a brief court bow. Not a time to show disrespect, with his soldiers there ready for disciplining a slave.

But, I thought, again, I might be immune from normal treatment. He wouldn't come here and speak unless he wanted something.

I shrugged. 'I thought I would paint it to show people what it's like.'

'*Paint* it.'

'As Messer Tommaso paints the hills of Rome, now he paints Rome, not generic hills that *symbolise* the city of the Empty Chair.'

'Freeman Rekhmire' said you were mad.' The Lord-Amir Hanno Anagastes spoke as if he had no concept that he could be either rude, or contradicted. 'Can you paint funeral portraits?'

I can charge him fifteen; twenty, perhaps. More money for me to save towards freedom. Or perhaps buy one of those poplar- and acacia-wood boards I saw in the market, priced as high as bronze.

'Yes,' I said.

'Good. Freeman Rekhmire' said you have a neat hand.' He stared at the painting again, shook his head, and visibly dismissed it. 'I want a funeral icon for my granddaughter.'

The thought is always sobering. I bowed again, Taraco-fashion. 'How old was she, lord?'

'She would have been three, in the autumn . . . ' He lifted the tip of his stick from the hard-packed earth, and gestured away towards the sanctuary entrance. 'She's there. Her name was—'

'*There?*'

Surprise all but choked it back; I blurted it out, nonetheless:

'Do you expect me to paint a formal funeral portrait for a child you *sacrificed*?'

His stick hit the earth sharply. 'Don't blaspheme!'

For a long moment we stared, each at the other, under the shifting light of Carthage's Penitence.

Finally, I spoke. 'Lord-Amir, at home, many say the Penitence is a penalty for your child-sacrifice. Although indeed some say not – instead, that the people of Carthage killed some prophet, or sold him to his enemies and *they* killed him, and the Dark came here . . . But most say it is the dead children.'

'Ah. Ah, *that* story.'

He did not condescend to sound as if he explained, but Hanno Anagastes spoke while he stared away towards the sanctuary of Baal.

'When a child dies at birth, or soon after, we give them back to God. They haven't been alive long enough to have forgotten His presence, or truly left it . . . so they come here, to His sanctuary. Stillbirths, early miscarriages, children whose spirits die in the night for no cause.'

His pale eyes moved as he looked at me.

'Hanno Tesha is there. You will paint her.'

'I thought—' Saying the words aloud would cause him pain. *I thought those were the bones of children that you people killed!*

Stunned, I muttered, 'There are animals' bones in there too.'

Because sometimes you try to cheat the god; sacrifice a goat instead of a child—

'Children have pets.' Hanno's shoulders, under his layers of robes, were thin; so much became visible when he put great weight on his walking stick. 'Tesha's little marmoset will come here when it dies. I dare say she misses it.'

'They're *all* . . . ?'

He seemed to catch himself, as if becoming newly aware that he spoke to a slave. 'I desire it done within the week. A portrait for my grandchild. You may inform Freeman Rekhmire' I have given you this commission.'

'It's a graveyard?'

'Do you think we're *savages*?' His shrewd eyes fixed on me. 'I don't care what you do up in your Taraconian hills, goat-boy. Goat-*girl*. Bury your still-births outside consecrated ground, like as not! This is the children's garden. Think yourself lucky your master allows you this trade. I would have your head on the Palace gate, otherwise.'

Dumb, I bowed. I thought him momentarily on the verge of giving up his desire for a funeral icon, or his desire for one from me; ordering his soldiers to beat me, breaking fingers and wrist-bones.

Fury. I had seen no priests here since the day that one chased me. And it occurred to me, now: *perhaps he was no priest, but only a parent.*

The anger transmuted in Hanno Anagastes. He shook his head.

'They do say we gave the Prophet Gundobad over to be killed.' He spoke as if we stood in an academy of formal debate, and not a crematorium of the unborn. 'Centuries ago. Who knows? Who knows how long the darkness has covered us, or if this Penitence was even imposed for that, if we did? You will not be a slave for ever, I think.'

That startled me into looking into his face.

'If I were to buy you,' Hanno Anagastes observed, 'I should certainly manumit you in my will, and I am old and cannot expect to live long. An artist's talent should be used. You are wasted as a slave scribe. Shall I ask your master to sell you to me?'

This man wants to *buy* me?

I bowed my head with a sudden show of respect. That let me hide my face before he saw shock on it – where he would expect joy.

'I'll . . . ask him to speak to you, Aldra Hanno; thank you.'

He didn't move for a moment. His stick finally tapped the shadowed earth.

As if I had made a quite different statement, he said reluctantly, 'Very well.'

He knows I won't ask Rekhmire'.

I think he knows I find this offer suspicious.

Hanno Anagastes looked around at the graveyard. He said quietly, 'You should remember that punishments do not need a reason.'

It might have been philosophy; it might have been threat. I could tell nothing from his tone. He turned without farewell, and walked away between his soldiers, into the darkness.

I found my palette box cold, the waxes congealed; I dropped brushes and a smoothing-spoon, from sheer clumsiness.

This place should feel less bloody, less savage, less sad, if it is a graveyard – and it does, but I find it no less disturbing.

Disturbing, too, that a man wishes to buy a slave he doesn't want. Apart from one or two pieces of indifferent quality, I'd seen no paintings in the House of Anagastes. Certainly nothing of the New School.

This morning I'd let the house-slaves know (as I must) that I might paint at one of two places; an urge woke in me to move to the other. The hollow eyes of Baal's face would need to be repainted . . . *No, cannot be*, I thought, looking at the half-finished board.

To paint them with knowledge I'll need to paint them again, from the beginning.

It took me a while to cool my instruments, and pack all away; and a while longer than that to make my way down past the Bursa, to where guides shadow the rich merchants' houses, and offer to show their foreign guests the sights of Carthage.

A small sum to a man whose name Rekhmire' had given me as trustworthy would provide both a guide, and assistance in not being knocked over the head and robbed when I was lost in laying the wax and blending the colours.

'We can walk,' the man Sarus said, shouldering my easel. 'The first of the pyramids are close to the city.'

He was correct. We walked for no more than twenty minutes outside the walls before we came up from a gully, and I felt the dry tingle of the desert wind. My hair stood up on that part of my neck which in dogs is the scruff.

The daytime darkness of the Penitence shivered in the sky, veils of crimson and blue twisting away on the southern horizon.

A mile away, the first of the tombs of the King-Caliphs stood. *And I will need to be this far from it, to paint*, I realised. Or else how can I get the size of it in?

The pagan ancestors of Carthage built pyramids of brick, covering the sides with plaster facing. Great masses of colour shrouded the sloping walls, hues distorted by the auroral light – a hundred thousand men had been set to painting images so huge as to be properly visible only from a distance. Even under the Penitence, the pyramid facing me clearly showed a rearing lioness, the crescent moon visible on her brow: the image itself taller than Carthage's walls.

I found I couldn't paint.

Sometimes it's so. This new form of painting isn't a mechanical skill. With the panorama of light and darkness in front of me, I sat cross-legged on the rock; tinkering with the *cera Punica*, and letting colours impinge on my mind as I fruitlessly mixed them. Rubica, sinopis, orpiment, caeruleum: red, brown, yellow, blue. Nothing I can match to the real colours in front of my eye. The chill wind, and Sarus's sandals kicking up sand as he trod the immediate area, faded from my perception.

To paint an icon to represent the city of Carthage will be easy. Crenellated walls, blue-tiled towers, men in robes and pointed helms. And in a corner, indicating distance and heraldic importance, a tiny triangular shape.

To make Carthage resemble its unique self . . . to make that corner into the foreground . . .

I ate Carthage's fish-biscuit (which the poor eat); shifted a corner of my cloak under myself on the chill rock; and found I was thinking not of Taraco, but about Marcomir.

I'd walked down to the docks once to look at Donata's rooming-house – still open for business – and caught sight of Marcomir on his way to work at the customs hall. It would be no great hardship to wait between the windowless walls of some alley and hit him with a cudgel, and kick him until I ceased to feel pain.

The turn of his head, as I saw it, reminded me of the attraction of bodies. Which had been genuine, and mutual.

Gazing now at the plain prepared board on the easel – calcium sulphate and egg-white; tinted with blue to add darkness to the Penitence's colours – I wondered whether it would be revenge if I beat him. Or merely the prejudice of the normal man against the man who is effeminate?

But then, I am the last to think of myself as normal.

And I would have to know whether it was the woman-part of me that desired Marcomir, or the man-soul, or both.

The idea of leaving Donata and Marcomir to prey on travellers felt distasteful. Rekhmire' might be persuaded to speak unofficially to someone in his wide circle of acquaintances in Carthage, I thought. It could be hinted to Marcomir that his customs job depended on his mother's rooming-house sticking to legal ways of fleecing foreigners . . .

I doubt there'll be more penalty – it's not Carthaginian citizens they've been robbing, after all.

Focusing again, I realised that the veils of light picked out two men in the sweep of land, coming up by a roundabout way from the city. Trudging figures made minuscule by the pyramids.

I hitched my cloak up around my shoulders, aware that Sarus squinted into the dim distance with me.

The men forged closer, across rock and sand.

'It's the Egyptian.' The lines of Sarus's shoulders loosened. 'He don't look *worried* by the man with him.'

I suspected Sarus, with his worn sandals and habit of standing with his hands relaxed at his sides, had seen service in one of Carthage's many legions. Certainly he thought easily in terms of hostility and acquiescence.

The man with Rekhmire', as he came close enough to be seen by the torches I had put up to help me paint, I thought also to be a soldier.

And not a Carthaginian soldier: he wore a Frankish brigandine, and hose.

The sight of clothing potentially from home brought me up onto my feet. My cloak fell down behind, onto the rock.

'Ilario!' Rekhmire' raised a large hand in greeting, and finished with an authoritative gesture that sent Sarus off to patrol a perimeter out of earshot.

The walk had daubed the Egyptian with dust to the knee. Rekhmire' swatted sand from his linen kilt, and glanced at me from the sides of his eyes. 'I've brought someone to see you. This is Honorius.'

I managed the single word. 'Honorius.'

The man with Rekhmire' looked me in the eye.

'Honorius, your father. Hello, Ilario.'

12

Wind-flickering torches showed me the newcomer standing almost as tall as Rekhmire'. Thinner, though; bare-headed, and dressed as a common soldier – under the blue velvet shell of his brigandine I could see the outline of the riveted iron plates.

This Honorius had hooked the buckled strap of his helmet over the pommel of his sword, so that the steel sallet hung, if not conveniently, at least usefully inverted at his hip: his mail gauntlets stuffed into it for safe-keeping. His uncovered head showed hair cropped short in a Frankish cut, as often adopted by Iberian crusaders in the north. If his hair had been black once, it was grey now.

I heard myself sound ungracious. 'What do *you* want?'

I saw no likeness in his eyes, under the torches and the aurora's dim light. I have Rosamunda's eyes.

Everything else of his face – chin, cheek, broad forehead, prominent nose – was a more masculine form of my own.

If I sketched myself, I would need only a few lines to change it to Honorius's face. That, and age. Stand us together in the same room, and—

Father.

'*Well?*' I demanded.

Honorius grinned, not taking his eyes off me, but speaking to Rekhmire'. 'You were right. There's no doubt!'

I demanded of the Egyptian eunuch, 'Did *you* bring him here? From – Iberia?'

I couldn't help staring at Honorius. Plainly a knight. He seemed to draw himself up, but not stiffly; his body kept the lanky, relaxed attitude of a cavalry soldier. And he must be close on fifty.

'I was in Taraco.' Honorius's voice held a rasp under the surface: years of shouting to be heard over the scream of edged iron, and the hollow percussion of guns. 'I've been buying new estates in the west. This – man – sent me word that you were here. My daughter-son.'

He said *that* without hesitation.

I stooped, catching my board as a gust of desert wind would have taken it off the easel. 'And . . . what do you want?'

'I want to adopt you.'

Slowly, I replaced the board and straightened up.

'As an adult. Formally legitimise you.'

Standing this close to him, I could see a shining quality to his eyes, despite the poor light. As if there was water there, and it might overflow.

'You're joking.' I glanced at Rekhmire', who said nothing. 'He's joking, isn't he?'

Honorius forged on. 'I have no heir.' The grin broke out on his face again. 'Except that I do! I've spent nearly thirty years cursed; I could give no wife of mine a child that lived. And – here you are.'

'I was here all the time.' I stared at him. 'In Taraco.'

'My career's been in the north. I'd planned to come home to retire.' His hands, by his side, clenched. I realised that he wanted to embrace me – and that it was not revulsion which held him back.

'You were there all the time. If that woman had told me—' He broke off. 'All this is too soon! It'll take time to get used to. For both of us. What do you want, Ilario?'

I turned away from that demand, glaring up in a blind rage at the Egyptian. 'You sent him a message? To King Rodrigo's court? With all that's happened!'

Rekhmire', who had gazed off with every aspect of politeness at the distant pyramids, turned back to me. His light voice was calm.

'As you can imagine, there's been considerable gossip among the trading houses. I listened while I was buying scrolls. I heard that the King-Caliph's diplomatic envoy did arrive in Taraconensis – and heard that the court is duly in an uproar. And I heard about Messer Honorius, here, and how he had indeed returned from the north to estates near Taraco. I thought it a good thing to send word to him. That's all.'

Honorius narrowed his eyes, staring at the Egyptian as if he reassessed him. 'You "heard" much, it seems. You're not a *spy*, are you?'

I couldn't help but laugh. Tension dissolved out of me.

'He gets a lot of that,' I said gravely, at Honorius's questioning look. 'Messer Honorius—'

Honorius interrupted. 'Is it too soon for you to call me "Father"?'

He put up a sun-browned hand, covered with old white scars, and corrected himself:

'Of course it is. Ilario . . . I'd planned to stay a few weeks in Carthage; I'd hoped we could learn to know each other.'

He pointed a scarred finger at Rekhmire'.

'This man, your owner. Should he desire to stay here – or leave Carthage for somewhere you do not wish to go? – you need not be with him. I can buy your contract and free you.'

The offer brought me up short, although Rekhmire' didn't look offended.

There are sound legal reasons to be a slave at the moment, but that was not why I bristled. My spine stiffened. 'This collar comes off when *I* say it comes off!'

The man who is my father and the eunuch who owns me exchanged a look that, in the midst of our tension, was nothing less than thoroughly amused.

Rekhmire' shook his head. '"You try". I said that, didn't I? "*You* try!"'

'Oh yes . . . '

I stared from one man to the other. 'I'll earn my freedom. And when I've paid off my debt, then nobody owns me except me. Is that clear?'

Honorius nodded. 'That's clear. And I'm proud to hear my son-daughter say it.'

I blinked at that.

Buying my contract.

Buying new estates? I suddenly thought.

'Rosamunda told me you were poor!'

Hearing my own exclamation made my face heat.

'Not that I wish to know anything of your private business—'

'It's *our* business. Family business,' Honorius interrupted firmly. He rested his hand down against his scabbard. 'I was poor, when I knew Rosamunda. I've been quite successful as a soldier, since.'

'You don't dress like it.' I grew still hotter. *Why is my foot firmly in my mouth?* 'That is . . . '

Honorius smiled, openly amused.

'Master Rekhmire' advised me to travel as a commoner – and with a small household. Apparently drawing attention to myself is a bad idea.'

If he was willing to discuss household affairs in front of the Egyptian, that argued he either thought Rekhmire' had a right to be there as my purchaser – which I frankly doubted – or else, in the time he had evidently spent getting to know the Egyptian, he recognised Rekhmire' for my only ally here, and would not rob me of that reassurance.

Which says something about both his judgement of character – if he hires soldiers, he should be accomplished at that! – and his own character.

Rekhmire' observed, 'Master Honorius is, in fact, a Captain-General.'

Honorius's voice took on instant military authority. 'I've retired!'

'A man doesn't retire from his reputation.'

Rekhmire' bowed his head, self-possessed, and addressed me without taking his eyes from the older man's face.

'Ilario, your father recently resigned from leading the royal armies of the House of Trastamara against the Franks. He is credited with keeping the borders of Castile-and-Leon intact. This is that Captain-General Honorius Licinus, known as *il leone di Castiglia*: the Lion of Castile.'

Despite the dark light, I could see my father visibly shifting from foot to foot. His embarrassment in front of a son-daughter he never thought to have was touching.

Honorius shoved his hand abruptly through his cropped greying hair. 'Ilario. Go where you wish. With this Egyptian if that's what you want, so long as you're safe. I've no desire to interfere. You're my only living heir: everything will come to you in the end. But I hope that you'll come home to see the estates, when this scandal dies away.' He coughed, clearly embarrassed. 'I have a house in the city, too; I need not disturb you while you paint.'

Despite appearances, he may be no different to the rest.

'You don't want to be seen with a man-woman?'

His lips pressed together; his head nodded very slightly.

I had a lurch of cold sweat before I realised it was not agreement – only an acknowledgement.

'Frankly, Ilario, I'm too old and too influential to have to care!' Honorius appeared to catch a look from Rekhmire'. He stiffened, and rode over what the Egyptian began to say: 'I would be proud to be seen with you, Ilario. Whatever you decide, I hope you'll visit me, at the least, even if living with an old man would be too tedious.'

Rekhmire' interrupted my muttered rebuttal. 'I doubt Ilario's life will be *tedious*, no matter where he – she – lives . . . '

'Rome,' I put in firmly.

I caught Honorius's questioning glance.

As well to get this mentioned before any other plans are made.

'Rome is where Mastro Masaccio has his workshop – Tommaso Cassai, the painter of the New School! – I don't suppose you have much acquaintance with painters—?'

The lean, tall man showed an infectious grin. 'Had a few of them designing banners and siege equipment for me, in some of my companies.'

It stopped me dead for a moment.

'This – this is different.' I found I was waving my hands, gesturing at the board on my easel. 'Masaccio and the other new artists in Florence – they paint nothing except how the world *looks* to the human eye!' It was difficult not to pace on the uneven rock. 'Mastro Cassai must have a hundred men in a week asking to be his apprentice – but I've studied drawings of his frescoes, I've been using his techniques in my own work, I can show him; he'll see that *I'm* the one he should teach!'

Honorius unfolded his arms with a creak of the brigandine. Unexpectedly, he reached out and ruffled at my hair, despite my lacking only half a head of his height. I suppose he had missed the chance when I was seven.

If I didn't manage to conceal affront, it only made him smile.

'So, this Masaccio – that's who you want this scribe to sell you to?'

Not for the first time, I regretted my papers lost in Donata's hearth-fire. 'An apprenticeship will do just as well.'

Honorius looked apologetic. 'Excuse a soldier's rough humour. Messer Rekhmire' here told me something of your skills as a painter; I only intended to make a jest.'

This is my father! I realised anew; the shock of it seeming to come in distinct waves of surprise, joy, shock, and distrust.

I squatted down to pack up paints, brushes, bowls, pestles, charcoal, and all the other paraphernalia, giving me time to think. Because I must think, for once.

Abandoning the mussel shells containing my mixed pigments, I stood up again.

With a cold clarity, I realised, *Rekhmire' thinks I have a need for allies.*

Sarus's sandals crunched on the gritty rock, approaching. I signalled, sending the guide patrolling back off towards the north-west. He was used to me acting in Rekhmire''s name: he obeyed a slave's orders without question.

Carthage's naphtha glow whitened the black horizon.

I faced the Egyptian.

'You haven't told all of what you heard from Taraco. And you didn't go to the trouble of getting messages all the way to Taraco without a good reason. What else has gone wrong?'

Honorius folded his arms, nodding to himself. I didn't have opportunity or time to enquire into his look of satisfaction.

'Pessimist that you are, Ilario!' Rekhmire' snorted, but I thought he looked relieved. 'It seemed to me that I *should* search out news from Taraco . . . '

He hesitated.

' . . . If only because there have been several offers made to me, in these last few weeks. Very casual, but genuine offers – to buy my slave-scribe. And much as I admire your cursive script, Ilario . . . you're not that good.'

The grey-haired soldier Honorius looked massively affronted.

I realised it was on my behalf.

Despite the dread I felt at hearing the news, Honorius's reaction was oddly warming. If his newly-discovered son-daughter is a slave – well, then; he'll have me be the best slave possible!

'Lord Hanno!' I blurted.

The memory coming back vividly, I recounted how Hanno Anagastes had found me at the tophet in the morning hours, and what he had said.

'Four offers to buy, then,' I concluded, momentarily cheered by Rekhmire''s failure to conceal his surprise.

'And they've taken to approaching you directly . . . '

The two vertical pleats in the skin between Rekhmire''s eyebrows deepened, the fineness of the shadow's gradation so unlike the conventions of funeral portraits.

A look passed between him and the man who was my father.

'Damn Carthaginians,' Honorius grunted.

The Egyptian inclined his head, acknowledging the point. 'As I confessed to you when you arrived, Master Honorius, I believe I may have made an error of judgement.'

'What error?' I looked from Rekhmire' to Honorius. 'What's happening at home?'

The soldier shrugged. 'Doubtless the usual nonsensical court business, no different to Castile or any other kingdom—'

'It was my intention—' Rekhmire' looked uncharacteristically as if he hadn't realised he was interrupting.

Honorius waved a hand. 'Go on. Tell the boy. Girl.'

Honorius looked openly embarrassed by his confusion, which reassured me. He admits me hermaphrodite, without pretending I'm man or woman.

'It was my intention,' Rekhmire' repeated quietly, 'in Lord Hanno's court, with the Aldro Rosamunda, that I would break the threat to Ilario's life by breaking the silence about Ilario.'

Honorius gave a slow nod of acknowledgement.

'If more people knew of the secret than Ilario alone . . . then, I thought, there could be no point in murder to ensure Ilario's silence.' Rekhmire' folded his arms across his bare chest. 'Truthfully, I didn't expect the matter to travel very far, or make more than a small fuss. I thought Aldro Rosamunda hysterical in her insistence that disclosure would be disastrous for her. The dust would soon settle, I thought. It's possible that . . . Recent developments suggest . . . '

He looked increasingly embarrassed.

' . . . It's possible that I was not entirely correct in my supposition of what would result from Lord Hanno Anagastes' judgement.'

I cocked an eyebrow.

'Aldra Videric's a powerful man!' the Egyptian snapped. 'Aldro Rosamunda is his wife! How could she fear a scandal, and her husband the richest man in Taraconensis apart from the King? I assumed the end of it would be what normally occurs with the rich and powerful – any scandal concerning them would be hushed up afterwards; silenced, disposed of!'

I stared at him as he sliced the air with his large hand. 'You might have told *me*!'

'Yes, I might – and I would have been wrong!'

He drew a harsh breath.

'There are so many rumours now, in Taraco . . . If the scandal hasn't been squashed . . . Ilario, I may have ignored the way in which spite would be a motive for attacking you. Or there may be something else behind this—'

Fear and impatience made me rude. 'What *else* did you get wrong!'

The Egyptian took out a finely-woven cotton kerchief and dusted fastidiously at his hands. 'I underestimated the use Carthage would wish to make of a scandal.'

Honorius's narrowed gaze, that I saw returned regularly to our surroundings, scanned rock and desert and desolate valley as if the Egyptian's words didn't come as news to him. In the distance, Sarus lifted a reassuring hand.

Rekhmire' went on quietly, 'The diplomatic rebuke in Taraco seems to have been . . . more effective than one would ever have imagined. It is enabling them to make demands of Taraco. And as long as you're available to be questioned, Ilario – or for producing to order – Carthage can keep this scandal alive. Hence their wish to buy you.'

'I thought you said it would be hushed up!' I know the machinery of gossip in Taraco: I have no wish to take another turn as its focus. 'What does Carthage want?'

'To take advantage of the Aldro Rosamunda's stupidity.'

I must have looked as if I would interrupt him with another question: he gestured to me to keep quiet.

'The Carthaginians want grain,' he said shortly. 'Need grain. Look around you! Iberia is their grain-basket. The King-Caliph here rules over Granada and the south, with legions and a "governor" friendly to North Africa – Taraconensis would be a valuable addition to their lands.'

I stared, taken aback. *This is not the scale at which I have been thinking.*

Rekhmire' shrugged. 'The Carthaginians can't be seen to destabilise Taraconensis too openly. Not if they hope to send in their legions and a local governor in the future, to save it, when the kingdom is obviously too weak to stand against a Frankish invasion and needs the protection of Carthage.'

Cold in the desert darkness and sputtering torches, I asked, 'What do I have to do with this?'

'This is the confidential part of the letter I received, which I share with you because it concerns you.' His gaze weighed and judged Honorius. 'And your father. The Carthaginian diplomatic interview with King Rodrigo Sanguerra took place in private. The King-Caliph's envoy, one Stilicho by name, began by requesting that Lord Videric be extradited back to North Africa, to be put on trial for his crimes – since, obviously, Aldro Rosamunda had been acting on his orders.'

'They *what*?'

Rekhmire' faintly smiled.

'Oh, I doubt the envoy expected any agreement. And that demand met the reception it deserved! The next request was – that in view of the scandal, Videric should step down, and resign his position as First Minister.'

'He wouldn't.' I was sure of nothing so much in my life. 'Videric would never do that.'

'It seems your King Rodrigo pointed out that any responsibility was in fact Aldro Rosamunda's, not Aldra Videric's. To which the envoy replied that in such a case, where the woman had attempted murder, if only of a slave—'

Rekhmire''s amused gaze met mine, over Honorius's scowl; I thought that part of his information had come verbatim.

'—in that case,' Rekhmire' emphasised, 'the Lord Videric would certainly put his wife aside – the envoy said – and divorce her. To prove his own honesty. She ruins and dishonours Videric's own reputation. She's a murderess. And, after all, she's a barren woman; any bishop would give him an annulment.'

The ironies of that were not lost on me. Nor, I thought, on the Carthaginian diplomat they had seen fit to send to Taraco, and who doubtless had heard from Hanno Anagastes that I was Rosamunda's child.

Honorius had his arms folded, an impatient expression on his face. 'And? He was told he might take a shite on his request, I assume?'

Rekhmire''s smile slowly faded.

'My colleague from Zaragoza has no account of what passed between them then. Or, indeed, between Lord Videric and King Rodrigo, when they met privately, afterwards. But – the upshot is, Aldra Videric has returned to his country estates, leaving the capital, and taking Rosamunda with him. The post of First Minister is – unoccupied.'

'*What?*'

In the silence, I heard only the desert wind.

It seemed too much to take in. Videric has been First Minister at court all the years I was there – for all the years I've been alive, if I thought about it. No man would expect to see him leave. Any more than they'd expect the great palace at Taraco to fly away.

'Are you sure you've been told the truth?'

'As sure as I can be. It seems, incredibly enough, as if the King of Taraconensis gave Aldra Videric an ultimatum. To rid himself of a dangerously volatile wife – or to leave the court. And that Lord Videric chose, not power, but his wife.'

Slowly, reason began to penetrate my shock.

'King Rodrigo can't have scandal near him.' I pieced it together, the mentality of years as court fool returning to me. 'Especially if it's true that Carthage threatens him. Videric looking as if he ordered my death – is too much. The only acceptable choice would be blaming it on my mother Rosamunda ... And Videric won't put her aside? What hold does she have over him!'

'You would know more than I.' Rekhmire' shrugged broad shoulders. '*We* know the Aldro Rosamunda bore one child, but as far as the world is concerned, it's she who can't give Videric an heir. Any other lord would have had the marriage annulled as soon as he could. And, if for some reason he couldn't do that, he would have taken mistresses and legitimised his bastards.'

The family of Lady Rosamunda, the Valdeviesos and the Sandinos, are not particularly powerful; that much I discovered for myself over the years. Videric need not keep in with them. That he should choose to let Carthage manipulate him in this way, that he should reject his King's express order . . .

This is not how I am used to thinking of Videric.

Rekhmire''s voice took on a musing quality. 'He has already shown more than common bias by remaining married to a woman perceived as barren, and living without an acknowledged heir.'

I caught a look on Honorius's face. Evidently he feels he has unfinished business with my mother

The Egyptian scowled. 'I should have realised he'd be reluctant to put her aside, whatever the true reason for it is. And now, what I had expected to be a two-day wonder and then die away . . . does not.'

'She has some political hold on him.' It was a sure conviction, deep as the chill making itself felt down my spine. 'But that isn't the immediate concern, is it? What happens now?'

'It . . . may be wise if I take my scroll-buying business out of Carthage for a time.'

Rekhmire' smiled, evidently intending reassurance.

'I doubt that I'll be knocked over the head in a dark alley and have my slave stolen! It's not considered at all wise to offend the Pharaoh-Queen. However . . . I mistrust the spite of the powerful.'

'Ilario.' Honorius surveyed me shrewdly. 'Is it safe for you to come back to Taraco if you're under my protection? I know you don't know me well, but would you trust me that far?'

The impulse to agree instantly was strong.

I suppressed it.

Wryly, I thought, *Seeking fathers and mothers miscellaneously has not yet helped improve my life.*

'You've been away in Castile,' I said. 'Pardon me, Master Honorius, but I may well know Taraco more recently than you do. I don't think any of us should go there until it's known what's going on.'

Honorius did not look insulted. He gave a slow, considering nod. I thought him torn between desiring my immediate trust, and being pleased by a lack of impulsiveness on my part.

The wind blew dust across us in a skein. I'd find fine sand embedded in the drying surfaces of my pigments, I realised. Nothing to be done about it now.

I thought this was over!

Rekhmire' swore by a pair of gods, and busied himself cleaning grit out of his eye.

In the preoccupied tone men assume on such occasions, he murmured, 'What would you yourself suggest, Ilario?'

I offered him my water bottle. A shiver of realisation suggested to me that I might be being tested, here, by being asked that unemphatic question in the presence of more experienced men.

And that makes the difference between being treated as a freeman or a slave more surely than this iron collar.

'Your book-buying trade, Master Rekhmire'.' My mouth was drier than the desert air could account for. 'I'd suppose you can go to more or less any large city and still be working for the Pharaoh-Queen – ah – the Pharaoh-Queen's Library?'

Rekhmire' rinsed his eye, dabbing at the lid with his kerchief. The corner of his mouth twitched. 'I'd suppose that, too.'

He handed me the leather water bottle, and folded his now-wet and muddy cloth. Monumental and grave, but not quite restraining a smile, he added, 'Why do I have the impression that you're coming up with a reason for your master to go somewhere to your advantage?'

'Because that's how you taught me to think . . . '

It conjured a smile out of him, but that didn't last long. I squinted against the wind, conscious of Sarus distantly turning and beginning to head back to us. Clearly, he saw nothing hostile nearby.

We are the half of an hour's walk from any city streets.

I have not thought of this place as a wilderness before. Or even as an empty place suitable for an ambush. With Rosamunda out of Carthage, I assumed this would be at an end. Now – I do not even begin to see the end of it. Or the end of my connection with her.

But I'm done with letting her control my life.

The wind blew out of the south. A wind that will take ships out of the harbour here.

I crouched down, under the daytime darkness and the aurora that swept from blue to crimson, and set about finishing packing up my tools and brushes. As I worked, I glanced up at my father. 'Where will you go, Master Honorius?'

Flesh creased at the corners of his eyes. I couldn't see if he narrowed his gaze against the now-brilliant purple of a rolling aurora, or if he smiled.

'I sailed with only a few men, as Master Rekhmire' recommended – but I can send word north fast enough. I dare say a good number of my household guard would be happy to accompany us – since they've by now found out that farm-work has to be done every day . . . '

His tone made me smile, rather than his weak joke.

And – he's just offered me an armed escort. Because he's worried about my safety.

This man is concerned on my behalf.

On top of that realisation came another:

Rekhmire' . . . Rekhmire' sending a message to Honorius was not the act of a slave-master.

One outsider to another, perhaps?

Carefully wrapping boards in prepared cloth, I said, 'Messer Honorius, I'm sorry I can't call you "Father" yet. I would like that time together. But I'll go nowhere near Taraco.'

The soldier hid it exceptionally well. I know the shape of that face in disappointment, however, since it's my own.

Conscious of a tight feeling in my stomach, I continued. 'But, since you're willing, and if Master Rekhmire' agrees – would you send word to your household, and travel with us?'

Honorius grinned, and I could see what he'd been like as a boy. The cheerfulness informed the posture of his whole body.

'You're a scribe, aren't you? I'll pay your master, here, and *you* can write the letters to my people! Ah – if we're leaving Carthage . . . where are we going?' Honorius demanded. 'Where am I about to be dragged off to in my old age?'

It would have seemed crass to crush his optimism by saying *Let's succeed in leaving Carthage first.*

And now I get to see in what state *I* leave this place.

My bag stood packed, ready for me to sling on my shoulders. The pale ghosts of painted pyramids will haunt my canvases and boards. I glanced back and up at Rekhmire', to see if he would merely issue orders.

In the shifting crimson light, and with his self-control, he was unreadable. He said nothing.

He's waiting. Judging.

I straightened up, brushing dirt from my knees under the hem of my slave's tunic. 'Being a pawn in Carthage isn't safe. So we should leave. Why *not* take refuge in Rome?'

Rekhmire''s head tilted, chin jutting with an air of challenge, and Honorius gave me a watchful stare. Both men with their arms folded, they resembled a pair of gateway statues. I let neither of them get out an objection.

'Master Rekhmire – you can buy scrolls in any city. Your colleagues will write to you, I expect, or visit if you ask, so we'll discover what's happening in Taraco. Perhaps even before Carthage realises we're gone. I know that Rome's a backwater—'

It will not remain a backwater, not with Mastro Masaccio down from Florence to paint frescoes, and who knows what other painters of the New Art being commissioned to join him. But this is not the time to mention that.

'—no one ever travels to the Empty Chair, but that's what makes it safe for us! Or safer than anywhere else I can think of. Messer Honorius ought not to go back to Taraco just now. And, yes, you yourself could go home to Constantinople – to Alexandria, sorry – but that'll be expected. Those roads and shipping routes are the first places Carthage would look.'

Rekhmire''s brow creased. He exchanged a glance with Honorius. Both men relaxed, slightly.

'Safer!' Honorius grumbled good-naturedly, looking as if he quite liked the prospect of adventure.

The Egyptian nodded. 'Well, certainly safer than Taraco or Alexandria, which are the first two places any agent of Carthage would go looking for us . . . '

I caught up the bag of tools and slung it across my shoulder. 'So, then, if trouble is coming, we'll be out of the way of it! We'll leave Carthage, travel to the Empty Chair, stay there – I can seek out Master Masaccio, and you can make sure we're better informed. We'll have Master Honorius's soldiers. What do you say?'

I couldn't help a crooked grin.

'What could possibly go wrong?'

Part Two
The Empty Chair

1

'All of these paintings are rubbish!'

Master Masaccio swiped me a sharp tap across the back of my head. 'What's *this*?'

Slave reflexes stopped me hitting back.

'My head? Mastro?' I added, somewhat bewildered.

'Exactly. Your head. And how big is it?'

I could only stare, confused. *Is he saying that I'm conceited?*

'Eyes. Nose.' Masaccio pointed at my most-prized painting – done not face-on, as encaustic wax funeral portraits are, or profile as bas-reliefs are shown, but in a three-quarter profile: a woman sitting with her head turned as if to the life.

'Ear,' he continued, pointing. 'Mouth. Chin, even. Where's the *head*?'

He swatted the back of my head again. It stung.

'Do you even *know* how large the skull is, compared to the face? How much head there is above the eyes and behind the ears? *No!* None of you amateurs do! Because you think the *face* is important, and you don't paint what you *see*.'

I had chosen my study of Rekhmire''s cook, back in Carthage, to first show to Mastro Masaccio, because I was abominably proud of that portrait. I wondered why, given the stiff lines and lack of any proportion – her head now appeared to be cut off flat not far above her eyebrows, and there was no swell of skull behind her ears.

Why was this not *apparent to me while I painted?*

'Rubbish!' He flicked casually through my stacked boards. 'Complete rubbish!'

The voice of Tommaso Cassai, nicknamed 'Masaccio', sounded completely certain.

'Masaccio' in the Florentine tongue can mean 'clumsy, bad Thomas', 'Thomas the blunt', or 'Thomas who is rude' – but not 'Thomas who is a liar'.

'They can't be!' Shocked, I reached to grab the portrait, set out on his wooden easel-frame. My peripheral vision caught Rekhmire' holding out his hand – and pulling it back, evidently thinking better of assisting a collared slave in public.

The dizziness that went through me threatened to make me fall or puke.

Doing either will be bad.

I swallowed, hard.

Masaccio snorted. 'Complete trash.'

I could only stare.

'You have not even *promise*! See, here—' He rapped his knuckles against the heat-glazed wax of my painted acacia boards. I winced as the sound echoed around his high, cluttered workshop. 'This "city wall with tower". Straight out of a pattern book! And these figures. You've painted men on tiptoe!'

'Like every fresco I see in a church!'

The colours swam in front of my eyes. I ignored the doe-eyed faces and jewelled belts and robes and looked at these my images of men.

Flat, facing out at the viewer, lined around with black. The tips of their feet pointed down in front of them.

'How else?' I said, bewildered. 'The body and face painted as if a man faces them straight on. And the feet are painted as if seen looking down from above. Everybody understands that! How else is it to be done!'

The bearded Florentine painter shook his head, looking up at me. 'You are an untutored barbarian. Perspective. Perspective, boy!'

I bristled at that but couldn't bring myself to say *I am no boy.* I'd intend *I am full-grown, adult,* but it would bring the truth too forcibly to my mind – here in this city where I am determined, now, to pass for male.

'What about the light?' I demanded. 'The . . . '

Words deserted my mind. I pulled out and stuck at the front a treated lime-wood board. Colours shone, encased in wax. Behind the painted masonry walls, I'd coloured the skies of Carthage under the Penitence. *I wasn't thinking of men, but of landscape—*

I stared at the painted city walls.

It's true.

These might be the walls of any fortified town in Iberia. Pattern-book style: 'this icon signifies a city'. At best, the architecture is a little in the Visigothic style. But as for it being specific – being Carthage, that great city of the King-Caliphs, rather than Zaragoza in Aragon, or Taraco, or—

No. There's nothing.

Why haven't I seen this myself!

The skies outside the workshop's great clerestory windows showed autumn grey. Brighter by far than the Penitence, but I felt as if the cloud's weight settled into me. The colour washed out light, energy, hope.

'Well . . . *this* is not without some merit.' Mastro Masaccio held at arm's length a small board I had left half-done. 'This is what you saw, no?'

Above the desert, above the regular sides of a small triangular pyramid, veils of green light rippled. The aurora. I remembered standing with the scent of the heated bronze pallet and liquid wax in my nostrils, staring up, feeling as if the curtains of Heaven were about to be drawn back.

'But—' Masaccio pointed at the triangle. 'No! *This* is not what was in front of you!'

The walls of the pyramid outside Carthage had been too large and detailed to cram into that small area.

'But it's what I know is there. The tombs of the King-Caliphs—'

'But you could not see all of it. Not with all this sky!'

'How can I paint what I see, if I don't paint what it means?'

The small, dark man nodded, as if I had finally said something of note. 'And that is the question of the New Art. Come. See. Here.'

Ignoring my supposed 'master' Rekhmire', he led me past the work-benches where the pestles and porphyry slabs for grinding colours stood interrupted in their cleaning. It was a large workshop: it was, nonetheless, crowded to the oak-beam rafters with the gear of a painter – rods of thin silver, for drawings that would oxidise brown on prepared paper; stoppered bottles of pigment after pigment, colours so rich that I all but tasted them; a squirrel-hair brush in the process of careful construction; a hundred differently shaped brushes hanging from their hooks; pots of bone-dust, size, and every type of varnish you might imagine . . .

Ranks of stacked paintings stood against the room's far wall. He pulled one out – surprisingly, painted on gesso on canvas, I realised, rather than on wood.

'This is a study for a fresco. I've done many for chapels – sermons on walls . . . This one, this is in Pisa.'

I caught a glance from the side of his eye which didn't match his emphatic tone. As if waiting to be judged, even by a slave who's asking to be his apprentice.

The painting's background was a flat gold, like any church icon. Likewise the discs of haloes, behind the heads of saints and angels. But the Empress-Mother in her green robes, and Her Divine Child . . .

'You've painted statues!' I blurted out.

It was true enough: the painting's flesh had the look of glossy pearl-white stone. Round enough to be tangible.

'They're . . . ' I realised I was making vague hand-gestures, as if I could capture the nature of the woman and naked child more easily that way than in words. 'They're . . . weighty.'

He frowned – but not from anger. Concentration, perhaps. 'I'm making mass out of value changes . . . Yes, it's too heavy here; flesh might indeed be marble. But once edge is abandoned, then depth or lightness of tone must take the place of outline . . . eh!'

He made hand-gestures of his own. It felt as if we both sought a vocabulary not yet created, or one *being* created, here in his workshop, and back in Florence; hammered out on the anvil of the New School's art.

The light and shadow of the Empress-Mother's face was as if I looked through the board at a real woman sitting on the other side of it. If this is done only by varying tone, hue, brilliance . . .

'I can't see how you do it!'

Masaccio grinned. 'Look, boy, I understand why you have come to Rome. I see you have the exact same ambition that I do: to be the best painter in the city of the Empty Chair, at the centre of the civilised world. But the difference is, *I* am Tommaso Cassai. And you are not.'

Rekhmire' raised an eloquent eyebrow, which I thought might query Masaccio's location of the civilised world's centre. I didn't allow the Egyptian the time to speak.

'If those—' I gestured briefly at my stacked boards, carried so carefully from Carthage to Rome. 'If those are trash, teach me otherwise.'

'No,' Masaccio returned instantly. 'You have not the talent. Look at you, how old?'

'Twenty-four.'

'Twenty-four, and what have you done?' He spoke arrogantly for a man who looked only three or four years my senior. 'These are mediocre. It would be better if you had done nothing. You've spoiled what little talent you had on mundane, trivial work. Do you even draw?'

The abrupt question startled me. 'Yes.'

'How long since? When did you start?'

I shrugged. 'I don't know. Always, I think. My foster-father used to hit me for wasting time drawing with a stone on the walls, when I was a small child.'

The sharp points of flints had been good for scoring lines into the crumbling plaster walls of Aldra Federico's villa; I could still feel the sensation in my fingertips.

'I drew the horses that the men unsaddled in the stables.' I added, 'It wasn't until I came to King Rodrigo's court that I learned the encaustic technique for pigments in wax.'

Masaccio grunted. I thought he sounded surprised, as if it was not what he expected to hear. Hope pierced clear through me; I felt my fingertips prickle and go cold with it.

'Still,' he said thoughtfully, as if holding a conversation with himself, 'you have all the old dross embedded in your technique. How could you unlearn that?'

'You did!' I burst out.

He stared at me.

'*You* must have unlearned the old school of painting,' I emphasised. My chest hurt with the tightness of my breathing, as well as the bandaging that flattened my small breasts under the Frankish fashion of thin, tight doublets. Holding the gaze of his black eyes, I added, 'If you can do it, so can I!'

'You're too old, now.' He turned aside, dismissively. 'You should have been drawing each day, every day, since you were ten.'

'I did – from before age ten—'

'I would have you spend six years grinding colours; then you would learn mixing, and it would be another ten years before you would be allowed to work on any painting to come from my workshop. No.'

Rekhmire' made a quiet interruption behind us. 'I've said that I can pay sufficiently for an apprenticeship. But is there no other work my slave might do here?'

His level tone made my temper flare. I clamped down on it. Masaccio turned back from the workshop tables. His eye had a look of interest in it – but not for me.

The planes of the tall Egyptian's face, and his disproportionate hands and feet, made him an automatic object of interest. His linen kilt looked not so out of place here as I'd imagined it would – and I realised why. Rekhmire' might be one of the Old Testament patriarchs scattered about the place in Masaccio's sketches. His size and height gave him the same gravity.

'You are a man of Egypt-in-exile. Castrato?' Masaccio hazarded.

Rekhmire' gave a social bow. 'We are not here to speak of me. In the matter of my slave here . . . might he begin as a servant?'

'I have all the servants I need.'

'Then, some other way in which he might aid you here, and meanwhile learn from what he sees—'

The Florentine interrupted with an over-loud laugh. 'I couldn't even use him as a model! His hips are wide enough for a woman!'

Another man wouldn't have noticed it. To the untutored eye, I look wiry: a man of medium height. I saw Mastro Masaccio looking at me in the way that a painter looks at the body and bones of men. His gaze lingered on my crotch, where the Frankish fashion for tight hose necessitated a cod-flap covering the bulge of my male genitalia. His gaze lifted to my chest.

He gave an absent nod. ' . . . And the shoulders of a man.'

I found my hand going up to smooth the fine down of hair on my cheek, sparse as it still was after my unshaven travelling. *I am a man, see: how could I be otherwise?*

Rekhmire' caught my eye, his gaze disapproving. I set my mouth.

Masaccio shook his head at me. 'You could model for neither man nor woman. Or both!'

I stared at him. Frustration kept me rigid. No use to plead. Nor bluster – not with a slave's name-collar resting around my neck.

I need him to teach me how he paints.

I need him to teach me how he sees.

'Wait!' the Italian said.

He approached me where I stood between the work-benches and easels. He squinted with the practised gaze of one used to perception by north light. I fisted my hands to stop them shaking.

'You have a Spanish colouring,' he said.

I nodded, stiffly. 'I'm from Taraconensis, in Iberia.'

'That would be well. A touch swarthy. And the rest of you . . . '

His head rose and fell as he studied me. I sweated. Any moment now he'll see – because he is a man who sees – what I am: hermaphrodite passing as male. And then I'll be beaten, hunted through the streets; perhaps burned at the public bonfires the Franks love so much—

'Cardinal Valente has paid for a painting of the Betrayal in the Garden.' Masaccio's black eyes closed to slits; sprang open again. 'I have no model for Judas.'

He smiled up at me with white teeth.

'Until now. A man who looks neither a man nor a woman – or looks like both! What could be more monstrous? Or more fitting? Mastro Rekhmire', I'll take your slave on as a model for the Great Traitor. Is that a deal?'

2

Rekhmire' took a deep breath as we stepped into the narrow street outside the workshop. 'There is a man who deserves his name!'

The control Rekhmire' could exercise amazed me. My hands were vibrating. I took an equal breath, to see if it would calm me too. 'You were happy to stand there and have your slave insulted!'

His mouth twisted as I mentioned the subject of slavery. It might have been amusement, or some other thought in his mind.

Not able to hold back, I spat out, '"Judas!" The Franks think of Gaius Judas as a villain! It's adding insult to injury – I'm a bad painter *and* their Great Traitor!'

Rekhmire' laughed ruefully. He glanced down at me as he shook out his Frankish woollen cloak, and swung it around his bare shoulders. The garment sat oddly with his kilt and sandals, and the reed head-band around his brow.

'Ilario. He was testing you. To see what mettle you have.'

'I know.'

'Yes.' This time Rekhmire' inclined his shaven head as he put up his cloak-hood. An acknowledgement?

Stepping out into the fine rain, he added, 'I haven't seen you – restraining your impulses in that manner, before.'

I threw my own cloak across my shoulders and followed Rekhmire' between the heavy, high buildings. 'He wanted to see if he could drive me out.'

'I congratulate you for the realisation of that.'

In the chill air and the failing rain, I could feel my face burn. To assure myself, privately, that I need to be less impulsive is one thing. To hear it from another—!

Rekhmire' gave me a disarmingly friendly look. My temper subsided.

We walked back towards our lodgings. I glanced up at the narrow sky. In the twelve interminable days it had taken to get an interview with Master Masaccio, I'd slogged morning and evening around every column and temple and atrium, bath and forum and amphitheatre, of ruined Imperial Rome. My eyes dazzled at first with the proportions of thousand-year-old architecture. Now—

I miss Taraco's heat. And Rome is failing.

'Well.' I stretched my arms to the rain, feeling spine and tendons realign. 'It puts off considering how I would live here for the seven years of an apprenticeship, as things stand now.'

Rekhmire' answered my look with one of his own, that was particularly reassuring.

'Master Honorius has twenty-five years he wishes to make up for: he would pay your apprenticeship unhesitatingly.' The Egyptian shrugged. 'And I did not lie: I would pay to have a slave trained. Although the painter would treat a freedman better.'

'All of it leaves me indebted,' I remarked.

The upper floors of most Roman buildings have crumbled away. Leaves dropped past my face with the rain, falling from shrubs embedded high in the brickwork. There was not one high wall without a tracery of weeds, or tiny rooted saplings. My fingers ached to draw the rotted shutters showing the sky through empty window-frames. And reproduce the texture of skin-tight moss on fallen monuments. Or attempt to.

Neither of these men would regard it as a debt, but – and then there is Carthage—

The moment's inattention cost me my balance. The surface of the street was in no less disrepair than the buildings: cobblestones out of their holes like teeth out of an old man's jaw, and slippery in the wet. I stumbled out of the way of a two-wheeled *cisia*-cart, lurching into the Roman men and matrons crowding the narrow streets, and found myself shoved back against Rekhmire' with curses.

Rekhmire' steadied me, his sandalled feet padding between dips and puddles with a flawless certainty that in another mood would have made me grin.

'You may be certain,' the Egyptian remarked. 'The Mastro would not have given you a job of any kind if he had not seen something in you.'

'*Ahh!*' I came to a dead halt in the street and slapped my hand against my forehead. The crowds parted, not amiably; and flowed around us.

Rekhmire' looked genuinely alarmed. 'What is it?'

'Sculpture! I should have told him! *I paint statues!* Instead of being a model, I could . . . '

Rekhmire' shrugged as he met my gaze. In that moment I saw it had both occurred to him as a choice and been dismissed.

'"Old art." Would it impress Master Masaccio, do you think, that you can practise that skill? Or would he think it merely something else on which your time is wasted?'

I grunted.

The Egyptian didn't press for an admission that he was correct.

Which would have been less irritating had I not realised quite how correct he was.

'This place is *shabby*,' I complained, as we began to walk again. '"Holy city." "Centre of the civilised world!" There's nothing here but – but – an empty chair. There's no centre of power here.'

The Egyptian looked silently down the several inches between our heights, and raised his eyebrow. He won a grin out of me.

'All *right*. I'm *in* Masaccio's workshop. Even if only as a model.'

I can watch. I can *learn*.

'Carthage's curse is darkness,' Rekhmire' murmured, slowing at the end of the street, next to the Tiber River. Looking for the entrance to the alley that led to our lodgings. 'Rome's curse is an empty Papal chair. History can lay a heavy hand on the present.'

'Yes, I know.'

He shot me a glance. I wondered what had come back to him, in that moment. I see Rosamunda's face: the face of my mother when I tell her that I *know* she planned to kill me when she abandoned me as a baby.

I have acknowledged that it happened. And now it has no influence over me. No, none.

'Messer Egyptian?' a voice called.

Rekhmire' turned with a smooth power in his movement. He didn't carry a sword, any more than I did; Frankish religious law not permitting it within the city walls. As a eunuch bureaucrat, I realised, he might not be trained in arms.

In a brawl, his tall, powerful body would go a long way to defending him. *And I have been trained to be a man.*

There seemed nothing to justify apprehension. No bandit or Carthaginian spy was visible. Only a small, elderly man in clerical robes, his hands tucked under his arms against the chill. He looked as though he had been waiting.

I moved my hand away from my dagger.

'A message from Cardinal Corradeo, Messer Egyptian,' the elderly man said in a squeak, wiping moisture from his nose. 'He will see you tomorrow, when it's convenient to you; an hour past noon, perhaps?'

Rekhmire' bowed with his hands crossed over his chest. 'My compliments to your master. I will attend on him at that time.'

His hands came down and out, and with that movement acquired something in them. I saw him palm a coin into the secretary's hand, and the little man bobbed his head and hurried off.

I cocked a brow at Rekhmire', in much the Egyptian's own fashion.

He smiled. 'There are forbidden books here, that the Franks themselves may not read. I hope to copy some for the Royal Library, at home. Being already a heathen, how can I be harmed by the sight of them?'

The look of innocence accompanying his last words made me grin.

'A Cardinal—' I stumbled over the unfamiliar church title. '—is truly prepared to let you into forbidden archives?'

81

The Egyptian began to pick his way down the street with the delicacy of a cat that dislikes getting its feet wet, incongruous in such a large man.

'On the one condition. That if I find anything relating to lifting the curse on St Peter's Chair, I turn it over to him. Corradeo is hoping I'll see something he won't, because he supposes I have knowledge from the Royal Library. I doubt that will happen.' Rekhmire''s expression under his shielding hood took on a faux innocence. 'Oh, and I must let him take the credit for whatever I find.'

That made me chuckle.

A thought wiped amusement out.

'Will you need me as a copyist?'

'No. I think it will take quite enough to persuade them to let one man in. I'll have to do my own copying.'

I was unsure whether that was generosity on his part, so that I might go to Masaccio's workshop, or useful truth; and while I frowned over it, he stopped, and pointed me towards our lodgings.

'You go on, Ilario. I realise I intended to pass by the Alexandrine house again, and see if there are letters for me.'

Which would make once every two days that he had gone to his embassy in this city, I calculated. Regular as a water-clock.

'You think your "colleague from Zaragoza" will have written to you yet? Or anyone else?'

'I have hopes.' Rekhmire' pulled his hood further down, against the rain and men seeing his face. 'I don't otherwise know whether to take this lack of news to be reassuring – or a silence before a storm.'

3

Outside the tenement lodgings, the scent of sweating beasts filled the rainy air. The horses of a *carrucas* snorted – the four-wheeled cart which men use to carry baggage and cargo to the sea-coast at Ostia Antica. Beyond them, similar muscles straining, men wrestling with roped boxes. I felt the shapes of the thick arched necks in my fingers.

One deep voice pierced the noise:

'*That* one first! Then these crates here. It shouldn't take you fifteen minutes!' Honorius's gaze shifted from the work-crew to me. He beamed. 'Ilario!'

The boxes had the marks of the small artisans' workshops, up behind the cathedral that housed the Empty Chair itself. Rosaries, for the most part: made in light materials like pearl-shell, attractive in Iberia for their foreignness, and usefully no different in structure whether one worships *Christus Imperator* or the Frankish heresy.

'You got everything packed up in time?'

'Yes. Get 'em taken down to the warehouses in Ostia and stored.' He spoke with satisfaction, stepping back to eye the cart with the vision of a man used to calculating bombard and baggage loads. 'Old mercenary company habit: trade light items . . . When the Egyptian gives me word it's safe, I can start exporting back to Taraconensis. All his letters from "book-buyers" in Iberia – if he's not a spy, he damn well *should* be!'

I gave my father the best innocent-slave look I could muster. 'He gets a lot of that, too . . . '

Honorius snorted, and turned back to settling payments with the carters, still laughing. I went into the house, hugging my secret news to me since I would not tell him in company; stumbling on the tiles in the inner rooms, blinking in the indoor twilight.

I set about igniting oil-lamps, the light blossoming up the plaster walls, and returned to some of the tasks I had left half-done before going out.

'Casserole?' Honorius remarked hopefully as he bustled through the low door, shaking rain from himself, and looking over my shoulder with ease. He frowned as I pressed the last of the clay seal around the edges of the pot.

'Not unless you plan on eating charcoal . . . '

'Spent my life in military camps, remember?'

Through a laugh, I explained, 'Charcoal for drawing,' and shifted the heavy pot over to the oven, where it could sit in the banked embers through the night. There were twelve of the small wired bundles in the pot; I thought that should last me my first month in Masaccio's workshop. 'By morning, I'll either have my own willow-twig charcoal, or . . . '

'Or—?'

'Or lots of crumbly little bits of wood.' I straightened up, one hand in the small of my back. 'Used to take a pot down to the baker's in the square at home, at the end of the day when he'd finished working. He'd always let me put it in his ovens overnight. That was vine charcoal, though. Better for drawing.'

About to leap from that to Masaccio, and my news, I saw my father looked distant. As if he remembered those few of the Taraconensis hills that will bear terraced vines, and the taste of the grape.

'I never know . . . ' Honorius frowned. 'Whether I should *expect* to see you play the housewife and bake meats. Or whether you don't cook when you're dressed as a man. Or whether you don't cook at all. I don't know what your nature is. Are you determined to keep up this charade?'

He jerked his thumb at me.

At my clothing, rather.

Frankish doublet and hose, in the Italian style, and not the slave tunic of North Africa's climate, which is worn equally by male and female.

I couldn't keep asperity out of my tone. 'I would have thought you'd prefer a son. Don't men want that?'

Finding your long-unknown, long-lost son-daughter is one thing. Travelling together can be another. For some reason, while it didn't bother him who turned my head in the street, how I dressed was an abrasive matter between us.

Honorius spoke bluntly. 'I'm not ashamed to have a ladyboy as my heir. But *you* seem to be ashamed, here. Is that why you pass as something you're not?'

I sat down at the table, leaving him standing over me.

'I have to be man *or* woman. It's not safe to be both in Frankish lands.'

Or in most other lands, outside of specific roles such as Taraco's court.

I strained my neck looking up at my father. His blue eyes were pale enough to be grey indoors, even with the room's shutters still open. I would need a highlight on the cornea, and a catch-light in the white, to make his eyes stand out emphatically enough in a painting.

'As a woman, I wouldn't be permitted to paint. And to be a woman and a slave . . . Legally, that makes me an animal. So I keep part of me hidden and play all the man.'

Normally he would have sat down companionably with me; I knew by this how disturbed he felt. He scratched at his hair, leaving himself with the curled short tuft on the crown of his head that everything – removing his linen-lined helmet; standing at a wind-ridden ship's rail – appeared to give him.

'A woman . . . It's not *that* bad, their life.'

I couldn't help giving him a raised brow. 'You would know?'

'Ximena – my late wife—'

I said nothing more. No man – or no man like Honorius – desires to listen to anything that would make him think his wife unhappy. Less so when there's no mending it after death. She might have been happier than most women, but that was based on supposing him as good a husband as father.

'I try to think of you as a son and a daughter in the same body,' he said earnestly. 'Is that not what you'd have me do?'

I wanted to say *You're doing well*; what fell out of my mouth was, 'You don't need to try so hard!'

Nothing on his face showed him affronted, but I saw it in the lessening curve of his spine and the movement of his shoulders.

Biting off each syllable, he said, 'I have missed twenty-four years.'

And I. Bitterly frustrated by not finding the right words, I managed all that I could put into speech. 'I'm – very glad you answered Rekhmire''s message.'

The line of his shoulders released itself. He dropped down onto the opposite bench, smiling across the table. 'So am I.'

I had rested my hands on the table to feel the grain, where much scrubbing clean had raised it above the surrounding soft wood. I registered my fingers in peripheral vision, stained with wax and umber and red lead, and looked up to meet Honorius's eyes.

I couldn't help beaming. 'I didn't tell you yet – Masaccio accepted me into his workshop. *Only* as a model. But—'

'Ilario!' He slapped his open palm on his thigh. 'I didn't like to ask when you came in; I thought . . . But this is wonderful! A beginning—'

'*Eightfold GODS!*'

The street and inner doors slammed, so close on each other that it was one blast of sound and cold air. Rekhmire' ducked to miss the low beams of the tenement-house ceiling. He threw himself down on the wooden bench beside Honorius, hurling an armful of scroll cases to the table-top.

I caught two before they could skitter to the floor. 'Good news, then?'

Rekhmire' gave me a look that would have melted glass in a Murano workshop.

One of Honorius's fists banged a ceramic bowl down in front of him, and the other a bottle of wine.

The Egyptian inclined his head in a way that told me, at least, that he was both pleased and surprised.

'*Finally*, news,' he corrected, untying his cloak at the throat, and wiping his hand over his shaven head.

'From home?'

I should have stood to serve him, but found I couldn't.

'Some of it.' Rekhmire' poured himself a bowl of wine. 'Sahathor sends me every whisper, rumour, and gossip; but of hard facts—! Heh and Hehet of the infinite spaces! How much *rubbish* the man writes!'

His large hands twisted the tops from cases and swept scrolls open, anchoring them that way with ceramic pots and jugs. Honorius gave me a glance. I gathered my father to be much amused by the bureaucrat's unbureaucratic swearing.

And to be waiting with as much apprehension as I felt.

Rekhmire' sat back, resting his large hands on the heap of papers. He looked from my father to me.

'There has been no time to write to Alexandria and get a reply, but I have consulted with some colleagues in the embassy here. I have not told more there than I thought any man should know, nor mentioned your names. Simply put, it isn't in Alexandria's interests to have Taraconensis destabilised, and Carthage made stronger. I would be no man's favourite if I said my error in Hanno's court might lead to that.' He flicked a gaze to me. 'Including you, I know.'

Any resentment had gone, I found, startled. 'You did the best you could at the time, with the knowledge you had.'

Rekhmire' reached across the table. His hand closed briefly and surprisingly over mine before he leaned back again. 'In the event that the Pharaoh-Queen communicates personally with me through the embassy, I think that the message will scrape the ears off the side of my head . . . '

'Let me write back to her.' I couldn't help smiling at him. 'I'll tell her it wasn't your fault. And my marvellous cursive hand will win her over.'

Since I knew that monumental gravity well by now, I could see how much humour he hid.

'I can only hope the autumn weather prevents a too-speedy delivery of post . . . '

'So.' Honorius indicated the scrolls with a wave of his hand. 'Where do we stand?'

I reached out for the last crumbs of cheese on one plate, although I could barely swallow. If I could paint their faces, in this remarkable mix of day-lit oil-lamps and rain-light coming in through half-shuttered windows . . . My master, the bureaucrat; my father, the soldier; myself, the artist. Because I will be an artist, I reminded myself. No matter what word comes from home.

From outside I heard the shouts of the *carrucas*-drivers. And the spatter of rain.

'Videric *is* gone from office. It's confirmed from many sources.' Rekhmire' traced a line of hieroglyphs on one sheet. 'There are no public rumours about Aldro Rosamunda's attempt to kill you, Ilario. The Lord Videric is supposed caught with his hand in the treasury chest, or in some other way under the King's displeasure. The Carthaginian envoy has taken ship back to Carthage . . . '

Honorius grunted, picking up a heel of loaf and tearing shreds of crust off it. 'Putting some distance in, so that if the King's tree falls, they're not caught shaking the trunk.'

Rekhmire''s smile was a rictus twitch. His oval eyelids were stained blue, I realised; with a lack of sleep that I thought only I had suffered these last few weeks. He rubbed hard with his thumb along the ridge of his brow.

'Ilario . . . Like it or not, you're still the key to this. These, here, these are the stories that are being spread around by Lord Videric's supporters. You'll see they all say, one way or another, that he's retired to his estates because he's *ill*. Not thrown out of his position as First Minister, but in bad health. Why would he claim sickness?'

I shook my head.

'Because,' Honorius rumbled, scowling, 'a man recovers from sickness.'

The Egyptian gave a swift nod. 'Quicker than from scandal. Videric's men are evidently preparing the ground so that he *can* return, in the future, without his dismissal or resignation ever having to be acknowledged. Why would King Rodrigo be willing to have Aldra Videric back as his First Minister?'

Grudgingly, I admitted, 'Because he's good at what he does?'

'That, too. And also, other kings and princes *believe* Taraconensis stronger while Videric is Rodrigo Sanguerra's minister. But, no.' Rekhmire' picked up a knife and began doodling the point under certain of the written glyphs. 'No, I think what has happened . . . is that Aldra Videric has found it possible to promise King Rodrigo something.'

I knew I would not like what I next heard. 'What?'

'A word overheard here, a whisper there . . . One can make a supposition from them. Suppose,' Rekhmire' leaned forward, lowering his voice. 'Suppose that this difficulty went away? Suppose that Lord Videric was able to say, "It's all lies, my wife did nothing, *I* did nothing: look at where this story comes from? Carthage would make any ridiculous claim, if it enables them to weaken this kingdom." How many men in Taraconensis would believe it a scandal cooked up by the King-Caliph, to make the King distrust his most necessary minister?'

I shrugged. 'Knowing the court, and given that men believe what they want to believe – most of them.'

Honorius downed a mug of wine, and wiped his sleeve across his mouth with a rasp of stubble. 'But the problem with that is – oh.'

Rekhmire''s chiselled lips soundlessly and satirically mimicked the *oh*, but I thought his smile more self-mocking. 'Yes. The problem for Videric is that Carthage has a witness. He may or may not know that witness is not in Carthage, now. But . . . '

Rekhmire' put his hand down flat on one letter. The unrolled end of the scroll was in cipher, and not one of the basic ones that every scribe learns.

'But, for reasons contained in these letters, I think that what Videric has promised the King is the life of Ilario.'

His gaze moved to me.

'Or, more specifically, the death of Ilario. If Aldra Videric can make this problem go away, then in a few months he can come back and take over his position again, and blame it all on Carthaginian rumour. But for that to work . . . Ilario, I believe he needs your death very urgently, now. Because he sees in it his way back to power.'

4

There was a coldness in my stomach. A round wooden bowl nudged my hand: I looked up to see Honorius offering it to me, filled with red wine.

The taste was only superficially warming.

'What I can gather from *Carthage*, on the other hand . . . ' Rekhmire' tapped his fingertips together, and I guessed that he changed direction to give me time to gain composure. ' . . . From Carthage, we have little enough to fear as regards harming you, Ilario. They have reason to wish you alive and well and in their hands, so they can keep the scandal-pot boiling nicely; all you have to fear from *them* is abduction. That way they keep the muck-raking alive, keep Videric out of office, keep King Rodrigo off-balance, and begin to convince the Frankish kingdoms that Taraconensis is ripe for a crusade.'

Honorius nodded. I realised he would be used to this scope of discussion, from his life in the north.

He reached to top my wine-bowl up, and said gruffly, 'He's right. The worst they'd do is kidnap you.'

The surface of the wine rippled. I realised I shuddered. *The shit and piss of the slaver's hall briefly real in my nostrils again.*

As if he could read my mind, Rekhmire' said, 'You have men who would seek you out, now, and free you.'

If it had not been Rekhmire' standing in the shadows. If I had not been reckless enough to demand to be taken seriously as a scribe . . .

I stood up from the table, crossing to the window, leaning between the open shutters. The rain felt cool on my scalding face. Twilight comes early among these tall Roman tenements. The wetness brought out the stink of dung, ripe fruit, sour sweat, horses.

My urge to pull back from the reassurance of these men comes because a slave can never trust anybody, and far too many will pretend to be a friend in fair weather.

You trust them or you don't. And if you have not known your father more than two months, well, the Egyptian has proved himself to feel – what was it he said in Hanno's court? – fellow-feeling. Friendship.

I wiped rain off my face and turned back, groping my way to the table since the waning day blinded me to the lamp's softer light. Shadows leapt up as I sat down, banging table and bench, and I clearly saw both men watching me.

Rekhmire' interlinked his large fingers in front of him. 'There's nothing to say it's known where we are. Believe me, I've sought to be sure of that! Because whereas I could safely refuse to sell you in Carthage, as a cousin of Ty-ameny—'

Catching the question in Honorius's eye, he added:

'We in the bureaucratic service are customarily called "cousins of the Lioness Throne". And in Carthage, that carries influence. But if they should discover us in Rome ... I think Ilario should not go out unaccompanied, if we ever have reason to think any man from Carthage has succeeded in finding us.'

Honorius jerked a thumb at the door to the side rooms, and looked questioningly at me. 'You want me to send the lads out with you?'

I could hear some of them at dinner; even recognise a few voices. I had sketched the small grizzled sergeant called 'Orazi' (none of the household guard being able to pronounce his proper Armenian name), and Attila and Tottola: twin hulking Germanic peasants become expert men-at-arms. Also a man named Berenguer, who stuck in my mind for how deeply he appeared to resent the company of an Alexandrine eunuch; one Saverico, an ensign who resembled one of the cathedral's boy-singers at home in Taraco, but must surely have more martial qualities somewhere about him; a handful of others ... All making cheerful conversation in the room beyond, which they had adopted as their barracks, as if it did not concern them that their captain would drag them halfway across the Mediterranean on an apparent whim.

The majority of Honorius's thirty or so men were faces to me, whose names I tended to confuse. Coming to the Empty Chair, only one name had had my attention: *Masaccio*.

'I think Ilario would be better off without an escort.' Rekhmire' sounded bland. 'Wiser not to draw attention to ourselves if we can avoid it.'

Bland, I thought, and nothing at all like a man protesting, *Mercenary Frankish soldiers, out from under their captain-general's thumb: I give it two days at best before all of them end in jail as drunken sots and Ilario with them!*

I couldn't imitate Rekhmire''s smooth insincerity without a give-away grin. 'I can just see that lot masquerading as body-servants! And fellow-slaves. And scribes.'

'All *right*.' Honorius glared. He failed to conceal a smile, and shook his head. 'But, damn it, I'd feel safer if you had armed men in attendance to protect you.'

'Anonymity is a good defence.' Rekhmire' spoke with the sound of long experience.

'Bloody big sword's a *better* one!'

I couldn't restrain laughter. Apart from his being my father, Honorius is an easily likeable man.

Concern abruptly chilled me. 'Aldra Videric. If he finds out I'm in Rome. He might know *you're* here. You won't be his favourite, either.'

Honorius snorted an obscenity.

'The Lord General Honorius won't be in great danger.' Rekhmire' looked over at me as he emphasised my father's title. 'Even his word and facial resemblance mean nothing if you're dead, Ilario. It would be Lord Honorius's word against Lord Videric's. And I suspect your father counts as a foreigner after having been gone for so long. The story's hearsay. Ilario ... you're the only living proof that Videric's wife attempted to kill a slave who is her own offspring.'

He shot an apologetic look at me, as if his chess-master weighing of the pieces might have offended.

'In a way, removing himself from court is a wise thing for Aldra Videric to do. Until the King of Taraconensis names a new First Minister – and none of my correspondents say he seems ready to do that – there's nothing to say that Videric doesn't *still* hold that position. But if, now, he were to go to his King and say that all can be blamed on Carthage – then King Rodrigo would refuse the idea, because Ilario can arrive at any time out of the blue, and prove Videric a liar.'

'I could talk with Videric.' The expectation of being in his presence again made my stomach twist, both with fear and rage. 'Tell him ... '

Tell him what?

Rekhmire' spoke while Honorius was still visibly weighing his words.

'If things are as we see them, then Aldra Videric is in circumstances where he *must* desire your death, leaving aside any personal vindictiveness. When the dust settles, he can take up the reins as chancellor of Taraconensis – *if* there's no possibility of a witness to Aldro Rosamunda's actions. With no witnesses, men will believe him if he says it's all Carthaginian propaganda. Is there an Iberian who doesn't know that Carthage wants to re-conquer the Peninsula? But that relies on no witness ever appearing to prove Carthage's accusations. It's in Lord Videric's interests now for you to be dead, Ilario. For you to be dead, and as soon as possible.'

'*Turds!*'

Had there been anything inexpensive and breakable, it would have been very relieving to throw it. Since there was neither, I settled for fetching one of the empty benches a kick. The oak left a throbbing bruise on the ball of my foot.

'I just want to *paint!*'

I held up both hands, stopping dual interruptions.

'I *know*. I am aware of the circumstances! But King Rodrigo knows me. Videric knows me. God's burning Hellfire, *Rosamunda knows me*! All of them know I have no intention of being used as a tool, by Carthage or anyone else; I – just – want – to – paint.'

Rekhmire' and Honorius exchanged looks.

'They can't afford to think they know you.' Honorius shrugged. 'It's like that in battle. Doesn't matter if the enemy's a man you've known for years. To achieve your objective, you have to take *all* precautions. If the Egyptian here's right, Videric thinks it's necessary for you to be dead.' His forehead corrugated. 'I still can't credit that Rosamunda would try to kill you.'

'You knew her twenty-five years ago—'

I didn't remark that she had done her best to make sure I died then, too, albeit without actually killing me.

'—That doesn't mean you know what she's capable of now.'

Honorius broke his bread into smaller and smaller pieces, eventually chewing and swallowing one. There was silence in the room except for the tearing of the crust.

It was broken so suddenly by a rap on the outer door that all three of us visibly startled.

One of the men-at-arms exchanged inaudible words outside the house; the door opened, and a rain-soaked soldier entered, removing papers from the breast of his cloak and laying them down on the table beside Honorius. I thought they might be bills of lading from the carts, but Honorius frowned, and began immediately to unfold them.

Rekhmire' caught my gaze, and stood. I joined him at the window, affording my father privacy. I watched the torch-lighter failing to ignite the pitch-torches on the taverna wall opposite, as the last light faded from the drizzling sky.

The Egyptian murmured, 'Rome is likely safe for a few months. Perhaps longer. If you ever spoke of Mastro Masaccio to Lord Videric or Lady Rosamunda—'

I nodded, mutely, seeing the expectation in his expression. Is there any man or woman to whom I *haven't* extolled the New Art?

'—Then they'll expect you to be travelling to Florence. Although I suppose they'll eventually receive news that he's staying in Rome, now. I don't know how to manage your apprenticeship under these circumstances.'

'*Dismissed.*'

Honorius didn't raise his voice, behind me, but the intensity of it brought me swinging around, away from the window. The inner door closed behind his lieutenant's back, and the man-at-arms who had been lighting further oil-lamps scurried out after him.

The lean man was on his feet beside the table. A bundle of untied papers covered the planks before him. He cocked his head in my direction: a grey-feathered raven.

'Message for me,' he grunted. 'Just had my aide take my token to the bank for funds – *this* was there for me—'

He threw down a scroll, with its red wax seal cracked open.

'"Message"?' Rekhmire' scowled, shoving his way back to the table. 'You surely left no word of where you were travelling!'

I thought my father might hit him.

Hastily joining them, I as hastily interrupted:

'How could any man know to send you a letter in Rome?'

'Read it if you like—' Honorius gulped his wine messily, wiped his hand down his doublet, and jerked his chin in the direction of the scroll. 'Wasn't sent to me in Rome. Didn't write to me *here*. Seems there's a copy gone out to every major branch of the Fugger moneylenders. I would have found the letter wherever I went, whenever I next drew on my funds.'

The Egyptian choked off a laugh, his eyes bright. 'Clever!'

I demanded, 'Who's it from?'

Honorius scratched at his cropped hair as if lice troubled him, and snapped a glance at me. 'Ask yourself, who can afford to do a thing like that?'

Videric might think of it. But if it were Videric, Honorius would have said.

'The King!' I said, simultaneously with Rekhmire''s reading aloud of the superscription:

'His Grace, Rodrigo Sanguerra Covarrubias, Lord of Taraconensis.'

5

Rodrigo's wise to use bankers, I thought. Taraconensis maintains ambassadors living at foreign courts, rather than having embassies like the Alexandrines, and the King wouldn't want every ambassador knowing his business if it concerned Carthage.

'But . . . ' I frowned. 'The King doesn't have any reason to connect you with me! Unless Videric's told him.'

'For once, it's not about *you*.'

Honorius gave me a grin that was both sardonic and reassuring. It melted away as he scowled down at the parchment scroll.

'It's about me. When I have the time, I'm cordially requested to come to court – and reading between the lines, he suggests I have the time right now.'

'To court? To *Taraco*?'

'Exactly. And why would King Rodrigo want to see me so badly?' Honorius turned his head, giving Rekhmire' a suspicious glare, clearly supposing him to have the answer, I think for no other reason than the book-buyer's general fluency with politics.

Rekhmire' sat down abruptly on his bench.

'I . . . imagine he thinks you're conspiring with the King-Caliph against his throne.'

'*What!*'

My father's indignation rang off the plaster walls. Despite the seriousness of the situation, I couldn't help smiling. His sharp glare made me drop the expression as rapidly as any of his new recruits.

Rekhmire' glanced up from the document, his lustrous eyes soot-dark in the lamp-light. 'I confess, I . . . well, at first, *I* had expected you to be a political rival of Aldra Videric, Lord General.'

'You gave me my son-daughter: enough of the "Lord General"!' Honorius's fist struck the flat of one of the oak beams above his head, loud enough to make a man-at-arms look around the inner door. Honorius gestured without looking and the soldier vanished. No man would argue with him in this mood.

'Why on God's earth would I rival Videric? It's been five-and-twenty years since I've seen Rosamunda—'

'*Political* rival,' Rekhmire' emphasised, his voice gentle. 'Why would it be so surprising? You've made yourself rich in foreign wars. You can expect to live to a fine old age. Why not come home to be – First Minister, even, in Aldra Videric's place?'

Honorius gave a startled bark that I recognised, after a second, as laughter.

'True enough,' Rekhmire' agreed, 'and I knew it within forty minutes of meeting you face to face. But King Rodrigo can't be expected to know that. Has he even seen you?'

Honorius slowly seated himself. 'As a young man, at court.'

'Then look at it from the King's position. Licinus Honorius. A rich man, with a considerable reputation—'

The Egyptian bowed his head respectfully; Honorius snorted.

'A considerable *military* reputation,' Rekhmire' emphasised. 'And a man who's been gone from his country for upwards of a generation. The King will only remember you as a young man, if at all. Say you sit on the throne of Taraconensis, you hear a man is coming home and buying land, and therefore means to stay in your kingdom; he has wealth, therefore can have influence, and his reputation will draw men to him. And having been – how many months had you been home?'

Honorius sounded reluctant. 'Three. Four, perhaps.'

'Having been a quarter of a year in Taraconensis, has not yet come to make his formal submission to his King—'

'I was buying an estate! And getting it in order! And sorting my men out; the ones who wanted to come back from the crusades and settle – parcelling land out to them, sorting out cattle and horses, arranging a monthly justice-meet for—' Honorius heaved a great sigh and slumped forward onto his elbows, on the table. 'I put it off. I don't like courts. Bunch of back-stabbing, lying, shit-eating toadies – it's why I preferred being on campaign to being in Alfonso's court. I kept thinking I could ride over to Taraco in the spring . . . '

Rekhmire' raised an eloquent eyebrow. 'And yet you sail to Carthage.'

'*You* know why I did that!'

'*King Rodrigo Sanguerra doesn't!*'

'I have never given my King any reason to doubt my loyalty!' Honorius thumped his fist down on the table, making every green-glazed jug and wooden spoon jump up. Over the clatter, he snarled, 'Ask the Kings of Aragon and Castile and Leon, ask His Royal Majesty Alfonso: I have *never* broken my word once given; why should I conspire against the lord of the kingdom in which I was *born!*'

I found myself wincing. Not as a slave does, from fear of a beating, but with the stunned appreciation with which one watches a mountain storm, or the great waves crashing on Taraco's shores in winter. Such primal loyalty is overwhelming.

'"Chancellor Honorius"!' Honorius snarled. '*Ha!*'

Rekhmire' had warmth in his gaze, I saw: amusement, and affection, as if the older man were a protégé of his, whom Rekhmire' was proud to see justify himself.

Christus Imperator! Rekhmire' found my father for me; I believe he feels a responsibility for Honorius being a good man.

There was something in that that spoke to friendship between the Egyptian and myself, but I put it aside to consider later, concentrating on Honorius where he sat and fumed:

'Who could imagine *me* wanting to be First Minister!'

'A lot of men want to.' I vividly recalled life at court. 'Most men, possibly. And I spent long enough in Taraco to know that no one's considered above suspicion.'

Honorius shot me a scorching glare from glass-grey eyes. 'I suppose *you* think I'm conspiring with the King-Caliph!'

It was possible. As a thing that some other man might do. *I'm not fool enough to think I know all fifty years of Honorius after two months in his company.* But having held Honorius's sallet while he puked over the ship's rail off Sardinia (which he assured me was commonly how bad weather took him), and having seen how he nonetheless cared for his household down to the youngest squire and kitchen-boy – and, more significantly, how little his mind ever turns from battle tactics to political power – I know this is not a possible thing for Licinus Honorius to do.

Honorius looked at me with a plain appeal on his face.

'I believe you!' I couldn't find words to explain what I knew he would see as cold rationality, and not faith in my father.

Rekhmire' came to my rescue. He tapped the paper. 'At worst, King Rodrigo Sanguerra suspects that, when the Carthaginian legions march up from Granada to offer their "protection" against crusading Franks, riding at their head will be Aldra Licinus Honorius – either as "adviser" to the King . . . or as a Carthaginian puppet-governor.'

'Rubbish!' Honorius sounded almost imploring. 'Ridiculous!'

'I've known you these past weeks; I suspect you have fewer political ambitions than any man alive—'

'Damn *right*! I just want to live in peace, on my estate, breeding my blood-line of horses.' He lifted his head, gazing intently at me. 'Looking after Ilario, if my son-daughter will let me.'

Rekhmire' upended the last of the Frankish wine into Honorius's bowl and pushed it at him. 'But you're not commanding the kingdom of Taraconensis. And if you were you'd look at it differently.'

Creases indented Honorius's forehead. The word *commanding* had been carefully chosen, I realised. Seeing the intent expression on my father's face, I realised that he knew it too.

'I've had my own problems with under-officers.' Honorius stared down into the reflections of his wine, and back at me before I had time to hide my expression. 'Surely a man who's been king as long as Rodrigo Sanguerra will *know* this is not what it seems?'

'No. He won't.' It was not news I wanted to give. 'His Majesty Rodrigo will tell you that endless suspicion is how any man stays king. Whether that's right or not, I don't know – it's certainly what *he* thinks.' I calculated the time that Honorius must have first arrived in Taraconensis. 'I think if I hadn't been busy with being kicked out as the King's Freak, and planning my voyage to Carthage, I would have heard rumours about this myself.'

Honorius looked torn between rage, anger at himself, and sorrow. Incised lines made his creased face seem older: a premonition of how we would both look at sixty.

'If I'd known you were there, Ilario, I would have come if I'd had to walk barefoot.'

'Well, that might have convinced Rodrigo you weren't rich and a problem.' I grinned. 'Except that, as my mother told me, you and I would have been seen together, and the gossips and rumour-mongers would have rung the cathedral bells in celebration!'

It cheered him a little, evidently. He set to prodding the letter with his forefinger, as if the royal seal would change into something less troublesome.

'My mind isn't made up.' He frowned. 'As to whether the bank will inform King Rodrigo Sanguerra where his letter was collected, because he's a king . . . or whether that makes it certain they'll refuse to say, because they bow their heads to no king. With the money they handle, they don't need to.'

The Egyptian moved his large hands as if they were the balance of a pair of scales. 'Could go either way.'

Honorius wiped his upper lip free of wine, where silver stubble already began to show after his shave.

'I think my way is clear, in any case.'

I didn't want to ask, but couldn't keep silent. 'What will you do?'

Honorius pushed his bench back as he rose, with a squeal of wood against floorboard. Circling the table, he sat beside me and rested his hand on my shoulder. 'I have to go back to Taraco and set the King straight on this.'

'I—'

Rekhmire' leaned towards us, cutting in as if he thought I would explode: 'He's his own best witness, Ilario.'

The Egyptian is a swift and good judge of character. I grimly reminded myself of that. Honorius's fingers dug into the fleshy part of my shoulder. As I have often done in court, I set a curb on my reactions.

'In that case – I'm going back to Taraco with you. As for Mastro Cassai . . . there'll be other Masters.'

'You are *not*!'

Rekhmire''s voice echoed simultaneously: '—not!'

Honorius's other hand closed on my arm. 'If the Egyptian here can make *me* see why Videric needs you dead, the argument has to be convincing to anybody. Even you, Ilario!'

Frustrated as I was, I had to smile at him. 'You're not as much of a blunt soldier as you make out.'

'I'm not a politician. However—' Honorius smiled somewhat grimly. 'I survived twenty-five years of the Frankish armies trying to kill me in Navarra and Leon. More to the point, I survived Castile's court! I'm not familiar with Rodrigo's courtiers after all this time, but I can take enough men to protect myself until I can see the King and clear up all this nonsense! But if you think I'm taking you back to Iberia, where Videric has every reason to *need* you dead—! And you can't even trust Rosamunda—'

I had shown Honorius my sketch-books on the voyage to Rome, pointing out my foster parents Federico and Valdamerca, and my stepsisters, and Father Felix. He wanted to know if he would recognise Rosamunda's face after so many years, but I could not show him. Every drawing I made of her, I burned in Carthage.

'No, I can't trust my mother. I can't trust Videric either. But I want to come with you.'

He gave me a small shake, as if he knew how much a slave gets used to being beaten, and would not wake such memories. 'Let me watch my back without having to look out for yours.'

He must have seen me look half-convinced.

'If you were killed, so soon after we've met, and the fault was mine—'

'All right!' I gave consent ungraciously, not able to help it. 'I'll feel the same. All of this is my fault.'

Rekhmire' had moved to rummage among boxes and baskets on the shelf beyond the hearth. His voice came clearly back. 'No.'

He straightened up with a differently shaped bottle. I recognised brandy. The Egyptian snagged wooden drinking bowls no smaller than we had used for wine, and rejoined us at the table.

'No,' he repeated, pouring the spirits. 'Aldra Videric's fault, in fact. Perhaps the Lady Rosamunda's, for her adultery. Just possibly, the Lord Commander Honorius here, for being a foolish young man in love, and helping her break her marriage vows. But everything that was done to cause this was done long before you were born, Ilario.'

I caught Honorius giving Rekhmire' a grateful look.

'I'll go back by land,' he muttered to me. 'Damned autumn storms are too much for my gullet. You stay here, study with Tommaso Cassai, and I'll leave some of my men with you—'

'Not unless you *want* to mark me as a target. Having a private army will draw unwanted attention and wrong conclusions.'

From his glare, I deduced we would have that argument again before his departure.

Before he could continue to wrangle, I said soberly, 'Unless you're planning to sell your estates and settle in another kingdom, you need to make peace with Rodrigo. I don't like it any better than you do, I don't suppose. As to Videric, I'm safe enough here at the moment. I . . . What else can I say? I wish you could stay? I don't know you well enough yet, after a lifetime apart?'

Honorius blinked fiercely. Of my three fathers – Federico and his commercial foster care; Videric, who, deep as he may be embedded in my life, is only a murderous step-father; and my blood-father Honorius – Honorius is the one I am least used to and feel I might understand best.

I wish I could say, *Stay a while longer*.

'But you're right,' I concluded, and said what I immediately realised he hadn't voiced, but had run in my reasoning in tandem. 'If the money-lenders do tell King Rodrigo where you picked up your letter, then Videric will hear about it. I don't care if he's on his estates, in Ethiopia with Prester John, or sailing the seas of the Moon – he'll hear the information. And he may, he just *may*, hear who's with you.'

Honorius was nodding as I spoke.

'Lectured by my own damned son-daughter! On politics!'

I opened my mouth to protest *Father!* and caught the glimmer of humour and aching sadness combined in his expression.

'*Somebody* evidently has to,' I remarked.

He closed with me, ruffled my hair into complete disarray, and embraced me as the Franks do, his lean muscles corded with strength. Unlike most, he touched my flesh as if there were no difference between it and anyone else's.

He stood back, grinning at how he'd dishevelled me. 'I don't plan to waste time. If it goes well, I'll be back by December.'

'Back?' I was suddenly and surprisingly light. 'You won't winter over in Taraco?'

'As far as that whoreson mule-fucker Videric is concerned—' Honorius spoke in a surprisingly even tone. '—I'll be travelling to my estates, to winter over, after I've visited the court and King Rodrigo. Fortunately, this lot of bone-headed layabouts who sponge off me are used to campaigning in bad weather, so we'll just take the Via Augusta straight back to Italy.'

He grinned like a soldier, relief under the surface. It took me a minute to realise that it must be because I looked pleased at the prospect.

'I don't seem to have lost the habit of travel, retired as I am. Of course, it's always easier without five thousand armed men along for the ride, not to mention a baggage train . . . '

In one of which I might have ridden as King Rodrigo's siege engineer, had my past decisions been different. *Would I ever have stood in my father's presence and known him?*

Honorius switched his gaze to Rekhmire'. 'If you're not here, leave word in that embassy of yours, and make sure they know who to pass it on to. I'll find you.'

Rekhmire' raised a hand, palm out, in a placating gesture. 'I swear, if I think there is the slightest danger, I will ask for asylum in the Alexandrine embassy.' He raised the drinking bowl of brandy in my direction. 'I may even take my slave with me ... '

Honorius relaxed into a grin. I made a mental note to thank Rekhmire' for the diplomatic skills of a book-buyer.

'I *may* even go,' I observed. 'Assuming I'm not busy being Judas.'

'Judas – oh. A model.' Honorius rested his hip against the table and raised his brow at me, doubtless considering his son-daughter and heir ornamenting a chapel wall in fresco.

'I suppose if I'd had the raising of you,' he said wistfully, 'you'd do as you were told.'

He intercepted Rekhmire''s stare.

'Ah. Silly of me ... '

Between them they raised my mood sufficiently that I could put Videric and Rosamunda to the back of my mind, treading firmly on any cold chill of fear that prodded my belly.

Honorius returned to the subject of Gaius Judas the following noon, when his men-at-arms – entirely unlike the layabouts he cheerfully called them to their faces – had four more *carrucas*-carts packed with their baggage, ready to leave Rome.

Rekhmire' made his own negotiations with a junior officer I recognised from his particularly wide-set eyes, and handed over a sealed scroll-case. Honorius drew me into the shadow of an awning on the far side of the street.

He rested his hand on my shoulder, the sun glinting off his articulated metal gauntlet. 'Convince this Bad Thomas he needs an apprentice, won't you? Think you'll do it before I get back?'

It's easy to take anything as rejection under such circumstances. Harshly attempting humour, I said, 'You mean you don't want me home for seven years?'

He cuffed my ear with the very tips of his fingers, so the gauntlet didn't catch me. 'Idiot! Nothing to say *I* can't stay in Rome a few years, is there? If – you'd want that?'

I nodded. After Rosamunda, Videric, Valdamerca, Rodrigo, silent assent was all I could manage.

'I want you with this Thomas Cassai, or some man as good.' Honorius absently rested his hand down on his sword-pommel as if it were part of him, his tone blunt. 'You need a trade. You tell me you don't want to be King Rodrigo's siege-engineer – I don't blame you. Battle's sickening enough. But I'd like to see you succeed at something. A man-woman needs a trade other than Court Freak, if they're to retain any self-respect.'

I blinked against the sunlight. Honesty, even without malice, is painful.

But not all pain is bad.

'That's what I *like* about you.' I smiled at my father. 'Your tact. December?'

Honorius hugged me as if I were a boy, and kissed me squarely on the brow as if I were a daughter.

'December!'

6

Mastro Masaccio burst out in a great guffaw.

I stepped away from his wooden painting-frame fast enough to lock one heel back against the other. I came to an abrupt halt.

Gasping, all but overbalancing, I shot a look from him to the drawing – *Is it damaged? I was only—*

'I didn't mean to touch it!' I protested. 'I was just brushing . . . away . . . brushing off . . . '

'Brushing off a fly.' His grin was wide and white, he having most of his teeth still. He walked briskly forward to stand beside me, gazing at the sketch of Judas, seated, in which the head and hands were now mostly complete.

Four fingers of space away from his rendition of my hair on my shoulder, the blow-fly sat motionless on the canvas.

I stared at it, more closely.

'It's . . . '

I looked back at him. Masaccio had the rough-skinned knuckles of his fist pushed into his mouth. He bit down, spluttered, dropped his hand away, and went off into peals of laughter.

' . . . *smudged,*' I said grimly.

While the Mastro finished his fit, I peered closely again. At such a small distance it was coal-dust and white pigment, and charcoal spotted in as the shadow the beast would cast.

And if I move here, then the shadow will be wrong . . .

But to a man standing before the easel, in the way that a man stands to view a picture, the illusion is absolute.

Wiping at his eyes, the Florentine said, 'The one great master, Giotto, played that trick eighty years ago. It still works. If a master plays it.'

Masaccio is an arse.

But – I understand his ambition. He's come to Rome to be the best. How can I *not* understand that?

More stiff and suspicious than I wished to sound, I said, 'It only works if you stand in the right place.'

'Ah.' His black eyes glinted. 'Ah, you see that, do you?'

I had no hope of him answering, but I scooped Judas's blood-red cloak up around me and asked, regardless. 'How do you *do* that?'

He glanced around the workshop – emptier at the moment than I'd seen it in two weeks, with his brother Giovanni gone back to Florence, and yet another assistant sacked – and stroked his hand over his tight curly beard.

'Go and sit for me again. I'm not done.'

'*I* am.' I bent down to catch my ankle as I lifted my foot, balancing like a heron, and stretched the muscles of my leg in tension against my arm. 'I have cramp, Mastro. You may as well tell me while I rest.'

'"Rest"? What are you doing but *sitting*?' He shook his head and snorted. 'And not half an hour by the clock at St Martin's, either. Every man and woman I ask to model is the same!'

I eyed him stubbornly.

He wants to tell me!

Fifteen days of being St Gaius *Tradditore* (as these Franks occasionally call their Judas), in twenty-odd positions. Masaccio's looking for a way to do this fresco in the style of the New Art, and he wants to tell another man who will understand him . . .

I attempted to look like just such a man.

Masaccio's finger stabbed out at the study on canvas. 'Tell me what's there.'

The air in the workshop was cool enough that sitting made my flesh freeze. I rubbed at my arms under the centurion's cloak while I moved around the sketch. The knowledge that I was being tested would have made me sweat on a less cold day.

When this is made into a fresco on a church wall, it will look more like a real man you'll see in the streets than any usual icon. *Why?*

'Here.' I pointed at the flurry of fine lines where he had drawn the figure of the Betrayer. 'It follows those, somehow . . . I don't know why.'

I got the confession out with difficulty, my fingertip close to the canvas, almost marking the canvas. There is nothing like those lines in nature: I wasn't sitting as Judas among converging wires in the air.

'But something about them,' I finished my thought, 'something means you can . . . distort things, so that they look more real. I don't understand! How can a distortion represent things more truly?'

Masaccio smiled, reaching past me; prodding with his fingertip at a central point that was perhaps one-third of the way up the canvas. 'Perspective.'

'It all . . . it . . . ' I drew with my finger in the air, inwards. 'All . . . points.'

'Comes down to that one point. And ends. That is the vanishing point. Simple one-point perspective, here. You may *know* what's beyond it – the other side of that box, or the far side of Judas's arm – but you can't *see* it. So I don't paint it.'

'And the distortion—'

'You see the world distorted.' He waved his hands. 'Every man does! Foreshortened, shrunk, extended, compressed. Every man sees the world from his own perspective. Two ends of a building measure the same, but the one that's far off, you see small. And I, I don't paint what you know must be there, I paint what you see!'

'What *you* see.' Meeting his angry gaze, I shrugged. 'Don't you choose the point I'm looking from?'

'As much as I can.' He nodded. 'I know where my paintings will be seen from. I know when the light will be best. If I put the point in the right place, every man will see the painting correctly.'

Experimentally, I took a pace to the side; then back. 'What happens if I don't stand here?'

'Then it's incorrect. I can do only what I can.' He scowled and nodded, as if, I thought, he would happily have nailed men's feet to the floor if it meant he could control their gaze. He reminded me in that moment of Aldra Videric.

'But I don't see how you . . . ' I leaned in. Where my sketched hands clasped together over the hilt of the Roman gladius, he had drawn only parts of my fingers and hands, and those parts curved and distorted.

This is a fingernail – although I can't see all of it. How is it that I know what it's *intended* to be?

'Go, walk!' Masaccio waved one hand extensively in circles above his head, which meant (judging by the last fortnight): walk around the workshop, don't knock over the bowls of ground bone-dust, or steeping parchment glue, or untreated canvas; don't step on the packing-crates, don't disturb the brushes in soak, do *not* spoil the expensive pigments.

He had taken my complaints of needing a break seriously since the third day, when cramp knocked me off the wooden box doing duty for the Tree, and spasmed me far enough along the floorboards to knock over his easel.

'Mastro—'

'Ach! Go, while I think!'

I caught the tip of my tongue between my teeth. The small pain reminded me: controlling my impatience got me here. Wait until he's willing to tell me more—

Cramp snagged a ball of muscle in my calf. 'Ah!'

I pressed the sole of my foot down against the floor, pushed at the knot of pain, and swore under my breath. Remembering to swear quietly, because swearing by the proper Christian saints will call attention in this heretic country—

Foreshortened, I thought, out of nowhere.

The nails on the hand are drawn foreshortened.

In the same way that if you look up at Rome's crumbling roofs, the wall and pillars of the building beside you are foreshortened. So, when a man looks at the hand from this one perspective, from the front, the nail appears distorted in that way.

And . . . *that's* what you do with feet. Not shown from above, so that you look down on the man's feet at the same time that you look face-on at his body. All parts, everything, shown from the artist's sole viewpoint. And so the feet are foreshortened, *also* seen from the front.

It's not merely perspective. Men often draw naturalistically – as the Egyptians do when they draw a torso seen full on, but a face in profile. It's perspective seen not from many places in the same painting, but consistently from one—

A glance across the benches showed me Masaccio bent over his steel engraving tools, talking under his breath.

Not a moment to interrupt. *But I can tell him I understand; I understand at least the beginning of his principles!*

I grinned wildly. I could have jumped and danced, if not for the cramp. Bending and rubbing at the muscle, I made my way to the back of the workshop, stamping on the wooden floorboards only when I was far enough off not to disturb the Florentine.

Digging my fingers into my locked flesh brought my head upside down, into odd positions. I gazed at objects – at boxes, at poles, at flat boards and canvases; at statues standing at the back of the workshop; at the slant of the half-open door to the courtyard.

Each one has its own distortion of its actual measurements and dimensions. Seen from each man's eyes.

Realisation filled up my vision. As if things rounded out before me, I saw how a man might draw lines converging to a single point, and place on them a simple regular object like a packing-case, or as complex an object as the statue of a man. They will appear larger or smaller, in themselves *or in their parts*, according to how close or distant they are!

I am no provincial amateur; I can *see*—

The cramp had been gone for some minutes by the time I stopped standing with my lowered head cocked sideways. I straightened up, feeling a heat in my cheeks not entirely due to bending over. If any man sees me, he'd think me mad!

Any man but one.

I turned, sweeping the rubbed velvet cloak around me, to look for Masaccio.

I had assumed that he would be anxiously waiting for me to get back into position. I was shocked to see him still bent close to the wooden frame, fractionally altering charcoal lines.

Perhaps he's nearly done with Judas?

Suppose this is the version he wants? Supposing it's right? Then he won't need me any more.

The chill of apprehension didn't paralyse me. Galvanised, instead, I moved forward to the middle of the workshop, waiting for Mastro Masaccio to notice me.

His head lifted.

I said, 'You have statues here.'

His oval lids blinked over his black eyes.

Masaccio remained blank-faced for all of a minute before his lines of concentration relaxed. His gaze swept the cluttered rear of the workshop, where indeed unpainted stone stood.

He gave me a very Florentine shrug.

'Oh, well, what will you? This is Rome; this is a new market for me. Some things I must do to bring immediate money in, for pigments and the rest—'

I knelt, with the Judas cloak sliding off my shoulders, and pulled at my leather travelling bag with half-numb fingers. I sprang up in time to interrupt him:

'*I* can paint them. Look. These are samples, that I did in Carthage. I could . . . if I painted the statues, *you'd* have the time to do the real painting!'

I felt the weight lift as he took one of the miniature busts from my outspread hands. It was the head and shoulders of a man of Carthage, carved in the local fashion. I had shaded the folds at the neck of his gown, and put tints of light into his curled hair and beard.

'Adequate.'

Masaccio nodded, as if his praise were nothing remarkable.

'All right. I have other work to do. Yes. Start tomorrow.'

'I – *Mastro!*'

He interrupted. 'Don't spoil the stonework. I'll take the cost of the pigments you use out of your wages.'

He gave me a level look as I was about to open my mouth and protest *But you don't pay me!*

The money will go to Rekhmire'. At least in the first instance. As will any losses.

That was a less welcome thought, but it couldn't sadden me at the moment.

'I'll need wax. *Cera Punica.* I can bring my own tools!' Suppressing the urge to dance on the spot, I said, 'Which statue shall I start on?'

'Any.' He shrugged carelessly. 'They're all overdue. But don't hurry so much you spoil the work.'

I thanked him, stumbling over the words, growing redder and hotter at the ears, hearing myself sound like a fool.

Am I in fact *thanking* this man for a chance to do what I'm weary of – old-style painting of monuments, graveyard statues, garden ornaments?

Yes. I am. Because it means I can stay on here!

Masaccio turned to his easel again. My heart hammering in my chest, I walked around to the back of the workshop.

The statues stood unpainted, although some had been treated with an undercoat of plaster and egg-white. Many were copies of Classical works. Sculptors mostly do not have the skill, now, to make them as fluid and lifelike as a millennium and a half ago – men and women stood flat-footed, carved face-on, stiff in the shoulders. I walked between them, reaching out. The unforgiving hardness of marble bruised my fingertips, and I had no care for it.

Side-stepping round a badly proportioned gladiator, I turned my head and found myself looking into the face of the most beautiful woman in the world.

'Oh . . . '

Someone is doing for stone what Masaccio is doing for paint!

She stood out for her workmanship from among the crowd of statues – saints, hermits, cardinals, and the occasional bust of Gaius Julius Caesar, Hannibal Barca, or Platon. I doubted the statue's model could be more than fifteen or sixteen years old. The Carrara marble was of such high quality, and the workmanship so good, that it had caught the heaviness in her oval eyelids without drowning out the sparkle of liveliness in her eye.

I ran my finger over the cold smoothness where the corner of her sculpted mouth turned up delicately, and her lips were just parted.

'That's a bride-piece.' Masaccio's voice came from behind me. He ignored how I jumped. Something showed in his expression; I couldn't put a name to it.

I stuttered, 'Should I start here? With this one? Or—'

'Why not? Yes.' He gave a curt nod and turned away.

Have I displeased him?

The thought faded away. I ran a finger along the icy stone of her rounded shoulder. She had been carved naked, as was common in the Antique past. The statue already had draped over it a long, light pleated tunic, which it would wear when displayed in public. Flimsy white linen, caught in around the stone waist with a knotted cord . . .

The hem had caught under the cord at one side. The rucked-up material left unclothed the curve of her lower thigh, and the soft, baby-fat contours of her knee, and her lower leg.

I crouched down, to gaze up at her. As Masaccio was inadvertently teaching me: *look at what you are to paint from all angles.*

If wax and paint could only make stone live! *Look* at her . . .

She gazed over her turned-back shoulder, as if to speak to someone behind her. I got up and walked around to her right side, to look her full in the face. Her eyes were stone-blind, as the eyes of unpainted statues are.

But wax and colours will give her the most exact copy of a young girl's eye, focusing on the world. *If* I have sufficient skill.

I *must* work on her first!

A striped linen cloak or mantle had been draped from one of her hands, so that it fell to pool and gather around her feet.

I stepped back, getting all of her in view.

The mantle she held didn't drape both her feet. It fell to the floor beside one foot.

Something about the proportions made me frown.

I don't know what I'm seeing. Is she not complete?

I knelt down.

The carving of her foot was not unfinished.

Down to her ankle, she was a young woman. But, from her ankle down, the sculptor had given her skin the texture of hair.

Smooth, silky – the pelt of an animal.

Beneath her ankle, she had no human foot. She had the carved hock, the beast's foot, and the split hoof that belongs to a goat.

7

If Rome was shabby, the Vatican palace was shabbiest of all. I made a habit of meeting Rekhmire' outside it in the late afternoons, after siesta, when the light became too bad for painting or reading or copying, and there was no hope of a messenger or letter arriving from Taraco that day. Although I knew it soon yet, even if my father Honorius had changed his mind and gone all the way from Ostia Antica by ship, rather than joining the land road.

The Egyptian's eyes showed red-rimmed as he lifted his hand in greeting. His clothes stank of lamp-oil. 'Ilario. How does your colouring of the bride-piece statue go?'

He habitually copies from so many libraries that he must be as much a scholar as bookseller. Having worked up courage enough with that thought, I asked him the question I badly needed answered:

'Master Rekhmire' – am I painting a demon?'

'The statue itself?' His brows shot up. 'I'd imagined that a Phoenician superstition, not an Iberian one—'

'No, *not* the statue itself!'

With the goat-foot explained, his large, lined face relaxed into a smile.

'No demon. A god, perhaps.' Rekhmire' shrugged at my expression. 'The temples at home are filled with animal-headed gods. A foot would not be unusual. And one of the Attic gods has a goat-foot, no?'

'Pan.'

'But, Attic work here . . . '

Rekhmire' pointed up, with a finger that showed ground-in ink to the second knuckle. Stumps of sculpture stood along the roof of this great cathedral, next to the Vatican. Rome's Classical gods shared a minimal presence with the many saints of the Green Christ.

The Egyptian snorted. 'They're not a people who love their Classical heritage. I'm finding scrolls by Homer and Sappho stuffed in damp corners, sole surviving copies eaten by rot – but the hagiographies of their Frankish saints are preserved under crystal, and copied and *re-*copied. A god's hoof on a statue would be . . . odd.'

I frowned. 'Then . . . could it be symbolism?'

He arched his plucked brow at me.

'Symbolising something physically monstrous,' I continued the thought. 'A club-foot, perhaps.'

'Being lame is hardly monstrous!'

'Not to you. Or in Iberia. The Franks are different. And if this statue is to advertise a bride . . . They wouldn't copy a physical deformity in stone. They might symbolise that something *is* there. As a warning.'

'A warning.' Rekhmire''s expression held distaste.

'Just as well they're not making one for me.' I didn't add: *Or you.*

He smiled sardonically. '*Does* the work go well?'

I thought for a moment, and nodded.

'Good.'

Rekhmire' didn't say more, perhaps for fear of unnerving me, but I knew what was in his mind. Masaccio won't want anything coming out of his workshop to be done badly. His name will be on it. So he must trust me to do this. And – I must do it well. Do it better than I've done any work before now.

'This isn't difficult.' I could feel her icy marble texture in my fingers. 'She's the most beautiful thing I've ever seen. I swear she tells me herself how she ought to be painted.'

'Despite the club-foot?'

'Despite the club-foot.'

Rekhmire' smiled. 'I should be careful if I were you, Ilario. None of the Classical stories of men in love with images end well.'

I blushed red.

He laughed out loud. 'My slave *is* infatuated!'

'My master can go fornicate with a three-legged donkey!'

Men of the Egyptian's mass and bulk shouldn't snicker; it leads to a perceptible loss of dignity on their part. Even if they do appear unmoved by that.

The following day I had a loss of nerve and ground up no pigments, merely taking up some of my old lime-wood boards and using the backs for drawing exercises – something I could be sure Masaccio would never reprove me for.

The Florentine merely grunted when he saw me. 'When you've finished there, you may as well do something useful.'

Matching size and angle and inclination of line can only be done for so long before the eye tires. At last I set down the boards and charcoal, and wandered over to Masaccio's other bench.

'You can do the cheese glue for the panel work,' he observed. 'You mix the cheese with powdered lime . . . '

He pushed a plate of decidedly rotten Roman pale cheese across the workbench.

'It works better if you crumble it with your fingers.'

'Cheese glue.'

I looked at him.

'If I were a younger apprentice—' I stifled choking and the urge to gag, as I fully smelled the cheese. '—I *might* be taken in by that one!'

I'd had enough in the scriptorium at Taraco, as the youngest apprentice, being sent down to the vellum store for a long stand and other traditional red herrings.

Masaccio hefted a piece of painted board up from where it was propped against the side of the bench. Covered in plaster dust, it had obviously been removed from some altar wall.

'Got this out of a chapel at Pavia . . . '

It was an ordinary altar painting of St Lawrence roasting on his griddle, done in the ancient style. There being few pieces of suitable flat wood large enough for such an altar panel, it was made of six separate boards glued together, and then covered over with linen as a ground for the pigment.

Masaccio rested the edge of the board on the lip of the workbench, holding it there as he stroked his beard with his free hand. 'Been up in the chapel three centuries, according to the monastery records – but who trusts them? A long time, certainly . . . '

He picked up a mallet, hefted it, and abruptly lifted his arm and smashed it down with all his strength.

The mallet-head sounded loud as a gun exploding. It landed squarely on a visible ridge in the painting that marked a join in the planks. I winced and stepped back from an anticipated fragmentation of splinters.

The wooden panel didn't break.

Masaccio stared down at it, rubbing his thumb over the small dent in the shiny surface. He scratched at it with his nail.

'Cheese glue,' he remarked. 'Once it's well set.'

Wordlessly, I reached for the plate and began crumbling the sticky wet cheese into the lime-dust, taking great care to get neither close to my eyes, and leaning back as the mess began to bubble and minutely sputter.

At the short afternoon's end, Masaccio invited me down to the taverna at the end of the street.

I accepted with no hesitation.

Technically, Master Tommaso Cassai's people are at war with mine. The Crusades still grind on, somewhere in the north of Iberia, on the Navarra-Castile border where Honorius fought: he had told me stories. But it still seems more than a world away, here in Masaccio's Roman workshop – which, Masaccio let slip, had taken only a bare month to become as cluttered as it was; he having come down from Florence just at the beginning of the autumn.

I finishing tidying and sweeping up and found him waiting impatiently at the door. But for all that, he was the first to open his purse at the tavern.

'You've got bad news for me.' I looked up from the bench where I sat, and then back at the leather jack of ale. 'You must have!'

His black eyes glinted. He drank, wiped his mouth on his sleeve, and lowered his voice below the chatter from the packed tavern-room.

'On the contrary, Spaniard. I'm impressed with your work on stone.'

He didn't pause long enough to let me take that in.

Shooting a sharp glance my way, he said, 'That's why I'm going to include you on the work I'm doing now – it's suddenly become a rush job, and I need another set of hands. Think you can work at the Egyptian embassy?'

If I'd drunk any ale, I'd have choked.

The ridiculous thought came instantly into my mind: *Rekhmire' has arranged this!*

I couldn't help asking. 'It's nothing to do with my master, is it?'

Masaccio looked bewildered.

'Your ... ' His expression cleared. 'Oh, the Egyptian castrato-bureaucrat. No; this is a contract from before I met your master. They have a statue they need painted before it's shipped out; suddenly it must be shipped in three weeks' time ... ' He shrugged. 'That's patrons for you.'

I looked down. Drawn in ale, the wet lines of a man's face glistened on the grain of the wood – one of the soldiers sitting by the hearth in ragged jack and hose, half his jaw gone to a combat wound. I rubbed my hand across the absent work of my fingers. 'Mastro, my drawing exercises. Are they well, in your estimation?'

'You're progressing.'

'I . . . ' A refusal wouldn't come out: my throat constricted too tightly. I breathed deep. 'I think I'm just *beginning* to learn perspective. Mastro, if you want me to do another statue—'

I couldn't hold it back.

'I don't want to be left doing nothing but stone-work! I want to learn more of the *real* art!'

In the dark curls of his beard, the white glint of a smile showed. 'This statue's different, Spaniard. You'll see.'

I took up the jack, drained it, and got to my feet, gazing down at Masaccio.

He gave a brief nod and led me out into the dark afternoon.

The streets of Rome aren't lit as Carthage's are; they don't have the use of naphtha. Nothing is so black as city streets between monumental buildings. I stumbled in Masaccio's wake, treading wetly in dung and less reputable rubbish. He walked as if it were clear daylight. But that was merely an excess of self-confidence.

Past one more bend in the Tiber, an island lay in the middle of the river. Mastro Masaccio spoke to the guards on the bridge, who let us across, and he strode on without looking back at me, up the steps of a Doric-pillared Roman mansion, and knocked without hesitation.

The hen-tracks and pictograms inscribed on one side of the door read (if I had it correctly from Rekhmire''s teaching), *Embassy of Alexandria-*

in-exile. And on the other side, in Latin letters, the city's name from before the conquest: *Embassy of Constantinople.*

I wondered if I might see Rekhmire' at this outpost of Egypt-in-Europe. *I must tell him I've been here.*

Light blazed unexpectedly into my eyes as the doors opened. Inside, the mansion was full of brilliance. Masaccio talked, laughing, to ruddy-skinned men in linen kilts. I rubbed at my streaming eyes as we went inside.

Lamps and candle-stands stood every few feet along the corridor, and, in the room they took us to, stood side-by-side. The heat and sweet scent of beeswax stunned me into a faintly nauseous state.

'It's not natural light,' I protested, when Masaccio came back from ushering our guides out through the square-pilastered doorway. 'The colours won't be right!'

'Apparently, this is the light they're to be seen by in Constantinople.' He shrugged, walking towards a sheet-covered monolith standing among pots, brushes, and pallets. I was pleased to see a brazier-box and slabs of Punic wax. The sheet would no doubt come off to show the statue in question.

Masaccio grinned lopsidedly. 'Behold!'

The white cloth fell away. I found myself gazing up at a statue of a man seven or eight feet high, made of fine white marble – and of brass.

'I've—' *seen one of these before*, I stopped myself saying.

In Carthage.

Rekhmire' is prone to lecture me about tact. It was hardly tact that allowed Mastro Masaccio to present me with his 'surprise'; I stood stunned by more than the statue's presence. Remembering Hanno Anagastes' house, and a glimpse of a similar metal-jointed statue that stood head-and-shoulders taller than an average man. Although Hanno's had been of yellow sandstone, not marble; and unpainted, rather than decorated as this one would be.

If there are any men from Carthage here – if they know of Rekhmire' – of me—

Desperately desiring to speak to Rekhmire', I examined the stonework, stumbling to make suitable exclamations. The statue towered taller than me by four-and-twenty inches; stood carved naked, and with its arms posed hanging at its sides.

Masaccio pointed at the legs and lower torso. 'Much of the flesh, I've done.'

Ruddy Egyptian flesh colours made it seem as if the lower part of a man indeed stood there, rounded out into life from the white stone.

'It will take many hours of skilful work to complete it well.' He gave me an uncompromising look. 'And I will have it done well.'

The arms and head and upper chest remained not coloured as yet, and I found myself sizing up the job as he talked, and nodding agreement.

The sculptor had carved every muscle, tendon-cord, and bone under the surface of the stone skin, and the brass-smith had chiselled the arm- and shoulder- and knee-joints with the same skill.

Masaccio broke what I realised had become a silence. He stroked his hand over his mouth, barely hiding a grin. 'They shipped it here to be painted by the world's best painter.'

Is that – can this be coincidence?

'Is it going back to Carthage, after?'

He shot me a look that suggested I ought not to hazard guesses about the origins of such statues.

'No. It's going on to Constantinople. A gift for the Pharaoh-Queen, Ty-ameny. With the name of my workshop on it, *and* the master's brush. So if you mess it up, Spaniard, I'll have your bollocks!'

I stifled a grin at what I knew in that last respect and he didn't.

And . . . If Carthage *knew* I'd come here, I would have walked into this embassy at Masaccio's heels and found Carthaginians ready to arrest me.

Not everything in the world concerning Carthage can revolve around Taraco. Or even me. They must have their business with powerful kingdoms such as New Alexandria . . .

Exhilarated, I squatted down by the boxes where my brushes and other tools were set out. *Calami* rush-stalks; the *rhabdion* that is spatulate at one end and round at the other; large and small brushes; different heating-irons. I reached forward to rake up the brazier that was heating coals for the pallet box.

Squinting up, I saw how foreshortened my view of the statue in fact was; the thighs and hands enormous, the neck and chin tiny . . .

The Florentine painter said, 'And you must make certain to do the details under the arms perfectly.'

Mastro Masaccio smiled when I looked at him.

'What for?'

'Because it'll show!' His tone implied *Obviously, you idiot!*

I stood up and touched the immense, chill marble. I couldn't push my fingertips between the statue's torso and the inside of its arm.

'I don't think—'

'You can't reach there?' Masaccio gave a short nod, and then lifted his chin, looking up into the carved marble face of the statue. '*Golem, lift up your arm.*'

The stone statue's arm noiselessly swivelled at the shoulder-joint and elbow-joint, and lifted up and forward from its body.

8

Masaccio's laughter peeled out loud enough that half the embassy bureaucrats came to peek round the door, before he ushered them away.

Obstruction blotting out the candle-light – a soundless, heavy motion passing my face—

I stood up from where I had ended, crouched against the room's far wall.

I dimly remembered muscles that flexed and sprang by instinct, putting me with my back to the masonry; and instinct and training also had a reed-cutting knife clenched in my hand.

Little enough good *that* would have done me.

I gazed up at the more than life-size statue, breathing heavily. 'So! It's a joke. I don't see ropes, or pulleys – is there a man inside?'

It looked solid marble, but it might be no thicker than a running-bird's eggshell; I have seen men who can carve stone or ivory to such thin perfection.

Masaccio rapped his knuckles against the polished smoothness of the statue's biceps. 'No one inside. You *are* a barbarian, boy! Have you never heard of Hero of Alexandria, who made a walking statue of a man? Now, evidently, someone has re-discovered that Classical science—'

'A *walking* statue?' Every muscle, as I relaxed it, shivered with cramp. I flexed my fingers. 'A walking *statue*?'

'—And re-discovered it in Carthage, by my best guess.' Masaccio frowned, concentrating, clearly not realising I'd interrupted. 'Although these Alexandrines are none too keen to talk about who shipped it from there; it might have been made elsewhere . . . What? Do you call me a liar? Look at it!'

I had not the slightest desire to approach the now-motionless carved shape of a man.

Except that I'll still be expected to lay colour onto the surface of that marble.

There being tools about the place, I picked up a mallet of soft wood as I approached, and – poised to spring away in an instant – rapped it against the statue's pectoral muscles.

The *thunk* of solid marble echoed through the low-roofed room.

The statue did not move.

Masaccio spoke loudly but calmly, as if to a deaf but only slightly dangerous animal. '*Golem, pour a drink of wine into the cup for me.*'

Its joints moved.

Soundlessly, it lifted a knee, flexed at ankle and toe – with a flash of light from the yellow brass gears – and it was walking.

A soft grating of stone against tile became the only noise in the room while a man might count a hundred.

The golem-statue stalked to the niche where the wine jug stood, lifted it, and poured liquid from the jug into an alabaster cup.

Surely the strength of that hand will crush—

The statue swivelled about, stopped; then moved with the same unchanging pace to Mastro Masaccio, and halted with an arm stretched out.

He took the cup.

I saw Masaccio's fingers were not steady.

The carved features of the statue's over-large face did not move: neither stone brows, nor mouth, nor eyes.

'How does it see?' I breathed. And flushed, not thinking to have spoken aloud.

'How indeed? There is some secret science of the ancient peoples, here.' Masaccio suddenly dipped his head, and threw back all the wine at a gulp. He stared up into the stone man's face. 'Which you cannot tell us, friend, can you? It can't speak,' he added to me.

The Egyptians had gone some way to decorating this Roman mansion in their own style. The house of the Lord-Amir of Carthage Hanno Anagastes was not too unlike this one: striped stone at the door arches, and red-and-yellow friezes along the walls. I thanked Christ the Emperor for that slight familiarity, disoriented as I felt.

There again, if I'd been longer in the house of Hanno Anagastes – would I have seen *his* statue move?

'Am I expected to touch that?' My voice sounded high, womanish. I made an effort to force it low. 'Paint it?'

Masaccio's glance was impatient. 'Unless you wish me to hire another assistant?'

'No!'

What else can I say? No matter if it belongs to Carthage, and I should stay away from anything belonging to the King-Caliph's people – I can't miss this!

Masaccio said, 'It obeys a man's commands, if told to by the Alexandrines here. That means my voice will be heeded, but yours not. If you need to paint where you cannot reach, you must ask me.'

'And I should say nothing of this, outside the workshop?' I pre-empted his speech.

His brilliant dark eyes summed me up. 'You'll take the formal oath as my apprentice.'

All I could do was stare.

'Your master'll permit it,' Masaccio added. 'He was anxious enough to get you apprenticed. Are you Frankish Christian?'

This not being a time to lie, I admitted, 'I was brought up in the faith of Christ Emperor.'

He dismissed a thousand years of religious schism and warfare with a wave of his hand. 'Same thing.'

I put the flat of my hand up against his palm as he raised it, feeling the heat of his paint-marked skin.

'Swear by Jesus Christ and the Holy Mother to give me your fidelity as my apprentice.'

'I swear by Christus Imperator and the Wise Holy Mother to be your true apprentice.'

'Good. I'll have you on the executioner's block if you fail me.' Masaccio nodded. 'Are you ready to begin?'

The reality of judicial punishment made me startle; only then did I think, *But I haven't asked Honorius.* Not for the first time, I wished him present to advise me. And Rekhmire'. Cold with apprehension, I thought, Should I have taken this step without consulting them?

Masaccio brought me to see this: he had no intention of letting me escape without an oath.

My gaze fell from the statue's face – but to look at its shoulders was no more reassuring. Reckoning by eye, now, I made it seven feet and two hands high. Carved proportionate to a man, it was almost a giant.

'Three weeks,' I said.

'I likely could finish it myself.' Masaccio's brows dipped in concentration. 'But I want no part of it hurried. And they're not paying me enough to have all of it *pel suo pennello*: from the master's brush alone. You'll still sit for me as Judas in the meanwhile. Cardinal Valente won't wait while I finish this.'

That momentarily took my attention from the golem-statue. In most Frankish church icons they represent Judas as he was in his Hebrew robes, before he joined the army and gained Roman citizenship. Robes would have suited me. But this Cardinal had chosen a depiction much closer to our own: Judas, under his Roman legionary name of Gaius, debating with the priests of Mithras. And wearing his military cloak, *lorica segmentata*, and a centurion's 'skirt' of leather straps.

Modelling that made me uneasy. Even changing to baggier hose in defiance of fashion hadn't rid me of a feeling that my hips and belly *must* show broad as a woman's. And there are no women in Masaccio's workshop.

I shifted, casually now, to a stance that I thought more concealed my feminine arse.

Masaccio lifted his chin confrontationally. 'You won't mind working night and day, will you?'

I couldn't help but smile through my fright. Monstrous the golem might be, but such a challenge to an artist's skill—! 'Where do you want me to start?'

He had me begin with fingernails, oddly enough. No foreshortening. Merely the laying of ground-work colour, where he had prepared the surface: then shading and wash, onto a solid surface; highlights to be brushed on when dry.

I pushed dry-mouthed apprehensiveness away. *The statue doesn't move, save at command.*

After a day or two of touching it without harm, fear gave way to sheer exhilaration. Fascination – how can such things be?

I found myself working at all hours of the night. Since the golem-statue could be painted during the evenings, the shortening daylight hours of autumn could be spent on other remunerative work. Judas. And the statue of the goat-foot girl.

Masaccio had not yet approached Rekhmire' to countersign the apprentice's contract – I would have had the Egyptian shouting at me if he had. I desired urgently to talk to Rekhmire' about the stone golem, but I thought that he would also regard my verbal oath as binding. Which meant I could not.

I bit my tongue, and concluded at the end of two days that Rekhmire' – in and out of the embassy as he eternally was! – must by now have found out all there was to know about the stone golem. He said nothing. *But that need only mean he respects my oath.*

Carthage had passed the golem straight to the Alexandrine embassy, it appeared, with orders to get it painted and sent on to Constantinople. I had merely to be careful of meeting stray Carthaginians before the statue was shipped out. I thought one or two times that I might have been followed in the street, but nothing came of it – and hermaphrodites are sometimes followed for reasons unconnected with politics, even when disguised as men.

Or, I thought, it might be Rekhmire' keeping a watchful eye open.

My opportunity to speak came when we were both all but asleep in the pungent Roman night, and Rekhmire' got up to open a shutter, and stare for some minutes at the waxing moon.

'In Lord Hanno Anagastes' house,' I got up on one elbow, 'I saw a statue – a man, done larger than life-size. I meant to ask you. There were rumours among the other slaves, that it moved. Walked. Like a man, I mean.'

The moonlight showed me Rekhmire''s expression: the lift of his brows, and faint amusement.

'That's the Lord-Amirs of Carthage for you. The Royal Library has had Lords arrive in person, to study the scrolls of Hero of ancient Alexandria-that-was. If they could match his engineering feats, the

Franks and the Turks would indeed have cause to fear Carthage's armies . . . '

'You think Lord Hanno's statue moves?'

'Single wonders of such a nature are . . . not unknown.' His face fell half into shadow. 'Although "not unknown" does not mean "not dangerous".'

I kept my satisfaction concealed. *I have managed to say nothing that breaks my promise of secrecy.*

'And on the subject of the Turks . . . ' Rekhmire' turned back to gazing out of the window, changing the subject more clumsily than he customarily did. 'I have found a document in the Vatican library that I think has been lost – mis-filed – these two hundred years.'

Monochrome light reflected from the dome of his shaven head; the planes of his cheeks. I reached for the board beside my pallet and, for all my sleepiness, began to sketch him in that profile. 'Document?'

'A Turkish traveller's account. I presume, ignored because written by a foreigner. But, depending on whether it is a forgery or not . . . it is an eye-witness testimony of the Prophet Gundobad's death.' Rekhmire''s brows came down. 'And it contains the actual words of the curse that Gundobad spoke. Those were unknown until now. Whether the cardinals might at last begin to break the curse on the Papal Chair, if they knew . . . '

'*Is* it genuine?'

His massive shoulders shrugged. 'I am attempting to find other supporting evidence. So far, there's none. Then again, the Vatican has a library half the size of ours, and with no competent custodians whatsoever. It is a task of years!'

I lay back down. Rekhmire' continued to gaze from the unshuttered window, frustration plain on his large face.

After I had slumped asleep as Judas a time or two, Mastro Masaccio took to letting me doze on a couch at the back of the workshop. My eyes shut, often, gazing up at the face of the marble girl. I had the preparation of her body done, ready to paint, colour, shade and highlight. But for that rest—

'I need to ask you a favour,' I said that dawn, as Masaccio and I returned from the embassy; he holding up a flaring pitch torch to scare off street toughs. The shadows in the hollows of his cheeks and eye-sockets danced with the torch and wind.

'And that is?'

'I've prepared all the stonework for pigment, and sewn the bride-piece's clothing . . . ' I had, to his sardonic amusement, also brought in a goat from a woman living in the next street, so that I could adequately paint the symbolic foot from life. ' . . . But I can't go on with the painting yet.'

His chin came up combatively. 'Why? Aren't I paying your master enough?'

'I need to see her face.'

'*I* need you not to waste time on that piece of . . . '

When he said nothing more, I added cautiously, 'If it's a bride-piece, does it not need to look like *her*? So far, according to instruction, I know her fair-skinned and fair-haired—'

'Yellow.'

I stared as he unlocked the heavy wooden gates of the workshop. '"Yellow"?'

'Her hair is yellow as a marsh buttercup.'

His back spoke a volume or two as he stalked in ahead of me, but I hadn't the language to read it.

Direct, I demanded, 'Who *is* she?'

'A whore.'

That startled me. The sun was not yet risen: I'd picked up and lit a candle-stump, preparatory to lighting the shop's oil-lamps; I all but burned my hand as he spoke. 'A *whore*?'

Masaccio's expression was hidden by darkness. He spoke quietly.

'A woman who *said* she loved me – she got me the commission on the strength of it. After the bride-piece statue was painted, I was to go to her father and . . . But before it was even carved, she told me she'd changed her mind. No marriage for Tommaso Cassai. A painter wasn't rich enough for her. The whore! For *her*. And *her* family!'

If we had been outside in the street, he would have spat.

'Perhaps her family stopped her,' I said. 'Women have little enough choice, commonly.'

Masaccio's laugh, in the closed-up workshop, was harsh and ugly. 'Defending her, boy? You don't know her! Why – you're in love with her yourself!'

'No—'

'You're red, boy!'

'I'm not!'

'Just from her image!' He laughed the more at my denial. I stifled protest.

'Well.' He shrugged. 'All I want is the money for a job done. If you need to see the bitch's face for that, well, see her. It's nothing to me.'

From his tone, money was far from all that concerned him. And evidently he could see that thought in my face, bad light notwithstanding.

'Here!' He scrawled quickly in charcoal, on a splinter of lath. 'Here's the address; I've drawn you where she lives. But mind, I can't spare you more than an hour from Judas – and the Egyptian embassy.'

9

I ran all the way.

The Paziathe mansion stood solid, dark, and grim, for all the gilding the morning sun attempted to lay on its masonry. It looked startlingly well-built for such a shabby district. Iron bars were set into the stone, covering the lower and upper windows.

What have they to lock up? They don't look rich.

I smiled wryly at that. They're well enough off to hire a sculptor and a painter to advertise their daughter for sale.

Who'd be a woman, in the Empty Chair? Thank God – Rekhmire''s eight of Them! – that I can pass as a man.

A sleepless night had left me gritty-eyed. The sprint across Rome, past the Forum and the amazingly narrow Via Sacra, to this outlying district, woke me fully. The mansion stood near a park, if the oak trees ahead of me were any guide. Clean, chill air hissed in my lungs. I felt the palms of my hands hot and wet.

I am Mastro Tommaso Cassai's apprentice, I rehearsed in my head. *Come to make colour sketches for your daughter's statue.*

'Old Aranthur's more likely to let *you* in than me,' Masaccio had called after me as daylight cleared his head, temper making him scowl.

Rekhmire', when I diverted my way past our lodgings, was out; gone already to the Vatican library. It would have eased my mind to talk to him, although I could not say why.

An elderly servant came out of a side door of the mansion, pulling a cloak around his shoulders.

I let him walk off before I went to the same door and rapped, using their bronze door-hammer cast in the shape of a Sacred Boar.

The iron-studded door was made from thick enough wood that I heard no footsteps approaching. It swung suddenly open, startling me.

'What did you forget?' In the doorway, a girl put her hand up to her face, shading her eyes from the sun; hiding her features from me. 'Oh! I'm sorry! I thought you were Father, come back! I shouldn't have answered the door!'

Her voice sounded musical, textured, distressed.

I do not need to see her face.

I watched the curve of those fingers into her palm as she shaded her eyes. I have seen them beside me for days on end. And the fold of her elbow, the curl of her hair.

Masaccio had given me her name, unwillingly enough. My voice half-broke in a boyish squeak. 'Madonna Sulva Paziathe?'

She took a step back. The movement had all grace in it. Both her bodice and her skirts were dark enough brocade to look black in the house's shadow. A hood or veil covered all but the edges of her braided bright hair.

She glanced around, as if looking for her servants.

'Don't be afraid!' I stuttered it out. She might as well have said it to me.

'I'm not supposed to—'

'I'm a painter; I come from Masaccio – I mean, Master Tommaso—'

She lowered her hand and glared at me. 'Tommaso Cassai?'

Now I could see inside the taffeta-cloth veil that framed her face. Her hair had been pinned up beside her temples in a myriad small braids. Enough of it was left unbound to flow over her shoulders. An unmarried woman's style, I guessed, even among the Franks.

And it is not the colour of buttercups, but the exact colour of the outer part of a candle's flame.

Her face. I'd need to use every skill I possessed to make that cream-pale face glow, as it did in the eastern sun. Shadow the faintest violet under her eyes; touch the crisp line of her lip with pink—

'Tell Messer Cassai to leave me alone!'

'He will! It's . . . I'm painting your statue. I needed to . . . ' A thunderstroke would have left me more articulate. 'To see you.'

Another woman might have blushed, pretending modesty. I was myself trained to behave that way, from time to time, at the court of King Rodrigo. She only opened her lips in a soundless *oh* of realisation.

'I'm Ilario,' I added, and hesitated too long over giving a family name for it to be natural. 'You don't have to be afraid. Mastro Cassai doesn't intend to come here. And I only need to make sketches.' I burbled. 'Match colours.'

She glanced back over her shoulder into the depths of the mansion. 'Father won't allow me to ask a stranger into the house.'

I was about to swear I would come back – any day; every day; whenever it would be convenient to see her – when she reached back into the darkness, and brought out a silk-fringed mantle to put around her narrow shoulders.

'We'll go into the garden.' A tiny curve of mischief lifted her lip, just as the sculptor had caught it. 'My maid can chaperone us. Hathli! *Hathli!*'

A dark-featured round woman with an incipient goitre came to the door with remarkable speed. She said nothing, only nodding at her mistress's commands, but her lips folded together, and I had no doubt what she was thinking.

122

'Madonna Sulva.' I followed them inside. 'I know Frankish women are more free in their behaviour than my people, but—'

'You're not Frankish?' Her eyes widened. 'That's exciting. I never travel. Tell me! Tell me what it's like where you're from.'

I told her of King Rodrigo's court as the maid accompanied us through corridors – to which my eyes were night-blind – and out into a central courtyard. Frail sun gleamed. Bay and basil grew in pots. A walled pool held the glint and flicker of carp. The girl gazed up at me from under her hood.

I let the leather sack of my tools fall at my feet, on the flagstones. *How can I ever reproduce you in pigments!*

'Messer . . . Ilario?'

'Ilario Honorius,' I finally managed. I will not use *Valdevieso*.

Sulva Paziathe had that heavy curve of flesh under her lower eyelids that was the plumpness of girlhood vanishing. It ought to have been ugly. All of her face *should* be ugly: her brows are too heavy, her lids too wide and oval; the philtrum under her nose too long, so that she doesn't show her teeth when she smiles.

But all these things together in her are . . . beautiful. She's rich as cream.

'This way,' Sulva Paziathe said. 'Here.'

She walked on, out across the courtyard. The woman Hathli hooked her arm under Sulva's, as if it were a thing of common use and no moment.

The girl is limping. Lame.

Sulva Paziathe pointed to the stone surround of the pond, and a marble bench beside it. 'We'll sit down. Hathli, you can walk over *that* way for a while.'

They exchanged a look. I guessed at history between them. There would be other servants about here, I could surmise that much. Men-servants. Men-at-arms, if the house still hid wealth under its shabbiness.

The older woman shrugged her own mantle about her swollen neck, toga-like. Her skirts swept ochre and umber leaves as she crossed the courtyard to be out of ear-shot.

'Now.' Sulva's eyes as she looked up had a mischievous gleam that it would defeat me to put into marble. 'You can tell me the things I shouldn't hear! What's it like, to travel from Iberia? And from – Carthage, was it? North Africa?'

She named it as if she named the Moon.

Numbed, I did as court usage had taught me; held out my hand to the young woman, so that she could steady herself as she sat down on the stone bench. Her flesh felt warm enough to be almost hot. At the touch of smooth skin, I felt as if that heat went through me in needles – and, simultaneously, as if I couldn't bear *not* to have the contact of her hand.

Marcomir had been planes and angles and male sweat: this girl was tactile beauty.

She stumbled, sat awkwardly down, and lifted up her head to gaze at me; her fingers still resting on mine. The brocade of her dress was woven with bronze thread, and oyster-shell black, and deep blue. Her skirts were rucked up where she had sat clumsily.

I couldn't help but look. And blushed bright red. *She'll think I'm looking to see her lame foot. She'll be embarrassed by her deformity*—

On her right foot, her silk slipper was strapped into a wooden patten, three or four inches high, to keep her out of mud or damp.

Her left foot had neither slipper nor patten; they could not have fitted. Only a sock-like silk cloth wrapped round it.

The fabric could not conceal the underlying shape from me; not now that I'm used to drawing the skin, muscle, tendon and bone that lies under men's clothes. Her foot was a twisted ball of clubbed flesh. It had folded back on itself, into a stump. I guessed she had either no toes at all, or else only vestigial ones. Her ankle was knobbled, under the concealing silk.

I looked up, meeting her gaze.

With a heartbreaking gentleness, she said, 'I'm . . . not allowed to go out into the city. People would . . . Tell me what it's like, far away?'

For all her brave words, she stared at me, terrified; as if my silence judged her. And as if one word of judgement could shatter her.

How alone, how isolated, she must feel, to invite a stranger in. To risk scandal, insult, mirth, disrespect.

Regardless of the wet leaves on the flagstones, I went down on one knee beside her, gripping her chilled hand tightly.

'Sulva . . . ' I watched her expression. 'Let me tell you how it's been for you. There is no more than one of you in the world. You are unique. Men think you something monstrous, but you're not; you're a soul like any other. All your life, you've been alone, finding no other like you. No one has ever spoken to you normally, as men speak to one another.' I took a breath. 'You are— As you *are*, you're more beautiful than anything I've ever seen. But they keep you here. Hide you away, for fear.'

Sulva put her free hand up to her face, gazing at me over the tips of her fingers. I saw her biting at her full lower lip as she hid it.

I said, 'Your father thought it right to commission a bride-piece. If you will have me, I'll speak to your father. If you will have me, I'll marry you.'

10

On my way back to Masaccio's workshop I stepped aside to our lodgings, hoping to bring the news to my Egyptian master.

'*You've done what?*'

Looking up at Rekhmire''s aghast face, I spoke doggedly.

'I've told Madonna Sulva Paziathe that I'll marry her. And she's agreed.'

He opened and shut his mouth soundlessly. Under other circumstances – when it didn't incise a sudden line of fire through my belly – I would have found it comic.

Rekhmire' caught his breath. 'And did you tell her that you're *not a man!*'

Now is not the moment to explain why Sulva Paziathe so desperately needs to be rescued.

I slammed the lodging-house door behind me as I left.

The door to Masaccio's workshop opened a quarter-hour after I'd got back, and let Rekhmire' in.

Masaccio didn't look up, being fixated by how the light fell on Judas's hands, where the Betrayer held the Spanish sword that drew no blood.

Rekhmire''s voice echoed up to the rafters. '*And* have you told her family that you're a *slave*?'

Masaccio looked up, startled. He grinned in the anticipation of scandal.

'I need a rest-break!' Hurriedly, I dropped the prop-sword, draped the velvet cloak in folds over the box, and strode across the room to herd the Egyptian back out.

I closed the workshop door on the painter's outraged complaints.

'Have you?' Rekhmire' demanded, voice echoing across the cobbled street.

'No!'

I was breathless with striding after him through Roman alleys.

Twenty feet below, the Tiber sluggishly flowed. I stared down off the bridge. Hadrian's fortress-crowned burial mound reflected here and there in the water, wherever the currents beneath let it appear still enough on the surface.

'As your owner—' Rekhmire' came to a sudden halt. '—I can easily refuse permission for you to get married!'

'*I* was hoping you'd come to the wedding.'

Rekhmire''s fist thumped down on the sandstone coping of the bridge parapet. '*Are you mad?*'

Now is not the time to tell him that I'll tell her, when the time's right.

Leaning on the coping-stones with my chest heaving, I managed an equable reply. 'Her father finds my proposal acceptable.'

Silence.

'It seems he thinks a fine upstanding young painter – *apprentice* to a painter – is completely suitable for his daughter.'

I shrugged.

'Of course, if she wasn't deformed, he wouldn't accept it. He's probably been wondering since she was born how the Hell he's going to get her married off.'

Aranthur Paziathe's face came back to me. My fingers ached to sketch the deep lines at the corners of his mouth, and those etched across his forehead. Small, dark, contained: I had no idea how such a fair acorn could drop from that oak.

'Her father may wonder, too,' I said aloud. And, at Rekhmire''s bemused look, explained, 'Whether her mother played him false . . . '

'Ilario—'

'I can let her stay locked up in that, that *prison*, crippled, until she grows old. Or I can get her out of there.' I watched emotion shift in Rekhmire''s dark eyes. 'And you know what? The club-foot isn't ugly. It's the thing that makes her beautiful.'

'You *are* mad.' He muttered something under his breath: a string of Alexandrine god-names. He began to pace, on the dusty surface of the bridge, turning with a sharp twist every three or four steps.

He stopped, facing me. 'You haven't thought about this.'

'Yes. This time I have.'

'If nothing else, *your* father's permission—'

'No need; I've long been of age. And Honorius isn't here. Besides . . . ' I remembered Honorius's creased face, seeing me for the first time. The joy in his eyes uncontaminated by disgust. 'I think he'd approve.'

'And back at the court of Taraco—!' He gestured with his large hands, as if he presented every incident between Carthage and Taraconensis, and my part in it, for my inspection. 'A wife is a hostage to fortune!'

'So are you! So is Honorius! So is any friend I might make, or my Mastro!'

I know well enough that, once out of Rome, my company might be dangerous.

'You're—' Rekhmire' cut off whatever he had been about to say. 'And

126

her father, he'll be happy to have you marry her by the Arian Christian rite, will he?'

That made me frown. 'I don't suppose they *are* worshippers of Christ-the-Emperor, here. No . . . That doesn't matter. I can marry her by the Frankish rite.'

'Amun and Amunet! *How can you marry her when you're half a woman yourself!* You're—'

'—A freak? And what's she, Rekhmire'? What's she!' I hauled in breath. 'She's the same as *I* am—'

'You're property. My property. You're a slave!'

'You think you're going to stop me doing this? Have me arrested! Because you're going to have to put chains on me to stop me helping her!'

Rekhmire' threw up his hands. In the purest dialect of Rome, audible to every man within fifty feet, he exclaimed, '*You stupid bitch—*!'

I brought my bags, the rest of my tools for the encaustic wax technique, and my bedroll, and put them on the couch at the back of the workshop.

Masaccio raised no eyebrow; he only harried me harder with modelling for the Franks' Great Betrayer, and painting the Alexandrine's miraculous moving golem-statue. He asked no questions about the Paziathe family.

It was twelve long hours, well into the evening, before I could get away to meet Sulva again – and then it was her father I found myself speaking with, not her.

That didn't come until the following morning.

'You haven't changed your mind?' I hardly dared look down into her face, that held the round newness of youth and too much knowledge of suffering.

Sulva gripped my arm for support as we walked. She lifted her head, pretending a wicked glint in her smile. 'No – not if you promise to take me travelling after we're married!'

Not only is Rekhmire' legally paid my wages for working in Masaccio's shop, not only will those wages be the only way to pay passage on a ship, but by law his permission is needed for me to travel anywhere.

We'll reconcile him to the idea, I thought, grimly determined, and smiled down at Sulva Paziathe. 'You can travel wherever you like. As far as Constantinople! As far as the lapis lazuli mine in Persia!'

She stifled her laughter with her fingers, for all we were outdoors.

A walled park lay behind their mansion. Grassed paths wound among ancient oak trees. Aranthur Paziathe and one of his middle-aged sons walked twenty yards ahead of us; Hathli and another maid dogged our

127

footsteps, half that distance behind. The only respectable way in which a betrothed couple may meet and talk.

I am not under the illusion that she sees in me anything but escape from her prison of a mansion. How can she? But does that matter? Once she has her marriage lines, she's free; a woman can have greater freedom posing as a respectable widow than she can as wife or daughter.

She can make her choices, then. And if she *does* decide she'll stay with me . . .

I pushed muddy oak-leaves aside with my foot, hotly aware of the pressure of her hand on my sleeve. All the wealth of the household went into her brocade bodice and skirts. I had been excusably mistaken when I thought her father a servant: he dressed the part, at least. The family was not rich.

Sulva broke the silence. 'Which is your local church, here?'

'My local—?'

'For reading the banns.'

In the cathedral of Taraco, the King's Freak prayed by the King's side. Now, I pray less often than a man ought. I didn't desire to explain why.

I said, 'I haven't been in Rome long enough to have a local parish. Won't your father speak to your family priest?'

'No.' Sulva looked up. I suppose my face showed surprise. She spoke hesitantly. 'Father said I had to tell you. I hope you won't . . . We're not followers of the Christ of the Frankish people. You and I will have a private ceremony later, and be married as my family custom is.'

I glanced ahead, at Aranthur's rigid spine. 'Later?'

'First, we should be married properly, in public.' Her eyes were serious and sad. 'So no gossip gets about. Believe me, it's best.'

My suspicion became a sudden certainty.

'You don't worship the Green Christ at all, do you? Not as Christ-the-Emperor, or Christus Viridianus, or any other way?'

She glanced ahead and behind, as if looking for help from Aranthur or Hathli.

'I don't care who a man prays to,' I added.

I caught the tiny movement of her head. Assent.

'We're Etruscan,' she whispered. 'We were here long before the Romans! We have our own gods. People don't . . . It isn't good to be a heretic here. But it's worse to be a heathen. Outside the city, we have a place to celebrate ceremonies: the villa in the trees . . . You look *relieved*,' she exclaimed.

I let out an explosive breath. 'It explains why your father's willing to let you marry *me*. I suppose local families know you are – what you are.'

Her face hid expression no better than glass hides sunlight. I watched wonder and realisation and desperate hope go across her features. If I could take her to Masaccio's shop, now; work on the statue—

No. Not with how he still speaks of her as a whore, because she didn't return his desire.

'Heresy doesn't worry me.' I shrugged. 'Let men pray to what they will. And if your people are, what is it, "Etruscan"?'

'Yes. The Rasenna. I did pray to the Frankish Christ, once! For a small miracle. For a healing.' She looked down at her foot as she walked.

'That doesn't worry me either,' I said. 'But – wasn't your father willing to let you marry Tommaso Cassai?'

Into her silence, I added, 'I know how poor I am. I suppose I do look . . . respectable.'

The word almost choked me with irony.

'But so is Masaccio,' I completed. 'And more so. He has the reputation of being a fine painter, a friend to the architects and painters of Florence – Brunelleschi, Donatello. A man with an abbot for a patron. Wasn't he a better prospect for your father to approve?'

Sulva's lips pressed together at the centre, and turned up at the corners, giving her exactly the smile of her statue. 'My father thought Tommaso Cassai a respectable man. But . . . after I knew him better . . . *Mas accio!*'

She emphasised the sounds of his nickname: the pejorative *-accio* ending. *Bad Thomas.*

'He was rough, and rude, and spiteful sometimes, and I told my father I wouldn't marry him!' Sulva watched me, her expression anxious. 'You think badly of me, now?'

'I was just thinking . . . ' I let her wait. 'Of how we can find a priest here who'll let us into his church to marry.'

'Oh!' She swatted lightly at my arm, and this time she didn't stifle her laughter.

The old man glanced back at us. I saw his concern fade into a disgust at youthful horse-play.

Sulva's light-heartedness ceased, abruptly. Her eyes, under her oval lids and long lashes, lowered with doubt.

'This is Rome.' I wrapped Sulva's hand more securely over my arm, steadying her on the slick leaves. 'It contains the most worldly priests on earth. You arrange your ceremony at the – villa?'

'The villa in the trees.'

'And I'll see there's a marriage here first. Is that what you would like?' Her smile was painfully raw in its joy.

11

Restlessness swarmed inside me, needing wind on my face to disperse it.

Masaccio swore and sent me off for an hour, for fidgeting as I sat.

I walked around as much of the ancient parts of Rome as I could encompass. Because who knows how much longer I shall be able to stay in this city? *I have plans to make.*

Must I leave Masaccio's workshop. How *can* I? There must be a way to manage it all!

At the bottom of one green valley, a great white marble arch stood – a gate to and from nowhere, covered with the triumphs of a general whose name no man remembers. I walked to the domed chapel of the Vestal Virgins: so small it seems impossible any woman could ever have lived inside. And I walked uphill – all Rome seems to be up a steep hill, or else down one – to an amphitheatre half-buried in the ground.

Row upon row of empty windows pierced the oval surrounding walls. Inside the roofless amphitheatre, and around an equally half-buried column (carved with Roman soldiers overcoming long-haired barbarians), all the earth was covered over with cob-walled, thatch-roofed houses; crammed up against each other, chickens and children running in the dust between them.

The sun burned down on my head. Even in the late months of the year, the high hours after noon are not well spent outdoors. I put away my charcoal and the board I always took with me to sketch on – put them away without regret; nothing of the monuments I had drawn was of any merit. In one corner of the board, I had managed a line or two that gave a hint how Sulva's cheek and shoulder looked when she turned her head. *This, only, I will keep.*

Closer to the Vatican, the buildings were mostly of ancient stone or brick. I welcomed the shade in the narrow passages. Seeing an open taverna, I ducked inside. The sun-blindness cleared from my gaze and I thought; *Luck is with me.* Sitting over my wine, I watched half a dozen clerics drinking and talking.

Over the next hour, two left, and a number more came in. It was strange to see no man in the robes belonging to a bishop's staff, but after a while I saw the green cloth robes of friars. And a friar would be sufficient.

'Where might a man go for a special marriage licence?' I asked my man, after I had chosen him and spent some time in drinking and conversation.

The priest, a Friar Sebastian, as he had introduced himself, looked at me shrewdly and wiped his finger across his upper lip. 'Time is too short for banns?'

He sketched a curve with his hand. I understood him to intend a woman's great belly, when she is about to have her child.

'I must leave Rome on business,' I improvised, the words coming fluently. 'My master, who is a painter, is sending me to Venice to buy blue pigment.'

Friar Sebastian nodded at that. In Rome, one evidently finds priests who understand the painting trade: how the colour blue is made solely from lapis lazuli, and how lapis-stone can only be bought at its one port of import from the East, Venice. He can probably quote me how many ducats the ounce – four for the good, and two ducats for the inferior stuff!

'I don't know how long I'll be gone,' I added, 'and my betrothed's father is anxious that I wed before I leave.'

His lip quirked up. My hands itched to draw that worldly smile. Let him conclude what he will: scandal is nothing to me. But I should encourage him towards silence, I thought. In case Sulva ever desires to return to Rome.

'A licence might be acquired,' Friar Sebastian remarked. 'By, let us say, tomorrow morning? I don't see how it can be done earlier. There will be fees, of course.'

'Of course,' I said flatly. I put down on the taverna bench between us the sole silver coin I had. It had been sewn into my cloak-hem since Carthage. But he need not know that. 'There is a down-payment. What church shall I come to?'

'To St Mithras Viridianus. By the Catacombs,' he added, seeing me look blank. 'You've not been long in the Empty Chair, have you? There again, so few people move into the city these days.'

He did not add, *in our ruin*, but the sigh that followed his words clearly implied it. Among the things I had seen in my walks were the great number of permanently closed churches.

'I consider Rome beautiful beyond all cities,' I flattered him, 'having found a bride in it. What hour shall I come to the church? There will be myself, and the bride, and her father and family.'

And no family of mine.

Nothing I do here can get me into *more* trouble with Aldra Videric, since he already needs me dead—

I jerked my thoughts away from Videric – and Rosamunda – and found my mind momentarily turning to Honorius. And Rekhmire'. Who before this I had imagined would stand in for family, were there the need.

'Tomorrow morning, before Matins.' Friar Sebastian reached across the ancient stained wood of the table. 'Now, let us finish this wine, shall we?'

12

I suppose every man asks himself on his wedding day, *How did I come to be here?*

Not so many will be confused about whether they ought to be the bride or the groom.

My confusion was not aided by a night spent largely sleepless – Masaccio had not thought it odd I should stay in the workshop when we returned from more hours spent covering square inches of stone golem with the accurate colours of skin. I lay awake, watching slivers of the moon's light cross the floor.

Rekhmire' did not send a message.

Nor did I.

How *did* I come to be here? I thought, walking in the pre-dawn mist through the wet, clean streets of the Empty Chair. It made me smile to myself – if wryly. Had I known the ship from Carthage would bring me to Mastro Masaccio, and sitting endless stiff hours as model for a man he thinks a traitor . . . That might have amused me, given what names the Aldra Videric must be calling me now. Had I known it would bring me wonders: a statue that moves of itself, a club-footed girl with a beauty so much greater for its imperfections . . .

I looked up as I reached the lodgings that had been mine and Rekhmire''s.

'Your master's already left for his work!' the woman from the next floor up remarked as she came down the stairs. She gave me a grin. 'Late night, was it?'

'Yes . . . ' Thinking rapidly, I improvised the look of a man frustrated in some effort. 'And I need to get my things, and I haven't his key—'

'Oh, that don't matter; I can let you in. Quintilla leaves the key with me most mornings.'

It was that easy to make an entry into the familiar low-roofed rooms, with the bustling woman at my back.

She nodded, as if to signal I should get on. I began grabbing at random among the men's clothes I still had here. *If she won't leave—*

Another woman came down the tenement stairs, carrying a slop-bucket; the two of them leaned either side of the door, and entered into conversation. Neither looking at a harmless slave.

I reached under his mattress, lifted the loose floorboard that Rekhmire' had indicated to me – 'Should we ever be in need of help, either of us' – and took, by feel, a handful of the coins that I knew were there.

No matter that he told me they were there to take – *Now I am a thief*.

Even worn baggy, I was finding Italian hose too close-fitting for pockets. I dropped the coins into my shirt-sleeve and tightened the draw-string; nodded to the two women, and left.

Friar Sebastian greeted me at the very door of St Mithras Viridianus. The coins vanished into his robe as if I had never stolen them.

His hand came out again.

'I had not appreciated the particular nature of the family,' he murmured.

I fumbled again in my sleeve, counting tiny ducat-coins into his hand until his face showed agreement. He nodded and led me in. I barely noticed the ornamental stonework, struck through with a sudden panic fear of poverty.

The back of the church was part of the catacombs themselves. Each wall I passed as he led me towards the altar was hollowed out into an ossuary. Morning's light through the round-arched windows couldn't combat the sticky darkness clinging to piles of bones, behind stone bars. Brown and yellow skulls stared out at me from their empty orbits.

'Ilario?' a soft voice said.

I had arrived before the rood-screen. Sulva stood to my right side, a veil covering her face. The bleached flax was transparent enough that I could see her eyes. Her irises the colour of turquoise-stone.

I smiled at her.

I can pass as a man; I can work; if I paint, I can sell my canvases and boards. Somehow, we'll contrive.

The rood-screen was not made of carved wood as they commonly are in Iberia. Like half the churches in the Empty Chair, it was built of brick or masonry, covered over and decorated with mosaic. On the other side of me, Aranthur Paziathe glared at the mosaics of the Bull and the Tree; barely hiding his affront.

I could not help studying the mosaic's antique style. Do men still know, now, how to make that blue, that green, that gold?

The crowd of men with Aranthur, who I took to be relatives, stood in a tight fearful group.

'Will we go to your country?' Sulva whispered to me, hardly audible. 'When we're truly married? I should like that.'

I would not, I thought grimly. Matters will have to be safer before that can happen.

And there will have to be a mending of fences before I can bring her to Rekhmire'. Or to Honorius, if the Egyptian won't be reconciled. This will take some thinking out . . .

Heated flesh touched mine; Sulva's fingers crept into my hand. Startled, I gripped her tightly. She gave me a tremulous smile.

'They say,' Aranthur emphasised the word enough to hint at complete disbelief, 'that the heretic Gundobad would have devastated the whole Frankish world, if Saint Heito hadn't stopped him. By which I suppose they mean, *his* heresy would have supplanted *their* heresy.'

It was a Frankish name I had not heard. '"Heito"?'

Aranthur Paziathe stepped forward, stabbing a walnut-coloured finger at the mosaic panels that hid the altar and Friar Sebastian praying.

Beside a figure burning on a bonfire – which must be Gundobad the Prophet – another man was depicted. His dress was antique, and white deer's horns sprang from his brow. That was enough to make me raise my own brows. What superstitions *do* the Franks believe?

'That's Saint Heito,' Aranthur's voice rumbled. 'And this man, burning, this is the Carthaginian's Prophet Gundobad, who cursed Rome and brought about the Empty Chair . . . They say Heito prevented him doing worse. Here is Pope Leo, whom the mob tore to pieces, and blinded and castrated. Pope Stephen the Fifth, whose horse trampled him, three days after he took the Papal Keys. Pope Paschal the First, who was struck by a levin-bolt. Pope Eugene, killed by a bust of St Thomas the Doubter falling from the front of St Peter's in a storm. All in the space of three months.'

Beside me, Sulva whispered, 'Father!'

Aranthur grunted, staring down at a patch of sunlight on the miniature glass tiles. 'Valentine, Gregory, Sergius, the second Paschal. They haven't room enough here to show all their dead popes! And they blame it on this Gundobad, when they must *know* that the true Gods find Frankish priests an abomination! . . . It didn't take long for the cardinals to become fearful. Their conclave has sat these two hundred years; it will never elect another pope – or not one who will consent to serve.'

'*Father!*'

Sulva's embarrassed whisper got his attention just in time for him to step back, and be standing beside me as Friar Sebastian arrived from the altar. I recovered my expression as best I might. The true Gods?

'Who,' Friar Sebastian enquired, 'gives possession of this woman?'

I glanced at Sulva – and found her looking back at me; her expression finally an exact copy of what I thought my own must be.

I paid little attention to the rest of the ceremony, only speaking in the right places, and signing my name where it was desired. Sulva Paziathe, now of the family Honorius, made an ink-mark with her thumb in the registry book. I had a hard job not to flinch every time a door opened somewhere in the church.

I wouldn't put it past Rekhmire' to walk in and proclaim: 'This ceremony is void: this slave has no permission to be married!'

Not until we walked out into the still-cool morning air did I draw an unrestricted breath.

'Sulva—'

A two-wheeled *cisia*-carriage stood waiting: Aranthur swung himself up into the seat, and peremptorily gestured for her to follow.

She put her hand up to my cheek in evident farewell. 'It won't be long now.'

'"Won't be long"?' I was bewildered.

'I have to be . . . ' She searched for a word. 'Purified. After *that*.'

She nodded at the front of the church. Friar Sebastian waved at us, cheerfully, too far away to hear what she said.

'You come to me in three nights' time.' She put her veil down, her gaze still on me through the translucent cloth. 'It's outside the walls. You'll have to travel secretly. Etruscans aren't supposed to leave the city without a permit, but one of my cousins will come and bring you to the villa in the trees on the third night—'

'"On the third night"?' I stared. 'Why didn't you tell me this!'

'Wasn't it obvious?' Her brows dipped down, a little vertical fold of flesh between them. 'I thought you'd know! You're a heretic too!'

How old is she, sixteen?

Hardly surprising if she forgets, or makes assumptions . . .

Gently, I touched my thumb to her forehead, smoothing the skin. Hathli gave me a sour look. I smiled down at Sulva. She smelled of musk; I supposed her veil to have been perfumed.

'A different kind of heretic,' I said softly. 'No matter. I'll come to you.'

Her skin flushed with a colour that I could never have caught in marble, not to make it lifelike.

'The custom is . . . that there are no lamps,' she said, in a hurry. Her gaze dropped. 'All will be in the dark. For the . . . wedding night.'

Quickly, she turned away, took Hathli's hand, and made an ungainly jerking movement that got her up into the *cisia* vehicle. The driver touched the horses with a whip and it moved away – no faster than walking-pace; the relatives and servants hurrying behind it, leaving me alone. Sunlight dazzled my eyes as I stared after them.

The sound of wheels on cobbles clattered into the distance, fading under street cries and the sounds of two men having an argument, and a barking dog. All the morning noises of the Empty Chair.

I smiled. *I am a married man.*

I stopped smiling.

I am a married *man*.

It will be in the dark. She desires it because of her foot, but *I*—

It was not until that moment that I realised. A wedding is not legal until consummated. And, until now . . .

Until *now*, I haven't thought to wonder what will happen when I come to her bed.

Standing alone in the street, I realised: I've become so used to passing as a man that I never once thought about the danger of discovery!

What have I done?

What have I become?

13

I strode back through the early morning to Masaccio's workshop.

I felt the pull of the lodging-house – a desperate need to speak with Rekhmire'.

But I doubt I'll get good advice from a man who calls me *bitch on heat*, I reflected, face burning at the memory of the tall Egyptian shouting just that across the bridge at Castel San' Angelo.

If she does not desire it, I will not touch her. We can lie about the fornication that legally seals a marriage.

The Egyptian thinks me besotted. He has no idea of the world a woman finds herself inhabiting.

'Your master's been here for you,' Mastro Tommaso Cassai greeted me as I came in. He jerked a thumb at the couch where I'd left my belongings. 'Took your bag back with him.'

Rage flared through me. 'Why didn't you stop him?'

For once, Masaccio didn't answer in words; he pointed. At me. I stared, for a moment; then reached up to touch my neck.

My fingers encountered my iron collar. I have grown so used to it resting there that I forget it. The engraved words would be plainly visible to him:

I am ::ILARIO:: owned by ::REKHMIRE'::

In Carthage, they only need to fill in the name-blanks; the collars come ready-chiselled with the remaining form of words. Now I had taken my cloak off, any man might see it. I wondered if Friar Sebastian would have objected in the slightest, had he noticed it in church. Perhaps he would have charged me more.

'I'm sleeping here tonight,' I said, in a tone that let Masaccio know I was not inclined to listen to joke or reason.

He shrugged. 'Sleep in the street if you like, boy. It's all one to me. What have you done to upset the Alexandrine?'

The tension brought truth out of me. I pointed at her statue: the goat-foot coloured like life, the face a white marble blank.

'I've married Sulva Paziathe. My master doesn't approve.'

'You've married— You've *married*—?'

The Florentine shook his head furiously, as if he cleared a bee out of his ear. His black eyes glinted at me.

'Did I hear you right? You, you are speaking of – you *married that bitch*?'

Had I been at Rodrigo's court (and had it been a day there that I was dressed as a male), I should have thrown a steel gauntlet in his face, or simply found a sword and stuck it through his belly.

Having only a dagger, and an immense respect for Masaccio as a painter, if not as a man, the red blur had washed through and past me by the time my hand touched my belt.

Masaccio noticed none of that. He grated incredulously, 'How is it she'd marry *you*?'

I shrugged lightly, and walked past him to throw the cloak I carried onto the couch. 'Perhaps because you only saw a pretty face?'

His voice dropped; he sounded like a man in a taverna ready to begin a fight. '*I loved her.*'

That stopped me. I looked back at him. 'I'm sorry.'

He blinked.

'Married you?' he repeated, after a moment.

Yes, me: is that so strange?

Well . . . yes.

'When are you – when did you—?' He stopped, and looked at me. 'Is the ceremony done?'

'This morning. Just now. At dawn.' I intended him to hear the finality of that.

'Dawn?' He echoed me, stupidly. The pupils of his black eyes altered in the light of an oil-lamp left burning on the table. 'But – you want to sleep here *tonight*?'

Flustered, I said, 'Yes. But—'

'So you're lying. Or else – eh, she's *using* you, isn't she? The bitch! You fall in love with a pretty stone face. And she sees a fool who'll marry a whore! And be fooled into not sticking his prick in her!'

'*She is not a whore!*'

The bearded man straightened, chin coming up. 'I know more about her than you do. Boy. All you see is a pretty face, you know *nothing* of her—'

'Then how is it *you* don't know why I have to sleep here until the third night? Or don't you know the customs of the Etruscan people?'

The workshop echoed my defiance.

Silence succeeded it.

My back ran with sudden cold sweat.

'Etruscan?' Masaccio stared in shock. 'That . . . would explain much.'

He gazed at me, his expression shuttling through unreadable emotions and settling on disgust.

'One of those people. And the whole family—? Yes, of course. Of course. I always *knew* there was something wrong about the Paziathe.'

Bewildered, I watched the Florentine shaking his head. I wanted to ask: If you still loved her, as indeed it seems you do, how can you go from that to this, in a matter of moments?

And – what have I said?

'It's a good thing your baggage is gone,' Masaccio said with harsh contempt. 'Model for Judas! *Judas!* Go. Leave! Get out of here!'

'What?' I said stupidly.

'You're fired. Go. I don't want to see your face again. Out of my workshop, now!'

He made flapping gestures at me, like an old woman shooing hens, that made me burst out into shocked laughter.

'*Out!*' His hand dipped down: he caught up a pestle from a mortar on the bench, and threw it.

The heavy porphyry implement hit the door-frame beside me in a shower of red pigment; thudded down onto the floorboards; left a dent in the wood.

I stopped laughing.

His hand scrabbled for another missile.

'I'm going!' I slid my foot back, pushing the door open; caught it and swung it closed behind me as I darted through.

Something solid hit the inside, hard enough to dent the planks.

Masaccio's voice raised in incoherent rage. I couldn't make out what he yelled; I could hear the raw fury. I took a pace or two back into the narrow cobbled street.

The threat of violence faded from my muscles and tendons.

'Mastro, you *won't* fire me.' I realised that I found myself not so bereft as I might have expected. 'Not until Judas is finished and on the church wall.'

Give him a day or two . . .

Should I try to warn Sulva? That I've said she's . . . Warn her of what? What can he do?

Like the Jews in Taraco, I guessed, it would be no real secret which families in the city were Etruscan.

Masaccio can only spread gossip. But words are a dangerous enough poison.

The impossible-to-paint blue of mist and sunlight grew in the sky overheard.

Thirty paces down the narrow street, I realised: I am still left with nowhere to sleep tonight. Or tomorrow.

'Then again,' I said aloud, 'I don't have to sleep.'

Tonight will be a night or two before the full of the moon. That will give me monochrome light enough to walk the city streets, go from district to district, draw sketches in return for jugs of wine in tavernas. I could do that tonight and tomorrow, and on the third night, share the hours of darkness with Sulva in this 'villa of the trees'.

I looked up from placing my feet between scattered mule-dung, and recognised where instinct had taken me. The road down to Castel San' Angelo.

I turned to go back, and stopped.

'No,' I said aloud.

Whether I need to sleep or not, whether I can hide or not . . .

No, I will not hide from anything I've done.

And whatever mess I've made – I'll clear it up.

14

'What are you doing?' I asked.

Rekhmire' looked up from where he sat cross-legged on the tenement room's floorboards. A small box-shrine stood open in front of the Egyptian.

'Praying to the gods of the primordial water, and the gods of invisibility. Heh and Hehet. Amun and Amunet.'

'Oh. Oh . . . I mean – God and Goddess of the primordial water, yes, but a god and goddess of *invisibility*?'

He stared at me, saying nothing.

Uncomfortable, I walked into the room and sat down on the low bed, watching him all the time.

'Your gods are all twin gods, aren't they? Paired. Are they male and female?' I added rapidly, before he could speak: 'Maybe they're hermaphrodites! That would be something, wouldn't it? Hermaphroditic deities. Maybe I should do that. Should I be "Ilario" and "Ilariet", do you think?'

He winced – at the butchery of language, too. 'Ilario. What do you want?'

'I want to apologise.'

His head came up. Without looking, but with a seamless movement, he closed the box-shrine. The click of painted wood sounded loudly in the tenement room.

'"Apologise"?'

'I'm sorry,' I said. 'I'm sorry I stole money from you. I'm sorry I didn't take your advice – although I couldn't, and I know I'm right in what I'm doing. I'm sorry I quarrelled with you. I'm sorry I've done so many things without . . . well, talking it over with you.'

Rekhmire''s face stayed impassive. 'With your master.'

'With my friend.'

'You're in trouble.'

Anger flared in me – but I caught, in time, the almost-imperceptible note of amusement in his voice.

Shakily, I smiled back at him. 'No. Well, yes. But nothing I can't sort out with carefulness and attention.'

'That would be something new . . . '

I spoke in the same tone as he. 'Be careful, Egyptian – I'll be Mastro

Tommaso Cassai's apprentice again in a couple of days; you don't want to speak disrespectfully to someone associated with such a superior man.'

'Threw you out, did he?' Rekhmire''s impassive face slipped into something close to a grin. He recovered himself immediately. I thought I should like to paint him amused: the liveliness of his expression setting off the monumental gravity of his features.

'You might throw me out, too.' I took a deep breath, hoping he didn't notice. 'I have married Madonna Sulva, after all.'

The Egyptian nodded slowly.

'It'll be—' I searched for a word. 'Complete. Three days from now. There's an Etruscan ceremony. I don't know if they allow strangers, but if they do, I'd like you to be there. As groom's man.'

His eyebrows rose up at *Etruscan*; at *groom's man* his eyes widened so much that I momentarily saw white all around the blue-brown irises.

I said, 'I'm sorry.'

His monumental features shifted. He nodded acceptance. 'I, also, apologise. I am sorry to have called you a bitch.'

That startled me; I could only stare at him.

Rekhmire''s lips quirked. 'There are people to whom I am only a man when they're pleased with me. At their *dis*pleasure, I become a gelded thing neither man nor woman; a monster, a freak of the surgeon's knife. I ... didn't intend to speak to you in that same way. I'm sorry for that.'

I have been given more than was owed to me, I thought, and for a moment couldn't speak.

'It's possible there'll be trouble,' I said, finally. 'Masaccio didn't know her family were Etruscan until I told him. I'm not asking for help. Only to talk things through. When I can see what's right, then I'll do it.'

'I can see we have a lot to discuss.' Rekhmire' got to his feet in one smooth, heavy movement; for a moment reminding me of the stone golem. 'Meanwhile ... meanwhile, we accept each other's apologies, I see, and – come with me.'

'What?'

He swung up a cloak from the foot of the bed, wrapping it around himself, largely concealing his Alexandrine clothes. One hand checked the purse tied to his belt. He thrust the room's door open. 'This way.'

I walked past him, through the doorway, out onto the staircase; half wondering if he would shut it behind me.

He did shut the door, but with himself on the same side of it as me, pausing only to turn the crude iron key in the lock.

'That won't keep Quintilla from snooping,' he murmured, 'but we shan't be out long. Come on.'

'But – we ought to – *but*—'

I found myself facing his back as he moved away down the stairs.

Out in the street, I must half-run to keep up with his strides. A shower of late morning rain left puddles the length of the alley. Our cloak-hems grew soaked and black. He strode from alley to street, and street to lane, until we crossed a great ancient square, whose wide empty geometry I ached to sketch, and came to a small shop set under an awning. A bald-headed, short Roman man stood with his arms folded, looking out disconsolately at the weather that would keep away customers.

'You are a notary?' Rekhmire' demanded.

The man straightened, and nodded.

Rekhmire' said, 'Good. Somewhere in your shop you will have the form for a deed of manumission. Draw it up. I am formally freeing my slave, here.'

He pointed at me.

'What?' I stuttered.

Coins changed hands.

The man went back into the dimness of his shop. A moment later, I saw the blossoming of lamp-light, and heard the stropping of a quill on paper. Rekhmire' took two steps across the antique pavement, worn into dips by millennia of passing feet, and grabbed me by the upper arm.

'What,' I managed to get out, 'are you *doing*?'

'I'm stopping you pretending to be helpless!'

The grip of his hand was firm, but not painful. I looked up at him, a head taller as he was. This is not so different from how I saw him in Carthage, at the slaver's hall. Only now a Frankish cloak covers the linen kilt and the woven reed head-band, and his sandals are crusted with mud, not dust.

'Pretending.' I couldn't manage to make it a question.

He nodded at that, and loosed his grip. I stood for a moment, feeling the first drops on my face as a heavier rain began to fall. It swept in a veil across the great paved square, and misted the ends of the arcade of shops. I felt, also, the weight of the iron band, resting on the linen at the neck of my shirt. It rubbed, by the day's end. I had seen few enough other slaves in Frankish Rome; most of them with evident foreigners.

Rekhmire' rumbled, 'It's long past time you took off that collar. You're no slave.'

'Alexandrine slavery is different?' I put forward, to see what he would say.

He was unstoppable. 'You and I do not behave as master and slave.'

I met his gaze. 'I don't have the money to pay you for my freedom.'

Recalling where I had got the money to pay Friar Sebastian, I felt my face heat until I must be scarlet to look at.

He shrugged. 'Then owe me a debt, as one free man does to another. The notary here can draw up the terms of that. I am not your conscience, to forbid you to do this or that. I am not master of you in any way. I won't let you hide behind that. You are to be freed, now. Whether you wish it or not.'

144

I couldn't help smiling at that. He gave a brief smile in answer. For a moment there was no sound but the pricking of the notary's iron pen on vellum.

'I understand why you're doing this,' I said. 'I have decisions to make, to clear up this mess.'

Rekhmire' inclined his head. 'And you must take them, not I for you.'

I touched the cold metal at my throat for the last time.

'Here's my first decision, then. I'm going back to Mastro Masaccio, to apologise to *him*.'

15

It took me more than twenty-four hours to get him to speak to me.

The clock at St Martin's chimed six on the evening of the next day. Masaccio came out of the workshop door, throwing out water from stained bowls he was evidently swilling clean.

I stepped back out of the way.

Instead of *I apologise*, which he had not yet allowed me to get out at all, I said, 'A woman with her poor taste is a fool, Mastro. But you will forgive her for that.'

Framing it so was the sacrifice I made in hope of reconciliation. His lips moved, half-hidden in his beard. I thought I might touch his vanity. Now I saw I had touched his humour.

'You're right,' Masaccio said. 'In both.' He upended the last bowl and watched it drip.

On impulse, I said, 'Would you like a drink at the taverna, Mastro?'

He grinned at me, showing white teeth. 'No drinking until we're done working. Do you know, I actually *fell behind* yesterday, with you not there at the Gyppos' house? There must be some use in an assistant after all!'

If bigoted, it was still a remark that reached out for reconciliation.

He looked the nearest he might come to shame-faced, which was momentary. I bowed acknowledgement, after the fashion of the court at Taraco. If it's work that will reconcile us, I'm willing. Tommaso Cassai is not a man to apologise for anything.

More tools and pigments than three men could carry had been piled on a two-wheeled flat hand-cart.

'You push,' he said, unsurprisingly, with a more relaxed grin, and walked beside me. The cart jolted at every shove. Why I should feel so light-hearted at Tommaso Cassai's fast-ended anger, I wasn't sure – until he began talking, as we walked through the streets to the Alexandrine embassy.

'You *will* be a painter. One day.' He waved his arm in a gesture that brought a tearing-metal bray from a donkey tied up by a pot-shop. 'That's more important than women! That stuff you brought with you from under the Penitence – trash! And who but *I* could have seen the little that wasn't? That showed talent? I do flatter myself I can see promise.'

So blankly it must have been comic, I said, 'You can?'

146

'You're beginning – just beginning – to learn. Or to know what it is you *don't* know!' Masaccio's smile was dizzying. He nodded to the guards on the embassy door, and talked to them at high speed as I wheeled the loaded hand-cart down through the building, towards the room that we worked in.

He thinks I have talent. He really thinks—

I stopped in the doorway.

Having not seen it for two days, the impact of the stone man on my senses was profound. I could only stand for a moment, and gaze up at it; patchwork flesh and marble as it appeared to be. 'I . . . *really* don't understand this.'

'Why should you?' Masaccio shrugged, seized the handles of the piled-high flat cart, and with a physical strength I had not expected pushed it ahead of himself into the room. He began to untie the tarpaulin that covered it. 'I ask myself: is it a machine, or is it a miracle? But I am not priest-ridden, like most Franks, so I have no doubt. *Men* made this. What I don't know is how!'

I put in: 'Or why.'

'"Why"? It's a servant! What else could it be?'

'When I was in Iberia, the King—'

Whom I need not now, or ever again, call *my master the King*, odd as that feels.

'—King Rodrigo Sanguerra had me trained in the techniques of siege works, thinking I had some talent for that. Mobile assault towers, to be used against walls. Catapults, mangonels, scorpions, trebuchets, ballista . . . cannon. Mastro Masaccio, you say a machine is a servant. I have little enough training. But if *I* can wonder what would be the killing ability of a dart-throwing machine, were it powered in the same way this stone man is – then so can any man wonder.'

'Weapons of war?' He cocked a brow at the golem, his expression thoughtful.

'Stone can't be hurt like flesh.'

'Who knows what hurts it? Is it in pain now, frozen as it stands? What does it feel?' Masaccio tapped his finger against his red lower lip, half-hidden in his curling beard. 'It sees nothing, but is not blind. You will have seen bats after dusk, avoiding nets and traps and walls. Does it see with their blind senses? If I were to carve a whistle that only dogs hear, would it come to that call?'

He shook his head, his gaze as he stared up at the golem's face frighteningly intense.

'Could I paint an image of the world, as this golem perceives it? Perhaps. If I truly understood it . . . But I don't know,' he finished. '*I don't know.*'

'You might go to Carthage.'

It was the obvious suggestion; it might excite suspicion not to make it.

Rekhmire''s Eight grant that he doesn't ask me to come with him!

'To see if I can find out who's making them? And how? That will be kept a secret. Guilds and trades . . . '

Masaccio shook his head. 'I never refuse knowledge to a man unless he's stupid enough that he can't benefit from it. Other men keep their secrets tight to their chests. And, I am weary of that. Very weary.'

'Mastro—'

He lifted a hand and pointed at the golem, interrupting me. 'Which is why I intend to do something about it. You'll see. Now, paint!'

He would say no more while we worked. Egyptian slaves came around two or three times to replenish the lamps with oil. Each time I felt a qualm. Masaccio did not comment on the weight of metal gone from my throat.

Being Masaccio, I thought, it may be because he hasn't noticed.

The sensation of lack was keen, to me. And watching the collared embassy slaves made me frown. Whether or not Alexandrine slavery is less onerous than the Carthaginian kind, they are still slaves.

Then again, they need not take decisions for themselves.

Evening wore on into night; overseers came to the door; Masaccio went to speak to them – to tell them we must continue working, I guessed. There looked to be less painting done than I'd expect since I'd last put brush to the stone.

I wonder if he spent time drunk in a taverna?

It might explain his tolerance of the thought of Sulva married, if wine had numbed him.

There were no windows in the low-ceilinged room. I did not always register the chime of the water-clock, but I guessed it to be past midnight when Masaccio put his brush down with finality. He cocked his head, listening. I could hear nothing move in the mansion. He opened the room doors. There was not even a sound of the guards.

'I had a friend in the Florentine militia,' he said, apparently out of nowhere.

In answer to my stare, he added, 'Who told me a thing that's certain. Soldiers would rather drink than guard! If there's one man on the door, now, I'll be surprised. A gift of wine may work a miracle.'

He grinned, his expression febrile.

'Mastro, what—'

'Didn't I say, I intend to do something about my lack of knowledge?' Masaccio put his hand flat on the unpainted part of the stone man's chest, looking up at it. 'This is the only golem I've ever seen. If I let this chance pass, I think it'll be the only one I *will* ever see.'

He turned to look at me.

'And that's why we're stealing it.'

For a moment, I couldn't speak.

I shot a glance at the unloaded hand-cart.

Masaccio nodded, without my needing to say anything; his lips stretching in an excited, enthusiastic grin.

'You planned this!' I accused.

The Florentine spoke amiably. 'It would be difficult to do it *without* planning.'

'You – you can't—' I put my single brush down with too much care. 'Mastro, I mean, you *really* can't. They'll work out who did it. They'll know where to come!'

'I have a cargo-boat moored down at the Tiber, ready to be rowed to Ostia Antica.' Masaccio shrugged. 'From there – well. Never mind. You shouldn't know more.'

Florence! flashed through my mind with absolute certainty. He'll take it home with him, to the city he calls *Fiorenza*.

'And all we have to do is get it down to the river. Come on.'

He made a beckoning gesture, as if I should fetch the hand-cart to him, and turned his thoughtful stare back to the immense statue.

I don't think the wheels will take it.

I didn't say it aloud. There was no necessity.

I blurted, 'Even if the guards are drinking, they'll still be at the entrances! We won't get as far as the front door!'

'Mother of God, boy! The wine's drugged, of course. Fortified with spirits – and poppy.' He stepped past me, impatiently grabbing the handles of the cart, and pushing it around behind the statue. '*Golem, lie down!* Here! *Golem, lie down here on the cart!*'

Stunned, I realised: This is why we've brought no rope and pulley. He knew it wouldn't be necessary.

I flinched back from the impossible movement of the stone man. Swivelling at the joints of hips and knee, turning about; the great marble hands reaching down to grasp the sides of the cart . . .

The stone man lowered himself carefully – comically carefully – back down onto the flat bed of the hand-cart.

The sound of protesting wood creaked through the room.

Masaccio put his lower lip between his teeth, biting hard enough that blood ran down into his beard.

The wood sang – and held.

He gave a sigh and a nod.

The Franks, in their practise of trades, are very expert at estimating, by eye, weights and volumes – which they must be, since (unlike Carthage) they have no common unit of measurement. A barrel and a bale in Rome are not the same as a barrel and a bale in Venice. Masaccio had judged this weight just bearable by the cart. *And so it is. Just.*

'Now, we push it.' He showed all his teeth in a grin of triumph.

'We—? I—?' By an effort, I stopped myself stuttering. I lowered my voice, every nerve tense against some Alexandrine coming down the corridor, entering the room, finding *this*. 'I'm not going to do it!'

'Afraid, *boy*?' He sounded too jubilant for his insult to sting.

'It's theft.' I found my face heating at his stare. 'I'm not a thief!'

A voice in my thoughts whispered sardonically, *Would that that were true* . . .

'The world needs this,' Masaccio said soberly. He reached out to draw the tarpaulin over the marble man laying flat on the cart.

Its feet lay nearer the floor than its head, because of the way it had placed itself down. As the golem vanished under the oiled cloth, I thought: That foreshortening, that perspective – I could *draw* this, now, and stand some chance of doing it justice.

'Who knows how it works?' Masaccio said, tying off a cord. 'Who knows what else could be done with it, if we *did* know?'

He looked at me, as if for the first time he saw me: Ilario.

'Wouldn't you rather slave-work was done by stone men, than by men of flesh and blood with iron collars around their necks?'

'How can I answer that? Of course I would!'

'Then lend a hand here.'

'But it's not that easy!'

Masaccio ignored me and bent to the cart's handles, half crouching. He got the weight of his body on a line through foot and calf and thigh and hip, and thrust forward.

By some miracle the wheels creaked and began to turn. The cart began moving from that first forward jolt.

Almost automatically, I stepped forward and reached for one of the cart-handles.

Before I could touch it, the end of the cart rolled out of the room. The feet of the stone man passed over the threshold of the room, out into the wide embassy corridor.

Cords snapped. The tarpaulin slid away. Stone grated on wood.

A strut somewhere in the cart gave way. A sharp *crack!* echoed flatly in the room.

The stone golem sat up.

My mouth opened on a breath, a warning shout: '*Ahh—*'

Too swiftly for heavy marble to move, the stone man sprang off the hand-cart, landing with an impact that jerked dust up from between the floor tiles. One of the tiles cracked under the weight.

The body of the stone man swivelled. It took too quick a step forward. Its marble hand shot under Masaccio's bearded chin – and closed.

He made one sound: a wheeze.

His lips stretched in a rictus grin, all his white teeth exposed. The handles of the cart dropped out of his fingers. His hands came up, locking around the golem's stone wrists. He kicked, furiously; slammed a boot at a knee-joint—

The statue lifted him, one-handed, into the air.

I sprang forward, grabbed at the painted marble wrist and knuckles, heaved—

And moved nothing.

'Let go! Let go of him! Golem, let go of him! *Golem, let go of his throat!*'

The cold brass joints moved unstoppably under my palms.

Masaccio choked.

His eyes bulged. His lips moved; his jaw worked.

Soundlessly.

Stone fingers clenched around his larynx. He couldn't speak a word.

His skin above his beard darkened, grew dusky blue; his eyes shone red as they filled up with blood. His fingers lost purchase on the stone arms. One flailing hand clawed towards its face. He caught me a sharp, dizzying blow with the other.

I stumbled; scrabbled down on the floor for a weapon.

'Help!' My voice echoed flatly in the room; outside; in the corridor. *'Somebody help us here!'*

The haft of a mallet slotted into my palm. I straightened up. With all my strength, I brought the mallet up and slammed it down on the metal wrist-joint; hit it, hit it again—

The golem's hand flexed closed.

I heard a distinct, sticky, hollow *click*.

I know that noise – it is the noise a hanged man makes, when the rope snaps his vertebrae apart.

Masaccio's feet drummed rapidly, briefly, against the stone man's thighs; and stopped.

His body hung from the statue's hand. Every line of his flesh was drawn down by gravity; limp as a rabbit in a poacher's hand.

I leaned forward, choking, bringing up acid and bile.

Still holding Masaccio's body out at arm's length, the stone golem swivelled around to face me.

Every muscle in my body instantly weakened; my thighs quivered.

The golem stepped lightly forward, arm stretched out. Masaccio swung limply in its grip.

The golem brought its other hand up.

Up and forward.

Towards *me*.

I broke out of the frozen, powerless daze; jolted violently back as the golem's foot came down on pigment-bowls, crushing them flat.

The stone golem's outstretched marble fingertips swung, reaching out for me; brushed past my forehead—

The mere touch slammed my head over to one side. Sharp, solid pain blinded me.

I staggered backwards, spun around, and ran.

16

Masaccio's dead!

Rain and panic froze me.

Grazes stung my knees, through abraded hose. My hands shook, cut where I had fallen on stones. The pitch-dark of the city hemmed me in. Lost. *I am lost.* And Masaccio—

I shook wet hair out of my eyes. A distant glimmer showed the barred, closed door of a taverna. I snatched a torch from its socket under the high awning. The light let me see enough to finally recognise streets as I ran, feet pounding the broken pavements. My head pounded with pain.

He will know; Rekhmire' will know what to do—

Masaccio is dead.

No mistaking that; no hope of a doctor's help.

I have drawn men hanged, by the justice of King Rodrigo's magistrates. They kick; choke. They loose their bowels; they hang, when their necks break, with just such a boneless immobility.

'Masaccio!' I howled, at the freezing rain.

Rekhmire' didn't answer his door; I hammered on it with the butt-end of the torch, yelling. Shutters slammed open over my head

The woman Quintilla bawled something down.

Gasping in a breath, I held up the torch so she might see it was me. '*Rekhmire'!* Wake him! Let me in; *I'll* wake him!'

'He's gone.'

Coldness flooded through me. I stopped – stopped breathing, almost.

'It is you, Ilario?' She leaned out of the window, peering down. 'If you want him, you'll have to follow him. His people came.'

Stupefied, I echoed, 'His people?'

'The other Egyptians. The Gyppies that live in the embassy house? One of them came banging on the shutters and woke everybody up; he's gone with *them.*'

Soaked, winded, I stood in the dark square; staring at the light spilling out through the embassy door.

Cold sent shudders through me. Rain slicked my skin.

I walked forward into the brilliance.

'You!' One of the linen-kilted guards reached towards his sword. 'It's the painter's apprentice; hold her!'

Egyptians see with the eyes of a different culture, I thought numbly. I'd never realised.

The Alexandrines are used to seeing eunuchs. So if they see a Frankish man who's 'wrong', they don't take him for a castrato as Romans do; they think him a woman. Even if that's equally inaccurate.

I didn't move as men rushed up either side of me.

'I want to see Master Rekhmire'. Take me inside, to him.'

Inside, nothing had changed in the time – minutes or hours – since I ran.

The end of the flat-bed cart still projected out into the corridor. Men milled around it; soldiers, diplomats, men whom I didn't recognise. My escort shouldered me through, into the room.

It smelled of dying.

The half-painted marble man stood in the centre of the floor, as motionless as if it was the statue it seemed.

Rekhmire' straightened up from examining its hands.

'*Get away from that!*' I snarled.

The Egyptian looked at the golem, looked at me – and walked across the room to where I stood.

'We're not safe in the same room with it!' My voice shook.

A sheet covered a body on the floor. I hadn't realised Masaccio was so small a man. It was his vital spirit that made him seem taller than he was.

'Ilario?' Rekhmire' glanced from me to the shroud. 'Tell me what happened here.'

I couldn't stop myself looking towards the stone golem. 'It killed him.'

A tenor voice interrupted from behind me, speaking Egyptian-accented Latin. 'The painter's apprentice? That's your slave, is it? Good! I'll have her tortured for information.'

Rekhmire' didn't take his gaze from my face. '*He* is a freedman. – *And* a freedwoman. In any case, free.'

The tall, fat Egyptian man behind him, wrapped in a night-robe evidently snatched up at random, swore in his native language. His voice rose higher than tenor.

'Ilario.' Rekhmire' spoke in a deliberate, soothing voice. 'This is Lord Menmet-Ra. Tell him the truth of what happened here. You will not be punished.'

I must close my eyes to do it, but I told the castrato Menmet-Ra all.

'I didn't know,' I finished, 'what Masaccio planned. Or I would have stopped him. *Somehow*. I would ... He would still – be alive—'

In the silence, I opened my eyes. The sheet covering Masaccio was rucked. I felt a foolish impulse to smooth it down.

He's beyond discomfort now.

'How could the Florentine *do* that!' Menmet-Ra snarled, thumping one heavy fist into his other hand. He was little shorter than Rekhmire', I now saw, but much broader; and with more of a belly of middle-age on him. His brows were soft and fine below the dome of his shaved head.

He drew his foot back as if to kick the corpse.

I made a jolting movement forward, and an inarticulate sound.

Rekhmire''s hand closed over my shoulder.

The Ambassador swung away from the body, leaving it untouched; spat another string of god-names that must be curses, and glared at Rekhmire'. 'If he hadn't struggled, it wouldn't have killed him!'

Cold sweat covered my skin.

'Who *wouldn't* struggle?' Rekhmire''s mild tone held an acid edge. 'Who wouldn't run? Menmet – Pamiu—'

He spoke the second word in the tone of a nickname. I suddenly understood: They know each other well.

'—How much trouble will this mean?'

Menmet-Ra let out an explosive sigh. 'Precisely as much as you think!'

'Well, then . . . ' Rekhmire''s face altered; I knew him well enough to know he was thinking fast and deeply.

Menmet-Ra glared up at the half-painted marble face of the golem. 'It was a precaution! To stop it being stolen! To stop *itself* being stolen. It should have held onto a thief. Who would have dreamed that the *painter* . . . '

Rekhmire' lifted his head, looking at the Ambassador. 'You go, Pamiu. Send your men away. Nothing was seen; nothing was heard. I'll clear up here myself.'

If I'd had emotion enough left to have been surprised, I would have felt shock. I stared dumbly as Rekhmire' and Menmet-Ra conversed quickly, in low tones, and parted, each with a grip to the forearm of the other.

The servants and soldiers vanished so quietly they might never have existed.

All this Alexandrine-decorated Roman mansion could have been drowned in sleep – except that, stupefied as I was, even I could sense the tension quivering in the air. The haste for the body to be dealt with, a scandal to be averted.

My knees loosened.

I went down on the tiles with a thump, beside Masaccio's body. Reaching out, I drew the improvised shroud more neatly over his face.

That shifted the cloth, exposing his hand.

I took it in mine and sat holding the still-warm flesh.

'Ilario.'

I did not look up. 'I thought . . . I know we joked . . . I thought you were a book-buyer who just carried messages, sometimes, or wrote – observations. You're . . . more, aren't you?'

'I am a man of some experience. And an old friend of Menmet-Ra.' Rekhmire' rested his hand on my shoulder, conveying reassurance,

154

warmth. 'At the university, we called him "Pamiu", "Old Tom-Cat" . . .'

The smile in his voice faded.

'If Pamiu must take official notice of this, there'll be scandal. Who knows what, then, will be uncovered? Better if it's handled out of sight.'

I squeezed Masaccio's cooling fingers hard enough that it would have hurt him, had he lived. These hands, these very hands, with which he painted—

'Because the golem *murdered* him? *That* will be a scandal?'

'Politics.' Rekhmire' spoke with a deliberation that acknowledged grief, while he himself stood aside from it. His heavy lids shrouded his eyes, and lifted again. 'In Carthage, they translate "Lord-Amir" as "scientist-magus". This is a political matter. According to Pamiu, the stone golem is their gift, and it shouldn't be known to have passed through Rome on its way to Alexandria-in-exile.'

'Carthage *again*.' The irony bit hard.

'As matters stand, Rome should not be *seen* to be friendly either to Carthage or to "Constantinople".' Rekhmire' used the foreigners' name for his own city with distaste. 'I have friends in many of the Alexandrine embassies,' he added. 'People gossip. It is not ever difficult to know what must be going on.'

Stunned, dizzy, I said, 'Masaccio's *dead*. That thing murdered him!'

Rekhmire' touched the icy hand of the stone golem. It gave me equal chills.

The Egyptian said, 'If I understand rightly, it has no will of its own. It no more murdered this man than the runaway cart which kills a child in the street.'

'*He was a genius.*'

My voice came back flatly from the walls. I hadn't realised I was shouting.

'There's *never* been a painter like him; now it's all – gone.'

'Painter. Yes.' Rekhmire''s gaze for a moment seemed absent. 'Let me see . . . Mastro Masaccio was painting a triptych, wasn't he? For Cardinal Valente. So one, at least, of the cardinals will be interested in his death.'

His gaze sharpened as he caught my eye.

'It would be – better – if the Conclave of Cardinals weren't drawn towards this embassy. Or towards Alexandria. Or Carthage. It would be *best* if Master Tommaso Cassai had died a natural death.'

A flash of memory put the living Masaccio before my eyes. Lips drawn back. Spine arched. Held out at arm's length, by a stone statue.

I swallowed. Between my hands, his flesh still held tepid warmth. But it felt too soft, with none of the tension of muscle that belongs to a living man.

Carefully, I placed Masaccio's useless hand back down at his side. 'I don't like the idea of hiding this. Masaccio's dead! Someone ought to—'

'Pay?' Rekhmire' prompted gently.

'Why did this happen!'

My cry went unanswered. Rekhmire' shook his head. I had a sudden flash of memory, of Hanno Anagastes, whose house looked so like this one, speaking to me in the graveyard of children. 'You should remember,' he said, 'that punishments do not need a reason.'

Later, I wondered if he had been speaking of the 'punishment' of living in a body that is both man and woman. Some things have no reason, they only are.

And yet Masaccio *did* this, I realised. If ignorance killed him, still, he chose to act.

With the sensation of Masaccio's dead skin still imprinted on mine, I must force myself to be calm. To think. Because something must be done, done now, and what will it be?

Do I stay here with Rekhmire' and his people? Do I run out into the Roman streets and call for the Watchmen? Tell the cardinals?

The golem is only a machine.

And will it do good for men to know that Masaccio died a thief?

I looked down at his motionless fingers.

'What would be true justice here . . . isn't clear to me.' Slowly, feeling all the pain of my bruises, I got to my feet. 'This is too much. Too sudden. But I'll tell you one thing I can think of. Masaccio wouldn't want his name associated with scandal.'

I looked up at the Egyptian who was no longer my master.

'If people heard he was a thief – that Mastro Masaccio had been killed while doing something criminal – that might smear the New Art. I know what he'd think. That patrons might then not want to buy paintings from artists who are following his techniques. Because men are fools. And everything he's worked for; how he tried to reform painting, re-birth it – would be dead. Gone. The New Art would be . . . finished.'

In the periphery of my sight, the golem's blank white eyes stared without knowledge or remorse.

'I'm hardly impartial,' I said. 'But . . . I don't think I can let that happen.'

17

I had no need to uncover Masaccio's face. The blue, crushed, swollen flesh was imprinted in detail in my mind. I glanced around the room; then back at Rekhmire'.

'How can we make *this* look like a natural death!'

Rekhmire' frowned. 'I don't know.'

'You don't *know?*'

His lip twitched. If a man had not lain dead on the floor beside us, I think it would have been a smile, if blackly sardonic.

'You expect much of me, Ilario. This isn't easy . . . Help me put him on that.' Rekhmire' nodded at the flat-bed cart.

'*What?*'

'Would it be the first time a man's been brought home drunk from the taverna like this? On his own cart?' The Egyptian shook his head, answering his own rhetorical questions. 'Whatever we do, first we must take him away from here. Quickly.'

I nodded, and knelt. Masaccio's cheek felt colder. But still soft. Bodies stiffen some time after death.

The water-clock chimed.

It's not an *hour*, yet!

How can I believe he's dead?

It felt almost as if, should I sufficiently refuse to believe it, Masaccio might *not* be dead. All this might yet resolve into some nightmare delusion.

But that false hope often accompanies sudden death.

As if he still breathed, I gently eased my hands under Masaccio's armpits, waiting for Rekhmire' to lift him at the knees.

We put him on the hand-cart. Rekhmire' reached out to shift his limbs. I protested; cut myself off. The Egyptian arranged Masaccio's body on its side, cloak-hood drawn across to shelter the blue, bruised face.

With the macabre humour that comes with death, I felt a terrible grin stretching at my mouth. 'He *does* look dead drunk, not dead.'

'The Eight grant the Watch think so, if we meet them!'

The handles of the cart moved easily as I lifted them. Iron wheel-rims gritted over rush mats laid down on the way out of the room.

I didn't turn my head to look back at the stone golem.

Let it stay half painted: half-statue and half-man. It's all the monument Mastro Tommaso Cassai will have.

There was no rain outside. The air was damp and clear. A swollen moon hung high enough to guide us in the fetid alleys.

The cart makes it too easy, I thought. He should be more of a weight.

This is not how he expected to come home. Nor the burden he expected this cart to bear.

'We *might* claim he died of plague.' Rekhmire' spoke quietly, walking beside me. 'That would keep people from viewing the body . . . But a Roman physician would need to sign the certificate. No physician can look at him. There's no disguising an evident death by violence—'

'Murder.' My bare hands clenched on the cold wood. A sudden jolt went through me. 'Master – Rekhmire' – I've just realised! There'll be witnesses to say that he and I quarrelled. People will say, Masaccio loved the girl first . . . There'll be enough gossip to make us enemies; justify me having battered Masaccio to death. *I* could be accused of his murder. Easily!'

Rekhmire' shot me a glance from those oval, dark eyes. Even by the guttering light of the one embassy torch, I could read his agreement.

'I want to *grieve* for him!' I exclaimed. 'Not to have to think of – of . . . '

'Yes, I understand. But we must think of it all.'

This is all I can do for him now. Save his reputation.

The workshop door was locked.

Masaccio wore his purse tied to his belt. I felt inside for the key. My fingers brushed against his bare wrist as I withdrew my hand. His flesh felt cold as Carrara marble to the touch. Stiff, stuck in one position, undignified, absurd.

Yes, he *is* dead. I don't want to believe it, but he is.

Hot water tracked a single runnel down my cheek.

'All that skill, lost. The first *painter* for eighty years—' I couldn't keep my voice male-sounding, or level. 'He won't paint anything else.'

The workshop doors creaked as Rekhmire' opened them. He came and took the cart handles from my hands, pushing the vehicle quickly inside. I saw how the moon's light cast shadows from each individual cobblestone paving the street. Masaccio might have been able to paint that tenuous, deceptive light.

'His brother!' I exclaimed. I kicked the door closed as I followed Rekhmire' in. 'Giovanni Cassai! He went back to Florence, a few weeks ago. He'll have to be told. He can't get here in time for the funeral, but . . . '

My thoughts outraced my words.

Rekhmire' gave me a keen look and prompted me. 'Yes?'

'Wait . . . '

I looked around the shadowy workshop: at tables, easels, pestles, stacked boards and canvases. The crate upon which I had sat to be Judas negotiating with the traitorous officers of Mithras.

Masaccio didn't know he was leaving all this for the last time tonight. I pushed the thought aside.

'I think I begin to see . . . It's not important what he died of. Plague, accident. Whatever lie. What's important is that no one *sees* him; that he's buried. Quickly. Yes?'

Rekhmire' nodded. 'But I gather he's not unknown in the city, and without a physician to certify the death—'

'I know a priest who'll bury him without one.'

'You do?' Rekhmire' looked startled. 'How can you be certain this priest won't merely report a murder?'

'Friar Sebastian married me, illegally, to an Etruscan woman.' I shrugged. 'And so he's susceptible to . . . '

The Egyptian had no hesitation in completing the thought bluntly. 'Blackmail.'

18

The smell of newly-turned earth is pleasant in spring, when planting crops. Although life in Rodrigo's court has not led me to have much more experience of it than watching other men strew seeds from their aprons.

In grey autumn, turned earth is merely clammy and cold. And it smells of corpses.

That thought might have been imagination.

The dawn wind blowing across the churchyard would have brought tears to my eyes even had I not had cause to weep.

Friar Sebastian did not gabble. He read with haste, undoubtedly, but still with a gravitas that gave Tommaso Cassai his due. Grave-diggers stood back towards the wall of the church. A scant half-dozen of Mastro Tommaso Cassai's Roman neighbours stood in front of Rekhmire' and I, around the foot of the grave. I did not know how gossip had brought them the early news, but it had. As his apprentice, I had been commiserated with on his sad, accidental death. Rumour differed as to whether it might have been a stroke brought on by drink, a fall in his workshop, or sudden illness.

I let my grief shelter me from any importunate questions.

This burial is just barely in time.

The prayers were unfamiliar in form, although much the same in content as I would have heard in Taraco: Judge this soul mercifully, and let the cold earth lie easily on him.

Under cover of the Frankish priest's intonation, Rekhmire' murmured, 'Your friar would be unwilling to do this, I think, were he not aware that we are about to leave Rome.'

'"Leave"?' I stared blankly.

'What else?' Rekhmire' had his gaze fixed on the coffin. 'Disruptive as that may be, we *must* go.'

'But Honorius is coming back here. We *came* here to hide from Videric and Carthage—'

'We came here because Rome was your painter's Grail-Castle.' Rekhmire' seemed at home with the Frankish metaphor. He kept his tone low. 'And now Rome's a place where Carthage and Alexandria are about to have a quarrel that will spread beyond their embassies, and involve the city authorities. The cardinals know my name. If they hear the name of the painter's apprentice, when they speak to the embassy . . . Too great a likelihood that Carthage will hear that my slave is in Rome.'

Now he did shoot a glance my way, his eyes bright with the cold wind, and his expression a complex mixture of grief, irony, and annoyance.

'Tommaso Cassai was an impetuous fool,' Rekhmire' said, his voice low. 'Which even you won't deny, Ilario. Do you think this friar would give in to threats of exposure *unless* we were leaving? It's that which makes this the easiest way out of the situation for him.'

Rekhmire''s forehead creased in concentration.

'I'll need to pass the Turkish document over to Cardinal Corradeo, or I doubt he'll allow me to go. I'll visit the Vatican immediately after the funeral's over. Can I rely on you to find us a boat for Ostia Antica?'

Leaving Rome?

The thought made me blink against the sliver of unbearable fire that was the rising sun. Shadows fell out of the east. I could have painted three of us about the grave: priest, eunuch, and another who is not a man. For better composition, I would have Friar Sebastian move to *there* . . .

No composition. No Masaccio. No apprenticeship. What is there to keep me in Rome?

Rekhmire' whispered urgently, 'I know you are no longer my slave, but will you pack belongings for both of us?'

The world snapped into focus around me.

'I can't leave.'

'*Can't* leave? When you could be arrested for murder?'

'What about my *wife*?'

Rekhmire' stared at me.

'I can't leave Sulva!' I made a movement somewhere between a shrug and a shiver, in the freezing morning air. 'Maybe . . . She liked the idea of travel. Maybe she'll be willing to leave Rome. But I have no money—'

Rekhmire' waved a dismissive hand. 'This woman. You're not legally married, you said?'

The third night is tonight, I realised.

'No, not until tonight, by their law. But I gave my word; I'm married in my eyes. *Yes*,' I got in, before Rekhmire' could interrupt, 'I have a lot to tell her! I will. She can do what she chooses, then, but— She *needs* to escape that prison of a house. I can't avoid that on a – a legal technicality.'

My heart beat out long, silent moments.

'That would mean not leaving until tonight. That's unwise. But—' Rekhmire' cut himself off.

A smile broke the monumental, forbidding surfaces of his face; out of place at a funeral.

'But that's not my decision, is it? Freedman. Freedwoman. *My* decision is only: will I wait for you, or will I leave now, alone?'

True as it was, I found it disconcerting.

'Ilario?'

I mentally shook myself, and looked up at the tall man by my side. 'What's your decision?'

He shrugged. 'I'll wait. The library will hide me a day longer – or so I must hope. Ilario, we must both stay out of sight. If the authorities arrest either of us, it will be of no use to appeal to the embassy. Pamiu can do nothing but disown me. And, now you are *not* my slave, he can do nothing for you; you're not an Alexandrine. We must be careful. And lucky. Ilario?'

I rubbed at the ridge of bone just under the skin of my brows. It felt tight. I touched the drying scab of blood where the golem's fingers had caught me, and winced.

Rekhmire' turned back to face the end of Friar Sebastian's praying. His murmur came softly to me:

'Inadvisable it may be – but I see that I will risk one more visit to my countrymen in the embassy. Injuries to the head are unpredictable. Potentially dangerous. You're hurt. I trust none of these Frankish butchers. You'll see a proper Alexandrine doctor before we leave.'

'Rekhmire'—'

'*No argument!*'

In the chill of the funeral, it was a moment's warmth.

19

The doctor, as it came about, was a short, round man – an essay in curves – with the confident manner of the professional physician. And while he nodded a greeting to Rekhmire' as to a friend, his eyes lit up when he saw me.

'This is Siamun,' Rekhmire' introduced me, folding his arms and leaning up against the Roman interior wall that some Egyptian hand had covered with cartouches.

'*This* is a professional consultation,' Siamun said, shooing him out through the door.

The physician Siamun prodded, poked; looked into my eyes; had me unlace my doublet and remove my shirt – *and* the bandages that bound my breasts. I did it all with no more than a sigh, rubbing my forehead against the insistent ache. He's a doctor: of course he will want to see this. What physician wouldn't? How many hermaphrodites will he see in his career?

It wouldn't have surprised me to see him taking notes.

'Your facial hair,' he murmured, 'it has been less dark than this, yes?'

I stared at him. 'It's my *head* that hurts.'

'But to answer the question?'

Sitting solely dressed in one's hose doesn't promote recalcitrance. My fingers were touching my cheek, I realised. Only a very little wispy hair. I had hoped it made disguise as a man more convincing. 'Yes, it's darkened, of late. My brows, too. I thought . . . I'm just growing older, yes?'

'And you perhaps have pains, here?' He reached down with a spatulate fingertip and tapped my knee. 'And other joints of the body?'

'Only when Masaccio makes me sit—' I began with a laugh; I ended in a reedy, thin croak. Constriction in my throat made it impossible to complete my words.

When Masaccio, who is *dead*, makes me sit for too long.

The doctor reached forward and took my right breast in his hand. He squeezed, firmly.

I yelped. 'What the hell—!'

'I apologise; I intended no hurt. Take off—' He gestured at my woollen hose, as if he couldn't find the Frankish word. 'Take off these, please.'

Not being laced to my doublet now, my hose were falling around my hips in any case. I finished their removal, and looked away as he felt at my belly, took my small penis in his hand, and then probed in with his fingers to find the cavity that lay behind it. The colours in the cartouches blurred. I stared as bas-reliefs of chariot warfare; winged gods; the fall of Old Alexandria to the Turks ... Faces painted in profile, to the left or right; men's muscular chests painted face-on. Eyes elongated with kohl ...

'Are you done yet?' I said harshly, self-conscious with the weight I'd put on eating Roman food. *My arse is truly a woman's, now!* 'Is looking at my belly-button going to tell you what's wrong with my cracked skull?'

Siamun straightened up from palpating my abdomen. His round, brown eyes fixed on me. 'Your skull is not cracked. Fortunately, you're bruised.'

You could have phrased that better!, I thought, grinning despite the pain in my head; but he hadn't finished.

'However,' he added, 'you are pregnant.'

20

The physical effects of shock are inescapable.

I learned that early on, being trained in the arts of hunting and war. A fall from a horse can leave you with more than pain or a cracked skull. The mind itself becomes stunned.

I have to see Sulva.

No lights showed at the barred windows of the Paziathe mansion.

Rekhmire''s hand at my elbow steadied me. Night had come. Clouds covered the full moon. No eye could distinguish detail below the rooflines. I found myself too numb to realise, except vaguely, how lucky that was.

Rekhmire''s voice spoke in the dark. 'This will conceal us from passers-by.'

From time to time, as we walked here, Rekhmire' had spoken quietly to me; but by the time I worked out what he had said, the moment for answering seemed to have passed. I did not think he mentioned Carthage, or Videric, or the golem, but it might be that I just didn't hear.

How is it I didn't realise that things were worse than I knew?

'It was Marcomir.' I interrupted Rekhmire'. 'If I'm – if it's not far advanced—'

He echoed Siamun's words: 'Four months.'

'Then it has to be Marcomir. There hasn't . . . been . . . anybody . . . '

Rekhmire' touched my arm, his voice a breath. '*Look*. There.'

The darkness gave up a figure holding up a pierced iron lantern.

Rekhmire' murmured, 'Is it the right man?'

Chiaroscuro: a face in light and shadow. Illumination made a hollow darkness of the eye-sockets.

I remembered his features from St Mithras Viridianus. 'It's one of Sulva's cousins.'

Rekhmire' lifted his voice. 'The groom is injured. I am here to help.'

His air of authority quashed any possible question. The cousin gave an uncertain nod, and beckoned. He turned away from the direction of the mansion. Towards 'the villa in the trees'.

The night blurred in my eyes.

We must at some point have passed a gate and left the city of Rome. If there were watchmen, I didn't see how we avoided them. The Etruscans, the 'Rasna'; they must be used to doing this . . .

For a mile or more, I recognised the Via Aemilia: that ancient road that runs north the whole length of the Warring States. Paving stones were cold and slippery under my shoes.

Broken earth. A track.

I lifted my head to find that we walked under trees, off the road.

Sulva's cousin spoke tightly, his voice breaking the long silence. 'Follow that path.'

Where he pointed, a broad, well-trodden trackway went off between mature oaks. In summer, no light could have penetrated the leaf-canopy. Now, as the clouds began to shred, full moonlight shone intermittently down between the bare branches.

The Etruscan man folded his arms. He made no further move to accompany us.

Rekhmire''s hand gripped my forearm. I realised that he had taken the iron lantern; yellow light dazzled in the corner of my eye.

'I don't need help!' It came out more harshly than I intended.

'You are still uncertain, from the wound.' In the lantern's light, I saw him glance at my forehead.

'You needn't worry.' I attempted to sound conciliatory. There is no obligation on Rekhmire' to come here. 'But I need to get there *fast*.'

We walked a distance.

Twigs crackled under my feet.

The noise became submerged by sounds I felt I ought to recognise, but could only find both familiar and unknown. I frowned. Rekhmire' swore under his breath, missing his footing. I thought I heard the faint sound of a reed.

'*Music?*' I blurted out.

Rekhmire' gave a sharp, preoccupied nod. 'It must be the young woman.'

I thrust out of my mind the thought *How shall I tell her?*

Because, now we're near, if I think about that, I shall go back.

Ahead, the trees began to thin. I caught sight of a slope rising up in the distance, out of the wood. On it, something that might be a villa. Bare branches all but hid a sloping roof. Splotched pillars – because painted, I realised, but the moonlight is showing only black and white.

The thread of sound grew strong.

Rekhmire''s voice was no more than a whisper. 'That – I think that is an aulos. An Etruscan flute. What . . . ?'

I stepped between two oaks, and found myself entering a wide clearing. The double melody sounded stronger.

Over it, regular, rhythmic grunts echoed through the frosty air. Deep, echoing sound. Music . . .

Branches creaked behind me in the wind. The remainder of the cloud-cover shredded away from the moon. Silver light splashed every leaf and twig, every bramble, every frost-curled fern. The moon hung full-bellied enough to make me wince, until the sight before me wiped that thought away.

I shuddered to a halt, staring.

'Sulva's come out to meet me . . . '

She is not alone.

'Kek and Keket and all the *Eight*!' Rekhmire' exclaimed.

Sulva stood in the centre of the clearing, perhaps thirty feet away. She held a double-piped flute to her lips. Two strands of melody wove in the moonlight. A mantle draped her shoulders; tiny braids kept her flowing hair back from her eyes.

Ten or twelve giant wild boars clustered around her.

They rootled beside the skirts of her long pleated tunic, their pointed ears flicking each time the melody altered. *Wild boars.* Not the small, black shapes of domestic pigs – what trampled the leaf-mould in the clearing ahead of me was huge, lean, and razor-backed, with curved tusks glinting in the moonlight.

Men call that light deceptive, but it was clear enough for me to see the testicles hanging between their back legs, and the breath rising up from their mouths. As they passed in front of her, their shaggy shoulders stood as high as Sulva's breast.

I breathed out. 'I don't believe . . . '

The boar is the most dangerous beast of the hunt; its ferocity and bad temper make it a favourite among heraldic devices. Here are no horses, no men, no weapons. Here is only a sixteen-year-old girl. And, if we were this close, ordinary boar would attack. They would have attacked *her* before now . . .

Rekhmire' spoke as if we sat in our lodgings over a scroll. 'As I recall, there is a legend attached to the aulos. That the Etruscans could play it skilfully enough to entice wild boar out of the hills, and bring them tame to the huntsman.'

Sulva lowered the flute from her lips. She slid it into a fold of her mantle, and from another fold brought out something white. Bread, I saw.

Her eyes bright, she offered the food in her hands; her gaze fixed on the beasts.

The wild boars gruntled. They reached up their snouts to her, and took old crusts from her fingers with the greatest gentleness.

'Sulva.' My voice came out a squeaky croak.

Her head lifted; her glance went past the Egyptian without pause. '*Ilario!*'

The boar furthest from her – and closest to me – swivelled his head around, staring. The gaze of his tiny wicked eye jolted me.

He turned his head back towards the nearest tree, and took a branch the size of a man's wrist between his jaws. Effortlessly, he bit down.

A sharp *crack!* sounded as the living wood split in two.

I shut my eyes.

The golem's closing hand.

Masaccio's face.

'Ilario . . . '

Sulva stood alone. Silent, but for the suck of mud against sharp trotters, the wild boar were moving away, fading into the moonlit trees at the clearing's edge.

Stumbling on the black, broken earth; pushing my way between the silver arcs of brambles; I closed the distance between she and I.

Sulva smiled.

It was painful; strained; embarrassed.

'What—' I started. 'Why—?'

'This.'

She pointed at moonlit stones I had not noticed buried in the bracken.

'This is the boundary. Beyond here is the villa in the trees. If you pass . . . '

Human feet sucked out of the mud. Rekhmire' came forward to stand by my shoulder, his sandals encrusted with wet churned dirt. He suddenly stilled.

I followed his gaze, downwards.

A flash of white.

Sulva's tunic was kilted up, to be out of the freezing mud. On one foot she wore a patten over her slipper, as before. The other—

The other shone white as an animal's pelt shines in moonlight.

She stepped forward on her perfect goat's foot.

I could only stare.

She ignored the fact that I was not alone. As if she had tensed herself to speak, and could let nothing stop her now, she blurted out, 'I prayed to the Christian priests for healing! They perform small miracles, sometimes. I thought . . . '

Her beautiful voice came clearly through the frost-bitten air:

'But I didn't receive Grace. Only a glamour that makes this seem to be a club-foot when I'm not in the forest.'

The moonlight shone undeniably on her.

Miracles.

Grace.

Glamour.

Frankish superstition!

I shook my head; laughed out loud; clapped my hands over my mouth. Just another strange occurrence – and how can I protest that, when I'm already one myself? As well be born with an animal's foot as the organs of both man and woman—

Rekhmire''s hand closed on my shoulder. 'Ilario.'

'I understand what this is. Sulva's . . . come to give me a choice. Haven't you?'

She gazed up at me. 'We are the Rasna,' she whispered. The people of Etruria. We're *old*. And these things happen in our families. The Christians' legends of satyrs . . . Will it matter to you so much?'

'Sulva . . . ' I could barely speak.

'Only your people consider us married. We have yet to lie together.'

She means we have yet to lie in bed, in bodily communion.

I felt my mouth twist. 'No, there's been lies between us. Believe me!'

Whatever the truth of her disfigurement is, she has come to warn me. To give me a chance to back out of this marriage. Because she is honest. While I . . .

Reaching out, I took her cold, crumb-dusted hands in mine.

They are still warmer than the dead.

'I have to tell you something,' I said.

She parted her lips slightly, as if she would have protested, but said nothing. No man could have painted her.

'No man could paint the moonlight on your face,' I said aloud. 'And I am no man. Sulva, I have to explain, tell you; somehow. I'm not a man. Or, I *am* – but not in the way you think I am.'

Her pupils contracted and expanded as moonlight varied between the clouds. '*Not* a – I don't—'

The confusion in her voice flayed me.

She frowned. 'Are you like your master? Him, there, beside you? A gelded man?'

I glanced back at Rekhmire', and saw in the dim lantern light that his expression was wretched, as if he hurt for me.

I shook my head hurriedly. 'Not my master, my friend. But in any case, no. I'm not a eunuch.'

'You're not a *woman*—'

'No! Yes! Sulva!'

My hold on her hands tightened. She gasped. I loosed her slightly.

'Listen.' I could barely get words out. The shock that numbed me at the Alexandrine embassy thawed – and I regretted it. I would sooner be numb, for this.

I shivered in the cold moonlight and frost.

'This is a night for myths, it seems. Have you heard of Hermaphroditus? The nymph Salmacis loved him, and Zeus answered her prayers by making them one flesh, man and woman joined in the same body. But this isn't a myth. I'm hermaphrodite. I'm both man and woman. I have the body of each.'

Sulva blinked, as if I had dazed her with a blow. 'I don't understand.'

I folded my fingers tightly around Sulva's. Pain coursed through my body.

'There's more. I must tell you it all. Listen to me! You know that I've been travelling. When I was in Carthage . . . In Carthage, I went to bed with a man. A man called Marcomir.'

'You're telling me you're a boy-lover? A sodomite?' She still looked beautiful when she was puzzled.

This is not something I ever wanted to say to my wife.

'Sulva. I'm telling you that I'm pregnant.'

She took her hands out of mine and put them over her face, and wailed like a child.

I did not wail – her grief was not mine to interrupt – but I wept.

21

'Is it true?' Aranthur Paziathe demanded.

The pictures on the walls of the villa were yellow, red, gold. Green ferns. Blue fountain-water. Either painted, or put on in mosaic. Men in primitive togas, dancing with their hands high. Pale naked girls in forests. Augurs before altars. Haruspices painted looking into the entrails of birds. The figures all drawn to depict, not what a man sees, but what a man knows is there.

The feet all pointing down.

'Tell me! *Is it true?*' Aranthur shouted.

'Oh, it's true! I've seen!' Sulva's eyes seemed literally to flash. In another frame of mind, I could have wished to capture the effect in wax and pigment.

'Yes,' I said. She has seen.

It had not been how I had imagined being in her bedchamber would be.

In her painted rooms, in this hidden villa, she assumed a brittle attitude that we were all girls, and so I might as well undress and show what I was.

Sulva frowned deeply, shaking her head. 'She's got a belly on her. *He* has. Not so big, but how he didn't *notice*—' She turned on me. 'Didn't your *bleeding* stop?'

I saw Aranthur wince at the mention of women's mysteries. Rekhmire' told me Etruscan women had freedom, in ancient times; I caught the echo of it in Aranthur's daughter's speech.

'Bleeding has never been a regular occurrence for me.' I felt cold, as if the house's warmth couldn't penetrate the night's frost. 'I thought – the travelling – the change of city – I'm sorry.'

Her hand flashed out. Her small palm cracked across my face.

Rekhmire' stirred, where he leaned against the wall by the door.

I shook my head, warning him back. A bruise on the cheek is hardly sufficient recompense for what I've done to her. It seems there are some hurts I can't cure.

Aranthur grated, 'Monstrous! A man, *pregnant*. A woman who's a man. Sulva, leave the room.'

He stood up from his high-backed oak chair. Simultaneously she stepped away.

Before I could protest what that told me – that, like other fathers now, Etruscans have come to beat their daughters – she noisily began to weep. 'I will *not*!'

The room felt oppressive, the ceiling low for a single-storey building. The windows opened only out into the central courtyard. Just outside, folding chairs stood under the colonnade of pillars. I had an urge to walk out there; to find the forest; to run.

He turned on me. '*You*.'

'I lied,' I admitted, before he could choke out anything else. 'I'm sorry. She's still virgin. She can marry—'

His expression stopped me.

'We have to abide by Rome's legal code.' Aranthur began to pace. 'That is the bargain made in Alaric's day. By Rome's law, my daughter is married to you. So it doesn't matter that by Rasna law she's still unmarried and virgin.'

The room was dominated by a long dining table; not polished, but covered in bright embroidered linen. He left his own chair and walked down past the length of the table, and paused with his hands resting on the back of another chair.

Aranthur's own throne-style wooden chair, carved all over with acorns and galls, stood at the head of the table, like the Romans who supplanted them. *Pater familias*, head of the house. All the other chairs were made out of curving slats, with a leather seat.

He rested his brown gnarled hands on the chair-back and gazed at me. 'Do you *know* what would have happened, if you had married Sulva by Roman and Etruscan law?'

All the answers I could think of were mere lists of disaster. I shook my head.

He pulled the chair back towards himself, and looked down at it for a moment.

I noted without in the least wishing to that the interlocking curved slats were beechwood, polished with linseed oil; that the shapes of air between the parts would make an excellent drawing exercise.

'You would have taken her away,' Aranthur said quietly. 'Even if you had never left Rome, you would have taken her away from *us*. That happens so often in this generation . . . She would never have come back. It would have swallowed her. She would have dressed as a Roman matron, not a *puia* – a wife. She would have prayed at a Roman church.'

I started to correct him, and stopped. If the details are here and there inaccurate, the picture is nonetheless true to life.

'She would never have associated with her family, after that,' Aranthur said. 'There would have been an empty chair at this table. It's our custom. We would have kept it for her. To remind us.'

I repeated, inadequately, 'I'm sorry.'

'*That's* what you're sorry for?' His head lifted; his eyes met mine. 'Sulva would have been *safe*.'

I stared.

He jabbed a finger at me. 'Not one of us, not part of this family any longer, no; not part of our people – but *safe*. And we would have honoured that, and sorrowed for it, with an empty chair here. Because I . . .'

His voice broke.

'I would have known that next time there were rumours of Etruscans poisoning wells, or Etruscan merchants cheating their Christian customers, or the city fathers needing a scapegoat and the Inquisition needing bodies for burning – *Sulva would have been safe*. As a Christian wife, a Christian mother. Not Rasna; not part of our *lautun*, our family. Lost to me. But safe.'

His hands slammed palm-down on the back of the chair.

'And in time, I would have added *another* chair, for the Etruscan husband who would never sit at this table! And then *more* chairs, on feast days, for the children she would never bring back here. In time, how many chairs would I put out for grandchildren?'

His torrent left me speechless.

'But you are *not* the young Christian man you made yourself out to be.' Aranthur Paziathe clenched his fists. 'You are not "he". And so she is *not* safe.'

My head felt clear. Pain will do that, sometimes. 'I'm sorry I lied. I will do what I can—'

'What *can* you do?' The old man pointed at my stomach. 'You have a *child* there. And you a man! And it a bastard!'

I let that one pass.

'Sulva can still be safe. It's as I tried to explain. Mastro Masaccio is dead, and I'm leaving Rome. If Sulva comes with me, I'll look after her—'

He slammed both hands down again on the carved back of the chair. 'You? What life can *you* have? You'll always be what you are! Sooner or later, men will know that. What life can she have with a— But no. No. I am not the bad father you think me. Ask her what she wants. Ask Sulva!'

He stamped across the room to his daughter, ignoring how Rekhmire' stepped fluidly back out of his way. He swung Sulva around.

His shout ricocheted off the illustrated walls. 'What do you want out of this?'

Sulva lifted her chin. Her eyes had red rims. Her skin showed pallid in some places, and blotchy in others. No man on earth would pay me to lay those colours on her statue.

That she should look that way, because of me, wrenched at my gut.

Abrupt, Aranthur demanded, 'Do you still wish to marry this man?'

She gazed about the room as if blind – a *lautun* room, I thought, remembering Aranthur's word. Where the family comes together. Where they can be what they are, themselves, instead of hiding, as in Rome.

I spoke to her. 'I'll look after you. As I promised. You – need not be wife in anything but name.'

'In name?'

Sulva swung around, staring.

'I thought you wanted to *marry* me.' Her eyes brimmed over: water ran in quick streaks down her face. 'Don't you love me? I thought you fell in love with me!'

Stupid as wood and fog, I said, 'I thought you wanted to escape. I thought you needed rescue.'

The room held absolute silence.

'"Rescue"!' Aranthur ended his pacing around the table back at his chair. He sat down suddenly, seemingly swallowed by the polished oak throne. 'A man my age has grown too old for the kindness of the gods. "Love". "Escape". "Rescue"!'

'This is my *family*.' Sulva sounded bewildered. 'Why would I need rescue? They love me. Even as I am. Ilario, I thought, you . . . '

Aranthur, brown face pulled by strain, spoke as if to himself. 'You Romans, you call it the *disciplina etrusca*. The sacred books. The *Libri Fatales*. They tell the truth of it! An old man is a body with barely a soul in it. This is my punishment, for having a daughter when I was already old.'

Punishments come for no reason.

With my gaze fixed on Sulva, I said, 'I'm not a Roman. Nor am I a punishment.'

I forced the configuration of my body out of my mind.

'I will do what I can for Sulva and for you: I swear it.'

'What can *you* do!'

Rekhmire''s sonorous tenor broke in. 'More than sit lamenting foolishly about "punishment", for one thing!'

I startled. 'We agreed – this is my business to settle.'

'Oh, so it is, it is.' He waved a large hand, and resumed leaning against a mural of a god springing from a furrow. 'But not for nothing do the Romans call the Rasenna the most superstitious men on earth!'

I turned back to Sulva. 'You're the most beautiful thing I've ever seen. Even with your foot. It seemed such a crime to keep you locked up in that old house.'

I broke off, sick at my stomach, watching how she looked at me.

'And as to love . . . Sulva . . . I knew you wouldn't want me.'

'"Want"? *Want?*'

Her expression changed, features tensing in a scorn that was absolute. 'I *want* a husband. Who loves me! Not some freak—'

'Aren't you a freak, too?'

174

It was no attack on her, only pain. My heart hammered, and my pulse all but blinded me.

'Your foot— Shouldn't that make you . . . shouldn't you feel *more* sympathetic? Because of that? And because your people are persecuted?'

'"That"?'

She looked down at her skirts, then up at me. 'That's why I want a normal husband! Isn't it all the more reason why I should want someone normal?'

She clenched small fists in front of her.

'I didn't ask to be like born this! I didn't ask to be born Rasna! And you – I wanted *children*—' She cut me off, before I could speak, with biting scorn. '*My* children!'

I followed her gaze, down. I had done, without knowing it, what I have seen women do: put my hand flat over my belly, as if I protected what was inside.

Sulva sounded shrill. 'You'll give birth to monsters. And father monsters on *me*! I'm sick with being called a monster because I'm Etruscan; I don't want a double burden!'

I held up both hands, watching her anger abate a fraction. 'What *do* you want?'

She changed in an instant; as cold as the ice on the brown, dead oak leaves outside. 'I want you to go away, Ilario. If you're missing for seven years, the Romans will have you legally declared dead, and I can re-marry.'

So many emotions crowded her face: spite, malice, hurt, hatred, and grief. I understood every one of them.

'And I don't want to waste time,' she added, caustically. 'The seven years can start now. Tonight. Just *go*. Man-woman!'

This is because she thought I loved her.

And if I were to claim, now, that I *do* love her, this pique would disappear. And she'd think she can forgive me.

Very careful in my words, I said, 'Sulva, we could still appear to be a family. You, I, and the child. You *must* want to get away from this life.'

'You don't understand our ways.' Blurry-eyed, bewildered, she glared at me and wept. Her contorted face seared me. I have put those colours there.

So I will have no family. It seared me. I put the thought of my own body out of my mind, and turned to face the old man. 'I will do *anything* I can. I swear it.'

'You've done enough, girl!' White showed around Aranthur's eyes. I saw the realisation come to him. 'You have! You've brought everything down on us! The painter, dead – questions— All this will come out— They'll trace you to us—'

'Then let me help!'

'No.' Aranthur's hands closed over the ends of the chair-arms, knuckles whitening against the patina of ancient polish. 'We must shut up the villa; move from the Roman house to the one in— And you, you can't help. You can't even help yourself!'

Spite and malice flickered in the deep creases of his expression.

'You're a monster carrying a child. The *Libri ostentaria* talks of such things. Even if you *could* carry the bastard to term, it would kill you when you came to birth it. You leave us to our troubles, she-male! You'll be too busy finding a back-alley abortionist.'

22

Silvery scales collect on unwashed human skin.

I picked with a fingernail at my swollen ankle. The thought surfaced: I should do something about this.

Bathe? The mental comment had something of Rekhmire''s acerbic tone about it. It stirred my sluggish mind.

Footsteps sounded on the dhow's deck, and the flap of the makeshift canvas shelter lifted. For a moment, I didn't look up. The water- and wind-scoured planks held a grain whose pattern I could trace in patches of sunlight, losing thought for hours. Now, only faint light from the outside shifted with the lift and swell of the sea.

A weight settled on the palliasse beside me. 'We're in for ill weather, they tell me.'

Rekhmire' rested his heavy arm around my shoulder.

Whether it was the comfort a man offers a man, or the comfort a man offers a woman . . . Rekhmire''s tenor might have belonged to a deep-voiced woman if I closed my eyes.

After a moment, something unclenched inside me.

I shifted, albeit awkward and ungainly, stared forward, and looked out of the shelter at the Adriatic. The cloth walls made all converging vertical lines, leading the eye towards the small opening. Outside, I saw the dhow's wet rigging. And a ship's rail that rose up above the horizon and fell below it. A sky the colour of a three-day-old bruise.

'How far are we from land?'

The Egyptian shrugged, which movement sent a tremor through me also. 'Too far to reach a port, or so the sailors say. Apparently we may run before this storm.'

Rekhmire''s hand closed loosely over the ball of my shoulder; his fingers large enough to encompass it. Had I been intending to draw anything, the Egyptian's hands would have been a suitable subject.

'Well, then.' He drew a breath. 'You will remember the Turkish document? I took it to Vittorio, Cardinal Corradeo, as we were leaving.'

'What . . . ?'

It was so poorly transparent an attempt to distract me – and from *this* man – that I must respond, despite myself, out of embarrassment and charity.

'What . . . happened? Is the Empty Chair to be cured?'

Rekhmire''s eyelashes flickered. I could all but see the other image form behind the lens of his eye with those words. Aranthur Paziathe, his hands gripping carved oak-wood—

Hurriedly, I said, 'And we can expect another Frankish pope, can we?'

'Not in my lifetime!'

'No?'

I met his gaze for the first time in many days, conscious of something other than numb misery and fog. Roused by his trivialities – by his design. I braced myself for the effort to reply:

'It wasn't true? The Turk wasn't truly there for the Prophet's death? Or . . . his scroll was a forgery? Or . . . knowing the words of the curse . . . doesn't help?'

Rekhmire''s unconscious shifting of body with ship, and the ship moving with the water, seemed soothing.

'If there *is* any such thing as a curse,' he remarked. 'But no, that's not why. Cardinal Corradeo took it away to be prayed over.'

A certain cynicism in his tone implied I ought to know why he phrased that so.

'He's a cardinal,' I objected, almost roused to asperity, had I sufficient strength. 'He's *supposed* to pray about things! What makes you think he isn't going to revoke the curse? And do – whatever the Conclave of Cardinals do when they elect a new pope?'

Rekhmire' smiled whimsically. 'Do you know where the Franks get their cardinals from, now?'

My ankle itched: I scratched at it again.

'From among bishops?'

'No. The death of all those popes discouraged men from Episcopal ambition. Only your Iberian and North African church *has* bishops, now. And the Franks would never elect a heretic bishop as pope . . . '

Rekhmire' held up a long dirty finger:

'The Franks have, these many years, depended on abbots to run their church. I'll tell you where they get their cardinals. Since they have no bishops, they rely on *abbots*, retired from their monasteries – "Cardinal Corradeo" was "Abbot Vittorio", not so many years ago.'

It began to concern me that my thoughts were so fog-ridden.

'Rekhmire', have we got any food?'

Rekhmire' leaned forward and bellowed through the open canvas flap to one of the crew. I felt a sudden and new desire for water. Or ale, or bread. Cheese. Solid plain food.

'So the cardinals used to be abbots. And . . . ' I paused expectantly.

Rekhmire' sat back, and left one hand resting heavily on my shoulder. 'And – they have absolutely *no* interest in putting any man on Peter's Chair who will bring back the bishops! The abbots control the Frankish church. They desire it no other way. As for the College of Cardinals –

178

electing one of the cardinals pope would mean one of them gaining more power than the others. So they prefer things exactly as they are.'

It had the feel of machinations at the court of Taraconensis. The familiarity was both nostalgic and ironic.

'So "prayed over" means "quietly taken away and lost"?'

'Corradeo has his reasons.' Rekhmire' waved his free hand illustratively. 'Decentralised power is obviously best. Look at Carthage and the Arian heresy. *They* have bishops – and they have the Penitence! Obviously God made a *felix culpa* out of Gundobad's curse, and is protecting the Frankish lands from the evils of Episcopal power . . . Or so the Cardinal says.'

My chest hurt. Wonderingly, I realised I had laughed. 'So, you having unearthed an eye-witness account . . . '

'Corradeo was remarkably happy to hear that I was on my way out of Rome, and not liable to return.'

Rekhmire' shook his head, chuckling.

'He can have a sub-committee of the other cardinals pray confidentially over this. It'll take them years, and the scroll will still be suppressed at the end of it. However, Corradeo did allow me a copy – on the firm understanding that I lose it in some dusty corner of the Royal Library, where no Christian scholar will ever look for it. It's not scholarship as I know it. But it does lead to original sources being preserved, rather than destroyed. Will you eat?'

Startled, I realised one of the Macedonian captain's crew-members squatted outside the deck-tent, balancing on the lifting and falling planks. I nodded thanks, and took the dark bread and ale. My movement disturbed the long shift I wore for warmth, and I realised how much it would benefit from rinsing, even if sea-water would make it scratchy against my skin.

Blackly, I thought, *Who else but I should wear a penitential shirt?*

Not Sulva Paziathe. Not Tommaso Cassai.

'And besides,' Rekhmire' added, pouring ale from a lidded pewter jug, 'Cardinal Corradeo is happy because, in the absolute meaning of the word, he need not lie if someone asks for the document to study. The Vatican library *doesn't* have a copy.'

Through a mouthful of bread, I found myself laughing.

Twice in a half-hour?

The food went swiftly, despite the swell's increase. Rekhmire' got up to claim more, and crept back under the deck-shelter with loaded square wooden plates. His platter cleaned remarkably fast, I noted. He stretched out his arms – no easy task in the combined space – and knocked open the canvas flap.

The salt-heavy wind blew in cold against my face, shocking more than skin and nerve awake.

'Rekhmire'. Where is this ship going?'

He wrapped long arms around his knees, and squinted at the rail and ropes outside. 'Venice.'

'*Venice?*'

Shock further broke the clouds surrounding my mind. I had assumed – beyond questioning – that it must be Alexandrian Constantinople this ship made its heading for.

'Why? Did you get more letters from Iberia? From Carthage? What . . .'

Hot liquid spilled over the lower lids of my eyes: I had not known until then that I would weep.

'Masaccio.' I wiped the back of my hand across my face. 'He said, once, he'd send me on a buying trip to Venice. For *lapis* blue. I made an excuse of it to that heretic priest that married me to Sulva . . . I never expected— Why *Venice?*'

'You were not in a state to give directions.'

The Egyptian shifted to sit closer, cautiously reached out, and combed his fingers through my tangled hair. His delicate touch worried knots undone without causing me pain. He made no other consolatory attempt, speaking with a bureaucrat's dry self-possession:

'In one way, this resembles our leaving Carthage for Rome – no man will expect us to travel anywhere else *but* Alexandria. So they will not look for us in the north. And there were considerable rumours of Carthaginian agents in Rome asking questions, the last week we were there. I left a trail I think will take any astray . . .'

His gaze, surveying something with inner satisfaction, left it and came back to me.

'Truthfully—' His bronze skin was a little darker on the high surfaces of his cheeks. 'Menmet-Ra, old friend that he is, called in a favour I could not honestly refuse him. He desires to stay in Rome, but *some* man must go north and sort out the Alexandrine house in Venice, after the ambassador there died this last autumn. Rather than Menmet-Ra being uprooted from his comfortable nest, he sees no reason why *I* need not return to Alexandria by the longer route . . .'

Much longer, I reflected, with the copied maps of travellers' itineraries in my mind's eye. The port of Venice being at the northern head of the Adriatic waters, and Constantinople way past the Greek Islands to the east.

'I thought it safer. The diversion's not uninteresting.' Rekhmire' absently set forefingers and thumbs to the knottier tangle of hair over my ear. To have his stare so close on me, but not meeting my eyes, felt oddly intimate.

He added, 'There seems to be some confusion with a printer of woodcuts. And whichever of Ty-ameny's book-buyers has been left as caretaker of the embassy. And rumours of a device—'

He cut himself off abruptly.

'No.' His large hand tilted my head back towards him; I hadn't realised I had turned away. '*Not* the golem. That will leave Rome by ship, Menmet-Ra was giving orders as we departed—'

There seemed no way to control the tears that collected inescapably in my eyes, blurring my vision, running hotly down my cheeks and neck. I shrugged out from under Rekhmire''s grasp, crawled unsteadily to the tent-opening, and ducked out under canvas and ropes.

Straightening up on cramped and blood-starved legs sent me staggering to the ship's rail. And not only that: my body's balance of gravity felt altered, as if I carried it in the now-visible curve of my belly.

You will be too busy seeking a back-alley abortionist—

'What "device"? Something else from Carthage?'

Rekhmire' came up beside me, perfectly steady on his bare feet despite the deck's pitch and yaw, a bundle over his arm.

'No. Something from the Frankish North. Burgundy or the Germanies, Menmet says. I have a report to read on it, when I cease the profession of nurse . . . '

He smiled, unwrapped the bundle, and it became a heavy woollen Frankish cloak, which he threw about my shoulders. One of his powerful hands grasped the rail behind me, serving as a brace while I settled the warm swathes of wool around me in toga-fashion.

My own hands were cold enough that this was not unlike clothing a sculpted marble figure. I could think of nothing but Masaccio. *I saw him die.* And now I'll explore the New Art on my own, because from what he told me, none of it has spread to the Venetian state.

In peripheral vision, I saw Rekhmire' frown. *Is that against grief, horror, bereavement?*

The Egyptian turned his head away from the wind, droplets of salt water dampening his shaven head, raising his voice a very little above the wind.

'Ilario – listen to me. Aranthur was not kind in what he said. But there is some truth there. Too much to ignore. If you continue to carry this child . . . But then again, it's very rare for a hermaphrodite *not* to lose any child by miscarriage, long before birth . . . That would be an ill thing to have happen to you, yes. But, forgive me, better than the other. If you *do* carry a child full term, it may rip you apart. You're not made for it.'

If my throat is stiff from disuse and private weeping, it's not for that.

'Your doctor *said* I carry Marcomir's child in my belly.' I wiped sea-spray off my face. 'I have no motherly feeling. If it quickens . . . But I feel no different from before.'

'You might *die* in labour!'

The sea-wind smelled of cold depths. The deck under my feet dipped deeper. Cries came from the crew; the steersman and captain shouting orders.

Rekhmire' bent down so that he could speak close into my ear. His voice sounded high with tension.

'I desire that we find an Alexandrine physician to manage the business. There will surely be one in Venice, attached to the Alexandria house. But it needs to be done sooner, more safely . . . I can order us put ashore at wherever we can get a ship east. The Dalmatian coast, perhaps.' He sounded distracted. '*Soon*. Before – if it is not already too late!'

'I made my decision in Rome.' I hadn't realised until I spoke it aloud.

'Suppose you carry it long enough that you're damaged when— what?' he interrupted himself.

He might have narrowed his eyes against the lashing water, or at me.

I faced him on the swaying deck. 'The doctor may be in error. If I *am* with child . . . If my body sheds this, well then, it's done. If not, then not. There's – what did you call it? – "the operation which birthed great Caesar". And that's my decision.'

'Don't you understand, you stupid—!' Rekhmire' cut himself off, I think caught between epitaphs, and lifted up his large hands. 'Your body is talking, not your mind; your mind is as absent as a woman in child-bed!'

My temper snapped. 'A eunuch gives me advice on procreation, does he!'

Rekhmire' straightened, towering over me. 'I'll speak it slowly. You. Could. Die.'

That he cared both warmed and puzzled me. Who would ever have thought that the man who purchased me would become so close?

'Rekhmire'—'

The deck shifted under me; came back at a slant.

I staggered two steps down the rail; grabbing at it.

One of the square wooden plates slid out of the tent-shelter and skidded across the deck towards the scuppers.

Rekhmire' bent and scooped it up, grabbing my arm with his other hand, and hustled us back towards the canopy. As I fell on my knees on the deck, I began dry-heaving.

Sea-sickness, that I had never suffered from in the seas between Iberia and Carthage, now emptied me and dried me out, until I could barely leave my blanket-roll.

I lost track of time, though I know that at some point the Egyptian demanded and got space for us under hatches with the cargo. In extreme physical misery, two things stood out in my mind. That Rekhmire' tended me, feeding me sips of water when nothing else would stay down. And that my belly remained distended, swelling and thickening even as I grew worn and thin. Once I bled, but it soon stopped, and did not happen again.

I dreamed of each precise fold of the sheet covering Masaccio's dead face. And of having to compulsively touch each one, before practising the charcoal drawing of cloth-folds to improve my use of tone. No more than that, but it made me wake myself crying out with horror.

The dhow *Iskander* ran south before the storm, lost itself among the first of the Greek islands – lost our armed convoy escort with the brass cannon, against pirates – and beat back against the tempests that came down one after another across the Adriatic.

And was driven repeatedly away from coasts and any ports by appalling seas.

'It is at least good we're where no man can search for us,' Rekhmire' observed, sodden from head to foot, and wincing every time the ship yawed. He looked across at me in the faint light leaking into the hold. 'It may be the agents from Carthage investigated the whereabouts of the King-Caliph's golem, rather than one Ilario, but—'

'Carthage won't be a concern if we drown.' *Nor will my belly.*

I wondered if Honorius had settled matters with King Rodrigo yet – and tried not to wonder if I would die before I saw my father again.

Days became a week, two, three.

I crept up on deck from time to time, suffocated by the creaking, shifting dark of the hold. The skies were filled with violet lightning, of a colour that I despaired of ever being able to paint; the crew screamed stories of sea-monsters; and one black noon I saw how such tales begin, with an optical delusion of the kind that men in the deserts call *mirage* – this time of a ship, an apparent sea-mile distant from us, with an impossible number of lateen sails making a tower of triangular shapes above the hull, and the whiskery face of a monster painted on the prow. Some trick of the storm-twilight made it seem immense, ten times the size of any mortal ship: a vessel that could belong only to giants.

I watched the geometric shapes merge into a squall, and remembered enough to sketch a line or two of the 'ghost-ship's' curious painted monster on damp paper with crumbling charcoal, before the next blast of the tempest made that impossible. It was the first time I had picked up charcoal since Masaccio died.

I let the sea take it.

The storms broke.

The clouds clearing, I could see that the stars in the night sky were not those of late autumn, now, but the constellations of deep winter.

The look-out sighted landmarks known to lie south-east of Venice.

I could no longer wear my doublet and hose. The hose would not stretch over my hips, nor the doublet lace up over my abdomen.

The Egyptian vanished into a far crevice of the cargo hold, and emerged with salt-water-stained cloth that unrolled itself and proved to be a shift and over-dress of soft linen and embroidered silk, respectively. As cargo it was ruined. Dried out, I could lace it loosely over my high belly and wear it.

I haven't worn skirts since the King's court in Taraco . . .

We were past the Republic of Venezia's guard and customs ships and the Lido before I came uncertainly up onto the deck.

'There.' Rekhmire' pointed.

Wind blew in my face from the rising sun. I squinted, seeing the sea and a great sky full of light; colours all so close to each other's shades as to be impossible to paint. Haze hid islands, ships' masts, and a glimmer of chimneys, roofs, and *campanile* . . . The lagoon's flat coastline was barely distinguishable from the water or the hazy air.

'Venice,' Rekhmire' said.

Painters, sculptors, architects, scholars . . . But all of the old schools.

I wondered where I might go, now Rome was closed to me, and noticed Rekhmire''s gaze sliding down to my bulge. So, as I came on deck, did that of the ship's captain. And the sailors.

Eavesdropping on gossip allowed me know that they supposed me a young woman who had come on board disguised as a man. The Egyptian, since a eunuch could not beget a bastard, figured as my protector only.

Venice's ships and spires began to solidify out of the dawn mist.

The beauty oppressed me. I went below, called for hot water, and shaved the last wisps of beard off my chin. In the event that Rekhmire''s hypothetical agent of Carthage did find his way to Venice, I wanted him to see nothing of the man who had been in Rome.

As I came back up on deck, Rekhmire' stepped in close, his linen kilt bright in the new sunlight. He towered over me, speaking quietly.

'Ilario. No argument. I'm sending for an Alexandrine physician as soon as we're docked.'

'You're not my master!'

'If I were still your owner, I'd *order* you—' Rekhmire' checked himself, an appalled expression on his face. 'Amun and Amunet! Thank the Eight I *don't* have to order that!'

For all my predicament, I couldn't help but laugh. 'Thank you. But I've dealt with my own problems all my life: I'll do the same now.'

The sun's warmth eased me, in body and temper. Dawn broke red over the islands and the lagoons, the winter geese rising up into the cold air. Hundreds of small ships poled and rowed their way past us as the dhow *Iskander* sailed in towards the mouth of the Grand Canal, and the dock at the steps of St Mark's Square.

Of course, Venice is a navy port, I thought, looking at the bigger trading vessels and the armed galleys. And much larger than Rome—

'But I wonder,' Rekhmire' continued soberly, as sails were furled above us, and small boats rowed out to ferry passengers ashore. 'You were a slave all your life. In your King Rodrigo's court – I know it was worse than you pretend. You have little *experience* of taking decisions.'

I winced, and thought of Marcomir in Carthage. 'I have some experience.'

'Yet you refuse to take responsibility for saving your own life.'

'*I've taken my decision.*'

I scooped up my small roll of belongings and let Rekhmire' offer me his large hand to steady me as I climbed down into a black boat.

From the flat level of the water, everything rose up to tower above me. Islands surrounded us; the sea hidden beyond a distant barrier. The oarsman sang in a thick patois as he poled us towards wide steps. Rekhmire' had the pinched expression of a man who will continue a conversation the moment he is not overheard.

Mooring-posts for boats jutted out of the water all along the quayside, in a clutter of straight lines and diagonals.

Trying to keep my balance as I disembarked, I found my gaze lifting from the murky depths of the lagoon, to steps rising up from the quayside to a piazza, and ancient red-tiled roofs. Chimes from a bell-tower deafened me as much as sheer visual complexity confused my eyes. I stared up at a Classical pillar on which a lion and a saint – San Marco? – wrestled for supremacy against the eggshell-blue sky.

Someone pushed against me. I staggered, shoved away from the moored boat by men's shoulders as they bustled past. Rekhmire' stepped ashore behind me, passing coins to the oarsman.

My share of the voyage will have to be added to the debt I owe for manumission, I thought, blinking at the stench of sweat and still water. Sailors I recognised from the dhow *Iskander* loped ashore and into the crowds. I saw porters, Venetian merchants, men and escorted women, unescorted whores, hand-carts and loaded mules, children running up with their dirty palms extended, bright eyes and teeth feverishly directed at me . . .

The Egyptian scattered a handful of small coins, which they pursued. I rested my hand by habit on my belly. *Orphans beg*, I thought, staring past the Riva steps at the facades of Gothic palaces, rising seemingly directly from the waters of a canal. The funnels of a thousand chimneys filled the skyline. I went to walk forward – and stopped.

In front of me, on the Riva steps, a familiar face resolved itself out of the crowds.

A lean man, on the tall side, his grey hair cropped down almost to baldness. Wearing military boots, and the high-collared cloak of the Iberian nations . . .

I stared at Honorius.

My father Honorius—

His eyes grew wider and wider. He glared at me. At Rekhmire'. At the moored ships—

And back at the Egyptian book-buyer.

'How *dare* you get my *son* PREGNANT!'

Part Three

The Most Serene

1

They call the city of Venice *La Serenissima*: 'the most serene'.

Honorius bellowed again, loudly enough to turn men's heads all the way across the Riva degli Schiavoni.

'*How* could you get her pregnant!'

He hesitated.

' . . . *him* pregnant?'

Rekhmire' gaped, struck speechless.

I snorted, sudden dry laughter overtaking me. 'It's a long story! But don't blame Master Rekhmire'; it's not his fault.'

'Oh.' Honorius looked at me. And back at Rekhmire'. 'Ah. Sorry! Thought you must have lied about—' Honorius grabbed illustratively at the crotch of his hose. '—You know?'

'In fact, no!' Rekhmire' appeared thoroughly flustered. 'Did you get my letter?'

I turned about, to stare at him. 'You wrote a *letter*? To my father?'

The Egyptian looked completely caught out.

Honorius spoke grimly. 'Oh, I got your letter. It caught me up when I'd got as far as Marseilles. *"Ilario and I are travelling from Rome to Venice"*. *"Ilario might welcome a father's company"*. And then I see Ilario like this! How *else* was I to read it, retrospectively, except *"I've got your son-daughter with child"*! *I* didn't know you and Ilario were fornicating—'

I put a hand up. 'I'm not. We're not! If we were, it *still* couldn't be Rekhmire''s child. And this—'

In peripheral vision, I saw many interested faces where the quayside steps went up to San Marco square. Brightly-dressed Venetian crowds, watching the entertaining foreigners shout at each other.

'—This is too public.'

Honorius nodded agreement, took a pace forward, and held out his arms. I stepped into his embrace. He felt solid, muscular; smelling of cassia. Used for a month and more to wind- and wave-noise, his silence made a welcome respite from the sudden human chatter.

Since it warms me to find him here – I believe I must have missed Honorius's company since Rome.

Now I was in skirts, the Captain-General of Castile and Leon seemed taller, although my true height was no less. The wool of his cloak was damp with dew under my hands. *From standing here since dawn?* I wondered. How long has he been waiting here?

How long has he been in *Venice*?

'I understand.' Honorius's voice growled beside my ear. 'It wasn't the Egyptian. How did this happen? Tell me! Were you attacked?'

The picture is all too plausible: a man-woman freak held down and raped by some gang of drunken thugs, just to see what would happen.

'No. The father's in Carthage. I'll explain later.' I stepped back, straightened my own shabby cloak, and managed a smile. 'If you ever visit the baths with Rekhmire', I'm sure he'll convince you of his credentials! As for this pregnancy—'

Honorius's stunned expression made me think he had not yet considered any of the medical aspects.

'—We'll speak about that later. Rekhmire', where's this Alexandrine embassy?'

Honorius spoke before Rekhmire' could, his lean weathered expression turned abruptly grim. 'Wait. The shock put it out of my mind – Master Rekhmire''s letter isn't the only reason I'm here.'

He raised his hand, signalling. Eight or nine men in Frankish helmets and Iberian brigandines shouldered towards us on the crowded steps; others moved in from further away. My heart went straight into my mouth.

No, I *know* them. That, there, is Tottola: the massive one. And that, the Armenian sergeant, Orazi—

I knew the other faces from Rome, also; my fingers having directed charcoal in the shape of a brow here, a nose and eyelid there. Even if most detail was hidden now by burnished steel sallets and the visors of burgonets.

'Your men – they didn't go back to Iberia with you?'

Honorius gave a further motion with his sun-browned hand. The men-at-arms fell into a loose, outward-facing circle about us.

'Those of my men who were weary of travelling, I sent on to Taraco and my estates. They can make my excuses to King Rodrigo. These men – these followed me in the Navarra wars; they'll follow me now, without question.'

'That doesn't answer *my* question!'

Honorius busied himself pulling on his gauntlets. One of the soldiers – a junior ensign; Saverico, if I remembered his name correctly – moved up, holding the Captain-General's sallet.

The mirror-polished curve of the steel reflected all the Doge's palace, and the wooden scaffolding that cloaked the building's walls.

Honorius dipped his head, putting the helmet on, and met my gaze as Saverico buckled the strap under his chin.

'Your foster family, Ilario – Aldra Federico, and his wife Valdamerca, and their daughters, and entourage. They're here, in Venice. They have an assassin with them. I believe he has orders to kill you.'

2

The teeming, shouting crowds of Venetians washed up against us like seas around a reef. I could only stare.

'What?' I managed.

'Ilario—'

'A *what*!'

My foster family: Aldra Federico, who has been a social climber since before he sold me to the King at the age of fifteen; Valdamerca, who rules her husband with iron will. And their daughters: Matasuntha, married and gone before I was of an age to know her, and Reinalda and Sunilda. Who are likely enough, now, to be respectable married women themselves. As I would be, were I wholly a woman.

I put them behind me when it seemed I had found kin in Rosamunda and the Lord Videric. Federico would have exploited my position as King's Freak – had I let him.

'What are they doing in *Venice*?' I turned from Honorius, to meet Rekhmire''s puzzled expression. 'How could they know I was coming here! *I* didn't know I was coming here . . . '

Honorius's eyes narrowed against the fretwork sun, bright even in winter, reflecting up from the lagoon's ripples.

'Your foster father Federico claims he's looking for "the New Art of the Italian city-states", to take back to Taraconensis. Apparently it's become the latest court fashion.'

The weight of irony in his tone could have sunk the *Iskander*, and several other ships beside.

'The assassin isn't Federico's own man,' Honorius added briskly. 'As far as I can discover, he's one of Aldra Videric's hired murderers.'

That made better sense of the matter. I nodded in understanding.

My father added, 'Videric got the man into your foster father's entourage. With Aldra Federico's knowledge, or without it; I don't know. I ran into them at Marseilles—'

'Marseilles?' Fear and realisation struck hard. 'Christus! You haven't answered the King's summons, have you? You came *here*, instead of going home to Rodrigo!'

Exasperated, Honorius declared, 'King Rodrigo Sanguerra can *wait*. When I left Rome, I had no idea that the Aldra Videric might employ others of your family against you. Now I know, matters are changed.

Your foster father sees himself as some kind of ally – lackey, more like! – to ex-First Minister Videric?'

'Very likely.' I agreed, dazed.

Familiar armed men jostled close to us, Honorius's badge sewn to their sleeves. Swords in scabbards; some of them carrying bows, and poleaxes. Fully-armed mercenaries ... I looked at Honorius. At Rekhmire' – plainly as stunned as I. Back at the soldiers.

'An *assassin*?'

A sigh came from beside me. Rekhmire' observed, 'It appears this isn't to be the restful stay in Venice that I had hoped for ... '

'JESÚ CHRISTUS IMPERATOR!'

Heads turned all along the quay, and on the nearer small boats in the lagoon.

'*Gaius Judas Tradditore!*' I added, neatly merging both sides of the Green religious schism. 'An assassin!'

Rekhmire''s smile covered a degree of concern. He touched my arm.

'I apologise,' I said, more stiffly than I intended. 'Clearly, you'll be better off lodging in a different part of the city—'

'Conceivably in a different city.'

His tone was light; steel underneath.

And if he's that determined to keep it a joke, I can't talk sense into him here.

I glanced about, questioning our destination now. The opening of the Canal Grande immediately took my eye – as it draws every man's gaze on entering La Serenissima. A prospect of red roof-tiles, funnel-shaped chimneys, and plastered brick walls rising directly out of the canal water ... plaster the colour of oatmeal and mustard, red chalk and pale sand.

I have only ever seen one painting of Florence: a fresco done on the walls of a chapel in Zaragoza.

Venice is the same, only taller.

Some of the stone-fronted palaces stood five and six storeys tall, not counting their attics and dovecotes. I saw bridges, innumerable bridges; and the sea omnipresent in harbour-basin and canal ...

Turning away from the laden boats, and men bustling everywhere, I found Rekhmire' sending an unobtrusive stare around the San Marco steps. I trusted him to see anything out of place that Honorius's plain soldiers might miss.

Videric is sending hired murderers to Italy.

With my foster parents.

And I thought I had nothing to do but come here and die in childbirth ...

'"Alexandrine Embassy"?' my father queried.

Rekhmire' raised the hood of his cloak, and gave me a glance that was evidently my cue to do likewise.

'My intention is to take Ilario to the Alexandrine house here, at the Campo San Barnaba, in the Dorsodura quarter. The late Ambassador

Pakharu died of cholera last autumn; the embassy's closed for ambassadorial business, but I have the Pharaoh-Queen's permission to stay there while I go about my own affairs.'

Rekhmire' regarded the soldiers.

'Being closed up, it may be safe. I think no man will willingly risk attacking us under the protection of the Pharaoh-Queen.'

'I'm not so sure.' Honorius grimaced. 'But, better than my lodgings. Videric's man isn't a fool. He's been watching. He knows where I stay.'

The same anger against pursuit that I had felt in Carthage rose hot in my throat. 'You know who it is?'

'I've been travelling with your foster father. I have an educated guess.'

'*Travelling* with Aldra Federico—!'

'I'll explain all when we're safe.'

The mass of people looked thickest towards the square of San Marco. Any man might approach us there covertly.

But in deserted streets, we'll be vulnerable. And in skirts, I doubt any man will lend me a weapon.

'Perhaps I should have disguised myself as a man again,' I remarked acerbically. 'A very *fat* man. I suppose the sole advantage is, your assassin won't be expecting to kill a woman.'

Honorius gave a snort at once sardonic and approving. 'Glad to see you taking it so well!'

'If you're watched, we should go,' Rekhmire' cut in. 'I advise walking – if we take a boat, we'll pay four times on the Riva what we should elsewhere, and the gondoliers will be bribed to say where we went.'

Honorius gave a shrug and a nod, of the kind indicating trust. 'Lead the way, then.'

The Egyptian strode off; the armed escort breaking our way with him, cresting the crowd. I stumbled after, feet coming down awkwardly among trash on the trampled mud and stone.

It was not the common feeling after being on board a ship. Even considering the month or five weeks it had been since I last trod land. There, the earth seems at once too rocking and too solid, and strikes hard up under the soles of the feet.

Now, my balance felt different; I no longer walked from the shoulder, but from the hip. The centre of my weight carried lower. I could neither achieve the female glide I had been taught in Taraco, nor walk like a man.

An assassin.

There have been the usual 'hunting accidents' and badly-disguised bandit-raids among Taraco's nobility; I'm used to the idea that not all accidental deaths might be natural. But that I should be followed by a man, or men, ordered to kill *me* . . .

At least Rosamunda's motive was personal.

The shadow of a tall brick tower fell across me – a beacon, or

194

lighthouse, I thought at first, and then realised it was a bell-tower, facing the sea – and the vast expanse of the San Marco square opened up. Sun blazed back from marble and ornamental facades; from the gilding on the Green Basilica. Before I could memorise more than a dozen astounding architectural details (since Honorius scowled at my groping in my baggage roll for my drawing-book), we were through the crowds, and striding briskly into alleys, between tall houses where plaster fell from the underlying brickwork. Weeds rooted in the crumbling mortar.

The black canal at my left hand reflected a series of windows rising up on either side, all shutters thrown open. Loud conversations in the Venezia dialect passed across the gap above our heads. I caught a balance and strode fast enough to catch up with Honorius.

'Where *is* my foster father?'

Honorius glanced about so casually that any man not much around soldiers might have been deceived into thinking him relaxed.

'In a hired palazzo, halfway down the Canal Grande. Little weasel keeps saying how regrettable it is that Chancellor Videric had to "give up" his position! There's a formidable woman with him who I take to be your foster mother.'

'*Formidable.*' I couldn't help a snort. 'This from the Captain-General of the House of Trastamara! Yes, that will be Valdamerca.'

My father grinned, and then looked grim. 'Two girls – young women. One of whom has your assassin with her.'

'Not Matasuntha, she'll be at home with her babies. It must be 'Nilda and 'Nalda.'

Who, to be truthful, I have not expected to encounter again, after being sold to King Rodrigo.

'Why would one of my sisters have a hired killer with her?' I persisted. 'And *do* you know who it is?'

'One Ramiro Carrasco de Luis, by name. He's here as their secretary.'

Honorius gave the name the familiar accents of Taraconensis. Nostalgia and homesickness unexpectedly stabbed through me.

Honorius walked as men of the sword do, all the weight loose from his shoulders, all the balance in the column of his spine. I ached to draw him. A rush of chill in my belly reminded me of other business.

'I doubt either young woman knows what Secretary Carrasco is . . . and I believe Carrasco's the last possible candidate. I've taken care to err on the *generous* side while getting rid of agents of Videric,' Honorius added, with a smile at the lift of my eyebrows.

His expression faded to seriousness.

'I'm a soldier, I know when the enemy's about – and I'm not the only man who's spent his every morning here watching the ships dock.'

A brick hurtled past my head, smashing into the building two yards ahead of me.

I brought up my baggage-roll, protecting my head. Chunks of plaster ricocheted from the cloth-wrapped wood and down across the earth, knocked free from the wall by the impact. Rekhmire' jumped in front of me. Honorius gave a harsh bark.

The soldiers skidded to a halt just on the canal's edge.

Out across the filthy green water, in the crepuscular light, two men stood in a knife-pointed black boat. Its covered central section seemed empty. One of the men, standing at the boat's rear, rapidly poled it towards a side canal.

'Hey! *You're* not a girl!' The other, shorter man lowered his hand from the throw. I saw his chest expand, breath punching a self-righteous tone across the increasing gap of the canal: 'You're a skinny ugly *boy* in a *dress*! With a pot belly! Who the fuck let *you* out into the streets?'

The German soldier Tottola raised a crossbow.

I saw the Venetian man's face change colour even across twelve yards of plague-ridden canal water – which will protect from swords and poleaxes, but not from the bolt of a bow.

I grabbed Honorius's wrist. 'Wait!'

He closed his mouth without giving an order. The boat silently glided on, moving only by impetus now; the boatman frozen. The shorter man stared blankly at me, no regret on his face.

I sighed. 'I *do* make an ugly woman. If you're planning to shoot every man who yells at me in the street, you should stock up on crossbow bolts.'

'This has happened to you before?'

'*Woman built like a stonemason!*', I remember from Carthage.

'Try asking Rekhmire' what it's like being a eunuch inside Frankish territory . . . Yes. It happens all the time. Or it's "whoreson catamite", when I'm wearing doublet and hose.'

Honorius wrinkled his nose, either at the smell of the water or his thoughts. He gestured with his free hand. Tottola removed his bolt, lowered the crossbow to uncrank it, and unhitched the bow-string.

The black boat vanished with rapidity into the side-canal. Distant voices raised in something unintelligible: relief, anger, or further insult.

'If I didn't want to keep us out of sight of the Council of Ten, I'd have both of them up here for the lads to beat bloody.' Honorius consolingly placed my hand on his arm and patted it.

Having come to know him somewhat, I thought he would do exactly the same if I were in male dress.

My heart hammered unusually hard. *Too much talk of assassins: I'm unnerved!*

It took until we had crossed the Canal Grande by a most splendid bridge, and passed into Venice's southernmost quarter, for me to steady myself. *Dorsodura*, they call the area, for the hard rock under it. It seemed poorer than San Marco: tall dank beam-and-plaster houses surrounding us. Swallows might nest under those eaves in the spring. For now, the water breathed off pure chill.

Rekhmire' strolled a few yards, hands clasped behind his back, frowning at a junction of three side-canals and streets. 'Yes . . . This way.'

He led us, rapidly, over two high-humped canal bridges. I gripped Honorius's elbow, assisting my balance on the slick cobblestones and mud, cursing skirts and pattens and the balance of my body.

It was easy to shift my concentration. 'Tell me why you're here in Venice – *now*, Father!'

'We were approaching Marseilles.' The retired soldier's lips pressed momentarily together. That thin line altered all the other lines of his face. 'The weather was bad enough that I'd decided to give up and take a ship the remainder of the way home, rather than continue riding west on the Via Augusta. While we waited for the tide, a messenger caught up with the Egyptian's letter for me. And while I was pondering *that*, one of the men brought me news of another large party of travellers, this time coming up from Iberia and riding east.' He shrugged. 'I've learned to follow instinct – I decided to wait a day or so. As soon as I saw them, I recognised them from your drawing-book in Rome.'

Honorius's expression abruptly reflected the fear that he might have committed an intrusion.

'I forgot I drew them,' I mused, and added, amiably, 'I didn't know you were so interested in my notebooks.'

'Oh. Well. My son-daughter's work . . . You know.' He collected himself. Giving me a look of surprising self-deprecation, he continued. 'So I established the travellers' names – and struck up an acquaintance. Two noblemen from Taraconensis, meeting abroad – I behaved like a garrulous retired soldier. You wouldn't *believe* how amiable I can be! Talked about campaigns in Navarra. Bored them rigid. *But* – they took me for no more than a busybody and a fool. Evidently, there are no rumours about me being your natural father, yet.'

The soldiers' boots echoed loudly against the walls of a small paved square. Ropes strung between upper windows held frost-stiffened shirts, hung out to dry. The succession of white shapes receded above our heads. Momentarily I missed the *Iskander*'s sails.

'I discovered their proposed route. Florence, Venice – and Rome. That was suspicion enough for me. Your Aldra Federico told me he was looking for painters of the New Art, to hire and take back to Taraco, to work for the King. I thought he must be looking for one artist in particular . . . ' Honorius's eyelids lowered in covert amusement. '*I* said to Federico, what a coincidence, *I* was going to buy art for my new estates; why didn't we travel together . . . '

Honorius spoke as briskly as we walked. I noted him not out of breath, despite our pace and the cold air. My own chest hurt. Five weeks idle on a boat helps no one.

'So, all of us ride back towards Italy, up the Via Augusta – if I'm correct, Aldra Videric sent three murderers after you. I've some experience with spies in the Crusader camps,' Honorius added, before I might interrupt. 'I had my sergeants drink with Federico's servants. Then at Genoa, there was an unfortunate brawl between my soldiers and some of Federico's men. You know what soldiers are like.'

His look of innocence would have deceived no man in the court of Taraco. I thought it not intended to. Only to impress on his son-daughter the depth of his concern.

'Honorius – Father—'

He gave a deprecating wave of his hand. 'Federico put two of his men on a ship back to Taraconensis, since they were too injured to perform their duties. I suppose they may report to Videric. But deaths would have looked suspicious.' He made a face of self-disgust. 'Ramon the cook, and the big mule-handler; they were no more than petty paid spies. Probably Videric keeping an eye on his own hired killer. The third man – this Ramiro Carrasco – we failed to entice into a fight.'

Honorius glanced down at me.

'I left Federico where the road to Venezia turns east. They were going on towards Rome, and *that* was safe enough, because I knew from the Egyptian's letter that you'd left the Empty Chair. But damned if they didn't turn up again, here, three weeks later! Rome didn't have what they wanted, maybe Venice has better artists, *ad nauseam* . . . I've been hinting that they should leave, try Florence; but no.'

'They may have heard rumours in Rome.' I saw him catch something in my tone. 'I . . . will have explanations of my own to make.'

Honorius glanced about with eyes that seemed permanently narrowed against sunlight, even in such cavernous streets as these. The houses rose six storeys above us.

'I hope that damned Egyptian spy knows where he's going – if this *is* a short cut to the Campo S. Barnaba—'

He broke off, and stared at me closely.

'*That's what it is!* Ilario! You're not wearing a collar!'

'I'm not a slave now.'

A broad slow beam spread over his face. '*Good!* How did Messer Rekhmire' finally persuade you?'

One of the men-at-arms ran back out of an alley ahead of us, swung around, saw Honorius, and began shouting. His voice shrilled high and urgent. Berenguer: a corporal – I recognised him by the glint of sunlight on a Frankish-style sallet, rather than his face.

He urgently pointed at the buildings on the far side of the narrow canal. The Navarrese-accented words went straight past me, my ear not attuned.

'*Hackbuts!* Ambush!'

I stepped forward.

Hard arms caught me around the waist.

The world lifted up beneath me in tongues of fire and flame.

In the same moment, a body struck me hard between the bones of my shoulders, sending my head flying back against an armoured chest. I cracked my skull against the metal, hearing a muffled thud. Disoriented, I felt the world tumble—

The tackle bowled me over, face-down and flat.

Hard, damp earth slammed against my hip and elbow and knee: I made a vain attempt to brace myself, terror stabbing instantly through me, every instinct trying to protect my belly.

Stone hit the knuckles of my out-flung hand.

Mail-clad arms buffered me painfully across one breast and my hip, preventing my belly from striking the ground.

Honorius's tall, narrow body wrapped around mine.

Noise fractured the world, loud enough that my teeth snapped together, catching my tongue; my skull jolting on cervical vertebrae. Not one noise, but a dozen in succession, and then more: a row of explosions, stabbing my ears. Concussion snatched the breath out of my lungs. Heat swirled in the air.

A hail of bits, rubbish and trash, fell down across me.

'*Charge!*' Honorius's voice rang through my head. Deafened, I barely heard him shouting military instructions. If I could have clawed myself beneath the cobblestones, I would have.

I stared at masonry, pale as honey. It was a wall that I had been borne painfully down behind. The stout curved parapet of a hump-backed bridge. Canal-water a yard away from my left hand.

Shock fractured images. Armoured men running past; sun on sallets and axe-blades. One man – Aznar? – his arm upraised and mouth open, shouting orders. Splinters of black wood fountaining down from above, against a blue sky. Doors and shutters slamming.

Mud and stones were cold under my body. The heels of my hands bled, gashed. Honorius's knee pressed down, planted in the small of my back: he yelled incomprehensible commands.

'Get – off—'

Hands turned me. Honorius's anxious face peered down into my face. '*Are you hurt?*'

The winter cold bit me: I stared down the length of my body as if I could not own it again until I saw it unhurt. No limbs missing, no parts mutilated.

'Not hurt. I— What are "hackbuts"?'

'Guns!' Honorius's crouched figure lifted; he stood and waved his arm, calling three curt directions. Fists on hips, he stared breathlessly over the bridge and canal. 'Frankish for "arquebus". They're running! No balls, these hired bravos!'

His exalted grin gave way to a frown.

'I half expected an ambush – should have thought of emplaced guns.'

A brilliant silver-grey smear caught the sun beside me, on the masonry of the bridge wall.

Lead, I realised.

The mark left by a flattened bullet, made of lead poured into a mould in a craftsman's manner that is very like the acts of craft in a painter's workshop.

I couldn't help but mutter my thoughts aloud. 'Jesú! I may have been in danger from the golem, but when I was working for Masaccio no one was *shooting* at me!'

'Golem?' Honorius sounded startled.

A shrill whistle cracked the air. I jerked round.

Sergeant Orazi strode back towards us, lowering his fingers from his lips. A heavy falchion gleamed in his other hand. I've sketched similar blades in butcher's shops. His had the same webs of red liquid across the flat of the steel, as if he had been unjointing animals.

The rest of the escort re-formed with him, sending insults and crossbow bolts after what must be running attackers. Honorius's curt unintelligible snarl brought them to order.

A few yards away from me, in the middle of the bridge, the young ensign Saverico sat up, felt his head, winced, and blushed as he climbed back up onto his feet.

Hoarsely, Sergeant Orazi shouted, 'That's right, Ensign, fall over at them – that'll scare any enemy!'

The little man shot a keen glance from one man to the other. Checking, I realised. They chuckled at his caustic remark. One of the older men ruffled Saverico's hair, where he had lost his helmet in the melee. The younger man glanced about and winced as he bent over to retrieve it.

Honorius snapped his fingers. 'Don't drop your guard!'

Two soldiers trotted up and knelt down beside me, one with a shield and the other with a crossbow, both scanning the canal path and open alley entrances all around. The shield-man couched his sword as if he were a hunter about to receive boar. The building on the far side of the canal was a warehouse: I could see under its eaves and into the empty arcades where our attackers must have hidden.

'Are you hurt?' Honorius took hold of me by the shoulders, eyes narrowing intently against the light as he studied me with a battlefield gaze. 'Can you *move*?'

Too loud, because deafened, I bellowed, 'Yes!'

I have only bruises. Surrounded by soldiers in mail and plate armour, it is not the time to mention nightmares that my hands will suffer an accident; dreams that wake me from sleep in the cold-sweats. Or the past fear that any slave-owner will realise my dread of being mutilated.

I flexed my fingers, and pried gravel out of the heel of my right hand, watching the slow welling-up of blood.

Aiming at a normal level of sound, I muttered, 'Unless this festers, it's nothing to worry about.'

Honorius tilted his head towards Sergeant Orazi.

'We hurt 'em,' the small man observed. 'Hit right after the first volley. Piled straight in, went right through 'em! They can run better than they can shoot. Four blood-trails leading off. No bodies. They may have taken their own. Whoever was in charge . . . ' He shrugged.

Honorius helped me onto my feet, demanding, 'A feint? Are they estimating our strength first?'

'Looks more like they thought they'd take us all out first time. They put everything they'd got into that.' The Armenian sergeant shrugged again. 'If they'd hit us without Berenguer's warning, we'd all be dead.'

Saverico scratched in his dusty curls and added something under his breath.

I could swear he just said: 'Lucky hermaphrodite or not!'

'"Lucky"?' I blurted out, staring down at the ensign who seemed barely old enough to be a page.

'We're alive.' Honorius chuckled. 'That's always lucky . . . '

I opened my mouth to make a comment about superstitions, and shut it again.

Honorius felt in his leather draw-purse, and handed me a white silk handkerchief, indicating I should bind my hand up with it. After a moment, seeing I couldn't tie a knot one-handed, he took over. The two pairs of armsmen he had sent out into the immediate area trotted back, faces red despite the winter chill, shaking their heads at the officers' questions.

'*This*,' Honorius observed, with some self-satisfaction, 'is why I bothered to send scouts out in front of us . . . In front, to the flanks, and behind! So far as that's possible with less than a dozen men here.'

I said, 'This Carrasco – is serious.'

Wisps of smoke drifted up from the colonnades of the warehouse, blue in the still air and sunlight over the canal.

Abandoned slow-match. The smell caught in my throat.

My ears still whined from the volley of shots.

Honorius, reaching down to the bridge coping, fingered a demi-sphere blown out of the sandstone. The inner surface showed perfectly smooth.

'I didn't expect hackbutters. But I was watched. If they weren't fools, there'd be *something*. Even if they can't know of Master Rekhmire', or what way he'd direct us to go.'

The excitement attendant on survival burned through me: I turned to look for Rekhmire', to share it with him.

His tall, bald figure wasn't among Honorius's soldiers.

Honorius glanced up, his expression faintly questioning.

At the same moment, the other one of the large, silent Germanic bodyguards, Attila, muttered, 'Aldra Honorius?' and pointed.

3

Honorius swore.

Rekhmire' lay face-down a few yards away on the slope of the bridge, in shadow, slumped at the foot of the parapet wall.

A snub-nosed trickle of liquid ran out from under his legs. Black, as I stared at it – turning bright scarlet in seconds.

The colour of blood when it meets the air.

Pooling under him—

'*Rekhmire'!*'

With no consciousness of moving, I was on my knees on the cobbles beside the large Egyptian. Reaching out—

'No.' Honorius's grip on my shoulder stopped me dead. 'Sergeant?'

The Armenian squatted between me and the sun, and felt with startlingly delicate fingers under Rekhmire''s tilted head.

An aeon later, he said, 'Be all right to move him, I reckon. Carefully. Caught his head on the stonework here, see?'

Blood on the gritty masonry. Rekhmire''s shaven head had a reddened, bleeding patch just below the crown. Honorius's hand ceased to hold me back. Fear choked me; I didn't reach again to touch Rekhmire'. I have seen men die of a snapped neck in such a way.

His eyelids creased without opening. His face formed a scowl. Still unconscious, he whined in the back of his throat.

The Armenian looked up from where he lifted the hem of the linen kilt, and soundlessly exposed the Egyptian's knee to his commander, and incidentally to me.

Jagged black skin and red flesh bulged open on the cap of Rekhmire''s right knee.

Something white showed in the depths, like meat chopped to the bone for cooking. Crisp black patches stank of burned hair. In the wreckage of the knee-joint, I saw a translucent carmine washing over broken shards of bone.

We could all be dead, here, now—

Honorius's harsh voice cracked out above me. 'You men. Carry him. *Don't* drop your guard because you think they won't be back!'

Two of the soldiers dropped bill-hooks to the earth, knelt and swiftly knotted a cloak between the shafts

Frightening: how often they must have done this, to be so proficient—

Stooping, the two men seized the unconscious Egyptian under his arms and one knee.

Rekhmire''s monumental features convulsed: he screamed. The shriek cut through the officers' orders; men talking loudly in the exhilaration of having survived an attack. A cautiously opened door banged shut, with the sound of bars slotting into iron brackets; no chance of calling on any of Dorsodura's inhabitants for a surgeon—

Rekhmire''s scream cut off.

I sprang up beside the bodyguards hoisting him onto the makeshift stretcher, grabbed at the Alexandrine's damp, cold hand, and found him limply unconscious.

Eight protect him! I wish I knew the proper prayers—

Pain cut deep lines even into his unconscious face. Breath hissed between his rounded lips. Blood on his chin— Where he bit through his lip, I realised. Not wounded in the lungs. Oh, Jesú, but suppose the wound turns poison?

Blood soaked through the green wool cloak under Rekhmire''s shattered leg, spattered to the earth, and marked the dust.

'Bind that up as we go!' Honorius harshly ordered.

Saverico obeyed, his helmet still off, his brown curls seeming shockingly unprotected. He crammed cloth against the bleeding knee and yanked it tight, and Rekhmire' did not cry out, did not move—

Breathing. The lift and fall of Rekhmire''s dust-marked chest was just perceptible, to my eye and to the hand that I rested down on his sternum as we moved off. Breathing with an erratic jerk and fall.

'This needs a physician right now!'

'The embassy. The Campo San Barnaba. That way.' Honorius signalled. '*Go.*'

Rekhmire' became conscious before we had staggered a mile through the Dorsodura quarter.

I realised it only as his fingers closed about mine, where I gripped his hand as I walked beside the makeshift stretcher. Large, powerful, the skin oddly smooth for such a masculine hand – it clenched tightly enough around my right hand to make me yelp.

'*Ke'et*—' He slurred the word, rolling his head in the dip of the woollen cloak, and opened clear eyes to stare at the sky. Roofs would be passing him, I realised, glancing up to follow his gaze.

His eyes clenched shut: he screamed, and swallowed the noise into his throat.

'Can I help?' I let Honorius and the soldiers make our way, concentrating only on the man bundled between the staff-weapons. 'What can we do?'

A wavering, high-pitched noise came out between his gritted teeth. It put the hairs on my neck upright. His free hand clawed at his waist – at his belt and purse, I realised. *Does he have something in his purse?*

I freed my hand from his, yanked his belt-buckle open, took the leather strings of his purse and snapped them apart.

The purse fell into the crease of cloth at his hip. Rekhmire' hauled up the leather belt from around his waist, doubled it over, and thrust the leather between his teeth. The hinge of his jaw moved as he bit down.

Berenguer staggered; Rekhmire''s uninjured leg knocked against my side; he made a stifled whinny, like a horse in pain, that turned into a high muffled scream.

The bundle of linen around his leg blotted red, dark red, and clotted black. Blood dripped, leaving a trail down the road. A pair of wild dogs took up following us, thirty yards distant. We crossed another canal bridge. I looked back. The dogs licked the cobblestones on the path behind us.

'Are we close? Is this it?' I hated to demand anything of him in his agony. 'Rekhmire'?'

The whine in his throat cut off.

White showed under his eyelids – only white, in a fish-belly curve that made me shudder, even while I thought it best thing for him.

Honorius argued with his scouts. I took another cloth from Saverico, and tied it as tightly as I could around Rekhmire''s knee. Blood made my hands all the red earth colours. It dried itchily. My head swum with dizziness; I felt cold to my fingertips.

I have seen worse on the field of tourney. Have seen men crippled there. Have fought.

But this is Rekhmire'.

His jaw clenched again, the pain visibly bringing him back to consciousness. Bone moved under the skin. His teeth sheared into the belt-leather. He rasped out a noise of agony.

Sick and cold, I looked away from the jolting cloak, swinging under its heavy burden.

The alley opened onto a deserted campo, and a barred-up church.

'This should be San Barnaba,' Honorius announced, looking around.

A high wall took up all one side of the square, broken only by a single gateway.

All of that gateway, from the bell-tower occupying the tiny arch above, to the narrow gate itself, was closed up with interlocking wrought iron.

4

The bars had been rubbed down to be re-painted. Rusting a perceptible orange now, they were still solidly set into the stonework. No entry by climbing, or pulling a bar loose.

I seized the embassy's rope bell-pull, jangling the bell that hung inaccessibly high. *'Alexandrines!'*

No answer. Honorius stood head-to-head in a muttered conference with his soldiers. I peered through the iron gate into a disused garden, cypress trees growing like tall, skinny black quill-pens.

No, not disused – a garden that some man had marked out around a central well, and then it had never been planted. The dead Pakharu? Nothing more surrounded the Roman-brick well-coping than bare earth, empty tubs, abandoned stepladders, rakes, shovels, wicker baskets.

I got out, 'He said the place is shut up – but there's a caretaker.'

My father bellowed, stentorian. 'Hello the house!'

Humped Roman roof-tiles and small grilled windows made it look like any other of the rare Classical houses in Venice. All the walls were whitewashed plaster, except on the frontage, where a fine pattern of lines and diamonds showed the unplastered areas prepared.

How long has the work been left like this?

'Should we go looking for a barber-surgeon?' I gripped the rails. Winter made them burning cold. 'But these Franks can't doctor—'

A woman in Egyptian dress and Frankish cloak came out of the cloister forming the front of the embassy building.

Her steps caught and faltered, seeing us. I saw her look past me.

She ran towards us, twisted a key in the squealing iron lock, and flung the gates wide open.

'We need a physician—' Honorius began.

The tall, elegant woman in Alexandrine silks fell on her knees in the mud, seizing Rekhmire''s large hands in her own.

He groaned, eyelids moving.

'No!' I squatted and grasped her surprisingly strong wrists, pulling her hands away from his. 'Is there an Alexandrine doctor here?'

Rekhmire''s long lashes flickered. The book-buyer opened his eyes and frowned, evidently confused to find his ex-slave and a woman apparently holding hands across his supine body.

'Ilario?' His eyes moved away from me, the lines deepening in the skin, showing pain and confusion. '*Jahar* ... ?'

'Neferet.' The woman emphasised the Alexandrine word, an odd long-suffering quality in her voice. She looked up. 'Is any other man of you hurt?'

Honorius shook his head. 'No worse than we can deal with.'

Rekhmire' shifted and stiffened. The cloak and weapon-shafts supporting his sagging body gave him increasing pain, I could see it. His teeth clacked together; he shivered as he spoke. 'Jahar – Neferet – we should – out of sight, quickly—'

'Rest.' The woman pulled her hands out of mine, and stroked a gentle finger along Rekhmire''s brow. She stood. I copied her, as she glanced at us, and then back at the Alexandrine House.

'Inside!' The tall woman ushered us quickly into the embassy grounds, her large hands clasped in front of her. She glanced down at Rekhmire' as she walked. She had the oval eyelids and grave long upper lip of a pharaoh.

'My name is Neferet.' She spoke to Honorius, his armour marking him out as a knight and man of rank. 'I'm a book-buyer for the Royal Library ... '

She guided the soldiers under the cloisters; I saw we had arrived at the house's main door.

' . . . There *is* no physician here. Ours returned home after Ambassador Pakharu died. I'll ... find you the best Frankish doctor I can.'

Without opening his eyes, the supine Rekhmire' gritted out, 'Butchers!'

It was clearly a known macabre joke between them: the tall Alexandrine woman smiled at it with long acquaintance.

The house's interior hall was all carved beams and painted brickwork, ceilings higher than I had imagined. Frankish rather than Alexandrine style. I blinked, to become accustomed faster to the dim light. Neferet glided forward, issuing a stream of orders to Honorius's soldiers – I saw no house-slaves – my father merely catching Sergeant Orazi's glance and nodding consent. Boots clattered: I made out a wide staircase as Honorius's men carried Rekhmire' up it.

Saverico, his helmet discarded, had his head bent around so far he might have been trying to see his own spine. His fingers wrenched at the buckles down the front of his brigandine. One of the older men, Aznar, came forward and took the weight of the steel-plate jacket, while Sergeant Orazi brushed the boy's hands aside and undid the buckles.

They unpeeled him out of the brigandine like a clam out of its shell. Something fell to the tiles with a hard clatter.

Saverico, seeming uneven on his feet, nonetheless bent and snatched it up, and held it triumphantly.

A deformed, flat ovoid of metal – *of lead!*

Saverico cheerfully waved the bullet that had flattened itself against a back-plate of his brigandine. '*Told* you I didn't fall over!'

Orazi ruffled his hair affectionately. 'So you didn't. Keep that one to show your grandchildren. Of course, if you get one eight inches lower, you won't *have* grandchildren . . . '

I lost the noise of their affectionate insults, my hand stealing to the high curve of my belly. Barely less than flat, but under it . . .

One of the oak doors across the hall opened; a man came out, calling to the Egyptian woman.

Much my age, I thought. Four- or five-and-twenty. An Italian of some well-born variety; dark-haired, well-dressed.

His gaze swept the jabbering hall, past Honorius making rapid ceremonious and chivalric introductions to the Alexandrine Neferet, and his eyes locked with mine.

He stepped forward, an expression of shock on his face. 'But – I *recognise* you! Master Ilario!'

5

'It's possible that I've had entirely too many surprises for one morning!' I muttered.

Honorius hadn't noticed. He had his head bent – not so far down – talking to the Egyptian woman, evidently conferring about doctors. I heard the shouts of the soldiers upstairs, sorting out a sick-bed. My impulse was to push the Italian man out of my path to Rekhmire'.

But he knows Ilario!

I don't know him.

There is a dagger on his hip, but no sword.

Assassin? If this man knows my face and name—

The Italian gave me a smile replete with self-confidence. 'You're *Judas!*'

It took my breath. I stepped back, accidentally, into the light streaming in through the still-open main door. The Italian man gained a clear look at me.

A blush like a fourteen-year-old page-boy's went up his face, reddening him from his round doublet collar to his brown curls.

'How rude of me!' His words tumbled over each other on their way out, as if he had once stuttered, and trained himself out of it. 'I apologise! That must be your . . . brother? You are Messer Ilario's sister?'

Presumably he apologises for mistaking me for a man.

I had a momentary, slightly hysterical, desire to assure him that the reverse error is no improvement.

He wore Florentine fashion, I realised, as Masaccio often had. Striped parti-coloured hose and skin-tight doublet, the shirt itself of better quality than I could afford. Likewise his shoes, and the small brimless felt hat. I didn't recognise him. And I would at least have remembered that nose, I thought. Which he would need to grow into, like a puppy growing into its paws.

He may have been one of the visitors to the workshop in Rome: there were many. That might be how he knows me.

'Excuse me,' I said steadily, keeping a grim hold on emotion, 'my friend is hurt; I have to go.'

Honorius, passing me on his way to the stairs, gripped my elbow once and tightly. 'Come up in a minute, when we've got him settled in a bed! The damn spy won't want *you* seeing him in pain.'

He was gone before I could question or object.

He gave no glance to the Florentine man.

The Alexandrine woman's husky, pleasantly-musical voice interrupted as I stared after my father. 'Dear Leon!'

I turned to find her giving the Florentine man a look I've rarely seen bettered by Iberian chatelaines with eight hundred years of the blood of Castile and Aragon in their veins.

'Make our friend feel at home; she'll wish to be with her sick friend here – won't you—?' She left the questioning gap with which polite people demand one's name.

We didn't discuss this, I realised; hearing by the evidence of his bellows that Honorius had reached the first floor of the Alexandrine house.

Names are fiercely gendered in the Italian languages. With this belly, I felt inclined to thank Christ Imperator that my saint's day is that of St Hillary – a name which has so many variations, both male and female.

'I'm Ilaria.'

And I must tell Honorius and Rekhmire' that.

'Neferet,' the Alexandrine woman returned, as if I hadn't retained her earlier, less-formal introduction. 'And this is Messer Leon Battista, of the Alberti family; a lawyer, newly returned graduated from Bologna.'

She stood an inch or so taller than the Italian; her gown and layered petticoats (in a dozen consecutive shades of blue) shone with gold thread, her hair was caught up away from her ears with pearl combs, and kohl lined her eyes. The gauze scarf wound around her neck and pinned up to the pearl combs just about resembled the hair-covering that Venice requires of modest women.

Reminded of that, I put my cloak hood back, feeling myself shabby in water-faded silks.

Leon Battista stared the more keenly, making no apology for it. Something about his gaze struck a note of recognition in me.

'I see the differences now,' he announced. 'Are you and your brother twins?'

I smiled amiably, not lying in speech, but allowing him to draw the wrong conclusion. Faces do differ in context. The jolt of meeting someone who recognised me reverberated through my body. Outside of Taraco, it's not something I have been used to.

Leon beamed at me. 'Tommaso never mentioned his Ilario had a sister. But then, I don't suppose he ever noticed anything but his paints!'

Pain showed abruptly and incongruously on his youth-plump face.

News will have had time to travel here by land, while we were on board ship. And if this man was Masaccio's client, or friend . . .

'I must tell you, Madonna Ilaria – no,' the Florentine interrupted himself. 'Let it wait: you have more important matters. But may I beg a word, soon? And I have some thoughts about the art of painting . . . Perhaps we could discuss them, at a later time?'

A painter, yes – that's why I recognise that weighing stare.

A slave learns to intimate the slightest sign of jealousy; however, I had no need for the talent. Neferet put her hand very firmly over Leon Battista's arm and showed me all her white teeth.

Moved by sheer contrariness – and a wish to delay feeling helpless in the presence of Rekhmire''s sickening pain – I nodded at Leon Battista. Who I suspected Honorius would assure me was no potential murderer. 'Would it surprise you to learn that I also paint, sir?'

He shook his head, beaming under that great hawk-nose that went so incongruously with his boyish curls. 'The skill should be accounted a mark of honour in a woman, as it was in ancient times. Wasn't Martia, Varro's daughter, celebrated for her painting?'

I felt unaccountably warmed, despite not knowing either name.

'Painting shows the noble intellect in a man,' Leon continued, somewhat earnestly, over the clatter of soldiers' sandals, and the outer door banging shut and open again. I heard men bawling addresses, where possible surgeons and doctors might reside.

The Florentine added, 'Why not also in a remarkable woman? The only true requirement is nobility of mind – the ancient Greeks knew this: this is why it was forbidden by law among them for a slave to learn to paint. To be worthy of painting, a man must have a free mind.'

The darkness and the sepia horizons of Carthage come back to me, and the heat of encaustic wax. I do not forget the weight of a collar about my throat. Or the man who removed it.

'Nobility of mind occurs in the strangest places,' I offered. Neferet stretched her lips; the Florentine Leon Battista coloured again, seemingly susceptible to blushing.

Rekhmire''s voice cried out, muffled, somewhere above my head.

Why should I care if my father thinks the book-buyer's pride will be damaged by me seeing him in pain? Why am I standing down here as if I were a respectable unmarried Venetian female? Is the compulsion of mere clothing so compelling?

'You'll excuse me; I'm needed.' I smiled apologies to Neferet.

Messer Battista bowed lithely enough to convince me he might be Florentine or Venetian nobility by birth.

I grabbed at my skirts so as not to tread on the hems as I strode up the stairs.

Honorius clattered down towards me, Orazi at his heels, and brushed his hand over my shoulder as we passed, as he might have done to a mercenary recruit. 'Look after him, will you? I've told Attila to give him a little of the woman's poppy-juice—'

There was something more – *'I don't like to without a sawbones' word'?* – but he was across the hall and out of the Alexandrine house by then, massive wooden door slamming behind him.

If the assassin's attack was disrupted sufficiently well, no man will have watched to see where we went. No man will be watching my father now.

If not . . .

Rekhmire' lay sprawled on his back, on a low bed that had evidently been hastily dragged closer to the small room's window, for the better light. I would have walked softly to avoid disturbing him – but the soldiers, briskly moving about and making a field-hospital of the place, shook the floorboards with their tread. I saw him wincing each time, no matter that his eyes were closed.

Seeing how he sweated, I went into the room and sat down on the edge of the bed, and wiped his forehead with a clean kerchief.

'How badly does it hurt?'

He blinked, black pupils widening under the poppy elixir's influence. '*Fuck* . . . '

'That's much as I imagined.'

If there was anything to be said for the flat and doubtless flea-ridden Frankish pallet acting as his mattress, it was that it didn't dip under my weight and shift his wounded leg. Rekhmire' bore my ministrations with immense dignity.

'This Neferet. You know her? Can we trust her?'

I asked to distract him, more than anything; his hips moved against the bed, as if he continually shifted to find some comfortable position on the linen sheets, and as continually failed. And because I did not want to say, *Are you going to die?* or hear his answer.

'Neferet is – an old friend – a cousin—'

The room's door banged open: Rekhmire' winced. Honorius, in a swirl of cold air from outdoors, cursed and caught hold of the door's edge before the wood could reverberate back into the doorway.

'Got you a doctor!' He beamed, reaching up to unbuckle his sallet, scratching his fingers through his cropped grey hair as if the helmet-lining irritated him. He bent to cast a knowledgeable eye at the blood seeping through Rekhmire''s bandages. 'Found him by a Free Company man's word. He's from Edirne. He's a Turk. He'll be here inside the hour.'

6

Each minute took days to pass, even if I counted their number on my racing pulse.

'Inside the hour' – it's close on midday! *What's the delay?*

Rekhmire''s forehead grew hotter under my fingers. He lay in a rigidly tense stillness, flinching as men clumped across the house's uneven floor-boards, on this and the ground floor.

I wiped his sweat away. The thought of what any physician might say made me sweat, also.

Suppose the physician wants to butcher the leg off?

Or says *Nothing can be done: he'll die?*

'By the Eight!' Rekhmire''s voice sounded thin. He slitted his eyes weakly against the winter light flooding in through the leaded window. 'Turkish physician. Slaughter me anyway, I'd think!'

'Just because Alexandria and the Turkish Empire share a border?' I forced a smile. 'He'll make you suffer first. Maybe poison.'

The corner of Rekhmire''s mouth twitched, recognisably a smile of his own.

Dare I give him more of the poppy elixir?

I dared not look at the knotted bandage over his wound. The sheets were sodden now, under his leg.

'Rekhmire'!' Neferet's husky feminine voice sounded. 'I have your physician.'

She entered the room after Honorius, together with a tall, spare man in robes and trousers; all of them followed by another man in Turkish dress, who stood a head taller than Attila behind him, and must duck under the ceiling's exposed oak beams.

'This is . . . Bariş, I believe.' Neferet gave me the look that, when I was a slave, I would have taken as a cue to leave the room.

Being freed, I merely continued to sit, and looked up at the thin Turkish doctor. He appeared to be in his middle years. His head was swathed in scarlet cloth, not unlike the rolled hats of the Franks.

'Bariş.' He pointed at himself. And at his companion, who was setting down a large ash-wood box with a leather carry-strap. 'Balaban.'

It might have been the giant's name; it might have been a description of medical tools. I bit the skin at the corner of my fingernail, worrying at it.

There was a brief interchange that I thought included Visigoth and Alexandrine Latin, as well as medical Greek; Honorius jerked a thumb at where the small man Orazi stood by the door, and added, 'My sergeant speaks most of the Turkish languages . . . '

'That may help.' Bariş looked down, his knife-nosed face in profile, and gave Rekhmire' a polite nod. He stumbled, evidently not familiar with the language. 'Master . . . Rekhmire'? My commanding officer is here, Venezia, recovering from a wound and sea-sickness, or we would have left for Edirne before now. Your good luck, I hope.'

Rekhmire''s hooded lids came down over his eyes for a moment. 'You're from a Janissary regiment.'

The Turk nodded, his teeth white as he smiled. '"Bariş" is not my given name! The soldiers call me that. It means "peace". Either because I refuse to take up weapons and fight, or because I bring peace to many as a doctor . . . '

My father was smiling, I saw, and Orazi and Attila; Neferet looked blank and slightly upset.

With a ghost of his normal demure irony, Rekhmire' said, 'I hope your patients don't *all* die . . . '

'Do I look that poor?' The Turk signalled and his servant brought the wooden case forward.

'The Janissaries are soldiers?' I queried, and at Honorius's nod, couldn't help a sigh of relief. 'Good! This is a gun-shot wound. Madama Neferet had to send away the Frankish doctor she found about two hours back. He said gunshot wounds are poisoned—'

The tall Turk snorted, his face becoming lively. '*Poisoned!* Astarte's bloody hand! You'd think the Franks never saw a wound made by anything that burned before. If they'd seen a man left black by Greek Fire . . . '

Rekhmire' barely managed to lift his finger, but it stopped the physician's enthusiasm.

The Egyptian raised an eyebrow at me, dignified despite laying flat on his back. I swayed a little where I sat on the side of the bed. I suspect I was much of his own colour.

Rekhmire' murmured, 'It's not the moment for that discussion, I think. One forgets how clearly you painters see in your mind's eye . . . '

I know the techniques to make size and gesso and pigment mimic flesh blackened at the edge and red-raw underneath. Masaccio was teaching me them for the Church martyrs. I just have no desire to think of them while the bundle of linen around Rekhmire''s leg weeps blood and yellow matter onto the sheets.

'Balaban, go and boil water; bring it when it's just warm.' The Turk bent over Rekhmire''s leg, not touching the rough bandaging. 'Master Honorius, I will work easier if you take most of your men away. Leave me a servant.'

The Turk Bariş nodded in my direction; clearly judging Rekhmire' content to have me there.

The other Janissary, Balaban, returned with water while Neferet was still arguing; both my father and the doctor capped her protests with the unsuitability of a woman being present at the physician's work, and the door closed on her voice arguing, 'But *Ilaria*—'

Honorius walked back from the door, the window light illuminating his face, shaking his head. '"Ilaria".'

With the Turks present, I would say nothing. I found my fists clenching while the physician and Balaban, between them, carefully soaked the bandages around Rekhmire''s leg and eased them off, crusted with congealed blood as they were.

Fresh blood stained the sheets. Bariş bent over and peered, his ship's-prow nose barely an inch from the Egyptian's flesh.

'You were lucky.' He straightened, pushing his hand against the small of his back. 'The shot was below your garment. If it had gone through your clothes, it might have carried street-filth into the wound and poisoned it. I would say it was a shot from long range—'

Honorius, dragging up a joint-stool and sitting at the foot of the bed, shook his head. 'Emplaced ambush, close range. I think they botched the second volley through haste – my lads were bearing down on them.'

Bariş gave him a look which spoke of more kinship between mercenary and Janissary than there was foreignness between Iberian and Turk. 'How did you know, Captain, they were a small enough number to be overwhelmed?'

Honorius's smile was frightening. 'We didn't.'

The physician harrumphed a little. He leaned down again to study the wound. 'You see, the cap of the knee is broke with a crack? This was almost a spent round. I say the man panicks, perhaps double-charges his arquebus.'

'*Double?*' Rekhmire''s voice echoed mine as I exclaimed.

Honorius shrugged, chin on the heels of his hands, as if his poring over the Egyptian's wound would tell him as much as the physician's.

'It's not difficult. You panic, you forget there's a charge in the gun, you load another ball and powder – the second charge goes *phut!*, at the front end, with a lot of smoke, and very little power.'

'Balaban.' The Turkish doctor signalled. His servant took one tray out of the wooden box and offered up the second one underneath.

The light gleamed on a metal instrument, not so unlike a stylus. I saw Physician Bariş dipping his hands in a second bowl of water, muttering a prayer to Astarte. Immediately after, he began to probe into the wound.

'It struck at the side, see?' His spoke loudly enough to conceal Rekhmire''s gasp and cry. 'A very small wound, here, and then a large one, where part of the lead ball has torn free. Stone shot would have been better, but . . . here. Hold out your hand, Master Alexandrine.'

Droplets of sweat ran down Rekhmire''s face. His whole body felt hot, radiating against me where I sat next to him. He opened his fingers as if obedience were automatic.

The Turkish doctor dropped a ragged dark shape onto his hand.

'A keepsake!' Bariş smirked. 'Your bullet. There. Now . . . there are pieces that splash off. Can't have that . . . That *will* poison the wound . . . '

He pulled out five or six smaller bits of lead, no larger than orange-pips, and added the hardened droplets to the collection in Rekhmire''s palm. The Egyptian closed his hand convulsively.

'Think of it as dropping an egg . . . ' Physician Bariş's voice sounded absent with concentration. 'Most sits as a mess in the middle, some bits spatter. Lead ball is no different. And some of the bits are embedded in your *other* leg. Hold still!'

Rekhmire' reached across his body with his free hand. Belatedly, I realised what he wanted, and put my hand into his. He squeezed hard enough that only experience as a slave enabled me to conceal the pain. *But I would not show it, now, and not for fear of a beating.*

'You are lucky,' Bariş repeated. 'A professional soldier would have kept his presence of mind, and re-loaded properly; I'd be sawing off your leg, and not hoping to patch it. An underloaded lead ball is not the worst wound in the— *Ah*. That, I think, is the last piece. Now let me look at what we have. Balaban, more water.'

Rekhmire' swore in a whisper so quiet that I could make out none of the words. It was a continuous stream of sound. The Turk took other instruments from his box, delving into the bloody wound, prodding at bone and muscle. Rekhmire''s ruined knee appeared swollen, now, white at the edges, as if the meat were too large for taut skin to contain it.

I could not look, despite how much professional curiosity might oblige me to. Much as I might want to attend an autopsy, to know what it is under a man's skin that affects what a painter shows . . . this is in no way how I wished to come by the knowledge.

Rekhmire''s forehead glistened, hot to the touch. 'Well?'

'Hmm?' The physician Bariş straightened up. 'Oh – I've seen misload injuries before. This, not enough to kill or amputate, enough to put you out of commission for a few months. But the operation will be difficult. The bones need to be put in their proper places, to knit, but then it must also move, afterwards, as a joint. I think it probable you will limp, after this.'

Rekhmire''s hooded lids blinked. 'Badly?'

Not a question I had expected the Egyptian to ask. *He's not so vain as to care about that—*

But he's a book-buyer: he's in the habit of travelling.

Rekhmire''s frown turned into a wince as the Turk began to re-dress his knee. I thought it brutal handling, to my eye, but I may have been prejudiced.

'This is the worse break.' The Turk stood back, finally, and illustratively rapped the front of his own knee, in his worn woollen trousers. 'Once the operation is done, you spend six weeks with your leg tied to a plank while you lay in bed. Or you get used to being a cripple. I'll attend you, all the while my captain's here. And I regret, the operation will cost; I must buy supplies, and in winter that's difficult.'

I spoke to Honorius before the Egyptian could. 'You're always saying you want me to take some of your money – I will. For this. I can owe you, and pay you back as soon as I get a commission.'

Rekhmire' opened his mouth: Honorius glared him into silence and turned back to me.

'Of course.' Honorius's rapid agreement came in the dialect of Taraconensis. 'Let's hope it isn't more than I have with me. If I visit a banker, every man in Europe will know where I am.'

'Captain-General,' Rekhmire' began stiffly.

'Shut *up*, Egyptian.' It was the same tone he addressed to his men-at-arms. And the same smile.

Rekhmire' hissed in pain and reluctantly nodded.

I spoke across them, to Physician Bariş. 'Doctor. This operation needs to happen as soon as possible.'

'Clearly. Now—'

I couldn't identify my father's expression while we debated, but it came to me as we made final arrangements for Rekhmire' to be operated on. *Honorius looks proud.*

There was a back-and-forth of words as the doctor packed away his urine flask and probes, and stood back for his large companion to pick up the box. The Turk measured Rekhmire' with an eye I thought not unfriendly, given the long-standing rivalry between Constantinople and the Turkish Empire.

'I will come early tomorrow, when I have collected supplies, and we have all the morning's light.'

It was more than I could do not to speak up. 'Doctor Bariş. What are the chances of a full recovery?'

'If not dead of a sickness after the operation?' He spoke as bluntly as any military man. 'Half and half. If it doesn't go bad, it will take long to finally heal.'

Lines showed around his narrowing eyes; he shot an uncomfortable look at Honorius and – to my surprise – at me.

'The Egyptian's got an equal chance of being crippled. But I don't like the look of how you're carrying your belly at all – your chances are maybe worse.'

7

I gave them all the coldest look possible, which, after nine years in King Rodrigo's court, I had perfected. '*I* don't need to see a doctor.'

Honorius's expression clearly weighed up Rekhmire''s immediate need against my later one.

The white of his eyes showed momentarily all around his irises.

I believe he's just realised what childbirth may mean for me.

'We'll talk,' Honorius said, his tone both commanding and noncommittal, and meant for me as much as for Physician Bariş.

Honorius needs to catch his breath as much as all of us.

And to prepare to be one of those who holds down Rekhmire' during the mending of his knee.

At the Alexandrine house door, Bariş gave an apologetic shrug. 'I had thought this house was shut up after the foreigner died. It was said you had your own physician here. If he's gone, will you also need a midwife found?'

Honorius held the door for him. Neferet and I gave identical shrugs, I was annoyed to note; she as unwilling to talk about her nesting in the closed embassy as I was about my belly.

Immediately after the morning's ambush, with Rekhmire''s agony echoing off the walls of endless squares and across innumerable bridges, my back had prickled with apprehension. Every tendon in my body pulled taut – as it now did again. Can we trust this Bariş not to gossip?

I thought of mimicking a forgettable, skulking, idle slave, but that might not work as well in Frankish or Turk lands as it does around the Mediterranean.

Honorius inclined his head, every inch the Iberian knight. 'Master Bariş, you'll be well paid for your trouble.'

For your silence, I translated.

Honorius accompanied Bariş and the giant Balaban as far as the iron gate, while I stood watching from the door, and returned looking satisfied with himself.

'We'll stay holed up here.' He took my arm, escorting me in as a man does a woman. 'I doubt the Aldra's man will try ambush again on the streets, and this house is defensible. Most criminals, banditti, hired thugs; they don't want to take on soldiers. Word will get around. If our "friend" gets to hire a second gang of ambushers, I'll eat my gauntlets . . . '

His effort to put me at ease made me smile, and then sober. 'Do you think he was at the ambush – this Ramiro Carrasco?'

'I couldn't make out their captain's face. But we can hope!' Honorius glanced around the Alexandrine house, or all that could be seen from this entrance hall. 'It took me long enough to find the Janissary doctor, and I was visible on the streets. While we were searching – this is the first time in three weeks that I haven't caught sight of some bastard skulking about behind me. Either Ramiro Carrasco can't find a man willing to play spy, or, God grant it, we hacked his head off in the confusion of the fight.'

I understood, belatedly, why men might carry their dead away from an ambush. It leaves us uncertain.

The shock of the attack still made my heart shake. The bruises Honorius's armour left in my flesh showed now, coming out green and black. I clenched my fists, and unclenched them, forcing the tendons and muscles to relax.

'This.' Honorius put his fingertips gently on the swell of my belly. 'We must speak of this.'

A muffled cry upstairs made me look in that direction.

'Yes. Not yet.'

The lean man frowned, but he allowed me to walk away from him and climb the stairs.

'I have my own decoction of poppy,' Bariş observed, the day following. 'It's stronger than you Franks use. It should make the surgery on your knee less of a painful butchery than you would otherwise find it.'

I found I felt sick.

'We use straps,' the Turk added, setting out his sharpening stone and instruments in the lid of his case, 'and you have three men to hold the leg still. Balaban, and those two of your soldiers like him in size.'

Honorius nodded, calling for Tottola and Attila without arguing about it.

As preparations began, Honorius stabbed his finger at me. '*You* don't get to do this. Belly! God He knows what it would do to a child in the womb, to witness blood like this!'

'That is *nothing* but superstition—'

He seized me by the scruff of my silk bodice. I dug my heels in, so he should not thrust me out and bar the door behind me.

'I'll go if Rekhmire' wants me to, not otherwise!'

A sensible interior voice asked what a slightly-built man-woman with no medical training might do, apart from witness Rekhmire' humiliated by his lack of control over his own pain. Stubbornly, I reminded myself: It's not my decision to take.

'You will leave when *I* say.' It evidently defeated Honorius that he could neither make himself use force on a pregnant daughter, nor beat the obstinacy out of his son. He fumed. 'I have no *idea* how I'm supposed to keep you safe!'

Rekhmire''s voice interrupted from the bed. 'I want Ilario here.'

Honorius turned his head and stared at him.

My bowels twisted, as if I would need to run to the necessary-house before long.

'You do?' I sounded startled, I realised.

Rekhmire' met my gaze. His eyes were bloodshot, but the irises still glowed the colour of old brandy where the light through the window caught him. He gave a pained, gentle smile.

'You've got a cool head.' He made a movement of his lips that would have been a wry shrug of the body, could he have moved that. 'I want to know what's done to me. Even if I weren't out of my mind with poppy-juice, I wouldn't be capable of seeing it. You sit here, right here next to me, and draw it. Then I can look, when I'm recovered.'

I held out both hands to him.

'And your fingers will stop shaking as soon as you sit down with a drawing-board.' There was a hint of the brusque master I had met in Carthage, offset by the deprecating humour in his gaze. 'Will you do this?'

I didn't hesitate.

'Of course I'll do it if you want me to.'

I drew with charcoal, so that when my hand shook, it was easy to erase the mistake. I copied the shapes of bone and gristle and stitches, in the clear north light, highlighting with good quality white chalk. I shut my ears to his howling pain.

8

I have never been so glad in my life as when his skin was sewn up and the surgery was over.

Over the next few hours of the morning, I sat anxiously, dreading that Rekhmire' would wake up a different man than before the poppy had stupefied him.

Making copies of the surgical drawings occupied my hands. I drew them out with pen and lamp-black ink, with a spare copy also for Physician Bariş. (At which he smiled, and remitted ten per cent of his fee.) And then I had nothing to do but sit beside the sick-bed.

As the largely silent Attila dosed out smaller and smaller amounts of tincture of poppy, Rekhmire' ceased to wake and slip into drugged sleep at regular intervals, and woke fully.

At midday, becoming conscious, he snarled at me to help prop him up against the low bed's headboard. I had sent the men-at-arms away, seeing how he flinched as their heavy tread on the floorboards jarred his leg, even bandaged and bound securely as it was between wooden planks. It occurred to me that I should call them back to restrain him.

But he'll be quieter if allowed some part of his own way.

I put my drawing-board and ink-pot down. Eventually, Rekhmire' sat white-faced and sweating, supported by bolsters.

'Cursed, stuffed, *moth*-eaten Frankish furniture!' he snarled, staring at the hangings of the bed. He shifted uncomfortably on the mattress, and made disgusted attempts at removing the blankets. I wasn't sure of the wisdom of it, but I helped him anyway.

Tottola had come in earlier, deftly lifting the woollen blankets and putting down a framework woven of willow-branches, that held the covers suspended up over the Egyptian's right leg. Head down and muttering almost inaudibly, he confessed the weaving skill was his own.

Rekhmire' now sniffed, grabbed at the wooden frame, and attempted to push his large and now ungainly body out and off the side of the bed.

'*Not a chance!*' I grabbed his wrists; each muscular enough that I could barely close a hand around it, as long as my fingers are.

'Copulation!' Rekhmire' spat out, in a pure Alexandrine accent, and shifted his hands to grip me, instead, while I eased him back onto the mattress. 'I intend to get up— Copulating diseased male dogs!'

'Don't move your leg, damn it—'

'Go bugger a bastard mule!'

'I can see this is going to be an educational experience. Learning a lot of useful Egyptian phrases ... ' I attempted to stifle a grin, and found myself needing to wipe wet eyelids. I rubbed my face on the shoulder of my dress.

'You're not hurt.' Rekhmire''s taut tone kept it from being a question. 'I didn't ask before – was any other man ... ?'

'No, no injuries. We're all well.' I let go, and went to push back the shutters, allowing more light into the dark Frankish room, and giving myself a clearer view of the Egyptian's worrying pallor.

'There was a doctor? A Frank?'

'That's the one your cousin Neferet threw off the premises ... ' Momentarily, I recalled the face of the Egyptian doctor in Rome – Siamun. For all his ability to see me as an interesting set of organs, and lack of tact, I would have trusted him more with Rekhmire''s injury than the Sorbonne-trained Burgundian that Neferet had thrown out.

' ... Then Honorius found a Janissary. He's good. And coming to check on you again this evening.'

The human body breathes, moves, speaks. As a slave at sick-beds, I have seen how very easily it falls prey to hot infection, thickened lungs, brain-spasms, and inexplicable deaths in sleep. *I do not want to see the Egyptian die.*

The clouds outside the window shutters shifted, winter sunlight brightening as if a shutter had been opened in a lamp.

Rekhmire' pushed himself further upright, his colour changing. 'Find me something I can use as a crutch.'

'You can't get up!' I spoke with no more patience than was to be expected under the circumstances. 'You've just had your leg blown open and sewn closed!'

'I need to talk to Neferet!'

'However important it is, it can wait!' I sat down heavily on the edge of the bed. So what if it makes the Egyptian wince? That in itself should tell him to *stay still!*

'When did you start work as a book-buyer?' I demanded.

Rekhmire' gazed at me with dark pupils reduced to pin-points, every line denoting stubbornness showing clearly in his face. Both his eyebrows shot up.

He answered the question, to my surprise.

'Sixteen. I was apprenticed to old Nebwy.'

People moved about in the house below. Nothing sounded urgent. I continued: 'What else have you done?'

'Ilario—'

'What trades? Occupations?' I didn't move from the bed, despite Rekhmire''s continual fidgeting to shift the covers, since I didn't trust him not to attempt to leave it again. 'Nothing, am I correct?'

His mouth set in a familiar obdurate line.

'So,' I said, 'that would mean that for, what, half your life, you've been wandering around the Mediterranean lands. And Asia. And the Frankish countries. And Christus Imperator knows where else!'

Rekhmire''s glare was less impressive when delivered sitting up in bed.

'Oh, but I'm sorry I took your collar off you! What's your point, Ilario?'

'"Ilaria",' I corrected, and saw I wouldn't need to further explain that. 'Rekhmire' – when did you last stay *anywhere* longer than a few months?'

He frowned thunderously. In the voice of a man running out of his store of patience, and not much inclined to look for replenishment, he demanded, 'What precisely do you mean by that?'

I reached forward and shoved a supporting bolster more firmly against the side of his ribs. 'I *mean* that you're going to be a God-awful invalid!'

It reassured him, so much was immediately visible.

I could all but see his thoughts on his face – 'Ilario would not joke with me in this particular manner if I were dying.'

The Alexandrine eunuch, well aware of his build and six-foot height, imitated the pout of a small boy. Clearly it was designed to make me laugh in turn. Regrettably, I couldn't help a spluttering giggle.

'You look ridiculous!'

'You'll be sorry when you have to nurse me.' He beamed, glancing about the room. 'I believe I shall ask Neferet to bring in a truckle-bed, so that you can sleep here – in case I need a drink of water during the night.'

'There's a canal outside your window,' I assured him. 'Although if you drink from it, I think all your troubles might be ended, judging from the smell.'

Rekhmire' grinned. '*Ilaria*. Listen. If you let me lean on your shoulder, I can very likely walk—'

'*No!*'

The Alexandrine woman Neferet glided into the room as I gave vent to a bellow entirely too rough to be female.

She raised a brow in a manner that left me in no doubt she and Rekhmire' were fellow countrymen. And fellow bureaucrats. She swept her robes about her with one long-fingered hand, and seated herself gracefully on a linen-oak chest near the head of the bed.

As if I were no more present than a slave, she addressed Rekhmire'. 'How are you, now the surgery's over?'

Rekhmire' grunted.

Brightly social, the woman persisted, 'And how is Lord Menmet-Ra?'

She did not call the plump ambassador to Rome *old Pamiu*, I noted. Or not in front of me.

'He's trying to avoid promotion to here!' Rekhmire' snapped testily. 'Ty-ameny wants him to take over in Pakharu's place. The last thing Pamiu wants is an ambassador's place where he'll have to *work*. I imagine he thinks it was overwork caused Pakharu to drop dead at his desk, and not the fever!'

Neferet chuckled. Her behaviour seemed more free than a Frankish woman of Venice: I wondered if this was always so in Constantinople.

And wondered also whether Rekhmire' might like me to interrupt this conversation. *Since she's plainly come up to get whatever she can while pain and the poppy makes his tongue unguarded!*

Standing and passing behind the woman to close the room door, I gave him a questioning look.

Timed while Neferet poured him water, he returned the weak ghost of a wink.

Neferet helped him to sip, and then clasped her hands under the folds of robes in her lap. 'Rome may be a backwater, but I understand the food is good there. Menmet-Ra would like that.'

The line of Rekhmire''s shoulders altered enough to tell me his pain was increasing.

Bluntly, he demanded, 'Where's your guest? The German Guildsman?'

A memory of ship-board conversation on the *Iskander* came back to me. I watched Neferet's large, long fingers creep out and play with the string of faience beads that hung from her belt. 'Guildsman?'

Rekhmire''s normal equable expression dissolved into a scowl, either provoked by the pain of his wound or using it as a credible excuse.

'Yes, the man who claims to have invented a writing-*machina*! This "Herr Mainz" from the Germanies! The man Pamiu wishes me to see. The man your *employer* Ty-ameny urgently wishes to speak with!'

He struck the side of the bed in exasperation, and with worryingly little impact.

'You must have seen the messages, Neferet! I know that the Queen wrote to Ambassador Pakharu before he died; it will have been in the papers you cleared up and sent home—'

'Did she send you to check up on me?'

Neferet's expression held shrewdness and some dislike, but I had no idea what to attribute to the situation, and what to past interaction between them.

With the silent deference of a slave, I went to make up the fire in the hearth, relying on those movements to make the woman, at least, automatically forget that I was present. Lumps of sea-coal dirtied my fingers; I wondered what nature of marks one might make on paper or wood using it.

My back was to the bed. I heard it creak as Rekhmire' leaned against the headboard.

'The embassy mail hasn't had time to catch up with me, these last few months. What I know, I know from Menmet-Ra. He asked if I would come here—'

'To check up on me.' She re-emphasised the words.

I turned my head to watch covertly, and saw that her every limb was stiff.

'I didn't ask for Pakharu's job! I didn't ask to be here when he died! Sacred Eight, I'm a book-buyer, not a diplomat! All I've been able to do is shut the embassy down, and tell the Venetians that the Queen-Goddess will send a replacement when the weather allows travelling. And deal with some minor essential matters myself. I'll be *happy* to hand over to Pakharu's replacement – whether that's Menmet-Ra, or any other man, or you—'

'Me?' Rekhmire''s voice was a dry squeak. 'I've no desire for an ambassador's post!'

'Really?' The Alexandrine woman leaned forward, sitting right on the edge of the linen-chest. 'Is that why you're here before Pakharu's sandals are cold? Travelling in *winter*? Because you're not looking for a promotion into the diplomatic service, and out of book-buying?'

Her pronounced features were all drawn up in concentration as she studied him: the light from the window would have made her a wonderful study to draw. Kohl emphasised the narrowing of her eyes as she searched his face.

Some kind of conclusion came to her; the moment of decision was obvious.

She rose to her feet with fluid grace. 'I'm sorry; I shouldn't speak to you like this while you're injured—'

'Neferet! I really have *no* interest—'

'You sleep, if you can; I'll come up again later.'

Her sandals clacked across the oak floorboards. The door shut behind her.

I poured a mug of Frankish small beer and moved to offer it to Rekhmire'. The brightness of the sun showed me droplets of sweat coalescing on the skin of his forehead, trickling down his temples.

'She's not going to tell you about this Herr Mainz,' I observed. 'Whoever he is. Who *is* he? Is it the man you mentioned while we were on the *Iskander*?'

He drank, and closed his eyes briefly. 'Is that an effort to take my mind off pain? Or merely vulgar curiosity?'

'Both,' I admitted. I added, to make him laugh, 'But mostly, vulgar curiosity.'

The Egyptian smiled faintly, opening his eyes. He shook his head when I offered to help him hold the drink; the pitch-lined leather cup shaking dangerously in his hands, liquid all but slopping onto the sheets.

'Apparently—' Rekhmire''s voice sounded weak, but familiarly acerbic. 'According to Menmet-Ra, all the Eight bless his name and loins—'

I couldn't help a snicker, even if he hadn't been trying to provoke it.

Rekhmire' continued dryly: 'According to him, as I mentioned on the

Iskander, there's a man here in Venice who claims to have a *machina* that will print out written books, as easily and as clearly as woodcuts. This German Guildsman, Herr Mainz, is that man.'

Most of the picture-dealers I'd been to in Rome kept a stock of several thousand woodcuts ready to sell, since they were so popular and so cheap. The idea of a *book* being so available ... I blinked, dazed, wondering how sick I must have been aboard ship not to hear this when Rekhmire' told me.

I reached out to take the Egyptian's tipping cup, and Rekhmire' blinked himself back to awareness.

'Naturally, Ty-ameny of the Five Great Names wants Herr Mainz to come to Alexandria. Think of such a print-making *machina* at the Royal Library! Ambassador Pakharu died before it could be arranged. Menmet-Ra told me Neferet hasn't answered messages he sent in the autumn, but she *is* only a book-purchaser, and not a member of the diplomatic service; she can do no more than be a caretaker. Menmet-Ra is clearly hoping someone else will be posted ambassador to Venice if he delays long enough in Rome ... '

I must have looked blank.

'Ensuring the golem is sent to Alexandria.'

'Of course. You said: I remember.' I would not bring it to my mind's eye, I swore. And found myself vividly conscious of every delicate cog and piece of gearing in those polished marble and bronze fingers. Marble slick with scuffs of drying blood.

'This Herr Mainz may be a charlatan.'

Rekhmire' evidently sought to use the subject in turn to distract both me and himself from our different pains.

'I've seen men who claimed to set letters in the same way a woodcut can be printed off, but never one that wasn't slower than a good copyist, or more likely illegible after the tenth copy.'

I smiled. 'My job's safe, then.'

Rekhmire' punched at his pillow. 'The *profession* of scribe is safe. The chance of anyone ever employing *you*, with your habit of annoying marginalia ... '

'My ambitions are crushed.'

It made him smile, but with more lines of pain in it than I wanted to see.

'The Janissary says some men stop breathing if they take too much poppy,' I said apologetically.

He nodded, the scored lines in his rounded face not diminishing. 'True. Or else they're left buying poppy to take for the rest of their lives. The pain is not as bad as it was.'

The spots of dampness on his brow, and spotting his stubbled scalp, called him *liar*. I kept my mouth shut.

Rekhmire' switched the direction of his thought with no apparent warning. 'You should show yourself here in Venice. Go to the squares, the palazzos, the markets. Let Neferet take you to the salons. Show yourself alive – as soon as possible. It puts a small obstacle that any of Videric's murderers will need to avoid.'

'It's the Council of Ten who rule here, isn't it?' I took over Neferet's linen-chest to sit down. 'If they ever catch and question the men who ambushed us, I suppose Videric's name would eventually come up?'

Rekhmire' narrowed his eyes, looking slightly impressed. 'Which is what we have to thank for the *Iskander* not being boarded as soon as we docked, and our throats slashed there and then.'

I found I was resting my hand on my belly and the salt-stained silk skirts. 'I'll go out. If I must. But we can discuss this later—'

'You need Frankish woman's dress. My purse is on the chest, there. The Merceria will have tailors and cloth: buy clothing.'

I pointed at the wooden framework over his leg, half-uncovered with sheets and blankets as it now was.

'That evidently affects the memory,' I explained.

Rekhmire' looked bewildered. 'What?'

'*I'm not your slave any more!*'

The lines of pain on his face were cut by the creases of a deep, appreciative smile. 'A little louder, please – there may be some man on the mainland who didn't hear you!'

'Just so I'm heard in this room!' Restless, I got up to walk from door to window, and window to door again. 'I don't have money to waste on Frankish women's clothes!'

He gave up the argument too easily. 'You might see if Neferet has anything she'll loan; she dresses in Frankish fashion when she has to.'

I had made a sketch or two of the exotically foreign woman, during Rekhmire''s restless periods of sleep, marking her deeply reddish-tan skin, satin black hair, and large eyes. Generously built, with a high brow and flawless carriage, she carried herself regally enough that I felt short, mannish, and laughable in her presence.

Somewhat satirically, I said, 'I don't think her gowns are going to fit me.'

'Pin up the hems. I see you haven't been looking with an artist's eye.'

'No, I doubt I *am* looking with an artist's eye! Consider yourself lucky I'm looking at all!'

Rekhmire' grinned, seeming unoffended.

I demanded, 'What am I missing?'

Despite pain and dishevelment, he looked infuriatingly smug. If I hadn't known it another of the Egyptian's attempts to cheer me, I would have quarrelled with him there and then.

'Listen.' He held up one long, spatulate finger.

Voices came in through the open window. I leaned out a little, between the shutters. In fact we were overlooking the walled garden, and not the canal directly, I found. Neferet was speaking with the Florentine lawyer Battista, and one of Honorius's men-at-arms.

I stared at her, and then back into this room, dim by contrast. Her national kinship with Rekhmire' was immediately apparent; even if he was all curves, and she all angles. It spoke itself in the tint of her skin, the long-lashed dark eyes, the large and elegant hands—

Large hands.

My head whipped around: I stared out of the window.

Rekhmire'. Neferet. Rekhmire'.

I stared from the one to the other, comparing this line with that.

'*But!*' I protested.

Rekhmire' threw his head back and laughed out loud, even as he clutched at himself in pain.

'*But* – she's the perfect woman!' I protested. 'I could paint her so!'

'She . . . doesn't have anything of what you have,' Rekhmire' said mildly, rubbing long fingers into the top of his thigh, massaging bruised flesh. He showed me all his teeth in a smile. 'Or, indeed, what I have. She was Jahar pa-sheri, when I knew my cousin first—'

He used the term as I'd heard him before, speaking of the Pharaoh-Queen Ty-ameny's bureaucrats.

'—and Neferet is a true eunuch.'

If I'd picked up anything about Alexandrine habits in Rekhmire''s company, and at the embassy in Rome, it was that it's common for Egyptians to take different names at different parts of their lives.

And that *pa-sheri* means 'son of'.

Rekhmire' added, 'Neferet chooses to dress as a woman in Venezia. And be one in all ways.'

Now that I looked, her softly plump shape had the appearance of being sleeked down under her robes by a corset. She was subtly too rounded at the shoulder and chest. The Egyptian woman stepped out of my view, under the colonnade at the front of the house; I heard the door open, and her voice and the soldier's diminish inside. If I listened with attention, her voice was low for a woman, and sensually husky: she might be a male alto.

'Christus Imperator!' I muttered, leaning back from the window ledge. 'Does *anybody* ever leave Egyptian Constantinople with their cock and balls intact!'

Rekhmire' choked.

I lurched to rescue the pitch-lined cup, taking it and setting it down on the chest. Rekhmire' wiped the back of his hand across his mouth, wincing between laughter and pain. His eyes spoke a volume or two.

'*Many* do!' he protested, when he had control of his voice. 'Neferet's an old friend as well as a cousin; she's not as intimidating as she seems, and she'll be happy to make you feel welcome in Venezia.'

'I suppose one of us should tell her about "Ilaria".' I managed a creditable imitation of his brow-raising. 'And as her old friend, "cousin", and my old master – that would be you.'

He thanked me, but not with the sincerity a man ought to use. I practised my sweetest feminine smile.

A thought intruded, pushing the mutual amusement aside. 'Is that why you never concerned yourself about my – condition?'

Rekhmire' laughed. It became a cough and a wince. The sweat of pain was back on his forehead; I regretted raising the matter. He snorted.

'Because my friend's made himself known as a girl since he was old enough to speak? As far as Neferet's concerned, she's been convinced since she was four that she has a woman's *ka* – a woman's soul. I've never doubted the strength of her opinion. And, truthfully, she lives a woman's life far more easily than a man's. But you – a matter of the body . . . and I would like to think that you and I get on rather more amiably than Neferet and I. Good a person as she is, we were jealous of each other as children, and it took some years to grow beyond that. It still comes out at times.'

He sweated. I sat on the edge of the bed again, to wipe his forehead with a clean kerchief.

'I don't know if it's a matter of the body.' I avoided meeting his eye as I spoke. 'It felt easy enough to live a man's life in Rome. Harder to be a woman here – but then, a woman's life *is* hard, almost everywhere. Restrictions are worse than obligations. What part of the soul is this *ka*?'

I doubted Father Felix, or any of the other clerks at the court of Taraco, would consider me competent to take part in a discussion concerning the soul. *But I'm willing to try, if it takes his mind from how he hurts.*

He fell asleep during his explanation.

The Janissary doctor Bariş came several times, twelve hours apart, worried for a time over the heat of the skin sewn over the wound, and then relieved. I let Honorius speak with him – he got more honesty, both being military men. After three days, he announced his visits could become less frequent.

He spoke with one eye in my general direction. I refrained from making myself scarce.

After a considerable pause for study, he observed, 'Five months, or a little more. Too late for measures of removal, without you die.'

I nodded, finding no voice.

Bariş gave me a smile strangely effective as reassurance. 'Then we concentrate on birth. Early or late.'

9

'*I don't care!*' I snapped, five days later. 'I'll move my bed in here and you'll have to watch me give birth! I'm *not* having you put any weight on that knee yet. You don't try to walk! Understand?'

'Yes, master . . . '

Rekhmire''s assumption of a slave's manner was too accurate for him to have been a freeman all his life, I thought, or even an Alexandrine bureaucrat-slave. He cocked an eyebrow at me. At my belly, in particular.

'I apologise,' he corrected himself. 'Yes, *mistress.*'

Since an appropriate insult eluded me, I reached down and ruffled the wheat-coloured bum-fluff that was growing on his scalp now he hadn't been able to get up and shave.

'That would carry much more weight,' I observed, 'if it didn't come from someone so closely resembling a dandelion!'

The Egyptian's eyes narrowed to slits, giving him the evil look of some ancient stone monument. 'Ask me if I wish to purchase you as a slave again – just *ask* me . . . '

'Not a chance!'

It made me grin to see him cheerful. Even if, to a degree, it sprang from being comfortably isolated in this sick-room from all responsibility.

'All those punishments you never subjected me to, *master*, and now it's too late . . . '

'Clearly.' He folded his arms and gave up the evil glare in favour of a blatant attempt to gain pity. 'But, as I recall, I never threatened *you* with anything so dire as being present at a childbirth. You're a cruel . . . '

'Yes?' I watched him trapped between gendered grammatical phrases, and was for the first time honestly amused.

' . . . I don't know. But whatever it is, you're a cruel one!'

I shifted my drawing-board to show him my work in silver-point. 'No, "cruel" would be drawing you when you're pouting.'

'Much as you may *think* you're amusing me,' Rekhmire''s smooth face might just have been concealing a grin, 'I assure you, I don't pout!'

'The silver-point drawing does not lie . . . This isn't bad. Of course, you don't have much choice about staying still for the modelling.'

'*Ha!*'

The sound of a book-buyer in full-throated outrage was something I'd missed. I grinned, and watched him fail to suppress a snicker.

'I can tell you're feeling better,' I added. 'So can everybody else. But you're still getting your food on wooden plates . . . '

And his drink in turned wooden drinking bowls, too; well-made Frankish ware. The beautiful grain of the wood was hardly the point, however, and by the Egyptian's shame-faced look I guessed he knew that.

'I only threw a bowl at you once, yesterday,' he protested. 'And it was completely called for!'

'Because I called you a bad invalid? You *are*—'

The drinking-bowl was at least empty when it bounced off the low ceiling-beam.

We sniggered like small children for a while.

I welcomed that, too. After the third and fourth days of his incapacity none of the Frankish servants would enter the room. Honorius's soldiers had had plates thrown at their heads with a frequency that frankly amused them, and caused them to openly admire the book-buyer.

But since I knew by now how little Rekhmire' likes to display temper, I could estimate the fear and fury that must be driving him.

'I assume you'll be walking before the birth . . . ' I added cross-hatched shadows that failed entirely to round out the drawing of his hand. 'I wouldn't mind if you were there.'

I looked up at Rekhmire'.

'I . . . hadn't intended to say that.'

The Egyptian briefly nodded. 'I'll be there.'

It had become second nature by now, I realised, to push the ballooning fear away, before it robbed me of all breath, and to assume a fatalistic stance.

My body will dictate when I deal with this. There's nothing I can do.

Close my mind firmly to the future as I might, I couldn't ignore a dislike of spending Honorius's money and living on the Alexandrine house's charity.

I doubt any workshop master would hire me for a job. But that doesn't mean I won't try to find one.

It surprised me that Honorius didn't attempt to stop my search.

'No man's seen Carrasco, or any other man watching us.' He shrugged. 'And besides, the lads and I will be going with you . . . '

I thought he preferred to see me outside the sick-room from time to time. The weather remained a dry cold without snow. I was willing to go out only because Rekhmire''s wound appeared to be mending both faster and better than even Bariş had anticipated.

No man in Venice appeared to teach the New Art. Which was no surprise, but no less infuriating.

On the next failed attempt to find employment, I thought it no coincidence that Honorius and I and a dozen of the men-at-arms ended up going back to the Dorsodura quarter by way of a campo that held pigment shops. I feasted my eyes on the rows of wooden boxes full of colour, and the small amount of unearthly and glowing four-ducat blue.

'I *would* go for a job picking the ashes for lapis lazuli.' I displayed my palms to my father, and we matched finger against finger. 'Women have small hands; they tend to be employed at it. But it's a job that goes nowhere in the industry, and my hands are in any case suspiciously large for a woman.'

I bought red chalk with Honorius's money and came away.

'I won't be a parasite.' I could not sufficiently voice my frustration. 'I don't have enough money left from Rome to support myself. And I owe Rekhmire' for the sea-voyage, leave aside what I owe you. Yes, you'd pay to have me apprenticed to a master here, if it could be managed safely, but this is a backwater – there's no one here who can teach me anything.'

Honorius pushed his lips together in a silent whistle.

I snapped, '*What?*'

'I like a man who's determined in her opinions!' Honorius grinned. 'But leaving aside the hypothetical genius we'd evidently have to find as your workshop master—'

One of the older men, Fulka, chuckled. I sneered at Honorius, since he evidently invited it. The Lion of Castile beamed warmly at me.

'I don't want you in a workshop.' He sobered. 'Even if any man would hire a pregnant widow—'

I winced, both at the necessary public pretence, and the brutal but true statement.

'—how would you explain the dozen or more soldiers there *with* you? You'd be too open to attack in a workshop—'

'I won't be locked up in the embassy!'

'No.' Lines wrinkled at the outer corners of his eyes. 'I see a lot of you in me. I'd hate Sergeant Orazi to be continually hunting you down after you climb out of windows.'

The Armenian grinned at me with his remaining teeth.

'As if I'd do a thing like that.'

'Trust me, you'd do a thing like that.' Stopping at a chestnut vendor, Honorius rubbed his palms and held them out to the iron brazier while his men bargained.

The roast nuts burned my fingertips and mouth, peeling and eating, but were worth it for the hot, dry taste.

Walking on, Honorius observed, 'Remember you're not the only one in danger. That whoreson Videric will bear a grudge. He will have heard the part played in all this by Master Rekhmire'. I'd as soon the Egyptian was tended by someone I implicitly trust.'

Is it too early for this untried trust between Honorius and I?

I can feel in flesh and bone the tension of his body covering mine, while the flames of arquebuses blasted over our heads.

Honorius's sand-coloured brows lifted in faux-innocence. 'And ask yourself who you think Master Rekhmire' would prefer as a nurse – you, or a bunch of hairy thugs from Castile?'

The eponymous hairy thugs grinned their agreement.

'I *could* ask. And he'd probably go for your crusader veterans!' My basic knowledge of nursing extends no further than patching up a beaten slave.

Honorius had an air of being much pleased with himself.

'Which of us can ensure the book-buyer doesn't make a cripple of himself, by assuming he's fit enough to get up and wander around Venice tomorrow? *And* the day after. And the day after *that*.'

There was enough nodding and murmured agreement among the men eating their roasted chestnuts that I realised, *They've adopted the royal book-buyer as a mascot. Along with the 'lucky hermaphrodite'* . . .

'Rekhmire''s got enough common sense to stay off his feet while it's necessary.'

'While there's spies in the city, and he's looking for this German Guildsman he keeps yelling at the Egyptian woman about, and he knows you've been ambushed once already?'

I settled for an irritated grunt.

Honorius said, 'You have the best chance of keeping him from crippling himself. And, while I want you under my eyes until we've removed this spy of Videric's, I think also that you feel you owe the Egyptian a debt, and would like a chance to repay it.'

I found myself giving Honorius a startled look.

Begin with the fact that Rekhmire' bought me, and never treated me as slaves are treated in Iberia. And that, even if he upset my life like an overturned cart, he intended well. He took me out of Rome when he had no reason to; when any other man would have abandoned me to my own business. But, more to the point, he is a friend who lifts my heart. If he cheers me whenever I see him, it only seems reasonable that I would want to do the same in return.

'I'll do what I can,' I said. 'Maybe I can sell some of my sketches while I'm here, though. There ought to be some money I can bring in.'

'I'll give you a commission.' Honorius held up both hands, palms out, as if to forestall an explosion. 'No, listen to me! The chapel at home needs rebuilding; I'd have to bring somebody in to fresco it. I've seen your work books. If you're not good enough now, you soon will be. And if what you paint is amateur—'

'You won't pay me?'

'I'll pay you half, for the time and work. But – worse, to you – if it's rubbish, I'll have another artist in to rip it out, and re-do the plaster and fresco. Do me a proper one.'

233

Fresco has to be done right the first time: there are no second chances. For all Masaccio's teaching, I'm nowhere near practised enough.

I wondered if I could talk my father into painted wood panelling without him realising that. *Probably not. So I must merely be honest.*

'It need not be fresco,' Honorius added. 'I'm open-minded on the medium.'

I suppose a man does get to be a reasonable judge of character when taking on soldiers for his companies. Or else my father is coming to know me.

'What subject do you want for the painting?'

'One of the soldier-saints. To be honest, I'd like it focused around St Gaius. A triptych, maybe. That would give you the joining, the betrayal, and the exile to the East.'

He seemed certain enough, which is a bonus in a client.

I could have wished my first patron not to come from nepotism, but I'll hardly be the first artist to begin that way. And I detected the steel under his surface – if his son-daughter produced anything inferior, no man would ever see it.

I'll make it good enough to take his breath away!

'There's no hurry,' I said, 'but I'll start some compositional drawings, so you can be thinking about them. What?'

My father stopped grinning like an idiot, said, 'Nothing,' and began grinning again.

Good enough that when he sees my work, he won't even be able to *speak*, never mind laugh.

'Ilario?' Honorius didn't correct himself, either because it would draw attention to my gender, or because he hadn't noticed.

'What? Oh.' I was walking with my hand high on my belly again, I realised, although it was scarcely less flat than before. The archetypal pose in which to paint the Mother of Christ Imperator. If without the toga and tiara.

With resolute optimism, Honorius said, 'I acknowledge you. I'll acknowledge my grandchild when it's born. If you want to claim the father in Carthage, I'll help—'

It must have been clear on my face that I pictured him and his household guard breaking down the doors of Donata's rooming-house, and beating Marcomir senseless.

'I have enough money even to hire lawyers,' he said mildly.

I smiled.

'I don't want Carthage involved,' I said, after a moment. 'They're too interested in me as it is . . . But thank you.'

Honorius patted my shoulder. 'One day you'll realise that you don't have to thank me for anything. I'm your *father*.'

I wasn't in a bad enough mood to mention Videric and Federico, my other experiences of paternal affection.

'I'll nurse Rekhmire',' I said, affecting a sigh.

Honorius smiled. Our gondola waited at the edge of steps, by the arc of a bridge leading over an ice-fringed canal. Honorius's men occupied both it and the wider oared boat beside it. I allowed my father to help me in.

Sitting, I hauled my skirts into some semblance of tidiness, arranging myself on the padded velvet seat in the stern; looked up, and saw Sergeant Orazi go down with a feathered shaft hanging out of his back.

'*All'arme!*' Honorius bellowed in the local dialect. '*To arms!*'

A flood of men – twenty, thirty, more – poured out of the nearby alleys, splitting into plainly practised groups. One group pushed the boat containing the majority of Honorius's men out into the centre of the canal, where it circled aimlessly for all one of the men attempted to paddle, and another to rack his crossbow.

I had only time to see senior Ensign Viscardo leap into the black water and start swimming grimly towards us. Honorius scooped me up off the seat with a powerful tug unexpected in a lean man, and dropped me in the bottom of our boat, turning back to command the brawl. Sparks shot into the air where two blade-edges slid down each other. Windows flew open overhead; banged shut again.

I managed to crawl forward, the skirts an intolerable obstacle where I kept kneeling on them.

One of our oars had fallen in-board. It was solid hard wood, perhaps twelve feet long, with the blade painted indigo and white on either side; far too cumbrous to wield as a staff-weapon, as I had with the iron candle-stand in Carthage.

Kneeling up, I squinted, spotting which man on the canal-path was plainly directing the operation.

A cloaked man wearing a Venetian white half-mask that covered him down to his lower lip. A plain expressionless mask-face . . .

Blank as a golem, I thought, as he loped towards the edge of the canal, calling out brusque orders.

I hefted the oar, found its point of balance, stood straight up in the rocking gondola, and cast the oar as a man casts the javelin in Taraco's Roman games.

The man turned, just as I fell forward from the impetus and landed on my hands and knees in the boat.

His movement shifted him enough that only the edge of the oar's end caught him – but the blow was to his temple. I heard the *thuck!* clearly over men shouting and metal scraping against metal.

The man's legs went out from under him: he dropped like a sack of meal.

'*That* one!' I yelled to Honorius, pointing. '*There!*'

A scuffle of swinging blades intervened. Men in blue livery with Honorius's badge swayed past me, in a rough and tumble that was more beer-house brawl than battle-line. Honorius's voice rose up from the back, shouting as much. The hired assassins fell back, routing into alleys and across the square

I stared along the edge of the canal.

Bare. No fallen man

I don't suppose he fell in and drowned.

No, that would be too easy. Either he recovered, or some of the men abandoning the fight piecemeal dragged him with them when they ran.

'Was that your Ramiro Carrasco de Luis?' I demanded as Honorius jogged up, calling his own men back.

'Couldn't tell. Didn't get a good look at him.' He panted, scowling at me. 'You shouldn't be doing things like that!'

'Why not? Oh.' I found myself with my hand resting on my belly. *Again.* I felt no different to how I ever have. 'It . . . doesn't seem to have done any harm.'

Or any good, depending on how you look at it.

'Has to have been Carrasco,' Honorius grunted. 'If the Council was letting thieves' bands get *that* big, we'd have heard gossip about it – Ilario, where do you think you're going?'

Sergeant Orazi swore as one of his men extracted an arrow-head from between the plates of his brigandine. Orazi didn't seem hurt; more embarrassed. Viscardo was probably in worse case, on hands and knees on the path, puking up dirty water.

Making my way with care down the rocking boat to the padded seat, I lifted my gaze to Honorius.

'This has gone on long enough! You know the way to Aldra Federico's palazzo, don't you? We're going there. *Now.*'

Honorius and his sergeant, who had been exchanging glances with far too much exaggerated tolerance in them for my liking, both looked disconcerted.

'Or,' I remarked into his silence, 'I can find the way on my own.'

If I were wholly woman, the words *crazy pregnant girl* would have passed Honorius's lips. But he and his soldiers sensed also the knight's training I have had in King Rodrigo's court, and that confused them.

Honorius grumbled, signalling to the gondola oarsmen.

'And *what* do you propose to do when we get there!'

10

Travelling along the Canal Grande, I failed at memorising details of the facades, for Honorius's protests. He had a look on his face which I suspected his officers must have seen, in a command tent, on crusade.

'It's too dangerous for you. You can't go anywhere *near*—' He broke off. 'Damn, that was stupid. Whatever you had in mind, you'll do now, won't you? Those skirts are deceptive.'

His sergeant smirked.

'I don't know what *you're* so happy about,' my father muttered, 'since I happen to know you owe Attila twenty ducats!'

'A bet?' I didn't know whether to be offended or amused.

'Orazi here bet you'd go haring off after Carrasco on your own. Attila—' Honorius nodded towards the large man at his oar. 'He wagered you'd want an escort.'

'They both bet I'd follow him?'

Honorius gave me the 'raw recruit, you don't know enough to lace up your own sandals!' look.

I huddled back into my cloak, uncertain how I felt about Honorius's men-at-arms knowing me well. On balance, I found it reassuring.

'This Ramiro Carrasco de Luis,' I offered. 'You have to have some sympathy for the man.'

Honorius choked. '*What!*'

I smiled sunnily at my father. 'You say Carrasco's hired by Videric. He thinks all he has to do is assassinate some young man. What could be easier? Take a young man out drinking and whoring, stick a knife in him when he's dead drunk, and there he is – dead. Only now Ramiro Carrasco finds out that reputable young *widows* tend not to go out whoring and drinking . . . '

The youngest officer, Ensign Saverico, snickered. Since I was facing forwards, I saw the other soldiers grinning. Honorius very wisely didn't turn around in the gondola to castigate them. He knows a losing battle when confronted with one.

'If Rekhmire' weren't recovering so well,' I added, 'I doubt I'd be so sanguine about chasing down the man who attacked him.'

'Attacked *us*.' Honorius humphed. 'What's to stop Ramiro Carrasco sticking a dagger in you as soon as you walk up to him?'

'Six heavily-armed men with more axes than sense?' I made a show of counting heads. 'I beg your pardon. Eight. Oh, except you don't have an axe . . .'

Ensign Saverico apparently choked on something. Sergeant Orazi whacked him hard in the middle of his back-plate.

' . . . Besides which, I don't know what the Doge's Council do when they catch public murderers, but *I'd* bet it's painful and disgusting and better avoided.'

Honorius shook his head, but whether in agreement with that statement, or despair over my attitude, I didn't know. Long ago, I discovered that a minor joy of wearing skirts is baiting respectable men. I wasn't sure if I was amused or annoyed that it worked with my father.

'That's Federico's house.' Honorius pointed towards a landing stage, over the pale green ripples of the canal. 'Be careful—'

Having gathered up my skirts beforehand, I was able to step ashore the moment the gondola touched the canal-side, before Ensign Viscardo could throw a line around the mooring-post.

The impetus of my foot pushed the boat. It drifted back away from the quay.

I heard Orazi curse behind me. And the slap of rope falling onto water. *Pole-axes and crossbows aren't the way to solve this.*

We had turned into a small side-canal – the access to this five-storey building for tradesmen and others who wouldn't disembark at the main jetty. I found myself on a paved quay with Gothic-arched windows in front of me.

Ignoring the shout from behind, I walked towards the narrow door, approached by six or seven stone steps.

On the top step, a dark-haired man in a cloak sat with his head resting down on one hand.

He looked up as I approached. A red and rapidly-darkening swollen lump showed on the left side of his forehead, bleeding from a narrow split in the skin. He blinked, his gaze glassy.

I walked up the flaking steps and smiled at him. 'That looks as though it hurts.'

I pulled a linen kerchief out of my sleeve.

The man sat and stared up at me.

I licked the kerchief and reached down to dab it carefully against his swelling flesh.

He hissed a breath, blinking, eyes focusing.

I showed him pink stains on the yellow cloth. 'Not so good. You may need a physician. Although it seems Venetian doctors are usually worse than the disease.'

'Indeed.' The man plainly agreed by reflex and instinct, not conscious thought. He had the curly black hair of Taraconensis, and skin the colour of old ivory, where it wasn't swelling and turning bruise-blue. Brown eyes showed so dark that pupil was barely distinguishable from iris. Under his cloak, the plain red doublet and hose he wore were servant's quality, not fitting him well; I concluded they were not his.

He didn't desire to come out dressed as Federico's family secretary.

'Who are you?' He struggled to get words out, squinting up from the steps. The sun must be at my back. He could see even less of me than I anticipated. 'What are you *doing*?'

'Don't be foolish. You know who I am.' I licked my kerchief again and gently cleaned around what looked like a splinter, driven shallowly under the skin of his forehead. 'This is going to hurt: hold still . . . Got it! You, your name is Ramiro Carrasco de Luis, and you – work for my mother's husband.'

He winced under my hands, wide-eyed.

I saw him visibly think to use the pain of the splinter's removal as an excuse – and then dismiss the idea.

'You're . . . '

'Ilaria.'

'Ilaria.' He emphasised the feminine ending very slightly.

'That's right.' I could hear voices, not far behind, on the quay; evidently my father and his men had achieved a landing, and were disagreeing over something.

Whether or not to interrupt the mad hermaphrodite, probably.

Ramiro Carrasco de Luis flushed darkly, high on his cheeks. He glanced dazedly at the armed men. I was uncertain whether or not he registered their significance.

'Madonna Ilaria . . . sorry . . . I'm – only a servant; I'm secretary to Aldra Federico's daughter—'

I managed an expression that stopped him stumbling out with a false story. He looked at me foolishly, his mouth open.

'You have an interesting face,' I said. 'Who should I ask for permission to draw you?'

Carrasco appeared thoroughly flustered. '*Draw* me?'

'I'm sure you were told I'm a painter . . . '

It isn't easy to exert any impression of authority sitting on your arse on a doorstep. I could have told him that myself. Every time he attempted to rise, I pressed down on the bruised flesh of his brow with fingers and kerchief.

He caught his lip between his teeth, bit down, and failed to suppress a yelp.

'Madonna Sunilda!' he managed to get out. 'Would give any permission. Or her father! Madonna, I don't understand what – why—'

'You should use witch-hazel for that bruise.' I straightened up, folding my kerchief neatly, and put it away under the bronze silk and brown velvet of my sleeve. Borrowing clothes from Neferet had its advantages. I reached up and put my large, lined cloak-hood back.

'It's nice to see a face from home.' I grinned at him amiably. 'Even if it does belong to someone who's been sent to kill me. I'm sure we're going to be *great* friends, you and I!'

It took me a minute, perhaps two, to wave and get Honorius to stop grousing at Sergeant Orazi and approach.

In that time, Ramiro Carrasco de Luis sat with his mouth open and couldn't seem to speak a word.

Other servants showed us inside.

The palazzo's tall rooms were decorated in the Classical style, ceilings plastered so that the structural beams didn't show through. I had no eye for the decorative work, or the carved ash-wood door frames and wall panelling.

After going so long without speaking to my foster father – *What am I to say to Aldra Federico, now?* And if Valdamerca's with him, or my sisters . . .

The servants threw open the doors to a great gallery overlooking the Canal Grande.

It was full of people.

11

Most were middle-aged men; most were in Frankish gowns and hose. Rich Venetians.

Honorius muttered, '*Fuck*,' under his breath, and straightened his shoulders. 'You do pick your moments.'

I looked for the horse-face and dark hair of Valdamerca, for the fiend-sisters of my childhood, and saw none of them. *Only a male gathering*, I realised, as Aldra Federico looked up from the servant who directed his attention to us.

He hadn't changed – still a good-looking middle-aged man, as curl-haired as Carrasco. He washed his hair in henna, I suspected. He must be in his middle sixties by now, but seemed fifteen years younger.

Federico stepped out of the crowd with a formal smile. 'Welcome! Ilaria!'

The smile took on an avid edge, that he must imagine he was keeping concealed.

'My dear! When I invited Venezia's artists, I'd no idea you'd hear of it! But welcome! I had no idea you were in the Serene Republic!' Federico waved a careless hand. Following his gesture led my eye across the throng.

I glimpsed the Florentine lawyer Leon Battista, talking to soberly-dressed older men. No Neferet, that I could see. No other man I recognised.

How do I broach the subject of Videric sending a paid murderer to kill me?

I caught the moment that Federico's pupils widened.

Rosamunda's voice sounded in my memory. '*As soon as you stand in a room together.*'

I saw by Federico's open stare at Honorius that at least one secret was now out in the open, to be gossiped about.

Best court manners returned as if I'd never left Taraco. 'You know Captain-General Honorius, he tells me. I was certain, sir, you wouldn't mind him accompanying me; he's a fellow art-enthusiast.'

'Not at all . . . ' Federico spoke absently, his deceptively sharp gaze still anatomising Honorius's features.

Is Federico interested for any other reason than gossip and scandal? Is he Videric's man, now? Useless to guess. He *would* be interested in scandal, in any case; I'd known that since he took me to court at fifteen.

As to whether he now reports back to Aldra Videric . . .

'*Honorius!*' A large, floridly blond man lurched between the conversing groups of Venetian men, rolling up with a blast of brandy on his breath. He slammed a hand on my father's shoulder, which somewhat to my surprise didn't knock Honorius over.

'Had no idea you were down this way! Not looking for a job, are you?'

The retired Captain-General of Castile and Leon smirked, looking down at the Frank. The fair-skinned man was in his late thirties, I estimated. Both men allowed themselves to be served wine, in Venetian-made glasses. Both looking as if they shouldn't be holding the delicate spiral parti-coloured glass stems. And for the same reason, I realised. *They're both soldiers.*

'Ilario.' Honorius didn't correct his suffix. 'This is Messer Carmagnola. We commanded troops together up in Aragon. He's running Venice's land forces now – isn't that right? Carmagnola, my daughter Ilaria.'

The piggy red eyes of the Captain-General of Venice surveyed me with subdued lust. Subdued out of deference to Honorius, I realised.

'I'm a mercenary; I do what I'm paid to do.' Carmagnola grinned, took my hand, and kissed it. He wavered, falling-down drunk.

Honorius slapped him on the shoulder in return. 'You beat the Milanese!' He spoke expansively to me. 'The current Doge has been in power these five years: he wants a mainland empire. I think our Carmagnola's going to give it to him. Are you being treated all right here, boy?'

My father gave an expert demonstration of a man concealing that he is not entirely sober – which, since he hadn't yet drunk from his Venetian-made glass, would give this Carmagnola and my foster father Federico the reassuring idea that Honorius had been apprehensive before he arrived. And so more likely to put a word wrong, here and there.

'Doge Foscari's very good to me,' Carmagnola slurred. 'Everybody is.'

The law I learned a long time ago in Rodrigo's court – *always* speak as if you are overheard – seemed to apply here, despite the talk around us being philosophy and the arts, rather than politics, or anything else the authorities might not like. I glanced about, uneasy.

The Frankish man Carmagnola leaned forward and prodded Honorius's shoulder with a weather-beaten finger. His nails had been chewed down so much, and plainly so consistently, that they had grown back a little deformed.

'Is it true Carthage is sending the legions into the Iberian coast? You know – where you always said you came from. Taraconensis.' He stumbled badly over the name.

Legions!

Social mores dictate downcast eyes for women; I was glad enough of it then, or else I would have given away my shock. If this man is a captain for Venice's Council of Ten, he's involved deep in Frankish politics, and North African affairs too. And what he says is a confirmation of all Rekhmire"'s concerns over Carthage.

'Legions?' Honorius spoke mildly enough to rouse my suspicions, if not the drunken mercenary's.

'Lord God, *you* know Carthage! They've got to have their import grain! Give 'em half an excuse and they'll take over any farmland outside the Penitence—' Carmagnola waved the hand that held his fragile glass; expensive wine slopped on his doublet's velvet cuff, and the so-fine flax linen of his shirt under it. I wondered numbly if I could accurately reproduce that stained translucent effect in oils.

'Didn't the government in Taraco fall?' Carmagnola added, visibly pulling himself together, glancing over at Federico. 'Or a king die? Or *something*? Honorius, I know you always said there was no career for you there – no wars.'

My foster father Federico shrugged, at his most diplomatic. 'There haven't been wars in Taraconensis – wars *involving* Taraconensis – in twenty-five years. Our noble Honorius needed to travel north as far as Castile and Leon to make his name.'

Honorius bowed with the lack of subtlety of a blunt soldier. I doubted Federico would believe that role now, with me standing beside a visible blood-father.

Carmagnola, apparently as if he forced his senses to obey him through the wine-haze, said, 'Taraconensis has a border with the Franks, doesn't it? Only a short one, where the Via Augusta runs between the mountains and the sea, but still a border. Carthage would love a land-route into Europe.'

I assumed the stupefied expression of a woman confronted with politics.

Given that Federico still thought of me as a King's amusing freak, he might credit my lack of interest, too.

I took a polite step back. A woman on the edge of any group is easily ignored; I wondered if I could use that to avoid the urgent questions Federico would doubtless have for me.

Bad weather will have delayed messages. How recent will this Carmagnola's news about Taraco be? Do mercenary commanders have better means of communication, even in the months when war is impossible?

Lost in deliberation, I missed my moment – Leon Battista appeared at my elbow without sufficient warning for me to avoid him.

'When may I see your brother?'

Whenever you like!

I managed not to smirk at my thoughts. If I did, Leon would put it down to feminine frivolity.

'He, ah, went into Dalmatia for the winter. Can I help?'

If one ignored his boat-prow of a nose, it was possible to note that Leon Battista had small, keen eyes. He studied me for a longer moment than was polite, and steered me a step aside from the crowd.

'It was you, madonna, wasn't it?'

'Me?'

With all else – with not being able to step outside the Campo San Barnaba without expecting an ambush – I have forgotten to think up a plausible tale for Neferet's Florentine.

'You.' Leon's hazel eyes shone bright with two catch-lights from the sunny window. 'There is no "brother". You disguised yourself as a man to work in Masaccio's workshop, didn't you?'

I managed to reply without hesitation. 'I wore men's clothing in Masaccio's workshop, yes.'

That much is certainly true . . .

'You will excuse me.' Leon's voice held subdued excitement. 'I'm here on business, but I saw you, and was suddenly sure . . . '

He had a roll of papers clasped in one hand. He noticed my interest, glanced about, and on a sudden pushed them into my grasp.

'These are common enough in Venice.'

The top one was a manuscript news-letter – composed of foreign news, propaganda both political and military, and stories of horrid crimes and murders, and the state executions they inevitably led to, all described in minute detail. Murders of husbands by wives appeared especially popular.

'I brought them to circulate, useless as they are. All bell-tower politics,' Leon Battista sneered. 'No Italian city-state ever cares about matters further away than the ringing of their own *campanile* can be heard! But I pass them privately because the Council of Ten would ban them if they could,' he added. 'The Doge thinks it's only one step from circulating manuscript news to having women preaching, pagans in the Senate, and the baptism of cats and horses!'

Most of the letters purported to have been written by some 'foreign visitor' to Venice. I turned my head sideways to squint at the penmanship, recognising the Venetian style.

'This is something I never considered when I was looking for employment! Although I suppose they hang the scribes, as well as whoever dictates the news-letters?'

Leon narrowed his hazel eyes, evidently not decided on whether I had a morbid sense of humour, or whether I made some attempt to feel out his political stance. Before I could add a joke to push his mind in the one direction, he reached out to extract one sheet of paper from the sheaf in my hands.

I held on to it, having a better grip than a woman.

'What's this?' I turned it about in my hand, adding, not too quickly, 'I don't speak your Florentine Italian.'

The relief in his expression was brief, but I caught it.

'This? Oh – I have bought some foreign letters to circulate, also. This is a similar letter of news, but for Florence.'

It's true I don't speak the Italian language of Florence. However, months in Masaccio's workshop, puzzling out the notes Tommaso Cassai left me, mean that I read a little of it.

Enough to enable me to make out 'Cast down the blood of the Medici Duke!' and 'Make this a true republic!'

Dangerous, I reflected.

I wondered who he had come here to meet, and pass these papers on to. *Not that it matters*. If I know little about Venice's politics, I know even less about those of Florence, but any invitation to depose a duke is rarely welcomed by a ruler.

It was not that which made me retain the paper.

This one was not written by a scribe.

The letters showed round, black, even, and as clear-edged as oak-gall ink and the sharpest quill could make a line. No smudging – I pushed the pad of my thumb across the page.

'How long did this take to make?'

Leon Battista's wariness vanished, seeing me involved in the manufacture of the news-sheet rather than its contents.

'As long as it would take a man to count to thirty.' He grinned at my expression. Relief may have moved him to speak out more than he intended. 'The setting up of the letters takes longer, to begin with.'

'Like a woodcut.' Masaccio had talked a little to me of that, and engraving.

Leon nodded. 'But then ... this is neither the first nor the five hundredth sheet made.'

Which makes the sharp clarity of the edges more than remarkable.

'How many in Florence can read?' I mused aloud.

Leon Battista shrugged. 'Enough that if you nail a news-letter to a door, one man can read it aloud to a dozen before the Duke's guards arrive.'

Too much of a coincidence, that Leon Battista would have something printed of such quality, and that Neferet knows of the existence of the Herr Mainz that the Pharaoh-Queen wishes to see.

'Can I keep this?'

Because I know Rekhmire' will want to see it!

Leon shook his head. 'I'm truly sorry, madonna, but you know what the authorities are like about news. I take enough of a risk conveying letters myself; I wouldn't forgive myself if I put you in danger of being thought a spy.'

A flicker of movement in my peripheral vision: Ramiro Carrasco de Luis.

The sleekly muscular dark man made an unobtrusive presence in Federico's apartments, acting as major-domo to pass on orders to the lower servants. He had taken a necessary handful of minutes to change out of his muddied and blood-stained clothes, reappearing in a charcoal-black Italian doublet and hose, of a quality remarkably good for a servant. But then again, it would be like Sunilda to want her secretary to appear smart.

The secretary rolled his eyes, evidently overhearing Leon Battista.

I said amiably, and a little loudly, 'True. Venice can be full of dangers.'

Leon frowned. If not for Carrasco being a servant, and therefore invisible, the Florentine might have noticed him flush, and deduced that I'd landed a dart in a vulnerable place. Which might lead to further undesirable conclusions.

Without showing haste, I changed the subject back. 'The printing is very fine.'

'Yes.' Leon didn't look guilty, which gave me some hopes for him as a conspirator or insurrectionist, or whatever he was to Florence.

He did bite at his lip, as he looked down at me. Momentarily, his gaze was distant, as if he could not help where his mind turned.

'Masaccio . . . Tommaso . . . ' He spoke in a sudden rush. '*Is the child his?*'

I might burst into laughter, or tears, or punch the Florentine.

The moment of decision must have given him the impression I was distressed.

'Madonna, I'm sorry! Forgive me for hoping that there was at least something left of my friend.'

I smiled forgiveness, as women do, and sought a way to distract him. 'How did you know that "Ilario" was not a man?'

His lips quirked in a very small smile. 'You know too much about painting for a normal woman, Madonna Ilaria. I doubt that comes from talking to a brother – you're too passionate about it, and you use Masaccio's very phrases. He must have been the master you learned from.'

Leon's expression was so seriously intent that I again desired to laugh. The thought of eavesdroppers sobered me. It was difficult not to stare around at the nobles of Venice that Federico had gathered under his roof.

What Leon evidently thinks a romantic, adventurous tale will be looked on as criminal by the Council of Ten, especially if they find out the whole of the matter.

A movement signalled Honorius's approach.

I looked Leon Battista in the eye, with what I thought he would read as defiance and shame. Speaking in an undertone, I said, 'Master Leon . . .

246

I can only ask you not to reveal what I've done. The child isn't Masaccio's. He never knew I was with child. I went through a marriage ceremony in Rome. Then . . . then the bride was deserted by her groom.'

My father hung back until Leon Battista had finished his apologies, protestations, reassurances, and promises that he would come to the Alexandria House in the near future, to further put my mind at rest.

Arm linked implacably through mine, Honorius steered me steadily towards the doors.

'And you say *I've* been too much under the Egyptian's influence!'

'I said nothing to Leon that wasn't true!'

'But you said it so he'd hear a lie!'

'You recognised that,' I said mildly, 'so I blame Rekhmire', because mercenary commanders are blunt, unsubtle, unpolitical animals . . . '

He laughed, hard enough that he choked. 'Ah, you *have* been talking to Carmagnola. The man's as much a conspirator as any damn courtier – we're better off out of here!'

I could only agree.

'Ilaria!' My foster father Federico reappeared. 'You're not leaving?'

'I have business elsewhere.' Honorius's smile was amiable and intractable in equal measure.

Nothing need be said out loud, I realised. Here I am. Here is my face on an older version of myself. If Federico's a pawn of Videric, he has scandal to pass on; if he's an ally, then Honorius's men-at-arms downstairs are adequate warning.

And as for Aldra Videric's assassin . . .

I glimpsed Ramiro Carrasco de Luis behind Aldra Federico, and guessed it to be the secretary who had prevented us slipping away unnoticed. He gave me a very swift, covert stare.

'Foster father.' I confined myself to a modest female's demeanour. 'I know you'll understand that, for my work, I have need of a trustworthy and discreet artist's model. May I borrow Secretary Carrasco from you?'

Federico put his hand through his curly hair, dishevelling it enough that the baldness of his crown became visible. His expression was extraordinary.

'You don't need to worry about disgrace,' I added. 'While I'm dressed as a woman, I have a duenna at all times – Madonna Neferet, the Egyptian representative in Venice. Well, her, or her women-servants. And Master Honorius loans me his honour guard when I go out.'

Seeing neither of the men with me react to 'dressed as a woman', Federico demanded bluntly, 'What about when you dress as a man?'

Either he's unobservant, or I don't show as much as I feel I do.

Valdamerca, he said, was out at the Merceria with my foster sisters. She was always the more intelligent one in the family. And she has a woman's eye for such things. One look at my very minutely larger breasts . . . *Thank God it's just Federico!*

'I don't dress as a man in Venezia.' I met Federico's suspicious gaze. 'For a while, it's easier to be a woman.'

He snorted. 'Oh, well, it would be! No need to work for a living, or defend yourself, or trouble your head with business.'

Work for a living? What do you think your household's women servants do?

'This drawing, though . . . '

'I have a commission.' I need not even lie about it. 'I need to make sketches for a chapel fresco. I haven't yet decided on the treatment of the subject, but the Franks seem to have a certain attitude to Judas – St Gaius – that I'd like to explore.'

Ramiro Carrasco had evidently been educated well enough, or been around enough Franks, to pick up the reference. His face was as blank as the wooden panelling on the walls.

'Tomorrow will do, to start,' I said briskly. 'If you don't need him, foster father?'

It occurred to me that the difficulty with Aldra Federico always seeming a little shifty is that it made it impossible to know if he was being more so, now.

'Oh, you can take him – you and Sunilda always did squabble over your toys.' Federico managed an unpleasant smirk. 'I'll have her send him over.'

Departing publicly enough that Federico couldn't ply me with questions, I promised to come again when my foster mother and sisters should be present, and allowed the Aldra's servants to show us out to the canal jetty. The salt wind off the lagoon caught me with a razor-edged chill.

Ramiro Carrasco de Luis, as my father and I passed him on the way out, turned his head away, incidentally giving me his best profile. Which was, at this moment, quite definitely not the left.

12

Knowing how little Rekhmire' liked his mind unoccupied, I gave him the story while I unpacked my chalk.

'Messer Leon Battista has letters not written by a scribe's hands . . . ' Rekhmire' tapped his thumbnail against his teeth.

His bed had the occupied air of the long-sick. Rumpled sheets and blankets were covered in scrolls, among which I saw the accounts of the Alexandrine House, as well as several military treatises loaned him by my father. He snarled absently at the willow-withy cage supporting sheets over his strapped leg.

'You're certain?' he queried.

'There was a nick in the "e".' So small as to be all but invisible, except to an eye used to drawing letters. 'That made me think of woodcuts, where an error's repeated in every printing. These letters were printed that way, I think. Every "e" had the nick.'

'And Messer Leon is Neferet's . . . lover, one assumes.' Rekhmire''s eyebrows lifted, which together with his unshaven skull gave him the air of a ruffled buzzard-chick. 'If Leon Battista of the Alberti family has found a man who prints letters, and it's *not* the German Guildsman that Menmet-Ra is after, then that is a remarkable coincidence.'

'Surely Leon wouldn't have let me look at the letter if he'd known his printer is wanted here?'

'It may *be* such a coincidence. In which case he wouldn't know.' The rounded brows snapped down. 'Or he may not have been told all by Neferet. I'll keep an eye on her. Matters may be opposite – you say Leon Battista was unwilling to let you see what is, after all, seditious writing. He may feel he needs to keep Neferet safe in ignorance.'

'Or Neferet provided him with this German Herr Mainz.' If Neferet was Rekhmire''s friend, it was up to me to state the obvious, and save him sounding as if he condemned her. 'It's not possible to travel anywhere in this weather. She may think the German can't go to Alexandria yet in any case, so he may as well help Leon.'

'By getting embroiled in Italian Peninsula politics!' Rekhmire''s fist came down too weakly on the bed-frame. 'They *burn* the authors of sedition here!'

He heaved a sigh, his body slumping at the end of it.

'We therefore proceed with great caution. If anything should come to you, be certain to tell me. If this is *not* the trail of Herr Mainz . . . then I have nothing at all to follow.'

'I'll listen out,' I promised.

His gaze through the leaded window at the cold sky became distant. 'You will not have seen the Great Library. Walking past mile on *mile* of scroll-cases . . . Do you know what there is, every few yards, on every floor in the Library?'

I shook my head.

'Sand buckets. Blankets. Against fire. So many of those scrolls are the sole copy. Our scriptoria work through the night as well as the day, but . . . can you imagine? To have as many copies as a printer's *machina* could make?' His voice took on a pained quality. 'And then – never to lose the last copy of a book, ever again?'

Ramiro Carrasco de Luis arrived at the Alexandrine House the following day, in a fine wool cloak against the winter rain, under which he wore a charcoal doublet so dark as to be almost black, the metal tags of his points all silvered. His shoes had small fashionable points, and his hose fitted his legs as close as another skin.

Not the clothes in which to control an ambush, I reflected, and put up with half an hour of the man preening when I ordered him to sit on an upright wooden chair and lift his head, as if he gazed up at the Tree.

Finally, I abandoned coal and chalk and tinted paper. 'Remorse.'

Ramiro Carrasco's head snapped down. He gave me a startled look. '*What?* Madonna,' he added hastily.

This was in part a response to the glare from the duenna whom Neferet had provided: a round, elderly Venetian woman who evidently didn't hold with handsome young foreign men. And in part a certain natural sense of self-preservation, since Honorius detailed off-shifts of his more intimidating household guard to sit in my room as I sketched.

Over the last weeks, the soldiers had dragged home a few unfortunate men they suspected of being spies for Lord Videric. 'In the way that a cat brings dead birds home to its master,' Rekhmire' commented, although these men tended to be only half-dead. After questioning them, Honorius donated the wounded men to the city's charitable hospices, where they could be more easily watched.

If what he learned is true, Aldra Videric might have more men than Ramiro Carrasco in Venice.

Or Ramiro Carrasco might hire men in order to give us that impression.

'You're St Gaius.' The white chalk had managed to mark not only my hand and my cuff, but the front of my bodice, and my lap. I shifted the drawing-board, and thought it just as well I'd borrowed old clothes from one of Neferet's Frankish servants. 'St Gaius – *Judas*, according to the people who pray at the local chapels here. You're looking up at the man you betrayed. Whether it's Christus Viridianus on the Green Tree, or

Christ the Imperator, it's all one. He's been hung up and broken, on your word; bones broken but no blood spilled; he's *dead* – and it's your doing. So stop looking as if you're wondering how many girls are staring at you . . .'

Ramiro Carrasco de Luis blinked, and then essayed a small smile. 'As far as I know, just the one, madonna.'

I let his smile die in the coldness of my reaction, and under the granite looks of the duenna and soldiers.

'There's a difference between staring and studying,' I said.

He appeared bewildered, and put out.

I added, 'And I'm not sure you'd like *me* staring at you . . .'

Carrasco opened his mouth to make some gallant protest, evidently recalled I was not entirely a woman – *or* a man – and blushed like a court page of fourteen or so.

I told Rekhmire' I could keep him off-balance. So far, I'm right.

'Studying close enough to draw detail,' I mused aloud, 'tells me things. You may dress well, but you didn't start in the literate class of servants. Your bones say you were hungry as a child. You're very clean: that means you'd like to keep the position you've earned. And then there's that nasty lump on your head. Somebody seems to have hit you, perhaps as you turned towards them, but clearly not with a fist . . .'

My hand moved as I watched him; I couldn't help making the briefest line sketches, trying to capture his successive expressions.

I can see why Videric would choose him as a spy; he barely gives away anything.

But a spy doesn't normally suffer the close inspection of an artist's model, and I could see every minute flinch, and tiny sheen of sweat under his hairline. At my last comment, his large, limpid brown eyes met mine – and I had been right to want to paint them.

'*Somebody* hit me?' His tone struggled with incredulity, and with outraged dignity, also; which is not what one usually sees in a servant. Someone has praised him above his merits, and he's wanted to believe them.

'A regrettable accident,' I said briskly. 'It would have to be, wouldn't it, messer? Anything else would mean reporting to the Council of Ten that I have my suspicions about who headed the gang of brigands that attacked the representative of Alexandria-in-Exile, and the noble retired Captain-General from Taraco.'

I had thought he would give away annoyance, if anything got through his poker face. Instead, I found my chalk and coal giving shadows and highlights to eyelids and pupils that showed, as they went down on paper, an expression somewhere close to desperation.

Now *why* would he . . .

'Isn't that appropriate for the nobility?' Ramiro Carrasco's tone sounded acid, although he returned to the pose of staring up at a hypothetical Tree of Grace. 'The merchant-princes of Venice are entirely happy to look after the interests of the landed princes of Iberia.'

'You ought to talk to a friend of mine, a lawyer . . . ' I rubbed at coal-dust with the pad of my thumb, and achieved a gradation of tone so impressive I abandoned it for fear of ruining it. 'He's all for containing the power of princes. He wants to do it with law . . . '

'The law's nothing beside armed power.'

'That depends on how many people agree to behave as if the law were a real thing.'

Carrasco's face had changed yet again when I looked up to take the line of his jaw.

Is he amused?

As if he spoke to an equal in status – and I suppose he did, if you rank 'King's Freak' against 'paid assassin of Aldra Videric' – Ramiro Carrasco explained, 'I thought *I* was a cynic.'

'Oh.' I smiled. 'For all I know, you may be. I prefer to think of it as recognising how the world really functions. You see a lot of that, as court fool.'

He blinked, fractionally fast, as he did every time I spoke with blatant honesty and appeared not to care I had an audience. I suspected he had realised that the old woman was very deaf. And that Honorius keeps his trusted soldiers well informed.

'Really,' I said. 'What would be the point of me pretending you haven't been told these things?'

'I, ah—'

'In the same way that I know you've tried to have me killed twice.'

I nodded at the ugly lump on his forehead, turning purple-black and green in about equal parts, with a scab beginning to form on the cut.

'I don't know whether or not you know *why* you have those orders. If it's assumed that I've told you . . . well, it probably will be assumed I've told you *all* I know. That puts you under a death sentence, if you weren't before.'

The same over-rapid blink was all that gave him away.

'Madonna . . . ' His shoulders, in the Italian-fashion doublet that showed every broad muscle, relaxed a very little. 'What comes next? The bribe? After the threat? You *are* attempting to get me to change sides?'

I found I was biting at the end of my tongue, while I took the shape of his short hair, tapering back to the nape of his neck in a servant's crop. Even the shortest hairs still had a curl.

'No, Messer Ramiro . . . that would just be silly. No one trusts you, and you must have realised at the beginning of this that you'd be wanted dead at the end. By your employer, if no other man. For some reason, you must think that's worth it . . . Or that you can escape. You can't.'

I flicked up a gaze and caught him staring at me with absolute fury. It was gone in a second, but I held it in my memory long enough to

252

put it on paper. Staring down at the constellation of heads and facial features on the *caput mortuum* tinted surface, I wondered where his ferocious outrage stemmed from, what it meant.

How I might use it.

'Don't blame me,' I said quietly. 'I certainly don't blame *you*. I'm sure you have your reasons.'

Ramiro Carrasco looked completely bemused; whip-lashed back and forth.

'The Franks revile Gaius as Judas,' I added. 'He betrayed their Green Christ with a kiss, and they say he'll be the last man still in Hell, when all the other damned have been redeemed and released. But you and I know the story goes differently. *Someone* had to make the betrayal, because He needed it. The world needed that act, for Him to redeem them. And Gaius was the only man with courage enough to do it – *because* it was necessary.'

Carrasco closed his hands on the chair, knuckles shining white through tension-stretched skin.

'Don't move.' I smiled at him. 'I've got you exactly where I want you.'

The expression I managed to get down on my sketch paper was notable.

A thunderous knock sounded on the outer door. One of Neferet's other servants got up from where she had been sitting by the fire in the antechamber – able to observe us through the doorway, not close enough to overhear, and in any case chatting with two more heavily-built soldiers in brigandines that Honorius had insisted also be present. She padded across the chill floorboards to answer the knocking.

'Madonna!' she called. 'It's Messer Leon.'

I had no chance to say I was busy; Leon Battista of the Alberti family bustled in, brandishing a sheaf of papers in one hand, smiling broadly at me, and ignoring the duenna and the Iberian men completely – both soldiers and assassin.

Leon must assume Carrasco is another Venetian I've called in as a model; obviously not one of freeman status – no, what do the Franks call it? 'Yeoman'?

While I tried to remember how the Franks divided up their society, the artist-lawyer walked up and laid the papers beside me. Hand-written, I saw; covered with diagrams. I picked the bound sheets up, turning them to look at one of the drawings.

'I invented that.' Leon Battista sounded proud. 'Did Masaccio use one in his workshop? Or outside?'

A drawing of a frame of wood, with lines crossing it.

Cloth, I realised. But spun with a heavy thread at every inch-mark, so that the translucent linen was crossed with a grid.

'See.' Leon held his fingers as if they framed a square, absent-mindedly putting a startled Ramiro Carrasco in the centre of his view.

'Now imagine you have it held still, by some means, and that you see all against these lines. How much *easier* is it, to see where your perspective must be drawn?'

I glanced from the papers to his hands, visualised – and wondered if one might use drawn wire, as the men-at-arms used to repair their mail. A wooden frame, strung with taut wires laterally and vertically, like the strangest of musical instruments.

I realised that I was now taking no more notice of the assassin than Leon had.

I shot Ramiro Carrasco a womanly flirtatious grin, that I thought might unsettle him, and added, 'I wonder how long it would take to build one of these?'

'Your "brother",' Leon prompted.

'Masaccio never mentioned it, that I knew,' I said honestly. 'You knew Masaccio . . . '

'I'm his executor.' Leon drew himself up a little; I could see the pride in him. And also see why Masaccio would choose a friend who was both a lawyer and an artist to draw up his last testament.

I said all I could think of. 'You will not have expected it to happen so soon.'

'No. Nor he.' Leon lifted his head, with a little shrug. 'He was often used to add to his will, or take things out . . . He wrote me a letter, and asked me to bring this to Ilario if the man was still living then.'

At *this*, he indicated the bound sheets.

'They're mine, in fact,' he added, almost shyly.

'What is it?'

'A draft of something I was working on. Masaccio was to read through it, and tell me what he thought should be added, but I don't know if he did before . . . ' Leon Battista picked up the papers and smoothed them, looking at the writing. Which must be his, I realised.

Leon Battista said, 'I follow the ancient scholars on how it is that the eye sees things. I'm trying to devise a way for the New Art, for the artist's eye to truly see what is there.'

Ramiro Carrasco chuckled.

I looked up. The Iberian man might never have made a sound. His expression was as demure as any servant in the presence of a master.

'*Truly see what is there.*'

He thinks Leon takes me for a woman.

If I had not been used to such conundrums in Taraco, I suppose I might have blushed.

Leon Battista looked irritated at the interruption.

I said carefully, 'Masaccio wanted my brother to have this?'

It was painful to have to lie, even though Leon Battista insisted on keeping my 'secret', as he conceived it.

More painful to think that Masaccio never knew who he had in his workshop as his apprentice.

'Tommaso wrote to me that Ilario might benefit from reading it. Might learn.' Leon looked embarrassed. 'He also wrote that Ilario would benefit from meeting *me*, but . . . that was mere kindness on his part.'

Having the assassin present at that moment of humility was awkward, although Leon Battista took no more notice of Carrasco than if he had been furniture.

'I wouldn't object to sketching outside,' I said, standing, and looked back at Ramiro Carrasco. 'Are you permitted to come tomorrow?'

The Iberian secretary-assassin spoke demurely. 'Aldra Federico permits it.'

And what am I to make of that? Aldra Federico would happily see his foster son-daughter dead in a backwater canal? Aldra Federico is too stupid to know why one of Videric's men is travelling with him? Or why Videric wants the King's Freak found? Not after the scandal when the Carthaginian envoy arrived – and now he's seen Honorius and I together.

Leon held the door open for me to leave with him.

Glancing back, I caught an expression on Ramiro Carrasco's face.

The assassin, now realising what he has been looking at without seeing. The gentle curve of a pregnant belly . . .

Ramiro Carrasco looked deeply confused.

He's not the only one, I reflected, resting my fingers on Leon's arm as the lawyer led me out towards the campo.

I wonder if he will succeed in getting this news back to Lord Videric?

And if it will make Videric willing to let Nature assassinate me, rather than his paid murderer?

13

It may have stemmed from having a killer in the house. Dawn light reflected up onto the room's ceiling from the canal, making bright fractured crescents on the plaster, and I woke from a vivid dream of Rosamunda.

Rosamunda, much younger, with her womb full of her child; giving birth, and then – what? – being forced up from child-bed, still bleeding, to be wrapped in a cloak and led out into the snow, and told to leave the new-born on the chapel steps?

Or was that a lie? Did the midwife show her what was between my legs and did she turn away? Did she hide her face and let Videric give the orders to dispose of the thing as a foundling? Knowing all the same, by the snow and the winter cold, that it would die before being found?

I lay listening to Rekhmire' grunt in pain as he slept. My body stayed motionless under the flat of my hand.

If anything quickens in my belly, it's too faint for me to feel.

And I can hate Rosamunda, since she had every reason to expect to get up out of child-bed.

As a slave, being a shameless snoop aids survival at court, and indeed anywhere else. Privacy is for freemen. The absence of a collar, I found, couldn't convince me differently.

Rekhmire''s voice echoed out of his partly-open door:

'You will not walk out of this room!'

I winced, because as statements go, that one is so easily proved untrue.

Since it was Neferet who'd come upstairs earlier, I expected Neferet to come striding out of Rekhmire''s room. I froze to the spot at the head of the stairs, unable to decide whether it would be ruder to enter and demonstrate I'd overheard them quarrelling, or to appear as if I was eavesdropping.

'What in the Eight's name are you doing keeping the Queen's offer away from him!' Rekhmire''s voice sounded high, cracked – as out of control as I'd ever heard him. 'It's there in the ambassador's papers! "Bring him to the Library; Ty-ameny will give him all the funds he wants." You couldn't miss seeing it!'

Impetus carried me on until I stood in the open doorway.

I might have been modelling nude for both roles of the Whore of Babylon's seduction-dance, and neither one would have looked at me.

Rekhmire' sat just on the bed still, his strapped-up leg dangerously close to teetering off the edge of it. Neferet had her back to the window, so he must squint against the light. Her arms were folded tightly across her just-too-wide-for-proportion chest.

'I need Herr Mainz!' Her heel dug at the floorboards. 'He can go home in a month or two—'

'He can end up in the Council of Ten's dungeons in a week or two!' Rekhmire' hit his fist against the feather-stuffed pillows. 'You've got him printing sedition for that boy of yours—'

'My "boy" is the man who'll bring the Alberti family back to power in Florence.' Lines dug in beside her mouth and nose, and I saw how she would look when she was fifty. 'As opposed to your *pregnant* boy, who does nothing to earn her money except scribble drawings!'

Rekhmire' pushed forward, missed his grip, and the plank on which his leg was bound slid forward and cracked one end down on the floorboards. I winced, automatically inclining forward, and then stopped as Rekhmire' slapped Neferet's offered hand aside.

He leaned, both hands on the splint, not touching anywhere on his bandaged leg, never mind his knee.

'If Ilario is in trouble, it's my fault.' His voice was stiff. 'I did something ill-advised in Carthage—'

Neferet snickered.

Rekhmire''s scalp and face turned a dull plum-red.

Dropping her hands to her hips, Neferet drew herself up, still smiling. 'I'm not that stupid – the day *you* sire a child is the day *I* give birth to one!'

The line of Rekhmire''s body folded forward from the hip, losing tension. He sighed. 'Whatever it is you're mixed up in, it must be bad. You used to do this when you were a boy – pick a quarrel until everyone else had forgotten the question. You've just grown better at picking tender spots.'

'I was never a boy.'

Rekhmire' corrected himself without the shadow of malice or contempt. 'When you were a girl with prick and balls.'

The older Egyptian nodded. She sat down on the oak chest under the window, with the graceful movements that it occurred to me she would have had to learn. Just as I was trained in them.

I was trained to move as a woman does, *and* as a man does. The difference between myself and Neferet being that neither one of them seems natural to me. A woman's movements are restricted, a man's exaggerated.

Neferet sighed and rubbed the heel of one hand into her eye. 'Talking of women born into the wrong bodies – will the scribe survive child-bed?

257

Should I keep the Turkish physician on retainer? Or are you just making her comfortable until the time comes?'

I couldn't see Rekhmire''s face. Mine felt numb and swollen, as if any expression would emerge caricatured.

'Neferet . . . ' Rekhmire' straightened, leaving his leg propped between himself and the floor as if it were not part of him. 'Stop this. Ilario is with me because I took an ill-advised action in Carthage. Cousin Ty-ameny will be happy to rip me open for the wider political aspects. Don't *you* start on anything else.'

'Ill-advised' – *the politics of the matter? Or buying me?*

Nothing stopped either of them seeing me in the doorway, except that I was so still. Hearing these things, I couldn't move. Only the blood went to my cheeks, knowing that within moments I would be mortified by discovery.

'You have the apparent right to question what I do with Leon.' Neferet's voice took on an ugly, uncontrolled rasp. 'But you think – *Cousin Ty-ameny* will think – that it's acceptable for you to abduct a boy-girl she-male, who's a magnet for Carthage and Iberia.'

'*Jahar.*' Rekhmire' used the male name as if it were both challenge and appeal.

'Why did you have to follow me here? What business is it of yours!'

'You're right: it's *not* my business. I'm here as a favour—' Rekhmire' grunted emphatically, trying to shift his leg. 'A favour to Menmet-Ra—'

'Oh, I might have known! Fat old Tom-Cat doesn't want to leave Rome, so he twists you around his little finger until you come nosing in here!' Neferet grinned triumphantly. 'And another report goes back to Ty-ameny and your name gets written up in phoenix gilding! Great Sekhmet, don't you ever get tired of creeping around the Pharaoh-Queen?'

The strain of the tilted plank obviously hurt him: I was frozen between helping him and hearing Neferet's words spill out. Lines cut deep on Rekhmire''s face.

Neferet turned back to the window, the morning's light showing gold thread in the weave of her linen over-dress. It was not true gold, I thought.

'Just because you're happy to run around doing favours for an old friend from the *scholarium* . . . ' Neferet unlatched the shutters, opening them to the winter air. I could hear the tolling of church bells, deep in the mist; the sound of a passing bell, for some man drowned or dead of plague.

'You'll run anybody's errands, Little Dog. What I'm doing here is *important.* In Florence they have laws to permit the burning alive of men who copulate with other men – twenty years ago they burned hundreds, under this Duke's father. And *they* decide who is a man.'

'And your Leon has of course told the Alberti family here in Venice

258

that you have a woman's soul, but not the womb to give the family an heir . . . '

Neferet spat out a piece of fishwife-Greek and I couldn't blame her; if Rekhmire' had spoken to me in that self-satisfied tone, I would have punched him.

'Leon loves me!' Neferet finished. 'Barbarian Frank he may be, but I had to come a hundred leagues from Alexandria to find a man who sees I am the woman for him!'

Her cry was equal parts pain and pride. In the same way, I didn't know whether to shed tears, or take up the refuge that cruel laughter would be.

Rekhmire' stubbornly dropped his chin down. 'Yes, I would happily see the Inquisition out of Fiorenza. And every other Frankish city! But Alexandria carries no weight against the believers in the Green Christ, or any man who chooses to speak for him. You of anybody ought to know that it's essential for Ty-ameny to have this German Guildsman. If he can do what he says he can do – and he won't have written it down, will he? There won't be more than sketch-plans; the secret of it will be inside the man's skull!'

He waved a hand, as if he indicated the passing bell.

'So easy to lose everything! It need not even be a competitor who wants him out of the way. An accident, a brush with cholera . . . Then it's *gone*, can't you see that?'

'I need him.' Neferet's voice was flatly stubborn as she stared down at the canal, three floors below. 'Leon needs him.'

'And why could this not happen next year? Let Herr Mainz come to Alexandria *first*.'

I was fascinated enough to breathe; shift, as men do when not sitting for painters or sculptors – and immediately both their heads turned.

Not next year, I realised, seeing her undefended face. Because for all Neferet says he loves her, she doesn't believe Leon will be here in twelve months' time. Not without the scribe-*machina*. She thinks he only stays because of that.

I don't know Leon well enough to know whether that's true or false. I know Neferet just well enough to be sure she'll hate me if I speak my guess.

'How long have you been spying there?' Neferet turned from me before I could answer, spitefully prodding at Rekhmire'. 'Training her up, are you? To listen at doors?'

Rekhmire' gave me the look of a disappointed pedagogue. As if, for a few denarii, he'd demand I stand up straight and apologise politely.

They reminded me so much of Sunilda and Reinalda before their coming-of-age feasts that I had to stifle a smile.

Stepping inside the room, I said equably, 'If you don't want people to

259

know these things, I advise not quarrelling at the top of your voices with the door open.'

The Alexandrine woman looked taken aback. The same expression showed on Rekhmire''s face.

Her voice hostile, but subdued, Neferet demanded, 'What did you hear?'

'Nothing that was my business. A lot that wasn't. You can probably be heard as far as the *kitchens*.' I exaggerated. 'And Visigoth Latin and Alexandrine Latin aren't that different. I'd have a word with Honorius about his guard, if I were you – you know how soldiers gossip.'

Rekhmire' and Neferet exchanged the kind of look that only a childhood spent quarrelling over the same toys will give you. I suppressed a smug grin at successfully uniting them against a common outsider. That doesn't come from Rodrigo's court, but from thirteen years of scrambling for a place with 'Nilda and 'Nalda.

'Pushy little thing, isn't she?' Neferet's long upper lip quivered, in the way that Rekhmire''s does when he suppresses a smile.

'Ilario, pushy? What would give you an idea like that?' He turned a pitch-coal eye on me. 'Help me up with this leg.'

'Your will is mine, O master.'

'One can only live in hope that some day that will be the case . . . ' Rekhmire' looked pious enough to make Neferet and I grin; she less willingly than I.

I slipped into the room past Neferet, and studied the position the book-buyer had got himself into. He abandoned the pose, braced himself on his hands, and shifted his backside towards the headboard as I lifted the plank and splints, taking care not to touch his leg at any point.

'Fornicating Carthaginian goats . . . ' He used the cuff of his Frankish morning-gown to wipe his forehead, immediately darkening the blue velvet with sweat. Without a word, Neferet poured him a drink from the pottery jug and passed it over.

I had a moment to wonder how the green glaze was done on the jug, and whether it was possible to reproduce the room's curved and monochrome reflection. Rekhmire' and Neferet spoke at once.

Neferet gestured elegantly, ceding. 'I'll leave you to talk to her.'

'I thought you might!'

The Alexandrine woman avoided the *sotto voce* comment, gliding out of the room with an elegance I envied now that all my weight was high and forward.

'I won't insult you by asking for secrecy.' Rekhmire' cradled the cup on the blankets in his lap. 'The Hermopolitan Eight know, we're aware enough of each other's lives. I *will* ask you to curb your immediate indiscreet tendency to leap astride the nearest horse and gallop off in all directions . . . '

'You have an over-inflated idea of your skills as a judge of character.'

I imitated him as closely as I could, and was rewarded by one of those quaking giggles that robbed his monumental gravity of all dignity.

'I wonder,' he said, regaining composure, 'whether it's too late to return to that Carthaginian slave-dealer and ask for a refund?'

'Much too late.'

It's a narrow step from macabre humour to thoughts that make me shudder – that Rekhmire' was in Carthage by the merest chance, and might never have bought me, is one of those things.

The Egyptian said quietly, 'You should never have been sold before. By your Aldra Federico, I mean. You were *freeborn*. Of two freeborn parents, even if not legitimate – but your father would have acknowledged you. Granted that was unknown then, but the sale itself is invalid. If you are ever back at the court of Taraco in anything like peace, you might ask Honorius to have lawyers look into that and void the original bill of sale to Rodrigo Sanguerra.'

Ever since I realised that Rodrigo's manumission documents burned in Donata's fire, there has been a nudging discomfort at the back of my mind – that even Rekhmire''s manumission of me in Rome was not valid, because it did not cover the years before he bought me.

'I take it back,' I said. 'You're a reasonable judge of character.'

He snickered and patted my shoulder; it might have been friendly mockery, or consolation, or – knowing Rekhmire' – both. He gazed levelly at me.

'Are you prepared to have a look around on my behalf? If you'd stayed my scribe, I would have begun this with you. Now you get a choice. I hear you keep your escort busy enough, taking your drawing-pad out. I swear I heard *Tottola* yesterday talking about "egg tempera fresco" . . . '

'He *asked*.' I may have sounded injured.

'And now he knows. Quite a lot, apparently, for a man I've never been convinced grew up knowing how to cook his food . . . '

The picture of Tottola and Attila in the depths of some German forest untouched since Varus's legions went missing, growing up on raw rabbit and fish, was all too easy to bring to mind.

'They'd like you thinking that,' I said, sitting carefully on the edge of the bed. 'They cultivate the reputation. People think if they don't speak, that means they must be stupid.'

'Not a mistake any man will make with you, scribe . . . '

The combination of Pharaonic dignity and angelic innocence was a sure indicator of whether he meant a compliment or insult.

'If *I* were about to ask someone a favour, *I* wouldn't insult that someone . . . '

'No, indeed.' The innocence increased.

'So what am I about to do?'

'Take your drawing materials out. You have an excuse to go

anywhere. The soldiers will doubtless complain about this cold, but you do Honorius a favour by keeping them keen-edged.'

'Oh, I'm sure I do . . . '

And I'd hear all about it, too, now that the variegated group of men – all of whom had been with Honorius a decade and more – had got over their shyness at the General's son or daughter turning out to be a son-daughter. It had been easier, or at least *quieter*, in Rome, when they'd been in awe of the phenomenon of the hermaphrodite. Familiarity had now brought matters down to, *Oh, it's just Ilario.*

Which I supposed has its own comfort.

I gave Rekhmire' a hard stare. 'It's not like I know how to do any of this . . . stuff . . . that comes with being a book-buyer. What am I looking for?'

Rekhmire' smiled. 'Listen. Watch. Don't ask questions, if you can avoid it; they *will* always sound awkward. If nothing shows up, that's what sometimes happens. And—'

'And?'

'And,' Rekhmire' said, 'if you can find the German Guildsman Herr Mainz, you can tell him I'd very much like a word with him.'

My freedom in Venice lasted ten more days.

14

It was Leon Battista who ended it.

Departing from one of our discussions while drawing Ramiro Carrasco, Leon remarked, 'I know your father is careful of you, in your state of health – but will you come to any of the Carnival festivities, with Madonna Neferet and myself? It would be my honour to show you how we do these things in Venezia.'

Wisdom fought desire. I could hear the arguments before Honorius voiced them. And I thought Carrasco's ears were keen enough to have overheard Leon.

'I think,' I said, 'that my father will say that Carnival is too dangerous a time for me to go out of the house.'

My guess proved accurate.

I argued only half-heartedly with Licinus Honorius. Part of me, at least, agreed with him. *I have taken my pitcher to the well twice already in the Most Serene Republic . . .*

The Alexandria House immediately felt as if it became a cramped prison.

Granted, there was no room to set up a full painter's workshop – but I could still work. I found myself missing the space in Masaccio's workshop . . . even missing the stench of fish glue being rendered down for size, and the permeating odour of varnish. Or in Tommaso Cassai's case, fifty different experiments with varnishes, to see which did not blue or yellow the pigments in his tempera painting.

'I've given up colour, for now,' I observed to Rekhmire', speeding my pen to try and catch his features before the angle of the light changed.

If I flicked through this particular work-book, I could see him become less gaunt, less pained, more himself, over the past weeks.

'Colour's a snare and a delusion.'

The Egyptian smiled. 'If not colour, what's left?'

I glared at him. 'Tone. Value. Perspective. The proportion of one part – every part – to every *other* part. How things grow short and fat when you foreshorten them—'

Rekhmire' felt at his nose.

'I even gave up drypoint,' I said, ignoring the implicit joke. 'I've been using a reed pen, so that I don't get trapped into fine detail. I do what

Masaccio said: observe, observe, observe . . . But it's knowing what I'm looking at.'

I was beginning to accept Masaccio's death. Or at least, I could bear to recall his precepts, and speak of them without tears or shudders.

Honorius entered, and stood behind my back for some time, observing me draw.

'Isn't he supposed to be smiling? He looks more like he's bawling his head off!'

'Since when did I ask for your opinion?' I blotted the reed pen dry, so I might cut it to a sharper point, and gave my father a frustrated smile. 'I'm still planning compositions for yours. I take it you want the donor's right of appearing in the picture?'

'He does,' Rekhmire' put in hastily. 'Sit down, Captain-General – it's the Lion of Castile's turn to be told off every fifty heartbeats for fidgeting!'

They continued somewhat in this manner while Honorius called for a drink, and Ensign Saverico bought a jug and drinking bowls. My father sat on the wooden settle facing the window, light falling on him unobstructed, and I began to draw.

The results were beyond bad.

I stared at my fingers, flexing them. I couldn't blame the black chalk, even if this batch *was* too hard and somewhat particulate, making for scratchy drawing. Sometimes the closer the subject is to the artist's heart, the less well it is painted.

I need to direct that artist's eye that Rekhmire' had me point at Neferet, and turn it on *il leone di Castiglia*.

Changing black chalk for willow charcoal, I smudged the paper where there were shadows on Honorius's face, and lifted part of it off again with rolled bread-crumbs, to lighten it. The shift in values was pleasingly gradual.

'Have you thought more about how you want to see St Gaius?' And then, particularly because my father must have spent so much time close to the Frankish border, 'Why St Gaius, *Judas*, of all the soldier saints? Why not Michael, or S. Bellona?'

He pushed his fingers through his hair. His nails were not bitten like Carmagnola's, but pared neatly down.

'I wanted something . . . ' He struggled for words. 'When you're fighting . . . Men die. That simple. And if you're giving the orders, they die because of you. You send men out to fight as a feint or diversion, when you know that, even though we'll win, these men will all die . . . All, to a man.'

Tottola came in with more wine at that point, and lifted his thick brows, and nodded to show assent.

'That's what soldiering is,' Honorius said. 'Who dies last. And someone has to give those necessary orders.'

He paused. I began a new drawing.

'St Gaius didn't kill himself,' he added softly. 'After the Lord-Emperor was dead, he went East, to the Turks and Persians and Indians, and beyond. Could you paint him when he's deciding that?'

'No.' I didn't hesitate. 'No. Not yet. I've had to forget every way of painting that I knew, and learn again. Ask me in a year. Better – in a year I'll make an altar board of St Gaius for your chapel, and you tell *me* if I can do it.'

My father slowly nodded.

He set his drinking bowl down and came to look over my shoulder again, effectively cutting off the drawing, but he spent long minutes studying what lines there were.

'I wish I could call up faces as you do.' His fingertip moved high above the paper's surface, mirroring the line of his jaw and ear. 'I made good friends when I first went north. Many of them. I can see them, in the eye of my mind; men I fought beside. We loved each other like brothers; *died* for each other. The last of them was killed at Candlemass, last year, and I decided I was done with fighting.'

He removed his hand, staring at what I had drawn of his face as if it could tell him something.

'I felt no grief when Antonio died. *None*. A man I knew for twenty-five years . . . Nothing. Then I knew I could either continue as a successful captain, and never mourn any butchered man of mine, or I must *stop*. I told King Juan the following day that I would be returning to Taraconensis.'

I rubbed my charcoal-black fingers on a rag, turning my skin grey. 'How can you command for all that time and still grieve when men die? How could you bear it?'

'War is horror. Let no man tell you otherwise. But if this is war, then at least it can be prosecuted with the least possible waste. I did not desire to turn into one of those commanders who gets their troops killed carelessly, and then hires more and does it again.'

After a moment, when I saw he wouldn't say more, I remarked, 'And I thought St Gaius was going to be easy!'

Honorius chuckled, as I thought he would, and leaned his arm across my shoulders. 'I mean to get my money's worth out of you, son-daughter!'

The desire to urinate thirty times a day, along with aches in joints and a general feeling that my body was becoming unfamiliar to me – and God He knows, it was unfamiliar enough as a human body before this! – left me in a foul temper.

'*Out!*' Honorius bellowed, on the second morning of Carnival season, when my ill-temper rubbed up against Rekhmire''s until the Egyptian so far forgot himself as to quarrel violently with me.

'Tell *him* to stop shouting!' I snarled.

'*I did not shout!*' Rekhmire', loudly indignant, slammed his hand down on the side of the bed and flinched. 'I may have raised my voice. I do not "shout"!'

'Then *I'll* leave!' Honorius snarled, and stalked out, slamming the door hard enough to rattle the scroll cases, pestles and mortars that stood on the shelves.

Silenced, I looked at Rekhmire' in embarrassment.

The book-buyer huffed out his breath, and looked at me from the corners of his eyes.

'He's a lot like you,' Rekhmire' said after a moment.

'Ha!' I was torn between the compliment and insult, both implicit in the Egyptian's words. I waddled over to sit in the wooden armed chair by the fire.

'I wish I thought I'd do half as much with my life as he has. Do you want to play another game of chess?'

'Not until you learn enough skill at it that the whole experience isn't a worse tedium than this!'

I left it a minute, and looked at him from the corners of *my* eyes. An unfamiliar eye wouldn't have seen it, but I read a degree of contrition on his face.

'Suppose you teach me chess,' I offered, 'so that I get better at it.'

Rekhmire' shrugged and nodded. It was an attempt to indicate that he didn't care either way, and a not hugely successful one.

'That might be better.' He waited for me to edge the chair over to the bed, and set the chessboard up on the cover. 'Thank you.'

'You're welcome.'

He smiled, almost shyly. One of the soldiers, Vasev, I think, currently shaved him in the morning, so he was back to his neat self. You would not have known he stayed in bed for any other reason than apparent idleness.

Which means he must be good at concealing pain. Considerable amounts of pain.

I wondered where and why he had learned it. Which for some reason turned my mind to Taraco's court, and I turned it resolutely away.

Sixteen moves into the game – with Rekhmire' explaining extensively at each where I might have done better – Honorius stomped back into the room. Evidently his body-servant had only got his cloak from him; his boots tracked slush across the floorboards and old dried rushes.

'Strange pick-pockets they have in Venice!' Honorius snorted. 'Most thieves cut your purse to take something *out* . . . '

I must have looked bewildered.

'Here!' He tossed his leather purse to Rekhmire', who caught it out of the air with a wince. 'See what you make of that.'

I eased my belly by leaning back from the chessboard. 'What's happened?'

My father looked down at his leaking muddy boots as if surprised to see them. 'Saverico!'

With one hand resting down on Saverico's shoulder as the man drew each boot off in turn, Honorius went on:

'The usual thing in the Mercaria, I thought – knocked aside by one man, purse cut off my belt and passed to a second. I chased them into the back alleys, thought I'd lose them; my fault for not taking one of the lads at my back. Then I saw the purse by the first bridge, where they'd dropped it. The money was gone . . . There's now a letter in it.'

Rekhmire' lifted his head from peering at the unfolded sheet of paper. 'This is an approach from Carthage!'

'That's what I thought, yes.' Honorius dropped down onto the hard wooden settle and wriggled his feet in front of the fire, as if that would dry his hose faster. He shot me a sharp look. 'You may have been right back in Rome. The King-Caliph thinks I'm interested in betraying King Rodrigo.'

'Or he'd like to have evidence that you would.' Rekhmire' carefully re-folded the paper along exactly the same lines. 'Either would help Carthage. You'd make an equally good figurehead governor, or distressing evidence of further internal dissent in Taraco.'

'The King-Caliph can sodomise a male goat!' Honorius said, in passable Carthaginian Latin. 'But that isn't the point!'

'Ask the goat!' Rekhmire' surprised the life out of me by murmuring. He nickered almost precisely like a horse when he stifled his laughter. It was silly enough that amusement bubbled up irresistibly in me, and I had to put both hands over my mouth.

'This is the subtle wit of the Alexandrines, evidently,' Honorius muttered, and tried hard to look as if he were not pleased to have reduced the large Egyptian to a quaking mass.

Honorius looked back at me, after a moment or two, and the laughter left his face.

'The point,' he said, 'is that this message has been delivered to me *here*. There are agents of Carthage in Venice. They must have arrived a month or more ago – travel's impossible now. If they know where I am, they know where *you* are, Ilario.'

Rekhmire' looked annoyed, plainly feeling that he should have been the one to say this.

'Carthage has no reason to hurt me,' I pointed out. 'The reverse, if anything. They need their witness alive and well.'

'That's as may be, but I don't fancy hiring a pirate fleet or a company of mercenaries to haul your backside out from under the Penitence!'

I smiled. He stopped glaring and looked embarrassed.

'Rescuing the maiden in distress?' I raised a brow at him, as much in Rekhmire''s manner as I could imitate.

'Carthage can have you!' Honorius snorted. 'In fact, I have a better idea – when I offer my services as local Carthaginian Governor of Taraconensis, I'll offer to sell them my son-daughter at a very reasonable price! Then there'll be no North African interference in my government, because you will have driven them all mad . . . '

I whispered solemnly to Rekhmire', 'You can see he *is* cut out to be a tyrant.'

The book-buyer, having been perilously near a sulk, abandoned it and gave me a smile; perfectly well aware that I attempted to entertain him into a better humour.

'That will stem from commanding armies,' he said as if Honorius were not in the room. His gaze grew sharper, directed at me. 'And your peace-making talents come from your years as Court Fool.'

If anybody would know that there's more to the position of Royal Freak than a quick tongue and a dual set of genitalia, it would be Rekhmire'.

'Rodrigo didn't like his nobles to kill each other – well, more than was absolutely necessary. And not at court.'

'Ilario!' Honorius rapped his knuckles against the wooden seat of the settle, as if he called a meeting to order. 'This settles it. You don't go outside at any time with fewer than two guards – and Lady Neferet can get used to my men doing guard duty in this building.'

Rekhmire' rested his fingers on the folded letter. 'What will you do with this?'

Honorius grunted, stood up, and slipped the paper out from under the Alexandrine's hand. 'You reminded me – I was on the way to the privy!'

Rekhmire' gazed at the door as it shut behind Honorius.

'And this is the man the Carthaginians wish to make Governor of Taraco . . . '

He gave the particular secretive smile he had when something amused him, and directed it at me.

'Not that I say the people of Taraconensis wouldn't benefit from being ruled as if they were a company of mercenaries.'

'I could say the same about the book-buyers of Alexandria!'

We went back to chess. In the short intervals while Rekhmire' considered his moves, I regarded the world beyond the leaded glass window, where the rain had now turned to sleet.

Videric's spies. And now spies from Carthage.

I said nothing of Rekhmire''s injured leg, in the same way that he made no reference to my swelling abdomen.

Neither of us debated the possibility of a winter voyage to Alexandrine Constantinople. Between storms by sea, and washed-out roads, mud, flooding rivers, avalanches, and landslides, there's little enough travelling done in this quarter of the year. Which should have comforted me – if we couldn't move, neither could any other man. But it persisted in seeming to me that things weren't as simple as that.

Rekhmire', being as keen a reader of expressions as drawing was making me, echoed my thoughts aloud. 'Likely we have trouble enough already here in Venice.'

Honorius, re-entering the room in time to hear it, scowled at the Egyptian, and then at me as he squatted to warm his whitened fingers at the hearth fire.

Abruptly, he said, 'Let me adopt you.'

'Will that make me safer? Or merely give you the illusion of having authority over me?' I grinned at his expression. 'I'm half inclined to think life was easier as a slave.' I looked at Rekhmire'. 'You wouldn't buy me again, would you?'

'Sun-god's egg, no! You were far too much trouble!'

If there had been anything breakable and moderately inexpensive to hand, I would have thrown it at him. Neferet stored only expensive knick-knacks in the embassy, and art that she said would repay the investment within a few years (which I personally doubted). I was reduced to glaring at the Egyptian.

'I was a better slave than you were a master!'

Rekhmire' and Honorius swapped looks. They had the effect of making me feel closer to fifteen than twenty-five.

'You see?' the Egyptian remarked. 'Nothing but trouble. And insolent, too.'

I grinned at him, and ambled to the window. If I could, I would paint the darkening sleet-streaked sky, with the serried ranks of wide-capped chimneys spouting smoke bent over by the wind.

'*And* you two gang up on me,' I added.

'Self-defence!' Honorius.

'Self-preservation!' Rekhmire'.

I snorted. 'If I had a *job*, I wouldn't have to sit here and listen to you two old codgers every day . . . '

Rekhmire' sounded offended. 'I'm not old!'

The retired Captain-General of Castile and Leon distinctly snickered.

'Isn't it Carnival?' I said sourly. 'You two should take that act on a *commedia* stage.'

Rekhmire' pointed a large, blunt finger at me, his expression changing. 'Yes. Carnival. Masks. Parties. Riots in the streets. Boats overturned. Could anything make life easier for an assassin?'

'Well, I'm already making it as easy as I *can* . . . '

I grinned at the Alexandrine's expression.

'They say "keep your friends close and your enemies closer", don't they? Ramiro Carrasco can sit next to me any day he pleases. He knows that. He just can't kill me. He knows that, too. It may,' I speculated, 'be driving him slowly insane.'

'I sympathise!' Honorius rumbled, but I could see that he was suppressing a smile. He had confidence in his men-at-arms.

As a slave, one grows used to living with no privacy. I had envisaged life as a freeman or freewoman significantly differently: plainly that was an error. It had taken a distinctly female fit of hysterics to keep Sergeant Orazi out of the garderobe with me. Two men slept in my room at night; one across the door, and one under the window.

'Federico will assume I'm only to be kidnapped.'

Honorius frowned. 'He must know that's ridiculous!'

'He'll know nothing he doesn't want to!' I snorted. 'There are plenty of pleasant lies Federico can tell himself, if he wants to. That Videric merely wants me kidnapped, not killed, say. He's capable of believing Videric only wants to lock me up in some back-country fortress, like an errant daughter.'

I wiped my hands free of charcoal on a rag, and realised it was a lost cause. My oatmeal-coloured woollen bodice and skirts were comprehensively smudged with black.

I got a look from both of them that silently informed me it was a penalty of wearing skirts.

I know that.

'If I don't get out of this house, I'll go mad! I know where Ramiro Carrasco is—'

'You don't know where every thug he's hired is!'

Honorius straightened up and looked at me with a hurt expression. 'I've told you, you can go anywhere you want to—'

'If I don't mind taking six hulking great Taraconian farm-boys with armour on their backs, and a Venetian woman with a face like a *prune*!'

The retired Captain-General put his hand over his mouth. I realised he was hiding a grin.

'*What?*'

'You really do sound like a woman when you put skirts on.'

Rekhmire', appearing to study the chessboard, grinned.

Honorius's gaze went up and down me, in a way that I am used to. More soberly, he said, 'You don't walk in Venice on your own. Not dressed as a woman. And not because of Carrasco. You *know* what cities are like, for a woman—'

'Why do you think I dress as a man in Frankish countries!'

'—and if you're hurt when you're alone, every man will say that you *deserved* it. Do you understand me?'

My hand rested on my abdomen again, I found. The obstruction to me wearing doublet and hose here in Venice, because my body has so evidently the shape of a womb, and not a man's belly.

As if we were alone in the room – which spoke volumes for his trust of the Egyptian – Honorius asked, 'Has it kicked yet?'

I shook my head. *It may be dead*, I thought but didn't say.

The lean ex-soldier drew in a breath, and stared into the low flames of the hearth-fire.

'My wives – both of them lost children early on. I suppose I know the signs. I don't . . . I don't know whether to hope to see them, with you, or hope not to.'

He shot me a look that, after a moment, I realised was to see whether he was hurting or offending me.

'The Egyptian says you could die of the birth,' he added.

I glared at Rekhmire', where he sat with his leg strapped uncomfortably to the ash-wood plank. 'The Egyptian should keep his damn mouth *shut*!'

'You weren't going to tell me?'

I faced both men. 'It hasn't quickened. It's more than five months. I don't feel anything. Except fatter and off balance. It's not a baby to me – and it might not be a baby,' I added. 'It might be a monster. Look who it's been fathered on.'

Honorius stood up and put his arm around my shoulder. Which I would have shaken off, had I not found it unexpectedly comforting.

'Skirts make you want to weep more,' I said, pulling out Neferet's kerchief, and dusting my nose hard. '*I* blame skirts.'

'Oh, so do I.' His grip tightened.

'Will *you* get a bad name if I go walking around on my own?'

'Yes. Of course.' He looked as hangdog as a man used to commanding armies can. 'But I worry about your safety, not that.'

'I'll take the Eight-gods-damn-them escort, then!'

I suspected I would narrowly escape being dragged back by the men-at-arms themselves, none too keen on being reprimanded by Honorius in the mood he would have been in.

Honorius steered me to sit down beside him on the settle, the hard wood not comfortable under my aching joints. Rekhmire' looked up from under his eyebrows, tipped his king over, and began to set up a new game.

'What I need to do,' I sighed, 'is talk to someone about what happened in Rome.'

Honorius gave me a look and a nod, both straightforward and accepting. Rekhmire' placed a row of pawns. He has heard this before, or most of it. My father . . .

I leaned my shoulder against the shoulder of Honorius. 'It involves more than you think. More than you'll be able to repeat. But I trust you. And I need to tell someone how it is that Masaccio died.'

I stayed indoors throughout Carnival.

271

Leon and Neferet came in after midnight every night, flushed with wine, and shaking gold-tissue streamers out of their hair. I tried not to sound as bad-tempered about it as I felt. Each campo had its own particular festivities, and a *commedia dell'arte* team set up in the square by the Alexandrine House for several days in succession.

'In Taraco, I would have been allowed to watch *that*,' I muttered at Honorius. 'Even if the King's Freak were dressed in skirts on that day.'

'Ilario—'

'You want to know where the assassin is?' I demanded of Honorius. 'I'll send a message and invite my foster father here, with Sunilda and Reinalda, and I'll make sure Ramiro Carrasco is with them. If he's here, nothing's going to happen!'

Rekhmire' began an objection.

'Nothing will happen,' I repeated, 'because Sergeant Orazi and the other men will happen to *him*. If he so much as looks at me funny. Am I right, Father?'

Honorius matched the Egyptian for gravity, clasping his hands lightly behind him, and rocking on his toes. 'She's right.'

'She's always right,' Rekhmire' muttered. 'Ilario, I suppose you want to draw the actors?'

'That too.'

I did draw them. The swaggering captain who played up to that portion of his audience consisting of the Iberian military, and won himself a great success, with Honorius slapping at his thigh and laughing until the tears came. The wily thieving servant, smarter than his masters – at whose appearance I shot a look at Carrasco, and was rewarded by something very like a blush. The woman—

There *is* only one woman in the *commedia*, and unlike the others she goes bare-faced. Except that her uncovered face represents Young Girl, and is as much of a mask as the others.

And the plague doctor, with his long-beaked leather mask, pretending to drink all of his urine flask at some turn of the plot that depends on the Girl's pregnancy.

Rekhmire' saw me put my chalk down. Barely audible over the shrieking, guffawing crowd, he queried, 'Ilario?'

I put my mouth close to his ear. 'Nothing. Lend me a cloak. It's cold.'

It *was* cold – a white rime of frost outlined the bricks, carved wooden house-beams, and well-trodden earth, and gave the *commedia* artists more pratfalls than they planned for. But it wasn't the winter that chilled me.

Mummers came next, from some northern country. From the Alexandrine House's upper windows, by torch-light, I watched them play the Frankish Sacred Boar's ceremony.

No one played the aulos flute.

The day after that, we were back to masked revellers; and so it went on, for what seemed like weeks, and was in fact nearly a month, until Ash Wednesday cut all short, and there was only a sludge of papier-mâché masks left floating in gutters and canals.

Frankish Lent being a time for austerity, I was glad to be in Neferet's house. She muttered something unusually low-voiced about 'superstitious Europeans!' when an official from the Council of Ten called to ask why the household didn't attend church. She told him that the servants certainly did attend, she and her colleague Rekhmire' were preparing to sacrifice to the gods of darkness and invisibility, and didn't mention my name at all.

'We need a young man and a young woman to eviscerate on the altar, for the requisite entrails,' Rekhmire' said, far too mildly. 'Thinking about that, *you* . . . '

'Could do both?' I threw an old paint-sponge at him. 'Have I mentioned how *very* much I dislike you?'

'Daily. Hourly.' He grinned, which was a startling expression on that monumental face. It turned rueful. 'If that young officer was as devoid of humour as he seemed, I may have to spend some time explaining to Doge Foscari that Alexandrines don't, in fact, practise sacrificial rites . . . '

'Wouldn't it be easier just to eviscerate someone?'

The knock on the door came with such fortuitousness that I couldn't help remarking, 'Ah. Carrasco. Come in . . . '

Ramiro Carrasco de Luis was shown in by Sergeant Orazi. Carrasco looked at Rekhmire', clearly more than a little bewildered by the Egyptian greeting him with a snort of amusement.

I smiled. Videric's man had been far too close to recovering his mental balance, now he was used to sitting as my model.

'Come in,' I repeated. 'Sit down, Ramiro. Take your hose off.'

'I *beg* your pardon!' he yelped.

Rekhmire', who had been rising to his feet, exchanged a glance with the sergeant and the other soldier, Aznar, and sat back down on the settle. 'I'll stay for this session, shall I?'

Ramiro Carrasco was looking satisfactorily aghast.

I beamed at him. 'Judas – St Gaius, rather – should be in Roman legionary uniform. I need to make some studies of your legs and feet. Do you have suitable legs?'

Carrasco muttered something unintelligible, and glanced around the room as if he would much rather not have been under the eye of the Egyptian and two of Honorius's crack troops. He shot me a glance in which I thought I discerned some unflattering disgust. As if this might have been titillating if I were a woman, but a man-woman was merely revolting.

'Stand there.' More harshly, I pointed. When he had rid himself of boots and hose, and wrapped around himself the cloak that I had put out for him, he stood not far from the fire, pale-skinned muscular legs on show. He was moderately hairy, but his feet were well-shaped – few people have actually well-shaped feet – and I lost myself in capturing their dimensions from various angles.

Not every man can retain his self-possession when bare from the thigh down. Ramiro Carrasco held his cloak around him with one hand, and stroked the narrow, clipped beard that he had taken to growing in this Frankish city, and eventually looked perfectly at ease.

Rekhmire' stirred, and departed to check Neferet's current stock of imported scrolls, and advise her on what should be sent back to Alexandria when the ships could sail again – not that he needed to give the advice, or she to hear it, but it gave them an excuse to pore over the finer points of papyrus, ink, ancient treatises, and rare finds with which they could make each other jealous.

Consequently, Leon Battista stepped in for some moments, on his way back from visiting Neferet, and studied the wood-and-linen frame I'd made up from his plans, scribbling some alterations down on a scrap of paper as he watched how I used it.

Without giving away my small reading vocabulary of the Florentine language, I had to think carefully how I would phrase it when I asked.

As he put the perspective frame down, I said, 'This is hardly my business, except for living here in this house – is it really wise, to be passing around letters that the Council of Ten have banned?'

'Some things have to be done.' Leon looked intensely at me. 'As for Florence – my family has been so long exiled from it . . . If Taraco were— If Carthage sent legions in and occupied your homeland, would you not do the same thing?'

'No.' I rubbed my thumb over the line of Carrasco's thigh, hopelessly botched, and began again. 'It's different for a slave. But you're not occupied – *Florence* isn't occupied. It's a quarrel between rich families—'

Leon crumpled the paper he wrote on, glared, and the door slammed behind him before I could find anything to say.

I found Sergeant Orazi and the soldier Aznar, and Ramiro Carrasco, looking at me with identical expressions.

'That . . . could have gone better.'

I ended the day's session because I tired of Ramiro Carrasco's grin. Which was not unlike that of Aznar, or Orazi.

The sergeant murmured, 'Could have told *you* that! Ma'am . . . '

'Suppose we go for a nice walk?' I muttered. 'All six of us?'

I managed to see quite an area of Venezia in what fine winter weather there was, by walking to places in which Honorius's soldiers might take an interest. This covered areas from Dorsodura to the shipyards – the Venetian Arsenale being the fifth largest in Frankish territory, as Aznar decided I needed to be extensively informed – where I decided it wouldn't be wise to sketch, given the number of guard-towers. And back, past the Doge's palace, to an area containing a number of commercial armouries.

By way of a fair return, Honorius's household guard were possibly the most well-educated soldiers in respect of church frescoes that you could find in a hundred-mile radius. I suspect they were pleased when my sixth month made me tire more easily, and desire to stand for shorter amounts of time gazing up at paintings.

It was the first time I had spent a period in close contact with men who were very much of an age with me (the sergeant excepting), and who were prepared to treat me as Honorius's son-daughter without anything in the way of questions. Berenguer was loud-mouthed and lectured me on the way I ought to behave as a man who was 'handicapped by being partly a woman'. Viscardo and Fulka and the others treated me as I was dressed, but with much less of that attitude common in Rodrigo's court: that a woman who can talk like a man is as amazing as a trained jackdaw – or that a man who can speak as a woman must be an effeminate catamite.

True, the same loud-mouthed Berenguer made a comment or two about 'men with no balls'. But a single look from Rekhmire' taught him an instant lesson in tact. The Egyptian pretended to no skill with a sword, but he didn't need to – it was an article of faith among Honorius's soldiers that he could break most of them in two with his bare hands.

'Torcello,' I remarked, on a morning in February when the first stirrings of spring were perceptible on the wind, and put my hand on my curved stomach, looking up at Honorius. 'I want to see the frescos on the island of Torcello. Before I can't walk more than fifty yards at a time!'

15

'Frescoes—' Honorius glanced over his shoulder at the bare garden in front of the Alexandrine house, where his guards had been a moment before. 'Look at that. Not a man in sight!'

Neferet, walking outside at that moment, smiled down at me. 'Ilaria, Leon will act as your escort, if you like. And I'll come with you. I like the idea of being out of the house.'

'So do I.' Honorius put his hand under my elbow as we walked back into the house to prepare. 'I'll detail off men to go with you. I suppose you want *me* to keep Aldra Federico and the damned assassin busy?'

'Ramiro Carrasco's useful. The longer we keep him writing messages to be sent back to Videric, the longer it'll be before Videric sends more men here.'

Honorius harrumphed under his breath about how many others we might not know of – though they would likely be hired men, by his opinion, and worth little without Carrasco's motivating presence.

Rekhmire' stumbled off the last stair as we came in, one crutch firmly under his arm as a support, and the other skidding on the oak floorboards. Honorius steadied him with one hand, at the same time notifying him of the proposed visits.

I picked up the dropped scroll Rekhmire' had been carrying under his arm. 'I wish you could come with us.'

The Egyptian cocked an eyebrow at me. 'Torcello?'

'Island. On the far side of Murano and Burano.'

He snorted, amused, hobbling towards the warmest downstairs room – which in the Alexandrine House is the kitchen.

'Is it a monastery?' He answered his own question before I could. 'No. Does it have old scrolls or books? *No.* Does any man live there now the bad air brings plague? No—'

'It's winter! There's no plague in cold air. Besides which . . . ' I adjusted my pace to keep level with him, avoiding his crutch impaling my foot. 'You could hold my hand, while Neferet holds Leon's. So I don't feel so – superfluous.'

'Not even for that.' Rekhmire' smiled. 'Charming as the thought is. *I* intend to stay here, and check over this stock that Neferet is so slow in sending back to Alexandria. By a brazier. With wine. In a room that's warm.'

'Coward!'

'At your service.' His round features curved into a grin.

But he was persuaded to leave the vast inglenook fireplace in the kitchens to bid us farewell, and my last sight was of him swinging his immobilised leg between the two crutches, and with difficulty waving a hand.

Leon Battista helped Neferet down into the low, wide boat that was to take us across the lagoon to the island of Torcello. His smile was brighter than the winter sun, and Neferet smoothed her white-and-lapis Alexandrine robes around her, gazing up at him with an affection that held no cynicism at all.

'Careful!' She caught my hands in hers as I sat down on the stern seat beside her. 'Ilaria, you really should take more care. The baby . . . '

This 'baby' is likely a dead stone within me.

Sergeant Orazi, at the prow, gave the order to cast off and row. I adjusted my borrowed bronze and gold robes around my shoulders, and the thick winter cloak over them. Neferet brushed my fingers aside to assist. Of all of them, she never had any hesitation in calling me 'Ilaria'.

I muttered, 'The baby will kill me. Or die at birth. Or turn out to be a monster. Rekhmire' must have told you what I am.'

She looked at me less coolly than I expected. 'You're a woman, Ilaria. Oh, I know, you may have a vestigial penis – but you're a woman, truly.'

Ensign Saverico, who happened to be sitting on the bench in front of me, coloured a bright red all up the back of his neck. Somebody choked; I thought it might have been Orazi. Certainly the sergeant looked back with an expression that spoke a desire to have the Alexandrine under his orders.

'Neferet – I'm not a woman!' I held up my hand, as she started to object. 'Yes, I'm woman enough to have conceived from some man's seed. But I'm also a man. I stand up to piss!'

Her calm demeanour didn't crack. Berenguer's neck went purple: he leaned forward and put his head into his hands, despite the rocking boat, *I don't want to be here!* written clearly in his posture, for all I couldn't see his face.

That made me grin. 'Believe me both. Not one; not the other. I'm – Honorius's son-daughter.'

'You behave like a woman,' Neferet contradicted. 'I've seen you.'

'I'm not permitted to behave like anything else here!'

'You couldn't if you tried!'

I felt a desire to smack her. And to take her around Rome, to the places I frequented as Masaccio's apprentice.

'Your body doesn't matter.' Neferet peered intently into my face. 'The spirit matters. The *ka*. The soul. What you truly are. Your *ka* is female. Like mine.'

I opened my mouth, and shut it again. Who knows how many of Honorius's men know that Neferet is the same as Rekhmire'? This is not the moment to educate them.

My drawing skills had improved enough that I'd borrowed a mirror from Neferet and achieved several charcoal and red chalk self-portraits. Drawn as a woman, you could see the male in my bones. Drawn male, I looked too effeminate. I drew as I saw myself in the mirror, and came back to my sketchbook to find Sergeant Orazi and Attila arguing over whether I'd drawn a man or a woman. Both their arguments seemed to come down to 'But it's *obvious*!'

Neferet, tall and elegant as she was, made a better woman than I. With her throat covered – since her male shape there was noticeable – and ignoring her too-large hands, she showed in my drawings much more of a female than I ever did.

'You won't be able to avoid the matter, once you've had the baby,' Neferet added. 'I know a Green priest, Father Azadanes, who's very adept. You could think about having your vestigial – *organs* – removed.'

Saverico put both hands over the cod-flap of his hose and crossed his legs.

It was unkind but I howled with laughter, slumping back against the padded stern seat and ignoring how both of them – for different reasons – glared ferociously at me.

'I need nothing removed!' I stated. 'It's not a matter of being one thing or the other.'

'Your *ka* is female.' Neferet sounded utterly stubborn.

'Fine,' I grumbled. 'My *ka* is female. My cock is male!'

If she had ever been inclined to abandon female decorum and punch me in the eye, I thought that was the moment.

I took the moment to be one in which shivering, huddling down in my cloak, and asking Saverico if I could borrow *his* cloak, too, to put over my knees against the spray, was a good idea.

Torcello had a thousand-year-old church, the stone throne of the Emperor Attila, a fresco which even I had to grant wouldn't teach me anything, and broken capitals from Roman pillars, scattered in the grass down by the landing place.

'The style is nothing new.' Leon Battista straightened up from studying the church's fresco 'torment of the damned', completely unmoved by their pain. 'The architecture – this is the old Roman style . . . '

I abandoned Neferet to be lectured on architecture, taking my sketch-book out of the church and back towards the boat. Ruins covered the sparse turf, embedded in the earth. I crossed my legs and sat on one fallen pillar, drawing another; the layers of petticoats doing something to keep out the cold.

Under the petticoats, I had put on and pinned up an old pair of countryman's breeches, mostly unbuttoned. It might make me look fatter than my pregnancy, but it was, thank Rekhmire''s Eight, *warm*.

I grinned to myself, thinking of the Egyptian's firm refusal to be rowed out to the island of Torcello. *He's not wrong*, I acknowledged, squiggling a line that was more acknowledgement of the acanthus leaves in ancient marble than an actual drawing. Notes for a drawing, perhaps.

My fingertips, where they protruded from the gloves I had trimmed for the purpose, were a whitish-blue that didn't argue well for control of red chalk, or charcoal.

'Learn all about naves and pediments?' I remarked as Neferet and Leon walked back down the slipway towards me, she with her hand tucked into his arm, and both of them flushed more than the winter chill would account for. 'Barrel vaults? Apses?'

Leon gave me the look a man would give a cheeky younger sister. 'Your appetite for knowledge being so inexhaustible, of course?'

'I needed to sit.' I tapped the front of my cloak. 'You don't want knowledge of swelling ankles . . . '

He agreed with unflattering haste.

It was a spring day come unexpectedly in the latter stages of winter, the sky a deep blue, and the sun warm when the wind fell, and if one did not discard a cloak too hurriedly. Even the lapping water looked deceptively blue, and not so bitterly cold.

'It's past three. We should think of going back.' Neferet shaded her eyes with one gloved hand, looking down the strand to where our soldiers and oarsmen were squatting around a driftwood fire and cracking obscene jokes in a dialect I hoped she would not understand. Leon caught my eye.

Much speculating about who does what and to whom, I attempted to put into a look. Leon nodded, fractionally.

His glance went past me, to the lagoon.

The creak of oars, that had been present in the back of my mind for uncounted minutes while I drew, became louder.

I scrambled down off the fallen Roman pillar, feet numb and prickling, and grabbed onto the carved marble to avoid falling over.

Orazi appeared at my elbow. I realised he must have been no more than fifteen feet away from me, he and his men watching the island with care.

A large shallow-draft row-boat grounded on the strand, and a man leaped ashore, waving towards us what I suspected he intended to be a reassuring dismissal.

His hat was a Venetian version of a Phrygian cap, banded with embroidery in the same blue and white as his tabard. I registered the blue tabards of his oarsmen, and the blue-and-white painting on the blades of their oars as they lifted them from the water.

He's an official of some kind—

Six armed men jumped onto the slick beach behind him. In the Doge's livery.

'In the name of the Council of Ten and Doge Foscari!'

I glimpsed in peripheral vision our own oarsmen, and the rest of Honorius's men, jogging towards us. I looked at Neferet. Her reddish-brown face was grey.

We are short in numbers – Attila must have left with Tottola and Fulka again, patrolling the grounds of the ancient church.

Leon Battista took a step forward, as if he were the only man present and therefore ought to control the situation.

I spoke before he could. The cold air made my voice harsh and much too low. 'What do you want?'

The Venetian in the Phrygian cap raised his eyebrows. 'Not you.' A pause. 'Madonna. Now—'

His head turned as he looked from me to Neferet, back to me, and then at the Alexandrine again. I felt my face growing hot. The official said nothing, but I considered what I might use in the way that I had used the oar with Ramiro Carrasco.

'Leon Battista Alberti.' The man's voice grew confident as he looked at the obvious man amongst us. 'By order of the Council of Ten, you're under arrest.'

'I'm *what*?' Leon sounded stunned.

'You're coming back with me now.' The official lifted his arm in what must be a pre-arranged signal.

I started to walk forward – Viscardo caught my arm, and Saverico stepped in on my other side – and the six men split up.

Two walked to Leon, and took him by each of his arms. The other four trotted to our boat, leaned over the side, and thrust with iron spikes – spikes long as a man's arm; a tool used for something, but I couldn't tell what.

They smashed through the bottom of the boat in seconds.

The oarsmen running up halted as if a wall had appeared in front of them. One small, spare-bodied man swore and spat, railing furiously against the Venetian official.

'*Council of Ten!*' the official repeated.

The two of the official's men that held Leon thrust him forward, towards their boat. I wrenched free, pushed past Orazi, and Neferet's long-fingered, broad hand closed over my elbow:

'You don't argue with the Council of Ten! *They'll take you too!*'

Leon sat down in the prow of the boat. His gaze rested on Neferet. He did not call out. Not a word.

The official stepped aboard. The men who had wrecked our boat thrust theirs into the lagoon, lurching up over the side and onto their rowing benches as the water deepened under their hull.

I looked at Neferet. At our broken boat.

'They can't just—!'

'They *can*. This is Venice. If someone's denounced him . . . ' She blinked, blind gaze turned in the direction of the boat. 'I don't have enough influence. Not for this.'

Squinting at the lagoon around Torcello, I saw no other craft. The blue-and-white-painted boat receded into the haze, oars delicately picking at the surface of the water like a skating-insect.

'Is there . . . anything we can do?'

'Appeal to the Doge.' Her eyes showed hazy, like the distance. 'But, foreigners. The Doge doesn't like . . . '

'My father knows the mercenary Captain-General of Venezia. He can probably kick Carmagnola into supporting us. What—' I wondered if she would tell me what I thought was the truth. 'What did they arrest Leon *for*?'

Neferet shook her head, gazing in the direction of the city of Venice. 'It really doesn't matter, you know.'

Attila's and Tottola's boots hit the soil hard enough to kick up divots as they pounded around the church's end-wall, and out onto the strand, outpacing Fulka and the few other men-at-arms who trailed panting behind. Orazi signalled his men into a defensive circle around us. I saw the oarsmen clustered, complaining vividly in low growls.

Orazi stared at the smashed hull on the island's beach.

'They can't . . . ' the Armenian sergeant began.

Neferet spoke as if he should already know what she said. 'They're the Council of Ten. They can do anything they like. *Foscari* can do anything he likes.'

'We,' Orazi scowled, narrowing his eyes against the last of the winter sun off the water, 'can see if the boat is capable of being mended. You were right, madonna,' he added, to me. 'No one lives here or comes here now. Not even peasants. There's no help to be had.'

Pain crunched the muscles of my belly.

A streak of something piercingly hot and wet ran down the inside of my leg. An almost-welcome warmth flooded my thighs and breeches and petticoats. Steam went up white into the winter air.

I had a moment to think in agonised embarrassment that I had pissed myself through fear – and another roll of muscle-pain all but closed over my head.

I grabbed Neferet's arm, shaking in panic. A snap of Orazi's fingers sent the men into armed stance: swords and bows at the ready to face whatever might be approaching. Neferet winced: my fingers dug into her arm, clenching the wool of her cloak.

Another cramp creased down my belly, following the wet and heat, sharp enough to make me gasp.

I don't bleed upwards of twice a year, and sometimes not that. This is different from women's cramps – but only in intensity, not in kind.

Orazi's blue-grey eyes opened in frank amazement.

'Jesu Christus!' I prised my fingers out of Neferet's arm. 'My waters broke!'

Pain washed over me; I lost long moments to it. My vision blurred, I thought – and I realised that it was mist on the late afternoon surface of the lagoon.

'Use the wreckage of the boat,' Orazi bellowed. 'If we can't row it, we can set it on fire as a beacon! Someone'll come.'

Specks moved in my field of vision.

It took me sluggishly long to decipher what it meant.

I pointed, and dug my other fist into the side of my body, against the dragging, grinding pain that washed through me.

'Someone *has* come.'

Light-headed and sweating, I watched a long shallow boat streak towards us, propelled by four standing men with oars. The failing light didn't let me accurately count the number of men in the main body of the boat. *I would be surprised if it were less than a dozen.*

Help or harm?

'I thought,' Neferet stuttered. 'Rekhmire' *said.*'

'Carrasco's out of town with Honorius and Federico.' Narrowing my eyes didn't bring me a clearer view. The oars knocked up foam from the lagoon water. Ramiro Carrasco might be being dragged round a mainland villa in Sunilda's wake, or he might be sitting fifty yards away from me in the boat.

I blinked. 'The light's bad. We could run.' Nothing I'd seen on Torcello made me think that would last long. *But* – 'Orazi, could we shut the doors of the church? Stand a siege inside? The windows are small, and those doors are solid oak—'

'Yeah. Best option.' He turned and gave quick orders. There was no milling about as men obeyed him; Honorius impelled his men to discipline even in his absence. I saw our oarsmen had vanished. Run. *I wish I might do the same!*

Hobbling with the pain, holding Neferet's arm, I let her inch me away up the foreshore. She glanced impatiently about; frightened, angry, frustrated. If I'd been shorter, or not pregnant, I think she would have picked me up and run.

But she doesn't seem to think of doing anything that a woman of her height and build can't, despite her male aspects.

Neferet peered back towards the lagoon, and slowed her steps. 'We're too late.'

The boat altered course, hissed up the pebbles on the foreshore and disgorged a band of men who pelted up the bank in a straggle.

Running to get between us and the church.

I stopped, legs aching, leaning one hand against a fallen marble pillar. No use in trying to race. Thirty heartbeats and they had us out-manoeuvred.

Orazi and Saverico and Tottola dropped back, swords out, yelling orders to the other men-at-arms – who spread far enough apart that their line would block attackers without bringing them close enough to cut each other.

The lessons of the Sanguerra sergeant-at-arms came back to me. *If a sword falls, I will pick it up.* Some acts stay bred into the muscle and bone. Even if that muscle is cramping so that the watercoloured late afternoon whites out into encompassing pain.

There will be swords falling, I thought grimly, counting the men now spreading out in a loose line before the church. Blocking us from refuge.

Thirty, at least. And we are, what, ten? A dozen with Neferet and I.

I suspected the men had known who they followed and how we were guarded: three against one are the preferred odds for beginning battle. If four against, or five to one, are impossible.

'All right.' Orazi's voice lifted a little. 'Here's what we're going to do. Vazev, Tottola, Saverico; you're going to feint like you're trying to break through to the church. The rest of you, we'll cut down to the beach and take *their* boat.'

I all but choked. I saw grins among his soldiers, too.

Orazi pulled the falchion from Attila's belt while the German furiously racked his crossbow, and pushed the sword's hilt at me. 'You can use a weapon.'

The weight of the blade-heavy cleaver pulled against my wrist.

He barked at Neferet. 'You?'

Even with the murderers closing in, she looked affronted at the insinuation that she might not be a woman. 'Give me a knife.'

Someone had a heavy, single-edged dagger with a bollock-hilt in ivory and brass, a souvenir of the Frankish Crusades, and a hand appeared and shoved it at the Alexandrine. I suspected whoever offered that particular weapon was entirely aware of why Frankish men wear it at their crotch, scabbard pointing down, the jutting two-lobed hilt blatant in its symbolism.

Neferet took the dagger, and I had a moment to look at each of the faces I now knew by name; to realise *they may end here, and so may I,* and to feel a burning fierce rush of fear and anger.

'I can't run.' I looked at Orazi. 'I'll move as fast as I can.'

There was a glimmer of contempt in his gaze, that I recognised as *Not a proper man,* before it vanished. The worst of it was that it was kind. Sympathetic.

'If it comes to it, we'll carry you.' His hand shot out and closed like a vice on my elbow, crushing muscle and nerve against bone, holding me bodily upright, ignoring my wet skirts. He abruptly glanced up the slope. '*Shit.* We've left this too late!'

The silhouettes of shoulders bobbed as armed men jogged down the slope from the church. Towards us. Attila let a bolt loose. Judging the range.

We shouldn't see silhouettes, I thought numbly.

The light's wrong!

The other half of the church's huge oak door banged open, and the light brightened still further from candles within.

A throng of men charged out of the church, and piled into the back of our first attackers.

Tottola said, 'What the *fuck*?' in pure Visigoth Latin.

Neferet raised her dagger.

Orazi yelled with the voice of a brazen trumpet, '*A Honorius! A leone di Castiglia! All of you, follow me!*'

Pain twisted my womb. Twilight blurred my vision. Orders, shouts, cries: all went up from the scrum of men desperately fighting on the turf in front of the church. In the light from the open door, I saw one man trip back over a half-buried Roman statue of a lion's head.

A sword caught the last true daylight, cold and blue. The man wielding it pushed it into the fallen man's throat, just into the soft part under the chin.

A hand went under my arms from either side.

My toes hit the earth. I tried to move enough to run, even to walk, but the two Germans Attila and Tottola lifted me higher and ran as if I were a sack of meal between them, sprinting down towards the beach. The pain in my shoulder-joints almost overwhelmed the pain between my hips.

'*Fuck.*' Orazi swung around.

My feet hit the sand by the lagoon. I staggered, taking my own weight on my feet again.

I smelled pitch burning. The boat the men had arrived in sent up flames too fierce to come from an accidental torch-fire. Coughing rasped the tender inside of my throat, and filled my eyes with water. *Our last chance, gone!*

The contraction buckled my knees.

Limp, I slid down through Attila and Tottola's grasp. Instinct wanted me up and pacing, but I couldn't force myself to my feet. Could only think *Pain, Jesu!*, as the waves of it bit down on me, burning into the pit of my belly.

On my knees on the fine sand and shells, I stared back at the ancient round roof of the monastery. Below that perfect curve, torch-light poured out of the doors, and fell like honey.

It fell on grass turned black by twilight, fell glistening on spreading blood, shone impartially on men huddled dead, and men shrieking and sobbing at mutilation and amputation, and men fighting who trampled over them all.

Pain made me weak-stomached. I vomited over the beach and my skirts, wet strings of mucus dependent from my fingers.

With so much death, I should think of the life I'm carrying under my heart, that I'm to give birth to. Except that it's never stirred, and the birth will kill me as dead as these men.

Five men ran shouting towards us, swords in hand.

Attila, crossbow racked again, shot the first one through the stomach.

The unwounded men skidded on the wet ground, boot-soles locking in the clinging sand – stared with doubtful expressions, in the light of the burning boat – and turned around and ran, so fast it resembled the acts of clowns in the *commedia*.

Attila raised his voice over the sick grunts of the shot man.

'Bugger's not dead.' He looked over at me. 'Did you drop my falchion?'

There was vomit on my right hand. The reason the fingers of my left hand hurt so much was that they were locked by cramp around the hilt of his sword.

I looked at it mutely. Attila squatted down and began to gently move each finger from the leather-bound grip, pushing his fingertips into my muscles and knuckle-joints, surprisingly gently. The cramp eased away.

Orazi prompted the men-at-arms in front of us into a loose half-circle, their backs to the burning boat and facing the church. 'What they doing up there?'

'Dead, hurt, or run.' Vasez grunted. 'Far too many of 'em run. If they get their shit together and come back, we're fucked.'

'That's "we're fucked, *Sergeant*",' Orazi rasped, and got the expected rawly-tense ripple of laughter from all. He shook his head. 'Now if we had *one* fucking boat in *one* fucking piece—'

A voice spoke up out of the twilight.

'There's a boat. Hidden thirty yards south. In the stand of willow.'

A convulsion pulled at my womb. The hairs on my neck shivered. *I have never heard a human voice sound like that in my life.*

After an appalling sound, the voice finished, 'But I don't know – when my men will come back for it.'

Orazi made a silent gesture, two soldiers picked up burning planks as makeshift torches, and he stepped forward with Saverico and Berenguer, all with naked blades in their hands. The small Armenian swore as his foot skidded.

The flickering light showed clearly what lay ten feet in front of me.

A man with fair hair and trimmed fair beard sprawled on the slope. He would have been flat on his back, but his face pointed directly towards me – because of the acanthus-flower capital of the fallen pillar behind him, propping up his head. A dark smear marked the marble. *Skull smashed?* I wondered, and then—

This is the man Attila's bolt hit.

I met the shining, too-bright eyes in his wet grey face.

I had not considered the kinetic force of a crossbow bolt, though I could tell you that of the stones from a trebuchet.

Chunks of bone scattered around him, as if his pelvic bone had not merely been pierced, but exploded. I thought at first the debris was stone, rubble, where the bolt had gone through him and struck the pillar. But the pieces showed white and scarlet, chopped like bones at a butcher's stall.

It was too cold to smell more than the throat-closing thickness of blood. Torn chunks shone, glistening like a display. His intestines bulged out under his ribs on one side; the same side that a leg lay motionless beside him.

It is his own leg, I realised. I had thought it could not be, because it lay in an impossible position. But it was not connected to his body. The rounded knob of a hip-bone glistened, exposed in the dim light.

Movement caught my eye – blood, bubbling up through the grass like water from a spring.

He can have only moments more—

'Ilario.'

The man's eyes caught the light of makeshift torches. He stared directly at me. His voice was numbed, and polite.

'Ilario ... '

It felt as nightmares do: frozen, implacable.

I pushed myself forward on hands and knees, no man breaking his own shock to help me. Wet skirts rucked under me. I stopped, crouched, a yard from that appalling face, and stench of shit.

He moved nothing but his eyes and his mouth. 'You. Ilario.'

'Yes.'

The fair hair and the breadth of his shoulders gave him something of a resemblance to Videric. I might have wished just this on Videric.

I spat out sour liquid. 'You were trying to kill me!'

He actually smiled.

If I prayed, it was to Rekhmire''s Eight. I want only a small miracle. Let him stay numb with shock. Let him feel nothing of what's been done to him.

Attila bent down, his mail sleeve flashing in the twilight, and stuffed a bundled-up mass of rags into the man's groin. The German's hand closed over the injured man's shoulder, and I saw the line of his back tense with the pressure he put into blocking the artery.

The dying man whispered, 'I stopped them killing you.'

The men who came running out of the church.

Attacking those who attacked us.

Led by this man?

His eyes showed pale. I saw the black gauze rag knotted around his neck. Men from under the Penitence often bandage their eyes when they first travel in lands outside the Darkness, because of the intense sunlight.

Under the mess of blood, his drenched clothing was Carthaginian.

He spoke again. *'Take the boat.'*

There are an unknown number of armed men in the dark winter twilight of Torcello. This man's. Videric's paid criminals. No man knowing who his enemy or friend is. Yes, we need the boat; we need to leave—

I bit back a groan as my belly contracted. It will be a ghost of pain beside his. I can control it.

I blurted, 'We can't just leave you here!'

By the burning spar's light, as Saverico held it lower, I could see that the man's eyebrows were blond, too. His lashes a dark sand colour. Laughter-lines on his face now cut too deep, in the intensity of agony.

'I was to take you to Carthage.' His voice faded to thread-thin. 'Your Alexandrine spy. Tell him he succeeded. All the way to Florence. And then I hit the ghetto walls ... Your Etruscan wife – is lovely.'

Saverico all but dropped the makeshift torch; Orazi swore. Fear turned my guts liquid. 'Have you hurt her?'

'Not even – speak to her. They don't let New Races in.' His eyes glistened. 'It took me too long to realise you ... Then, here ... Go ... so I know you live.'

I was to take you to Carthage. Kidnap me; my guess was correct.

Coming to Torcello with so few soldiers – I didn't realise how many people would find that irresistible bait.

Orazi gripped my shoulder. 'We're going.'

'What about him!'

He gave the Carthaginian a professional glance. Speaking directly to him, Orazi said, 'You can live two or three hours – but you probably don't want to. Want one of my lads to help?'

Attila shifted, where he gripped the man, but looked determined.

The Carthaginian agent looked as if he attempted to shake his head. An odd shudder went through him.

'No.' There was no resonance in his voice. 'You never know – what will happen.'

Orazi's expression was clear in the light of the burning boat. If he'd spoken, he clearly would have said he knew precisely what will happen. The numbness wears off and you die screaming.

'Every man should have his choice.' Orazi dusted his knees and got up, stooped to grab under my arm, and I gripped the hard edges of his brigandine as he pulled me onto my feet and I towered over him.

He jerked his head at Attila. 'Up.' Orazi widened his tone to include the rest. 'Find these fucking willow trees! Find the boat!'

Attila stood up, his arms soaked red beyond the elbows. I looked down. The Carthaginian agent paused, I thought, to gather his strength before speaking.

His face was utterly still. His chest didn't move.

His eyelids drifted down a little, leaving only a curved line of white visible.

The welling wetness at his hips no longer attracted the eye with its movement.

There must have been some moisture rising from the hot shining tissue, distinct in the cold air. It was gone now, all his exposed viscera dull. His ribs had barely moved in the shallow breathing of shock; now they did not move at all. My eye insisted that the rise and fall of his chest continued; my ear, that I could detect the hiss of his breath. *All illusion.*

There is no lack of motion, no silence, that is like death.

'Just as well.' Orazi jerked his head to call Tottola in on the other side of me. 'I would have had to tell somebody to do it. Couldn't have him telling those other fuckers where we've gone.'

He sounded faintly apologetic. I identified what else was in his tone after a moment. Gratitude.

Because this man attacked for his own reasons, to abduct me – but he kept us all alive. He must have secreted his men in the church crypt. And without that attack in the rear of Videric's other agents . . .

I crested another burn of the pain, and wondered if his sacrifice was useless.

'He may have papers.' It occurred to me in Rekhmire''s voice.

Evidently this was not unusual to Orazi in my father's service. He nodded, and gave Fulka brief instructions.

'He's painstaking,' Orazi said aloud. 'If there's anything, he'll find it. Are you all right?'

'It – hurts a little.' I couldn't decide if the surges came more frequently now.

Neferet jogged back, skirts held up, large bare feet muddy where she had kicked off her shoes to run in the winter mud. Fire and flame shone back from her black hair.

'There *is* a boat! We found it!'

'Thank Christ for that!' I looked wanly at her as another pang went through me. 'I don't want to give birth on this damned island!'

Neferet's eyes rounded, as if she hadn't realised until now. 'You're two months early!'

'I know!'

The death of the Carthaginian agent swept over me with an absolute horror. He had known what had happened to him; he knew what *was* happening as he died. But the knowledge had not helped him. His heart is cool and still in his chest even now.

Every word I had ever heard or read, between the Penitence and

Rome and the Most Serene city; every warning from Rekhmire' or physicians or Neferet's tame Green priest that she had brought into the Alexandrine House – all of it closed down on me like the metal jaws of a trap.

My body *will* do this. No matter what I want, or what I do. My body will labour and try for birth, and if common opinion's right, in a few hours I'll find out what the Carthaginian now knows.

The Carthaginian, and whoever else of these men lies back there in the darkness, not wounded, not hurt, not 'in danger, but may heal' – *dead*. Dead, and there has never been any appeal against it.

Orazi gave a sharp nod, and Tottola and Attila linked hands and wrists and scooped my body up between them, carrying me out to the boat. Neferet splashed heedlessly through the rippling water and climbed into the bows, so that she could help me in, and seat me among cushions and half a dozen cloaks on the stern bench.

Saverico wrapped a blanket around my shoulders; he shook as badly as I. He took up one of the oars and smiled – or I assume his grimace was intended to be a reassuring smile.

'You did well,' I said aloud – startled, because I am not the person who knows how to encourage others. 'You've known Honorius longer than I have – but I know he'll be pleased with what you did here. All of you.'

Orazi's callused hand closed briefly on my shoulder as he scrambled forward in the boat, past me.

'Which is *why*,' he said generally and aloud, 'you idle buggers are going to row like *fuck*! Because you all know what the Lion's going to be like if we lose his son-daughter now . . . '

It was a reminder of warmth, more than the thing itself, but I saw Attila wryly grinning, and Vasev reach enthusiastically for his oar. The Carthaginian agent's boat had been intended for three or four lances of men, and what is heavy enough to carry thirty is a bitch for ten or a dozen to row.

We have no dead or wounded, I realised, breathless with relief, as the last man-at-arms shoved the boat into deeper water and scrambled in. Brushwood burned as makeshift torches, winter-dry gorse popping and crackling, and smelling acrid.

My stomach turned.

The child didn't quicken – and it's been barely six months—

I must have said at least the last words aloud. Neferet corrected me: 'Seven.'

I tried to count up the time lapsed since Carthage, and doubled forward again, lost in a red haze.

If there's a time for womanly fainting, I reflected, this would be it.

The birthing pangs had the contrary effect of making me wide awake.

Conscious for every lift and fall of the oars, every spatter of cold water coming inboard as we were rowed past the cypress island, past the merchant ships, and after what felt like aeons, past the Arsenale, and towards the Piazza San Marco. The last light in the west showed silhouettes of Venice's roofs and funnel-shaped chimneys, black against the sky.

Neferet told me to count breaths between the pains.

I used what vocabulary I remembered from being trained as a knight in Rodrigo's court. No man has quite such a hand with an insult as a sergeant at arms.

'Not long,' Neferet said. And, 'Not long now,' Sergeant Orazi said, as the boat rowed what felt like infinitesimally slowly up the Canal Grande, and entered the side canals of Dorsodura.

Saverico began, 'Not lo—', and cut himself off in mid-word, at least giving me a smile as he did it.

The boat grated against the side of our campo, and Neferet leaped ashore in the dark like an Alexandrine eunuch, not a Venetian lady.

16

I could hear her screaming for assistance even as Honorius pelted out of the iron gate, and knelt down to help me from the wide stern bench. Between the cold, and stiffening against the pain, I could barely manage to stand on feet that were like blocks of wood. I flinched against the light of the soldiers' torches; held onto my father as he supported me in through the bare garden and oak door.

'Call the midwife!' Honorius bellowed at one of the ensigns, who left at a run.

'And Bariş!' Rekhmire', clinging to his crutch and the door-frame, shuffled with difficulty backwards into the hall. 'Go to the Janissary captain's lodgings. I've paid a retainer fee; Bariş will come! Ilario, you should do well enough, between the Turk and a midwife.'

The warmth of the Alexandrine House made me shudder after the night's biting chill. My cloak and sleeves glistened, sticky with half-dried blood. The Egyptian shifted his weight onto one crutch, and seized my shoulder with the other. I was used enough to obeying him as his slave that I inadvertently closed my mouth on what I had been going to say.

'Ilario. Whether the child is coming too soon or not – *you* will do well enough.'

His tone was firm and confident. If, as he met Honorius's gaze where my father supported me, it did not quite match what I saw in his eyes, I wouldn't question him. As full of fear as of pain, I only want to hear reassurance.

Neferet brought me to the room that was Rekhmire''s and mine, undoing every latch and lock in it, and let me sit on the larger wooden bed that was the Egyptian's, loosing the draperies. I sat with my back against the bolster, and gripped my bare ankles, and swore. The hearth fire spread heat; extra charcoal-braziers made the room warm – too warm, I might have thought, if, with the blissful sensation of heat soaking into my body, I could have considered anything as *too* warm.

The Alexandrine and her women changed me out of my waters-soiled clothing, into a voluminous light cotton shift. They undid my hair. It was not truly long enough to braid up, but they let it down in any case, and it hung around my face, turning into rat's-tails as I sweated.

'Where's Rekhmire'? Where's my father?'

Neferet frowned. 'Allowing men in—'

'Don't be ridiculous!' I barked the deep order. 'Do it!'

Honorius walked through the door with his hand on the shoulder of a Venetian: a rosy woman who looked somewhere between fifty and sixty. One of those midwives who has birthed thousands of babies and borne none. Rekhmire' followed, swinging himself adeptly on his crutches, in turn followed by the Turkish physician Bariş, who nodded a cheerful greeting.

Dual examinations stopped me from realising, until it was too late, that a green-robed and black-bearded Frankish priest also entered – Neferet's Father Azadanes. He and the Alexandrine women removed the chess-board from the table by the hearth, and set up a Frankish prayer-box.

'Son of a bitch!' Waves of pain rolled through me. The professional hands of Bariş and the Venetian midwife seemed unbearably clammy on my skin.

She and he stepped back to confer. Possibly to argue, from their lowered, intense tones.

'Closer together?' Rekhmire' eased himself carefully onto the side of the mattress, sitting with his crutches resting between his knees. 'Your pains, I mean.'

'Yes.' I gritted my teeth. 'No. I don't know. Perhaps. This will be over soon, won't it?'

'All I've read of first labours—'

'I can do without hearing that!'

The retired Captain-General of Castile sat down on the other side of the bed. 'How many of these people do you want here, Ilario? I can throw the rest out.'

My instinct is to hide in a dark place, like a beast wounded during a hunt. *Send them all away!*

I looked from him to Rekhmire', and back. 'You don't have to be here. You forget, I *do* know what men think about child-bed. If you wait outside, that won't distress me.'

The two of them exchanged a glance across the top of my head.

'I want to watch the midwife,' Rekhmire' observed in an undertone.

Honorius echoed: 'And the priest.'

They turned their heads in unison, looking at the dark, full-bearded man in the green cowl and habit, who was picking over the midwife's herb basket with her. Every so often the Venetian woman's gaze would stray towards me, but she never looked above the line of my now slightly swollen breasts.

The hours went past, as they do even when it seems impossible they will.

The warmth made me dizzy, I found.

'Could I have something to eat?'

The midwife immediately came forward. 'That can't be permitted.'

Bariş frowned. 'It's not uncommon, in my country.'

The argument went on long enough that, between the fierce pains of the contractions, my head sank back against the bolster, and I found myself all but falling asleep.

I closed my eyes until I could see only a line of the fire's golden flickering light. *My body should have expelled this in Rome.* Or before. To carry it so long, and now have it die – if it was ever alive . . .

Pain tires. I have found this from injuries, before now. I debated requesting my sketch-paper, to while away the time, but the warmth sank deeper into me, and I began to doze. It was not unpleasant, except where I would find myself riding up the crest of the pain, until it burst in a cramping wrench that felt as if it would tear my body open.

I did sleep a little. When I was next fairly awake, Rekhmire' had swapped to sitting on the other side of the bed, Honorius was deep in reminiscences of battlefield doctoring with Neferet's Father Azadanes, and the midwife was having what looked like a sulky argument with the Turk. I couldn't see Neferet. The clock's single hand showed it gone midnight.

'Eight hours . . . !' I sat up, appalled.

Rekhmire' propped more bolsters under me. 'In the courts of the Pharaoh, women walk about for their birth. Neferet's gone looking to see if anyone has a birthing stool, if you wish to try it.'

'Walk!' I snorted, and then squinted across the room at the midwife. 'What's the argument there?'

'She wants to give herbs to hasten the birth on. Or to stop it, in case this isn't time.' The Egyptian curved a large hand and rested it on my abdomen. The touch felt reassuring. 'Physician Bariş says you've dropped down; it's time.'

Whether the child can survive this or not.

Or I.

'I just want this over! And in God's name get them to stop treating me like an invalid!' I pushed myself more upright in the bed. 'Maybe your "pacing" has something to be said for it!'

Rekhmire''s solemn face split in a grin. 'I'm told that, after my mother birthed me, she got up and cleaned the house from top to bottom. My father aided her. You're just such another as she.'

I smiled. The mental image came to me of what she would have been cleaning. I stopped smiling.

'Gah!' A jolt of pain made me grunt. 'Teach me more of the eight gods' names, will you? I think I may need to blaspheme very loudly before long.'

In the warmth of the panelled dark room, Rekhmire' amused me by teaching me how one properly addresses all four duads of the Hermopolitan Ogdoad, under all circumstances, and Honorius went irritably in and out of the door until the midwife tried to banish him. He clearly had no intention of obeying, and took one of the clay lamps to the embrasure of the oriel window, where he sat and stared out at the Venetian night.

The Green priest's prayer-box was somewhat like Rekhmire''s own, but this one had in it a model of Christus Viridianus's mother at the foot of the Leafless Tree, the blood of the birthing red between her thighs, and the Eagle above and the Boar beside her. Father Azadanes set the female doll's legs wide apart. It seemed oddly obscene, even if she was wearing a minutely-sewn silk birthing robe. (Which I don't for one moment suppose the Mother of God had with her in the German forests.)

'It's – the superstition of sympathy—' Pain made me slow with words. 'That like can affect like. Rekhmire'—'

He shot a glance up at me from where he bent over, pressing his fingers into his healing knee. 'Less trouble to let him pray than to throw him out and have Neferet bellowing at us.'

'You are sure he's safe? Nothing to do with Videric?'

The Egyptian shook his head. 'Nothing. But if it eases your mind, Honorius will call the soldiers back. You couldn't be safer.'

'Draw the curtains.' I pointed up at the tester bed curtains, and realised my hand shook. *The enemy is not outside this bed, not tonight.* 'I don't think anything's going to happen for a while.'

I was accurate, and I could wish not to have been.

The hours of darkness went by. For some reason I expected to pass the child's dead flesh in the small hours of three or four in the morning, but all that happened was that the long cramps continued. Indeed, they began to lessen in frequency. I saw, between the curtains, Rekhmire' and the midwife speaking to one another. I was too tired to wonder what they said.

The slow grey light of pre-dawn illuminated in the sky.

Coal braziers burned black and scarlet, their scent contending with the winter air. I could not tell whether I was warm or cold. Neferet's insistence on having the shutters undone meant I could lay back in bed and look at the sky.

There is nothing left to do.

The long, slow, rolling waves of pain lifted me up, dropped me down, ebbed away, and slowly gathered again. It might have been a tide. I felt heat between my legs, and the midwife took soaked cloths away, but there was nothing else. When her fingers felt my belly again, she set her mouth into a hard and inexpressive line.

Bariş frowned, also, but at her.

Back at Federico's estate, much younger, I would sometimes aid with the lambing or the calving. It always frightened me to see beasts with bodies so different to my own. The weatherbeaten farm slaves handled their ewes and cattle much as the midwife offered to handle me, grease-slicked fingers poised to slide up the birth canal.

If her fingers were hesitant, I realised, it was because of the hermaphrodite organs she found when she raised my linen gown.

The Turkish physician Bariş caught my gaze and came over, shifting a bunch of cloth to cover my penis, and steered the midwife away with a hand to her elbow. I noted that this led to him sending Balaban for more water, and washing, even though the last of the dead Carthaginian agent's blood was long gone from my cuffs and his own hands.

'Ilario?'

Honorius's voice, I realised.

I had slid down the bolster. Trying to hitch myself back up, I caught a stench of human scent released by the movement. Sweat. Rank sweat. And blood of my own.

The pain didn't stop. I tried to concentrate on his words. 'Are they arguing *again?*'

Honorius smoothed black strands of hair from my eyes and forehead. 'You may have to choose. The midwife can give you herbs to bring on the birthing. But that will endanger the child, if . . . '

'If it isn't already dead?'

He held a wooden water-bowl to my mouth, and I sipped gratefully. 'I don't think it can ever have been alive. I've felt nothing.'

The herbs tasted bitter.

They did no good.

I lived through every hour between dawn and early afternoon, but have no great wish to recall them. They say the pain of child-bed is forgotten. This is a lie.

At one point, when the midwife and Neferet and Bariş and the priest were all screaming at each other – and I was too breathless to scream any more – I reached down, but could feel nothing different between my legs. It all stayed resolutely in my belly.

The memory of lambing returned. Dizzy, I wondered if they would try to pull the infant out bodily, which would fail as that always does, and if I would look white and blue and greasy, as dead ewes do when they die with their litter still in the womb.

'Remind me to have a word with your foster father.'

Honorius's voice sounded rusty and grim. I opened my eyes, realising I must have muttered aloud.

'Lambing,' Honorius added, with revulsion that sat oddly on a veteran of battlefields.

'Not my fault!' The midwife's voice rose self-righteously high. 'How can I help a monster give birth!'

Honorius's weight left the bed in a rush. By the time I had myself as upright as I could manage – leaning on my elbows – I glimpsed him hauling the woman out through the door. It slammed. Voices rose from the hall.

'"Monster".' I shrugged. 'She's not wrong.'

Neferet's Frankish priest, Father Azadanes, peered myopically at me from where he stood on the other side of the bed. 'Madonna Ilario, shall you and I pray for this child? And for you?'

I had not sufficient concentration to be rude to him. 'If you wish.'

For all the pain, I felt as if I were being kept from a job I badly needed to do – manual work, like a slave in a mine or on a farm. I could feel it in every sinew, every muscle: *I need to get up* now *and work!*

Pain rushed through me, hard enough that I crested it yelling, as I was taught to yell on the impact of my sword or axe in knightly training. Once: once more: once again—

'Nothing!' I snarled, frustrated. Looking up at Honorius and Rekhmire', I asked, 'What's Physician Bariş's advice?'

Honorius was white to his mouth. 'That he should act as a surgeon.'

I think I have known since Rome that it would come to this.

I saw Father Azadanes praying by the hearth.

'I don't care what the Church says about the pains of sinful Eve in child-bed . . . If you cut me open, I want poppy.'

Pain and poppy together made me hallucinate a Carnival mask on Bariş's face. The long-beaked leather mask of the Plague Doctor, in lapidary detail. If I could only see so well when I draw with a silver rod . . .

I must have struggled to get out of the bed. Hands pushed me down. I stared; felt myself writhing, sweating—

Honorius held my right shoulder in an immovable grip; nothing to suggest him fifty years old. Decades of soldiering have worn him to rawhide strength. Rekhmire''s hands pressed less heavily down on my left arm, where he sat on the bed, and I felt it when his own pain made him shift.

Each time the poppy took hold, I dropped into intricate, lengthy, narrative dreams, that took years to pass in my mind, and only moments by the burning-down of the marked candles.

Bariş set up a sheet that draped my knees.

I almost laughed out loud. I have *no* desire to see what's going on! And, for the others here – what do they not already know about me?

Another rolling wave of pain made me grunt, biting down until I drew blood from my lip; the small pain lost in the arid, scraping, swollen agony in my womb.

The poppy made clear in my mind the paper on which I drew Rekhmire''s flayed knee. Every fibre, tendon, shard of bone; and rivulet of blood among the so-fine hairs on his skin. There is no one present who can draw me. And no one who can draw these images from my mind.

Time slipped, as it does in high fever or pain; I caught myself cursing, and then lost interest and energy in it. The Frankish priest stood by the physician's shoulder, I saw, but I was not sure that Bariş knew it. All his attention fixed on something below my line of sight.

Below the raised flax-linen sheet – spattered with perfect ovals of blood.

I opened my mouth to ask how he did, and a constricting pain shattered my pelvic bones, and tumbled me into a state where time didn't exist.

Father Azadanes' bushy black beard moved. Anger boiled through me.

'No prayers!' *I want no final rites from a Frankish priest! I don't want the rites at all—*

Bariş straightened up, wiping a bloody hand across his forehead. His dark skin smeared brilliant red in the sunlight that shone in through the window. *Is it afternoon? Another morning?* I did not know.

The Turkish Janissary's eyes narrowed. He didn't look down at me, but at the two men either side of me. 'If it comes to a choice, which shall I save? The baby or the – mother?'

Honorius and Rekhmire' spoke together, both in the same breath:

'The mother!'

I saw Honorius give the Egyptian a look, to which Rekhmire' remained oblivious.

The mother. A faint feeling grew in me that I ought to protest that. I ought.

The obligation seemed no more and no less than that: obligation.

A dribble of water ran down my forehead, narrowly avoiding running into my eyes. The stench of some herb or other startled me into jerking my head back against the bolster. The cuff of a green habit brushed my chin as the hand drew back. Azadanes' deep bass rumbled, 'Blessed mother, blessed infant, *Mater dolorosa, Sancta Mater—*'

I growled a protest, and a grinding pain sliced at my body; took me enough by surprise that I could only reach up and grab wildly – catching my father's arm, and Rekhmire''s shoulder – and grunt as something was lifted out of the cavity of my body.

The physicality of the sensation so amazed me that I had no memory of the physician's actions after that. Something seemed flaccid; moved. The Janissary physician reached down, I speculated, *How many times on campaign does he deal with childbirth!*, and there was a great gush. His hands as he lifted them were vermilion.

'Gahh!' I said, or thought I said.

Honorius chuckled and ruffled at my hair.

Rekhmire' squeezed my fingers.

I snarled weakly, 'I'll never lie with any man again! And if I ever see Marcomir, I'll *geld* him!'

A face leaned into my field of view. Neferet's reddish-tan profile. She peered down behind the sheet, where I couldn't see, and then looked back at me. 'Ilaria, shall I have Father Azadanes also pray to remove those vestigial organs you don't need?'

'*No!*'

Someone yanked Neferet aside. *Rekhmire'*, I thought; since I could no longer feel the warmth of a body on that side of me. Chill struck on the other side, too, as Honorius leaned away from me, intently staring at something.

'Father . . . '

His lean, muscled frame sat back. His hands were cupped.

It must be something to do with me, I thought, or he would not be offering it. Am I to say farewell to my dead child? My chest was hollow, blown up suddenly with a grief that choked me.

'*Take* her!' Honorius whispered.

But I saw nothing, felt nothing!

I looked into Honorius's cupped hands. She was tiny. It took the breath out of me with a fierce tug, how very small she was. A miniature screwed-up face, pink and bloody and greyish-white, as if she had been lightly rubbed over with clay. I touched my thumb-tip to her face, before I knew I would do it.

Her small and perfect lips reflexively moved.

'It's alive!' I wondered instantly how long this would last.

'Look,' Honorius breathed.

The scrunched blue-purple-and-red face wrinkled itself up further under my gaze. She yawped, yawned, and settled into an undramatic breathy grizzle. A person, there before me.

'She's *alive*.' I put my hand out again, touching my fingers to her slick greasy-grey belly, where the swollen cord still lay. '*I'm* alive. What—?'

She lay on Honorius's brown hand, barely long enough to cover him from wrist to fingertip. If she weighed two Frankish pounds I would be surprised.

The priest's deep voice rumbled at my shoulder. 'Thanks be to God Himself for this miracle!'

Bariş muttered something under his breath in Turkish. I didn't think it was devout. My body moved with the tug and rip of stitches being put into my skin, but the poppy kept the pain at a distance, even though I felt it.

I let him move my hands when he came to tidy up the birth-cord. I could not stop looking.

'She can't live, surely?' I measured my thumb against her minuscule hand, and jolted with shock as her fingers momentarily closed on me. 'It's too soon. She wasn't due for two months.'

Honorius's hand began to shake: he steadied it by gripping his wrist with his other hand.

'Your midwife keeps saying "seven-month babies live all the time"!'
His voice was ragged, and his eyes ran over with sudden bright water.

The sheet shifted. I glimpsed a dark scarlet mess in the bed, that was either afterbirth or my inner organs. I thought I would feel considerably less well if it were the latter.

'She has black hair. Like mine.'

'The first hair is always black.' Rekhmire''s weight came down on the mattress, pressing against my ribs. He sat holding a clean cloth in his hands, dampened with Balaban's tepid water, and as Honorius continued to support her, the Egyptian began very delicately to clean the new-born.

He glanced at me. 'Do you want to do this?'

'It's . . . She's so *small*!' Her arm, as he lifted it to wipe the skin, was no bigger around than my finger.

Bariş reached over with a dry cloth, tucking it around the minute body. He scooped her from Honorius's callused palm, and put her against my chest. 'Sorry, madonna, it's a girl.'

I did not note the apology.

'Are you sure?' I stared down. It took no more than one of my hands to keep the new-born weight tucked against the warmth of my naked skin, on the slope of my breast. '*Are you sure?*'

'Of course. Ah.' Bariş nodded.

With Rekhmire''s help, and Honorius's hindrance, the Janissary doctor re-examined the child's nether end. I thought about long campaigns, and soldiers' wives and whores.

I do not care if the child is female or male: only let her not be like me!

'Girl.' The physician tucked the cloth napkin back, his fingers extraordinarily gentle. 'Very small. There is sometimes trouble with small and—' He tapped his chest. 'The breath?'

Fascinated, I nodded, and rubbed the very tip of my finger over her lower lip. '*Look* at her.'

The little mouth made a sucking noise.

Panic washed me hot and cold in one second. I saw in my mind the Carthaginian agent: how his chest stopped moving, how breath just – ceased.

'We have to find it a tit to feed from! We have to put it to one; it'll die!'

Bariş smiled at me. 'What? No. She doesn't need to eat until she shows she wants to. You think you won't be able to feed her?'

Seizing authority, he sent the priest out of the room, and directed Honorius and Rekhmire' to the fireside, since they wouldn't go further from me. Bariş set himself to examine my small breasts that, while painful, were no larger than before the pregnancy.

'Sometimes milk, this takes time coming in,' Bariş said finally, frowning. 'I can find you a wet-nurse? If you haven't one?'

Numbly, I nodded assent. The damp, warm weight in my palm

wriggled faintly – *so small!* – and settled her head back against my useless breast.

As Physician Bariş began to speak to Honorius about wet-nurses, Rekhmire' limped over from the room's door, propped himself upright on his crutches, and pulled the bed drapes fully back.

The child in my hand wailed faintly, rolling her head away from the bright day. Hastily, I shaded her with the fingers of my other hand.

Rekhmire''s brows dipped down.

'I know,' I said, dizzy with wonder. 'The chances of her living are . . . If she makes two months, I'll name her.'

Her hair was soft and dry now under my thumb, and I smoothed it down.

Rekhmire''s frown didn't lift. 'Azadanes wants to go through some Frankish Christian rite. To clean her soul?'

That would have been his business at the door, I realised. Throwing the Frankish priest out.

I shook my head, bemused. 'How can she have done anything wrong yet? An hour ago, she wasn't *here*.'

'Don't ask a man who worships the Eight . . . '

The small lashes on her cheek were perfect. As they lifted, I saw she had deep blue baby's eyes. *If she lives, they might be any colour.*

'You hold her, Rekhmire'.' I scooped both hands about her, supporting every part, waiting until the Egyptian settled himself on the bed. I placed her gently in Rekhmire''s large hands.

'It's strange.' I couldn't take my gaze from her. 'She never moved inside me. I never felt I was with child. She wasn't born to me in the normal way. She . . . Is she really from me?'

Rekhmire' smiled. He stroked his fingertip in her tiny lined palm. Her fingers could not grasp all his finger's circumference, but I saw her try.

'No one else here was with child. The evidence suggests she's from your womb. Or was that howling merely to entertain us?'

'I can't feed her.'

'You don't know that yet.'

'I know.' My conviction was irrational but strong. I took her back into the crook of my arm. 'See if they have a wet-nurse yet? Or at least if the kitchens would have any goat's or cow's milk?'

The door openly, briskly; I saw every man in the room startle. Ensign Viscardo's dark face made me sigh in relief. We are all as tight as an overwound harp-string here—

'What?' Honorius snapped, ferocious at an interruption.

Viscardo's eyes showed wide.

'Sir – it's Ilario's family!'

My heart physically jerked in my chest.

Which family?

The minuscule new-born let out a breath of a wail.

Viscardo's eyes opened wider, seeing me; he suddenly grinned like a boy, and as abruptly collected himself – although his gaze kept sliding sideways to the new-born child.

'Sir, it's Signor Federico, and his wife, and his daughters. They're here! They heard about the labour. They want to see Messer Ilario!'

Honorius looked completely blank.

Venetian servants, I thought. Since here it isn't slaves. The rumour-mill grinds just as efficiently. Federico and Valdamerca . . .

An ominous set of rising voices came from downstairs.

I pushed the sweat-darkened sheets into a nest on my chest, and settled the new-born where she could feel my heat and heartbeat. I looked up at Honorius and Rekhmire'.

'Can I have these sheets changed? Then, let them in.'

Viscardo nodded acknowledgement, barely waiting for Honorius's signal, and ran out.

'Ilario,' Rekhmire' warned.

'They can see me and *go away*.' I snorted. 'I'll be asleep in a quarter-hour! I'm exhausted. But I know Federico – he won't go away until he does see me.'

Tired as I was, I made the shift to the Iberian of Taraconensis, speaking both to Honorius and Rekhmire'.

'You know he won't go! Federico has come here to find out whether or not he can send a message to – to my mother's husband . . . telling him that I'm dying or dead.'

17

Neferet's servants worked around me, replacing the dirty sheets with clean cool linen that soothed my skin. The child lay in a makeshift wooden cradle – in fact, originally a small oak linen-chest – by the fire, with both my father and the Egyptian blocking all access to her.

Reclining up against the bolsters, I found myself unable to settle. Without that steadily pinkening small figure under my eye, how can I believe in a baby's existence?

Poppy-extract kept my scurrying mind numbed, as well as my body. I barely heard the shuffle of feet outside, that I knew must be Honorius's men-at-arms moving into position.

As the door opened to let in Federico, the invisible child proved itself far from inaudible. She sent up a hunger-wail that made my throat thicken and my eyes prick with tears.

'Ilario!' Federico bustled up to the foot of the bed, gesturing for the others with him to stand back.

I saw Valdamerca's long-nosed equine features at the back of the group; she caught my eye and gave me a grim smile. Reinalda's look was softer. She stood with her sister, her arm linked through Sunilda's, and had the same look as her mother. *Welcome to the sisterhood.*

That's right, I thought groggily. Carrasco told me. Reinalda married, a year back; she has a baby. Sunilda, no, she's not . . .

Bariş's voice came from the far side of the bed. 'Don't trouble her long, sir. I've given her a drink for the pain, and she'll sleep now.'

Federico waved an impatient hand. He frowned a little, looking down at me.

'If I'd known . . . ' he began slowly.

'If you'd known I could be put to stud,' I said acerbically, 'you would have included that when you sold me to King Rodrigo. Right?'

'You do me very ill.' He made a gesture, as if he would reach out to me, but didn't complete it.

'Signor Federico.' Honorius's brusque tones came from the hearth. He interrupted a minute or two before I had told him he should, but I was grateful all the same.

Jesu! I can't breathe!

With the servants of Aldra Federico, and the retinue attending

Valdamerca and her daughters, and Neferet's women acting as chaper-
ones, as well as at least four of Honorius's soldiers, armed in mail, and
lining the walls, I found the room very much too crowded. Polite words
were spoken, the dozen or so people in the room congregating at the foot
of my bed, and then moving towards the cradle. I wondered if I could
pull the bed-curtains and fall asleep without anyone noticing.

As I thought of it, a figure stepped alongside the bed, running the
curtain soundlessly along and blocking off much of the view of the rest of
the room.

Sunlight shone in on Ramiro Carrasco's black curls. He gave me a
strained smile, reached for one of the loose pillows that lay on the bed,
and pushed it down over my face.

18

Ramiro Carrasco has not seen me as a man!

It was the only thought in my head.

I couldn't breathe. His hands pressed cloth and a bulk of goose-down feathers into my mouth and nose. My vision blacked into sparkles.

My chest hurt as I tried and failed to pull in air.

It can happen just this easily! – because people are busy for a few minutes looking at the baby, because these curtains are drawn—

'Ilario's heart stopped.' Even Physician Bariş will say so. The labour of having the baby. Too much for a hermaphrodite body. Even Rekhmire' will believe it. The midwife will confirm it. Ramiro Carrasco has nothing to do now but wait until my face is blue and then scream out an alarm that I'm not breathing—

And Ramiro Carrasco has never seen me dressed as a man.

The pillow blinded me towards the left field of my vision, but left a sliver of my right eye clear. Carrasco stared down at me, his expression curiously desperate as he bore down with his full weight.

I had time to think *Shouldn't I be the desperate one?* and ceased to claw at the pillow, and at his rock-hard muscles.

I let my arm fall out loosely to the side, over the edge of the bed.

Hard ceramic clipped the tips of my fingers.

My heart thudded hard enough to take the remaining air out of my lungs. My ribs ached with trying to breathe. And— Yes, this is where I saw one of the servants set down a water-jug. A brown-glazed pint jug, with a narrow neck, and two moulded loops for lifting.

My head throbbed under the pressure of his hands. I slid my fingers through the glazed loops at the jug's neck, gripped tightly, and locked my elbow. The weight pulling on tendon and muscle told me it was still completely full.

Lifting pottery and the weight of water together, barely able to see where I aimed past the pillow and his arm, I brought the jug round in a hard arc. And crashed it into the side of Ramiro Carrasco's head.

With all the muscular strength of an arm that, while it isn't male, isn't female either.

Pottery smashed. Water sprayed.

Pressure lifted up off my face.

For a moment I couldn't see – couldn't claw the pillow away from my nose and mouth—

A noise sounded to the side of me. A tremendous crash.

'*Ilario!*'

Clear air hissed into my lungs.

Rekhmire' stood looking down, pillow in his hand; there were the backs of four or five men behind him, low down, on the floor—

Kneeling *on* someone on the floor.

'Ilario!' A knee landed beside me on the other side of the bed; Honorius's lean and chilly hand felt roughly at my neck. Feeling for my heartbeat.

'I'm alive!' I gasped. Pain ached through my entire body. I hitched myself up on my elbows and gazed down past Rekhmire', at where Orazi and Viscardo and Saverico were kneeling on, and punching at, the slumped figure of Ramiro Carrasco de Luis.

'Don't kill him,' I added weakly. '*I* want to.'

Honorius gave out with a deep-bellied laugh, and ruffled my sweat-soaked hair. 'That's my son-daughter!'

'What—?' Federico stepped forward from the thunderstruck family group, boggling down at Carrasco. His shock looked genuine. '*What* did he . . . He can't have tried— There *must* be some mistake—!'

The door banged opened hard enough to bruise the wood panelling, Neferet and her midwife and priest piled into the room, together with those others of Honorius's men within earshot. Tottola and his brother between them completely blocked the doorway.

I felt tension infuse Honorius, through his hand on my scalp.

He looked across, caught Orazi's eye, nodded at Aldra Federico, and then at the door. 'Get them *out* of here!'

Federico blustered, Sunilda burst into tears, Reinalda threw her arms around her sister and led her out through the door. Valdamerca, tall enough to look Orazi in the eye, made a fist and punched at the sergeant's mail-covered chest as he and the two German men-at-arms bodily shoved all of my foster family out of the room.

The slamming two-inch-thick oak cut off Valdamerca's virulent complaints and protestations of innocence.

Still coughing and choking, I got out, 'I don't suppose they *did* know he'd do that!'

'They don't matter.' Honorius spoke with enough habitual authority that I didn't for the moment desire to question him. He beckoned with his free hand. 'Physician. Come and see to this! I want Ilario *thoroughly* checked.'

Rekhmire' stood back as Bariş bent over me.

I reached out one hand to the Egyptian, and one to Honorius on the other side, and squeezed both hard. 'The son of a bitch tried to *kill* me!'

Rekhmire''s severe face was grey, under the ruddy tone of his skin. 'We should not have let him lull us.'

Honorius turned back from confirming with the Turkish physician that, yes, I might have bruises, and yes, I had been constricted as to air, but in fact there was – as I wanted to shout – *nothing wrong with me!*

'Nothing that eighteen hours of labour doesn't put into the shade . . . ' I may have muttered that aloud.

Honorius pulled his hand-and-a-half sword half out of its scabbard, the noise muffled by the loud room. 'Finally. Finally, we don't have to worry about Carrasco any longer!'

Neferet, the Venetian midwife, Physician Bariş, and Father Azadanes all raised their voices, crowding around Honorius, impeding his sword-arm.

He ignored them, looking only at me.

I stared down off the edge of the bed, at Ramiro Carrasco de Luis sprawled supine on the floorboards.

Unconscious, by the trickle of blood staining his chin. Or perhaps he'd just bitten himself while mailed fists were punching him.

His face was bruised, bloody; his lashes fluttered a little and were still. I saw the pulse beating in his throat.

'You can't kill him while he's unconscious.' It was not a rational objection, but I could come up with no greater argument. My hands shook.

Trying to keep control of my voice, I added, 'Denounce him to the Council of Ten. Let them arrest him!'

For all I could see Neferet's face a strained grey, my bitterness spilled out:

'Put Carrasco in a Venetian dungeon! Let my noble stepfather Videric explain to Venice why his spy is in prison! Or let my damn foster father explain why his *secretary* just tried to kill his fosterchild!'

Rekhmire' had not let go of my hand; he must feel how I trembled. His own hand was not completely steady. The Egyptian looked down at me with a warm expression.

'That's my Ilario! Yes. Let's use this to cause as much trouble for the Aldra Videric as we can, shall we? And Aldra Federico, of course. Complaints, lawsuits, public gossip . . . '

By the time I rolled my head over on the bolster to look up at him, Honorius was reluctantly nodding. He shoved his sword into his red leather scabbard with the ease that only comes from long use.

'It's not a bad idea. But, Ilario, if you're hurt . . . If you just *want* me to do this . . . He's a dead man. I have enough influence here that I won't need to answer for it.'

Despite the storm of protests from the Venetians and the Alexandrine, I thought he was probably correct. Apart from anything else, the retired Captain-General of Castile and Leon is a friend of the successful mercenary general Carmagnola, whom the Venetian Council currently employs and won't wish upset.

Years in Rodrigo's court can teach many things.

I have a clear picture in my mind, in the hopes of later making a painting of it. Ramiro Carrasco's face as he held the stifling pillow over me. And his absolute and strange desperation.

'Don't kill Carrasco.' A sudden unannounced fear went through me, jagged as lightning. 'Is the baby— Did the *baby* die?'

That sent the crowd to the cradle.

I slumped back on the mattress, shutting my eyes. So small, born so much before its proper time . . . Likely she will have died when all this violence shattered the atmosphere of peace in the room. For one moment I was completely certain.

It – she – did not feel like my child. I could feel no love, no warmth, no attraction to her. A sheer wave of fear rushed through me; making my head feel as if it was swollen, and my vision black as grief.

'Here.' Honorius placed the carefully-wrapped warm bundle on my chest: it wriggled and thinly whined. 'She's here. She's just hungry.' A confused look went across his sun-burned features. 'I *think* she's hungry.'

His men looked amused, Rekhmire' gave him a look of sympathy, and the unspoken stare that commented 'Ignoramus!' came – I noted as I gazed around – from the midwife, Bariş the physician, the priest, and Neferet. I wondered at that last.

'I,' I said, 'don't know any more than you do.'

Rekhmire' gave a nod, and turned to speak to the midwife.

'Wet-nurse,' he said.

The men-at-arms dragged Ramiro Carrasco de Luis out by the heels of his boots, and I heard his head bang against every tread on the way down the stairs.

19

With a chair moved close to the window, and a blanket about me, I could avoid the worst of the draughts coming in around the cracked wood, and still gain a clear view of the blue sky.

Winter's heavy grey and sharp blue was softening, and the frost whitened the earth only in the early mornings and late evenings.

I kept the room warm for the baby, although the air outside in the middle of the day was temperate enough for me to cast off an over-robe.

While making my own way as far as the Riva was impossible, I heard from my father that ships from other ports already began to dock in the San Marco basin.

'Travel's becoming possible again.' Restless, I abandoned a sketch of my knife and plate – the elipse of the plate defeating me – going to lay on my bed that was now beside the hearth with the child's makeshift cradle. I watched Rekhmire' experimenting with a walking-staff taller than he. 'Messages. Men. We're not cut off. Or, soon won't be.'

The Egyptian finally settled on using just the one crutch, lodged under his right arm. He had abandoned the linen kilt of the Alexandrines for a tunic and trousers in the Turkish style. I suspected this was so that no man could look at his knee, now that the bandages were off it.

A clatter of rapid footsteps sounded. Rekhmire' shifted himself with difficulty to open the room door. The noise resolved itself into Neferet, wearing pattens that tracked mud down the passage past the bedroom. She gave a distracted wave of her hand, not stopping to speak, or pet the new-born.

'No news of Leon Battista,' I speculated.

'Still in the Doge's prison.' Rekhmire' thumped his crutch against the floorboards. 'As is your Ramiro Carrasco de Luis. A man I hope *rots* there.'

I felt no love for the baby – which convinced me I was the monster I had always assumed. A true mother would well up with love, knowing the child as her own.

If I felt anything, it was fear and wonder.

Amazement had me laying with her in the crook of my arm, tracing her perfectly-folded eyelids and dark lashes, and having my stomach jerk whenever her flailing hand intersected mine. I couldn't tell if her fingers closed of their own volition over me.

Fear made me watch like a patient falcon as her skin colour passed from blue-red to red to the normal shade – and panic when her feet stayed the peculiar blue-purple of the new-born. It took Bariş an afternoon to reassure me that this would change in several days, and I blushed at seeing the Turkish doctor after that, feeling a fool.

'I've been asked all questions!' Bariş gave me an aquiline smile as his fingers checked the red fontanelle patches on her skull. 'The fathers, they're the worst. "If it cries when it sees me, does that mean it's not mine?"'

I thought of asking him if he was ever asked that very question by mothers.

But that might lead to disquieting information about his previous Caesarian surgeries, and I had, if I was honest, no desire to know. I merely desired my burning belly to heal.

'She *doesn't* cry,' I said. 'Is she too weak?'

'Some of them don't.' He smiled down at her, lines creasing all his narrow face, and touched his finger to her perfect cheek. 'When she does, you'll be sorry you asked! Now, have I told you how to care for the birth-cord?'

Fear made me lay awake hour after dark hour in the night, waiting for her to wake, and Tottola or Saverico to bring up boiled cow's milk so that one of us might feed her with spoon and cup. After the first few days she turned her head repeatedly from the hired Venetian woman who had more milk than her own son could drink.

But she grows heavier on animal milk, I judged, weighing her in my two hands every day. And she did not have the stolid, lethargic look of those lambs that refuse to thrive. I wondered if I might judge her in the same way that one judges a beast, or whether humankind is different.

After five days, her birth-cord dropped off. It was the last of the landmarks Bariş had charged me to watch for: her bowels and bladder both proved themselves functional earlier, and I learned to pin cloth around her.

She was yellow for a few days, which the Turkish physician also dismissed as a cause for fear.

I felt fear of the darkness; fear of the cold winter nights with the damp blowing in off the lagoon; fear of every gossiping rumour of plague or fever. Her eyes moved under her eyelids as she dreamed. I wondered if she could dream of Torcello, and the sights and smells imprinted on me while she began her birth.

My time passed in small landmarks and the overhanging dread of death.

Days went by. I grew stronger. Neferet lost her womanly plumpness and grew gaunt with worry.

I knew Rekhmire', as well as Neferet, must be contacting all the men a book-buyer would know in this city – but Leon Battista was a son of the Alberti family, it seemed, and the Alberti family had been exiles in Venice these twenty years. If their accumulated interest couldn't move the Doge's mercy, I doubted two Alexandrines could.

Supine in bed, stitches healing, I studied Leon's treatise on vision as if some obscure sympathetic magic would ensure that the more attention I gave it, the more likely Leon Battista would have good fortune.

I blamed the Green priest for superstitious thoughts. Neferet's Father Azadanes claimed the baby's (and my) survival as his own Green Christ's miracle. I found the argument not persuasive.

'Sheer chance!' I said, when Rekhmire' had his prayer-box open, lighting incense to the eight gods within. 'Chance plays far too much of a part in the world for men to be easy thinking of it.'

Rekhmire' finished his ceremony with a bow of his head to the Eight, and clipped the box shut again.

'A man should always be polite . . .' He dusted incense from the front of his tunic and trousers, and used his crutch to cross the room, putting the prayer-box away in his oak chest. '. . . Especially to minor gods. The advantage of deities who control small things is that one need never worry about why evil and pain rule so much of this world – minor gods are obviously too weak to prevent it.' He hesitated. 'I don't know what the excuse of Father Azadanes' God is.'

I was inclined to smile at that, but very wryly. 'Heathen! Pagan. Atheist!'

Rekhmire' snorted. 'Make up your mind which!'

The tiny, warm, damp weight of the child on my chest became something I was used to, as I rested in the great bed in the Alexandrine house and regained my strength.

When I complained that I was strong enough, Rekhmire' invited me to move, and I discovered how badly the stitches knitting the walls of my womb could hurt.

I steered clear of Father Azadanes' company, weary as I was of hearing about his 'Green miracle', and how he attributed the baby's survival and mine to the Green Christ. It was difficult to avoid him, since he was much with Neferet.

Once, coming into a room more quietly than I realised, I overheard Neferet asking, 'But can't your God make *my* body mirror what my *ka* is?', and I backed out as silently as I'd come. Her – *his* – desperation hurt me.

The more so because of her jealousy. She watched the baby, in my arms; watched it avidly enough that, if I hadn't had Honorius with me, I would have been half inclined to offer it to her for adoption. Certainly no one would ever get past that lioness-of-Alexandria attitude to harm the child.

Physician Bariş, with a sombre face, came to tell me he doubted his surgery could mend a womb like mine so that it could conceive again. Especially since it had been such a remote chance I should conceive the first time.

I felt a rush of relief, and at the same time terror, looking at the miniature sleeping face and thinking, *This is the only one.*

'Tell you truth,' Bariş observed dispassionately, having finished his investigation of my healing surgical wound. 'I'm more surprised to see *you* live than her. Frankly, it's a miracle you survived.'

He looked confused when I muttered, 'Don't *you* start!'

The baby's small size continued to flabbergast me.

She was barely bigger than Honorius's hand when he caressed her in her swaddling bands. Although she didn't wear the tight strips of cloth for long – a day or so later, Rekhmire' muttered something about barbaric customs, and (with Bariş's help) overrode the Venetian midwife and my father. The baby girl was allowed to lay on my bedcover, only a swathe of linen around her, in the patches of sunlight that made her dark eyes close and open as slowly as if she were under the sea.

The stitches being painful for longer than I expected, I found myself frustrated in my desire to care for her. Neferet, unsurprisingly, took up every chance to feed or bathe her – somewhat more surprisingly, I had help from not only Honorius himself, but from Saverico and those others of the men-at-arms with younger siblings or their own children at home. Berenguer slid in and out of the room when she was a few weeks old, and left a fish carved out of ash-wood, that she might play with – or at least watch – in the shallow water of her bath.

I wondered much if there might be something wrong with her. But I kept those thoughts to myself.

After a few weeks, as she put on weight by the efforts of cow- and goat-milk, I found that I knew what her name ought to be, even if she still might not live to use it.

I spoke to Honorius one midday, when the rest of the house was still at their meal.

'With your permission – I would like to call her "Onorata".'

My father smiled and wept together, without shame.

'I feel nothing like a mother,' I said to Rekhmire', as the Egyptian handed Onorata back to me after she burped milk over the feeding-cloth on his shoulder. 'I can't put her to my breast . . . '

Looking up, I surprised concern on his face.

'But I feel I should protect her,' I added. 'Perhaps I should think of myself as Onorata's father?'

The Egyptian's brows dipped into a scowl. 'If it comes to it, I would suppose you both, in that sense. But why not a mother?'

Because I would not be Rosamunda if my life depended on it.

The thought of that woman, in Carthage or Taraco, still sends hot sweat down my spine, half the length of the Mediterranean Sea away from her.

Am I not supposed to understand her better, now?

'I have no idea how to be a mother. Valdamerca raised me as a slave.' I shrugged. 'But Honorius is a good father. If Onorata lives, perhaps I can be to her what he would have been to me.'

The Egyptian slowly nodded.

I don't know if Rekhmire' mentioned the conversation to Honorius, but one day after the year's early Easter, when I ventured downstairs, I caught the Captain-General of Castile and Leon drawing up dowry documents for his granddaughter, and another version of his will.

He blushed and put the documents away in his portable wooden writing-desk.

'I leaned to write a reasonable scribe's hand when I didn't have an ensign in camp who could do it for me.' He shrugged, ostensibly casual. 'I want you and Onorata to be wealthy when I die.'

'Now why didn't I think of that?' I nodded towards his sword, where it was wrapped in the scabbard's straps and laying on the window-chest. 'Pass me the sword and I'll be able to afford all the red chalk I could ever need . . .'

Honorius grinned.

'I'll haunt you,' he said cheerfully.

'You do anyway. I can't get away from you. You and the bloody book-buyer!' I raised my voice in case Rekhmire' should be near enough to tease, but there was no response.

And no crying baby, either. He often took her into his lap while he sorted scrolls, so I suspected the one absence answered the other.

Honorius neatly cleaned and wrapped up his quills and wax tablets and paper, stowing them away. He crossed the room and bent over to place another piece of wood on the fire in the hearth.

'I spoke through Carmagnola to Doge Foscari,' he observed. 'Apparently, Messer Leon Battista will come for trial, soon.'

I had wondered why matters would drag on for so long – until I worked out that the Council of Ten would want to know how it was that so very many identical seditious news-letters could be produced within a short amount of time. And since the name of Herr Mainz wasn't being bandied about Venezia, I guessed Leon had not yet spoken.

A slave has always to live under the threat of torture. It is a subject I have given some thought. The idea of Leon Battista having to undergo pain like that, unprepared as he must surely be . . .

Honorius put his lean hand on my shoulder. As if he read my mind in my face, he said, 'Neferet's seen him. She says they're letting darkness and hunger do their work for them. Given the Alberti family's place on the Council, even Foscari won't use outright torture until he can make it

312

seem there's no other option. And by then he'll be out of there. You like Leon Battista,' he finished, with an odd questioning note to his voice.

I nodded. Frankly, I said, 'I think he's a *fool*. But I don't have a city that I care about as he cares for Florence. Perhaps I'd do the same under those circumstances. Slaves don't have homes in that way.'

'No.' Honorius's hand gave my shoulder a final pressure. He looked at me with a smile. 'Have you thought? Onorata is freeborn.'

For my final examination before he departed, the Janissary doctor was visibly not certain whether to request a man or a woman as chaperone.

Bariş seized on Rekhmire''s muttered volunteering with gladness – likely because 'Alexandrine eunuch bureaucrat' trumped both in terms of respectability.

'You should tell the physician if you intend to have sex again,' Rekhmire' mumbled towards the end of an extensive examination, translating some of the medical Greek technicalities.

I raised both eyebrows at him.

A dark flush turned his Egyptian colouring something closer to brick-red than I had imagined possible.

'Whether you intend to fornicate . . . It's not as if you're breast-feeding, to avoid conception. I know he's said, ah . . . that it's all but impossible . . . but . . . You ought not to get pregnant again. That would be very dangerous.'

I grinned at him. 'You're not my master, Rekhmire'.'

Or a mother hen, I reflected, as he looked even more flustered.

Evidently pulling himself together, and ignoring my minor harassment, Rekhmire' faced the Jannissary doctor. '*Is* Ilario capable of conceiving another child?'

I murmured, 'Now there's a question I never wanted to hear . . . '

Bariş looked amused. Rekhmire' failed to.

'Because, you see, if Ilario is capable, then having sex as a woman could be dangerous, if not fatal.' Rekhmire' stuttered. 'Ilario, will you be content to have sex as a man does?'

'Uh.' I felt my cheeks heating; knew I must be red from neck to hairline.

'With – another *man*, that is? I suppose – of course – if you were to have sex as a man does with a woman—' Rekhmire' tucked his arms tightly across his chest and glared down at me. 'Doctor, can Ilario get a woman pregnant?'

'No.' Bariş shook his head. 'Never.'

He glanced from Rekhmire' to me, and back to the Egyptian.

'Because I have never, in my entire professional career, seen such a scarlet shade of embarrassment – I doubt this patient will ever have sex again!'

What concerns I might have had were, by that, and the expression on Rekhmire''s face, exploded completely.

I howled and clutched at my ribs.

Rekhmire' squirmed. 'I hardly meant . . . I had no intention of . . . ! I—'

'Go *away*, Rekhmire'.' I couldn't stop grinning. 'You're not my master, you don't have to force yourself to ask the doctor gynaecological questions! And Physician Bariş is right. At the moment, I'm debating between a monastery and a nunnery! Just so long as it's a celibate order!'

It wouldn't have surprised me had the Egyptian cited some of the more scurrilous rumours about Frankish monasteries and nunneries. Instead, Rekhmire' clattered his crutch against the floor and made a production of lumbering off. I wheezed with the first uninhibited laugh I'd had in months.

Bariş eventually ended his investigations under my skirts.

'You're healing healthily and quickly. Put no stress on that part of your body; avoid heavy exertion for the moment.' He signalled to the giant Balaban to pack up his medical chest. 'Might I have a look at the child? If you don't mind?'

I lifted Onorata out of the oak-chest cot, unwinding the nominal swaddling bands that loosely swathed her. Instead of crying, she beat thin perfect arms against me, and snuggled onto my chest in wide-eyed relaxation, apparently gazing up at the Turk.

'Can you tell? If she's normal,' I clarified.

He ran his finger down the sole of her foot, watching her small toes curl. 'I examined her at the birth.'

'Yes, but – I don't know what there might be on the inside.'

Bariş's ship's-prow nose cast a shadow across Onorata's body as he bent down, peering very closely.

'These things are so rare. Nor do *I* know, to be honest. And most "hermaphrodites" are men born looking in some way like a woman, or women who have what resemble the man's parts. Or nothing changes until they become adult, and then a woman merely coughs and testicles appear . . . I thought the *true* hermaphrodite was only a rumour. A fable.'

I sighed as he lifted Onorata with all gentleness, and laid her back on the wooden chest's bedding.

I put my hands to the hem of my shift. 'You want another look?'

'May I? The last occasions have been a little fraught . . . '

His voice became muffled as he bent down.

The iron instruments were cold, making me flinch.

In accented Alexandrine Egyptian, Bariş observed, 'You have little more than the eunuch has, as testes go! I *wish* I had you for an autopsy, to find out for certain whether this lump is testes or ovary . . . '

'Well, I'm damn glad you don't!'

Bariş gave me something perilously close to a grin, and gestured for me to pull my shift back down. 'A shame I go back to Edirne now my captain has recovered. You could put it in your will that I could have your body.'

Having pulled my shift down, I shrugged my way into the voluminous Venetian over-robe that Honorius had gifted me, and began to lace up the front of it.

'Firstly, I'm not dying! And, secondly, if I *do* die in Venice, not only will my friend Rekhmire' follow you to Edirne and kill you several times, each more horrible than the last . . . I, personally, will *haunt* you.'

The Turkish doctor called for a bowl to bathe his hands. Deadpan, he remarked, 'I begin to see the advantages in the Hippocratic Oath . . . '

Having washed, he took a wax tablet and stylus from an inside pocket of his tunic, and poised the one over the other.

'I may write to Ephesus and Padua with my findings,' he remarked, small bright eyes focusing on me. 'But I have a number of additional questions I wish you will answer, Ilario . . . Which only you can answer. *You* must know which is best – the male orgasm or the female orgasm? So, which? Or is it that you feel you only know what's normal for a hermaphrodite, and not for a man or a woman? How is your sexual appetite? When your man-parts are spent; is it possible to function as a woman until the male refractory period passes? Have you ever dually and simultaneously—'

Honorius walked into the room, perfunctorily rapping on the door.

'Oh thank God!'

Honorius ignored that. 'I need to talk to you. Alone.'

20

'Alone' meant three of us; my father sending one of his men for Rekhmire'. Four, if Onorata counted – blissfully silent, since asleep in her lidless oak chest.

Honorius himself served mulled wine into ceramic bowls. He sat on the joint-stool by the bed, set his own wine down on the stone hearth, and scratched at his hair until it stood up in tufts, giving him the semblance of a fierce, if ruffled, owl.

He broke the silence.

'A letter has arrived. Written to me.'

Fear stabbed under the joining of my ribs.

I ignored Rekhmire''s concerned frown and held out my hand. 'Show me!'

Silently, Honorius fished out creased papers from his sleeve, and held one out between two fingers. I took it.

'From King Rodrigo Sanguerra.'

If my sight blurred with shock, I still recognised Hunulf's penmanship: a particular curve on the 'd' and 'g'. He's long wanted my nominal position as scribe to the Sanguerra family.

I reached for the bowl with my other hand, welcoming the hot taste of spiced wine, and finding my fingers shaking only a little as I read.

'Translated freely,' I observed, 'it appears to say, "Get your arse back here before I sequester your estates *and* put your family under attainder"—'

Rekhmire' snickered, caught Honorius's glare, and glossed it: 'You see why I employed Ilario as a scribe.'

'No.' Honorius kept a perfectly straight face for a moment. He smirked as he took the page back from me and passed it over to the Egyptian. 'I grant you the accuracy of reading between the lines.'

'This isn't like the last one?' I speculated. 'Not a dozen copies sent out to ambassadors or bankers, so that one would get to you sooner or later? This came direct to Venezia?'

Rekhmire' did not even look up to see Honorius's confirming nod.

'It would appear that King Rodrigo knows where the Captain-General is . . . There are other channels by which information could pass, but I will point out that Aldra Federico – and Ramiro Carrasco, when he was at large – are both positioned to have told your King this. Or rather Videric, whom we may assume would tell King Rodrigo.'

Honorius muttered, '*Court politics!*' in tones of deepest disgust

I got up. It eased me to pace the room, despite the pull on my pink and healing stitches.

'This makes twice King Rodrigo's ordered you home.' I paused, bending down to touch the fluff on Onorata's head. 'And as we said in Rome, it's understandable. You retire, rich. You head home for Taraco. No man sees you. The first thing you do is leave again for Carthage—'

'That was to visit you!' Honorius looked mulish.

'I know that! You know that! The King doesn't know that!'

Onorata began grizzling.

Rekhmire' leaned his crutch against the hearth-surround, and lifted Onorata out of her cot into his lap. His arm supported her head with a professional care. I did not know whether to feel pleasure or jealousy that she subsided at once into whining mutters.

Voice soft and even, Rekhmire' said, 'Ilario's correct. King Rodrigo *doesn't* know. He has a foreign general come home – foreign, because twenty-five years in Navarra and Castile means no man knows you. You have the reputation of "the Lion of Castile"—'

The Egyptian pressed on when Honorius would have interrupted:

'—Whatever you think of your reputation, you have it. You return to Taraconensis, you ask your King for nothing, and you go to Carthage. *Exactly* when, as far as he's concerned, Carthage has just robbed him of his First Minister!'

My father spluttered.

I took the opportunity to speak. 'Either Federico will have written, or Videric will have told King Rodrigo himself, that you're my father.'

And if that interview took place between Videric and Rodrigo Sanguerra, I would like to have witnessed it. Between Videric's embarrassment at being cuckolded, and Rodrigo's ferocious temper at not having been told all this before, I thought I would have found it very satisfying.

Rekhmire' handed Onorata up to me and reclaimed his own drinking bowl. 'Which, of course, makes Videric all the more dangerous now. Viler things have been done out of fear than ever stemmed from anger or revenge.'

Honorius sprang to his feet, his fingers white against the green glaze of his wine bowl. 'I can't believe my supposed *King* thinks me disloyal!'

Watching Honorius's stiff back as he stalked over to the window, I doubted he would conceive of anyone believing him that.

I rocked Onorata gently in my arms. 'You didn't return from Rome at his request.'

'I—' Honorius spun on his boot-heel, pointing at Rekhmire'. 'Your messengers caught me up!'

The Egyptian nodded. 'Which is why I thought hard before I wrote. I knew it might look bad.'

Honorius set his jaw. 'I can sort this out ten minutes after I set foot in Taraco harbour – which I *will*, once I have assurances of my son-daughter's and grand-daughter's safety!'

Onorata stretched up her hand and prodded at my chin, although the contact may have been accidental. Judging by the slant of the light, she would be hungry soon.

'If I were Aldra Videric,' I said absently, playing catch-finger with the baby, 'I'd be telling Rodrigo Sanguerra that you came back from Castile with the express intent of talking *his* place as First Minister. I'd tell the King you're in alliance with Carthage. That when Taraconensis gets legions sent in to keep the kingdom safe from crusading Franks, the military governor they put in place of the King will be Aldra Captain-General Honorius.'

Honorius stared at me. Rekhmire' too, I noted.

'Rodrigo will be thinking that you *planned* to work with Carthage, to use me to get rid of Videric.' I shook my head. 'What? I was at court! I learned how all this works so that I could stay out of it!'

'Goddamn!' Honorius muttered in one of the northern Frankish dialects. 'Bloody goddamn . . . I swear you're right. Since the King doesn't merely threaten his anger—'

'What else?' Rekhmire' leaned forward on his stool, wincing at some pain in his knee-joint. 'There's more?'

'Oh, there's more . . . ' Honorius's lean body straightened, his hand closing around the remaining pages. Tendons and cartilege pulled taut under his skin; altered all the planes of light and shadow that made up his face.

'King Rodrigo Sanguerra is generously pleased to write me a *warning*.' Honorius's voice rasped. 'You may read it here, on this second page. He writes to tell me he's taken certain precautions for the safety of my new estates. In my absence.'

Honorius's forefinger tapped a tattoo on the paper.

'He's sent his royal troops in, to protect my lands against bandits – and against land-hungry nobles, who might jump in while I'm away. It seems that four hundred gentlemen and squires in the King's service are billeted on my land, in my castle – for which my estate naturally has to pay bed and board.'

His hand closed up, paper crumpling into a tight ball.

'Four hundred royal men-at-arms eating their bellies full at *my* expense! And I get this favour *because* I'm so loyal to the Crown! Rodrigo Sanguerra's doing me this favour because "is unwise to leave land unprotected in these uncertain times" . . . '

Rekhmire' had the look he wore during mathematical calculation. 'Will your estates support that many men? How many of your own are there?'

Honorius rubbed his brow hard. 'Thirty, thirty-five knights, and their lances? Say six or eight men to a lance . . . Three hundred-odd came home from Castile with me to settle down; act as my stewards, overseers, and the like. Marry local girls. I left most there when I came to Rome. Now – they won't dare disobey the King's orders. And they can't fight off four hundred men without a bloodbath on both sides.'

He stared, for a long silent moment; the flames of the fire were within his view but I doubted he saw them.

'And, no.' Honorius looked up at Rekhmire' as if he had only just remembered what he had been asked. 'My lands can't *support* four hundred extra men! They'll eat their way through the storerooms and the granaries, their horses will empty my stables, my stewards will run the coffers dry attempting to fulfil this responsibility . . . I left no man with the authority to go into debt on my behalf, but I won't be surprised to get back and find they've gone to the Etruscans or the Jews.'

He dropped the ball of paper to the floor and ground it under the heel of his boot.

'If Rodrigo's men-at-arms are anything like mine, they'll be living off the land inside a couple of months! That means the noblemen whose lands border mine won't be friends or allies of mine. Not if their fodder and crops are being raided.'

He glanced at me, with a sour smile containing admiration.

'King Rodrigo notes that, if I were disloyal, he wouldn't gift me this "small contingent" to protect my estates against insurrection from outside. *And* revolt from inside. Which means that if any of my lads protest, they'll find themselves accused of being rebels exploiting *my* absence! And meanwhile the King can go on draining away my resources and making enemies of my neighbours . . . Until I go back to Taraco.'

One of his hands made a fist: I noted how it thickened the tendons in his wrist.

'What I *resent* is that publicly Rodrigo will be seen to be doing something intelligent! In effect, he levies a fine on me that I can't refuse to pay. *He's* not having to support those troops himself, all the while this goes on. And no supporter of mine, if I have any, can point to the King being unfair, because he's *protecting* me!'

I echoed Honorius, quietly for the child in my arms. 'Goddamn!'

Rekhmire' replaced his wine bowl on the chess table. 'I begin to see why it's not merely Aldra Videric who's kept Taraconensis free and peaceful, this past generation and more! In every other man's eyes, King Rodrigo is doing something legal, something moral, to aid you. And meanwhile—'

The Alexandrine lifted one hand and mimicked a twisting motion.

Honorius laughed harshly. 'Meanwhile the bloody screws tighten, until my thumbs begin to bleed!'

My father threw himself down on the wooden settle, stretching out one long leg, and watching as I replaced Onorata in her cot. I hoped her doze would last.

'Ilario.' Honorius spoke quietly. 'There's no need for you to be concerned over this. I didn't come home from Castile poor. It'll take a year or two longer to get the estates in order, that's all. A good harvest next year or the year after and we're set.'

I rubbed my back as I straightened up. 'I can see why you never went in for politics. You're a really bad liar.'

Rekhmire' spluttered.

Honorius, with an unwillingly pleased look, said, 'I can deceive and feint on the field of battle. But you're right: I can't tell lies worth a damn. I see I should tell you the truth in future, you'll find it more reassuring.'

'I suppose that's one word for it . . . '

Honorius added, 'I'm not leaving Venice.'

He barely sounded stubborn about it. Twenty or thirty years of taking and giving orders – especially the giving – and even his common pronouncements tend to sound like statements of irrefutable fact. As for anything he thinks he's made his mind up over . . .

'You are leaving!'

It didn't sound at all impressive in my emphatic tenor. Perhaps because of the alto squeak that crept in, despite my efforts. I glared at the grey-haired soldier.

Not looking up from the page he studied, Rekhmire' observed, 'Going to Taraco might, now, be very advantageous – I know what I would do if I were in Rodrigo Sanguerra's situation. I would offer the post of First Minister to Honorius.'

'*What!*' I turned to face him rapidly enough that I had to bend over, hands pressing against my stitches through my petticoats. I breathed hard. 'You think the King should give Honorius *Videric's* job?'

Honorius exploded into a chuckle and glanced between us, as if we were there for his entertainment.

The Egyptian ticked off points on his fingers. 'It would provide stability for Taraconensis. They would have a First Minister again, and it would be a war hero – twenty-five years of service in the Crusades. King Rodrigo is seen to have a powerful man at his side. *And* it to some degree fixes Honorius under Taraco's standard – how can Captain-General Licinus Honorius sneak off to Carthage and claim to want to be the "strong governor" Taraconensis needs, if he's already King Rodrigo's first adviser?'

Honorius slapped his leg in evident delight.

I snorted. That caught my stitches, too. 'You're forgetting one thing. *Videric wouldn't let him do it!*'

'Possibly. But even Aldra Videric must now be conjecturing that the King gains no current advantage from listening to *him*.' Rekhmire' shot me a sharp gaze. 'I grant you the risk of your father returning to Taraco.

But consider this. Master Honorius was twenty-five years in Castile and Leon.'

Honorius gave me a small, silent shrug.

'And?' I was as bewildered.

'I had some communication with scroll-collectors in Burgos and Salamanca and Avila, before winter set in.' Rekhmire''s rounded features smoothed into a shrewd expression. 'They confirmed what I recall of Castile and Leon – a snake-pit of political alliances and betrayals. All of which, Ilario, your father has steadfastly ignored.'

If Honorius spoke, it would be to snap, *Of course!* I quickly gestured for Rekhmire' to continue.

'King Juan the Second of Castile has one infallibly loyal man,' the Egyptian said. 'Called Alvaro, Count di Luna. Who, because of that position as the King's favourite, is the most powerful single individual in northern Iberia. In more than two decades, Master Honorius never joined any conspiracy against King Juan's favourite. More: he never tried to strike up a partnership with Alvaro di Luna.'

'You think Rodrigo Sanguerra will draw conclusions from that?'

Rekhmire' handed the page of King Rodrigo's letter back towards my father. 'How many Caesars began as successful generals? A man with an army supporting him has always been dangerous. If the soldiers of a kingdom follow one man, tradition and law all make way for him. As far as I can discover, and as far as King Rodrigo Sanguerra's spies in Leon and Castile should be telling *him*, the mercenary commander Licinus Honorius has never given any of his kings one sleepless night.'

Honorius looked plainly embarrassed.

A low hungry whine came from Onorata's cot; Honorius quickly rose and scooped her up, letting her suck on his forefinger, and went over to the door to call for milk.

Rekhmire' directed a look at me that said *I have given him somewhat to think on.*

'He shouldn't go to Taraco!' I attempted to shove hands into breeches-pockets, which in petticoats and a Frankish over-robe is bound to be unsuccessful. 'Not with Videric as his enemy. And you shouldn't be encouraging him!'

'Ilario—'

I rode over Rekhmire''s protest. 'This letter may just be something to get him on the road home! Suppose that's all it is? Suppose it doesn't matter about Taraco, because he's not intended to reach home – Videric will have paid *banditi, masnadiere*, pirates, any kind of thugs!'

'It's possible . . . but Master Honorius is a soldier.' Rekhmire' came to stand at my shoulder, watching my father give orders to one of Neferet's women. 'Have you thought? If King Rodrigo takes his lands, and forbids him to cross the borders of Taraconensis – your father loses everything it's taken him twenty-five years to earn by battle.'

21

I found it impossible to persuade Honorius to leave Venice.

Appealing to emotion, to logic; simply shouting as loudly as I could without breaking my scar open – nothing convinced him.

He sat in silence while I coaxed Onorata to feed. The room's tenseness made her cry and throw her arms about, spattering milk. Eventually I laid her across my lap, to ease her of belly-cramps as the midwife had suggested, but it was an hour or more before she ceased to cry, and fell asleep.

That had proved enough to make Rekhmire' descend the stairs, no matter how awkward he found it, and Honorius joined him. I left Neferet watching over Onorata – since *her* appetite for the bawling, squalling thing seemed inexhaustible – and took refuge in a chalk profile of Rekhmire', while Honorius shuffled through his small company's accounts.

'I won't leave you unprotected,' he remarked, finally. 'I've three lances here. Even if I split them with you, that only leaves each of us inadequately defended.'

'*I* don't need protection!' The proportions of Rekhmire''s eye and nose in no way matched each other. I threw down the slate in disgust. 'You'd be the one going into danger!'

The argument went on for an hour at the least, becoming increasingly mathematical. Rekhmire' joined in, not disputing Honorius's tactical assessments, but digging deeply into the same question – which my father declined to answer: *How many of your men do you need to stay safe from danger on the roads?*

I stopped speaking and let them go at it, treasuring an idea that came into my mind.

When both fell breathlessly silent, I spoke again.

'The answer to "How many men?" is "All of them",' I said. 'It has to be. I'll tell you why. Father, your concern is that when Videric's spies see you and your men leave, they'll kill me—'

'*No*, you can't come with me!' Honorius interrupted. 'I've seen the sewing-work on your belly: there's no way you're riding a horse or being strapped into a litter – *or* puking your guts up by sea! I know how long it takes men to recover from battlefield wounds; you're still weeks from ready, no matter what the Turk said—'

'Yes, but I don't think anyone else knows that.' I walked across the room and rested my hands on his shoulders, standing behind his chair. 'Go with all your men, banners flying. Ensign Saverico is about my height and build, although he's fair-haired. Put him in my green travelling cloak and a skirt. Any spies will report to Videric that I've left Venice.'

'A battle double.' Honorius glanced up, the dawning of amusement in his gaze. 'Well thought of! But not good enough. Am I supposed to leave my son-daughter and Onorata to that whoreson Federico, or any other ruffian who can make his way to Venice?'

'You'll lose your estates!'

He looked away from me. 'My reputation – which you and the Egyptian both seem to think I have – should mean I have no difficulty in earning more money, and buying more land. If it's not in Taraco . . . then it's elsewhere.'

'You are the *worst* liar!'

Honorius grinned, and reached for the seal on a wine bottle.

'Honorius – *Father—*'

It was my first experience of a long and pointless argument as a free individual rather than as a slave.

It was no less aggravating, and I seemed equally powerless. True, no man threatened to whip me when I threw a shoe at Honorius's head. But that was solely because it made him laugh, and then wipe at his eyes as if he were deeply moved.

'Stupid soldier!' I snarled.

He crossed the room and put his arms about my shoulders. As ever, he seemed to have no hesitation in touching me. He wept a little.

'Must have been hanging out with too many damned English mercenaries,' he muttered, wiping his face. 'All the English are far too emotional, always have been!'

I stated it as plainly as I could. 'If you have to fight to be paid again, you might be killed. I don't want that.'

'I am going nowhere until you're safe!' He scowled at me. 'And – what *is* safe? If you and the child could travel, I wouldn't take you with me. You and Videric in the same kingdom? There'd be men waiting at every corner to cut your throat!'

'Then I'll stay in Venice!'

'That's no better!'

The tense silence snapped, broken by a diplomatic cough from Rekhmire'.

'There's Alexandria,' I said, and translated for Honorius: 'Constantinople.'

'"Constantinople."' Rekhmire' wrinkled his upper lip at the Frankish name for his city. 'I had wondered, if I can find Herr Mainz, or if the Pharaoh-Queen sends a new ambassador for Venice, whether I could wait a month or so until the weather is clearer, and then take a ship down through the Aegean to Alexandria. But, such a long voyage . . . '

Honorius scowled. 'Onorata is still very small. Travel might kill her.'

'Alexandria is far enough from Taraco that Ilario should be out of Videric's reach. And Ilario will have friends and protection there.' Rekhmire' had his chin on his hand, where he sat at the large table; his gaze only glanced across me.

'I won't risk such a young child,' Honorius grumbled.

He looked over at me, but I paid no attention. Fear turned my bowels hot and cold while he spoke to me, and I realised in a flash why.

If, in guilty waking moments, in the early hours of the morning, I held the unvoiced thought that it would be better, kinder, if the sickly child didn't survive – or better if the responsibility weren't left to someone as completely unfitted for it as I – the thought of someone else taking her made the bottom of my stomach drop away with fear.

All the time it was me, alone, there was no concern if I fell into debt and was sold back into slavery. I've lived as a slave before; I can do it again.

But slaves have no say in whether their babies are taken from them. Their children are sold on, and they never see them again.

'You're not rich enough to buy all three of us,' I whispered to Rekhmire', trying for humour and not achieving it.

'If it comes to it, I'm perfectly capable of embezzling the funds of any Alexandrine House,' the Egyptian said, as if it were not only obvious but sensible. 'However. I strongly suggest we don't let it come to that.'

He exchanged a glance with Honorius, as if both of them could come to a conclusion without words.

'Let the weather improve.' Honorius grumbled. 'Give it a few months for the child to thrive. I'll sail to Alexandria with you. Then, when you're safe, Ilario, I'll sort out Rodrigo Sanguerra.'

'Honorius.' Breathing deeply gave me some control. 'I read what Hanulf wrote, and I know what the King dictated to him. I worked for Rodrigo Sanguerra for nearly a decade. I *know* the man. *He won't wait!*'

Honorius smiled, lines spidering his face at the mouth and eyes. 'Let's sit, eat. Discuss this like sensible men. You can protest how you like, Ilario. I won't leave Venice while you need me.'

'Damn it—!'

The rest of the discussion was as fruitless as any I have ever had with a noble of King Rodrigo's court set on going his own way – and being a freed slave rather than the King's Freak did not appear to help me in the slightest.

Gazing at Honorius while he ate delicate flakes of white fish as if they were about to give way to famine, I thought, *Even his affection might fade if acknowledging me ends by robbing him of everything he's earned in his life.*

*

My body had returned to as normal a state as I thought it now could achieve, and I was watching Onorata blink sleepily at the spring sunshine from her cradle when Neferet bustled her way into the ground-floor room that looked out into the courtyard, an expostulating Rekhmire' and Honorius in her wake.

'Ilaria!' She had not given up calling me by a female name, as most of the household inhabitants had when not outside in Venice itself. 'Ilaria, I need your help.'

I have been your guest: that imposes obligations. I shot a look at the two men behind Neferet, who were both yelling loudly enough that I could understand what neither was saying. *Obligations, but not without caution.*

'What do you need?' I asked, standing up, my fingers resting on the wooden hood of the cradle.

'The Council of Ten are holding Leon's trial tomorrow.'

Neferet's face was lean, tight, intense. She fixed me with brown-black eyes, and what I thought was a flush under her reddish skin. 'They'll torture him; I *know* he'll be executed, because he won't say . . . anything.'

I wanted to interrupt with some commiseration or sympathy; she didn't permit it.

'His family have disowned him,' she said sharply. 'It's not worth their while to sink with him, is what they mean! I spoke to his father – no matter. We have to do something tomorrow – *I* have to – *you* have to help me!'

The Frankish season of Lent was on the house: I didn't suffer from diet restrictions, since I'd had to regain my health after the birth, but I felt the abstinence going on all around me, and had abandoned wine for the time. That was a mistake, I thought. *I have a feeling I could do with a flask of Falernian right about now.*

'What?' I began.

'He'll be convicted. Sentenced.' Neferet's eyes seemed to gleam in her intense face. 'I can't do anything about that: the gods they know I've tried! But he's bound to be sentenced to execution. I need . . . I would do this myself, but it's the one thing I can't do. I can't do it.'

She shook her head. She looked oddly dignified for a moment, the spring sun showing up every line worry had cut into her soft face over the past weeks.

'I can't think of any plea of leniency they might listen to, except this.' She stepped forward, reached out, took my hand, and closed her other hand over my knuckles. 'I need you to go to the Doge's palace tomorrow, and plead for his life.'

'*Me?*'

Neferet made an impatient sound. In the doorway, Rekhmire' and Honorius fell silent. My father's mouth was a white line. The Egyptian had his arms crossed firmly across his chest.

'You.' Neferet looked down the inch or two of height she had on me, into my face. 'You have to go to them, and plead your belly.'

22

If I stared as incoherently as I felt, it was no wonder she began to speak in slow, plain words, as if to a village idiot.

'Tell them this is *Leon's* child.' She jerked her chin toward the cradle, never taking her eyes off my face. 'Tell them he visited Tommaso Cassai in Rome. And seduced you, while he was there. You followed him here, pretending to be a widow. It's *why* you're here. You need a father for your child. You need them to commute the sentence from execution. It doesn't matter to what. Anything, so long as he lives! We can aid him later. But you have to go there and do this for him; it's the thing that *I can't do.*'

Rekhmire' came up behind her and put his hands on her shoulders. She didn't let go of my hand.

I could see the man under her disguise – or the false pale body that held her female *ka*, as she would say. She stood with a kind of exhausted, humiliated dignity, gazing down at me.

If I didn't much like her, still, pain for her wrenched through my belly. 'Of course I will.'

'I won't have you put yourself into danger!'

Honorius and I spoke at the same time.

Rekhmire''s great hand tightened on the shoulder of Neferet's long Alexandrine robe. His grave dark gaze met mine.

'You can take your father's armed escort,' Rekhmire' said. 'No man would think the less of you, not after you were attacked by a madman.'

The last few words let me know what story had been given out about Ramiro Carrasco's attempt to murder me.

Honorius glared. 'I don't like it! The boy Leon – nice enough boy – wouldn't have him in a company of mine, and the world doesn't need more lawyers – but I'm not risking my son-daughter for him!'

His protectiveness made me smile. It's frightening, because I'm not used to it, and what one learns to value, it may pain one to lose. But it still made me warm.

Freeing my hands, I bent over the cradle and picked up Onorata. She had grown, but she was still smaller than any new-born should be. I slid my finger over her palm, and she made an infinitesimally tiny sound and closed her small perfect fingers on me.

'I haven't taken her out of the house,' I said.

Honorius erupted into a fine amount of oratory, Rekhmire' speculated about what Alexandrine physicians might advise, and Neferet said nothing at all. She continued to look at me.

I have seen the expression before, on slaves' faces, before they break down and beg.

Hurriedly, I said, 'We'll take the midwife. And ... your Father Azadanes?' Who, privately, I thought would be of more use to Neferet as a friend than to me as a Green priest. 'And the wet-nurse. And the soldiers.'

My father gave me a furious look.

Knowing him, I knew that Neferet's distress had already lost him the argument he would still have with me.

I looked from Honorius to Rekhmire' – the Egyptian's expression heavy with thoughts I shared – and then at Neferet. 'You do know how small a chance this is, don't you?'

The Alexandrine eunuch dressed as a woman gave me that inclination of the head that, outside of Frankish lands, passes as a bow.

'I know,' Neferet said. 'Nonetheless.'

The great medieval palace of the Doges was in the process of being demolished – rather, demolished and re-built – so I spent my time leading us between scaffolding-covered walls, and treading close enough to the heels of the Doge's soldier that I wouldn't lose him as he led us inside. Every so often I looked inside the fold of my cloak to find Onorata still breathing.

No love connected us, but I would wake two or three times in the night, convinced she had died as she slept, and must crawl to the foot of my bed and look at her in her chest-cot, and feel her breath against my finger, before I could go back to sleep.

The Council guards escorted us into the main chamber of the Doge.

They will see through me.

The thought echoed through my head clearly enough to down out the ringing footsteps on the flagstones, and the echoes that came back from the Gothic vaults. I had no time to look at the ducal splendour of Foscari's half-rebuilt palace, in the new Classical style. I could only think *I will join Leon Battista Alberti in prison!*

I thought sardonically that I ought to have been barefoot, with my skirt hems worn to frays, and the baby in my arms wrapped in faded linen. That would make them believe the poor seduced woman come to get justice from her ravisher ...

Looking up, past the semi-circle of white-faced old men under Phrygian caps, all identical to me in this state of fear, I caught Leon Battista's eye where he stood between four armed guards.

His eyes bugged out of his head.

'He'll give it away!' I muttered.

Honorius gave me the same look he gave disobedient young recruits. 'Steady.'

On my other side – and I was beginning to wonder when they had constituted themselves my bookends – Rekhmire' leaned on his crutch and suggested, 'Will you take the baby?'

Honorius spoke across me. 'Not for a moment. Let them see us.'

I might not be a grubby-faced ex-whore with snow on my feet and a baby in my arms, I reflected, wondering if I could paint that in any way that these rich fat men would believe.

What they must see in front of them in this dark and torch-lit hall was a young woman in silks and satins, clearly of good family, her father in knight's armour, her Egyptian scribe at her elbow, her armed escort clattering across the stone floor behind us, and the nursemaid with the child two formal paces to my rear.

Like it or not, this stands more of a chance of presenting them a picture they'll buy.

'This is my daughter—' Honorius stuttered over the word, in a way I'd never heard him stutter over 'son-daughter'. '—Ilaria. I demand compensation for her! I demand justice!'

All of the ten men at the council table looked at Honorius, except for the middle-aged man with alert brown eyes who took in my appearance in an instant, and slightly lifted a brow.

'Messer Captain-General Honorius.' It was the keen-eyed man who spoke: I realised this must be Foscari. 'We have read the evidence you put before us. What claim have you on this man's estate, except the testimony of this woman?'

Onorata was wrapped up with swaddling bands, very loosely, for the look of the thing. Being fed, I had every hope she'd sleep and look sweet. With her arranged in the crook of my arm, I stepped forward and waited until Honorius finished repeating verbally what he had dictated to any number of the Doge's secretaries.

'Lords, seigniors, illustrious *Duca*.' I let my Iberian accent come out, and caught Leon Battista's eye as I looked up as modestly as I could. 'If the late Tommaso Cassai, artist in Rome, could speak to you, he would tell you about the truth of this—'

Yes: he'd tell you I'm lying in my teeth!

'—If you wish, I will swear an oath that Messer Alberti promised me marriage before he seduced me, and I therefore considered us betrothed—'

I said I would swear it. Not that it would be true.

Because I will swear myself black in the face if it helps. And if court life teaches you anything, it is how to lie with the greatest innocence.

'—I don't beg you not to punish him, illustrious sirs. Only to have mercy on my child. Who needs her father!'

329

And that may be true – or she may already be overburdened with a mother-father.

The man to Foscari's right said, 'We could order some settlement made out of the prisoner's estate?'

Honorius's hand closed around my elbow and gently pulled me back – but I had no chance of breaking his grip. He glanced down as he let me go, and stroked a fingertip over the baby's fine fluffy hair where it protruded from under her linen cap. I saw Doge Foscari register his smile.

That's useful: he sees that the baby's grandfather is willing to acknowledge her—

My thoughts were interrupted by a burst of deep-throated laughter from the councillor on the Doge's left hand:

'That is poetic!'

He was overweight, with the high colour fat men in middle age get. I stared at him, not knowing whether to wish him dead of a heart spasm on the spot. Foscari lifted his eyebrow again, as if he wished to seem slightly disconcerted; the other men on the council followed his lead by frowning.

'Poetic justice, perhaps.' Doge Foscari linked his fingers together on the polished dark table. The cabochon-cut rings he wore reflected in the shine, in dark incarnations of their colours: emerald, ruby, sapphire. I wondered which, if any, was the ring with which the Doge of The Most Serene Republic weds the sea every Easter-tide. The council put their heads together again and I couldn't hear anything they said.

Rekhmire' touched my shoulder, and Saverico took the baby out of my arm, returning her to another wet-nurse brought for the look of the thing. I dabbed at a damp spot on the silk brocade bodice Neferet had loaned me, and saw my fingertips shaking.

Not the time to be holding a child. Nightmare visions of her fragility assailed me, and I blinked them away, staring across the room at Leon Battista. At this distance I could see little enough – only that he seemed well-dressed, grubby, pale with his time in prison; but had evidently been kept in locked apartments, rather than down below us in the dungeons.

That will not stop them hanging him now, if they decide to.

We would look like a normal aristocrat family gathered in this justice hall. Even an Alexandrine secretary would not be so unusual. I wondered how many of the councillors were looking and wondering where the other representative of Alexandria was this morning. *Do they know she's his lover? Do they know 'she' should be here in place of me?*

Hot sweat gathered, and rolled down my back between my shoulder-blades. The canvas straps of the corset chafed under the sleeves of my bodice. For the first time in a number of years, I wished for a sword, and the memory of my knightly training.

'You paint, Donna Ilaria,' Foscari remarked, leaning forward and speaking plainly and clearly to me.

It may have been how he spoke to foreigners uncertain of the Venetian language. It felt as if he spoke to a child of eight or ten winters.

'I was studying the New Art in the studio of Tommaso Cassai.' Some truth must have rung in my tone, since that was the case. I saw two of the councillors speak to each other behind the chair of a third. 'Messer Leon Battista Alberti presented me with his treatise on the eye, and vision in painting. It is here.'

Rekhmire' walked forward and placed *De Pictura* on the table before the Doge, bowed, and returned to his place behind me.

Foscari shot a look at Leon Battista. 'The writing of this took you some time?'

'Yes, messire.' His voice sounded dry.

'And the copying, also, to have a copy that Donna Ilaria might have read to her?'

Leon Battista nodded, not speaking.

The Doge Foscari leaned back in his carved chair. 'Clearly, Donna Ilaria's father, Lord Honorius, supposed there to be a betrothal, all that time. Or you would not have been permitted to give such a gift. You do not deny this?'

Leon's chin came up. 'I say nothing.'

. . . And therefore, so far, not one of us has lied.

'I understand there has been legislation passed in Florence of late.' The Doge ignored a choked-off laugh from the fat man, and looked further down the table. 'Simon?'

The sleek man he addressed leaned his hands on the table. 'Indeed, seignior. They have passed laws legitimising prostitution. Messer Alberti will have heard.'

'They have done this,' the Doge Foscari looked blandly at Leon Battista Alberti, 'so that the young men of the city should become less interested in, shall we say, exclusively male pursuits.'

I fixed my eyes on a tile on the floor, following the ochre and red glaze's repeating geometric pattern. *I will not look at my father, I will not look at Rekhmire'!* 'Exclusively male.' Let Doge Foscari think the young woman is modestly pretending not to understand what is referred to.

Under my skirts, I have a womb and (as I ascertained privately once I was sufficiently healed) a functioning penis. 'Exclusively male' is considerably outside my experience.

' . . . And to further eradicate the sin of Sodom,' the Doge was saying. He had risen to his feet at some point; a ripple of light from the torches shot back colour from his jewel-encrusted brocade robes. Drawing him would be easy, painting the effect of that light and shadow unbelievably difficult. He held out his hands, plainly giving judgement.

'This is the sentence on Messer Leon Battista Alberti. Because of his

331

family's good name, and because of the lineage of the Captain-General of Castile and Leon,' a bow towards my father, 'it is considered just that the penalty of execution be commuted to exile. Messer Leon Battista Alberti shall have a month to leave our territories of the Italian Peninsula. But in the interests of holding up a good example, and discouraging that sin of Sodom which in Florence is so prevalent, and which threatens us everywhere, Messer Leon Battista Alberti shall hold to his promise of betrothal.'

Rekhmire''s arm quivered, where he had stepped close and now pressed against me. I felt his shock as clearly as I felt mine. Honorius frowned and opened his mouth. Out of sight, I dug my fingers into the palm of his hand, cutting myself against the edge of his plate gauntlet.

Foscari turned his head away and fixed an unrelenting gaze on Leon Battista.

'Because we will see justice done, you will be married in the presence of a priest. Before you depart from Venezia! I will call for a confessor now, and you shall be shriven clean so that you can marry. This child will have a father's name. This shamed maiden shall be made into a wife.'

Silence echoed through the chamber.

The Doge turned towards Honorius. 'It has been forty days: your daughter has been churched.'

Honorius took no notice of my nails digging into the thin leather glove he wore under his gauntlet. He bowed with the skill of a courtier, and spoke with the bluntness of a soldier. 'Yes, lord. She can wed whenever you desire.'

There is nothing else he *can* say, I admitted to myself. Anything else will smack of trying to win concessions, either from the Alberti family or the Doge himself, and this Foscari is likely to find some way to remove Leon again if he thinks his decision is being used for advantage.

The Doge looked across the vast chamber at me. 'As soon as you are wed and able to bear the journey, you will leave Venice and join your husband in Florence.'

Leon Battista choked. 'Florence!'

'You may join your family there,' Foscari said amiably. 'Other members of your family are also returning, I understand. We will miss them, after so many years in our Republic.'

The candlelight showed his face all innocence as he taunted Leon Battista.

'As I understand,' Foscari concluded, 'the ban against your family in Florence has been lifted. Your exile is over. There are already moves to make your father one of Duke Ludovico's councillors. Of course, the agitation and rabble-rousing will stop; it doesn't become the Alberti to act against their own Duke. As I'm sure your family will tell you.'

It was clear enough to me: the Alberti family have been given a place in Florence again – on the condition that they keep their insurrectionary son under control.

Leon was close enough between his guards that I read the realisation in his face. No more pamphlets, no attacking the Republic of Florence for its injustices, because the Albertis have a stake in the city again – as it stands. No more talk that might lead to revolution. The poor will stay poor, and at the mercy of the powerful.

Leon's expression closed. He bowed.

He might continue to think his family had sold him out. Or he might tell himself that ideals of good government are a naive man's illusions. I didn't know him well enough to know which way he would go.

Once again, I thought. I'm marrying someone – and I have no true idea of who they are.

23

'It's arranged.' Honorius threw off his cloak, and came to stand by the hearth. 'The banns will be read thrice, and then you'll be married.'

I sank further down on the settle, easing my shoes off. My toes were hot and cold at the same time, and I wriggled them in my stocking-hose, presenting them to the fire. 'Good! Tell Neferet she and Leon can leave as soon as we're done.'

Honorius nodded soberly. Rekhmire' shot me a questioning look.

Dear god, I thought.

He wants to know if I've told Honorius what happened in Rome—

'It won't be legal,' I blurted out.

Honorius turned his back to the fire, hitching up the skirt of his doublet and warming his backside. 'How could it be? I'll be honest, Ilario, I don't know if you *can* marry. As a man-woman—'

'I can marry.'

'What?' He suddenly frowned.

'This gets Leon safely out of Venice,' I said. 'But you should know . . . I went through a Christian marriage ceremony in Rome. To an Etruscan woman, Sulva. I was married: that time as the groom. This time, it will be the bride.'

I have rarely seen such an expression.

'Groom?' Honorius stared at me. 'Bride.'

'You should reassure Leon it's in name only,' I emphasised dryly. And then, as the thought occurred to me: 'Although it may not bother him: he's with Neferet, after all.'

His face made me itch to reach for my chalks, in the same way as I had wanted to in the Doge's hall. The difference being that Honorius, unlike Foscari, made me want to smile.

Rekhmire' crossed the room in answer to a soft knock at the door. Tired enough to watch without seeing, I barely registered one of the house servants pass a note to the Egyptian.

'Life.' Rekhmire' observed as he came back from the door.

'What?'

'Our assassin – Secretary Ramiro Carrasco de Luis. The Doge's Council have committed him to prison for life. I suspect he'll end up on one of those islands.'

The Egyptian's nod towards the unshuttered windows made me

follow his gaze. A small patch of blue sky showed between the buildings opposite. The canal reflecting the sky's light back to it. I thought how brilliant it would be out on the lagoon.

In which are isolated small islands, covered in cypresses, which they call lazaretto: quarantined islands for sufferers from leprosy, or prisoners who will never be released. Sometimes both on the same island.

If that made me shudder, I had only to remember the moments of not being able – because of another's physical force – to breath in air. Nothing kills human sympathy so fast.

'We won't be rid of him.' Honorius spoke without moving away from the fire.

'A life sentence,' Rekhmire' began irritably.

'Not *Carrasco*.' Honorius glanced down apologetically, evidently realising he robbed me of heat. He sat, beside me, his back nearly as upright as the oak settle's. 'Videric! Or, some other man, or men, *sent* by Aldra Videric. Videric *will* send more spies. More murderers.'

The tone admitted of no doubt. I glanced automatically towards the cradle in the corner of the room, to reassure myself that Onorata slept.

No matter that a child doesn't understand, I think she hears the tone of a man's voice . . .

'You're right.' I rubbed at gritty eyes. 'I saw them drag Carrasco off and was glad – that lasted, oh, a quarter of an hour. And then I realised that as soon as Videric stops getting what reports Carrasco was sending him, he'll send other men, to replace the ones who attacked us on Torcello.'

In my mind I have the flare of a striped cotton robe as a man turns, the clack of his war-sandals on tiles as he walks away, leaving me with a woman who he fully expects to murder me. *That's the last time I saw him*, I realised suddenly.

I ran for a ship immediately after my mother – after *Rosamunda* – tried to kill me.

I know he sent her after me. I know he will have sent others. But that's the last I saw: his face concerned with worry for his wife – and all of it a flat-out lie, to get me into the same room with her so that she could put a dagger into me.

It is more than three quarters of a year now. I wonder if that fair hair, that burly profile, look any different. If exile back to his estates at Rodrigo's order has made him look old. Or whether he merely bides his time, knowing that sooner or later one of the murderers he sends *will* kill me. And then the scandal may have the chance to die, too, and he may in the future come back to court . . .

'Carrasco's arrest solves nothing.' Restless, I rose to walk about the room, careful not to tread the hem of my petticoats underfoot. 'If no one else tells Videric, Federico will – because God forbid my foster father shouldn't be scrambling to be in favour with every faction he can find!'

335

Honorius seemed surprised at my bitterness. 'You know him better than I do. This Federico, I mean. Videric I remember as Rodrigo's Chancellor, before I went north for the Crusades.'

He looked a little bitter himself, and I wondered if his expression mirrored mine – or mine his.

'Ilario, you can't expect me to be unbiased. Videric blackmailed Rosamunda into staying with him instead of leaving with me.'

Much as I like the idea that Honorius is my father, it still jolts me that Rosamunda remains my mother.

And that that is irrevocable, no matter that the man I thought my father is only a stepfather – my mother's husband.

And a man who will send other men to kill me. I have considered this, wide awake in the Venetian darkness, while the campanile lets me know it is three, four, five in the morning.

Rekhmire''s crutch struck the floor with a hollow sound as he came to peer out of the window, at the narrow view afforded of the Campo S. Barnaba from this room. 'I'm told the Council's dungeons aren't good for the health. It's possible Master Carrasco won't be transported to the lazarettos.'

A breath of chill touched me that was not this winter cold. *If there were other Alexandrines here, I would suspect that was an offer ...*

'All the while Carrasco was here,' I speculated, 'Videric evidently felt he *would* kill me. He either doubted, or he sent the men who attacked me on Torcello to assist Carrasco. Now ... I have no idea how many men he can hire who would murder me for money, or where they'll be, or how long it'll take them to get to Venice – if he didn't give up on Ramiro Carrasco and send them weeks ago.'

I intercepted a look between the two men.

'You're right,' Honorius agreed as if the Egyptian had spoken. 'It's even more unsettling when that happens in petticoats.'

'What, when I prove I have more wit than a firefly?' I glared at both of them. 'Remind me *never* to dress up as a woman again, once I'm out of Venice.'

Rekhmire' gave me a crooked smile. 'Breeches or petticoats, you are still in need of a good beating. I regret I never took my opportunity as your master.'

Such jokes are a lot easier for the master to make. But, free, I can afford to smile at them, and I did.

His expression becoming serious, Rekhmire' stated, 'Aldra Videric will send more men: he cannot afford not to. More hired men who won't think twice about killing. Sooner or later, there will be a slip – even among your men, Master Honorius.'

I miss Rekhmire''s presence at the wedding, I realised, looking around the cold and gloomy Frankish church. He had been a rock of comfort when I went to Sulva, however much he may have disagreed with my reasons for that marriage.

'Man and wife,' Honorius murmured in my ear, as we walked down the aisle to the altar-rail, his baritone surprisingly quiet for a man used to shouting across battlefields. He proceeded to prove himself far too much in the Egyptian's company of late by adding, with black humour, 'Which one would *you* like to be?'

I clapped my hand up to my mouth, hiding a splutter of horrified amusement. I bowed my head, and hoped the looming members of the Alberti family would take it as feminine shyness. 'The Lion of Castile is about to come to a horrible end in the Most Serene Republic, I hope you realise?'

'Ah, what it is to have a dutiful daughter . . . '

He squeezed my arm with quite genuine encouragement and stepped forward to consult with the group of middle-aged men in dark velvet and miniver fur. I caught sight of Leon Battista at the back, his Roman nose all the more prominent for the gaunt lines of starvation in his face.

And that would be how they convinced him . . .

I wished again that I had Rekhmire' at my shoulder, to exchange looks of realisation, and to discuss, *sotto voce*, whether it would be wise to go through with this, despite Neferet's pleas.

A persistent wail echoed into the high Gothic beams.

Honorius took Onorata out of Attila's arms, displaying her in her swaddling clothes to the Alberti men. Unused to it, she found the bindings uncomfortable, and her crying had a determined edge. I bit my lip and stayed where I had been left.

'A girl?' The older Alberti sounded displeased. 'Well, there is no need to worry about dowries, she can always be put in a convent. There's time for a son later. At least this proves my grandson capable of siring a child.'

The significant look he shot over his shoulder at Leon led me to suppose he had made aspersions to the contrary. Leon's mouth set in a thin line: he did not look towards me.

I thought it was I who was making the sacrifice here. But I have no lover to object to my name being coupled with another's.

Honorius handed my baby back to the large Germanic man-at-arms, and Attila took a longer way down the church so that he might pass me, heels ringing on the flagstones, and let me look at Onorata as he passed. Her face was scarlet, her eyes screwed up and hot with tears. He touched a forefinger to the swaddling bands and gave me a significant look – by which I knew him off to remove them.

I have marked the sympathy between soldiers and small children before now, in Taraco; I had not ever thought I would be grateful to it when it provided me with at least six persistent and efficient nursemaids. Even if they are not half so enthusiastic during the small hours of the night, or when it came to changing breech-clouts.

'Madonna Ilaria.' The priest beckoned me forward to stand at Leon Battista's side.

S. Barnaba had nothing worth the looking at, its altar-piece was third-rate, and the Green priest – evidently hired by the Alberti family – rattled through the ceremony so fast that it reached the moment of commitment before I was ready for it.

Leon had no shred of prison dirt on him now, even the stench being eradicated in favour of soap and civet, but I could recognise the expression on his face. That of a slave who has been punished by dark and isolation, and found it full of unexpected monsters.

'Yes.' My mouth formed the appropriate words before I was aware I had made my decision. Consenting to wed this man, in name only, is nothing more than words to me. It is freedom to him.

I walked out of the church married for the second time in half a year. This time as the bride.

'We understand your daughter and the child cannot travel as yet.' The Alberti patriarch spoke to Honorius, without even a glance towards me. 'We will send our son from Florence to collect her, as soon as she may.'

The proper things were said, the Alberti men departed in a splendidly-decorated oared boat, and I noted Leon Battista slipping quietly off into the Alexandrine embassy ahead of us.

It took me a time to settle Onorata, she being too disturbed to sleep – eventually conceding only when Attila fetched a bowl of milk and a spoon from the kitchens, and sat by the fire to feed her with infinite patience.

I recall those hands, so much larger than my child's head, loosing the bolt that tore the Carthaginian agent apart. It will not be the first or last man that he has killed.

I made a sketch with coal and chalk, that was only broad shapes except for the features, but caught the difference between the two faces: one still unmarked and with deep clear eyes, the other with half a lifetime worn into skin creased with staring through sunlight.

Coming downstairs, I walked into Rekhmire' as he left the main room, and clutched at him to keep both of us on our feet.

A fragile Venetian glass hurtled through the door and smashed on the opposite wall.

Rekhmire' wouldn't be able to bend down with his crutch; therefore called for one of the Egyptian's servants to sweep up the fragments. I nodded towards the open door, hearing loud raised voices beyond.

'What is it?'

Rekhmire' finished steadying himself with a grip on my shoulder, and brushed himself down. 'It's Master Leon Battista. He says he cannot travel to Alexandria, it appears.'

Alexandria would be a good refuge for him – for us all, I thought. It was too cold to stand in this passageway, spring or not, and besides, I was curious as to the actions of my husband. I strode through the open door, Rekhmire' behind me, the cloth-padded end of his crutch stomping down on the floorboards.

Neferet instantly flung away from Leon Battista, where the dark man stood silhouetted at the window, and glared at me. '*Here* she is. The happy bride! No wonder you won't leave Venice!'

Slave or free, I can recognise when someone desires a mere target for their temper. Without venom, I reminded, 'You asked me to do this.'

She stalked out of the room, pulling the door behind her with a shattering crash.

Rekhmire' took some moments to arrange himself in the armed chair by the hearth; I took the settle, and after a moment Leon Battista walked to sit beside me.

'That's poor thanks for saving my life.' He spoke firmly, holding my gaze. 'I've told Neferet the marriage will remain in name only: she has no need for concern. Please don't take that as an insult – if I were not hers, I could seek for no better woman than you for my wife.'

Rekhmire''s luminous dark eyes caught mine. Whatever else Neferet might have said in her rage, I perceived that 'hermaphrodite' was not one of those words.

'I don't take offence,' I said, and attempted to sound as if I only changed the subject out of feminine embarrassment. 'I had expected you and Neferet to be on the first ship out for Alexandria-Constantinople?'

Leon Battista looked down at his hands. The knuckles were more prominent than they should be. He rubbed his fingers together.

'My family's exile is ended, on condition they rein in their rabble-rousing son.' His expression turned sour. He looked up, without lifting his head, and met my gaze through his long, dark lashes. 'Therefore, I have to be seen in Florence. *With* my family, carrying on the family's affairs, and not fomenting rebellion against the Duke.'

Rekhmire' leaned forward and prodded the coal with one of the fire-irons. He sat back with a grunt. 'The Alberti family expect Master Leon Battista to be in *your* company, Ilario, as soon as you may travel. Not Neferet's.'

The short walk from church had given me enough time to solve that problem. 'Tell them I *died*! Plague. Cholera. Anything! It happens all the time. You can safely tell anyone that, just as soon as I can leave Venice.'

Not before. I would be very surprised if the Alberti didn't have men watching their son's wife. And, by his expression, I had no need to spell that out.

Leon's mouth quirked. 'There's no need to condemn you to an early grave. When it becomes possible, I can prove our marriage void.'

'You can?' All the banns and church offices had been what I understand the Frankish marriage ceremonies to be. I could not help looking at him in surprise. 'How?'

339

Leon Battista took a deep breath. 'I married Neferet six months ago, in the autumn.'

My mouth was open, but I could make no sound come out.

'Although,' he added, 'for obvious reasons, I can't take Neferet to Florence as my wife – the family would insist on having a council of midwives to examine her, to confirm that she was a virgin before she married me, and capable of child-bearing. And that . . . '

'Yes, I can see that would present problems.'

The door opened; Neferet's women servants came in, followed by Neferet herself – she looked taken aback to see me still present, and she glared at Rekhmire', but since neither of us moved, she gestured for wine to be served.

After a warming sip of the wine, I had courage enough to look her in the face. 'Couldn't you go to Florence as Leon's mistress?'

The lines of her face spoke, *I don't know what business this is of yours!* more clearly than any word could have.

She nevertheless seated herself gracefully on one of the window-embrasures, reclining on cushions embroidered in the Alexandrine style. 'Think, Madonna Ilaria! Leon arrives *without* his new wife and infant child, but *with* a mistress – and a foreign mistress at that! How long before the family demands he be respectable?'

Something under a quarter of an hour after passing Florence's walled gate, I suspected, but didn't desire to say. Neferet's long-fingered large hands still faintly trembled with anger. No need to draw the lightning down on myself.

'If I go as a cook or servant,' she said, her graceful reclining pose stiffening with her neck, 'or anything else an unmarried woman may do, I will be assumed as a matter of course to be Leon's whore.'

Her head turned: she fixed Leon with a desolate stare.

'And I am *your wife*.'

Leon Battista sprang up, went to the window, and knelt down beside her. I thought it tactful to turn away and converse with Rekhmire' while Leon comforted her.

I drained my wine glass. 'No one would care in Alexandria, would they?'

'That they are man and man, not man and wife? Likely not; why should they? If they want to live as man and woman, and are discreet, Ty-ameny would permit it. Given Master Leon's interest in the arts and architecture, and the Classical writings, I think she would even forgive him being a Frank.'

There was a very faint teasing air about that last. I smiled briefly at him.

'But still,' Rekhmire' murmured, the amusement leaving his expression, 'Neferet didn't expect to return to Alexandria without him. That will hurt her.'

'*I would take you with me!*' Leon's voice rose. 'I swear by Christ on the Tree! If there was any way it could be managed—'

Perhaps the matter had been enough on my mind recently that I saw through it, in that instant, to an answer. As if I reached up and caught the tail of the lightning-bolt, and was instantly gifted with illumination.

Yes: this will work!

But she will not like it, I realised. It may work, but she will hate it and me . . .

I stood up, finding by that I drew Rekhmire''s and Leon's attention. Leon had one arm about Neferet's waist, where he knelt at her side. Neferet's large fingers were interlocked with his.

'You said it yourself,' I remarked, meeting Neferet's gaze. 'There's no role for an unmarried woman in a house in Florence. Or for one married to a *different* man, or to a widow, unless you could produce visible evidence of a husband. You wouldn't be trusted because you're a foreigner.'

Leon scowled, looking as if he would interrupt.

'*I* found Venice far more confining than Rome or Carthage,' I said, 'and in Carthage I was a slave! But leaving that aside: in Venice, I've been a woman. In Rome, I was,' remembering Leon's presence, I stumbled over, 'dressed as – a man.'

Rekhmire' gestured with an open demanding palm. 'And?'

I turned to the other Alexandrine. 'Neferet, couldn't you go to Florence—'

Some friendly deity moved me to add a phrase:

'—disguised as a man?'

She stared.

I added hastily, 'Nobody would think anything of Leon taking on an Alexandrine scribe as a secretary—'

'*Disguised as a man?*'

Neferet shrieked loudly enough that I had time to think I would, if I had simply said *go to Florence as a man,* either now be deaf, or have had something injurious thrown at me. And likely deserve it.

I snapped out, 'If I can disguise myself as a man, you can!'

I saw her turn the matter over in her mind. She knows, from gossip with Honorius's men-at-arms, that I was a thoroughly convincing young man in Rome. She has been telling me, all the while I've been here, that truly I am a woman. If I can pass as a man, therefore – why not she?

'I won't do it!' She stood up, trembling. 'It's undignified! And you—' She swung around, pointing a finger at Rekhmire'. 'You've never believed me anything but Jahar pa-sheri! You see me as a monster, don't you?'

Rekhmire', pale under his reddish skin, sat bolt upright. 'No more than I do Ilario!'

Frustration sealed her lips: she glared at Rekhmire', and at me, and turned on her heel to shout at Leon Battista.

The Florentine was still kneeling on the floor beside the window-seat. He looked up, without rising.

'Neferet – I really don't mind.'

Her hand made a fist, in the folds of her dress. She stared so intensely at him, her glance would have made glass catch fire and burn.

'What do you mean?'

He put a hand on the window embrasure and pushed himself up, making a face as his knees evidently pained him. The wet cold in the Doge's prison takes a long time to leave a man's bones.

'I don't care.' He walked over and took each of Neferet's hands in his own. 'Whether you're a man or a woman, whether you *dress* as a man or a woman – none of that has any importance. It's you I love.'

Neferet began to cry.

I had my arm under Rekhmire''s other armpit, acting as an additional crutch, and tactfully removed us from the room. I signalled as I left for one of the men-at-arms to guard the door – since there is an obvious method by which Leon could convince Neferet of his love, and if I were Leon, I wouldn't even waste so much time as it would take to reach the bedrooms.

Heading by common consent for the kitchen, where it would be warm, Rekhmire' shook his head as he walked, still gripping lightly at my arm.

'I haven't seen Neferet in a scribe's kilt in fifteen years. And then only when court formalities wouldn't let her get away with anything else.' He steered us towards the kitchen inglenook, with a wave to the cooks. 'Better send up the wine in wooden bowls – it's not like the house has much Venetian glass left!'

'You're glad for her.'

'Am I?' He busied himself with being seated, tucking his crutch beside him, and easing that leg into a stretch towards the fire. The heat of the fire, perhaps, cast a flush onto his cheek.

'She's your friend. You're happy that she's happy.' I winced at a dimly heard crash from the depths of the house. 'Or at least, if not happy, that she can be with Leon.'

'The Florentines will find her a trifle feminine, I think.' He gave me a sudden grin. 'But then, all we Alexandrine eunuchs are feminine males, according to common talk!'

I grinned back. 'I don't think you'd suit a Frankish skirt and bodice . . . '

In the hours following, Neferet's quarrel broke out from time to time, like an unquenched brush-fire – but it had little enough true heat, given that she would break off from her ranting to look in wonder at Leon, and her demeanour invariably softened after that. Since the Alberti were due to depart in two days, she had perforce to make a decision and pack.

I woke early on that morning, to feed Onorata, and to bid Neferet farewell. I found her in the atrium of the house – and for a moment truly did not recognise Neferet in this slim and straight-shouldered man, dressed in the short linen jacket and white kilt of an Alexandrine scribe.

'Ilaria.' She spoke with the pitch of her voice lower, a little husky.

Her skin showed smooth, under the linen. Her face looked curiously bare with only a line of kohl above each row of eyelashes. She had her hair cut short, falling to touch her shoulders, as one of the Alexandrine customs is, and a narrow braided reed-band holding it back from her eyes.

Honorius's men-at-arms, at the house door, could be heard greeting Leon Battista.

'Good fortune,' I said, a little hurriedly, not able to put all I thought into words.

'You too.' She – he – smiled.

It was a morning cool and damp enough for fog, rolling in with the smell of the sea about it, clinging to Venice's brick walls and Roman-tiles roofs, and filtering the sunlight to diffuse glory. At the gate of the Alexandrine house, Leon Battista awaited us. He greeted Neferet with no more than a companionable nod – something neither his servants nor the oarsmen of his boat would be surprised to see, in a man collecting a new officer for his household.

Their eyes linked. It was a different enough story that I thought *I hope they can be discreet.*

'This is a custom among my people.' Neferet opened a small folded cloth that she carried. I saw a glint of reddish black. She held up a braided loop, handing one to Leon Battista, and one to Rekhmire', and – after a fractional hesitation – one to me.

A bracelet, I found, clasped with gold, and made with braided shining hair. Neferet's hair, now that she had dropped her hair to man's length.

'Thank you.' Bereft of words, I could say nothing else.

Neferet, or Jahar, gave me a look with humour in the depths of it, and murmured, 'Think of it as a wedding gift . . . '

I stumbled though Leon's formal farewells, and watched as Rekhmire' limped forward on his crutch to give last departing words to both apparent men, all the while my thumb caressing the braided bracelet, and the damp fog pearling on my velvet over-gown.

I turned and went back into the embassy.

A few moments later, Rekhmire' stamped back inside – as well as a man walking with a crutch may stamp – blowing on his fingers against the damp cold, and swearing.

'What?' I asked.

'—Holy dung that hatched the cosmos-egg!' he concluded. 'Damn that woman!'

Having seen the boat depart, and Rekhmire''s salute to it, I'd thought all well.

'She still won't tell me where Herr Mainz is!' He made a fist, his face scarlet. 'Nor will Master Alberti. And they wait until *now* to tell me this!'

'Why won't they?'

'Some nonsense that the Florentine Duke will demand Herr Mainz, if he appears openly in Venice, and that at the moment, La Serenissima would probably keep Florence quiet by handing the man over. If they don't imprison him on their own behalf, and try to beat the secret of this printing-*machina* out of him!'

I shrugged, following the Egyptian towards the kitchens. 'If I were Herr Mainz, *I'd* certainly want to stay out of sight.'

'Sacred Eight, I want to *help* the man!' The padded end of the crutch thwacked the short, wide floorboards. 'Ty-ameny needs him; I want to invite him to Alexandria—'

'—Which, until the weather's better, is inaccessible by road, and no ship will risk these seas. So he can't leave Venice.'

'Sun god's *egg*!'

'You would have said precisely the same thing, if you were in Neferet's place.'

While true, it was not tactful; I was not in the least surprised when he stomped away towards the stairs, muttering under his breath. 'I could have hidden him *here*! Sent him to Edirne with the Turk! *Something!*'

I heard him calling for fresh ink as he vanished into his room, and guessed he intended a ciphered message to follow Neferet, and say this and more.

I reflected: If I were her, I'd make sure to drop the paper in a canal – or in the Arno, if it reaches her in Florence.

Florence, I belated realised.

My wife and my husband will end up living within the walls of the same city.

The man-at-arms Berenguer grinned at me, the following morning.

'Get your cloak, Mistress Ilario. You're being abducted.'

It said something for the state of mind to which constant threat had reduced me that I wore a dagger on my belt about the house – though the dress's hanging sleeves might have made drawing it quickly impractical.

One look at Berenguer convinced me I had no need.

'Abducted?'

'Sold,' he corrected himself, picking my winter cloak up from where it lay across the back of the wooden settle. He held it up, as a gentleman does for a lady. 'Betrayed by the faithless mercenaries employed by the foreign captain Lord Honorius . . . '

Berenguer might not have liked a hermaphrodite when he met me in Rome. He might from time to time still give me wary looks when the two of us chanced to be in a room alone together, as if I might leap on him, and seduce and rape him simultaneously. *But as for not trusting him to be faithful to my father* . . .

I walked across the room to stand with my back to the black-haired man-at-arms, letting him settle the woollen cloak around my shoulders.

'Who's buying me?' I inquired.

Berenguer somewhat automatically tied my cloak-ties for me and then stood back a little awkwardly and permitted me to raise the silk-lined and fur-trimmed hood myself. His sharp glance assessed me.

'The weasel-lord,' he announced. 'What's-name? The one with the horse-faced wife.'

'Federico. That's my foster father you're insulting,' I added, settling the folds of the green cloak about me. 'Accurately, I may say. Although Valdamerca has her charitable moments.'

Berenguer chuckled, at least partly with relief that his lord's son-daughter hadn't chosen to take offence when treated like a woman and spoken to like a man.

'Her husband's about to be *very* charitable!' He held the room door open for me, hand on the hilt of his bastard sword. 'Do you think you could look frightened for us?'

'Us', it transpired, were fifteen of my father's soldiers – Attila and Tottola without smiles, and therefore at their most intimidating; every man else in brigandine or breastplate, with swords or maces; even Saverico with his polished sallet under his arm, a red and gold silk sash tied from shoulder to waist.

A tall, thin soldier with his cloak hood raised proved, on lifting the edge of it, to be Honorius.

'Help,' I observed gravely. 'Oh, oh, I am being stolen away! Will nobody help a poor defenceless—'

'"Defenceless"', my backside!' Honorius brushed his knuckles against my cheek with open affection. 'I told Berenguer when he brought me this story – if we just take the money and hand you over, not only will we be rich, *I'll* have some peace and quiet!'

Under the cover of general amusement, and donning of cloaks over armour, intended to disguise the immediate passage of armed mercenaries through Venice's alleys, I asked Honorius, 'What in Christ-the-Emperor's name does he think he's *doing!*'

'Lord Videric? Sending your foster father to buy off my soldiers. After all, they're only common mercenaries.'

Over the less-than-sincere thanks offered by his men at that point, I managed to amend my question. 'Truly, I meant Federico.'

'Being desperate! That's what *he's* doing.' My father produced a short length of rope, wrapped it about my wrists in a false knot, and gave me the two ends to grip in my hands so that I looked sufficiently bound. 'I spoke to the Egyptian about this. He suggests that, if messages and travellers are getting through from the Peninsula, Federico will have heard directly from Videric. I think he's right. Whether or not Videric knows we disposed of Carrasco, he's clearly told Federico to move his arse.'

I nodded. 'Something was going to happen, now. It's inevitable.'

The sky above me was the colour of lapis lazuli ashes. The warm air shifted, bringing me the scents of cooking, canal water, and the lagoon. However cold it may still be, and how wet, the world is beginning to move again. If long sea voyages are still unsafe, there are the coastal routes. And some of the better-maintained roads, the Via Augusta included, will be open.

'Is Rekhmire' coming to make sure I'm properly sold?'

Honorius shook his head. 'He'd be recognised. I've requested him to stay here with the rest of the guard, and protect my granddaughter.'

I ignored a stab of disappointment. Because, injured leg or no, I will trust Rekhmire''s determination to protect Onorata above most men's.

'Videric will send more men to kill me,' I observed as we walked across the Campo S. Barnaba. 'True, the more men he hires, the more gossip, the more danger people will hear what he's doing – but I think he'll be willing to risk that, now.'

'Bandits. Pirates. Thugs.' Honorius grunted. He pulled the front of his hood forward. Dressed as a plain soldier, there was nothing to mark him out from the other cloaked mercenaries. 'Knew I should have brought more than three lances . . . '

'We're worth six!' Saverico grinned. Tottola slapped him on the shoulder, which all but sent the slight ensign staggering.

I expected a boat to be waiting, but we instead walked on into the mass of lanes and small squares, until we had left the Dorsodura quarter, and finally approached the Grand Canal. We emerged on the edge of that wide thoroughfare at the foot of the Rialto Bridge.

Berenguer glanced at Honorius for permission, and fell in beside me as we walked in under the wooden roof that capped the bridge.

'We've arranged a public place for the exchange.' Berenguer's grin showed two teeth missing, far back on the left side. 'Less chance of anybody cheating . . . '

The sides of the bridge were also walled with solid planks, but no man could see that except from the outside. Inside, too many shop-booths blocked the line of sight; goods piled up clear to the bridge's roof. We picked a way up the wide stone steps, between merchants and gossiping servants; groups of men purchasing goods or changing money; woman accompanied by male relatives or armed servants.

I shook my head, amazed. 'Federico approached you directly?'

Berenguer gave that kind of shrug that invites discrete admiration. 'Sent one of his servants. But I'd seen the man at that palazzo, when you went after the secretary. Told him I wouldn't talk to anybody but his master.'

'And Federico *agreed*?'

If that's the case, Honorius will not be so far from the mark if he describes my foster father as desperate.

'Yeah. Next time, sure enough, there's Lord Weasel – beg pardon, Lord Federico – muffled up to the eyes, and telling me that he knows we're mercenaries, we're for hire, and he can offer us a better contract than Captain-General Honorius—' Berenguer put up his hand, as if to say *you've heard nothing!*, and added, 'His *first* offer is, every man who comes in on this can get a place in Lord Carmagnola's Venetian army, and have a share of the plunder of Milan, along with Lord Weasel's hefty bribe—'

Attila stepped up on Berenguer's other side, towering a full head above us. He had braided his beard, but left his mane of hair loose; any man could believe him an eater of babies and easily hired murderer. He snorted. 'The General and Lord Carmagnola fought together, up north, so he'd have our arses skinned if we even *thought* about this!'

Berenguer grinned. 'Lord Weasel thinks we're too dumb to know that. So I ask: what will Lord Federico pay in cold cash? And he says: every man can have a safeguarded voyage to the mainland, a saddlebag of gold, and a horse to ride away on. All we have to do is bring him the General's son-daughter, so she can be put away in a convent, safe and sound!'

Ahead, at the top of the steps, I could see light. The open drawbridge section of the Rialto, that is winched up to let tall-masted boats through on their way up the Canal Grande.

'Kidnapped and put in a convent.' I glanced at Honorius, but he had already fallen back into the crowd of armed men, indistinguishable as their captain. Tottola moved in on my flank, a mirror-image of Attila's Germanic wildness.

Berenguer gave me an apologetic glance and took hold of my elbow. 'Lord Weasel, he sounded like he believed it. But if he's your foster dad, he'd want to, wouldn't he? This Lord back in Taraco, this Aldra Videric, he didn't mind sending men to kill us. I don't reckon you'd ever see the inside of any convent.'

'No.' My pulse jolted, chest feeling hollow. The muscles and tendons at the back of my knees pulled, walking up the steps, after so long recovering from Physician Bariş's surgery.

Berenguer scanned the crowds blocking the steps. 'Anyhow, I told Lord Weasel as how he'd have to give us gold. *And* a ship to get off this island. He bargained a bit, but he agreed. Normally, I'd reckon he'd tell the Doge we stole his money and have us taken up and hanged for theft, but he can't risk us talking. Not that it matters . . . '

The crowds became no thinner at the high arch of the Rialto Bridge. I found myself in the midst of cloaked men who might be conspicuous in their number. *But then, Federico will have brought household men-at-arms, too . . .*

Looking above the heads of the Venetians, I saw a mast and sails gliding past.

The creak of the winch and clatter of chains indicated the drawbridge was being wound down into place again.

'Deal is, half the gold when we hand you over; half when we reach the mainland.' Berenguer surveyed me, head to foot. 'Could you maybe look frightened now?'

I have over a dozen armed soldiers around me, and my father.

'No.' I shrugged. 'It would look unconvincing. He'd see that. I can manage "sullen".'

Berenguer's hand went up, tilting his sallet's visor to shield his eyes against the spring sun. 'We don't want him to run before we get the money . . . He's here!'

Gathered in the small open space between the sheltered Rialto and the drawbridge itself, we were not quite enough to block the general way. I saw Federico instantly, his white face visible under a brown felt hat as he approached from the Rialto's other side.

One man in his livery colours walked behind him, a middling-sized iron-bound chest clasped in both arms.

I bit my lip, preventing myself with difficulty from pointing this out to Berenguer or Tottola. *They see it too – and they are besides supposed to have betrayed you!*

Berenguer pulled at my elbow, striding forward onto the drawbridge itself. 'Come on, you!'

The planks did not shift underfoot, but I could see the green waters of the Grand Canal between them.

Only Berenguer and Tottola came forward. The dozen others remained on that side of the Rialto Bridge; I supposed by prior agreement. The urge to break out laughing almost overwhelmed me. If I could not manage fear or recalcitrance, I contrived to look exasperated – by way of thinking of my silverpoint drawing of Onorata back at the embassy, which I had spent three days on, and ruined with four unwise strokes just before the midday meal.

I looked across the short distance at Federico, and greeted him with a glare of hate. *He will expect me to have deduced himself behind this: who else is there in Venice now who can act on Videric's behalf?*

It may not be true in a week or two's time – but for now, there is only my foster father.

'Lord Federico.' I spoke before either he or Berenguer could, and heard my voice shake. With excitement, but I hoped he did not recognise that. 'You were never a father to me. But I didn't think even you could hand me over to be butchered like a hog!'

Tottola's immense arm wrapped around my upper chest, squeezing my tender breasts painfully if (I thought) accidentally. His other hand clapped over my mouth.

It was less violent than it looked, by far, but the sensation that he need only move the upper edge of his hand to stifle me made it easy to struggle. The German soldier's grip locked solidly around me.

Federico pulled off his brimless hat, ran his hands through disordered wispy hair, and pulled the hat on again. His skin was pale, dotted with sweat across his wide brow. He hissed, 'You will not be butchered! I have a promise of that! It is no more than giving you up to the life of a devout religious!'

Imprisoned in some cold stone nunnery or monastery, woken every three hours through the night to pray, and fed only on what we might grow – nothing of this appeals to me, whether in God's name or man's. But no need to argue the matter.

I took a long look at Federico, wondering if it could be marked on his face: this man that raised me, sold me, benefited by me – is he also willing to help murder me? Or does he genuinely force himself into a belief that this is no more than kidnapping?

In the dialect of Taraconensis – which I thought he might suppose these mercenaries not to speak – I asked, 'What hold *is* it that Videric has over you?'

Federico laughed.

He spoke in the same local variant of Iberian Latin, while he fondly shook his head. 'He has no hold over me! On the contrary, he values me.

He has for many years taken my advice on investing his gold – I have a nose for where the trade will go, and what items are best bought and sold, and when. The Aldra Videric would hardly be half so wealthy if not for my aid—'

'Why not make *yourself* rich?' I cut in, holding his gaze. 'Foster father, you forget. I know what the estate is really like. I know that Valdamerca keeps hens and sells the eggs for pennies when she's at home. I know how long it took you to save up Matasuntha's dowry.'

Federico waved an impatient hand. 'It will come – gold clings to gold! Do you think me rich enough to invest on my own? At least at first? Ridiculous! But Aldra Videric has the funds to invest, and I benefit, also.'

I wondered what tiny percentage Videric doled out to him – remembered I must seem to be scared of abduction – and decided I could risk no more questions.

He and Berenguer spoke rapidly in one of the Frankish tongues. I turned my head so that my hood drooped concealingly over my face.

More quietly than I had ever heard him speak, Tottola murmured, 'Not long now . . . '

Federico snapped his fingers briskly, and folded his arms where he stood. The serving man staggered out onto the Rialto drawbridge, iron-bound chest clasped in both arms. Berenguer stepped forward, taking a key from Federico's hand, and thrust it in the lock and twisted.

I caught the merest glimmer.

The reflection of light from true gold is unmistakable.

'Looks about right.' Berenguer slammed the lid down and turned the key again, and hitched the chest over onto his hip as if it weighed no more than Onorata.

Federico, turning away, reached out and grasped my arm just below the shoulder. 'Ilario, come with me.'

''Fraid not.' Berenguer pulled sword and scabbard together out of the straps of his belt, and lay the still-undrawn weapon flat across Federico's chest.

With one hand to the sword-hilt and the other gripping the mouth of the scabbard, he could have edged steel free in a moment. But because he did not, because no sword was actually drawn, no man looked at us or interfered.

Federico stared down at the red leather of the scabbard in pure astonishment. 'You have your first half of the gold! Three thousand ducats! You get no more until you set foot on the Veneto!'

'She's – he's—' Berenguer stumbled. 'Ilario's not going anywhere with you.'

'We have a *contract*!'

Berenguer showed his teeth. 'Yeah. We did. Sorry about that – we changed our minds.'

It will not be so easy, I thought. And caught the moment that the skin folded and creased at the corners of Federico's eyes. In his narrowed gaze I saw anger and fear. *The latter is far more dangerous!*

Berenguer jerked his head, the polished finished of his helmet blazing back the sun. The dozen and more cloaked men strode forward onto the bridge itself, surrounding us.

Something nudged my shoulder.

I glanced back – just sufficiently less tall that I could glimpse Honorius's features, under the drooping edge of his hood.

'Contemptible!' Federico's jaw came up: he glared at Berenguer. 'You may attempt to cheat me. But what of when I go to your master Licinus Honorius, and say how you were willing to betray him for money?'

A cloaked figure brushed past my shoulder. Lifting his hands, putting his hood back, my father remarked cheerfully, 'Licinus Honorius already knows.'

With another company, it might have been possible to deceive Federico into thinking that the Captain-General had merely discovered the betrayal, and averted it.

These men have fought too long together: there's no mistaking their comradeship.

Which means my foster father is aware he has been taken, lock, stock, and arquebus-barrel.

Federico drew himself up, remarkably unafraid for a man with one servant at his back.

'How unfortunate to find you engaged in something so dishonest, Captain Honorius. But all the same, I believe you won't stop me taking my foster child away from here.'

'You think?' Honorius cocked a brow, and nodded towards the railing of the drawbridge. 'Think again.'

Honorius had clearly not left all twenty of his remaining men at the Alexandrine embassy. Ten of them, I saw, occupied two boats moored to slanting posts just at the side of the Rialto Bridge.

Seated in the bottom of the wide-bottomed boats, hands manacled behind them, were twice their number of men – a mixture of household servants without their livery badges, hired bravos, and that kind of man who is a petty criminal or a mercenary soldier according to the season of the year. More than half had ears cropped, or 'T' for 'thief' branded on their foreheads.

Honorius called an order. The men-at-arms rowed back into the side canal from which I deduced they must have come.

I turned to Federico. He seemed self-possessed – except for the colour of his complexion. A man might have blown plaster-dust across his skin and got that same aghast white.

All the rage is gone out of him.

He might have been furious at the trick, as well as a raid of consequences – Honorius's men-at-arms being unnerving *en masse* – but there was no anger to be drawn from his expression.

Federico looked about – for his servant, I realised. When I too looked, I couldn't see the man. Honorius's soldiers must have permitted him to run. He could go nowhere that would harm us.

'Keep the money.' Federico spoke abruptly. 'I'm done.'

There was more than satisfaction in Honorius's smile.

Of course, I thought. Now Honorius has three thousand ducats: he need not betray his location by going to any banker in any city.

Except that he *must* go back to Taraco! I made a grim note to bring this to my father's attention, yet again. *Before Videric robs him of all he has!*

Federico moved almost unconsciously back, feet shifting on the heavy planks.

I stepped forward and caught the velvet of his doublet sleeve. 'You may give Videric a message from me—'

'Videric? No!' Federico laughed harshly. He looked down at my hand, not pulling out of my grip, and then back at me. A scarlet flush covered the pallor of his cheeks: he looked unhealthy, and feverish. 'That's it: I'm *done*. I have Valdamerca and my girls with me – Matasuntha's husband will have to take care of her. Let the King confiscate that pitiable shack of an estate! I'm not returning to Taraconensis now.'

I found my hand holding the fabric tighter, as if I could keep him from escape. 'What do you mean, not going back to Taraco now? When *will* you go back?'

Federico laughed.

I heard bitterness in it, but a surprising amount of relief, too.

'Not ever.' He spoke almost gently, and stiffened his shoulders as he looked around at our mercenary soldiers. 'Never. This is what comes of trying to improve on my orders. Aldra Videric suggested I bribe your soldiers merely to desert, and then permit the men he will send to deal with you. I thought, if I had you in my hands to bring to him . . . '

His gaze was directed at the green water below, stippled and criss-crossed with gold light where wavelets caught the sun. I thought he saw none of that.

His tight, controlled voice quivered. 'And he will expect me to pay it back out of my own pocket! He will call me a fool for failing, and ask me for three thousand ducats. Dear Lord!'

Federico shook his head, and took a kerchief from his doublet sleeve to wipe across his forehead.

Things will not have changed so much in the eight months I have been gone, I thought, and said, 'You don't have three thousand ducats in gold.'

'Nor if I sold the estate!' Federico wiped his forehead again, and opened his hand. The white cloth spiralled down, spreading on the canal water below as it landed, and gradually sinking. He stared until the whiteness entirely vanished.

'I'm done!' he repeated. Straightening up off the drawbridge's railing, he snorted – a sardonic sound, that might have been a laugh – and looked at me. 'No need for concern. I have a nose for business, and I've made enough business contacts while making my lord Videric rich. I won't starve. The Alpine passes in northern Italy will be open by the time I reach the mainland. I think that Flanders and all of north Burgundy have it in them to be even richer than they are now . . . And I'm done with playing lapdog for my Lord Pirro Videric Galindo!'

Federico rolled out Videric's given name and matronymic with relish.

More than taken aback, I could only say, 'I thought you were his man.'

'And what is the use of supporting a man permanently out of power? Yes, he has wealth; he can buy men to do his bidding. But he's not a power in the land now, and he never will be – Videric becoming King Rodrigo's First Minister again: what are the chances of that?'

The scorn in his voice was hard, dry, and, I judged, perfectly genuine. It left me blinking at him in shock.

Federico patted my hand, where my fingers were still clenched in his sleeve. '*You* may give Aldra Videric a message from me, Ilario, since I hope devoutly never to see the man again.'

'I'm hardly so keen myself!'

Federico surprised me by laughing out loud.

'Nevertheless, if you do, convey him my regards. Tell him, I hope his miserly testicles wither and drop off. That, when he dies, I shall dance on his grave. And that, if I had known a quarter – an eighth part! – of the trouble waiting for me when he sent me after *you*, I would have thrown myself down on the Via Augusta and let the mule-train trample me to death!'

The soldiers chuckled, behind me. I heard Berenguer choke back an outright guffaw.

Federico clasped my hand in his and turned it over. I did not resist him. His thumb brushed the scribe's calluses, and those left by sword-use, still not gone after months without training. He regarded the smear of black charcoal that came off on his skin with seeming amusement.

'Aldra Videric knows you well enough to know you won't abandon the New Art. Just a word of warning.'

He patted my fingers with his other hand, and released me.

Looking up at the hooded figure of Honorius at my side, he said, 'Satisfy my curiosity, Aldra. Is she your son-and-daughter? Or did some son of yours father him? Or is it coincidence?'

Honorius took the iron-bound chest as Berenguer passed it to him and patted the lid. 'It would take more than three thousand ducats to buy those answers.'

'Indeed – I suspect them not for sale.' My foster father regarded my father for a long moment, looking almost jaunty. 'I also suspect you aren't a man to shoot someone in the back. Do let me know if I'm incorrect.'

Federico nodded politely, caught my eye as he turned away, and shot me a look so complex I could not unravel in it all the old loyalty, old grudges, despair, joy, and risk. His boots rang on the planks of the drawbridge, and then were muffled on the stone of the Rialto steps.

His back would not stop prickling until he reached his own palazzo, I guessed.

Perhaps not until he's out of Venice and across the Alps.

And it is not we who he fears.

The men he will send to deal with you. I heard Federico's voice in memory as he shoved his way into the Rialto crowds.

'He won't be the only man watching his back, now,' I said.

And it is not only here we face danger.

I looked at Honorius as we turned to retreat under the covered steps of the Rialto. It is weeks, if not more than a month, since my father received his letter from King Rodrigo. And, apart from the likelihood that Rodrigo's men have eaten Honorius's estate bare, now, and raided the others nearest to it . . . it is never wise to have a ruling king as an enemy.

25

Winter has not ever been my favourite season – at Federico's old estate, it meant feet continually numb in freezing mud; at Rodrigo's court, if fires burned in great brick hearths big enough to stable a horse, and I had boots, still, there was more venomous gossip around the Yule fireside than at any of her time.

Now I watched for spring's signs with terror.

If they come for me, and this family I have here, who will look after my child?

Even if she survives, she'll become a foundling in turn.

Trees, such as they are in Venezia, remained reassuringly bare of branch. But close inspection showed buds on every twig of the hazel beside S. Barnaba, thick and swelling, even if with no green at the tips yet. Travellers crossing the S. Marco square wore the clothes of Greece, Turkish Tyre and Sidon, Malta, and every other port from which further ships daily arrived. The Merceria was piled high with goods of all kinds, the scarcities and excuses of past weeks forgotten as if unspoken. People walked with heads up, their backs not stooped over into biting winds, although the sea-cold still drove into our bones.

Rekhmire' was out every day, rowed up and down this canal and that, trying for news on whether seas to Constantinople were traversible yet. Or whether any man had seen a Herr Mainz, late of the Germanies. Attila taught him a phrase or two to speak to the few northern men in Venice. Travelling by gondola or other boat kept Rekhmire' from putting his weight on his injured knee. He still came back to the embassy swearing – although whether physical pain occasioned this, or frustration, I couldn't say with certainty.

'Just when I could do with Neferet's salons,' he grumbled, one day without cloud, when I noted it stayed light into the early evening. 'Your father can provide me with an introduction to Captain Carmagnola, but outside of the military world . . . I have never known a man so uninterested in politics!'

That was frustration. I grinned. 'Can I draft a reference from you? Rodrigo would like to know his throne's safe, I'm sure.'

'Safe from your father!' Rekhmire' grunted, and dug the tips of his fingers hard into the misshapen muscle about his right knee. He still wore Turkish trousers, on the excuse of cold; I had come to the conclusion

355

that it was he who didn't wish to see his healing injury. The Egyptian added, 'He may be distracted from that – it's conceivable that King Rodrigo Sanguerra may have foreign troops on the Via Augusta before July . . . '

Even when I set foot in Carthage first, under the hissing naphtha lights, I was obscurely comforted by the thought that Taraconensis lay behind me in all its familiarity. I might desire not to be in that kingdom, but it was reassuring to know my past lay untouched behind me. The thought that it might change – all of it – and the men of Carthage march north and take control . . .

'Nothing may happen until next year,' Rekhmire' murmured. I knew he saw me concerned.

'Assuming we see next year.' I shrugged. 'There's no arguing against geography – it will be possible to take a ship from Taraconensis to Italy before it's safe to sail from Italy to Constantinople. If Videric sends another Carrasco, or more men like those on Torcello island . . . how long before they can get here?'

Rekhmire' frowned, recognising the rhetorical question. 'You could persuade nothing out of Lord Federico before he departed?'

Two of Honorius's more disreputable-looking men-at-arms had followed Federico and Valdamerca and my foster-sisters to the mainland, undetected as far as it was possible to judge. Whether Federico was indeed planning to head over the Alpine passes when they opened, or whether he would go elsewhere, he was not seen to take any road that led in the direction of Iberia.

'I think he was telling the truth – he *is* done with this.' I looked about for my roll of cloth with charcoal wrapped in it. 'I wish I might say the same.'

My fingers desired to draw. There was a thought in my mind, but I could not see the shape of it. I went for my sketchbook, to study Onorata again while she was blessedly asleep in her cot beside the fire, and see if my mind would work while my fingers were occupied. Rekhmire' talked while I looked into the tiny face, transferring the shadows to paper

It could be twelve or thirteen years before I know. Before *we* know. Whether she gets her menses, or not. Whether she changes, and becomes like me – although I was always both. But fear hangs over her, nonetheless, with me for an inheritance. What *is* she?

I reached down, adjusting her woollen blanket, and pictured Neferet and Leon sailing to the mainland. The long road they would have to travel. And at the end of it, there are Masaccio's friends: Brunelleschi, Donatello, other names he often mentioned while I sat as St Gaius and listened to him detail their work in sculpture and architecture.

I carefully drew the line of my child's lip – and by the end of it, an idea appeared full-blown in my head.

*

356

Refusing Honorius's company in a way that he would accept was not easy. Likewise that of Rekhmire', despite his difficulty walking. On the excuse of shopping for a better quality of chalks, I managed to get their agreement that I would go accompanied by the two largest men of the guard: Attila and Tottola, of course.

Honorius reminded me, in their hearing, as I walked down with him to the gondola at the landing stage. 'That weasel-eyed bastard Federico may still change his mind and come back! He may think his quickest way to favour is to travel back to Taraco with your pickled corpse in a barrel.'

'Thank you.' I blinked. 'A charming image!'

Attila lumbered down into the blue-painted wide gondola, gripping each side in hands the size of hams. His brother paused – and offered me a helping hand down onto the stern bench.

I waved, eyes tearing up in the cold wind, and the gondola crept out of the Dorsodura quarter, and into the busyness of the Grand Canal.

26

With Tottola and Attila at my shoulder, I followed the guard down into the lower rooms and dungeons of the ducal palace.

It was clear why the Doge Foscari wanted to rebuild the palace. The lower we went down, the more the stone steps glistened with water and the walls with white nitrous deposits. A damp cold crept into my bones. I pulled my fur-lined cloak more securely around my shoulders.

There was a reason why I was wearing silk and brocade and was evidently warm – Honorius's soldiers might think it a desire to aspire above my social station, but it was not.

'Here,' the jailer said, unlooking a tiny iron-barred wooden door, with a squeal of ungreased metal. I put coins into his hand, and ducked low to enter. Attila muttered something at my back – he had not liked their swords being kept at the guardhouse before we were allowed into the dungeons.

'You're lucky this one's still here,' the jailer added. He was a plump man, with laughter-lines about his eyes; I could imagine him patiently playing with grandchildren, or explaining duties to a slow apprentice. The complete blank failure to register the men chained to the walls, I suppose one develops as a consequence of such work.

'Lucky,' he repeated, thumbing the small coins in his palm, and holding the door to with his other hand. 'When he come in, his head was all swole up; then he had a fever.'

Head swollen.

The sounds came back to me with hallucinatory clarity: Honorius's men striking him in righteous anger, dragging him down the stairs.

I am not the only one to have struck him on the skull, and that jug was heavy enough to crack bone.

I do not feel guilty.

The jailer stressed, 'Hot as anything, he was. If I hadn't taken pity and brought him water . . . That's why he's still here, see? No man wants to move him when he's got jail-fever, it's the risk *they* might get it.'

I stepped forward, towards the door. Another ducat made its way from my fingers to the middle-aged man's hand.

More cheerfully, he said, 'Tough little bugger, though! He was dizzy and falling over and raving for a week; it would have killed another man. Here.'

The jailer swung the oak door open, and I saw it as thick through as a man's hand is wide.

Muttering, the jailor felt in his pockets for flint and tinder-box, and set about lighting the torches in the cell. A curve emerged from the darkness: became a man's back, where the man slumped on straw on the floor. For several minutes I watched.

Ramiro Carrasco de Luis did not raise his head.

'I know what it's like,' I said.

He turned over, at last. I saw comprehension on his face.

Hoarsely, he said, 'Ilaria . . . You were a slave. You know what it's like to be chained up like a dog.'

'And now you know, too.'

The torchlight showed me his face clearly enough. His bruises were mostly healed. Fading scabs still covered the cuts; the swelling had finished going down over his right eye. Under his prison-filthy clothes, I suspected there would be other injuries; a cracked or broken rib or two, now probably healed.

Ramiro Carrasco rasped, 'Not so pretty to draw, now?'

'You'd be more interesting to draw now,' I said truthfully.

He flinched as I stepped near to him.

I wondered: Have you begun to learn what can happen to a man in a prison?

' . . . Although I don't know if I could use you for the beaten Christus Imperator in the same panel as St Gaius.'

Another flicker of expression that was almost a flinch. Painfully, slowly, he got to his feet. As he straightened up, I thought he might be doing it simply to stand taller than I was, and not be intimidated.

He blinked at me. I saw him realise that we were much of a height.

'I thought you'd come for a look.' He attempted a glare of moral superiority. 'Poke a stick through the bars.'

He spoke with his gaze on me, ignoring the jailer and Attila and Tottola as if they were not present. I admired that attempt at dignity.

'You think I'm petty enough to want to see the man who tried to kill me chained up in his own filth?'

That wasn't quite accurate: the cell had basic facilities of straw and a chamber-pot. But Ramiro Carrasco coloured up all the same; I saw that clearly in the torchlight. To paint a blush in that light would require skill.

'*I* would.' Carrasco shrugged. 'Why wouldn't you?'

'I didn't say I wouldn't. I'm as petty as the next . . . woman,' I specified, remembering the jailer behind me. 'You put a pillow over my face. I was terrified. I don't much mind seeing you here, terrified yourself.'

'I'm not afraid!'

He might be speaking the truth. What I saw, if I looked as close as an artist can, was not necessarily fear. It was very like the desperation I had seen in his eyes as he pushed me back against the bed. But mixed with hopelessness, now.

'Why did you want to kill me?'

He scrubbed his fingers through his curly hair, each as filthy as the other. 'I didn't *want* to!'

And that is the truth.

The realisation surprised me. I caught Ramiro Carrasco's eye, and the half-sardonic and half-frightened look there.

A smugness, at having told me a truth he thinks I will dismiss out of hand.

And something that isn't fear of execution, or exile, or dying in jail.

'Why did you try?' I ticked it off on upraised fingers just protruding from the fur of the cloak, wrapped warm around me in this freezing prison cell. 'Near to the Riva degli Schiavona. In the gondola. Across the lagoon, on Torcello. You *tried,* certainly.'

Temper slashed in his tone. 'I've been convicted! What more do you *want?*'

'I want to know why.'

I turned away for a moment, guiding the jailer aside, speaking quietly enough that I knew Carrasco couldn't hear me. The man nodded and left.

Turning back, I found Ramiro Carrasco with a face that stress and helplessness made white and drawn.

I held his gaze.

'Are you a man who can kill because he's promised money? I talk to my father about that. When he has peasant levies to train . . . it takes time to make a man kill another man. You have to brutalise him. Convince him that the man he's killing isn't human. You can make professional soldiers out of some men. Most of them still vomit their stomachs empty, after a battle. But . . . some men have no knowledge *here,*' I put my palm against my abdomen, 'that any other man is real. So they can kill without thinking about it. Sometimes they look like kind grandfathers.'

I didn't look to see if the jailer had returned. And was quietly glad that Onorata's grandfather has never become inured enough to the sight of a battlefield that he doesn't, even now, spend some nights not daring to go back to sleep.

Ramiro Carrasco stared away from me, into the darker corners of the cell. I reached out and turned his head towards me. He appeared surprised at the force I could exert.

I said, '*You* haven't that capacity. Which, for an assassin, is perhaps unfortunate.'

He only shivered. I thought he might protest against 'assassin', but he merely gave me a look as full of hot hate and rage as any I've seen. Behind me, Tottola stretched himself in unsubtle warning.

360

I asked, 'Why did you do what Videric told you?'

At the name of my father – my mother's husband – he first flinched and then laughed.

'Get out of here.' His voice had a harsh undertone in its whisper. 'You'll get nothing out of me.'

'I don't need to. I know Videric wants me dead. I know *why*. I know it was Videric who sent you with Federico so that you could get close to me. I know there was more than one man with you, and I know they didn't get further than Genoa. I know Videric will send other men, now you're out of it, because he really *does* need me dead. No, I don't need you to tell me any of that.'

Ramiro Carrasco de Luis blinked in the light of the torches. He wiped his wrist across his mouth. Sweat, smeared away, left whiter skin displayed. A waft of unwashed body smell came to me when he lifted his arm.

'I don't understand.' He was careful not to phrase anything as agreement with me. 'If you don't want to know anything, why are you asking me? What are you asking me?'

'Why you'd try to do it. Try to kill me. Why you feel you *have* to.'

I saw decision on his face.

He spoke again, in a dialect common in the hill close to the Pyrenees, which was unlikely to be understood much outside of Taraconensis, and his bright eyes watched me to see that I comprehended:

'It was a choice between you and my family.'

The simplicity of his statement was at odds with the ferocious contained emotion behind his eyes.

'I'm the first of my family to go to university.' He spread his hands, mocking himself. 'I have a lawyer's degree! My mother and father, my brothers, my cousins and *their* parents, they'll all serfs, still. Tied to the land. Owned by the man who owns the estates.'

No need to ask his name.

'You will think it very little of an excuse.' Ramiro Carrasco spoke sardonically. 'Nor would I, in your place – what are twenty people you don't know, compared to your own life? But *I* know. I know my mother Acibella de Luis Gatonez; Berig Carrasco Pelayo, my father; my brothers Aoric and Gaton, and my sister Muniadomna . . . my uncle Thorismund . . . my grandmother Sancha . . . And I don't know you. Why should I care about some *freak*?'

He spat the last word. I looked at him.

The hatred comes from helplessness. From being arrested, charged, imprisoned; locked away from being able to kill one Ilario Honorius. And knowing that, because of that . . .

'Blackmail's very like being a slave,' I said, into the cold silence of the dungeon. 'They can kill your parent or your child, or sell them away from where you are. There are never as many slave revolts as you'd think there would be. That's one of the reasons why. Do you know how long he'll wait without hearing from you?'

The question caught him by surprise. Carrasco shook his head before he realised. 'It's not – there's *not*—!'

I ignored the stuttered denials of something it was too late to deny.

The same odd feeling of fellowship came back to me. It is no wonder I could never hate this man. I nodded, absently, thinking, Perhaps this will not be so unpleasant to you – or perhaps you will find it unbearable.

I heard the jailer returning, grunting as he carried a weight down the passage. The torch showed him with tools in his hand, and a small block of steel-topped wood under his arm.

I took a leather bag of coins out of my cloak's inner pocket and passed them over.

'Do it here,' I said.

The jailer looked a little uncertain. I signalled to Attila and Tottola. Having spoken to them on the way, they knew what I wanted. Of all of us in the cell, I saw an expression of surprise only on the face of Ramiro Carrasco.

The two soldiers picked up Carrasco and held him down, bent over the anvil. Hands in Carrasco's hair held him stretched rigid. The jailer slid a slave's collar around Ramiro Carrasco's neck and cold-hammered a rivet home.

'This isn't legal!'

'You'd think so, wouldn't you?' I watched, arms folded, the cloak warmly wrapped about me. 'But Venice has always been able to put prisoners and captives of war into her galleys as slaves. It's legal to buy a prisoner as a slave in Venice. Provided you don't stay on Frankish territory. Perhaps they didn't mention that when you studied law? It's true all the same.'

He couldn't struggle in the two men's grip, but it didn't stop him trying. 'Why do you want me enslaved? What *use* am I as a slave?'

He hasn't realised what has happened to him, even though the collar is now around his neck.

Some don't. I have seen men whipped until the blood runs before they realise that their freedom has gone. That they're property. I wondered what it would take to make it clear to Ramiro Carrasco de Luis.

In Iberian I said, 'You'll know one thing about the law of slavery, I don't doubt. What happens when the owner of a slave is murdered?'

The chime of the hammer fixing the second rivet all but drowned his words:

'The household slaves are tortured—'

'Tortured. Why? Why not questioned?'

'Because it's assumed all slaves lie; it's a legal assumption—'

I saw it hit him.

If Ilario dies, I am a household slave; I will be tortured.

Not even because they assume a slave committed the murder, but simply that a slave will not be trusted to be honest *because* they're a slave.

Ramiro Carrasco looked up at me with wide dark eyes.

I watched him as I spoke. 'If something were to happen to me, if I were to die – even if it was merely from a sickness . . . Then, my slaves will be turned over to the authorities, and tortured to find out what they know. And Ramiro Carrasco the slave won't know anything about what killed me. But – interrogated men talk about everything they know, if they're subjected to enough pain. Everything.'

There was no need to say it aloud, in front of the jailor; I saw the understanding in Ramiro Carrasco's expression.

Everything. Including every order Aldro Videric ever gave you, when he told you to murder me.

27

Outside the Doge's palace, Tottola went to the Riva degli Schiavoni to summon a gondola. Attila crossed his arms, the end of the slave's chain-leash held in one hand.

Ramiro Carrasco blinked against the sunlight, weak as it was.

It was clear enough to show up the filth caking him. He did not, for all he wore the same clothes, appear much to resemble the sardonic secretary of my sister Sunilda.

Tears ran down his face, and he lifted both hands to wipe them, since his wrists were manacled together. I wondered if it was the brightness of the light.

He shot a dazzled look at me. 'My family—'

I gazed back coolly. 'As an owner, I can always *volunteer* my own slave for interrogation.'

He took a step forward and Attila jerked the links of the chain through his fingers. The iron collar came up hard against Carrasco's windpipe. I couldn't help wincing in sympathy; I know how that feels.

'Declared your slave . . . ' There was a degree of wonder in his tone. *No, he hasn't realised the truth of it yet.*

'You have to stay with me now,' I said, gently enough. 'What we're going to do with you, God knows. But you have to live with me, as my slave, so that if anything happens to me, all Videric's dirty little facts get spilled out into the open. It's a balance, a set of scales: if he kills me, everything comes out into the open.'

Videric may know me well enough to know I only want to be left alone. But whether he believes it – whether he fears having knowledge at large, in my head, not safely in a hole in the ground . . .

'You're my precaution,' I said. 'And since you have to be a slave for it to work – then you *are* a slave. You don't understand that yet, but I suppose you will.'

Attila rumbled a brief, 'Let me belt the cheeky bastard.'

Ramiro Carrasco opened his mouth. And shut it again.

'That's right.' I shrugged. 'If I tell Attila here to beat you until your bones break – and if he was the kind of man to do it – I could order it right here, and no one could stop it happening. *You have to understand this.* You don't have the legal protection of being a serf. You're no more human than a horse or a chair.'

It was not my words that had the effect on him, I thought, but the sombre lack of surprise from Honorius's soldier – a man whom Ramiro Carrasco would probably know, from his visits to Neferet's house.

'You . . . ' Ramiro Carrasco turned his head and looked at me. His back straightened. Even under the filth, he had a certain amount of dignity. I wondered how much experience of slavery it would take to curve his spine, and make him – as I sometimes still do – lower my head automatically in the presence of the free.

Ramiro Carrasco said, 'You may have stopped him killing my mother and father.'

'Yes.'

Because if that news were to reach him, he would turn traitor to Videric freely; any man would.

'But you had no way of knowing that I – that it was because . . . You couldn't know!'

I flicked back in the small hand-sewn pages of my sketchbook, abandoning an effort to draw the standing gondolier steering his craft in towards the steps. I found the page I wanted, and turned it towards Carrasco.

He looked down at his own face, in a preliminary sketch for Gaius.

'Look at that, Ramiro. Tell me that I *didn't* know you weren't doing this of your own accord.'

His collared neck straightened; he stared at me with fierce affront. '*Drawing* me? You couldn't know anything about me!'

Studying and reproducing the planes and features of a face, time after time, seeing how it subtly alters with each emotion . . . Once, I stopped midway through a charcoal drawing of Ramiro Carrasco, when I had put in the tone of his face, and only an outline of his hair. It made him look white-haired. I had thought, *This is how Carrasco will look when he's fifty.*

I stated, 'You've never killed a man.'

I saw the shock on his face.

'If you can fight with a sword, it's because you saw an arms master for a few weeks while you were at your university, and any new recruit would kill you inside two minutes. You were planning to stick a knife into me, because anybody can do *that,* surely? You've been delaying, delaying all the time, terrified that the Aldra would carry out his threats – I don't know what reports you've been sending back to him, but I know you wanted to convince him you were just about to succeed. All the time, just on the verge of success.'

The muscles that surround the jaw bone relax under shock. His mouth hung very slightly open. It wasn't fair that it gave him a look that was faintly comic. Under these circumstances, that could move one to pity.

'Yes, you could kill a man in self-defence,' I hazarded. 'No, you're not an assassin. And Videric wouldn't care what being a murderer would do to you. Why would he? Here you were – educated, so capable of taking a place with Federico; capable of being blackmailed, therefore controllable; capable of getting close to the man-woman Ilario. You were perfect. But just . . . not a natural assassin.'

Carrasco's voice cracked with desperation. 'Let me go back to Taraco! I don't even know if they're alive, if my father—'

'They're better protected from the Aldra while you're here.'

Videric would calmly and coldly work out that his weapon had turned in his hand, I knew. And would I put it past Videric to go into a white rage, and order his serfs slaughtered out of rage? It would be stupidity. But . . .

Carrasco stared at me. I read the same knowledge in him. Yes, he knows Videric well. And wishes he didn't.

'I can't guarantee anything,' I said. 'I'm sorry. I wish I could.'

'You're sorry?' Ramiro Carrasco's voice went up an octave.

By his side, Attila looked thoughtfully at the chain-leash's end. I shook my head. The exchange went right past Ramiro.

Carrasco spluttered, 'You're *sorry*? I tried to smother you!'

'Yes. I do remember.'

The caustic remark was very much in his own vein. It stopped him dead.

'Ilaria . . . You can do . . . whatever you like to me, can't you? If you want revenge for me frightening you . . . '

He didn't say *for hurting you*; he was perceptive enough to know which I would resent the more.

I shrugged. 'That's one of the things about being a slave.'

'And I can't . . . ' His dark eyes blinked against the spring sun, running clear water after the jail's permanent dimness. 'I can't thank you for perhaps saving my family's lives, either. Because you'll just think I'm trying to escape a punishment.'

'That's another of the things about being a slave.' I moved forward as the gondola came in to the steps. Looking back as I took Tottola's extended hand, I said, 'With slavery as you find it in Iberia, nothing honest can be said between slave and master.'

Attila thrust Ramiro Carrasco into the boat behind me, the chain drawn up tight enough that he had the secretary-assassin by the neck, iron biting into the secretary's prison-filthy flesh.

Honorius and Rekhmire' appeared on the Alexandrine house's jetty before we got within fifty yards of the landing stage. They watched in silence, one standing beside the other, as the gondola glided up and we disembarked.

'What?' Honorius pointed at the stinking and wet figure crouching in the bottom of the boat – wet because Ramiro Carrasco de Luis had not entirely believed Tottola wouldn't let go if he jumped over the side of the gondola.

Ramiro Carrasco coughed, shivered, and spat over the side, wiping his running nose.

The royal book-buyer chimed in, '*Why?*'

'I bought him,' I said – and watched comprehension spread over their faces.

28

'You're a wonder!' the Captain-General of Castile and Leon grinned, pulling me up out of the gondola and into his arms, and swinging me around in such a way that my scars pulled painfully – which I would not have told him for the world.

'Well done!' Rekhmire' gave me a pat on the shoulder, when he might reach me. 'Ilario – that was almost *clever.*'

'Why, thank you!' I mimed being offended, and gasped a little, under the impression my ribs might crack. Honorius released me. I added, 'All I need to do now is get word back to Videric, to tell him.'

A thought made me grin.

'A shame Federico decided not to go back to Taraco – I would like to have seen his face, when I asked him to carry the message . . . '

Rekhmire' openly snickered.

'Shall we go in?' I added.

'What about him?' Honorius jerked a thumb at my purchase.

'He's a slave, he has to be seen to be treated like one.' I glanced at Rekhmire'. 'I was thinking – along the lines of the Alexandrine model. Once we get out of Venice.'

The book-buyer smiled, and inclined his head.

Honorius continued loud congratulations while I introduced Carrasco to the kitchens and the soldiers, with stern words that the man should not be injured because valuable. I thought one or two of them entirely likely to give him more than a brain-fever, if left unwarned; attempting to murder a woman in child-bed is comfortably different enough from a soldier's killing that they can safely feel the utmost contempt.

Even if the woman is not wholly a woman.

The late frost bit at my fingers as I returned from the courtyard, having shown Ramiro Carrasco the iron bars on the gate. I sent him off to Sergeant Orazi to be found a place to sleep. Rekhmire' came up with me on my way to the main room, his steps more uneven now because of his less-than-successful attempts to use a walking-stick instead of his crutch.

'Out with it!' I directed, when we had reached the room and he had not yet spoken.

Honorius looked up curiously from a joint-stool by the fire, evidently equally desirous of hearing the answer.

'I admire your initiative.' Rekhmire' racketed over to the room's only armed chair, lurching like a town drunk at midday. 'To conceive of buying Carrasco – and to put the plan into operation—' He gave a faint smile. 'It's admirable. It's worthy of a book-buyer.'

'Spy!' Honorius rubbed his fingers hard under his nose, preventing himself from laughing. He had ceased to be entirely clean-shaven in the last few days, and was growing a moustache. I assumed he thought it would disguise him, at least to be less recognisable at a distance. It came out a little greyer than the hair of his head.

Having an ear for nuance, at least where the Egyptian is concerned, I smiled at my father, and turned back to Rekhmire'.

'But? "It's admirable" – and I hear a *but*.'

Rekhmire' sighed. 'But it won't work.'

29

The four words dropped into the room and brought about complete silence.

'*What do you mean, it won't work!*'

I checked the door and window by reflexive action. No Ramiro Carrasco; no guards or servants other than Honorius's trusted men.

'How can it not work?'

'Consider.' Rekhmire' steepled his fingers in the old way he had had in Rome. 'If you die, Carrasco is legally tortured, and Videric's secrets come out. If *Carrasco* dies – nothing.'

I stared at him. Able only to echo. 'If Carrasco dies . . . '

'Dies *first*. All you've done,' Rekhmire' observed, 'is given Videric a motive to have Carrasco assassinated before he kills you.'

Into the stunned quiet, Honorius's voice intoned, 'Shite.'

'I—' The inescapability of it flooded in on me.

'I wondered why he had been left alive,' Rekhmire' added, shifting uncomfortably on the hard chair. 'It wouldn't have been difficult to get a man into the prison to silence him. Evidently Videric didn't consider him a danger. If you've made him into one . . . '

The Egyptian shrugged.

' . . . You ensure he will kill both of you.'

'*No*.' I slammed one fist into my other hand. 'I thought it out, every step of it! It *will* work. It's a stand-off. All the while I have Ramiro Carrasco, Aldra Videric can't touch me!'

'All the while you *have* Carrasco,' the Egyptian emphasised softly. 'I grant you, it works while you do. But what you've done now is given Aldra Videric a reason to kill the slave before he kills you. And the easiest way to be sure of that, is to kill both you and he together.'

To come so close to safety – *so close*—

Despair went through me. I pushed it down, out of sight, so that the two men should not see it when I turned back to them.

Honorius clearly forced himself to sound encouraging. 'It's a good plan, while it works.'

Rekhmire' very briefly smiled. Knowing him as I did, I thought it was an appreciation of the irony of the assassin Carrasco now become the target.

Frustration washed through me. I thought it no metaphor, now, that men's vision goes red when they hate.

'It doesn't matter what I do!' I snarled. 'He'll never get back into power, the King will never take him as First Minister again, but Videric is just going to keep on sending more men! He'll send soldiers, he'll – I don't know – bribe a ship's captain to maroon me – send a proper murderer who's efficient enough to sneak through a military guard – *something*. Aldra Videric, he'll just . . . keep on coming. Keep. On. Coming.'

30

There has to be an answer.

I can't see it.

Venice, which had seemed safe enough while I knew the freeman Ramiro Carrasco's location and temper, seemed dangerous now.

I thought there might also be an outside chance that, as a slave, he could still be able to hire men to kill me. But given the risk to his extended family back in Taraconensis; I doubted he would attempt that.

But . . . I have no idea who else is here from Taraconensis. Who may be on the road here, of docking on a ship this minute . . .

No one knocked on my door. Honorius and Rekhmire' both knew me better than to think I would want companions. I curled up in the window embrasure, taking charcoal to a wooden board, and rubbing out everything I drew that I was unsatisfied with. Which was everything. Proportion, value, perspective: all eluded me.

Some time towards the evening, when the dusk came swiftly down, a servant brought a plate of food and a jug and cup. Not until I caught his individual way of moving in peripheral vision did I realise it was not a servant, but Ramiro Carrasco de Luis.

Not a servant but a slave.

I put the drawing-board down and stretched my legs, uncurling out of my seated position with spine to the wall. The secretary-assassin stood by the table, food abandoned, his expression awkward. I wondered why he was so ill at ease; whether I should be suspicious.

'I'll take it back.' Carrasco's resigned voice broke the silence. 'I'll get someone else to bring you a meal.'

Poisoning me will keep his family alive, at least, provided Videric keeps his word – even if it'll get Carrasco handed over for a judicial burning as a poisoner.

Unless they flay him, as a slave who has killed his master.

Ramiro Carrasco's face showed a faint pink colour that was not reflected warmth from the hearth fire. 'You ought to eat.'

He abruptly reached down to pick up the wooden plate. It had dark bread and pale cheese on it, and I could smell that what was in the jug was honey ale. All of which can be sabotaged, I suppose, if a man sets his mind and ingenuity to it. But then, what can't be?

Crossing the room, I caught hold of Ramiro Carrasco's wrist, took the plate out of his hand, and set it back on the table. He appeared surprised that I would be strong enough to arrest his movement.

'I'll eat,' I said. His skin felt cool in my grip. I released him. 'Who sent you? My father? The Egyptian?'

Ramiro Carrasco de Luis looked down at the floorboards.

There was enough light from the window and the hearth-fire to let me see he ferociously blushed.

I could scent him sweating, too, but there wasn't the cold sweat of fear.

'You got this for me.' I couldn't help smiling at his evident embarrassment.

'It's not – tampered with!'

'You got this for me. Because . . . '

He was not in the dark Italian doublet and hose that he had worn as Sunilda's secretary, and naturally enough he had no stiletto at his belt. I'd bought him, but who clothed him?

Honorius, probably, from the household guards' baggage. The rumpled woollen hose, and doublet with darned point-holes, both looked as if they might have been discarded by some soldier after long service.

Carrasco had enough of the freeman still in him that he stood as if the scruffy clothes were a humiliation rather than a fortunate gift.

'Because?' I prompted.

Some man in the house had cut his hair back to the scalp, presumably to rid it of prison mites. Under his leather coif, he was quite bald. The same long-lashed black eyes looked back at me that I had spent weeks drawing.

I doubt he really needed to have his head shaved rather than washed – but someone will have found it amusing.

Ramiro Carrasco looked down at the table top, and blushed painfully red over his neck and ears, that I could see where the coif was cut high. He muttered, 'You're right, you can't say anything honest between master and slave. I just wanted . . . You . . . I do *know* I'd be dead of sickness by now!'

I picked up the crust of dark bread and bit a corner off. It was yesterday's. Dry enough that anything would soak into it.

What? some part of my mind scoffed. You think he has a chest full of poisons in his bedroll, all ready to play the assassin again?

Although he only has to have had access to my painting gear. The poisonous paints will kill any artist, if a painter is foolish enough to lick their brush.

'If I were in your position,' I said, 'I wouldn't poison the first plate of food. *Or* the second. I'd wait until I was trusted, until people were used to me, until I wasn't noticed. Then I could be certain the food would be consumed . . . What? You think I was never sold to any man I didn't dream of killing?'

Carrasco flushed. 'I forgot you've been a slave.'

It would have taken counting on my fingers to get the right of it. 'I think I've spent more of my life formally as a slave than formally free. I know all the tricks. And it's not like I've forgotten how many times you tried to have me killed. Even if I do understand why.'

The look Ramiro Carrasco de Luis gave me was something to treasure, if one is not immune to normal human vindictiveness.

He stood with his balance on the balls of his feet, shoulders hunched a little. I thought he would have liked to brawl with me. He glanced at my hand, where I bit at the dark bread again, and looked remarkably uncomfortable.

'You will not allow me even to thank you, for keeping me alive—'

'You don't want to thank me. You just feel you ought to. I *have* saved your life.' I couldn't help grinning, momentarily.

'Ilaria—'

'You're another one who's going to have to be beaten into remembering "master".' I put the bread down, drank from the jug – watching him and seeing no reaction other than a flushed anger. 'Listen. You call *everybody* master or mistress. They call you . . . whatever they like. It's like a dog or a horse. If I don't like the name "Ramiro" I can change it.'

That brought his head up. His dark eyes glared at me. Names are important.

'As for thanking me,' I said. 'You're glad to be alive, but you don't desire to thank me for keeping you that way. You hate the fact that I rescued you. I'd guess you spend half your time wishing I was dead, and half the time wishing *you* were. And you don't wish to thank me for making you a slave – you find it humiliating, because you have more pride than any man *ought* to have. Certainly more than you have sense. Travelling with Federico and his wife and daughters, being Videric's man covertly, knowing what was really going on . . . that suited you. Being property, being a shield between Videric and the man-woman . . . No, that sticks in your throat.'

I watched Carrasco go as white as he had been red.

'She-male!' he spat out finally, intending it for insult, not description.

'Ramiro, I spent enough time drawing you to know you.'

He knocked the wooden plate off the table, stalked out of the room, and his footsteps died away while the plate still spun and clattered on the floorboards.

How many times is he going to be whipped or starved before he realises what he is, now?

One word could have started that process. I felt more sympathy than I wanted to admit with his position. Am I to be the first to cause weals on his back?

A shield.

Yes, I thought. And I must finally admit it: Rekhmire' and my father are right. It merely puts Ramiro Carrasco where *he* has to be killed before I can be.

There must be a solution.

I can't see it!

The night came; I slept deeply, aware of no dreams; and opened my eyes with a snap in the morning, mind suddenly awake and aware, everything instantaneously laid out before me as the light and shadow of a drawing sometimes is.

I hauled a man's doublet on over my night-gown and clattered down the stairs.

The smell of cooking permeated the house from the kitchens to the main room downstairs, overlooking the still-bald garden of the embassy. Evidently I had slept through men breaking their fast. Walking in, I found that the long oak table was cleared – of knives and plates, at least.

My father and Rekhmire' sat with opened boxes and crates about their feet. Some of the smaller crates occupied the table top, surrounded by heaps of straw. The window's light caught shining curves.

I recognised glass goblets, lantern-shields, beads, jugs; all such as I had seen on the lagoon-islands of Murano and Burano.

'Old mercenary habit,' Honorius murmured, as he had in Rome; studying the pattern of a blue glass goblet he held up. 'Venetian glass will make excellent export goods . . . '

The room's far door closed behind Ramiro Carrasco.

Rekhmire' and my father, at the bench at the long table, smiled their individual smiles.

'I know another slave who was impossible to train,' the Egyptian remarked, blithely provoking.

I met his gaze.

Rekhmire' stopped and looked closely up at me. 'What is it?'

Honorius hooked a joint-stool up to the table, in invitation to sit, his gaze narrowed expectantly.

'I have the answer.' I slide a crate towards me, picking one of the glass goblets out of the straw. 'I doubt you'll like or approve of it.'

Rekhmire''s dark eyes fixed on me, intent and intense. Characteristically, he said nothing, only waiting for me to speak.

I tilted the goblet, watching the spiral of coloured glass in the stem catch the light. 'I don't like it either . . . But I can see no other way.'

Honorius reached and took the glass out of my hand, and set it firmly on the table. '*Well?*'

'Videric isn't going to stop—'

Old habits coming back to me, I sprang up, striding to open the room's far door. No man was listening. I checked the door I had come in by, and left both open – since it's harder to eavesdrop at an open door.

'Bear with me, and listen.' I paced back, resting my palms on the table as I leaned and looked at them, across the crates and packing.

Honorius nodded. Rekhmire' remained motionless.

'And tell me where I may be wrong,' I added. 'Ramiro Carrasco is some protection to us, because he will implicate Videric thoroughly, should he come to be tortured. And I suspect, if Videric harms his family out of pique, Carrasco would turn into a willing witness for us. But – if Videric can send a man who kills Ramiro Carrasco before he kills me, that doesn't matter.'

'Masterly,' Rekhmire' murmured under his breath, and held his large hands up defensively as I glared at him. 'No, Ilario, please. Continue. I'm sure this has a point ... '

The waspishness reassured me. Rekhmire''s temper only verges on inadvertent rudeness when he is under great stress.

And that means the situation is as dangerous as I say it is.

Leaning with my hip against the edge of the table, I picked fragments of the straw packing out of one of the boxes, and looked across at Honorius.

'Tell me why you first went to Castile and Leon.'

Honorius looked as if he flushed, under the sun-browned skin. 'Your mother—'

'No.' I stood up straight. 'No, I understand *that*. Rosamunda didn't want to leave a rich man for a poor man.'

The bluntness must have hurt him, but he only nodded.

'You were a soldier. Why did you go *north*?'

Honorius's brows came down. 'Because that's where the war was! Still is, for that matter.'

I reprised the history of it, even though I could see a light of knowledge come into his eye. 'You couldn't have succeeded as well as you have in Taraco?'

Honorius shrugged. 'There wasn't going to be war in Taraconensis, I thought. I was right: there hasn't been a war on the Frankish border with Taraconensis for twenty-five years, to my certain knowledge. I knew if I went north to the crusades—'

I nodded, interrupting him, and set off pacing around the long table again, too restless to stay still. Rekhmire' leaned his head back as I passed him, intent dark gaze on me.

I said, 'We've both listened to the gossip in the salons. Every man seems to think Taraconensis so weak now, that Carthage might send legions in. So that the Franks can't press down from the north, take Taraco, and threaten North Africa.'

Honorius merely nodded. His frown was thoughtful. He had spent more than a little time talking over this with Carmagnola, I knew from my own observation.

'Ask yourself: what changed?' I held up my hand, stopping him speaking. 'And we know, of course. It started half a year ago, when Carthage sent their ambassador over and caused a scandal—'

Honorius scowled. 'You're saying *Videric* is the reason why—'

'Rodrigo had Videric as his adviser, his First Minister, all the time I was growing up at the court.' I ended at the head of the dark oak table, resting my weight on my hands. 'I *know* Rodrigo Sanguerra. Yes, he's a good king. But if you force me to admit it, I have to say – he would have been less good without Videric.'

I went on swiftly, before either staring man could interrupt me:

'Others think the same thing. How *true* it is – hardly matters. Politics is a matter of belief. And men believe that Taraconensis is weak because the First Minister has been banished from court.'

In the silence, I heard servants' voices distant in the kitchens, and Saverico out in the embassy courtyard, laughing like a much younger boy at some remark Berenguer made.

Honorius's scowl did not lighten. 'Ilario – what is this?'

'It's inescapable.'

I straightened up, facing both of them: the Iberian soldier and the Egyptian book-buyer.

'Aldra Videric needs me dead. If I'm dead, the scandal starts to die, and eventually Rodrigo can recall him to court. Videric's a rich man, a powerful man. He can afford to pay to send any number of thugs and murderers after me. And to arrange for any witnesses to be killed, after.'

I saw Honorius and Rekhmire' swap glances. Clearly, this is not a new thought to them.

I pulled one of the smaller crates towards me, running my finger across the grain of the beech wood. That soothed me enough to get words out:

'I know that Aldra Videric will not run out of money. And he's well enough guarded at his estates that it would not be possible to attack or ambush *him*. Nor will he forget this matter – the only thing Videric has ever had is his place at the King's side. He won't forgive losing it. He won't cease wanting it back.'

I took a breath, feeling an odd combination of confidence and swimming dizziness,

'I remain the obstacle. What Ramiro Carrasco can say might give Videric a moment's pause. But as far as that goes – as you say – he can probably arrange an attack by bandits that wipes out an entire party of travellers, just as soon as we leave Venice. He's rich enough to crew a ship and send men after me that way. I've thought of this backwards, forwards, and sideways. The answer remains: Videric's not going to stop coming after me.'

Honorius put war-worn hands down on the table. 'Ilario . . . naturally this must worry you. I can defend you—'

'Not indefinitely. And it puts you in danger.'

I circumvented Honorius's further words by pointing at the Egyptian. 'You too, Rekhmire'. You're a witness.'

With an unexpectedly hard note in his voice, Rekhmire' stated, '*I* am a representative of Alexandria-in-Exile and the Pharaoh-Queen.'

'Then go back there and be safe,' Honorius rapped out. 'This isn't your fight—'

The temperature in the room dropped ten degrees. Expression rigid, Rekhmire' said, 'Is it not?'

'Damn it, man, you know what I mean! You *can* leave, and so you should—'

'If I had not *interfered* at Carthage,' the Egyptian's voice bit down, cutting Honorius short. 'If I had not thought it so *wise* to go spilling Aldra Videric's secrets – your son-daughter might not be in such complete danger of being killed! Yes, you have every right to blame me for that—'

'I don't blame you!' Honorius jumped to his feet, waving his hands wildly. 'Ilario doesn't blame you!'

'It never *occurred* to me to— Will you two *be quiet!*' I yelled. 'And just for once *listen!*'

The silent room echoed to a tiny sharp snap.

I looked down. The serpentine stem of the goblet I had picked up had snapped neatly into two.

Gently, I put the parts of the glass down in the straw-lined crate.

'I have the answer,' I said, 'if you will *listen.*'

Honorius seated himself again on the bench, one hand resting on the table. As I watched, it curled into a white-knuckled fist. Rekhmire' steepled his fingers and gazed at me over his clean spade-cut nails.

'Videric will not stop,' I repeated. 'And I can see only one way to stop him eventually killing me. Killing *us*, I should say – he won't leave witnesses. And that one way is . . . We have to see that Videric gets what he wants.'

Honorius blinked in total bewilderment. 'But he wants you dead!'

I snorted a laugh, and wiped at my face.

'Apologies! No. Think. He wants me dead, but only as the means to something else. He desires to be summoned back from exile. He wants to be Rodrigo's adviser again. Videric wants to be the King's First Minister of Taraconensis.'

Rekhmire' stared at me with as blank an expression as I had ever seen on his face. 'And . . . '

'And – that's what we have to do.'

I looked from the Egyptian to my father, and from Honorius back to Rekhmire'.

'That's what will stop these attempts at murder. That's what will make us safe. I have to *help* my greatest enemy.'

Rage boiled up through me with the suddenness of thunder in

summer. I seized up the wooden crate of export glass, and hurled it two-handed and bodily towards the room's further wall.

It struck home with a vibrant, world-shattering crash.

'I have to *help* the man who's trying to kill me. And the only way to help Videric . . . I have to help him get what he wants. I have to put him back in power.'

Part Four

Alexandria-In-Exile

1

'*That* means . . . ' I broke the silence with some deliberation. ' . . . that I go back to Taraconensis, now, and negotiate this with Videric. Face to face.'

Rekhmire', bent awkwardly over on his crutches, and surveying the remains of the crate of export glass, shot a startled look at me. 'You do not!'

'Is it necessary to point out that you freed me in Rome?'

The Egyptian straightened up, monumentally prepared to rebuke me. Honorius rose to his feet, knocking his own glass over. Spilled wine spread in a pool of reflection that I wished I might paint.

The Lion of Castile snapped, 'You may be of age, but as your father—'

I stopped pacing and completed his words: '—You've learned to recognise a losing battle when you see one?'

'Don't you be cheeky with me, young Ilario!'

I swung around, striding back up the room, ignoring the pull of healing stitches. Low as the beams were, and cramped as these small quarters might be, movement was the only thing that eased my mind. Wearing one of Neferet's Alexandrine housecoats and a doublet is not like wearing Frankish petticoats. *I begin to feel more myself than I have since I came to Venice.*

I pushed open the panelled shutters, letting in cold spring air, and gazed down at the canal at the rear of the embassy. Brickwork reflected in the water. The sun stood high enough overhead to strike down between the tall buildings. Symmetrical ripples spidered off the water, too bright to look at directly.

'Tell me that there's *any* other way to do this!' Dazzled, I turned about; resting my back against the windowsill. I stared into a room now completely black to my eyes. 'Videric lost his place at the King's side because people won't allow Rodrigo to have a would-be murderer there. You know Carthage will have said Videric tried to kill me, no matter how much of it was Rosamunda!'

In the brilliance of the water outside, I see the Court of Fountains in Taraco, regardless of the heat there and the chill here.

'Videric will be devising plans to get back into favour. Which all depend on having me dead and forgotten. He'll send more men like

Carrasco. If we're in Frankish territory, he's long used to dealing with the banking firms and all the major merchants for King Rodrigo – he can pick up gossip about hermaphrodites, about painters . . . With Federico's reports, he knows as much about what I'm doing as *you* do.'

Honorius frankly scowled, I saw, as my eyes adapted back to light and shadow. He desired to contradict me. Clearly, he couldn't.

Rekhmire' seated himself on the bench with a grunt, and a clatter of crutches. 'It's true: Aldra Videric *would* be better returned to court as your King's minister. Carthage is under the Penitence, and Iberia is the grain-basket of the empire. Any excuse to take over more of its kingdoms . . . It seems there are too many people with confidence in First Minister Videric as a politician, and King Rodrigo's right hand.'

Which made me desire to spit out something bitter. Why hearing confirmation of my thoughts should create such revulsion, when I had been brought to admit the truth of the argument through long hours spent feeding Onorata and brooding, I did not know.

I stared both of them down: the sitting spy, and the standing General, whom I cannot afford at this moment to think of as friend and father. 'Who else can sort this out but me? If I go back to Taraco, persuade Videric that I'm not interested in having Rosamunda arrested for my attempted murder—'

Honorius interrupted by lifting his head and bellowing, 'Carrasco!'

While my ears still rang, Ramiro Carrasco came in, and shut the door behind him on the sound of a crying baby. He shot a frightened look around the room. The slave's look, which I know well: *What have I done? And: It doesn't matter if I did anything or not, am I going to suffer for it?*

He does learn fast.

'You.' Honorius seemed reluctant to call the assassin by his name again. 'Tell me something. How long might you live, if you stepped off a ship in Taraconensis now?'

They speak of men going white. It would be more accurate, I thought, feeling the shape of it in my fingers that itched to draw, to say that their faces go sunken. It wasn't possible to tell if Ramiro Carrasco the slave looked pale in this dim room. He did instantly look ten years older.

He snorted unsteadily. 'Minutes if I'm lucky! As long as it'll take the Aldra to send out his household men disguised as bandits. On territory he *knows*.'

Carrasco swung about, unslavelike, and shot me a look of appeal.

'My family – they'll be dead too! He'd leave nothing! You can't be thinking of—'

Honorius, apparently unmoved by Carrasco's disrespect in not addressing him as 'master', leaned his hand on the table, tapping a finger on the wood. 'Ilario's thinking of travelling back to Taraco. What about it, Ilario, would you take your slave?'

Honorius didn't take his eyes off Carrasco as he spoke.

That will be part of his continuing investigation into whether the man speaks the truth, I thought. As well as pointing out to Ilario what an idiot Ilario is . . .

Stubborn, I said, 'Ramiro Carrasco will stay with you.'

Rekhmire' leaned his elbows on the table, beside Honorius; his weight making the wood groan. 'So much for the slave Carrasco as your shield against Aldra Videric . . . '

'He can be that out of my company.'

I doubted the truth of it even as I said it. And kicked a joint-stool out of the way as I paced back down the length of the room.

Ramiro Carrasco blinked at me with the bewildered look of a slave realising that none of the decisions which will affect him are taken with any reference to what he thinks.

I could read nothing on Rekhmire''s impassive countenance. An unexpected pang went through me. *Who knows*, I thought, *what orders he'll receive from Alexandria, when ships can safely travel here from Constantinople?*

Orders that take precedence over this.

'And my granddaughter?' Honorius demanded, behind me. 'Do I sit in some place as yet undecided, with your slave and your baby? While you venture back to Taraco, walk up to Videric, and – watch your head go bouncing across the ground, because it won't take ten heartbeats for one of his men to "protect" him! He needs you dead, Ilario! What better excuse for instant execution than "Ilario wanted revenge and I had to defend myself"? You won't get a chance to speak to the King. Nor to any other man. Videric's informers will tell him what ship you're on, and some thug will hit you behind the ear with a cudgel and tip you over the quay-side before you get a foot off the gang-plank!'

I swung around. 'Then tell me some other way to do this!'

The shout bounced back flatly off the plaster and beams, silencing Honorius.

I leaned on the other side of the table, both fists against the wood, staring down at the retired soldier, my father. 'Videric must listen when I speak to him. How can I know, here, what it will take to get him back in favour? I don't know how King Rodrigo will ever be able to say, *Here's Videric, he's my First Minister* again. And if I don't go and ask Videric, face to face, I never *will* know!'

Rekhmire' raised his clear low tenor voice. 'If you will stop charging full-tilt into things—!'

Honorius interrupted, a burning look in his eye. 'I forbid this.'

Rekhmire' smacked one large palm against the side of his forehead. 'Amun and Amunet! The donkey can be led but not driven!'

Honorius snorted down his nose and glared at me. 'In my experience, the donkey can't be led *or* driven!'

My fingernails drove painfully into my palms.

A faint sound of Onorata's crying reached through the ill-shut door and clawed down the tendons and muscles of my neck, stiffening them. With an effort, I pushed away my urge to rush to her.

'You,' I said quietly, 'need not look after the child: I will. I may be no mother at all to her—'

And that's as well, when you think of Rosamunda!

'—But at least I know now how to be a father.'

I inclined my head in thanks to Honorius. He looked taken aback in the extreme.

To Rekhmire', I added, 'I know you have business for Constantinople; I can't ask you to go out of your way. I do thank you for what you've done for me. If you're going to Constantinople – to Alexandria – it would help me if you'd take Ramiro Carrasco with you as your slave. Probably Videric will have a harder time getting him murdered if he's there.'

Rekhmire''s mouth looked as if he'd eaten fresh lemon.

He turned his head, not to look at Carrasco, as I expected, but to exchange glances with Honorius.

'Fucking idiot!' The retired Captain-General of Leon and Castile waved an expressive hand. 'My son-daughter; not you.'

'Ah.' Rekhmire''s smile was that familiar all-but-imperceptible one that meant he was truly amused. 'Well, it is more generally applicable, after all.'

'Oh, ay.' Honorius nodded, hit himself on the chest with his fist, and then pointed a sword-callused hand at Ramiro Carrasco. 'Ilario's father, slave, and . . . '

'"Book-buyer"?' Rekhmire' suggested.

You could have scraped paint off acacia wood with Honorius's look of scepticism.

'Book. Buyer.' The soldier paced down the room and planted himself in front of me, with the light of the window in his face. His eyes narrowed, either against the brightness or his thoughts. He glared down the few inches difference between our heights.

'If you go marching back into Taraconensis, Videric will kill you! Yes, I'll agree: you're right that Videric needs to be put back at Rodrigo's side – with a collar on him, so he can't do too much damage! But this is not the way to go about it!'

The Egyptian snorted. 'You'll never tell him – her – Ilario! – that.'

Rekhmire' was being chronological, I thought, rather than mistaken in his gender.

I could see in his expression that same emotion I'd seen when he asked me how long it was after Rosamunda attempted to stab me that I fled Taraco.

How long was it after I met Sulva that I asked her to wed me?

Anger set me to pacing the room again. 'No, Taraconensis isn't safe. Nowhere else is more safe! Father, you said it yourself – Videric's had

386

Federico looking for me in Rome, and Florence, and Venice. If I looked for a local mastro in Bologna or Ravenna or Milan, now, Videric would find me. And none of that—' I glanced aside, taking in Rekhmire''s glare. 'None of it, no matter where I hide, will get me closer to putting Videric back into power!'

The silence after my words rang in the low-ceilinged room.

Honorius folded his arms. In the same moment, Rekhmire' also folded his. In another mood it would have made me burst out laughing – both of them scowling like pediment sculptures in Green cathedrals. As it was, it snapped what little temper remained to me.

'I bought that man!' I flung out one arm to point at Carrasco. He visibly startled. 'Because he is protection. Because all I want to do is be left alone to paint.'

The floorboards creaked under me as I restlessly shifted, gripping my hands together to deny that urge to frantic pacing.

'Because I have a child that, if it doesn't die of some childhood disease, or merely *die*, I need to protect. And now the sole and only way I can see to achieve that – is to go back and sort things out with my stepfather—'

Rekhmire' interrupted. 'Say if you leave Venice, take sanctuary in Alexandria—'

'There is no sanctuary!' I found myself making fists again, nails leaving white crescents against my skin. 'None that's more than temporary. Videric's been the King's councillor for more than twenty years. I know how courts work. Videric knows men in every major city in the Mediterranean and Frankish lands, and if he's out of favour now, he can still find some men who think that won't last. So they'll do him favours. Look out for travellers. Pass word back to him. He found me here; he'll find me again. If he can't kill me because of Ramiro here, then he'll kill both of us, and the only way I can see to stop this is to go back to Taraco!'

'But,' Rekhmire' protested.

The reasonable tone of his voice triggered my vision to a blur of rage. 'No, I won't hear more!'

Honorius drew himself up a little, at the table's end, inclining his head. He rested his hands flat on the wood.

If I painted him, I thought, it would be just so, with campaign maps under his fingers, and lanterns behind, illuminating the dark interior of a military commander's tent.

'Yes, this has to be done.' He fixed me with a direct look. 'But there is least of all any sanctuary for you in *Taraco*! I at least have an excuse, a need, to go home to my King. And I'll use that chance to talk to him; convince Rodrigo Coverrubias that I'd far rather see First Minister Videric than First Minister Honorius. But you – you have no reason to go home except to be murdered, and I won't allow it.'

There was no blustering father in his voice now. It was all confident

Captain-General; the commander who knows he will be obeyed because there is no other reasonable option.

More quietly, he added, 'Constantinople is still the safest destination – for you *and* that rat's testicle Carrasco.'

Honorius continued over Rekhmire''s splutter of amusement, and Ramiro Carrasco's glare.

'Let the spy take you to his city, until we can begin to solve this.'

Rekhmire', having looked sour as an early plum at *spy*, broke his silence with a sigh. 'Regrettably, I might need to send, rather than take.' He glanced up at Honorius. 'If I don't find Herr Mainz by the time ships can sail for Alexandria, then I suspect my orders will send me to Florence, to shake the information of his whereabouts out of Neferet. And Ilario is hardly welcome in Florence.'

Without ever having been there, I reflected.

Honorius gave the Egyptian a sceptical look. 'You won't be riding or walking to Florence until that knee's healed up. But in any case, when I leave for Taraco, I desire some man to look out for my son-daughter's interests—'

I pounced on my father's admission. 'You'll go back, now? Persuade Rodrigo to take his troops off your estate? Convince him you're loyal?'

Licinus Honorius gave me somewhat of an old-fashioned look. He sighed, shoulders appearing to relax their stiffness. 'Say I agree with you. That returning Aldra Videric to the position of First Minister is the only way to both end this and keep Taraconensis safe. Which of us, alone, is in a position to begin this? Not the spy—'

Rekhmire' snorted.

'—since King Rodrigo doesn't know the Alexandrine well enough to trust him as I do.'

I caught a fleeting look of embarrassed pleasure on Rekhmire''s face. The trust of the Lion of Castile is not given lightly, or hurriedly. Evidently he appreciated this.

'And not *you*,' Honorius snapped bluntly, glaring at me. 'Videric would show you your liver inside two days. That only leaves me.'

I could find no ready answer.

Turning aside, I directed Ramiro Carrasco to clear up the broken glass, and stood tearing at my mind for ideas while he did so and departed. Nothing came to me.

Honorius's hand rested on my shoulder with a sudden pressure that was startling.

'I'll go,' he repeated. 'As soon I have a safe refuge for you and Onorata. I'll go back to King Rodrigo – I knew that I would have to.'

I found myself torn between grief and joy. Joy that he could reconcile himself with the King; that he will not lose everything he ever earned – with his own blood – because of me. And grief, I reflected, because I will badly miss his presence, and because he may be going into more danger than we know.

Honorius turned his face to the window for a moment, as if he could pierce the buildings and the haze of aerial perspective, and see westwards all the way over the Italies, and the Middle Sea, clear to Iberia. His eyes slitted.

Turning back, my father shot me a look that, even in that dim panelled room, I could not mistake for anything but wry humour.

'To be fair . . . ' Honorius sighed, and put his arm around my shoulder. 'You realise, I hope? That this is the only way I might go home – and not kill Aldra Pirro Videric a quarter-hour after I set foot on Taraco dock?'

2

'*Kill—*' Breath left me. *I have not thought of this!*

Under the smile of Honorius's much-creased face, I saw frank amorality, that if I had to guess, I would attribute to stratagems on the field of battle.

'Ask yourself, Ilario. This man persecutes my son-daughter. Apparently he won't stop. What's the best way to ensure he will? A foot of steel through his ribs, and make mince-meat of his heart and lungs. The dead have no friends or allies.'

Honorius had the flat of his hand resting against his thigh, where his sword would hang were he not in the house.

A little weakly, I said, 'You won't kill him? Because – apart from needing the whoreson bastard as First Minister – they'd hang you for murdering a noble! Lion of Castile or not.'

'"Lion of Castile" would get me hanged with a silken rope,' Honorius mused, somewhat over-gravely. 'Or at least the charity of an efficient headsman at the block. I once saw an execution take twenty blows of the axe, and the man's head was still on—'

'*Father!*'

'—just,' he completed gruesomely, with an open, loving grin. 'No: I won't kill Pirro Videric. Much as the little shite deserves it. No: I won't get myself executed. Or even arrested. Yes: I'll talk as persuasively to His Grace King Rodrigo as I can. Are you content with that?'

'More or less,' I grumbled, with the intention of seeing if I could provoke a laugh out of him. It did.

'Very well.' He sobered, fixing me with a bright gaze. 'And now we must make plans for you and my granddaughter.'

I continued to pass nights broken by feeding Onorata. That would have given me time to think deeply on my father's proposed departure, and how long I might be safe in Venice, if I had not ended all but delirious with sleeplessness, and unable to think at all.

Seeing this, Honorius took it on himself to take at least one of the night feeds ('What, you think me not capable of feeding my own grandchild? How many brats do you think a mercenary baggage-train *has*?'), although he drew the line at changing her soiled cloths.

Rekhmire', while content to nurse a sleeping child as he wrote his

390

correspondence ready for sending east, lost his fascination for her as often as she puked or burped over him. Although I did find her in his company surprisingly often for a man who claimed to have no idea of what eunuchs and babies might have in common.

'The ability to bawl their heads off when they don't get their own way?' was not the politest remark I ever allowed to unwisely escape me.

Rekhmire' merely sniffed.

'*I* am not as sentimental as those great oafs of soldiers,' he observed, and then pinched at the bridge of his nose as if to ease a headache brought on by writing. Eyes still closed, he added, 'You have a dozen "uncles" for the child, who would take more care of her than an egg made of diamond – if only because they know Master Honorius would unravel their guts if they damaged his precious grandchild.'

He opened his eyes and glared at me.

'For the Eight's sake, take advantage of that while you can!'

'I will.' I nodded at the portable writing-slope on his lap. 'If you've correspondence I can help write, I will. Meantime, since I've forgotten the outside world exists, I'm going out to the Merceria.'

'Only if you—'

'—take half of Honorius's company with me,' I finished, ahead of the Egyptian, and found myself with a grin. 'I will. Can I run any errands for you while I'm out?'

Rekhmire' snorted, in a less than dignified manner, and rummaged among the scrolls and documents on the table beside him. '"Run"? I doubt you'll run anywhere until those stitches heal! But if you care to waddle about the city for a while, see if you can discover any more of these put up on walls?'

I took the paper he handed me. It was instantly recognisable: one of Leon's seditious hand-bills.

'You think Herr Mainz might be still here, and printing for someone else?'

'I hope so. I have no great desire to go to Florence . . . '

Despite walking about considerable areas of Venezia, with various of Honorius's guard, I saw no similar hand-bills. The following day, I conceived of asking among the scriptoria, on the pretence of looking again for work, but found no one familiar with the overly-precise lettering of the supposed printing-*machina*.

The following day brought sleet, slanting and chill, and took off every appearance Venice might have had of being in early spring.

My healed stitches itched, and still pulled when I walked, I found. Those of the soldiers I privately consulted assured me this was normal for edged-weapon wounds – which I supposed Caesar's cut at the base of the womb might best resemble.

I refused to wear wooden pattens, and that at least made walking easier, without trying to balance several inches above the mud.

Ramiro Carrasco can clean my shoes for me, I reflected, as I plodded over a high hump-backed bridge, treading in Attila's footsteps through the mire. *Ah, the evils of slavery . . .*

The thought that it might be a true evil took the smile from my face. *True evil, if I only think that slavery's bad when I am the one sold and enslaved.*

Leon Battista's hand-bill crumpled up in my hand as I clenched my fist.

I tugged off my leather gloves to smooth out the thick paper.

'Holy Eight!' I stopped suddenly enough that Tottola walked into me from behind, and I felt him grab my biceps with hands like iron, so as not to send me flying.

'What?' He looked down at my belly, under the long cloak, as he released me. 'You took ill?'

'No. But I realise I've been looking in the wrong places!'

I held up the printed paper illustratively as Attila strode back to us, his hand on his sword.

'Master Leon Battista had enough of these printed . . . It doesn't matter if no man recognises the print.' I rubbed my thumb over the rag-made surface. 'What I should have been looking for is the man who sold him this *paper.*'

'This the last workshop?' Tottola rumbled behind me.

'For today.' I pointed. A tabarra stood a few doors down the narrow street, torchlight reflecting into the mucky grey daylight and the half-frozen canal. 'You can wait for me . . . '

'We'll come with you.' Tottola didn't have the hint of a sigh in his voice. 'Both of us.'

I recalled Sergeant Orazi's advice, passed on to me at one point: that his troopers should be made far more scared of him than they were of any conceivable enemy. Between that and loyalty to Honorius, there was no chance the two Germanic mercenaries would leave me unguarded.

We entered the fifth warehouse that day; I took a half-hour choosing three variant colours of green earth pigment, and discussing with the workshop-master the advantages and disadvantages of various mixtures of size for wood and canvas.

'I need to buy more paper,' I finally observed. Attila and Tottola had become bored enough to amuse themselves by looming over the shopkeeper's apprentices and watching them pale – doubtless having been raised on Tacitus's *History of the Huns*.

'What kind of paper?' The workshop master stretched out his hand as I put a torn-edged sample into it. 'Ah.'

I fully expected to be told it wasn't familiar, or wasn't made by this workshop, or sold here – or else that they had only small quantities available in stock. Two of the parcels Tottola carried contained unavoidable purchases of paper.

The Venetian workmaster put the torn scrap of paper down by the edge of the terre verte pigment tub. 'Yes. Whoever recommended you here was correct: this is our make – I'd know that drying-lattice pattern anywhere.'

He straightened up, and spoke again before I managed to collect myself:

'I'd like to help, but we're out of stock. A customer came in at the beginning of Lent, bought up the whole stock; it'll still be a week or two before we have any more of that particular kind pressed. When do you need it by? Or can I offer you this other—'

'I need it now,' I interrupted, mouth unaccountably dry. *Whatever Rekhmire' can do as a book-buyer, I can do*. It's nothing but pretence and asking questions.

With what I hoped resembled genuine rich-man's petulance, I whined, 'Are you sure you don't have any left? Just a small piece?'

The man shook his head, as one will do when wondering at the vagaries of customers. 'He bought up all the sheets. Don't forget a sale like that.'

I looked brightly at him, as if the thought had just struck me, instead of being painstakingly constructed between Attila and myself in the gondola that brought us here.

'Where did you have the paper delivered to? If I could go and ask him if he has any left . . . even a quarter sheet . . . '

My heart thudded in my chest.

Here's where he says the man had it collected, they didn't deliver.

The works master reached down for a ledger, thumbed through it with agonising slowness – and halted his finger halfway down a page. 'You'd tell him we sent you? Like his custom again, if I can get it.'

'I'll make certain he knows.' I offered the carefully saved end-sheet of paper, and watched him write down an address.

Once outside, I took a deep breath of wet, freezing air – and realised Attila and Tottola were looking down at me with identical expressions.

'Escort me there,' I directed, with a look that plainly informed them I did not expect to come to harm in their company. 'But you'll have to wait outside. If this Herr Mainz knows Leon Battista got thrown into prison, I imagine he's somewhat nervous.'

'So I am!' Tottola muttered, as we set off towards the churches the master had used as landmarks while telling me directions. 'The General will have my balls!'

'And that Egyptian bastard will have *my* balls to go with yours – and his!' Attila muttered.

Tottola made no reply, but he looked worried. On a bearded Hun a head taller than any man in the streets of Venice, that is suitably impressive.

'Honorius expects you to guard me,' I said, the cold air welcome in my lungs after what seemed like weeks indoors. I stepped out more briskly. 'And "that Egyptian bastard" will be too busy being pleased, if this comes off, to even think about how we did this – *or* about your balls, Attila. Which, let's be honest, no one wants to think about . . . '

I said it much in the same manner as the young ensign Saverico might have. The large German soldier snickered. I thought Attila was more comfortable with the part of me that was young man than young woman.

Attila continued my arguing for me with Tottola as we trudged across campo, bridge, canal-path, and more bridges.

The address turned out to be a small shed at the back of a closed-up house. The house looked to have no occupants; the shed had two shutters propped open to let in the light.

I left the two mercenaries at the head of the alley.

There being nothing to be lost by a direct approach, I knocked on the shed door and opened it without waiting for an answer.

In the dim natural light that was all the illumination, a lean man with rough-cropped black hair turned away from a bench and towards me, both his hands laden down with long thin metal teeth that I thought Leon Battista would have recognised as type.

I spoke in the clearest Frankish Latin I could manage.

'You'll be the German Guildsman, Herr Mainz.'

I added rapidly, as I saw consternation on his face:

'The Alexandrine embassy would like to speak with you.'

3

At *Alexandrine*, a flood of emotions passed over his face. He stepped forward, into the better light. The lines of his face spoke of hunger and distrust, and of hope.

Irritably, he muttered, 'You ignoramuses still have it wrong! "*Master* of Mainz", not "Herr Mainz"! "The Master of Mainz" is still my title, even if expelled from the guild!'

'Ilario Honorius,' I introduced myself. Something in the shadows at the back looked very like a wine-press, if a great carved wooden screw might be combined with trays and racks, rather than a grape-tub. 'If I have your name wrong, how should I say it? It was Messer Leon Battista who called you "Herr Mainz".'

'Chicken-hearted Florentine!' The German came almost up to the door. With the dying light from outside, I could see his robe and hose were patched and worn. 'My name is Johannes Gutenberg, of the *city* of Mainz. Where is Herr Alberti? I have not seen him these many weeks.'

'Prison. Florence. Exile.' I gave the knowledge in chronological order, and briskly – what a man who has been lied to needs is the truth, blunt as it may be. 'Why didn't you come to the Alexandrine embassy?'

The German printer seized at his hair, knocking his black felt hat off the back of his head, and yanking his short crop up into hedgehog-spikes. '*You* ask me that! You, one of Alberti's lackeys! I could be in Constantinople!' Gutenberg choked out. 'With a patron! I could work with the best materials – the finest resources – and *you—*'

He spat on the dirt floor at my feet.

'Your petty little republic! Who is Duke? Who cares! Honest men can't work, or are killed, and then another nobleman, same as the last!'

I moved my foot. 'I don't disagree. But a clear explanation and less public noise might be of more use than a political discussion. Florence isn't my republic, and I'm not a servant of Leon Battista Alberti.'

And Herr Mainz must take me for a man, I realised, with my back to the open door's light, and cloaked as I am. Since he doesn't treat me as a woman.

'I'm from the Alexandrine embassy,' I persisted.

'The woman said, no messages; that she would not take even letters from me!'

That confirmed every suspicion. *Damn Neferet!* I wondered which of the sacred Eight one appeals to in such circumstances.

Honesty still remaining my best option, I said, 'Madonna Neferet was a conspirator along with Leon Battista; they both had their reasons for wanting you to stay here in Venice. They've both been sent into exile, now. The representative of Alexandria has been looking for you.'

He snorted derisively.

I brought out the hand-bill, hoping it would act as my credentials.

Tilting the paper to catch the grey light, I observed, 'I've seen nothing like this before. The edges of the letters are sharp as if they'd been cut.'

'They are.' Herr Mainz sounded smug.

I nodded at long metal stylus-shapes in his hands. 'But if your type is made from lead – I know lead—'

My mind clearly sees a silver-grey smear on the masonry of a bridge. Saverico's brigandine; Rekhmire''s leg. *This may be an even more dangerous use for lead.*

'I'm not ignorant,' I offered. 'Men have been talking about the dangers of a mechanical scribe, and if one could be built, since I was a child. Lead's soft. It deforms. The type would be crushed after printing a few sheets, the edges of the letters smeared.'

He gave me an abrasively close-mouthed smile, confirming himself secretive as other German Guildsmen, and no fool.

I took a breath, and pressed the limits of my authority.

'Alexandria wants you and your printing-*machina* in Constantinople, if you'll come. The Pharaoh-Queen may be willing to become your patron, if the printing works.'

The light gave Mainz – Gutenberg – oddly silver eyes. He looked stunned. 'I have not dared to go out, to search . . . The Doge's officers, here . . . '

I took a swift glance around the shabby workshop. 'What do you need to bring with you, to replicate this device in Alexandria?'

Herr Mainz looked at me for a long moment, turned his back, and emptied his handful of long metal type into a large canvas bag.

The contents of a rattling shallow tray followed.

'What I need? All of it!' Gutenberg freed one hand to tap the side of his head, without turning round. 'But all is here, safe, I do not forget!'

'No, but accidents happen to any man.'

He shrugged, as much as a man may who is rapidly tying up the neck of a sack. 'What, you'd have me tell my Guild secrets? The ratio of antimony and tin to lead, so that the edges of these letters stay sharp? Then what is stopping your theft of that?'

I could find no quick answer that I thought would convince him.

I squinted through the gloom. The *machina's* screw was turned by wooden shafts, thick through as a gondola's oar.

'We can send men back to dismantle the printing-*machina* and bring it.'

I glanced around, uneasy for no reason I could pin down, and wished for the first time in many months that I had a sword, and a more recent memory of my knight's training in Taraco.

'If I may, I'll call my father's guards, and we can go to the embassy now.'

I found myself glad of the grey cloud and sleet, that brought twilight in ahead of its time.

A gondola took us as far as the Canal Grande, and then another boat over to the Dorsodura quarter, where we reverted to foot. In a maze of small alleys and waterways that bemused my sense of direction, Tottola took one long stride and caught up, dipping his head to murmur:

'There are men behind us. Somewhere between ten and twelve, lightly armed, no armour except breastplates.'

Dread twisted cold in my belly. 'The Venetians were having his workshop watched!'

Attila, as closely attached to Herr Mainz's side as he might be without rope binding them together, spoke something in one of the Germanic tongues of the Holy Roman Empire, to which the printer responded.

Reverting to Visigothic Latin, Attila said, 'Council of Ten.'

Increasing my pace put a line of pain across my lower abdomen.

'I can't run,' I confessed, feeling my face burn hot against the cold wind. '*Get him to the embassy.* Don't wait for me. Once you're there, they can't touch him.'

The Germanic brothers exchanged a look over my head.

Tottola grunted. '*I'm* not waiting to see what the captain would do if we left you!'

He moved swiftly enough that it took me by surprise. As Attila and Herr Mainz burst into a run, Tottola scooped his arms under my shoulders and knees, and lifted me clear off the cobbles.

Abandoning the parcels of paper, and the ceramic pots of green earth pigment that shattered as they fell, Tottola clutched me against his chest and began to run.

'Bar the gates!' Attila bawled as he hustled Herr Mainz ahead of me. '*Turn out the guard!*'

Berenguer and Saverico hauled the iron trellis of the Alexandrine gate open, stood ready, and slammed it on the heels of our passing through.

The bare garden of the Alexandrine house filled with running men, Sergeant Orazi at their head. Tottola breasted the flood – and failed to put me down, despite urgent request. The house door banged open; we entered from cold to warmth.

Rekhmire', balanced on crutches in the entrance hall, shouted at me immediately he saw me. 'How could you leave this house where you're safe!'

Pointing out that I am most safe wherever Honorius's Hunnish soldiers are, I thought would not help me.

'I'm back here safely,' I snapped, as Tottola set me down on my feet like a child in the entrance hall. 'Even if the Venetians *are* on our heels!'

That turned out not to be a wise thing to say: Rekhmire' broke into a flood of Alexandrine Latin – much of which I understood, although I would rather not – and then into Pharaonic Egyptian.

A glance at Honorius as he stomped in from the gate showed him unlikely to help me with translation.

Not that I need it, I reflected, watching Rekhmire' balance his two crutches precariously in his armpits, so he could windmill his arms while he shouted at me. It all amounts to 'You can walk around Venice, I can't, and this gives rise to fear.'

'We have the officers of Foscari's council on our doorstep,' Honorius announced matter-of-factly. He surveyed the man from Mainz, where the German stood dishevelled and panting, and then turned his attention to me. 'And *you* found him, why?'

'Because I engaged in a paper chase!' I rearranged my cloak, that had been rucked up in the chase. In peripheral vision I saw Gutenberg blink as he caught a glimpse of my skirts. 'As to the Doge's men – I thought they had no idea of where he was.'

It had seemed reasonable, as we were rowed back, to suppose that the Council of Ten must be hunting for a large facility, a factory or a large scriptorium, or a workshop where woodcuts had somehow been made able to cut small letters. Not one man in a shed.

The Egyptian got out hoarsely, 'They surely must have failed to find him while Alberti was here, or they would have stopped him.'

Talking to Gutenberg in the gondola had given me somewhat of his background; I summarised it.

'He was setting three or four pamphlets a week. As fast as Leon could write them. They went off in bales on mule-back, to Florence. After Leon and Neferet left, he didn't have business contacts, and he heard the Doge's council wanted to speak to him and went into hiding.' I cocked my head, listening to raised voices at the outer gate. 'They must have found him and been watching him, hoping to pick up other conspirators.'

'Instead, they found us.' Honorius scowled. Noise rose louder from the gate. Evidently the Council of Ten weren't used to being defied by armed foreigners.

Honorius's household guard are not a large number of men, I realised, compared to how many soldiers the Doge of Venice might call to arms. *Suppose we end with Carmagnola outside the Alexandria House?*

Rekhmire' abruptly closed a hand over my shoulder. His eyes shone bright in the lantern-light. 'Listen.'

I could pick out nothing among the voices, strain as I might.

Honorius, when I caught his eye, shook his head bemusedly.

Rekhmire' secured his grasp on his crutches and swung himself awkwardly and rapidly out into the late afternoon twilight, seeming oblivious to the cold sleet landing on his bare head.

I barely caught Honorius's signal to Attila, to stay with Gutenberg, and then my father strode with me as I stumbled outside again in the Egyptian's wake.

Lanterns illuminated the gate area, but made the desolate garden even darker. The scent of canal-water pervaded the air. Voices lifted in screaming confrontation at the iron grille of the Alexandrine house, where iron bars had been dropped into sockets across the gate.

Words rang like brazen trumpets in the language of the lagoon, and in Visigothic and Frankish Latin – and in another tongue that I only recognised as I caught it for the second time.

'*Listen!*' I echoed, seizing Honorius's arm. 'That's Pharaonic Egyptian, I swear it!'

The mercenary soldiers made way automatically for my father, their faces grim under the lanterns, helmets and pole-axes and swords catching the light.

The circle of torches and lanterns beyond the gate was wider, and the Council of Ten's officers more numerous, but I hardly spared the Venetians a look.

In chiaroscuro, their reddish-brown flesh covered by lamellar leather armour, and with spears in their hands, a squad of some fifty or so men in Alexandrine clothing formed a double line towards the gate.

Down the path between them, across the S. Barnaba campo, a well-padded male figure strolled, not shivering despite his linen kilt and bare legs. His scarlet cloak flowed out behind him, light sparking from the fabric where droplets of rain lodged in the weave.

He stopped before the iron of the gate, a yard or two of space separating us.

His features took me back instantly to another city and another embassy. I found myself rubbing my hands one against the other, as if my skin felt still sticky from trying to pry stone fingers out of Mastro Masaccio's throat.

The Alexandrine cast a leisurely eye around, the uproar from the Doge's soldiers quietening as he did so, and ended with a nod of greeting to Rekhmire'.

'I'm sorry,' Lord Menmet-Ra remarked. 'Am I interrupting some-thing?'

4

He seemed so consciously pleased with his pose that a man could hardly resent it.

Inadvertently, I broke the silence. 'You're not in Rome!'

Heads turned. I blushed. *That sounded foolish!*

I had thought that, having drawn so many sketches now of Masaccio in ink or silverpoint or charcoal, I had begun to have difficulty in remembering Masaccio himself. This tall round eunuch in Alexandrine kilt and lapis-lazuli collar returned Masaccio's dead features intensely to my mind.

'Ilario.' He nodded to me.

'Lord Menmet-Ra,' I apologised.

The last time I saw the Alexandrine, he had been dishevelled and in a night-robe, Masaccio's blood staining the hem. The torchlight gave him stature, although he was still clearly fleshy. He carried an air of authority that he had barely seemed to in Rome.

He added, 'I was hoping to speak with you, Messer Ilario. I have a message for you, from the Pharaoh-Queen Ty-ameny.'

It may have been anticipation or dread, or only the icy wind, that made my eyes water and my throat ache.

Menmet-Ra turned back, raising his high tenor voice that rang over the darkening square.

'Go home, men of Venezia! This is Alexandrine soil – as much so as the ambassadorial warship in San Marco basin, that has brought me to your city. Go ask your superiors if they wish to offend the Pharaoh-Queen through her newest ambassador, before you rashly act here!'

Heads bowed together in the dusk; I heard whispered consultation.

The officers and men of the Council of Ten faded into the darkness, only boots echoing between the high brick walls to mark their departure.

The gate being unbarred with a clash, Menmet-Ra signalled his men to follow, and swept through with some gravitas, despite his body having the smoothness of fat rather than muscle. I did not truly note what words he and my father exchanged, but I stumbled dumbly in their wake, back into the house.

Established in a carved chair by the great hearth in the main room, the

Alexandrine looked unhappily at Rekhmire''s crutches, and then lifted his kohl-lined eyes.

'Ty-ameny says you must bring the German. As to the other matter . . . '

'Carrasco.' Rekhmire' spoke brusquely. 'Fetch wine.'

Ramiro Carrasco went out, wordless. Lord Menmet-Ra extended his hands to the fire. There were goose-bumps on his arms, despite the oncoming spring, I saw. The waters of Venice make anywhere cold, no matter if you're used to Taraco or Constantinople.

'Well, our cousin got me at last . . . ' He looked up ruefully at Rekhmire'. 'You see before you the newest appointee to the position of Ambassador in Venezia.'

'So I gathered,' Rekhmire' remarked dryly, seating himself on the oak settle by the fire. I took a place silently beside him, as quiet as slaves are when hoping not to be noticed.

'With a warship?' Rekhmire' added, one brow raised.

'Trireme,' the older man's light voice said. 'I believe the Queen, all praise to her ten thousand ancestors, thinks the Doge of Venice needs a reminder who rules the eastern seas, and not merely some few fathoms of the Adriatic . . . '

They exchanged looks that I thought in less professional men would have been broad grins.

' . . . And so no making my way here on hired boats,' the new ambassador concluded. 'I come with flags, banners, arbalests, a company of marines, and all to impress. Ah—' Menmet-Ra rose to his feet with the grace of a much thinner man. 'Lord Honorius.'

My father pulled the door closed behind him and Ramiro Carrasco, stepping forward, and giving the impression he ignored Carrasco as the younger man served wine into Venetian goblets.

'I've got my sergeant sorting your men into quarters. Just as well I'm leaving, or we'd be sleeping six in each bed!'

Honorius had discarded sallet and sword, and was in nothing more martial than a pleated doublet and hose. Nonetheless, as he crossed to the hearth and planted himself with his back to the fire, no man could have taken him for anything else but a soldier.

I knew my father well enough, now, to realise this entirely deliberate.

'I hear you want to speak with my son-daughter,' he added bluntly, flipping up the back of his doublet-skirts to take best advantage of the heat on his arse.

If the subject had not put a thrill of fear through me, I might have snickered at the Lion of Castile playing the blunt mercenary commander.

All but inaudibly, Rekhmire' murmured at my ear, '*How* long do you suppose it will take to house-train the man?'

His fellow Alexandrine heard, as I thought he had been intended to. Encourage him to underestimate the Iberian barbarian . . .

Menmet-Ra seated himself again, and spoke with deliberation. 'If you are aware of an incident in Rome, at which Ilario was present—'

Honorius nodded curtly. I chose it as my moment to interrupt.

'Lord Menmet-Ra.' I leaned forward on the settle, my gaze on him. 'The . . . statue. Golem. Did it go to Alexandria? Did anyone finish painting it? Is it still in Rome?'

Honorius's brows went down as if someone had pinched a thumb and finger full of flesh over his nose. 'Ilario, you will not go anywhere near that monstrosity!'

I had described Masaccio's death; I could not make him feel or smell what the reality had been like. Meeting Menmet-Ra's gaze, I saw under his self-possession, an identical fear to mine.

'The gift of Carthage,' the Egyptian ambassador emphasised slightly, 'is in Alexandria, now. The painting of it remains unfinished. I escorted the gift from Rome to Alexandria myself.' He paused. 'Not on the same ship with it.'

I might have laughed if I had not been moved to shudder.

Rekhmire' looked across and curtly signalled Carrasco to leave. I rose and took the wine glasses around myself. Not that it will make a difference to have Ramiro Carrasco hear anything – but I understand why Rekhmire' prefers his absence.

Lord Menmet-Ra nodded thanks and sipped at wine from a sea-blue glass. He looked up.

'I see you're made free now.'

He thus neatly avoided using the terms *freeman* or *freewoman* to me.

'In which case, I can now extend the request of the Pharaoh-Queen in person, to you, that you come to Alexandria—'

'No prodding!'

The words fell out of my mouth without my expecting it.

Rekhmire' put his hand lightly over his eyes. Honorius grinned.

'I mean,' I managed, 'that I have no wish to end with the doctors of Alexandria examining me.'

Menmet-Ra smiled across at Rekhmire' with the ease of long friendship.

'I've had too much of that kind of interest before,' I said levelly. 'Being hermaphrodite.'

Menmet-Ra's kohl-darkened brows went up. 'Ah! No. Although I dare say there are many of our scientists who would like to examine you. But my business with you is not to do with that.'

My business with you.

The golem's fingers a joint deep into Masaccio's larynx as he and I both tore with useless human hands at motionless stone.

No . . . I suppose that business was not going to be done with so easily.

The large, fat Alexandrine put the tips of his fingers together. With all the appearance of good humour, he said, 'The Pharaoh-Queen Ty-ameny has no hold over you, not being the slave of one of her people now. Nonetheless, she requests, if you can, that you come to Alexandria, and tell how it was that Masaccio died. There was no one but you and he alive in that room with the stone engine when it killed him. If you could bear witness . . . '

He left an encouraging gap into which I could speak my agreement. I looked at Rekhmire'.

The book-buyer shifted where he sat on the wooden settle. 'Ilario, you will understand that this "gift of Carthage" is partly an encumbrance, partly a dare – and, I imagine, the Queen's advisers are now afraid, partly a trap.'

'I understand.' It was too much to resist. I moved to lean on the back of the settle, and looked equably at Menmet-Ra. 'I *understand* that Carthage is giving this one of their golems to Alexandria because the thing can be used as a weapon – even if it hasn't yet – and the Lords-Amir are showing off. Daring you to discover how it walks and moves and obeys. Because they're convinced you won't be able to.'

The skin around Menmet-Ra's eyes crinkled. 'Masaccio hired no stupid apprentices, I note.'

It made me grin, until what occurred in Rome crashed down on me again.

'I'll be frank.' The Alexandrine ambassador glanced at Honorius. 'Since Rekhmire' reports you and your father trustworthy.'

Oh, does he?

The book-buyer was none too eager to meet my eye.

Menmet-Ra continued. 'Any gift from Carthage to Alexandria is likely to be a poisoned chalice – Lord Honorius, as a military man, you will understand this.'

Honorius inclined his head in the Iberian fashion, said nothing, but appeared to listen willingly enough.

'It is a concealed threat. Yes, they show us this one of their weapons, and leave us to guess at what else they might have devised. They show they're certain enough of no other man investigating the golem's secrets by giving us the gift of one. And the more our scientist-philosophers baffle themselves examining this golem, the more powerful Carthage grows in our minds . . . and the more fearful of them Alexandria is.'

Menmet-Ra looked up, addressing me directly.

'After the events in Rome, I made my report from your eye-witness statement. But it is still only my report. You were the one that saw. There are those at home who would have the Pharaoh-Queen turn down this "golem" – I think rightly so. Suppose it were to run amuck one day in the courts of Alexandria? How many could it kill, before it was overwhelmed? And, most importantly, if it has hidden orders that send it against Ty-ameny herself . . . '

I opened my mouth to speak the obvious suggestion.

'No.' Rekhmire' raised a brow at me. 'The Pharaoh-Queen – all worship to her ten thousand God-ancestors – is very nearly as stubborn as you are. There is no chance of dropping the thing into Alexandria's harbour!'

Menmet-Ra gave Rekhmire' a look I couldn't identify. 'The Pharaoh-Queen, all praise to her ten thousand God-ancestors, does not desire to look frightened in front of Carthage! Which if she refuses the gift, or sends it away, or visibly incapacitates it, she will. But it is *not* safe to have near her.'

The truth would not greatly benefit me, but I spoke it all the same. 'I don't know what else I can add to what I told you in Rome.'

'Nevertheless. She very much desires to speak with you,' Menmet-Ra said. 'As soon as you feel you might come to Alexandria-in-exile.'

'Thank you,' I got in, before Rekhmire' or Honorius could speak. 'But, obviously, I'll need to talk this over with my family.'

'Of course.' Menmet-Ra stirred himself, finishing his wine. 'I shall hope to speak to you again. Before I completely immerse myself in opening this embassy for business.'

His smile was amiable, but the sensation was odd: to hear that what has felt like my house belongs to this stranger.

Menmet-Ra added, 'And on that subject – I should speak to Neferet.'

'Ah.' Rekhmire' blinked, with the expression of an amiable lizard. 'I believe I also have matters I should discuss with you.'

Honorius spoke gracefully-extricating farewells, grabbed me firmly by the elbow, and I followed his lead in leaving the room.

'We'll talk it over,' Honorius muttered, 'but not near my export glass!'

'Sorry.'

He patted my shoulder, with a wry smile.

Glancing back as we mounted the stairs to his rooms, he added, 'This is no opportunity to miss – if Master Rekhmire' can persuade his ambassador into it, you might make your way to Alexandria on one of their warships. That would greatly ease my mind about your safety.'

I closed the shutters against the chill early evening, and plumped down on a linen chest, wincing as my stitches twinged. 'I imagine Rekhmire' will be escorting Herr Gutenberg and his mechanical copyist on that ship. Before the Doge decides he *can* search the embassy.'

'Well, then. It never hurts to have a highly-placed man in court, to introduce you to his sovereign.'

It took me a moment to realise that my father meant Rekhmire'.

But, yes, he is more than a book-buyer.

I watched Honorius put a taper to the oil lanterns. Swelling yellow light limned his hair and cheekbone.

'Alexandria is half a world from Taraco,' Honorius said thoughtfully. His eyes were lucid in the soft shadows. 'Outside Frankish territories, too. The Pharaoh-Queen won't need Videric's influence or friendship, even if he had any to give. And you're intelligent enough to answer her questions about that stone blasphemy and still avoid going into the same room with it. Of all the places for you to be, while I return home . . . ' He smiled at me. 'You may even learn something!'

'I've seen Alexandrine art. It's all toes-pointing-down. And chests face-on and faces in profile. The New Art's here, in the Italian cities!'

'So are Videric's informants,' Honorius said dryly. 'You know, I wonder if my estates at Taraco ought not to have some Alexandrine work, as well as Italian? I hear they make faïence tiles, and amazing enamel-work.'

I gave him a look. 'What would you know about enamel work unless it was on the pommel of your sword?'

Honorius grinned. 'I can learn.'

He brought bread and cheese, and another bottle of his better wine, and set them on a bench by us, reaching out for a braided-stem glass and tilting it against the light.

'I don't like dragging a youngling all around the middle sea,' he observed, and shot me a keen glance. 'Better she's with you, though.'

I am by no means so sure.

'And you need have no concern for money, or worry that you'll find yourself dependent on the book-buyer's charity.'

In another mood, that would have made me bristle. 'I'd sooner not be dependent on any other source – but I doubt I can keep myself and Onorata on encaustic wax funeral portraits in Alexandria!'

Honorius snorted. 'I intend to leave you half the household men-at-arms,' he added.

'We had this quarrel in Rome!' I chewed at the dark gritty bread. 'You'll make me noticeable—'

'That hardly matters now!'

'—and you'll rob *yourself* of men you need to have with you.' I met his pale eyes, and held his gaze. 'If you go to Taraco with only a small number of soldiers, Aldra Videric or Rodrigo Sanguerra will think the best solution to the problem you pose is a quick death, or quietly vanishing into one of the King's prisons. You must know this!'

'I want you to be safe! I should have bought you when you were still a slave. You'd have been so much less trouble!'

'I wouldn't count on it!' Rekhmire''s voice came from the doorway. At Honorius's beckoning gesture, he took the armed chair nearest the hearth.

Putting his crutches down, and allowing his forearms to rest along the arms of the wooden chair, he for a moment resembled one of the

Pharaoh-Kings of Old Alexandria, heir to a thousand generations of history. The lantern-light made sculpture of his face.

With an entirely irreverent-to-history gleam in his eyes, he murmured, 'I've given Pamiu much to think on, while he arranges this household to his satisfaction! Ilario, are you inclined to risk another sea-voyage?'

'To Constantinople?' I shrugged. 'I can tell your Queen Ty-ameny what I saw. I doubt it will help. It will tell her nothing except that the golem . . . obeys orders. And I suspect they know *that*.'

'You don't know what her philosopher-scientists will discover from what you saw.' Rekhmire' spoke in an eminently reasonable tone.

'I still say I should go back to Taraco and have it out with Videric!'

Honorius made a growling noise beside me, and I found myself in receipt of his 'you-lower-than-dirt-new-recruit' glare.

'Alexandria is your best choice.' Rekhmire' spoke unusually abruptly. 'If only as a shelter. A place to rest. To give you time to think, to plan, to—'

'—be prodded by every one of the Pharaoh-Queen's philosophers because they've never seen a true hermaphrodite before!'

Rekhmire''s brows went up. 'Oh, I wouldn't say *never*. You're not unique, you know.'

My temper was uncertain, but I managed to avoid that particular inviting trap, and grin at the book-buyer. Which, although less satisfying than throwing breakable objects, still pleased me greatly when I saw his startled look.

More because I desired to bait him than by way of serious argument, I said, 'You should let me send word to Videric, and meet him, and settle the matter.'

Rekhmire' snapped like a bad-tempered mastiff. 'Certainly, if you met, it would settle the matter – with a freshly-dug grave! Ilario, come to Alexandria.'

I grinned at him to let him know he'd been provoked. 'Maybe I should have left Venice with my husband.'

Honorius rested his chin on his sun-darkened fist. 'If Madam Neferet sees you in Master Leon's company he'll probably flay the skin off your face before you reach the Arno!'

I found the reference to Neferet as *he* unexpectedly jolting.

Rekhmire' drained his glass of the dark wine. 'Neferet had sufficient trouble before leaving Venice.' He caught my puzzled look. 'You heard none of the gossip? I suppose not. It was widely said of your wedding that Master Leon Battista had thrown Neferet over in favour of a "real woman".'

My father and I looked at each other for a long moment. He hit his thigh with the flat of his hand several times, straining to breathe. I bit down hard on the root of my thumb, not knowing whether I desired to laugh or cry.

'If they *knew*.' I shook my head.

'It would be additional danger,' Honorius said mildly. 'As if you needed it! The longer you stay in Venice, the more likely it is some rumour will be spread by the midwife or priest – although God He knows we bribed them well enough! Or a story will come north that you got married in Rome, and not to Messer Leon.'

Rekhmire' repeated, 'Come to Alexandria.'

Nothing but being contrary moved me to say, 'Give me one good reason why!'

He pushed himself to his feet. For all he stood like an Egyptian monolith, I thought he seemed oddly uncertain.

'I can protect you there.'

'Oh, you can?' I caught, out of the corner of my eye, a smile on Honorius's face. 'Why can you protect me in Alexandria? Why would you want to?'

Rekhmire' looked surprisingly pained.

'I think of you as a friend, not a master,' I said hastily. 'But shouldn't you be, I don't know, off buying more scrolls?' I gave him a slant look. 'Or finding more mechanical copyists for the Pharaoh-Queen?'

Rekhmire''s lips made a compressed line that spoke much of irritation, to one who knows the man. His gaze, when it met mine, was in part amused, and in part annoyed.

'I do have to escort Master Mainz back to the city—'

For Egyptians, I think, there is only one city in all the world. Without qualification, the words mean Alexandria-in-Exile.

'—and it is the weather for sea travel.'

I wondered momentarily whether the voyage from Ostia Antica had been dogged with sickness because I was with child. *If not, I swear never to set foot off land again!*

'Come to Alexandria,' Rekhmire' repeated, as if he would go on tirelessly repeating it like water wearing down granite. 'I can protect you.'

I looked him in the eyes. 'Why?'

Sounding momentarily confused, Rekhmire' said, 'What?'

'Why can a book-buyer for the Royal Library protect me?' I jerked a thumb at Honorius. 'I can understand it with the Captain-General here, and his thugs in livery—'

'Thanks!' Honorius grinned, as I intended him to.

'—but why do you say you can protect me?'

The monumental face smoothed out into complete immobility. It was possible to read nothing from him. I might have painted that face, or rendered it in marble, and no man could have got any clue as to his thoughts.

The Egyptian wiped his hands down his linen kilt and looked up from his chair.

'This may come as a shock,' he said sardonically, 'but I have certain

407

resources I can call on. Menmet-Ra will help with the voyage. You would travel under a pass-port of the Pharaoh-Queen's protection, which I would provide.'

'And you can do that because ... '

Rekhmire' began to look cornered.

I folded my arms and gave him a recalcitrant stare.

'Why should I trust you to get me – and my daughter – to Alexandria? What makes a buyer of scrolls so capable of that?'

'Ilario—' He bit off whatever he had been going to say, glared back at me, and snapped, 'Because I'm a spy!'

The room poised, full of silence.

'Ah.' I didn't look away from his gaze. 'Good. I did wonder when you might tell me ... '

Rekhmire' positively snarled at me. '*What!*'

Honorius slid down a little on the bench beside me, hammering at his thigh with his fist. Small tears easing out of the corners of his screwed-shut eyes. I couldn't make out what he wheezed.

'Father?'

The Captain-General reached for the bottle and glasses, tipping a fair amount of wine from one into the other. He pushed a glass at me, and held one out to Rekhmire', ridiculously delicate in his warrior's fingers, never mind the Egyptian's large hand.

Honorius lifted his own glass, as in a toast. He remarked cheerfully, 'I bet you don't get a lot of *that*.'

5

At Rekhmire"s suggestion, Honorius broke off from packing long enough to send ten men, inconspicuously, to pack up and bring back Herr Mainz's printing-*machina* from his workshop.

They found the anonymous shed stripped bare.

I supposed the Venetians might gain some knowledge from the construction of the *machina* itself, but the German Guildsman's satisfied smile confirmed that the metal type was key.

Since mercenaries must be expert at moving their habitation, and Rekhmire' I knew to be more than used to packing up as a book-buyer, I left the household to their skills.

Ramiro Carrasco entered the room I had come to think of as mine, just as I completed packing what art supplies I judged worthy into a chest for transport, and throwing out what paper I had wasted on unsuccessful rendering.

'You can take these down.' I indicated the ash-wood chests. It disquieted me how easy I found it to give plain orders.

Although some of that is the influence of men-at-arms, and not merely experience of slavery.

A faint fuzz of black hair showed under Carrasco's coif, growing back in. A blue mark under his eye was a bruise, and new. No great wonder if he didn't mourn the departure of my father's company for Taraconensis.

'I feel strange at leaving this room.' I looked about me, touching the green velvet hangings of the bed, and continued without forethought: 'After all, I gave birth to a child here.'

Ramiro Carrasco coloured from the skin at the neck of his shirt, clear up to his ears and scalp; a glowing scarlet translucency of the flesh that might as well have been a brand.

I refuse to be embarrassed that this man tried to kill me!

'I'll take these,' he muttered, squatting to lift one chest. He did not add 'master' or 'mistress'. I was willing to bet he owed his black eye to another such omission.

Shooting an apologetic glance, he added, 'Will I come back and help with the child?'

Onorata's blankets, clothing, and feeding gear still occupied the bed in sprawled heaps. She herself, in her lidless oaken chest, was beginning that restless shifting of her face that meant she would wake soon and be hungry.

'*Lord Christ Emperor on the Tree.*' I sat bonelessly and suddenly on the edge of the bed, hard enough to jolt my teeth, and found myself staring up at Carrasco as the only other adult present.

He put down the box, stepping forward. 'Is she ill? Should I fetch a physician?'

'What? No.' My knuckles were white, where my hands made fists quite without my own volition. 'I realised – I haven't taken her out of the city before. A *sea* voyage! Suppose it kills her? She's so small!'

Carrasco gave me a bright-eyed and unguarded smile, still a little russet from his previous embarrassment. 'You put me in mind of my youngest sister and *her* first.'

At *sister* he blinked uncertainly, evidently registering that I had dressed in doublet and hose for travelling.

'She's a small one, but she's thriving.' Carrasco squatted down by the oak chest, not touching my child, but looking at her with unselfconscious approval.

'How can you *tell*?' The Turkish physician had been extensive in his description of stools, rashes, fontanels, birth-marks, crusts on her eyes, and illnesses in general – but seemed to think I must know what constituted good health.

Carrasco lifted his head and looked at me, amazed. On the bed and its dais, I sat considerably higher than him; I felt it failed to give me any moral authority. He seemed momentarily entirely confident.

'She's growing. After the first couple of weeks, provided they grow and they don't get sick, they're all right.'

'Certainly she eats enough!' I might sound frustrated, I thought. 'Eats, sleeps, shits – I swear you could set a monastery clock by her! Every Vespers, Matins, Lauds . . . She doesn't do anything *else*. Do you think there's something wrong with her?'

Seriously, Carrasco observed, 'Your father should have hired you a nurse.'

He stood, and I saw him glance at the bed again, his flush reasserting itself.

'If I remember, madonna, she's two months old or a little less. She'll do more when she's older. They say she was early?'

Reckoning up weeks, it came to me that if she had gone full term, it would be now that she would have been born. Looking at her in that light, her minute hands and ears and eyes did not seem so undersized for a newborn.

I made to stand and found my knees still weak. 'How in Christ-the-Emperor's name will I manage when she starts moving about! Talking!'

If they were not my blood-kin, nevertheless, Honorius's most trusted men-at-arms had filled the place of family these last months. But without her grandfather, and with all the responsibility falling to me . . .

I wondered if the attempt to hire another wet-nurse would be worth my child's frantic roaring and screaming and obdurate refusal to feed.

My child.

'I can make you a sling, for the babe.' Carrasco shifted his weight from one foot to the other as I looked at him, and shrugged. 'Madonna. My mother used to carry the little ones that way. Left her hands free.'

The blush was not quite gone from his skin. The involuntary colouring spoke of shame. And if 'madonna' is not 'mistress' or 'master', it is still a respectful form of address for the women of the Italies.

If I didn't think Carrasco a man forced into violence by desperation – if I hadn't thought him capable of feeling guilt for attempting to kill a new mother – he would not be under the same roof as Onorata.

I managed to unclench my hands. 'Thank you. Yes. How warmly should I dress her, if I carry her in this sling?'

My erstwhile assassin stepped up onto the dais, sorting with quick efficiency through the piles of clothes, and laying out thin shawls, and a tiny fur-lined hood.

'If there's anything more odd than this day in my life—' I caught Ramiro Carrasco's gaze. '—I'm going to need to be better rested to meet it!'

He made a movement that was part shrug, part slave's duck of the head, and all amazingly awkward. To my surprise, he followed that with a smile.

'Shall I help you with her feed, madonna?'

'I can do that. You carry the boxes: I can't . . . '

He nodded, and took up the packed chests, and in the quietness of his departure, I began to ready the pottery vessel with a glazed spout that had proved the best thing for Onorata to suckle and feed from.

A scrape of wood on wood made me look up. Rekhmire', crutch lodged securely under his arm, had evidently just stopped at the open doorway. He smiled and came in, awkwardly dumping the scrolls under his free arm onto the bed.

'Are you ready?' He peered intently at Onorata in my lap, as she suckled at the pottery spout, but directed the question at me.

'Yes. No.'

Panic returned in a flood.

I did not let it alter my cradling of the tiny child.

'How am I to feed her on the *ship*! We can't be forever putting into ports to buy milk—'

Briskly, Rekhmire' said, 'It's a *galley*, Ilario!'

At my bemused look, he added, 'Built much on Venetian lines, I must admit, even if it is out of an Alexandrine dockyard. Three rowers to every oar, a full complement of marines, the captain and navigator and his officers, and I don't doubt a passenger or two beside you and I and Herr Mainz! With a crew of two hundred men, we'll be calling in at coastal ports for water and food every other day – the pilot's knowledge of that, and the headlands, currents, and landmarks, is what will take us to each port on the way through the Aegean to Alexandria . . . '

'Calling into a port every other day?' I had thought only of the deep seas the *Iskander* survived, in the autumn storms, not this coastal hopping from harbour to harbour.

Rekhmire' nodded. 'And even if not – you'll find, down towards the port side of the captain's cabin, the enclosure where they pen up the animals for slaughter during the voyage. The galley carries several goats in kid, and three nursing nannies, for the milk, and your father has added several more to that contingent.'

A smile touched his solemn face.

'I think Master Honorius would turn the galley into a livestock cargo ship, rather than think of the child going hungry.'

Evidently he would rather turn a joke than put into my mind the dangers of the whole ship sinking, should we encounter bad storms.

There are banker's scrips in my purse.

'I can't support her on my own.' The reality of that failure biting deep, I could hear an edge to my voice. 'Lord Emperor Christ knows what I'd be doing if I hadn't found you and Honorius this year!'

'Children should be raised by the whole family.' Rekhmire' brushed his thumb over her forehead, and down to her flared lips, that had latched onto the pottery spout with no apparent indication of ever letting go.

I snorted. 'Without all her soldier-uncles, I'll be hard put enough to feed her properly all day and all night!'

Rekhmire' turned his head, looking mildly at me. 'Does being no man-at-arms disqualify me from assisting?'

My face was a little hot. I satisfied myself that Onorata had done with sucking, and sat her upright to burp her, wiping off the resulting gob of milk.

'You have responsibilities . . . '

I detected something like pique in Rekhmire''s expression, I thought.

Experimentally, I added, 'But you know she falls asleep fastest when you read her old Aramaic . . . '

He put his ruddy-coloured finger to her palm, and her pale tiny hand clenched over his nail. 'You know very well she's working on a translation. Aren't you, Little Wise One?'

A slave is ill-advised to roll their eyes or be sarcastic; I was under no such restriction. 'Yes, *master.*'

A thought came into my mind on the heels of that.

'Do you realise – if she'd been born in Rome, you'd have owned her too?'

'Dear holy Eight!' Rekhmire' closed his eyes devoutly, and somewhat spoiled the effect by peeking out under his long eyelashes. 'Two of you. It hardly bears thinking of.'

Onorata burped again.

That, and Rekhmire''s expression, made me laugh, as he evidently desired. Taking my mind from the lives of slaves and their children when not free.

'The *Sekhmet* leaves at dawn tomorrow,' he added, retrieving his hand as Onorata abandoned interest in his finger. 'Are you ready?'

'No.' As ever, I found it more than easy to give him the truth. 'It terrifies me, to think of such a small baby on a long voyage across the sea. How can she ever survive it?'

If I expected baseless reassurance, I was mistaken. Rekhmire' thoughtfully nodded agreement.

'But,' he said, 'you're as far from Taraco, here, as you are from Alexandria-in-exile. So it would be no better for her to travel to your home country. If you could stay here, that would be best – but Venice is full of fever in the hot weather, and in any case, I doubt you can stay here in safety from your enemies. This is not the best choice, but I can think of no better.'

He softened nothing, but he did not lie.

I held the tiny solid weight of Onorata, marvelling at her dark lashes and scant feather-light hair. Like Herr Mainz – Herr Gutenberg – I have a need for truth, no matter how little varnish men put on it.

6

The dawn was not even grey in the east when the household stirred again for our departure.

Licinus Honorius I found in the makeshift Alexandrine bath room, when I came to tackle him on the final details of a military guard; two of his men-at-arms bringing in jugs of heated water to fill the porphyry tub.

Naked, he was thin and muscular, with white scars crossing every area of his body, in particular below the knees and elbows.

'Shins and hands. Targets.' He wiped himself down with a wash-cloth, as dignified as if he were clothed in more than soap-opaque water. 'You need not nag. I'll leave only two men with you – one as bodyguard for you, one for the child.'

In the last instance, when all else has failed, a bodyguard's duty is to interpose their flesh between mine and a weapon. I thought I could have refused it for myself. Not for Onorata.

'Who?'

'Tottola and Attila.' He stood, receiving the towel I handed him with equanimity. I wished I had ever thought to ask for a nude study of him: he would be ideal, I thought, for one of the more martial Prophets.

'They have the advantage,' he added, 'of looking nothing in the least like Iberian soldiers. I've told them to take off my livery badges.'

'You'll take all the rest?' I fixed Honorius with as beady a gaze as I might manage. Difficult to exert authority over a man older than I am, and besides my father. 'And take the Via Augusta?'

The skies will be clear, the stars able to be seen for navigation at sea, but not yet as reliably as in the summer months.

'*Yes.*' His exasperation was more reassuring than promises. 'Hand me my shirt. Besides, I have a surprise for you – you will *appear* to be travelling with me . . . '

The importance of secrecy regarding my whereabouts and destination was not lost on me; I could not, however, guess at his meaning. Honorius, dressed, grinned and led me through to the Alexandrine House's warm kitchens.

'No!' the Ensign Saverico's voice whined. 'I won't wear women's dress; I'd sooner be flayed alive!'

Honorius shot the boy a look that seemed to promise just that, and he subsided.

Saverico, in a dark wig – purchased from one of the local whores – and a gown I had borrowed from Neferet, was, it seemed, ordered to make himself visible on the short voyage to the mainland, and as they rode across the Veneto. He folded his arms across his bodice and blushed at me.

'Be cheerful,' I advised him. 'By definition, you need not make the most convincing woman . . . '

This time Saverico joined in the laughter.

'*You'll* travel cloaked,' my father directed me, with similarly no apparent expectation of being disobeyed. 'I don't want to be able to tell if you're woman or man!'

I thought it was Saverico who muttered 'Nothing new there!', but he was smiling, and I let him escape without retribution.

Honorius would have taken us by way of the S. Marco quay for a farewell, I knew, but the importance of my seeming anonymous argued a less public rendezvous with the Alexandrine galley. Honorius and I therefore parted in the bare garden of the Alexandria House, behind high walls, with only just enough grey light to see each other's faces.

'Let me say goodbye to my grandchild.' He took a whining Onorata into his arms. 'I'll miss her first walking and speaking.'

'Just as well, or her first words would be military curses!'

Honorius grinned like a boy. He pushed his ungloved hand into Onorata's tiny fingers. She shoved his thumb against her lips, making gnawing motions, the crying forgotten.

'I do wish,' I observed, 'that you might come as far as Alexandria and keep doing that!'

'She's biddable enough with her grandfather.' He smirked, sounding very smug, and ended with a sigh. 'If I trusted her in the borders of the same kingdom as Pirro Videric, I'd ask to take her home with me. I've raised no children from this age . . . Constantinople will be safer.'

Files of Alexandrine sailors and slaves moved past us, down to the other boats, whose oarsmen began to spider them out into the canal. I had a panicked urge to step back and leave the breathing, living child in Honorius's arms.

If I felt no rush of affection when I looked at her, I could still be taken by surprise by the intensity of my desire to protect her.

The same fear that drove me to think of rockfalls, floods, butchering free-company bandits, and thunderstorms, on the road to Taraco, and made me fear that this was the last time I would see Honorius, paradoxically argued that my daughter would be far safer with him than with me.

'I know nothing of children!' I muttered, staring at her darkening blue eyes. 'I'm not even a proper mother.'

Honorius's fingertip traced the amazing clarity of her skin, where he must feel the faintest fuzz, and moved to the whorl of her ear. I had drawn that shell often enough (before permanent exhaustion overtook me) to know every curve and kink of it. Sometimes I had drawn it by candle-light, when I sat awake, filled with fear, watching her breathe and praying I would not see her stop.

'If I hadn't seen before how soldiers are sentimental over children,' Honorius observed sourly, 'I'd wonder why I scarcely had a chance to hold my own grandchild!'

That was so much hyperbole that I couldn't help smiling.

Honorius continued, 'As for Attila and Tottola, the further advantage of those two is that they both have families at home. Young brothers, cousins; maybe a bastard or two. Between them they can likely change the babe's shit-rag if you fall for sea-sickness on the voyage . . . '

'That's good to hear. Although I was thinking of leaving the task for Master Rekhmire'.'

My father looked across the bare earth to the Egyptian, where he stood in close and rapid conversation with one of Menmet-Ra's slaves. All Rekhmire''s weight leaned onto his stick, although unobtrusively enough that only drawing it had let me know, through my fingers, how much he relied on that support.

'Can't think of a man better suited,' Honorius said urbanely. 'I owe the man too great a debt not to want to see him disconcerted from time to time . . . '

I grinned. Then, 'Debt?'

'He wrote to me to come to Carthage. He gave me you.' Honorius looked openly moved. 'And he's sworn that if, Christ the Emperor forbid it, you should die while in the East, he'll bring Onorata to me.'

That thought sobered me.

Most things that could be responsible for killing me would kill her too. I did not say it. *Honorius will know this.*

My father scowled reflexively in the book-buyer's direction. 'If he fails to look after you both in Constantinople, I'll show him the colour of his own spleen!'

I wondered briefly what colour a spleen was, and whether Galen had written anything on the subject. And realised that Honorius, if asked, might give me an answer based on far more empirical observation.

I didn't ask.

'It's time,' I said.

Honorius put Onorata into my arms, and held us both in an embrace. 'As soon as it's safe to come to Taraco, I'll send word.' He reluctantly released me. 'Trust no one who doesn't come with my authority. Any messenger of mine will inquire of the progress of an altar panel to St Stephen, and then correct to St Gaius if you query that.'

Wordless myself because of the constriction in my throat, I could only nod.

'And I want to see some drawings of your Gaius Judas,' Honorius observed, as cheerfully as he could pretend to. 'Give you something to do when you're lazing about in Constantinople.'

'Lazing.'

'Of course.' He unbuttoned the purse at his belt, and took out a bag of softer leather. 'You should be able to trust my banker, but just in case. These are all my rings. If you need money, sell them; it's why I give them to you. If you're afraid of robbery, don't hide them in the child's cradle, or your hair, or your cunny. It's the first place any pirate or bandit will look.'

I felt my cheeks hot. 'For a respectable military man, you know far too much about how to steal!'

'Used to taking precautions . . . ' His amused tone dared me to doubt it. 'Most often from being robbed by the men I was commanding!'

The men in his livery grumbled mock-outrage.

'There are three bracelets in here that look like cheap brass,' Honorius added. 'Which they are, on the surface, but scratch below and you'll find solid gold. Wear those at all times. And as I said, you may use my name for credit, whatever you need; you have letters to every banker I've had dealings with over the years. I'm good for sufficient funds to keep you safe and get you home. Understand?'

He fretted like a horse with a harness that galls.

'I understand,' I said, 'that you'd like to lock us both up in a Tower of Ladies at the estate, and perhaps let Onorata out when she turns thirty!'

I understand him to be as afraid as I am of those things in the world that threaten what we love.

Honorius cupped his hands over my shoulders, surprisingly gentle even though he must still find them too narrow for a son and too wide for a daughter.

'I know I can't stand between you and every danger. I know you can cope with all hazards. I merely . . . *wish* I might protect you from all ills and accidents, no matter how foolish that is.'

I shrugged, lightly enough to not disturb the baby. 'I understand: I feel the same way about you. And how old are *you*, Lion of Castile?'

Honorius laughed out loud.

'We'll both of us protect the babe, then.' He held her hand between the thumb and forefinger of his own.

The wind came up from the lagoon, heavy with the scent of silt and rot, and at the same time a warm and a chill breeze. Spring, and I am at last leaving this city: I feel as if a cell-door opens.

Honorius embraced us both again, and I turned away to carry out of Venice the child that had not existed as a fully-human living soul when I entered it.

The light in the east was the colour of Naples Yellow as we climbed into the boat that would take us through the canals of the Dorsodura quarter, and out into the basin where lord Menmet-Ra's *Sekhmet* was moored. My feet left dark marks in the dew on the canal-side flagstones. I had my hood up, and pulled well forward, and Onorata tied into a buckram and linen sling under my cloak. *I doubt any man might recognise us unless he stands next to me.*

The creaking of oars all but lulled me asleep, since I had slept so little before. A dim lantern let me see the baggage boat ahead, and from time to time a candle-lit window permitted me a view into some Venetian's daily life. I could not help but look back when I witnessed a woman pacing with her baby against her shoulder, the raw screaming audible through half-closed shutters.

Clouds bulked up before the sun could rise, keeping the small boat inconspicuous. I heard the water lap and drip. The turn of raised oar-blades just caught the light, letting me know the other boats still accompanied us. Wind in my face brought more than the scent of the lagoon – brought the open sea.

I only realised that we had rowed under the stern of the moored Alexandrine galley as it blocked the dawn like a mountain of darkness above us.

There was a pervasive strong odour of tar. And tar adhered to my hands when I climbed up the steps on the side of the ship, and onto the galley's stern deck.

On this high deck, I could not help a glance back towards the Riva degli Schiavoni. I saw lights enough that I knew men were working; loading cargo, unloading early fishing-boats. I heard no clash of arms. Saw no reflections of torches from armour.

If the Council of Ten has the Venetian soldiery there, certainly I don't see them.

Herr Mainz scrambled up the steps to the deck, the German men-at-arms behind him assisting Rekhmire'. Attila and Tottola wore identical fixed frowns, visible by the galley's lanterns – which might have been taken to indicate intense devotion to their duty, but I thought had more to do with the send-off the rest of the company had given them, a scant few hours before. Tottola failed to hide a wince when Onorata, impossibly hungry again, or else disturbed by the stink of the tar on ropes and deck-planks, began to cry.

The galley's captain showed every disposition to put me in a low cabin, close to the water-line, at the stern of the ship. Despite its prestigious and secure nature – it was, after all, where the captain kept treasure and valuable small cargo – I balked, after discovering I would have no light except through the hatch from the cabin above.

By the time I had argued strongly enough to secure the higher cabin, I felt an all but imperceptible life in the wood of the ship.

'I'm going up on deck,' I told Rekhmire'.

I had missed seeing the *Sekhmet* as we approached, so that I had no clear idea how a hundred and twenty feet of galley appears to the naked eye; I did not desire to miss our casting-off for Constantinople.

Rekhmire' followed me to the deck, jerking the padded crutch and shifting his weight with rapid efficiency. I kept Onorata with us in her sling, not simply because I thought she would otherwise wake, but because I did not feel safe leaving her without the German men-at-arms being over their temporary inconvenience.

Pale cool light flooded the arch of the sky. Venice lay spread out behind us.

'Ilario—'

The ferrule of Rekhmire''s crutch slipped on the deck.

His hand came down hard on my shoulder, and his fingers dug into the muscle there. I heard him curse under his breath, raggedly and with no restraint.

I stood perfectly still, Onorata clasped to my chest, until he caught his balance again.

'You'll be glad to get rid of that.' I nodded at the crutch as he straightened up.

Rekhmire' shut his eyes, as if he did no more than listen to the heave and grunt of the oarsmen, and the yells of the deck crew raising the main lateen sail above our heads. I saw one of his hands creep down to push at the muscle of his thigh. He still wore the Turkish fashion in trousers; I had thought it because of the cold.

'I was not about to say in front of Pamiu or your father.' Rekhmire' opened his eyes, focusing on the distant campanile of S. Marco behind us. 'But – if the Turk's diagnosis was correct, and if the physicians in Alexandria have no better treatment . . . Then it's unlikely I will ever walk again without this help.'

7

I am lost on this ship! I realised.

I signalled to one of Menmet-Ra's linen-kilted servants, requesting briskly that he take us to our cabin. Rekhmire' stomped in my wake. I said nothing while any man was within earshot.

The cabin's thick wooden door closed. The noise of running feet, men casting off ropes, and creaking oars drowned out anything a listener might have overheard.

'*Why didn't you tell me?*'

Rekhmire' blinked at me in his most feline manner.

'What should I have said? That I'll be lame?' His expression altered significantly. 'Does it concern you that I won't be able to act in defence of you, or Onorata?'

Frustration and some nameless emotion stifled any reply I might have formed.

A brisk knock sounded on the cabin door. Onorata jolted and began to grizzle. *Hunger,* I thought, although it might have been wind or heat. She did not feel wet enough to change.

'Come!'

At my summons, Attila walked in with a straw palliasse over his shoulder. He threw it down inside the door.

'One of us will be awake at all times,' he said brusquely. 'The other one will sleep across your door. We know you're the Lion's *son-daughter—*' He emphasised the first term. '—but we've got orders to keep you safe.'

His eyes were a remarkable pale blue, this Germanic mercenary, and he could not stand in this galley cabin without bending his head. I wondered at the change between Venice and his attitude here on ship. A matter of sole responsibility, perhaps, now there is only him and his brother?

'I'll agree to any defence, within reason. Consult with me first.' I waited until the tall German nodded. 'Do we have Carrasco?'

'In the hold, in chains, until you want him.'

Conscience might have pricked me. But I think Ramiro Carrasco quite capable of jumping into the S. Marco basin, as volatile as he seems now.

This cabin would belong to some junior officer, I guessed. For all my own protests, Rekhmire''s influence with Menmet-Ra had gained it; and you might sleep six men in it, if four of them lay head-to-toe on the floor, leaving the wooden box-beds for two others.

The Egyptian swung himself over to the far bed and sat down, wedging the crutch in a niche between bed and deck.

I do not know what to say to you. Except that, without me, you would not be injured.

Cherry-flower might be over-ripe and dropping from saplings hardy enough to root in the Adriatic ports we visited, and the day warm enough to go without a cloak at midday, but spring is still a dangerous season for travel.

I saw little enough of the ports myself, and little enough of the Pharaoh-Queen's trireme. One instance of being shown the higher stern cabins above me, where the captain bunked, and the helmsman followed the track of the lodestone in its binnacle, was interrupted by a frantic summons to feed Onorata, since she had apparently decided to take the pottery bottle from no hand but mine.

I likewise had little enough time to admire the breath-taking regularity of the sweeps, the oarsman not standing at their benches as the Venetians do, but sitting by threes, and drawing the long oars when the lateen sails were not sufficient, or we had spent too many hours tacking. There were arbalests set at weapons ports between every bench. And at the prow, where a Venetian war-galley would have the iron beak that served as a ram, I saw a sparkle of sun on bronze.

Herr Gutenberg came back with tar marking every item of clothing he owned, raving about a siphon and dragon's-head spout that would shoot Greek Fire at any enemy of Alexandria. I fell asleep upright on my bunk listening to him.

'Three month colic,' Attila muttered, when he woke bleary-eyed before his shift guarding the cabin door was due, and looked with some dislike at my child.

I sat with her face-down over my lap, rubbing at her back, in the hope that her wide-mouthed screaming might stem from a frustrated desire to fart.

I was appalled. 'It lasts three months?'

'It usually ends when they're three months old.' He dug a dirty fist into his eye as if he would grind it out of the socket, and yawned. 'Usually.'

That there was another part of the ship, I didn't realise until I wondered just where Rekhmire' had stowed Ramiro Carrasco.

Brief inquiry gained me the knowledge that, below the rower's benches and the line of cargo between them (on which the officers walked up and down to supervise), there was another hold. This took cargo or pilgrims, a man from Dalmatia on his way south informed me, and showed me down the steps to the galley's dark interior. They likewise had no light except what came in the hatches – but this hold ran the length of the ship from stem to stern, running off into darkness either side of me; pilgrims and other passengers sleeping with their heads to the hull and their feet to the middle, where their luggage lay as a central barrier.

White sand ballast filled the ship to the level of this deck, as the Dalmatian showed me when he took up a plank and unearthed his bottle of wine and his eggs, which he had stored there to keep cool.

The stench of the bilges, combined with the idea of food, sent me rapidly up to daylight before I had a chance to look for Carrasco.

If not for Honorius, I would be travelling there. I doubt Onorata would survive it.

In the cabin, Onorata was screaming again.

I put her into the sling and took her up on deck.

The buckram and linen sling encompassed Onorata, supporting her body and head, although I kept my arm under her until I should grow used to it. I brought my cloak around her, to shield her from the ripe brisk wind blowing from the pine headlands of the coast. Her tiny screwed-up features showed dwarfed in her fur-lined hood. I wriggled my finger in to touch her neck, and judged her neither too warm nor too cold.

Rekhmire' stomped to stand beside me at the ship's rail, in that open middle area around the mainmast that they call 'the market-place of the galley'. The crutch's ferrule scraped on the deck. He cocked an interrogative brow at the sling.

'Well thought of,' he approved.

'Ramiro Carrasco made it for me,' I said, taking the opportunity for truth.

The Egyptian scowled.

'It's perfectly harmless!' I protested. 'Safe. One of the things you learn in a large family, it appears.'

'If he were not a necessary shield to you—' Rekhmire' broke off, took a visible effort to collect himself, and gave it up. 'Have you lost your mind? Taking help from him? The man tried to murder you!'

His words brought the memory of Ramiro Carrasco in prison sharply to my mind's eye. '*I* came nearer to killing him. I cracked his skull.'

Rekhmire' snorted.

'Besides which,' I added, 'you need not either trust nor like him, but – *I need a servant!* And since he had to come with us, it might as well be Messer Carrasco.'

'Plain Carrasco the slave!' Rekhmire' corrected with a snort.

He stomped off down the deck before I could add more.

This voyage would be infinitely easier if those two men co-operated.

Watching Rekhmire's rigid back, I thought, *It won't happen.*

'Say what you like!' Exhaustion made me stubborn. 'I haven't slept in

422

twenty hours – *again!* – and you neither. Attila has to be on guard and Tottola asleep. There is no one else!'

'You'd trust Carrasco with your *child*?'

The note in Rekhmire''s voice was far closer to pique than to concern, I thought.

His heavy lids hooded his eyes. Had things been right between us, he would have made some joke regarding the necessity of strangling the bawling brat in any case.

'I don't *care* how trustworthy he is!' I raised my voice over Onorata's roaring. 'I have to sleep!'

The same went for Attila – curled up on his pallet, all of his clothing and blankets pulled over his head and wrapped about his ears – and for Rekhmire' himself. Spattered ink showed his failure to compose report-scrolls away up on the deck in a brisk wind. The cabin seemed full of something tangible, as if you could touch Onorata's hopeless wailing.

Blue patches marked Rekhmire''s eyes that were nothing to do with kohl. 'You *trust* that—'

Evidently an epithet escaped him.

'"Spy"?' I suggested sweetly.

'"Would-be murderer"!' Rekhmire' snapped.

'I just want him to sit here for an hour and watch her! Then I'll walk her on the deck again.' I thought my muscles might easily recover from their weakness after the Caesarean, given the amount of exercise I gained walking and crooning to the baby. 'I don't believe he'd hurt her.'

Rekhmire' threw down a stoppered ink-horn. 'You *cannot* propose to put your child into that man's care!'

He said considerably more, but tiredness blurred the edges of it. At this moment, I thought, *I* am a greater danger. If I sleep now, I'll roll over and suffocate the child; at least if Ramiro Carrasco has her for an hour, I'll be less exhausted.

'Besides,' I added, 'Tottola can watch him for an hour, instead of the door.'

I sent Attila to unchain Videric's spy and my slave.

Ramiro Carrasco had not benefited from his week in the hold, I saw, with those Alexandrine slaves not involved in rowing or sailing the trireme. He stumbled into the cabin half-awake and fearful, hair in spikes.

'You're looking after Onorata,' I said bluntly. 'Nurse her. Feed her if she carries on crying. You know how to do that?'

'Yes.' He looked stunned.

I did not dare not stand up to pass her over, dizzy as I felt. Carrasco squatted, not meeting my eye, gently taking Onorata from my arms into his.

I strung words together. 'If she sleeps, and Attila's awake by the next

423

ship's bell, get him to help you make her feed. Wake me if anything is wrong, or if you even *think* there is. Understand?'

Carrasco didn't rise. He unwittingly echoed Rekhmire', in a hoarse whisper. 'You'd trust me with your child?'

'If I thought you were a man even *capable* of harming my child . . . I would have sent a lying message to Videric, telling him I'd bought you,' I said. 'And I would have paid the Venetian jailer to cut your carotid artery while I stood and watched, to make sure.'

There was no threat in what I said. What threat could ensure the safety of Onorata? I saw him take in the reality of the situation, however, before I lay down and wrapped my cloak over my ears, and sleep came over me as black and dark as the sea beneath the galley's hull.

Before the *Sekhmet*, I would have thought it only possible to fear storms, sea-thieves, clouds that obscure the stars, and pestilence-banners flying from harbours we desired to put in to, for just so long.

Had I been travelling alone, this might have been the case.

As it was, I fretted from the Adriatic to the Aegean, week on week, and I missed the company of the book-buyer.

If Rekhmire' was much absent in conversation with the captain – a man originally from Rhodes, or Cyprus, or some such island – Tottola and Attila attended to their guard duty with considerably more attentiveness than when they had comrades to take responsibility from their shoulders. One always slept, one always woke; and they assumed a demeanour that made Menmet-Ra's returning slaves (when I could strike up a conversation) regard them as the worst kind of cannibal Franks.

The Master of Mainz never slept, or not in our cabin. I felt no inclination to blame him: *I* would have slept elsewhere if I could. Gutenberg busied himself with every aspect of the trireme he could investigate, from the Greek Fire weapon at the prow to the *bussola nautica* that indicates the position of the magnetic poles. I changed Onorata's shit-rags.

Onorata bawled.

Ramiro Carrasco sung her a lullaby that, after final frustrated inquiry, I discovered to be only the rose of the compass sung to a tune of his own devising. *Tramontana, Griego, Levante, Sirocho,* and so on to include all eight winds.

If it had not granted me sleep, I would have resented my daughter for attending more to the man who would have killed her than to her mother-father.

'"Ostro, Garbin, Ponente, Maistro" . . . ' Since she appeared soothed by only that lullaby, I learned the song by default.

Being in constant attendance on the child, I found myself taken for a woman, for all I dressed in hose. Attila pointed out that I might be a woman dressed in male clothing for travelling, as many do. That gave me pause to think of where I was going. If I had been on better terms with Rekhmire', I might have asked to borrow Alexandrine clothing.

For all I had been thinking of it league after league, the arrival at Constantinople nonetheless took me by surprise.

8

Harsh light blazed up off the water, and the land to either side.

'I dreamed of bears last night.' I blinked, surprised to hear myself sound morose.

Tottola glanced down from where he leaned on the ship's rail, at my right hand. 'That only counts if you dream *before* you embark.'

Attila's massive elbows came to rest on the sun-baked wooden rail at my other side. He murmured, 'Just don't sneeze, now . . . '

I managed a sneer at him, for his superstition, as well as I might for the jumping frogs of nervousness in my guts.

Other than leaving Rome – when I had other matters in my mind – I always observe the politenesses of travel that I was taught along with court behaviour. Step on board a ship with the right foot, never with the left. Avoid sneezing or coughing as one comes on board. Sailors have been known to tip a supposed bad-luck passenger overboard before now. But they're only ancient delusions: certainly I wouldn't go so far as to delay a voyage if I dreamed of bears or boars or any other Heraldic beast on the night before sailing.

'Besides,' I said aloud. 'That's the harbour: we're here now. If we sink, I'm sure somebody can fish us out . . . '

'Assuming they'd bother,' Rekhmire''s voice remarked, more amiably than he had for some weeks. He directed a shame-faced smile in my direction. 'Are you certain you wish to associate with us so closely?'

He claimed this land to be no further south than Taraconensis, merely much further east. I, having sweated the more as the ship sailed south past each Greek island, doubted him. Confronting him a week ago, I had borrowed what garments of an Alexandrine bureaucrat might fit me.

'I look like one of your people,' I said mildly, hitching at the wrap-around linen kilt that I wore. Over it I'd belted a sleeved robe – made from a single thickness of linen fabric, light enough to bear the heat of the morning but enough to keep my skin from burning.

And enough to hide my bare chest.

Rekhmire' didn't need to hide his. He had his braided cloth and reed headband tied around his forehead, this time over a voluminous hood or veil of flax linen, which held it so that his shaven head and his neck were protected against the sun.

'Pireaus and the last three Greek ports, they took me for an Alexandrine eunuch,' I added, smugly.

'That,' he observed, 'is why no one will bother to fish you out of the harbour. Far too many of us here as it is. Place is swarming.'

I failed to stifle a snicker. And thought myself regrettably comfortable in his company, for a man with whom I had not settled a quarrel. If we *had* quarrelled. And if I was certain over what.

Ramiro Carrasco shot me a puzzled look, standing holding Onorata among the baby's luggage. Which, if you leave out of the calculation any sketchbooks I may have brought on the voyage, or any Greek scrolls that found their way into Rekhmire''s hands, was the largest single amount of baggage in our expedition.

The crop-haired Herr 'Mainz' strolled past Carrasco, his gaze going between me and Rekhmire'. 'This. This is Constantinople?'

Rekhmire' murmured a phrase in Alexandrine Greek, and then added, 'Franks still call it that. We call it the cities of the Pharaohs of exile. Or New Alexandria, if that's easier for you, Master Johannes.'

The German guild-man nodded absently, his gaze still fixed on rocking water, packed hulls and bare masts, and the massive and monumental stone walls of the city.

I thought, I have seen nothing like it since Carthage, and Carthage's walls are no longer seen in daylight!

My hands itched to be at chalk and paper.

Rekhmire' was still talking to the German. 'How would you prefer to be introduced to the Pharaoh-Queen Ty-ameny? As Master Mainz?'

'It may be best.' The German didn't shift his gaze from the bright waters. 'The Guild in Mainz dismissed many of us when they threw out the patricians. If your Pharaoh-Queen will not think it odd?'

The German is as nervous as I, I realised.

Thoughts of Videric, deliberately pushed into the background all this month we sailed south, intruded back into my mind. Between that and the vista rising from the water beyond the *Sekhmet*'s prow – great walls decorated with painted bands and enamel, the ochre-coloured domes, the temples and the obelisks lining the skyline – I felt amazingly small.

And I have essentially come here – to ask for help.

I must be mad.

That thought was purely honest.

No one here will have any reason to help me, no matter what I can testify about the Empty Chair and Masaccio's death.

And here I may see again the thing that murdered him.

My fingers shook, cold despite the heat. I thrust one hand up each opposite sleeve, folding my arms, and leaned on the rail again. One of Menmet-Ra's slaves, by name Asru, giggled in a high-pitched voice, and I glanced aside from the magnificence of Alexandria to see her flirting unsubtly with Attila. She had one of her hands clasping at his arm, trying

427

to run her fingers through the thick fair hair that, unbound, fell to his waist.

Beyond her, Ramiro Carrasco de Luis, with the baby's baggage piled up in a mountain about his knees, cradled Onorata up against his shoulder. His hand, huge against her tiny cloth-wrapped body, rubbed at her shoulder-blades with two fingers. In an undertone, he murmured, 'There we go . . . '

Onorata's face screwed up. She jerked, and made a sound like a kitten sneezing.

A gobbet of something white and half-digested hit Carrasco's neck and doublet-collar about equally.

The baby's unfocused blue eyes returned to gazing out at sunlight fracturing off the water. The assassin, still supporting her by one hand and the sling, scooped at his neck with his fingers, dragging the mess out from between his linen doublet and his steel collar. He wiped his hand down his hose. I heard him heave a half-exasperated and half-satisfied sigh as I got to within a pace of him, and he placidly went back to stroking Onorata's shoulders, humming under his breath.

'Where did *you* learn to do that?' I demanded, since it was in no way the way I burped her.

He leaped as if I'd stuck a sword point in him. My daughter began to howl. Tottola and Attila put hands to weapons as one – assessed the situation instantly – and took an automatic pace away across the ship's desk. Away from a disturbed baby.

Red-faced, I muttered, 'Shit . . . '

'She's done that. I changed her.'

I glared.

Between distracting her and petting her, Carrasco and I persuaded Onorata that she desired to sleep more than she desired to scream like the fabled steam-ball of the Alexandrine philosopher Heron. I found it difficult to be soothing when I wished to strangle the man beside me.

I shot him a glance, and met harassed dark eyes. And snorted. 'Maybe I should light another candle to Rekhmire''s Hermopolitan Ogdoad. It seems to work.'

'Or it was colic, and now she's older . . . ' He rocked her a little, in her linen wrappings. She settled curled up onto his breast, nosing momentarily for something she would not get from him.

Or from me. I was momentarily bleak.

'Amazing,' Rekhmire' remarked, at my shoulder, 'how "wet-nurse" comes in the list of required talents for an assassin.'

The dark-haired Iberian immediately lowered his gaze.

He's picked up some slave habits, I realised. Among which is the necessity of hiding your thoughts from your owner.

'Give her to me.'

The solid, warm bundle in my hands felt so breakable that, even with

428

the sling, and Onorata tucked into the crook of my arm and with my other hand supporting her head, I couldn't convince myself that she was safe in my arms.

Ramiro Carrasco muttered something, and I looked up and raised a prompting brow.

He moved his shoulders under the patched doublet. His iron collar gleamed dully in the sunlight. 'Like I said, I'm the next-to-eldest in my family. I used to have to look after the young ones a lot, before the priest took me off to teach me my letters.'

Anger stung me. I have not paid enough attention to this before – or, I have, but the necessity of having more than one set of hands to look after Onorata made me wilfully ignore it. 'How long do you think I'm going to have an assassin near my baby?'

Ramiro Carrasco de Luis blushed like the schoolboy he would have been when his local priest singled him out as worth teaching his letters. 'You can kill me. Torture me.' He looked down at his dirty bare feet. 'Without needing to think whether anyone will ask why. They won't. Under these circumstances, do you think I'd take a step out of line?'

I thought him a long way from the sharply-dressed secretary who'd waited on Aldra Federico and Sunilda. The sun had bleached his doublet, and the foot-less Frankish hose. He went bare-headed as slaves do, his hair growing out short and shaggy. The labour the captain had also co-opted him into on the *Sekhmet* had hardened his muscles, as well as his palms and the soles of his feet.

I waited until he looked up, rubbing my thumb in small circles on Onorata's chest since she seemed to like the rhythm. 'I've known slaves who decided they had nothing to lose. Who felt it didn't matter if they were tortured to death, so long as they had that one strike back at the master they hated. You might wait your moment, and drop my baby over the side of the ship. Or just pinch her nostrils together. After all, it isn't a season yet since you tried to kill me.'

Shame made me hot even as I spoke.

This is gratuitous cruelty. Since I am ashamed of having not been sufficient for my child. Ashamed of trusting Carrasco out of sheer convenience.

Onorata stirred, whimpered at tension she must feel through my arms and chest. She reached out with one wavering starfish-hand.

With the automatic reaction that meant this must have happened a hundred times before, Ramiro Carrasco absently reached down and put his forefinger close to the baby now cradled in another's arms.

Onorata's hand closed around his finger, lifted her head a little as she pulled it to her mouth, and lay back mumbling his nail as she subsided into dreamless squirming.

'She's advanced,' Ramiro murmured absently, 'for three months. She holds her head up well—'

He glanced up.

Tethered by the infant's grip, wide-eyed, the Iberian assassin gave me a look of slave's terror.

'I didn't mean anything . . . Mistress!' Carrasco added rapidly. His gaze skidded up and down me, like a water-insect on a canal. 'Master!'

He grew used enough to seeing me in gowns in Venice to think of me as female. The eastern robe and kilt, which is male clothing in Alexandria, is enough like Frankish women's gowns to confuse him further. His eyes widened enough to show white at top and bottom.

I frowned, in sudden realisation. 'Have the ship's other slaves been telling you stories?'

He nodded.

That will go a long way to explain why he looks more ready to soil himself than Onorata does.

'It's not all lies,' I said. 'But Alexandrine slavery's different. I've been trying to follow Rekhmire''s model. It was the one I preferred to live under when he bought me.'

Ramiro Carrasco de Luis looked as thoroughly miserable as I have ever seen a man.

'You're right.' He managed to achieve looking me directly in the eye. 'Nothing honest can pass between a slave and a master. Anything I say, you'll think I'm ingratiating myself through fear of punishment. I wouldn't harm a child—'

Anger momentarily broke through, to be succeeded by despair.

'—but you'll think I say that for the same reason.'

I knew the secretary-assassin had not had particularly comfortable treatment in Venice; Honorius's men, who would have treated a slave with some decency, set out to make the life of the man who had threatened their commander's family a complete and total misery. The smallest things do it. A kick here, a spit in one's dish there; an accidental knock into a canal, after telling tales of monster- or plague-infested waters. They might have done worse if Honorius had not had a quiet word with them. The old skills of slavehood led me to be in a place to overhear my father order that they should not maim or bugger or kill the man.

But that was all he ordered.

I studied the peeling red and callused finger that Onorata firmly gripped. No great wonder if the university-taught lawyer had sunk into himself; kept himself to menial duties with his eyes always cast down. But . . .

'I saw you with Federico and Sunilda.' I spoke quietly enough that I wouldn't wake the baby. 'I'd say you were an expert at ingratiating yourself with people.'

The frustration and despair on Ramiro Carrasco's face was something I couldn't sketch with my arms full of Onorata, and that was a shame.

How have I become so vindictive? I wondered.

Am I so jealous, if my child appears to love him better than she does me?

I wanted to claw at my chest through the thin linen; claw at the small breasts that – ache as they might – would give not even one drop of milk.

'If I trusted you, I'd be a fool,' I said.

'So you would,' a powerful tenor voice interrupted.

I looked up to see Rekhmire' looming over Ramiro Carrasco. The Egyptian nodded to me. His gaze went to the finger that Onorata suckled on.

'Get the rest of the baggage ready for disembarking,' Rekhmire' added.

The secretary-assassin removed his hand from Onorata with a gentleness that did speak of younger brothers and sisters. He instantly slid off through the crowd of sailors and soldiers without another word.

If he had his shirt and tunic off, I wondered, how many weals would I see on his back?

'You can't trust that man.' Rekhmire' gazed, not at me, but at the massive masonry walls of Constantinople harbour gliding past. They dwarfed the other ships anchored here in the Golden Horn.

His expression would have seemed impassive to someone who didn't know him well.

Oddly enough, his overt bad temper reassured me. 'You got out of the bunk the wrong side this morning . . . '

Rekhmire' suddenly smiled at me. 'It's always a little nerve racking to see one's superiors again. Who knows what I've failed to report back in the last half year or so?'

The idea of the large Egyptian being dressed down by his spymasters here in Constantinople . . . I smiled. 'I'd like to hear *that* conversation.'

A sudden change came in the tone of talk around us. Rekhmire' frowned. I glanced around. Attila and half the ship's crew were looking over the port side of the boat—

No, every man looks in that direction.

Clasping Onorata, I elbowed my way back to Tottola's side at the rail, the book-buyer in his familiar place beside me.

Ships lined the quays at the foot of Constantinople's massive walls. The larger vessels anchored further out in the harbour. More of them moored here than there had been ships in Venice. Every kind of ship: cogs, dhows, bireme galleys. Warships.

At Venice, I missed the full-distance sight of the *Sekhmet* moored in St Mark's basin. At Alexandria, now – I found it brought home to me that the Alexandrine navy consists of more than one trireme.

'Six,' I counted, and took unfair advantage of Tottola's presence to tie Onorata's sling firmly around his chest. I hauled prepared paper and silverpoint out of my linen purse, to sketch everything from the high sterncastle of the nearest trireme to its triangular prow sail.

Yes, it came from the same dockyard as the *Sekhmet*. But to see the ship all at once, whole . . .

Six – no, seven – of the narrow vessels rocked on the gentle swell in the harbour. Twenty-three paces from prow to stern, if they matched ours: better than a hundred and twenty feet. And a mere seventeen or eighteen feet wide. Narrow, knife-hulled vessels, with bronze nozzles pointing out of the dragon's mouths at their prows. Oars spidering rhythmically into the sea . . .

Hand and eye moving between ships and paper, it took me a minute to notice that the smaller sails were set. On most of the triremes, a crew of oarsman was in evidence.

'They're not moored—' I caught the line of one galley's stern as she turned away from us: a heartbreaking beautiful swell up from the water, past the cabin ports, to the central stock of the rudder.

A few lines put in cargo cogs in the background, for the scale.

'Do they patrol the harbour here?'

Rekhmire' did not answer. I sketched the tracery of rope and sail against the sky, angry that I could not – because I did not know the use of each – draw it properly. If I had Mainz's freedom about the ship, I would know every function.

I hatched horizontal lines for the hull's reflection in the harbour and abandoned the page, turning to the next empty sheet, and the trireme that carried the lion-head of the Pharaoh-Queen on its mainsail. 'That's one *big* ship . . . '

At my ear, Rekhmire''s voice sounded oddly.

'No – no, it's really not . . . '

I lifted my head from the page, and saw what he must be looking at. 'That's an interesting trick of perspective.'

Close at hand, a hull with a rack of masts rose up against the background of Constantinople's walls as if it were a mountainside. A ship whose designation I didn't know – not a galley, not a cargo-ship – but which some trick of distance and light made ten times the size of every other ship here.

Unimaginably huge . . .

I watched as one of the Alexandrine navy triremes rowed to pass far behind the evidently foreign craft.

Attila swore. '*Christ Emperor!*'

I leaned out, ship's rail hard against my belly, healed wound forgotten. I stared into the light blazing up from the water.

Distantly I could hear the trireme's drum beating the pace. The oars lifted, dipped, flashed drops of sea water—

And the trireme did not slide out of sight behind the close-at-hand ship.

It glided *between* us and it.

Not something that is small, close at hand, seeming large. Something large, far off, that is vast.

'Not a trick.' Rekhmire' sounded stifled. His face showed blank shock.

As the ranked oars sent the trireme curving towards the stern of the foreign ship, I stared at the top of the trireme's mainmast.

The very top of the mast did not reach as high as the foreign ship's stern deck.

I judged a man standing in the crow's-nest of the trireme would still find himself the height of a house below the foreign ship's taffrail.

'I – wait!' I gripped Onorata almost too hard, finding myself with both arms wrapped protectively about her sling. 'I *remember*—'

Memory came back with instant clarity. Cannon-metal grey skies. Storm-lightning and rain shining all but purple on the heaving Adriatic swell. And seen from the deck of the *Iskander* . . .

'I've seen this before!'

Beating up against storm after storm in the Adriatic. And the sailors telling hushed rumours of . . .

'Ghost ships.' I breathed out. 'That's . . . '

'Not a ghost,' Rekhmire' completed, his hand coming down warm on my shoulder.

'But it is a ship.'

My eyes no longer lied to me. The ghost ship was moored far out from the quays, almost in the centre of the harbour. Each of the Alexandrine navy galleys patrolled around it: around the great walls of wood that rose from the water. A blue-glass shadow echoed it, as deep again.

Now I saw it again as it was – and how I had seen it at sea. That vast assembly of bare wood, ranked stark as a winter forest against the sky, would hold lateen sails. Sails piled higher and higher, one row on top of another, each bellied out in a tight curve against the wind. I had seen rank upon rank of them, rising up against the storm.

In this clear morning light of Constantinople's harbour, each spar showed the irregular edges that meant sails bundled and furled.

Below the masts was a great broad hull, with a flat prow. A hull that my eyes told me stood ten times longer, and five times higher, than any other ship in the harbour. The deck swarmed with men so tiny at this distance that I must believe the size of their ship.

As we inched past the ghost ship, I saw painted on the prow, in green and gold and red paint, a great spiked serpentine beast. Eyes were flat black-on-white discs, staring out across the Alexandrine waters and at us.

With shaking fingers, I made notes too rough to be of use. But copying the drawing of the serpent told me one thing.

Not in Iberia. Not in Carthage. Nor Rome. Nor Venice.

'Not the Turks, either,' I found myself murmuring aloud, thinking of the patterns woven into Bariş's tunic. 'I've seen much while searching out the New Art. That – that is nothing like any style of painting I've ever seen.'

9

Identical shock showed on each face. Honorius's two men-at-arms, the ship's sailors, Asru, Carrasco, Johannes Gutenberg. Rekhmire'.

Attila snorted out a protest. 'They don't *build* ships that big!'

Rekhmire' frowned and muttered words which I finally distinguished as a list of shipyards. 'Cyprus, Sidon, Tyre, Venice, Carthage, La Rochelle . . . '

He glanced up at the trireme's captain, on the sterncastle. I could see the man shaking his head.

'No. None of them.' Rekhmire' narrowed his eyes against the sun glittering off the water. 'Menmet-Ra said nothing of this. It must have arrived recently, therefore. Within the last few weeks.'

'Arrived here? You're likely right—' Onorata whined and mumbled. I stroked her cheek, hypnotised by the sight of the immense ship. '—but I think it's been in the Middle Sea longer than that.'

My drawing had gone, destroyed by weather, but I could recognise what I had taken for delirium and *trompe l'oeil*, in the Adriatic sea.

Rekhmire' tilted his head back. At this distance it was possible to pick out small figures of men on that impossibly high rail. Not possible to see any detail. He mused aloud, 'It will be – interesting – to know how it came to be here.'

'And if anybody can find out, you can!'

He gave me the same abrupt and undignified grin that he had sometimes gifted me with in Carthage.

It stayed quiet enough that I could hear ropes creaking overhead, and the sweeps groaning as the oars brought us steadily on towards our mooring place. The captain bellowed something obscene as our wake wavered, the rowers' attention being all on the huge ship. I realised we were listing, every man who could lining the rail on this side of the ship.

I shaded my eyes with my free hand. 'How many men would it take to crew something that size?'

'It's . . . remarkable.' Lines creased Rekhmire''s forehead; I could see them where his hand lifted his cloth veil as he tried to cut out the ambient light from sky and flashing wavelets. He looked back at me. 'But, if I may say so – not our first concern. We have matters to take up with the Pharaoh-Queen. Although it might be useful, perhaps, to mention to her that you've seen this vessel months ago.'

Our ship drove on steadily towards the mountainous masonry of Constantinople. I realised I had the jumping frogs in my belly again.

The ghost ship. Yes. But . . .

Sooner or later, the Pharaoh-Queen will call me in to bear witness to what I saw in Rome.

When this city had been built by the Romans and Carthaginians, it was called Byzantium. The Franks called it 'Constantinople' after one of their emperors, and added monumental grandeur to the place. But it was the last of dynastic Egypt that had taken the city and changed it to New Alexandria, long centuries in the past, after the Turks overran the Egyptian homeland.

It looked nothing like the harbours of Frankish ports, or Iberia, or even Carthage. I stared out at the squares of the city, lined with great inscribed obelisks; temples with masses of clustered pillars under great roofs; and the bas-reliefs that ornamented buildings – painted bas-reliefs, bright as enamel—

I could do nothing but stare as we docked and were greeted. A bevy of bureaucrats stood by, awaiting the galley's small boats. It occurred to me that if Menmet-Ra had sent messages indicating his success in finding the printer and the hermaphrodite, his messengers might have had better sailing than ours, and arrived here before us.

'Come.' Rekhmire' touched my shoulder. 'We'll go up to the palace.'

The Pharaoh-Queen Ty-ameny, otherwise Ty-Amenhotep, Lord of the Two Lost Rivers and Ruler of the Five Great Names, stood around four foot six in her bare feet, and wore a beard.

She *was* barefoot, I saw; a pair of gilded sandals having been kicked off across the rush matting on the faïence-tiled floor, and she reached up and unhooked the false beard from her ears as the mute slaves showed us into her bedchamber. Sunlight streaming in through the linen-draped windows spot-lit the small, black-haired figure as she turned and beamed.

'Rekhmire'! You're back.'

'Great Queen.' Rekhmire' lurched only slightly as he stepped forward, aided by his crutch. He bowed almost double, and put his free arm very gently around Ty-ameny, embracing her as one does a relative or close friend. 'I've brought you Ilario, son-daughter of Licinus Honorius, who is lately Captain-General of the Frankish thrones of Leon and Castile.'

Ty-ameny nodded briefly, with a quick and bird-like movement. Her arms were thin but muscled, and showed ruddy under the half-sleeved white linen tunic she wore. A heap of brocade and cloth-of-gold on the bed, spilling down the sides of the dais, had the look of formal clothing – and the braided beard hit the top of the heap with some force.

'I can do without one more formal audience!' Ty-ameny dusted her hands, and put small fists on her hips. In a tunic that came down to her knees, and with matt-black hair cut in a curtain that fell below her waist, she looked something between the beggar children and fisher-girls down on the dock, and – because of the quality of the cloth – a great lady. She strode across the mats to where a sunken area of the floor was lined with marble benches, padded with silk cushions. She waved one arm at her slaves.

'Good day to you, Freeborn Ilario.' This in halting Iberian. 'Please, sit. You should drink.' She met my gaze with eyes that were black as sloes, and smiled. 'Foreigners don't drink enough in New Alexandria, and then we have to treat them for heat-stroke.' Back in the Alexandrine Latin lingua franca of the eastern Mediterranean Sea, she added, 'Cousin Rekhmire', Pamiu tells me you've had my witness with you for *months*.'

She used the familiar for 'cousin', rather than the formal. I raised an eyebrow at the Egyptian book-buyer, taking a seat on the low couch as I did so.

Rekhmire' looked back at me, as innocently as any man might.

I wonder if Ty-ameny of the Five Great Names would mind if I kicked him on the ankle?

But I felt oddly cheered that he would tease me again, after the tension between us on the *Sekhmet*.

Slaves poured watered wine into golden cups, that were circled with cabochon-cut sapphires in the pattern called Horus-Eye. Rekhmire' offered his hand to the Pharaoh-Queen, and with surprising grace led her to an individual small couch. She curled her bare feet up under her as she sat down.

He shot me a glance as he thumped down onto the padded bench beside me, and smiled. 'Fourth cousin; nine hundred and seventh in line to the throne of the Ptolemies. Were you wondering?'

Ty-ameny made a sound that, had she not been in her thirties and the ruler of a great city, I should have described as a snicker. 'Has he been playing the humble scroll-purchaser again?'

'Oh yes.' I mentally rummaged through the rapid briefing he had dumped on me on the way up the Thousand Steps to the palace, while I was still more concerned with leaving my daughter yelling at Tottola. 'Yes, Divine Daughter of Ra.'

She had all of her teeth still, and they showed white in the pale-vaulted room as she smiled. 'What would it be in Iberia? "Aldra" – lord? "Altezza" – "Highness"? And every man in this room is higher than I am!'

Ty-ameny leaned forward, both her hands cupping one of the golden bowls, looking keenly interested.

'A man-woman – what do you call yourself? Hermaphrodite? If you'd consent to it, there are natural philosophers here who would dearly like to speak to you, after this matter of Carthage's gift is dealt with.'

Rekhmire' spoke before I could get a word out.

'No prodding!'

The Pharaoh-Queen's kohl-lined brows shot up into her straight-cut fringe.

With an effort of will I kept *I told you so* out of my glare.

Ty-ameny loosed her cup with one hand, and slapped her knee. 'Rekhmire', *what* have you been telling her! Him. I'm sorry—' She swivelled back to me. 'Which do you prefer?'

'Usually I go with what I'm dressed as, Altezza.'

She nodded thoughtfully. 'I suppose "he"; you're most like our eunuchs, after all.'

Rekhmire' said firmly, 'No.'

'No?' Her brows went up again, and came down. There were a few minuscule golden spots on the reddish skin of her cheeks, I saw; like freckles. She bit at a thumbnail, and looked at me with a curiosity that was so frank I found it difficult to be offended. 'I suppose not. You have both? And—'

'And you,' Rekhmire' put in smoothly, 'were far too curious back when I was made eunuch, never mind now, Ty-ameny of the Five Great Names.'

His face was monumentally solemn.

The Pharaoh-Queen gazed up at him where he sat, pursed her lips in a silent whistle, and gave him a surprisingly gamin grin. 'I'm in trouble if I'm "of the Five Great Names" . . . '

'Ilario didn't come here to be put in a specimen cabinet in your secret museum!' Rekhmire' spoke mildly, but anyone who knew him could see he was amused now. 'Kek and Keket!, but I wonder what Pamiu wrote in his report from Rome. Great Queen of the Five Names, this is a painter, Ilario, whose account of the gift of King-Caliph Ammianus of Carthage you should hear. What any of us have under our robes is nothing to do with the matter.'

The black gaze of the small woman switched back to me.

'No prodding,' she said meekly.

I thought Rekhmire', if he hadn't the control of a lifetime, would have been quaking; I could feel his arm quiver where it rested against mine.

I managed to say, 'Thank you, Queen Ty-ameny.'

She grinned, and signalled for slaves to pour more wine. Two men and two women came in. I noted that they took a reasonable pride in serving deftly, and didn't seem to be always on the watch against being hit.

'You're already in possession of delicate information.' Ty-ameny smoothed her tunic over her knees, and directed a keen black stare at me. 'I suppose the Carthaginians ordered their gift painted at Rome so that rumours would spread out among the Franks. I understand that Menmet-Ra allowed the Italian's apprentice – you – to come in and work since things were progressing so slowly?'

'I wasn't told why.' The memory of hours spent carefully laying on coat after coat of colour and tint brought me back Masaccio's face, laughing as he told me stories while he painted with intent genius.

'According to Menmet-Ra, your late master took so long, and kept breaking off to do so much other work, that Menmet-Ra feared he would run over the deadline Carthage had ordered. It would never do to insult the King-Caliph unintentionally ... ' The Pharaoh-Queen's eyes narrowed.

I couldn't think of Carthage.

The warm wind blew in scents of the Alexandrine harbour and the palace gardens, and linen curtains streamed in the breeze.

He didn't break off to do other work, I thought. Even if they assumed so. He drew the job out so he could study the golem. He died simply because he wanted an amazing thing for himself. He didn't want it to come here ...

The chamber was silent, I realised. I looked up from my wine cup.

'I understand that you were fond of your master.' Ty-ameny smiled sadly.

'He was painting things in a way no other man could. Maybe never will.' I felt the muscles tight between my shoulder-blades. 'Is the golem here?'

'The golem is in my throne room,' Ty-ameny said, suddenly tight-lipped. 'So that Carthage isn't offended at a rejection of their gift. That thing stands there – by my throne – already has blood on its hands – and I have no idea if it waits for some signal to run riot, kill everyone around it!'

'Couldn't you drop it in the harbour?'

She raised a brow at me, in a way that very much reminded me of Rekhmire' himself. 'You put much work into it, I understand.'

'Some of the best statue work I've ever done.' I steadily regarded Ty-ameny. 'If you can't push it into your harbour, I can lift a sledge-hammer.'

Her mouth quirked up at one corner, in a very distinctively sardonic smile. 'I understand why you might feel that way. It isn't possible, because of the situation between nations, to destroy it. We study it. And, as Carthage designed, we have not the slightest idea how it works! Months it's been here, and none of my philosophers can tell me how it moves, even. Not with all the resources of the Library. Someone in Carthage has made a breakthrough – House Barbas, my counsellors suspect. And Carthage won't share the secret ... '

Because of Rodrigo's purchase, I am both used to courts and great nobles, and used to being present at the discussion of policy. If Ty-ameny was treating me in the same way, it might be because she knew how long I had been a slave. Or else Menmet-Ra's report had been specific about my silence as regards what happened in the Roman embassy.

'I'll tell you everything I know.' I shrugged. 'It won't help you.'

'I shall still be grateful.' She inclined her head with a movement so suddenly graceful that I had no doubt that this woman had been on the throne of Alexandria since the age of four.

She shot a glance across to Rekhmire'. 'But you will have seen our problem? In the harbour? I thank the Gods you're home today! Now I have a man I can trust to deal with this. No—'

As he rose, she gestured to him to sit. Rekhmire' only steadied his balance on his crutch, shot her a silent intense look, and made an apologetic indication of both the crutch and – now he was in the formal Egyptian linen kilt – his visibly scarred knee.

'Oh, pah!' Ty-ameny said lightly.

I did not desire to be jealous of how bright his face grew at her words. Or resent that he never reacted so to any encouragement of mine. *But then, I am neither his employer nor his sovereign.*

Ty-ameny bent almost double with her hands on her own knees for support. The scars were still inflamed, I saw; ridges of pink and purple flesh that stood up twistedly about the cap and side of his knee. Some patches of flesh seemed to have healed white and hairless.

'I'll have my physicians look at it.' She straightened, seeming almost apologetic. 'May I send you on work, first? You can see it's urgent.'

My stomach turned suddenly unaccountably cold.

Of course, he is her agent, she can send him where she pleases—

Suppose she sends him away, out of Alexandria?

For some reason I had not envisaged being on my own here, in charge of a baby and Aldra Videric's return to power.

My court manners abruptly returning to me, I stood up and bowed, preparing to leave.

Ty-ameny held out an arresting hand. 'No, this concerns you – you particularly, Messer Ilario, if you would consent.'

On my feet, it was just possible, from the window of this great fortress tower, to see down to the harbour. And to see the top masts of one ship. One ship only. No other is tall enough to be visible. I sat down again.

'Cousin.' Ty-ameny faced Rekhmire'. 'You will go aboard and talk to these foreigners. No delegation has been successful so far, but I have every confidence in you.'

It was not what she said, I realised, but the casual competency with which she said it. She really does trust 'cousin' Rekhmire' the humble book-buyer . . .

'I take it your injury will not prevent this?'

He shook his head.

'And if you would agree.' She turned towards me, speaking with the utmost directness. 'I would like you to go aboard as one of the delegation. Posing as Cousin Rekhmire''s scribe, perhaps.'

Rekhmire' snorted. 'Ilario will go! Especially if it involves getting closer to some new painting or fresco or inlay!'

He has just informed the Pharaoh-Queen that she may offer me whatever terms she likes and still see me fight tooth-and-nail to get near the foreign ship.

I caught Rekhmire''s eye, and found the amusement I expected.

Ty-ameny leaned forward, addressing me. 'But you have a child, with you?'

Between Menmet-Ra and Rekhmire', no matter how discreet the latter might have been, I doubted there would be anything the Pharaoh-Queen didn't know about my private life. Privacy had not been possible for a slave in Taraco either.

That doesn't mean I have to like it.

I went on the attack. 'My daughter Onorata will be safe and guarded, Great Queen. But I have to admit, I don't understand – I was Rekhmire''s scribe in Carthage, and I did reasonable work. Good work, even.'

I avoided Rekhmire''s eye, suspecting I might find even more amusement there now.

'But I don't see why you want me to be his scribe aboard this ship. Rather than one of your own people.'

Almost absently, Ty-ameny stood and padded over to the window. She had to come much closer to the sill, short as she was, to glimpse the high masts down in the harbour. The sunlight glimmered on the straight black hair that fell in a cape over her shoulders and back. Her small hands clenched into fists at her sides.

'They've been here three days now ... My diplomats and philosophers have discovered nothing of these foreigners – not their name, not what weapons that vessel carries, nor the intention of its captain. I have every confidence that Rekhmire' will open negotiations in a manner that I can trust.'

She turned around, silhouetted against the bright light outside. I couldn't see her expression when she spoke:

'They will allow very few men aboard. I am told I could not risk myself in any case. But I desire to see what that ship is like – and have my Royal Mathematicians see it, also. Ilario, I understand from Menmet-Ra and from Rekhmire' here that you follow what the Franks call the "New Art". If you'll agree, I wish you to go aboard the ship with Rekhmire''s servants – and draw for me exactly what it is that you see there.'

10

Attila nodded a greeting, standing guard at the door of our assigned palace rooms.

Inside the chambers, I found his brother. Tottola might not wear his breastplate in this climate, but even in the palace he wore mail. He carried his gauntlets hooked by their buckled straps over the hilt of his bastard sword, banging at his hip. His polished steel helm – very like Honorius's sallet – sat upturned in his lap, with Onorata laying propped up in it as if it were a very odd cradle.

She followed his moving finger with her dark blue eyes, and cooed in a serious and attentive way.

Tottola had her naked, in the heat, and Ramiro Carrasco scurried out of our vast quarters with the jug and bowl he had evidently used to bathe her. She had been fed again, I realised, and felt a twinge at having missed it.

Onorata kicked her bare feet. Tottola sang under his breath, and continued with verses that she was thankfully too young to understand. Half her lullabies were marching songs. Lengths of linen padded the metal of his sallet, and protected Tottola's helmet-lining against anything unfortunate.

It was a habit he had picked up from my father, who delighted to find his grandchild small enough to cradle in his sallet. Every man, from Sergeant Orazi down to Ensign Saverico, seemed to think it was permissible to joke with their lord about the likelihood of baby-shit next time he put the visored helmet on . . . And soon, now, she'll be too big.

I took the opportunity to unstopper my ink bottle and quickly sketch tones on the rough paper to show her with Tottola's curving protective arm. 'I'll never understand soldiers . . . '

Rekhmire' offered Onorata his finger, which she batted away. He turned back to me. 'The child will be safe enough with them while we go aboard.'

It was not until I started drawing her that Onorata looked to me like an individual child. I had worried, in Venice and on the voyage: if you put her down among a dozen other babies, would I know mine? A mother is supposed to know her child. There is instinct – which I clearly did not have.

But I know the slope of her upper lip, and her grave, extraordinary stare.

There were sufficient drawings of Onorata in my sketchbooks that Queen Ty-ameny was convinced using me as her eye was sound. One could see how Onorata had grown since we left the Most Serene city of Venice.

'She'd be safer with Honorius,' I grumbled. 'Back home.'

Hot countries, plagues, the bowel-flux, flies, itches, irritations, rashes – if I sat down, I dare say I could come up with a list of similar discomforts in cold countries, too. Nowhere is as safe for her as I could wish. But here . . .

'Ty-ameny hasn't let any of them come ashore.' I nodded towards the window, nominally in the direction of the harbour.

'Her advisers were very keen on quarantine.'

'So no man's seen these strangers.'

'Except to say they're not Franks, or North Africans; they perhaps look like Turks or Persians, but then again, *not* like them . . . ' Rekhmire' repeated rumours frustratedly. 'They arrived three days ago: if it was a plague ship, the doctors who went aboard the first day would probably have sickened by now.'

The way I heard the rumour from Attila, who had been gossiping in the palace kitchen and barracks, Queen Ty-ameny had only got doctors aboard the foreign ship by threatening to raise the vast iron chain and keep the monstrous vessel out of the shelter of Alexandria's harbour.

If that ship had to arrive here, it might have waited until we'd come and gone!

I put a finishing smudge of shadow onto the drawing of Onorata, abandoned it, and walked out onto the balcony beside Rekhmire'.

He leaned heavily on the yellow stone balustrade, gazing down – very far down – at the glimmering blue of the harbour.

'Even if it weren't so large,' I said, 'that's a style of ship I've never seen.'

The Egyptian inclined his head.

'And she just . . . expects you to go and talk to these people?'

'It would be some other man, if I hadn't returned at the right moment.' Rekhmire''s eyes might have been narrowed against the sunlight. 'Ty-ameny feels she can trust me. If I fail, I shall only fail. I won't be a part of one or other of the court conspiracies, with my own ideas of who should be sitting on the Lion-throne.'

'And there was me thinking all this monumental grandeur meant a different kind of court to Taraco . . . ' Sometimes directness is the only way to knowledge. 'Why does she trust you? Because you're her cousin? Which, by the way, you never told me!'

'A fourth cousin is one of the very many.' Rekhmire' blinked mild eyes, apparently amused to be withholding information. He sharpened his gaze, and smiled outright. 'No, you have it right; she feels she has good reason. I had a hand in preventing one of the early assassination attempts, back when she was coming of age and taking power from the Regency Council. She knows I won't lie to her.'

'Given most courts I've visited, that would be invaluable.' I suspected there was more to it, that he'd done more than 'had a hand in preventing' whatever had happened – probably discovered the whole thing, I reflected. But if the Queen had so much confidence in her wandering book-buyer . . .

I was still holding a half-inch stub of red chalk. I held it up demonstrably. 'Will she regard this as constituting a debt?'

'For you to ask for help with the situation in Taraconensis?'

Frustrated, I shrugged. 'I'm thinking of asking somebody – anybody! – just how I get Videric accepted as the King Rodrigo's chief counsellor again. Because, worry at it as I may, I have no idea!'

The hour passed noon; the hot sun was too much for me. I turned and walked back inside, taking refuge in the stone room's coolness and shade.

Rekhmire' followed me in, sandals soundless on the floor.

A fan made of fine woven fibres, and hanging from a frame, moved two and fro in a leisurely stirring of the air. I opened my mouth to castigate the German men-at-arms for letting in a palace slave – and saw, in time, that Ramiro Carrasco sat bemusedly pulling on the fan's cord.

Rekhmire' went to the door, exchanging words with a servant there, and came back after a short time with a clear drink made of herbs, and with hacked-small chunks of ice floating in the jug. I realised myself thirsty in the extreme – which argued that we all must be, and I requested he find more, especially for the men wearing mail-shirts.

By the time Rekhmire' returned, I had experimented with stroking Onorata's palms and the soles of her feet with quick strokes of melting lump of ice. Feeling the skin of her belly, she no longer tended to the overheated.

'It couldn't hurt to have the Pharaoh-Queen in our debt,' I suggested.

The Egyptian smiled, levering himself across the floor and into the sunken area. He thumped down, took the baby from Tottola's hands as the German soldier proffered her, and put her into the crook of his elbow. Tottola made thankfully for the iced drink.

'She sends further word,' Rekhmire' added.

My traitorous child ignored me, even as I sat down next to the Egyptian. She waved her hands at him. He broke off to answer her in some nonsense-tongue.

'*What* did the Queen say?'

'How carefully we need to tread. They apparently don't desire too many men on board at one time.'

Tottola lowered the jug and wiped his mouth. 'Damned if I can see why not, sir. That thing's the size of a city! What can they be frightened of?'

Since they had evidently been allowed to advise Honorius, both the German brothers thought they should continue that habit with me – and, by extension, the book-buyer.

'The Queen will want to send as few people as possible,' I put in, stroking Onorata's scurfy curls. 'In case they take hostages. I'd expect a balancing act between men with enough rank to honour the visitors, and people who wouldn't be missed.'

Rekhmire' inclined his head. 'She's reluctant to risk her witness to the golem. But since you're the only practitioner of the New Art here, that leaves her no choice.'

Tottola made a noise like a horse snorting, and glared at Rekhmire'. 'I know the Lion of Castile – if you let Ilario come to harm on that thing, sir, don't bother coming ashore!'

At his raised voice, the baby stopped waving her arms, poised for a moment between bubbling with amusement and screaming in fear. Rekhmire' slid a large hand under the baby's arse, supported her head, and thrust her instantly towards me. 'She's hungry.'

It was a guess. I took her in my arms, heavy for the small size of her, and warm and faintly damp as she was.

'Ramiro.' I signalled him to leave the fan. 'Help me feed her. She might just sleep through until I come back.'

Rekhmire' was in the process of giving Tottola his impermeable bureaucrat expression. 'I refuse to take responsibility for Ilario – since Ilario doesn't just draw trouble like a lode-stone, but goes out specifically to invite it home with him – her—'

I might have protested at that, but my bodyguard was far too busy agreeing with the Egyptian.

'When you two have finished bickering like an old married couple,' I remarked, 'you'll be disappointed to know I plan to *ask* if I may draw things on the strangers' ship. *And* where I can safely draw. Nothing like being taken for a spy to make life interesting. Right, Rekhmire'?'

Under his ruddy skin, I could swear he went a darker red. 'I knew I should regret telling you that!'

'As if you had to *tell* me!'

I broke off, since Tottola was in the process of making a remark entirely similar in meaning, but more restrained by military discipline.

I was still snickering intermittently, and holding Onorata while Carrasco fed her, when two or three of the Pharaoh-Queen's eunuch bureaucrats were shown into the room by Attila.

If I heard anything of the hours of intense briefing, it fell back out of my head instantly. I was too busy reckoning up every item I could put in a scribe's leather satchel, that I could carry over my shoulder. All tools for drawing, since I doubted any man would let me heat the bronze pallet-box for encaustic wax painting. The leather snapsack to protect paper and papyrus from splashes as we were rowed out into the harbour. Silverpoint stylus, reed pen, ink, chalk, charcoal-sticks, and perhaps it would be worth taking a wax tablet: stylus-lines can be incised into the soft surface as well as the more normal letters and words . . .

'Ready?' Rekhmire' inquired. 'I tell you now: if you choose not to risk yourself because of the child, Ty-ameny will understand that.'

Much as I hate being any man's to beat or fondle, the life of a slave is at least easier in that one is ordered, not asked to decide.

I glanced around the great high-ceilinged rooms, beyond whose windows the white furnace of afternoon was cooling to early evening. 'I'm ready.'

The noise of the city rose up about us as Ty-ameny's soldiers escorted us down towards the quay. The sound was different to Venice, although I saw the trade was no less intense. *Different and familiar*, I felt. More like the Turkish cities along the Old Egyptian coast, and Malta, and Taraco, and Carthage.

One of the war-galleys sent in a boat. I sat upright, cooled by the occasional spray. The oarsmen rowed us through the encircling ring of triremes. I watched the touch of the sweeps, that kept each oared vessel with its Greek Fire siphon pointed at the massive foreign ship.

Hunched in the rocking stern, I practised a quick charcoal sketch of the serpent-decorated ship, to shake the stiffness out of my hand.

In a few minutes we, also, will be at the centre of that circle of potential Greek Fire.

I have barely been in Constantinople four hours, I thought, as my sandal touched the deck of the vast foreign ship.

My body was still adjusted to the motion of the sea under my feet. Every step up to the palace and down to the harbour again had felt as if I were slamming the soles of my feet into granite. The consciousness of the shift and dip of a moored ship would feel reassuring to me.

But there was no sensation of the sea on this colossus. I might have been standing on a wooden fortress in the harbour.

Two other eunuch bureaucrats accompanied Rekhmire'; one in my former job as clerk. They stood by his shoulders now as he spoke for a long time to the guards who surrounded us. I glanced briefly over the monolith's side at the plank and rope ladder, bobbing down an incredible distance to the ferry boat, and gave up that route of escape.

The ship's crew crowded close.

Freaks surrounded me.

No. Men.

But flat-faced men; men almost with the faces of village idiots. I have been, from time to time in Taraco, put in company with those born witless, or with no voices; only the ability to lumber about, grinning and groaning. Some of them can be remarkably gentle, given kind treatment.

The ones surrounding me now were barefoot, wearing high-collared belted robes. They held long thin-bladed spears, and carried short swords.

A ship of the mad, the witless. I recognised those odd, folded eyelids; the emotionless features. Shuddering and cold despite the evening's heat, I wanted desperately to tell Rekhmire' what I saw. *But no, it can't be; madmen couldn't sail a ship!*

Rekhmire' stood very upright, his back to me, speaking in a normal tone; trying as many languages as he could think of.

I knew what he must be saying: Hello, may we come aboard, who is your captain?

Did Ty-ameny's eunuchs get us this permission by the equivalent of point-and-mime!

Rekhmire' spoke again, with considerably more confidence.

I recognised the language, if not the words. Occasionally, I'd heard it in Venice, from traders come in not by sea, but over the long land routes from the lapis mines in Afghanistan and the east. A dialect something like that spoken by the Turks and Persians. I understood one word in five, if that.

The larger of the black-eyed men broke into a broad grin, looked up at Rekhmire' – just looked up: he was almost of a height with the book-buyer – and laughed out loud.

'*Gaxıng jiandào nî!*' he exclaimed, in a completely different-sounding language, and began to rattle off the Persian or Turkish dialect at an amazing rate. He gestured towards the stern of the ship.

The way to the captain's quarters? I wondered.

As respectfully as if he were still my master, I murmured to Rekhmire', 'Will you ask permission if I can draw as I go? Those spears look sharp.'

Cautiously, the Egyptian spoke to the broad man in belted robes that, now I could look at them closely, were not Persian at all. The fabric shimmered. Silk.

Absorbed in the play of light and shade in the fabric's folds, and what a difference it made to the colours of the blue dye, it was a minute before I became aware of Rekhmire'. He waved a broad hand, and gazed equably down at me.

'Draw something for this gentleman, if you please.'

I unfolded my drawing book, showed the stub of red chalk on an outstretched hand, and then – as well as I could with fingers that were shaking from the climb – managed line and tone that encompassed the shape of the ship's flat prow.

The foreign man scowled.

Or I thought he did; I realised I could read none of his thoughts for certain from his expression.

The man smeared his forefinger across one sheet of paper, smearing the chalk, and lifted it to his finger to taste.

His head snapped around; he rattled off something very quick, very emphatic.

Rekhmire' bowed, in the Turkish fashion, and replied. As well as that unknown language, I recognised some of the versions of Carthaginian Latin from the western coast of Africa. Evidently everything was having to be said two or three times, three or four different ways.

'He wants you to show his captain, I believe.' Rekhmire' shifted a gaze that took in all the Golden Horn, and the great fortress city – in which, now I thought about it, he must have been born or grown up. And now to find this huge, dangerous vessel and its unknown crew here, right here in the harbour . . .

Rekhmire' inclined his head to the stout man in silk robes, gestured his eunuch clerks to precede him, tucked his crutch neatly under his arm, and took hold of my sleeve with his other hand.

I whispered, 'They look like—'

'Yes, but they speak like men. Like you or I.'

Rekhmire' paused for a moment after that last remark, gave me a smile that only he and I would ever comprehend, and ducked his way under the wood and silk awning that protected the doorway into the poop deck cabin.

The ship's captain was no different to his officers and crew, I thought at first glance, except for his size; he stood well over six feet tall. His broad face shone sallow in the light through the ports. Looking up at us from a table full of maps and charts, his heavy brows dipped down; he had the same small eyes as every other man on the ship. And it was almost as if he had been facing into a desert wind, dehydrating; or had been hit in the face: the flesh of his eyelids swollen up and only narrow slits of sloe-coloured eyes visible.

A close-fitting black cap covered his hair, and his thin black beard was shaven at the sides, but fell down to touch his belt at the front. As he turned I saw his robes were slit at the side, and that under the plain ochre over-robes, immensely-patterned blue and red and gold thread shone. I could not have begun to guess at his age.

I leaned over toward Rekhmire''s ear. 'Ask him if he'll sit for me to paint him!'

With perfect aplomb, Rekhmire' remarked, 'Shut up, Ilario,' and bowed deeply in the Turkish fashion to the man evidently in command of this vast vessel.

The squarish man who had greeted us rattled off something, nodding at me, and the tall captain held out his hand.

Looking at the square-set officer for confirmation, I put the leather snapsack into the captain's hand.

He upended it on his desk, turning over sized parchment and tinted paper. Before I could warn him, he opened a stoppered ink-horn and spilled oak-gall ink over his fingers. He prodded messily and suspiciously at the sharp point of a stylus, until I warily showed him how it sketched palest grey lines on a paper prepared with fine-ground bone dust. I had no idea if he gained any idea of the connection between that and the older silverpoint lines in my sketchbook that had turned brown.

He flicked through the sewn-together pad of sketch paper with nothing I could read in his expression. It was not a new book, I realised, embarrassed, as he stopped momentarily at a few lines that held something of Onorata's sleeping face.

'Eh.' He beckoned, took my sleeve, and led me round the immense map table.

There were papers and brushes neatly spread out on his desk, and shallow white dishes. He tipped water onto a flat slate and took up a black stick, grinding one end on the surface as if he ground pigments. The brush he used to take up the wet blackness was not of familiar animal hair. I bent close, observing how he divided his pigment among pots with great or little amounts of water.

The scent was unfamiliar but distinctive.

He felt my sketchbook with his thumb, shook his head, and drew up a sheet of his own very fine, light paper. With a look of intense concentration, he dipped his brush first in water, and then less deeply in liquid pigment, and less deeply still in the deepest black. The curve of his wrist was very quick with that last: I just caught that he touched not the whole of his brush, but either side, in turn, very lightly.

Two, three, four strokes. No more than six at most, black, the brush held at different angles—

A shape glistened on the paper. Differential pigment made it miraculous: pale and dark lines drawn with the same swirl of a brush. Graduating from ink-black through pale grey to grey pearl.

Recognition snapped into my mind.

'Horse!' My voice squeaked embarrassingly.

As solid as if it lived, the mane and tail of a galloping horse shaped the wind. All its hooves raised off the earth, except for one – and that one, I saw as I peered closely, was not on the ground, but on the back of a flying bird.

It was as if he painted darkness and used it to carve light out of the page. A horse in such living movement that I almost felt it.

Rekhmire', his clerks, and this captain's officer all watched me.

There were other sketchbooks tumbled out of my snapsack; I fumbled one up, and thumbed through until I found what I wanted.

'There! Horse!'

Done months ago in Rome: carts setting off with Honorius's luggage. Here, a cart-horse with every muscle bunched and clenched as it began to shift the dead weight of the vehicle . . . Done in red chalk, or at least half-done; unfinished, but the study of the forequarters had some virtue to it, so I had not thrown it away.

The captain exclaimed loudly.

I suspected I'd learned the word *horse*, when I could get my ear around it.

He beamed down at me. I realised I was grinning back at him like an idiot.

Behind me, Rekhmire' respectfully spoke in the Turkish dialect, and the large foreign captain frowned thoughtfully. After a moment he jerked his head; I wasn't sure whether it was assent or negation.

'Cheng Ho.' He leaned down, looking into my face intensely. He spoke again: this time I might have represented it as 'Zheng He.'

Guessing, I copied Rekhmire''s bow. 'Ilario Honorius.'

He couldn't fit his tongue around the words. He planted one large hand flat on the page of my sketchbook. More exchange of words in a number of different languages took place between him and Rekhmire', while Zheng He – if that was a name, and not a rank – paged through my book of drawings.

Rekhmire' finally said smoothly, in Iberian, 'Zheng He, the Admiral of the Ocean Seas, desires you to show him what you draw before you leave the ship. I suspect he'll destroy anything that he doesn't want known about.'

A trickle of cold permeated my belly. 'Don't let him get any ideas about putting out the artist's eyes, along with the preliminary sketches.'

Rekhmire' muttered something. For a second I saw him look genuinely appalled, before a diplomatic blandness reasserted itself.

In that Iberian dialect which it was unlikely his clerks spoke, never mind these foreigners, he asked, 'Is that what you were threatened with in Taraco?'

'And it could have been done. Easily. Could you tell him I'm not a slave? Make sure you tell him that!'

Rekhmire' reverted to Turkish, in which I could pick out the word for slave and not much else. Then Carthaginian Latin, in an odd accent. After two or three exchanges with the large foreigner, Rekhmire' bowed, looked momentarily puzzled, and gestured for me to take back my book.

'The Admiral Zheng says every man is a slave. He himself is the humble slave of Emperor – "Zhu Di", I think. Zhu Di of the Chin. Or *of* Chin. He, ah . . . '

Rekhmire''s brows rose as the foreign admiral added something.

'He says, this is the first civilised country he's found in two years of sailing. Because the bureaucrats sent to meet him are slaves and eunuchs, as they should be.'

11

If we hadn't been in a foreign ship's cabin, surrounded by clerks and Zheng He's armed sailors, I thought Rekhmire' would have howled with laughter. When something hits his sense of humour, it affects him strongly.

'You can tell the Pharaoh-Queen she did something right, then.' I barely managed not to grin myself. 'Should I go draw things before he realises I'm – not exactly what he thinks?'

'That might be wise.' Rekhmire' bowed to the Admiral, and murmured, aside, 'Do try not to get killed while we're aboard.'

'This ship has more arbalests on its deck than your entire navy; if these people didn't *want* something, they'd be using them!'

His brow rose again. Why he would think – with Honorius for a father; with King Rodrigo's training – that I wouldn't take automatic notice of armaments?

The Admiral rattled off something in the oddly-toned language. He wiped his fingers on a cloth, surveyed his desk, swept up a small box and tipped the contents into his hand. Small gold-marked sticks, oval in cross-section, black and red – belatedly I recognised his ink-sticks. He let them slide and click back into the box, and thrust it into my hand.

He wants *me to draw!* I all but shouted aloud.

He spoke urgently again, and finished by pointing at the squarely-built officer, and then at me.

'*Dong ma?*'

That was *do you understand?* as plainly as I had ever heard it. I bowed. 'Thank you, Admiral Zheng He.'

I went out in the company of my minder.

An hour later, I had the smart idea of sending in to Rekhmire''s scribes to borrow more of their paper, since I'd run out.

I persuaded Jian (my guess at the pronunciation of the squarely-built officer's name) that this would do no harm. Talking to each other, each in our own languages, I'd added what I thought were 'yes' – *shìde* or *hâo de* – and an all-purpose apology, *duìbùqî*, 'sorry', to my vocabulary. If I hadn't found the word for 'no', that was because I found he didn't often like to use it. Jian would distract me, or misunderstand me, or carefully not hear me, if anything requiring a refusal arose. I wondered if that was him, or the Chin in general.

There was also *hùndàn*, but I suspected I hadn't been intended to hear that one. Certainly Jian hustled me away from the lower deck tiers where one of the anonymous oarsmen threw it after me. I stored it away for a useful insult, when I could find out whether it was on the order of friendly abuse, or something certain to start a fight to the death. It pays to find that out beforehand.

I smiled, thinking of Honorius; he'd appreciate another foreign oath. The ship was a marvel.

What I took to be other officers muttered, seeing me draw the outlines of sails and hull, and broke out into outright complaint when I sketched the swivel-based arbalests they had mounted on the decks, and the exact number of masts and cross-trees.

Jian screeched at them, highly-pitched as a hawk.

What he said, I didn't know: I suspect it was *Our captain sees no sense in hiding what any man in this city can see if they sail a dhow past our moorings!* Although that was not true of the interior cabins, with their great Turkish-style pillows on the mats instead of Frankish or North African furniture; or of the interminable storerooms and holds, that carried food and water enough to allow Ty-ameny's generals to make a guess at what crew the ship carried.

If it's under five thousand men, I'll eat my chalk, I reflected, and yelped and shot up into the air as a hand went up my linen tunic from the rear.

Whoever it was behind went over with a scream. The old reflexes of slavehood either keep one perfectly still under assault, because it may be a master, or lash out, because it may be another slave. My reflexes evidently didn't think I had a master on this ship.

I swung around to face a gang of twenty or thirty of the foreigners, as well as the one writhing on the deck and clutching his knee.

Before I could speak, the officer Jian beat his way through the crowd with the use of a short wooden stick. Thankfully, I saw he had a clutch of paper in his other fist. I stepped forward to take the sheets from him, and, as he yelled at me, to mime what had happened.

The deck around us sounded like a mews when the falcons have been disturbed; all high screeches that set the nerves and blood on edge. I slid my hand into my satchel, putting my hand on my pen knife – a blade less than an inch long, but made of such quality metal, and taking such an edge, that it would go through any man's jugular if I merely brushed his throat.

Jian thwacked two of the nearer sailors with his staff, kicked the man on the deck, and over his loud screaming, evidently ordered the others to drag him away. Whether to punishment or medical treatment was unclear. Jian swung on his heel, exclaimed '*Duibùqî!*' as clearly as he evidently could, and scratched at his tied-back hair, plainly puzzled at how to get through to me.

452

With as much of what I could remember of Turkish, Carthaginian Latin, and the Venetian trade patois, I attempted to describe the assault.

Jian finally beamed, and nodded. He tried several languages, before a combination allowed him to make himself almost understood. 'You are not a masterless slave?'

I opened my mouth to try every word for 'freeman' I could remember, thought of Rekhmire' repeating *we are all eunuch slaves here*, and settled for pointing at the main cabin. 'Master Rekhmire'.'

The Egyptian name puzzled him until I mimed someone taller, broader, and – with a chop of the edge of my hand, down at kilt-level – eunuch. Jian grinned.

I pointed at the steps leading up to the rear poop deck, gestured for Jian to sit, and tapped my chalk against the new paper.

I was still sitting there, drawing yet another of the surrounding crowd of sailors, when Rekhmire' came out to find me.

The sun stood further down the sky. The tide smelled of weed. Jian cleared the audience and I stood up, brushing fruitlessly at the chalk and charcoal that marked the front of my linen robe, and handed the latest sketch off to the remaining Chin sailor. He bowed, repetitively, and ran off. He might have been holding the paper upside down – I wasn't sure if these people could see, in any real sense, how I put things down on paper, but their desire for a souvenir from the mad foreign slave evidently overcame their lack of understanding.

'Are we leaving?' Buckling my leather case, and slinging it over my shoulder, I glanced hurriedly around.

Even if not allowed back on board, I have enough to keep the Pharaoh-Queen's philosophers happy. But – there is so much more—!

'For the moment, we leave.' Rekhmire' beckoned his clerks, and swung himself on his crutch with the appearance of calm, towards the side of the great ship.

Falling back on the Iberian no man would understand but us, I asked, 'Did you find out why they're here? Are they a threat? Did the Admiral tell you what they want here?'

The Egyptian reached out and rested his arm across my shoulders, letting me take a substantial amount of his weight. I was momentarily startled. Clearly he found this physically wearing.

But to Jian, it will hardly hurt to have us appear master and slave again. And that is how he will take this.

Rekhmire' gave me a brief smile all friendship and relief. I concluded myself not the only one glad to be leaving. He reached for the ropes of the cradle in which, it was evident, they intended to lower us to our own vessel.

Looking over the heads of the Chin sailors, he murmured, 'I *can* tell you why this ship is here in Alexandria.'

'You can?'

I let them tie us in to the leather sling like luggage, closing my eyes against the distance from deck to sea.

Rekhmire''s voice spoke Iberian in my darkness, as the ropes jolted and lifted.

'The Admiral was clear enough about that. Although other things are less clear. But I think I believe him as regards this. This ship is here, in this port – because they are lost.'

12

'*Lost?*'

The Pharaoh-Queen Ty-ameny gave Rekhmire' a look that could have melted Venetian glass, never mind smashed it.

My drawings lay spread out over the pink marble tiles of this one of her private chambers. She had questioned me extensively about each sketch. And now, when Rekhmire' answered her question . . .

'Lost,' she repeated flatly.

'Yes. And seeking a route back to this empire of theirs,' Rekhmire' said equably. 'Which, as far as I can make out, is called "Chin". Thousands of leagues to the east. Past Tana—'

That name was one I recognised, having often heard the Venetians mention it: a port in the north-eastern part of the Black Sea.

'—at the end of wherever the Silk Road goes.'

I think Ty-ameny and I stared at him with precisely the same expression.

'As for why they're here . . . They became lost during a storm; I'm uncertain where. But they can at least navigate well enough to sail towards the sunrise, and sailing east has finally brought them to Alexandria. It's clear to them that there's more sea beyond here.' Rekhmire''s nod indicated the vast window, and the eastern horizon beyond the Golden Horn. 'They think they can sail to Chin on the Black Sea waters. They have no idea that it's a closed sea. And that there's nothing but land beyond the easternmost Turkish ports.'

'And you . . . '

'I have said nothing of that, as yet.'

It would be strange, I thought, to have no idea of what the Middle Sea looks like.

True, no two charts I'd ever seen in a shop had ever got the shape of the lands the same – or put them in quite the same place, come to that – but the names of ports, the number of leagues and days' sailing between them, the knowledge of rocks and reefs and pirates . . . All these were, if not precisely known, still capable of making a shape in my mind's eye.

I imagined Zheng He and his great ship creeping along from headland to headland, as the trireme had, but with no pilot. Sometimes lost out of sight of land . . . losing his course if a storm made his lodestone useless . . .

As to where they might have sailed before they got here, what seas there may be between the Middle Sea and the place where the Silk Road ends – for that, I have no shape in my mind at all.

I thought of the Admiral's horse. Four or five curves and strokes of a brush. Like nothing I have ever seen.

Aloud, I stated, 'They're not lying if they say they come from very far away.'

The small Egyptian woman pulled her feet up onto the cushions on the marble ledge, tucking her legs under her. She leaned her chin on her hand. Ty-ameny of the Five Great Names might have been a robin's egg, with her freckles spattered across her nose. Certainly her eyes had the same lively bird-like look to them.

'They're lost.' She made the admission with clear reluctance.

Rekhmire' shrugged, in a way that made it clear that the magnitude of it didn't escape him. 'He and the interpreters and I aren't always in accord, but if I'm understanding Admiral Zheng He, his ship was driven through what I would guess are the Gates of the Hesperides, past Gades, some time last winter. Since then, he's been sailing about the Middle Sea.'

Including the Adriatic. The memory of what I had thought an optical illusion was strong. I wondered if Leon would add more in *De Pictura* on how you can have something directly under your eye and still be unable to see what it truly is.

'Looking for a way out.' Ty-ameny corrected herself. 'A way *east*.'

She frowned up at Rekhmire', who prodded with the ferrule of his crutch among the spread-out papers.

'Is it as simple as that?'

'Possibly.' The book-buyer glanced at the Pharaoh-Queen, a frown indenting his brows. 'Look at what Ilario's drawn. It's more than possible this Zheng He's been at sea as long as he says he has, given the clear evidence of wear on the ship. He has trade goods from Africa in his hold. *And* goods from the far southern coasts of the Persians. It would take a strong sea to sink that ship. He naturally wouldn't show me his charts, but it's possible he's come by sea from the land where the Silk Road ends.'

Since there was an obvious one unspoken, I appended, 'But?'

'But . . . He may be lying. Or exaggerating for threat's sake. Or – well.' Without asking permission, the tall Egyptian shuffled himself along the bench, settling ultimately on the cushions within an arm's reach of the Pharaoh-Queen.

She put her tiny hand on his arm. 'Well?'

Rekhmire' looked down at my spread-out papers, his brow creased with more than worry. 'Well, there is nothing here to confirm or deny it . . . but what the Admiral Zheng He claims is that when he was driven before the great storm, he was separated from the rest of his fleet.'

Ty-ameny did precisely what I did, I noticed a moment later: stared at the palace window overlooking the harbour, as if she could see through the city's massive walls, and the darkening evening, into the heart and mind of the foreign man aboard the foreign ship.

'"Fleet",' she echoed, a little derisively.

Rekhmire' linked his broad, large fingers, and looked down at his hands. 'Which he claims is made up of ships the same or similar tonnage to this one we have out there. He exaggerates, of course, because that is what a man will do. But—'

Ty-ameny slapped his shoulder, as if she were no more than a younger sister to him.

'How *many*?'

'His lost fleet,' Rekhmire' said, 'he claims to consist of two hundred ships.'

A silence filled the royal chambers.

Ty-amenhotep of the Five Great Names snorted, the sound remarkably like any camel's bad temper down in Constantinople's marketplaces.

'Two *hundred*? Oh, he might at least tell a convincing lie!'

She sprang up, absently turned on her heel, and paced with that control of the space about her that I have grown used to seeing among powerful men. Seeing the same gestures in a woman—

As I also rose to my feet out of respect, I realised, *Now I know how disconcerted men and women feel, when they lay eyes on me.*

'Two dozen would be bad enough!' she grumbled. 'And even two would pose a danger. Is it significant that this foreign admiral feels he must boast?'

One wall of this particular room was carved with bas-reliefs and cartouches in red and blue. At least some of the sculptors, I saw, had chosen to depict Old Alexandria falling to that Turk who had kept his defeated enemies in iron cages. Constantinople would never need, behind its vast walls, to be concerned with similar enemies. But more than one ship like Zheng He's . . .

Rekhmire' reached for his crutch, but sank back at her gesture. He confirmed my thoughts. 'Not only is Zheng He lost, but lost among men not at all like him. I think he lies and exaggerates no more than any other commander.' The book-buyer shrugged. 'But then, we have hardly been allowed to see everything on the ship.'

I had been permitted to bring only one thing away, apart from my drawings for Ty-ameny – a tiny cup, no larger than a child's hand, in which Jian had served me a colourless and fairly insipid wine. Showing it to the Pharaoh-Queen had gathered some admiration. The ceramic was light and translucent enough that when, as now, I put my finger inside the empty cup, I could see its shadow through the side.

Ty-amenhotep raised her voice to call for more servants to light sweet-smelling oil lamps; she and Rekhmire' spoke of court politics; and I sat regretting the terre verte pigment lost in Venice – using egg tempera on a gesso ground, I might have begun to make an attempt at capturing the glaze's pearlescent shine, along with its transparency. Although that is a task for a master, which as yet I am not.

Masaccio, making colour value into mass and form . . .

The master that should see this is dead.

I wondered, then, the word in my mind, whether the Master of Mainz would also be housed with us. Or whether the Pharaoh-Queen's 'Royal Mathematicians' – as she named her natural philosophers – would have him all night explaining his printing-*machina*.

Standing wearied me, but Ty-ameny continued her pacing. I rubbed my hand across my eyes, the darkness behind my eyelids welcome.

The familiar drag and click of Rekhmire''s crutches let me know he had risen.

I opened my eyes to see him join Ty-ameny at her window, overlooking the vast city.

'Sidon?' he suggested, naming a port that I thought somewhere west and south of us. 'They might leave their ship and march home along the Silk Road.'

'I wish they might leave their ship here!' Ty-ameny gave her cousin her gamin grin. 'But if I were the captain, I wouldn't be parted from it. Besides, can you imagine sailors asked to turn soldier and march all those thousands of leagues? Never mind what they carry as cargo.'

The lamp-lit chamber was comfortable, even if it dwarfed the book-buyer and the Pharaoh-Queen with its high ceiling and vast blocks of masonry that made up the walls. I felt not only at ease, I realised, but as if it were familiar.

Because neither Ty-amenhotep nor Rekhmire' take exception to my presence?

As Rodrigo's King's Freak, it never surprised me to be involved in court business in Taraco, although I steered clear of factions. That I could fall into the same pattern here, as Rekhmire''s scribe and Queen Ty-ameny's artist, felt similarly comfortable.

'Great Queen,' I suggested, into the perfumed silence, that was broken only by the noise of voices and vehicles in the city below. 'I think the Admiral desires charts. His officer Jian was speaking of them.'

She nodded, receiving the suggestion equably. 'Not to give too much aid at first – Rekhmire', if I send you with maps of the coast here, and the waters to the east; let him see land-maps that show the road to Aleppo and other Turkish cities. I think it's well this Zheng He begins to believe they're at the other end of their trade route with us.'

'Us barbarians.' Rekhmire' made the addendum gravely.

The Pharaoh-Queen gave him a look.

'That's what he calls us.' Rekhmire' smiled down at Ty-ameny. 'The Admiral Zheng He says their empire has lasted five thousand years. Older than Carthage.'

'Five thousand years of emperors? And two hundred giant ships?' The Pharaoh-Queen craned to look around the carved stone frame of the window, at pale light behind the gathering clouds. 'I suppose they have a trading colony on the moon, too!'

I risked mimicking Rekhmire''s equable look. 'That would explain why they don't look like anyone else, Great Queen. Or draw or paint like anyone else.'

Ty-amenhotep of the Five Great Names glanced from me to Rekhmire', and stalked past us, back into the room to flop down on the nearest seat. 'Cousin, either you've been too much in Ilario's company, or Ilario has been too much in yours!'

The book-buyer gave me a more relaxed smile than I had seen since we boarded the trireme in Venice.

He seated himself again on the marble bench, collecting silk pillows with his free hand and stuffing them behind his back. I joined him. He beckoned for my drawings, and ink and chalk-work, and the two of them bent over my efforts again.

Jian had taken some of the Admiral's scrolls out for me to look at. Delicate, as if the colour had been put on with spring water, or spring light. Language didn't allow him to explain how.

As well as sketching all aspects that I could see of their great cistern-shaped hull, I'd paced out the distances across the deck and made a quiet note of the measurements. Looking at the Pharaoh-Queen Ty-ameny as she scribbled furiously on a wax tablet, I thought her as capable as her Alexandrine 'philosopher-scientists' of working out the exact tonnage of Zheng He's ship. And the offensive power of the ship's cannon (cast out of recognisable bronze), and their engines that shot great long iron bolts (if I could judge by the ammunition stores).

Among the scattered papers I saw my drawings of two-handed ceramic containers, that might have been pots for oil or wine, but – from Jian's ardent keenness to remove me from their vicinity – I knew must be weapons as well. They looked as if they could be fused. Some parts of the hull stores had the distinctive scent of gunpowder.

Still, I thought, hauling my ankles up to sit cross-legged among the cushions beside Rekhmire'. Magnificent as it is, it's only one ship. It can't threaten to take on the navy here and bombard Constantinople's walls down . . .

Unless the rest of the hypothetical fleet turn up.

And then even Carthage and Venice will be pushed to hold on to sea-power in the Middle Sea.

By the window, a patch of moonlight progressed across the shining stone floor.

I watched it, in silence unbroken except by the rustling of paper. My hands felt oddly empty, since they held neither a stylus nor Onorata.

There has been little enough time, I thought, rubbing at the gravel that seemed to be collecting in my eyes. Little enough time since we landed, and all of it taken up by the Admiral of the Ocean Seas, but—

Sooner or later I must ask her.

Must ask the Pharaoh-Queen of New Alexandria, *How do I make the Aldra Pirro Videric into the First Minister of Taraconensis again?*

'—Ilario?'

The Pharaoh-Queen was turning back from dismissing a beardless fat man who I took to be a eunuch servant. By the sound of her voice, it was not the first time she had asked.

I straightened myself up beside Rekhmire', piqued that he had not used the elbow I was leaning against to nudge me into greater attention. 'Yes, Great Queen?'

'The hour's late.' Her eyes shone darkly in the many lamps' light. 'And it's a poor reward for you helping me with the foreigners' ship. But I need, urgently, to speak to you. Will you tell me everything that you experienced with Carthage's stone golem?'

13

We left Rekhmire' with a dozen of the Queen's Royal Mathematicians, checking calculations and speculations regarding the ghost ship.

A tall and unusually thin eunuch mathematician by the name of Ahhotep joined Ty-ameny at her signal, walking the palace's corridors quickly enough beside me that his linen robe flicked against my bare ankles. Two slaves took lamps ahead, light shading from terracotta to burnt-earth colours up the carved walls.

If I had been paying closer attention, I could have overheard what Ty-ameny and her black-haired adviser spoke of. Weariness and fear kept me concentrating on putting one foot before the other and falling over neither.

I wondered if Tottola had needed to call Ramiro Carrasco to feed Onorata, and whether she was asleep or screaming.

Cool air touched my forehead. It was not until I saw sky above a wide courtyard that I realised we had left the main palace. Obelisks blotted out stars and moon.

Ahhotep glanced back at me with a friendly smile. The moonlight caught the fine silver chain about his neck, that all the bureaucrats wore symbolic of their slavery. He pointed to one side and a dimly-seen frontage. 'The Royal Library.'

It might have been part of the palace or separate; I would not be able to see unless by daylight.

The pressure of air at my right hand was suddenly less; I guessed at an empty outdoor area, perhaps a larger public square. Our footsteps came clicking back from a nearer wall – except for Ty-ameny, barefoot and noiseless.

What caught my interest, through the ache in my muscles, was that Ty-ameny stopped by the vast doors of a final building, and dismissed her slaves, taking one of the lamps into her own hands.

The Pharaoh-Queen of the Lion-Throne can walk around at night without guards . . .

Either that argues a devout respect for the Queen, unlike that in other kingdoms, or – it belatedly occurred – her guards might merely be very good at keeping themselves out of sight.

Ahhotep opened a postern gate, bowing Ty-ameny and myself through. Inside, the lamp's inadequate light showed the curves of vast pillars, set close together. I could not see their tops. The eunuch mathematician took the lamp from the Queen and led the way forward, out across an open space tiled in red and blue and gold.

'Throne room,' Ty-ameny murmured, as if she too were reluctant to disturb the silence.

Ahhotep suddenly held up the oil-lamp.

I found myself facing the Carthaginian golem.

'*Ilario!*'

The female voice sounded sharp, but with concern. I fought to throw dizziness off and move in response.

Mosaic tiles were hard under my hands and knees.

I sat back, falling heavily to one side. Ty-ameny thrust a cloth at me. The eunuch Ahhotep returned out of the darkness with a bucket, and began spilling sand over something on the floor that the lamplight did not clearly show.

My throat felt raw. The taste of vomit was disgusting in my mouth.

'I ought to have realised!' Ahhotep sounded as if he were repeating himself. 'Great Queen, I'm so sorry! Master Ilario, how can I apologise!'

I dimly remember Rekhmire' once mentioning that the Royal Library kept fire-buckets of sand in every room. Evidently it was a practice throughout the palace complex.

I doubt he ever imagined them being used to cover up sick.

I pushed my heels against the tiny ridges of the mosaic, edging back. Wiping the cloth over my mouth took away some of the taste.

Only yards away from me, at the edge of the lamplight, stood feet too large for life-size – but skilfully painted in the colours of flesh.

The stone feet of the Carthaginian golem rested immovably against the floor. The shadows hid its height, but I glimpsed a curve of reflected light on its fingers, where its hands hung by its sides.

'I should have realised!' Ahhotep moaned again.

My own realisation was closer to *I wish to hit Ahhotep*.

The golem stood, half-painted, beside the Queen's ancient stone throne. Under other circumstances, the carved porphyry block would have been impressive in itself: a dark purple stone, the seat worn down into a deep dip by dynasty upon dynasty of Pharaohs. But the crystalline glitter in the rock could not take my eye from the painted golem.

Like a Venetian harlequin.

I'd forgotten we hadn't finished the face.

In the gold lamp-light, one blind stone eye looked at me. The other was painted to have the brilliance of life. Lustrous and brown and my stomach rose again, threateningly, as I recognised it – the evident model for the painted stonework was Masaccio's eyes, where he had begun to give its face some touches of a self-portrait.

I wiped the cloth hard across my lips.

If I'd thought anything, after Menmet-Ra's arrival at the Alexandrine house, it was that Ty-ameny must have had one of her craftsmen finish off the painting here. I'd even imagined asking, with insouciant gallows humour, 'What butcher did you get to finish this paint job?'

Instead I throw up, like a child.

'You know that it killed the master I was apprenticed to?'

Ty-ameny moved her bird-boned shoulders in a shrug. 'Yes. I regret that. *You* know, that if I had a choice, I'd wrap in anchor-chain and dump it in the Bosphorus!'

Ahhotep fumbled in the sleeves of his robes, bringing out a stylus and wax tablets. 'The diplomatic representatives of Carthage would notice, Great Queen, and we dare not seem afraid of anything they offer us. Master Ilario, anything you can tell us will be helpful. Don't worry what Lord Menmet-Ra may have reported before. Just begin at the start, in your own words.'

Climbing to my feet, I realised I recognised the gleam in the skinny eunuch's eye. *It is Masaccio's.*

I thought of Rome; the chill of early autumn. If Tommaso Cassai had had the chance to hear about this golem, would he have cared if it had killed a man before?

In all truth – no, he would not.

And this Ahhotep, black hair cut at jaw-level and wearing formal Alexandrine robes, might have been the Florentine painter's blood brother in that respect.

All my muscles tensed, every tendon; every nerve on edge.

If that thing moves, I will be out of this throne room so fast—

I thought it not impossible it might have connected itself to me, somehow, in the embassy at Rome; that my presence might move it to act.

Fear moved me to recklessness. I picked the lamp up from where Ahhotep had stood it on the dais of the throne, and held it close to the golem. This close, the light showed me every scratch on the bronze and brass metalwork of the joints.

The nobles of Carthage being what they are, Ty-ameny will have been put in possession of the words to make it move.

Even if she will not use them.

'The paint looks absurd.' Mimic skin and veins and hair as it might, you may as well put a ribbon on a boulder. 'This is nothing more nor less than a weapon, no matter what shape it is.'

Ty-ameny stepped lightly up the carved porphyry steps and sat on the throne, a yard from the golem. The lamp cast shadows in the sockets of her eyes.

'If we're very lucky,' she observed flatly, 'whatever madman wrought this in Carthage can only make a few of them. A handful. Not dozens.

Because if you see these on the field of battle, in numbers ... If I see them outside this city's walls ...'

Honorius had seen my one partial rendering of the stone golem (done out of memory), and instantly remarked, *A man armoured invulnerably at every point!* And after a pause, had added, *Who can't be stopped by wounds. Only hacked to pieces.*

I repeated this aloud.

Ahhotep looked as if he had suffered six weeks with a fever. Stress drew dark lines down from his nose to the corners of his mouth.

'I fear it badly enough, Master Ilario.' He put his hand on the edge of the purple throne, glancing at Ty-ameny. 'As her Great Name knows, I fear seeing this thing come to life and kill the Queen. Tell us what you know.'

I told him everything.

What I thought I could not remember, his questions prodded out of me. The night turned on, oil in the lamp guttering, until at last I was telling my story in the dark. I couldn't shut my eyes hard enough to prevent hot tears leaking out from under the lids. *Masaccio. Sulva.* And where is her bride-piece statue, now?

Ty-ameny became gradually silent.

I fretted. *I am telling her nothing she does not already know.*

An urgent need for sleep weighed me down, but I felt an unexpected sympathy for the Pharaoh-Queen – I, at least, need not ever see the monstrous thing again; she must have the golem beside her throne whenever she gives audience.

'Could it not have sunk on the ship coming from Rome?' I finally blurted out.

A new oil-lamp flared to light under Ahhotep's hands. By it, I saw that Ty-ameny smiled. She shook her head. 'Too many spies and gossips have seen it here.'

The gleam of light on stone disturbed me.

'It needs painting, Great Queen. Could it not be in a workshop, instead of standing beside the throne?'

Ahhotep came forward, one hand fiddling with his neck-chain. 'The Carthaginian envoy is expected. He will expect to see the gift where protocol demands it should be.'

'For the same reason,' Ty-ameny put it, with a gloomy cheerfulness that reminded me much of Rekhmire', 'we can neither set it in Roman concrete nor forge chains around it.'

'Can't you—' I waved a hand, frustrated. 'Restrain it secretly, in some way?'

'If there is such a way, none of my Royal Mathematicians have advised me of it.'

Silence fell. It had been quiet some time when I heard Ahhotep's sandals on the mosaic, diminishing away from us. Before I could formulate a question, I heard the creak of a door opening. A larger postern door, by the faint light that streamed in from it, wet and chill with dew. The sun has risen.

'From what you tell me,' Ty-ameny observed quietly, '*any* man may have the word that orders the stone man to act. I need not go to the trouble of banning all Carthaginians from the court, because they might send anyone. One of their own, or not.'

Raw-throated from speech, now, I nodded my agreement.

'I need to stay alive.' The woman pushed herself up, weight on her wrists, and stepped stiffly down from the throne. Unselfconsciously, she reached up to link her arm in mine, walking us both towards the door.

The flagstones outside were dry of dew already. The sky was a perfect infinite blue, and the sun not yet risen.

'I don't mean that I don't want to die.' She made a small smile, evidently a strain. 'Although I don't. But I need to live out this generation, and I need my daughter to rule the next one. And not just for Alexandria's sake.'

She looked at me with some concern.

'You need to sleep. But we'll go back by way of the Library – Ahhotep, go tell them we're coming – because there are things I need to discuss with you.'

Passing the building last night had given me no idea of its size. The lemon-coloured light of the dawn illuminated roof on roof, storey on storey, of the Royal Library; and I suspected that the obelisk-fronted door we entered by was only one of many opening into a library complex.

Inside, the stone of walls and floor shone pale, echoing daylight through the corridors and halls. Stepping over the threshold, I was hit by the scent of parchment, papyrus, scrolls . . . Plunged into memory of the scriptorium in Rodrigo Sanguerra's castle.

Our steps echoed. I followed Ty-ameny's small figure through gallery after gallery of leather scroll-cases, lost among squat pillars and vast square-lintelled archways. The rooms grew smaller and scruffier after a while, and the Queen called greetings to eunuch clerks already at their desks, doing reconstruction work on old papyruses. Cheerful voices called out from one chamber to the next.

About the time I thought we'd run out of building – and owned myself completely lost – Ty-ameny turned sharply right and loped up a flight of sandstone steps, that were less surprisingly worn away into a dip in the middle.

The arch at the top opened into a bright gallery. Carved windows opened into a piazza below us.

No books. No scrolls. *Because the light would fade them.* They want good light for . . .

'The printing-*machina*.'

The Pharaoh-Queen's subjects must have been working through the night. Herr Mainz – Herr Gutenberg – stood beside a wooden frame, gesturing expansively, and broke off to grin like a badger at Ty-ameny.

'Great Queen! We should have it finished before the end of today. Or at least the prototype.'

Ty-ameny strode up to stand beside him, not even as high as his shoulder. Her eyes glittered as she appeared to follow his report of his progress.

'You also know how this works?' she demanded of me.

Gutenberg stroked blunted fingers over a tray of metal type. 'Messer Ilario does not. No man but I, not even in my Guild.'

Storms on the voyage through the Aegean might have robbed Ty-ameny of her printing-*machina*; likewise the cholera and plague endemic to large cities. I thought perhaps Ty-ameny might persuade him to write his plans down, where I had failed.

Ty-ameny smiled at him. Her tiny ruddy-skinned hand stroked the printing-*machina*'s frame as if it were a blood-horse.

'Not the details. The meaning. That in the time the scriptorium takes to copy a scroll once, I can have you set the type to print the same words. And in the time it takes to copy a scroll *twice* – I can have five hundred copies, printed and ready!'

She wiped her fingers down her plain linen robes, seemingly unaware of the black grease.

Gutenberg very precisely explained, in a mixture of German and bad Carthaginian Latin, how it would take longer to set up his lead letters the first time than to copy them on paper, but after that ... Ty-ameny clearly wasn't listening. As Gutenberg went back to his machine, she took my arm, gazing up into my face, and pointed.

'You see that?'

I stared into an empty corner of the gallery.

'A bucket.' Embarrassed by memory of what happened in the throne room, I added, 'Master Rekhmire' told me – you have them in every room here, because of the fear of fire.'

I thought of Masaccio's cluttered workshop, full of wooden frames, canvas, pigments, oils, buckets of sand and water. The same principle, even if he had appeared to work in chaos.

Ty-ameny released my arm.

'Yes. We have buckets. Water and sand. And all the walls are masonry. And there are courtyards between various buildings in the complex, to act as firebreaks, and cellars below, insulated from one another by the living rock. Because these walls are piled high and stuffed full with papyrus, vellum, paper ... Everything flammable. Even our shelves are carved out of stone.'

Her gaze searched out Gutenberg's tray of lead letters.

'There have been minor fires before. We've lost scrolls. Scrolls that were the last copies of their work. And it doesn't matter how many clerks I put into the scriptorium, they won't catch up the copying of four thousand years of collecting. And one day, one day ... One day everything we have will burn.'

Finding myself close enough to the wall to touch it, I ran a finger down a seamless masonry join. 'You can't know that—'

Ty-ameny's head jerked up, as if she woke from a deep sleep or vision. 'I can!'

Ahhotep muttered something; she chopped her tiny hand down in a surprisingly fierce gesture. She turned sloe-dark eyes on me, and I was not conscious of her small stature.

'If there's no great fire, still, we're not as great a power as we once were. Conquerors will pass through with fire and sword. It will be Carthage or the Turks,' she added, with a flat pragmatic certainty.

I was unsure that Gutenberg understood her Alexandrine Latin; he straightened and frowned at her.

Ty-ameny paced to the window, and it did not change her dignity in the least that she must stand up on her toes to stare out at the city below.

'Cousin Rekhmire' could have told you this, but I see he has been circumspect. Still, it's not a secret among my advisers. We were a great empire – once. Now we have only one city, with no hinterland. The Turks have taken our old lands, and nibble away at our borders here. And Carthage is jealous of any sea-power not hers.'

Her hand gripped the sculpted frame possessively.

'I'd counted on having my reign and my daughter's before someone takes this city and burns it. Time enough to copy the most valuable volumes here – or at least some of them. I no longer believe we have two generations. I may be the last of the line of Pharaohs. But now I have *this*—'

She turned about, her gaze hungry on Gutenberg and the *machina*.

'Now – we can turn out a flood of knowledge! Copies of every scroll and book and document in the Royal Library – many copies. I'll send them as royal gifts to the kings of Francia and Persia and Carthage if I have to. I'll sell them cheap through Venice. This city will send out so many copies that no fire or war or shipwreck or disaster can ever destroy every copy of a work. This knowledge will *not* be lost.'

Between the Egyptian Ahhotep and Gutenberg, Ty-ameny appeared the size of a child. Speaking, there was enough desperate energy in her to make someone three times her size.

I should ask if I can paint her!

Hard on the heels of that came another realisation.

'You don't mean that Alexandria will fall some day in the far-off future, do you, Great Queen? You expect it in our lifetime.'

In her lifetime.

In mine.

In Onorata's . . .

'Soon,' Ty-amenhotep said. 'But I'll sell printed scrolls to the Franks, to North Africa, to Persia and the Silk Road. Pages for pennies. If not for the fact that men don't value what they don't pay for, I'd give them away! But every ducat that they earn, I swear I'll turn to hiring more scribes, and building more of Herr Mainz's machines!'

I grew up hearing stories of Constantinople as a city great beyond all cities of the earth, last home of Pharaonic Egypt, repository of occult knowledge, free market of traders from every country in Europe and Africa, and from impossibly distant Turkey and Hind . . .

Hearing a very little of the hollowness of that image in her tone, a shiver went down my spine. I thought of Alexandrine Constantinople's thick walls reduced to rubble and dust – but their inheritance, a river of knowledge, flowing out first to all the quarters of the earth.

Ty-ameny beamed at the German.

'We'll need many of these machinae. I think I can persuade my council to give you whatever funds you need. How long will it take you to train apprentices?'

'Herr Mainz' was reduced to a burbling, beaming mess in the next few minutes. I moved to stand aside with Ahhotep by the vast masonry windows, and smiled. It's pleasing to see someone get their heart's desire.

'Master Ilario.' Ahhotep had his elbows on the window-ledge, the dawn's brightness falling on his soft skin.

I followed his gaze. In that direction, I saw there was indeed an open square of sorts; a public plaza. Great wide steps led down to the city below – which made me conclude the squat black building that we faced, now, was that throne room of Ty-ameny's where the golem stood.

'Suppose,' the tall eunuch muttered, 'he has no time to set up printing machinae, because the stone monster has turned on the Pharaoh-Queen and killed her?'

I need not turn to look at Ty-amenhotep to remember how small she is, barely coming up to my breast.

All of us are that small in front of the stone golem.

'Would Carthage dare kill your queen? Other kingdoms would condemn them—'

Ahhotep shrugged. 'Evidently, if they *can* do it, they *may* do it.'

I protested, 'And you won't dispose of it, you won't chain it up—'

Ahhotep indicated the direction of the harbour with one long clean finger. 'Show ourselves afraid, and you'd see the Carthaginian fleet in the Bosphorus in a month!'

Frustration boiled up in me. I waved a hand at the library complex about us. 'Old Egypt was always supposed to be the heart of occult knowledge. Don't you have – I don't know – ancient Egyptian magic! Can't you bind the golem with invisible chains?'

Ahhotep looked at me as if I were a child. '"Magic"?'

Somewhat defensively, I muttered, 'My child was born by Caesarean in Venice; there was a priest there who swore *that* was magic—'

'Miracle,' Ahhotep interrupted. 'If I know Green priests. Miracle, not magic. Yes. The Franks do show a distressing capacity, on occasion, for circumventing what is possible.'

The eunuch stared thoughtfully at my lower abdomen, in the manner of a man pondering autopsies.

'I suppose,' he said diffidently, 'you would not be willing to let me see your scar?'

Once here, with Rekhmire''s favour keeping a roof over my head – and faced with a plain curiosity from Ahhotep that I must recognise from the mirror – matters seemed different.

'Prod away,' I offered, resignedly reaching for the fastening of my linen robe.

Ahhotep took me into one of the side-chambers of the gallery, making copious notes and little cries of excitement. I listened to Ty-amenhotep and Master Gutenberg, outside, discussing which manuscripts might best be set in type first.

I continued to worry obsessively at the matter of the stone golem.

14

I woke, finally, to Attila pacing the length of the immense chamber, soothing Onorata, singing some obscene song that he and his brother had concocted about 'Admiral Black-Eyes'.

I can only pray for her to remember none of this when she grows up!

He supported my baby's head well, but he walked up and down more roughly than I would have done. Every so often he stopped to show her bas-reliefs, and cartouches painted in red and blue on the walls. I was unsure she could see so far yet.

'I'll feed her,' I offered, staggering up and seizing a robe.

Her body was warmly solid in my arms; it was no hardship to sit on a couch by the wide windows, with a towel thrown over me, and let her coo and slurp over the sloppy gruel that Carrasco thought should be her introduction to anything other than goat's milk. Had we been going by the clock, it would have been an early evening meal.

The familiar drag and click of Rekhmire''s crutches let me know he had come into the room. He paused beside me to brush his fingers over Onorata's forehead.

Her translucent eyelids closed, hiding the blue of her eyes. They had begun to remind me of Honorius's eyes, though not as pale and wind-washed as the man who had sat around far too many military camp-fires.

'Ty-ameny would like you aboard the Admiral's ship at least once more.' He wiped his sticky hand on my towel, and smiled down at me. 'If you'll draw for her.'

'Oh, I'll draw.'

Rekhmire' thudded down onto the marble bench edging the room, and unexpectedly held out his arms for Onorata. I put her into his lap, and began to clean up myself and my surroundings, while he sat among embroidered cushions telling her stories of Lion-Headed Sekhmet (who apparently punishes evil-doers), and Ra Son-of-the-Sun, and the steersman on the Boat of the Dead.

'You don't need to draw,' he remarked. 'The Queen would consider any request about Taraconensis from you on its own merits.'

'I hope the brat pees on you,' I observed. 'And do you really think I *don't* want to go back on Zheng He's ship?'

'I was unsure.' He beamed up at me. 'But at least, while I'm holding your child, you can neither hit me nor throw things at me!'

I considered the bowl holding remnants of Onorata's food, narrowly dismissed the temptation, and by way of pointing out certain errors in the book-buyer's reasoning, threw a cushion that missed my baby and caught him neatly on the ear.

Anyone who lives at court – King's Freak, or merely in attendance on the ruling powers – knows the necessity for every least adviser to have his say. I watched Ty-ameny recede into a crowd of Constantinople's eunuch bureaucrats over the next few days, on occasion taking Rekhmire' with her. I confined myself to drawing on board Admiral Zheng He's 'war-junk', as I understood him to call it, and left others to study the sketches.

I spent considerable time, when it was not too hot, on the city walls, and at the gates leading down onto the quays. Drawing gate-guards while I talked with them, and merchants; children playing complicated games with pebbles, musicians crouching in corners and playing for coins, sailors coming and going from the moored vessels. Onorata, under her cradle's sail-cloth awning, seemed to take notice of the movement, I thought.

Neither Attila nor Tottola seemed adverse to duties involving sitting down. On occasion, both the German men-at-arms would accompany me. Attila sloped off to see the Alexandrine slave from the *Sekhmet*, Asru. Tottola, on his off-hours, seemed to be working his way through the palace kitchens.

Something over a week later, we walked back to the palace in time to sleep through the scarifyingly hot hours between one and five in the afternoon, and I found Rekhmire' usefully present for conversation. He fell in beside me in the corridor, not having been out to Zheng He's ship for two days, and consequently rested enough that he used a silver-handled stout stick instead of crutches.

'Those twelve ships.' I nodded in what would have been the direction of the harbour, if cartouche-strewn corridors and bright paintings of Ra and Horus and Sekhmet hadn't got me turned around. 'The Greek-fire ships. That's all the Alexandrine navy, isn't it?'

The Egyptian opened our chambers' doors for me, and looked on while I put Onorata down to sleep. 'I believe there are two the other side of the Bosphorus, patrolling Turkish shores.'

I crossed the room almost on tiptoe, so she would not wake and grizzle. Sprawling down onto the sunken bench beside Rekhmire', I showed him a page of my sketchbook.

'Some of your old cannon on the city walls are bound with leather.'

When barrels are cast, not poured, they soak leather and wrap it around the muzzle-loading brass cannon-barrels, so that they won't burst with the first shot. I'd seen more than a few at old fortresses in the Taraconensis hills.

I hated to think what Honorius would say if anyone expected him to fight without iron cannon.

'You do realise?' Rekhmire' reached for the jug and glass standing beside him on the sunken seat. 'That most visitors aren't allowed to go where you go?'

'I realise that either Ty-ameny implicitly trusts your opinion of me, or someone is going to put my eyes out with hot irons before I leave. In case I should draw images again, once I'm far from Alexandrine Constantinople.'

'Ilario—' He halted, Venetian glass of watered wine halfway to his lips. 'She trusts my opinion.'

'And now you can tell me why.'

'I have long been loyal—'

'*No.*'

On such occasions, mere reassurance in words won't do; I saw him read that in me.

'I won't risk judicial mutilation just because you *think* your Queen trusts you, and by extension me. *Why* does she trust you?'

Rekhmire' put his glass down. He reached for his stick, pushing himself up onto his feet. Before I could complain at his leaving, he laid the stick back down on the bench, and tugged at the belt holding up his linen kilt. He folded the cloth down before I could speak.

Against his ruddy skin, I saw an ancient white scar, as wide as three fingers, just above his hip.

'Come here.' He beckoned, and reached around to his back.

Half-turned away from me, he looked over his shoulder, and eased down the pale cotton.

I saw he had a corresponding scar on his back, a little larger and more jagged. Frighteningly close to his kidney.

'I was big at fourteen.' He didn't readjust his linen wrap around his hips yet. 'And Ty-ameny had just reached the size she is now, though we are the same age. She trusts me because the sword only went through me far enough to give her a purely decorative scar.'

Cold sweat dampened my tunic between my shoulders and under my arms.

'You put yourself between her and a sword.' A wide enough blade, by the injury. He would need an Egyptian physician to survive that! 'It went *through* you . . . '

Rekhmire' turned back around, facing me, and traced the white irregularity in his skin. 'Some lord had very carefully chosen a number of the Royal Egyptian Guard who could be persuaded to revolt against their young Queen. I passed that information on, but didn't trust the minister who said it would be dealt with. Ty-ameny . . . '

'Decided you needed a career as a book-buyer?'

'Something very like that.'

472

'Well.' I shrugged. 'I suppose my eyes are safe enough, then.'

The cold sweat didn't go from my spine. Even jokes don't make that thought easier.

I looked up at the large Egyptian. 'I can see why Ty-ameny trusts you as she does.'

Rekhmire' smiled sardonically. 'I tell her it's foolish. Just because a man takes a wound for you once, you can't trust him the rest of his life! But she refuses to listen. I am . . . therefore careful about who I tell her *I* trust.'

That made me feel unaccountably warm.

Onorata interrupted from her cradle with a cough. I listened until I heard her even breathing resume.

'She could die.' I gave Rekhmire' my hand to clasp, so he could sit down again with more ease. 'That's what wakes me up sweating at nights. Fever. Cold. Anything. Nothing.'

'True enough. But she can also live.' Rekhmire' nodded towards the bench on the opposite side of the sunken area, at the failed egg tempera painting of Zheng He's porcelain cup and those other drawings that littered the area – and would do until more of Ty-ameny's bureaucrats came to remove them for study. 'Remember your family is building up a debt. The Queen owes you much.'

I may have looked irritated.

Rekhmire' sounded faintly apologetic. 'You were in King Rodrigo Sanguerra's court: I need not tell you any of this. When the moment comes, then you ask.'

'*What* do I ask for? "Would Constantinople like to step in and sort out the court of Taraco?" No! Would King Rodrigo like that? Frankly—' I bit my lip as Onorata grumbled in her sleep, and added, much more quietly, 'Frankly, *no*! And it would be a direct provocation to Carthage.'

Rekhmire' nodded, and ground the heel of one large hand against his eye and socket.

He surveyed the resulting smudge of kohl on his skin with disapprobation.

'First things first. You may come to the next council,' he added, not very much as though it were a suggestion.

'How long before Queen Ty-ameny deals with the Admiral and his ship?'

I did not add, *And can listen to pleas for help from book-buyers' assistants?* since the renewed accord between Rekhmire' and I seemed to make that redundant.

'A week or so. Certainly before the end of this lunar month.'

15

The smell hung heavy in the air, rich in the back of my throat where I couldn't choke it away.

It was a hot climate, for all the stone walls about us. Necessity put us on the Library's upper floors, to get the natural light. But that made this hotter than the earth-insulated cellars.

'Shall I turn that over for you?' The philosopher Bakennefi nodded down.

It is hardly the first dead body I've seen.

Not even the first body cut to pieces. I once managed to attend a public dissection in the university at Barcelona, along with two hundred other students, in the hopes of discovering what those lumps and bumps one sees while drawing the human body actually are, under the skin – and what they look like when there is no such surface.

Perhaps, I thought, it's that this small old man was obviously a slave.

Masaccio said that in the same way one can't draw robes without knowledge of the body underneath, it's not possible to draw skin without knowledge of muscle, tendon, ligament, bones.

'Yes: turn him.' I managed to get the words out without bringing up the bile at the back of my throat.

Bakennefi carefully turned over the dead man's skinned hand.

I set about drawing the uncovered tendons and muscles of the palm.

This Bakennefi was Bakennefi Aa, 'eldest', out of the three brother Royal Mathematicians who ran this department, along with Bakennefi Hery-ib ('he who is in the middle') and Bakennefi Nedjes ('small'). He had a watercolour of the autopsy in progress on the vast stone slab beside him. He painted it as delicately as if the dead body were a book opened for his enjoyment. There seemed to me to be little connection between the carefully-labelled bright organs and the slithery mass in the opened belly. But that may have been because I deliberately avoided looking closely.

I swatted at one of the ever-present flies.

The hum of the swarm was loud enough that a man had actually to raise his voice to be heard, despite the twenty or so slaves with fans waving the air above the stone slab clear.

Bakennefi Aa gave a last prod at the opened palm with his iron-hafted pen. 'Do you know, I think this one's done with? He's a little more past his time than I imagined.'

Sheer cowardice made me turn away and set about putting brushes, reeds, scrapers and paints away with my chalk in the leather snapsack. If I had to hear the sounds of the cloth being wrapped around the dissection body, and smell the sudden wash of stink as slaves lifted it, at least I need not look.

And the worst thing is that these drawings will be invaluable to me.

'You are good.' Queen Ty-ameny's light voice spoke behind me. I startled hard enough to drop a brush.

'I wonder you don't ask me for a commission,' she added.

Scrabbling hurriedly on the Library's marble floor, I stood up again, clutching the brush, flushed. Ty-ameny was standing on her toes looking at my painting. She glanced at me for an answer to her implied question.

'Why not?' She wore a simple linen tunic edged with purple, and her black eyes looked brightly at me. 'Why wouldn't you ask? I might agree.'

I stuttered, 'I grew up in a court, Aldro.'

No matter how small and provincial it might have been.

'There are always factions in a court,' I added, packing the brush away in its wooden box, and slipping that into my bag. 'Aldro Ty-amenhotep, I've been used to being next to a King, most of my adult life. Not that I had any power in Taraco. But even a Fool who has the King's ear gets courted.'

'Perhaps even more so.' Ty-ameny grinned, and tilted her head up, watching me. As if it were a familiar story, she murmured, 'Pay attention to any one man, and before you know it, you're on one side, and there are other sides, all of whom have reason to hate you. And whoever you listened to first, they don't trust you. I wondered,' she added, 'why you've stood so much in my cousin's shadow while you were here.'

I couldn't help a smile in response to hers. Rekhmire' wasn't liable to give his loyalty to a stupid ruler.

'I'm too used to being a King's—' *pet*. I chose a better word. '— associate. Kings don't awe me. That's sometimes unfortunate. Other lords have found me disrespectful in the past, because of what I'm used to. And any court faction you like to mention thinks I can be bribed or threatened. I find it better to stay in the background, where I can't give offence.'

The buzz of flies diminished, most of them giving up now and circling to find the open stone windows. Two slaves remained, waving fans made out of huge white feathers, and concealing the kind of relieved boredom that comes with not being ordered to any dirty or difficult task.

Ty-ameny walked over to the window, her thin arms folded across her chest. Gold bracelets flashed back points of light that left dots across my vision. She gazed out at the blue sky – at the sun she gravitated towards, I suddenly realised, at any moment she might.

'Divine Father Ra!' she muttered, either in prayer or exasperation. 'Ilario . . . You've done good work for me with Zheng He. As one of my court painters, here, you could afford to keep your daughter.'

Having occasionally had an oak door slammed in my face, I recognise that feeling of shock. Even if this is from a door opening.

'But . . . Master Rekhmire' will have told you my business in Iberia.'

'In broad detail.' The Pharaoh-Queen Ty-ameny rested her elbows on the stone sill.

The spreading gardens below had the air of something Roman. A stone maze beyond a hedge looked darker, a mass of obelisks and pyramids that I thought must be monuments or graves. Momentarily I pictured the ancient junipers growing in the dark, in Carthage's tophet. If I painted Baal's face now, could I get it right? Now there's Onorata?

Ty-ameny shifted herself around, looking a considerable way up to see my face. Under that study, I reached out to the silver basin on the sill, water warmed by the sun, and began to wash blood and paint from my hands.

The Pharaoh-Queen said, 'And what are your intentions towards Rekhmire'?'

A slave thrust a towel into my hands and I dropped it.

What?

The slave passed me another cloth. Mute through bewilderment, I dried my hands and returned it. Not that the droplets wouldn't have been sucked up by the sun in a few minutes.

'Intentions?' I forced myself to calmness. 'To help him wherever I can, Highness.'

She put her hand up on my forearm. Her fingers were as small as a twelve-year-old girl's, and her palm sandy and hot.

'It would displease me personally if Rekhmire' were deliberately hurt.'

Bakennefi had also examined me, at Ahhotep's request; both of them had found something to criticise and cluck over in the stitches removed from my lower belly. I will always bear the marks. Now I thought I heard Honorius and Rekhmire''s voices spontaneously chiming together: *Save the mother.*

Ty-ameny's clear small voice said, 'Suppose his duties take him to a different land, now? Suppose he were to leave Alexandria tomorrow? With the foreign ship?'

There was a sharp pain in the pit of my stomach, keen enough to make me wonder if Alexandrine food might not be suited to it.

Mouth dry, I thought, *Interesting – I would sooner he didn't leave.*

Rekhmire' no longer owns me as a slave. He brought me to Alexandria because he needed to come here himself. Yes, he will help solve the problem of Aldra Videric, but – not, perhaps, personally.

I must look bewildered and stupid, I realised, but I could find no words for this realisation I would have preferred to avoid.

The Pharaoh-Queen studied me with a sparrow-like tilt to her head. I thought it an even throw of the dice whether she would accept my silence, or have one of the sandal-hurling outbursts of temper that Egypt seems to permit its female rulers.

'Great Queen.' I wiped my hand over my face. Spots of colour told me I had missed spatters; I doused my fingers in the bowl and wiped water over my skin again. 'I . . . would still wish to help him.'

She gave a decided nod.

'We should talk of the future.' Her features a mask of distaste, she raised her free hand a fraction. 'Elsewhere.'

The nearest slave crossed the room instantly and bowed, giving her a scented cloth. I avoided the slave's eye. Even with the stone surface sluiced down, the stink of the dead slave still hung in this room. If this slave dies of age or sickness here, will he end up opened on a stone table?

'Bakennefi Aa wouldn't mind a look under *my* skin,' I said before I knew I was to be quite so honest.

Queen Ty-ameny frowned at me over her silk kerchief.

'I do hope you're careful about taking food and drink around him . . . '

Rekhmire' entered the chamber just as Queen Ty-ameny of the Five Great Names doubled up, giggling like a schoolgirl.

I folded my arms.

At Rekhmire''s raised brow, Ty-ameny pointed at me, waved a hand weakly in dismissal of the matter, and shot me a glance with more genuine apology than I have ever had from King Rodrigo.

'It's hardly fair,' she murmured. 'I'm Alexandria's queen; how much free interchange can there be between a queen and any other man or woman?'

Before I thought, I said, 'That's what I tell my slave.'

Rekhmire''s rumbled louder comment drowned me out. 'That's why I freed Ilario, cousin.'

The tiny woman smiled wryly. 'Well, no man is going to free me from the throne. And I don't think I would let them. Very well: we need to talk. The matter of Zheng He must be settled soon – before there is more trouble from Carthage.'

16

Pharaoh-Queen Ty-ameny of the Five Great Names sat small and erect, among cushions embroidered in blue and gold with her lineal ancestor Ra the Sun-God of Old Egypt.

The Admiral of the Ocean Sea, at last on shore, sat on her right-hand side, on the ochre marble ledge of the sunken area of her Council chamber, Jian beside him. Rekhmire' was next to Ty-ameny, then I on Rekhmire''s left hand, with half the eunuch bureaucracy beyond me. Zheng He's other officers and Alexandria's sea-captains and army-generals, at the end of the great chamber, shared space with Ty-ameny's natural philosophers and Royal Mathematicians, who kept papers and instruments and charts beside them on the low seat.

The Alexandrines might be old, young, fat, thin, eunuch, or – occasionally – intact male. What they all had in common was an intensity of gaze when it came to Zheng He.

Absently, I began to sketch Ty-ameny on the virgin wax surface of my tablet. She wore a gold mask that included the shape of a beard; less hot, I thought, to tie over her face than the hair-replica. I put the lines of Zheng He in beside her to give scale. She barely came up to his shoulder. *She is the only woman in the room. If you do not count the half of me.* I pushed other concerns out of my mind.

Because if Videric can reach out to harm me in the middle of Ty-ameny's court in Alexandria, I may as well give up now.

In fact, there was little enough said over the next hour that had not been said between Rekhmire' and Admiral Zheng He on the great war-junk. I came to the conclusion that the Admiral wanted to hear it from the mouth of – as he called her – 'the Great Foreign Empress'.

Rekhmire' himself finally caught Ty-ameny's eye, and hauled forward one of the sea-charts.

'In fact, noble Admiral, it is as the Great Queen of the Five Name's captains inform you. That enticing eastward-leading sea there, vast as it appears, will not take you further than Turkish ports close to Aleppo. And if you have maps of the land routes between your home and those cities, you will know that they are still hundreds of leagues distant from it; perhaps thousands.'

And full of Turks and Persians, though Rekhmire' said nothing of that. Ty-ameny might suppose this foreigner ultimately an ally of those more eastern powers.

Zheng He grunted, leaned forward to study the map, and waved Jian's formal polite thanks aside, interrupting his subordinate. 'Yes, I see, but why would I believe?'

Ty-ameny's face behind the mask would be fascinating to draw, I thought regretfully.

Rekhmire' smiled, inclining his head. 'Because if the Black Sea were the way to your home, New Alexandria would be asking you to pay the fee to pass the Bosphorus, great Admiral. As we do with all vessels passing to trade in the Black Sea.'

'And you don't charge us a fee in any case? And send us through and keep silent about—' Zheng He waved a huge hand at the charts. '—this bounded Black Sea of yours?'

Ty-ameny's voice issued from behind the full curved mouth of the golden mask of Ra. 'There is a reasonable chance that you and your ship would afterwards return here.'

Her rich tone showed her definitely amused, to anyone who knew her.

Rekhmire' smoothly added, 'This is the only route into, and out of, the closed sea. Forgive the Great Queen of the Five Names if she doesn't desire to have you and your great ship back here angry at perceived treachery. That would hardly be worth anything we could extort from you now.'

Zheng He slapped his thigh. His officers obediently laughed. I saw a certain relaxation go through Ty-ameny's commanders. Having used up almost all the wax surface of my tablets, I set myself to detailing the embroidery on Zheng He's high collar, and the lines around his eyes and mouth that signified amused satisfaction.

'If closed sea.' He traced the lines of the Black Sea on the Egyptian chart before him – it was meagre with detail, I noted – before moving west to Alexandria and the straits, and the beginning of the Greek islands. 'Is this, you call it "Middle Sea", also closed? But no. Because we came in. And where there is a way in, there is also a way out.'

None of the Pharaoh-Queen's charts showed any of the sea or land west of Crete. That was in no way an accident. Zheng He's ship might navigate back from Alexandria, through the long straits after Marmara, to the Aegean. But after that . . . the natural direction for him would be south and east, but that would only bring him, eventually, to Sidon and Tyre.

'We have not yet,' Zheng He said equably to Ty-ameny's implacable mask, 'begun to discuss the advantages of trade between my land and yours, great Empress.'

Plain as the daylight outside the linen-shaded windows: *Now we merely argue about the price!*

I shifted where I sat, not able to talk to Rekhmire' now he was the main conduit of translation between Zheng He and the Pharaoh-Queen.

It should be possible to find the Straits to the western ocean simply by following along the coast of North Africa, I thought, but not if no man was willing to tell him how it might be done.

I saw instantly what Ty-ameny had to bargain with. Charts, yes, but charts are often inaccurate. What Zheng He will need to get back to the Straits between Iberia and North Africa is a pilot.

Something nagged at the back of my brain. I prodded and scraped my tablets clean, and fell to doodling Horus-eyes while the council continued with every man desiring his say.

Two hours later, there was a pause for wine and light food.

I took Rekhmire''s elbow on pretence of assisting him, and steered him into one of the alcoves, out of earshot of Ty-ameny and her generals socially chatting with Zheng He and Jian and the other foreigners.

Rekhmire' raised a familiar brow at me.

'Would you call this a crisis?' I demanded.

His brows came down, frowning. 'Potential. I think it defused by what we've done—'

'The *arrival* of his ship.' I clamped down on my impatience. 'No kingdom in the Middle Sea has anything to match it. Whatever port sees Zheng He, there'll be panic and crisis. Am I right?'

Rekhmire''s lips parted, very slightly; in any other man it would have been an *ah* of realisation.

I spoke before he could.

'Perhaps, cause enough panic that a King – no matter what difficulties he might seem to be having with his most trusted adviser – would find himself forced to call that man back to court?'

17

I held Rekhmire''s gaze.

'I comprehend,' he murmured. 'If it could be negotiated for Zheng He to sail to *Taraco* . . . '

My mind raced. I glanced back into the chamber, ensuring no eunuch or man of Chin was within hearing distance. 'King Rodrigo could take that as the excuse to bring Videric back from his estate.'

Rekhmire' stood very still, his face intent.

I urged, 'He *would*. If a messenger was sent ahead to explain to him . . . Look at that ship! Do you think any man in Taraco would be surprised if Rodrigo wanted his best adviser back to help him deal with it? Even *Carthage* wouldn't blink at that.'

Rekhmire' clasped his hands over the top of his stick. His intense gazed focused onto me. 'That – would be a beginning.'

My hands sweated. I rubbed them on my linen tunic. 'You think—'

'It would soon become apparent that the Admiral is no threat. The scandal around Videric's name might not be entirely gone. But, yes, as a beginning—' He interrupted himself. 'Carthage! If Carthage was to take the war-junk as an ally of Taraconensis . . . '

'Would that be good or bad?' I asked anxiously.

'Good, if it makes the Lords-Amir cautious about sending legions into Iberia. Bad, if it provokes them into doing that very thing out of panic.'

I found my hand clenching around the wood frame of the wax tablets, cutting into my skin. 'I didn't think of that.'

Rekhmire' stroked his hand down his hairless chin, his eyes narrowing. 'This is worth considering. Many ramifications – many . . . '

His monumental face momentarily split in a warm smile that was all Rekhmire'. And a nod that was pure professional cousin of Ty-ameny.

'I'll speak with the Pharaoh-Queen. It must be discussed through and through. Ty-ameny has no greater wish than you to see war start in Taraconensis, and bring every other kingdom in with it.'

He blinked eyes that caught the linen-sifted light, and shone the colour of brandy.

'It won't be a quick answer, I fear. Between Ty-ameny's councillors and the Admiral's advisers . . . But I'll have an answer. I will. Well done, Ilario.'

I watched him as he limped away towards the Pharaoh-Queen, my stomach fairly tying itself into knots.

True to his word, time passed.

In those occasional hours when I saw him out of council, he desired only to rest his mind, and this seemed to take the form of escorting Onorata and myself (with the German brothers) about Constantinople – 'A city,' as he said, 'where you can walk from Europe to Asia in the space of a mile.'

I did just that, dragging Tottola and Attila along with me in the evening's warmth, taking Onorata under a great paper sunshade from the Chin war-junk. So that I would be able to tell her, when she was old enough, that she had stood in Asian lands.

Which assumes she does not stay here, grow up in Alexandria-in-exile . . .

Both Rekhmire' and the Pharaoh-Queen Ty-ameny showed an interest in my daughter.

The book-buyer, finding me holding her on the room's balcony again one morning, bent over to study her more closely. Onorata was solidly asleep, one closed fist resting up under her fat chins, and I stroked with a forefinger at the dark hair slicked down on her scalp.

Rekhmire' straightened up. 'When do they get interesting?'

'They *what*?'

'Infants. Will she talk soon? Or move around more?'

I raised an eyebrow at him, as much in his own fashion as I could imitate. 'You don't know?'

'I'm a book-buyer, not a nurse!' Half affronted and half amused, he gazed down at me. 'Aren't you supposed to know these things?'

'I was the youngest. I expect Sunilda or Matasuntha could tell you. And I'm a *painter*!'

Tottola strolled in from the anterooms, evidently changing shift on guard duty, and gave the Egyptian a look that clearly inquired *And the thing that's so funny is—?*, without needing a word. He stripped off his mail-shirt and garments, abandoning them for striped linen robes that reminded me painfully sharply of Iberia, nodded respectfully to me, and fell instantly asleep on his palliasse.

Onorata began a grumble in her sleep. Rocking her in the crook of my arm, I discovered she found that motion no substitute for milk.

Rekhmire' offered her a blunt-nailed thumb, with no better success.

I said, 'I'll get Carrasco to make her feed.'

Rekhmire' made himself scarce.

Ty-ameny's interest was the authentic tone of the Alexandrine philosopher. She visited, a day or two after, and leaned forward from among the cushions, studying my child who had fallen asleep on a blanket on the floor.

How I'll ever convince anyone of the hellion she is, when she angelically sleeps in their presence—

'Is she normal?' Ty-ameny asked.

Any other woman, I would have slapped. It was the Alexandrine curiosity in her tone that restrained me, more than her rank. Although that carried its weight.

'It appears so, Aldro. Until she grows up, who can say?'

The small woman nodded, and leaned back.

Without requesting permission, I settled on the goats'-wool blankets beside Onorata.

Rekhmire' remained standing.

Ty-ameny complained almost sulkily, 'You're making my neck ache. Sit down, in Ra's name!'

Rekhmire' bowed as deeply as slaves do. With the help of his stick, he moved as if to seat himself on the stone ledge beyond her.

Her hand closed over his wrist as he passed.

Rekhmire' let her arrest him. I saw in a heart's beat all their history in the glance between them. I felt curiously shut out. Although the ruling of New Alexandria is no concern of mine.

Ty-ameny's cheeks darkened a little, as if the heat of the room flushed her face. She moved her hand to her chin, as if she would stroke the Pharaoh's false beard that she was not wearing today. 'It was a reasonable question!'

'Yes, Great Queen,' Rekhmire' said mildly.

The queen looked at him through narrowed eyes.

Without turning, she said, 'Ilario, I apologise for not asking that in a more tactful manner.'

I bowed, catching how Rekhmire''s face warmed as she spoke.

'Too many people have thought it a reasonable question for me to like it, Great Queen,' I said.

'I believe that was the reason I was just slapped down.' She spoke darkly, looking up at Rekhmire'. 'Isn't that right, cousin?'

'The wisdom of the everlasting Gods is spoken through the mouth of the Pharaoh-Queen.' Rekhmire''s monumental face broke into a smile that made him look twenty. 'Most of the time . . . '

'Stop towering over me, book-buyer. I can still shorten you by a head, any day of the week!'

'Of course, cousin.' Rekhmire''s bow was so elegantly proper that, had I been Ty-ameny, I would have thrown something at him. I saw her small fingers tighten around one of the cushions as she grinned. The large Egyptian moved, seating himself on the bench beside her, and under cover of smoothing out the folds of his linen kilt, shot me a reassuring look.

I envied them their closeness.

'In fact,' Ty-ameny added, with more gravitas than one might expect from a woman with the stature of a twelve-year-old, 'if it would set your mind at ease to have her examined, the best of my Royal Mathematicians and physicians will do so.'

I could manage only 'Thank you', but it must have been clear what I meant.

The next several days had all my attention on my child, who bawled dispiritingly whenever an Alexandrine picked her up, and looked at me as if I were the Frankish version of Judas.

All of them pronounced her normal, but let me know that the extent of their knowledge – 'Without dissection!', Bakennefi Aa cheerily remarked – must be limited.

Slaves continued to bring food to our quarters at regular intervals. I sunk myself into the enjoyment of palace living – since I did not know if I would ever live in a palace again – and on two days when it was too hot to go outside, or do more than lay down on the great bed on the dais in my chamber, I dozed beside Onorata's cradle.

I woke on the third day, bored.

Zheng He, on land, would not have barbarians on his ship while he was not there.

I had itchy fingers, and established myself under a striped awning on another of the palace balconies, with Onorata asleep in a hooded cradle, and a stack of old parchments and a stoppered flask of oak-gall ink.

The striped awning reminded me of Taraco. I began a letter to Honorius, got as far as *Honoured Father*, and the ink dried on my quill while I tried to think of what I could say that would do no harm if someone opened the letter.

'*Father*' is not harmless.

Nor was anything else I could come up with.

I turned the parchment over, shaping the quill with an evilly sharp pen knife that I hadn't been able to resist in Alexandria's main market square, both for its Damascus steel and its beautiful walnut haft, and set about sketching the lines of the aqueduct that came into the palace here. Arches of yellow brick cast shadows across a square. People came and went around the statue of a griffin-like creature on a plinth. A white mongrel dog paused long enough to cock its leg.

The sun arriving overhead, I took Onorata back to our chambers and our own balcony, and set about drawing the great harbour, and the mass of streets going down from here to the massive walls.

It turned into a study of Zheng He's distant warship, but the size of it made the perspective look wrong.

I checked it as mathematically as Masaccio and Leon Battista had ever instructed me, found it correct, and wondered, *What do I do when reality itself seems incredible, even by an accurate description?*

Chin on fist, I stared down absently into the harbour, looking for another subject. I might draw Onorata, if Rekhmire' wasn't already making smart remarks about how many drawings of the child he's expected to make comment on . . .

I began a listless study of another ship moored between Europa and Asia. Dwarfed by comparison with Zheng He's it might be, but the lines interested me – not a war-ship, or a fat-bellied cargo-ship, or a dhow, but a fast light galley with canvas-shrouded arbalests on prow and stern for defence.

My quill-point scritched at the treated surface of the parchment; I made a reasonable attempt at the sterncastle and rudder before I startled, and the pen blotted a great spurt of ink over all.

I have drawn a ship like this before, and when I did – it was a Carthaginian bireme!

'Agatha and Jude!' It was safer to swear by Christian saints in this city, if you were a foreigner. I mopped at the ink with my sleeve, but the thin cotton only absorbed most of the liquid, leaving enough to shroud the carefully-drawn lines.

'That will be the envoy,' Rekhmire' said, an arm's length behind me.

I started again, jerked my wrist, and sent a hooked line of ink through the harbour wall. 'Caius Gaius *Judas*! Stop creeping up on me!'

The tall Egyptian grinned, entirely unrepentant, and bent to stroke a fingertip over Onorata's brow. She wriggled a little, and settled deeper into sleep. Rekhmire' looked up and to the side.

'Shadow will be off this balcony soon. You'll need to take her in.'

'*You* take her in,' I muttered. 'This is the Carthaginian envoy? The one you expected? Why's he here?'

'As far as I know, nothing but a previously-arranged diplomatic visit. Ty-ameny's ministers are running around like drunken piglets,' Rekhmire' observed, in response to my querying look. 'Now the jaws truly bite – Carthage's envoy will expect to see their latest gift on display in the Pharaoh-Queen's throne room. None of the Royal Mathematicians can yet promise it won't do to her as it did to Masaccio. She has a choice of offending Carthage – which we can't afford – *or* afford to have them find *that* out! – or else put herself in danger of murder by the golem.'

The ink had dried on my nib. I scratched it against my thumb, wishing for treated wooden boards on which I could use encaustic wax, or Masaccio's expensive pigments, and try out designs for Honorius's altar-panels.

'No.' I looked up, blinking. 'She doesn't.'

Rekhmire''s brows, stark under his shaved head, dipped down, casting all his face into severe lines.

'If we smash the golem's limbs, or chain it, or immobilise it safely in some way, that would be no less offensive to Carthage—'

I interrupted him before his rising tone could wake Onorata. It was difficult to keep my own voice sufficiently quiet.

'*No*. They don't have to break the damned thing to stop it hurting the Pharaoh-Queen. I know how we can do it. I *know*.'

Rekhmire''s sceptical look had hope badly suppressed under the surface. 'You know?'

I ignored his stress on the initial word.

'I know,' I said. 'Cheese glue.'

18

'Cheese glue?' the Pharaoh-Queen of Alexandria said.

'Cheese glue.'

'*Cheese* glue?'

One of the Royal Mathematicians muttered, 'Cheese *glue*?', in an equally bemused tone.

Rekhmire' smoothly intervened. 'Hear Ilario out, Great Name of Sekhmet; I think you should.'

Ty-ameny's sloe-black eyes darted to his face. Whatever she found there was sufficient to have her not throw me straight out of the Royal apartments.

'Explain,' she demanded grimly.

'Cheese glue's made with limestone and . . . cheese.'

I shuffled a little where I sat, hearing the words as they must sound to her.

'Yes, it *sounds* foolish, but I know this part of my trade! The best kind is cheese that's gone bad. Great Queen, when I was in Rome, Mastro Masaccio had me crumbling cheese and limestone and mixing the glue. You use it to size boards for painting, especially if your board has to be made up of several smaller pieces. When it sets . . . '

In memory I still hear Masaccio's hammer.

'I saw examples twice, in his workshop,' I said, seeing the Alexandrines perk up at the sound of empirical evidence. 'Once of a six-part panel put together before the plague came to Europa, that a man couldn't break with all his strength. The other was more subtle, I think – an older board, that had a funeral portrait on it from Hannibal Barca's time. The wax was gone, and the pigments too, and the wood broken in many places.'

I held finger and thumb a half-inch apart.

'But the glue that had held the wood together, *that* was still intact! Where the worms had eaten the wood all away, the cheese and lime glue stood up alone, rigid, like a framework.'

I took a breath, realising the frown on the Royal Mathematician Bakennefi Aa's face was calculation rather than scorn.

'When it ages, it yellows, but initially it sets clear. Like glass. You would not ever know it was there.' My mouth felt dry. I swallowed. Rekhmire' remained silent where he sat beside me.

Either he desires me to have all the credit for this – or all the blame!

Ty-ameny's frown was now of a different kind, I saw. She asked, 'How would this help us?'

She's willing to consider it!

'The golem's limbs are articulated.' The memory of stone fingers was one I pushed aside almost by habit now. 'Each of the arms, knees, fingers, feet – they're all jointed, by metal gears. If you were to pour prepared glue into the joint mechanisms and let it set . . . '

Ty-ameny blinked as if dazed.

'And no one could see this?' Her black gaze snapped into focus. 'At a distance, say, of – Ahhotep, over there, beside the window. If I am here, and he is there, will he see this has been done?'

I considered it, heart racing, not wanting to seem too sure of myself.

'No,' I said at last. 'Not even if he knew what he was looking for. The joints are brass, they shine. The extra coating will shine the same way.'

The room of advisers was silent for the space of ten heartbeats; Tyameny put her chin in her hand. She gazed unseeing at Rekhmire', silhouetted against the white afternoon heat.

My voice creaked and dropped down into the lower male registers. 'At the very worst, it would give you warning, when the joints move and the glue shatters. There would be time enough to move away. If the cheese glue's allowed time to cure and set – the golem will pull itself to pieces before those joints will move.'

'Bakennefi Aa.' Ty-ameny gave the Royal Mathematician and his cohorts a look that indicated they should – as rapidly as possible – search out sources in the Library. As the three Bakennefi brothers bowed and left, she turned back to me.

'You know how to mix this? The proportions of each; all the ingredients?'

That amount of implied responsibility cut off my breath. My heart pounded in palpable thuds. I swallowed, I hoped imperceptibly, and nodded.

'You mix a batch,' the Pharaoh-Queen said. 'My mathematicians will run tests. But, at the same time – the golem will be treated with your substance, too. Where it stands, beside the royal throne; undertake the treatment there.'

She shot a glance at Rekhmire'.

'Plausible ways can be found to delay the Carthaginian envoy's formal audience for a few more days?'

'He's a diplomat, Great Queen, he'll expect it.'

The corner of her mouth tweaked up, although she nodded solemnly enough. Her gaze switched back to me.

'*Cheese* glue!' she muttered.

19

The envoy of the King-Caliph Ammianus of Carthage was received with the proper amount of ceremony, Pharaoh-Queen Ty-amenhotep giving the impression – as I note Alexandrines like to do – that she condescended to pay respect to a member of a younger and more barbaric civilisation.

Rekhmire', shielding me from the view of the envoy's entourage, murmured, 'If he *does* anything in public, he's a fool.'

The great audience hall had space enough to hide me, veiled and therefore female, among Ty-ameny's advisers. I hoped that if the Carthaginian envoy had been briefed at all, he would be looking for Rekhmire''s scribe, or at best the painter's apprentice from Rome, and not the pregnant woman of Venice.

Apprehension made my mouth dry.

Onorata lay newly-fed and grumpy up in our apartments, with Ramiro Carrasco and the German brothers and a squad of Ty-ameny's Royal Guard in attendance. I didn't trust the Carthaginians not to attempt abduction of my baby. Nor, evidently, did the Pharaoh-Queen.

Brass horns blared.

The crowds at the doors shifted.

I guessed the envoy's party had begun their way up the Thousand Stairs to the Daughter of Ra's palace. In the white heat of afternoon. Surely a calculated insult?

'He may well think that,' Rekhmire' confirmed my suggestion. 'But he's from the Darkness. The sun in the middle of the day addles the brains of any local man fool enough to walk out in it. What it'll do to a man used to twilight, and used to being out in all the hours of the day . . . '

'Any advantage she can get?' I speculated.

The bald man's lip quirked. 'Regrettably the Pharaoh-Queen could not find time in her busy schedule until this hour.'

Constantinople is worse than Taraco at midday. I'd made the mistake of going out drawing in the day's heat once and only once. The lines of silver-point on the treated paper scrawled off into flicks and trailing half-circles; and I had had to be brought home by Carrasco, of all men, and put in a darkened room to be fed cool water in drips.

By the time Carrasco found me, I had rolled under the edge of a cart at the side of the market square's infinite hot expanse. The air shimmered, the heat hit like a hammer, and I had sought out the only tiny piece of visible shade.

Ramiro Carrasco pulled me out by one foot and smugly carried me back to the palace over his shoulder. It might have left him scarlet-faced and gasping, but he evidently thought the moral ascendancy worth it. I felt too grateful to even resent that. If I had been fool enough to take Onorata out with me, she would be dead.

Picturing the unknown envoy, I knew that he would be craving darkness, cool, shade; that his head will throb, and his eyes pain him.

The crowd parted as the horns blasted out a flat raw sound.

Men stood silhouetted against the white sky.

The Carthaginian party moved inside, almost with unseemly haste. Perhaps a dozen men, most of them wearing Carthaginian plate armour – I winced in sympathy for the soldiers – and two in long white robes. The envoy and an aide, I guessed.

They stood for a long moment in the entrance to the throne-hall, long enough for whispers to start.

The taller of the robed men put his hand up to his face.

I realised he was unknotting the length of white gauze cloth he wore tied about his head, over his eyes. His entourage also.

Of course: they're Carthaginians, they must *know* what countries outside the Penitence are like!

His hawk-bearded face uncovered, the taller man bowed to his shorter companion, and signalled to the guards. They walked between impassive lines of the Pharaoh-Queen's Royal Guard, ignoring the ceremonial sarissas that the men held.

The Carthaginian soldiers had empty scabbards at their sides. I guessed there were halberds left at the palace gatehouse, too. They walked as stiffly as men in plate armour in high heat do, and I caught two of them exchanging a word and a grimace, exactly as Honorius's men might have done.

'You stay here,' Rekhmire' murmured. 'I must be beside the Queen, but I want you out of danger.'

I thought him angry that the Pharaoh's ban on armed foreigners in the throne room should extend to Attila and Tottola. And that I had insisted on being present.

'Rekhmire', I'm not *in* danger—'

'I can't protect both of you!'

He did not speak loudly, but the intensity of it stopped me dead.

'If it comes to it,' I said, as steadily as I could, 'don't throw yourself between anybody and a sword. I don't want you to do that.'

Rekhmire''s mouth twisted. He gazed down at the short, stout staff with a silver handle, that he had substituted for his usual crutches. 'You need not worry. It's not likely I'll be able to move fast enough to put myself between Ty-ameny and harm—'

His whisper was grim and somewhat self-mocking; I interrupted it mercilessly. '*Unless* you're right next to her. Don't think I don't know why you want to be at her elbow.'

'I can't be at hers *and* yours.'

His expression was frighteningly raw for a usually composed man.

He looks torn in two, as if he would literally divide himself up to defend both of us – and sell his soul to be the man of quick movement that he was before his injury.

'I'll be safe enough,' I said, indicating my female dress.

He desires to keep me as safe as his Pharaoh-Queen, I realised. As for what that means—

I don't know if he values my knowledge and political usefulness – or if he's as fond of me as he plainly is of Ty-ameny of the Five Great Names, who he treats like a brat of a schoolgirl.

Aiding him the only way I could think of, I said, 'Where am I safest, for you?'

'This side of the throne.' His eyes narrowed at the hulking apparent statue beside the tiny figure of Ty-ameny. 'I don't trust that thing not to come for you, Ilario. Far more likely Carthage intends it for her, but how do we know it doesn't remember you?'

'It doesn't remember anything. It's stone.' I thought of it killing. Nothing with feelings could act that way without *some* emotion showing, if only satisfaction at an order obeyed. 'It's a set of orders, waiting to act on command.'

Rekhmire''s look had something I recognised, eventually, as respect. If he hadn't seen the golem act in Rome, he trusted what I'd observed. That is a responsibility, too.

His hand closed once on my shoulder, and he ambled off, deceptively relaxed, sliding into the group of advisers around Ty-ameny's imperial purple throne.

The Carthaginians would recognise his role, I thought, assuming any of them had been on diplomatic duty for more than a week. But the ability to deter an assassination is also valuable.

Unless they're sure an attack will succeed; so sure that it doesn't matter how many men Ty-ameny has around herself, or how well armed they are, because hands of stone can bat swords aside without a second thought, and stone can smash iron, bone, arm, skull—

'Welcome our visitors,' Ty-ameny said aloud, her voice muffled by the gold mask and braided false beard she wore. Her herald stepped forward, rapped his serpent-staff on the marble steps, and began a lengthy greeting to the lords of Carthage and the representatives of his sublime greatness the King-Caliph of that nation . . .

The herald stuttered a couple of times and looked annoyed with

491

himself. He wanted to be nothing but imperturbable duty, a role rather than a man, I guessed, and not seem as on edge and apprehensive as the rest of us were.

' . . . the Daughter of Sekhmet and the Regent of Ra graciously allows you to present yourself to her.' The herald bowed and stepped back.

The shorter of the two robed men stepped forward, as if they were engaged in a formal dance. Which I supposed, in fact, they were.

Out of respect, the man put back his hood. It left his sun-reddened face exposed to the courtiers, with the white strip of skin where he had covered his eyes with cloth.

His tight expression suggested him aware of the comic tone of his appearance.

The man's features, which would otherwise have been handsome, tugged at my awareness.

Rummaging in one sleeve, I pulled out a folded sheet of paper and a remnant of willow-twig charcoal. The palace laundry could be excused for complaining at me, I reflected, while I looked up and back, up and back, marking the values of the ambassador's face on the paper.

With the tones and shape broadly in place I studied the sketch, while the initial diplomatic niceties droned on. And dabbed at the charcoal, smoothing it to a paler grey where I had drawn his hair in its long single braid.

With pale hair, that suddenly seemed like the white of old age, the face of Hanno Anagastes stared off the paper at me.

Under the drawing, I scrawled, *Younger son of House of Hanno???*, beckoned a page, and sent the boy off with it to Rekhmire'. As I watched him thread his way through the press of bodies, the ambassador's pleasantly resonant baritone rang through the throne room.

'I have a question for the great Pharaoh-Queen. Why do you consort with that ship of demons?'

Ty-ameny must love her ceremonial mask, I thought. No change was visible in her small figure, sitting with her gold sandals neatly together on a footstool set on the throne's step. Without a view of her features, her body was impassive.

The Carthaginian diplomat stirred a little in the silence that followed his words.

Ty-ameny beckoned her herald and spoke briefly into his ear.

The herald straightened and fixed the ambassador with a bland look. 'The Divine Daughter of Ra says her Royal Mathematicians have not yet finished determining what the nature of the ship and its crew may be.'

'It's obvious what they are!'

It was obvious to *me* that the man seized on the excuse of working himself up. He threw off the hand the taller man rested on his arm – which I was willing to bet they'd cooked up between them, back on the Carthaginian bireme.

He wants to be able to shout at Ty-ameny.

My body was suddenly and instantly cold, knowing the reason why he might need to do that.

'Even followers of false gods must be able to recognise the presence of corruption in their midst—'

The Pharaoh-Queen's captain of the guard shifted his gaze, just barely, to catch her orders. She lifted one finger, where her hand lay on the arm of her throne. He stiffened, made no further move and issued no orders, but I saw his nostrils flare.

The pale skin of Rekhmire' caught my eye, in a chiaroscuro against the black robes of the palace guard. Idly, he clasped his hands behind him, leaning back on his stick, standing squarely between Ty-ameny's throne and the stone golem.

He rocked unevenly back and forth on heels and toes as if this were nothing more than another trade delegation, political approach, or other everyday order of government. The Carthaginian man of House Hanno shot him a glance.

He won't care if the golem goes straight through you to get to the Queen.

If I'm wrong, I thought. If this stupid, stupid idea doesn't work – oh, Judas, he does mean to kill her!

The ambassador's voice was rising to a peroration. Ty-ameny leaned one slender elbow on the arm of her throne, chin in hand, as if supremely bored. I obsessively repeated Masaccio's ingredients and method for glue; wondering if a week in the creating and curing could make anything with a tensile strength greater than a spiderweb.

I was on tiptoe, I found, and straining my eyes to stare at the golem. Not a quiver of movement.

The joints glistened in reflected light from the piazza outside, but that could be the polished brass and bronze gears. The finished glue had poured like liquid glass in Milano's factories; poured in and settled around every cog, every spring, every wheel, every plate, every part of the statue that moved.

And that it did move had been confirmed by Ty-amenhotep's orders to it, shouted from thirty yards off, so that it exposed all its limbs and joints to us to anoint.

Alexandrine Constantinople – or the life of Ty-ameny, at least – depends on the tensile strength of glue, once set.

I bit my lip until the sharp pain of bursting skin gave me the taste of blood.

'—consorting against even the tenets of the heretic Frankish church—'

Rekhmire' turned his head as the page tugged on his sleeve. I saw him read the note; his lips moved, saying something to the boy. He returned his gaze to the ambassador, not looking over towards me.

Too professional to seek me out. Too concerned that I may be a target. But I realised I would find it infinitely reassuring to meet his gaze.

'—and it is treachery! Conspiring with slant-eyed demons against the civilised world! Treachery in the highest degree, without even the excuse of necessity of – Saint – Gaius – Judas!'

He hit the saint's Carthaginian and Frankish names heavily, with a hammer's rhythm.

That's it! That's the trigger for the golem's orders—

The son of the House of Hanno stared, white showing all around his eyes.

A faint click sounded, below the discreet mutterings of the courtiers about the discourtesy of this diplomat, and speculations as to what Tyameny would do about him. The faintest possible abrasion of metal against metal.

The surface of the stone quivered. Once, twice. And—

Nothing.

Nothing more.

20

The Carthaginian envoy stared at the stone golem.

The stone golem stared sightlessly into the distance, as if the palace walls were transparent to it, and it could see all of the city, the sea, and the walls of Carthage that lay so many weeks of travel to the west.

It still did not move.

I frowned, squinting. Most of the crowd were looking at the ambassador or their Queen; I doubted more than half a dozen of us were looking at the golem.

Nothing.

Holding my breath made my mouth arid as the desert around Carthage, and dread made me feel as cold. Stare as I might, I could see no more vibration in the stone limbs and body.

They *meant* it to kill her!

Rage soared through me, bringing welcome heat. The golem's response, minimal as it was, spoke of all the danger that Carthage's gift would have brought here – a poisoned chalice that the Pharaoh-Queen could not diplomatically set aside; a trap that would have stood statue-like at her side, until the right words from an agent of Carthage sent it into convulsions of violence.

For a moment I could smell an illusion of the carnage that this hall would have suffered; see the pale bodies marked with blood, and Ty-ameny's limbs and head pulled from her body in grotesque parody of a child pulling apart an insect.

'We are pleased to accept the new envoy of Carthage, Hanno Gaiseric.' Ty-ameny spoke up, her tone with something savagely restrained under it. 'And if the King-Caliph will accept a poor gift in recompense for this gift of his—'

Here she gestured at the motionless stone golem.

'—then I have drawings, documents, and divers other things concerning the foreign demons of Chin, which the King-Caliph's scientist-magi may find of interest.'

Hanno Gaiseric tore his gaze away from the golem with evident difficulty.

'The King-Caliph accepts with—' The word seemed to choke him: '—gratitude.'

Forty-eight hours later, Hanno Gaiseric went aboard the bireme and unexpectedly left the grand harbour; Ty-ameny's spies reported the ship heading unerringly and unstoppably back towards Carthage.

An hour after *that*, the Pharaoh-Queen announced Carthage's gift so valuable that it must be installed in the Royal Library. And Rekhmire' came back up to our quarters dusting his hands together, having lent a hand at mortaring the stone blocks and iron bars that irrevocably closed up one of the Library's lowest storage chambers, now buried well below ground-level.

'"Safe".' Ty-ameny shook her head, her unbound hair rippling over her bare shoulders. 'Yes. Yes, but – Carthage desired us to know we cannot engineer what they can. Very well, we have been lessoned . . . '

Even in her private chambers, wearing only a linen wrap in the afternoon heat, she kept the presence of the Pharaoh-Queen. Hanno Gaiseric's attempt at murder seemed only to have energised her. She smiled ferociously at Rekhmire'.

'I think, therefore, it's time to issue a lesson of our own.'

As ever in a court, it may have seemed that we were alone, but as soon as Ty-ameny lifted her hand, slaves and servants came with wine, ivory cups, small crisp biscuits, and a number of leather map-cases. A shaven-headed slave ordered the placing of a low table in the room's sunken-floor area, spread the maps with his own hands, and bowed to his queen as he left.

Each chart was bordered at top and bottom with brass, to keep them from rolling back up; I found myself wondering if there was a use for that in drawing.

Had I been able to pick them up to investigate, I would; in fact, my hands were occupied in sliding under Onorata to check she was still dry. The palace's smallest tyrant having decided she would spend any part of the day out of my company in screaming, I had no option but to bring her with me, and sit as much out of the way as possible.

'Here.' Ty-ameny put her finger on a point on the larger map, glancing at Rekhmire', and then to me.

She beckoned me forward. 'Let me hold the child.'

Reluctantly I got up and moved forward. 'If she wakes, she'll scream, Great Name . . . '

'She won't.'

The Pharaoh-Queen held out her hands, confident enough, I thought. *Of course, I am a fool: she has had three daughters.*

I passed Onorata into the wiry, muscular arms, and watched Ty-ameny smile down at her. The venal thought of a monarch as god-parent to my child came into my mind. But courts are cut-throat: Onorata will be better out of them . . .

'There.' Ty-ameny pointed with her chin. Rekhmire' spread out the largest map.

The Middle Sea, I saw. Or a version of it. The headland on the African coast could only be Carthage, given how close it was to Malta – the furthest edge of the Penitence – and Sardinia and the Italies.

Rekhmire' lifted his head where he sat. After a moment, I realised I was hearing, with him, the creak of slave-wielded fans, loud in the silence. He looked questioningly at the Pharaoh-Queen. Ty-ameny gestured them away.

There have been kings who would merely kill their slaves after, in case they had overheard what they should not.

The last slave left. Heat grew in the palace room, despite the open windows. I could still taste, in the back of my throat, the smell of dead meat. Ty-ameny clucked at my child, and I seated myself beside Rekhmire'.

I thought, not for the first time, *If I had been bought by any other man* . . .

As King Rodrigo's Freak, I was always spared the worst excesses of being owned. My time as Rekhmire''s slave has been far more like Constantinople's bureaucratic model than how life is outside of the courts of power. Compared to Ty-ameny's palace slaves, I have barely been in slavery; compared to the world outside Alexandria – labour, prostitution, either way worked to death – I have been closest to free. I watched the Queen stroke Onorata's bare ankle.

My daughter will never be a slave, no matter what.

'There,' Ty-ameny said, her voice low and even.

Rekhmire', as if his hands were hers, indicated cities on the North African coast, and ports at Sicily, Crete, and Rhodes.

'We'll issue a warning,' she said. 'The golem-*machina* is their opening shot. House Barbas has put this weapon into the King-Caliph's hand . . . I am told.'

She gave a sudden smile, looking from under her kohl-blackened lashes at Rekhmire'. He returned his 'only a book-buyer' expression of innocence. I bit the inside of my lip so as not to laugh aloud. With an inexplicable lift of the heart, I thought, *They are closer to brother and sister than cousins.*

'That being so,' she continued, rocking Onorata gently, 'King-Caliph Ammianus will continue to test us. Rekhmire', how many golem have they?'

'As much as I can now tell, no more than a dozen, we think. Ammianus keeps most, but his chief allies among the Lords-Amir have been given them as gifts.'

Hanno Anagastes, I thought.

I saw tears in his eyes when I gave him the funeral portrait of Hanno Tesha, although I'd had to put the lustrous brown eyes and sleek dark hair of cliché, since that was the only description of the child he could give me. Would he be capable of ordering a golem like the one in his house to kill men as Masaccio was killed?

Given what men do in war, yes. No question.

Rekhmire' leaned back, his fingers absently kneading at the muscles above his knee though the linen kilt. 'It's possible the King-Caliph will gift one to the Turkish Sultan. And to at least one of the Frankish Kings. As far as we know, we're first outside the Bursa-hill itself.'

'A warning.' The Pharaoh-Queen repeated it stubbornly. She darted a glance at me, keen and black, jolting me with the intensity of her attention. 'And here, I think, is where our business intersects.'

'Aldro.' I waited as respectfully as I might, for impatience.

Ty-ameny spoke while she watched my sleeping child. 'Rekhmire' has brought me knowledge of how Taraconensis appears to be unstable, and how your stepfather may be a solution to that.'

There is nothing she has not been told.

But I expected that.

'You have your own reasons for wishing to see Lord Videric in his place at court again.' The gleam in Ty-ameny's black eyes was in part serious, in part amused, and wholly elated. 'Chief among which, I imagine, is not continually anticipating murder.'

I answered the question she had carefully not asked.

'When I trusted Aldro Videric – when I thought he was my father, and a good man – I also thought he was King Rodrigo Sanguerra's necessary right hand. He's still that. Without being a good man.'

I caught a scowl on Rekhmire''s face, briefly wondered if I had spoken amiss, and found the Pharaoh-Queen nodding with approval.

'I had counted on forty years,' she observed, 'and, if I must, will settle for twenty.'

Before Alexandrine Constantinople falls.

It hit me like a falling boulder: in twenty years, my daughter could be twenty. A woman. Those identical baby-features, that have only a suggestion of her grandfather and I in the bones behind the skin, and the colour of her hair, will give way to a face uniquely hers, a mind uniquely hers.

Cold down my spine under the linen tunic, despite the heat of the room, I said, 'I grew up during peace – it guarantees nothing. But I know what war guarantees.'

Ty-ameny pressed her lips together, nodding. She looked like a girl cuddling a small sister.

She sat up, both her arms cradling Onorata, and the change was as sudden and different as the crack of lightning falling from heaven to earth.

'The King-Caliph Ammianus sees fit to send me a warning.' Ty-ameny's eyes glinted. 'It is my intention now to send a warning back!'

She lifted her arms, and I automatically stood and came to take

Onorata from her. The Queen of Constantinople knelt down by the map-table, like a beggar-child playing at marbles in the street. I moved to watch over her shoulder.

A little frown making a fold of skin between her brows, Ty-ameny said, 'The Admiral Zheng He and I are debating an agreement. I will loan him a pilot, and charts, to help him regain the ocean sea, and find his fleet, if they're not sunk. My captains suggest it will have been a storm around the West African islands; those are dangerous waters.'

The thought of more war-junks, no matter how few more there might be, made me shudder. Jian thought nothing of his crew numbering five thousand Chin men, as I knew from speaking to him. There are armies in the Frankish lands made up of fewer men than that. If they should decide to conquer a kingdom and stay here . . .

A little too intuitively for my liking, Ty-ameny remarked, 'I think the Admiral truly anxious to get back to his Emperor – this is not the first voyage they've made to foreign waters, and they've found only "barbarians" wherever they sail. Zheng He's words.'

The little smile curved her lip.

'We rank as civilised, having a proper eunuch bureaucracy. Although he cares very little for having a woman and a heathen on the throne. However,' she added briskly, 'he will agree to visit the port of Carthage, on his voyage back to the ocean sea.'

'Carthage?'

She gestured irritably for me to sit down, a moment before I realised that she had no desire to crick her neck looking up. I set Onorata cautiously into her sling around my neck (for which she was almost too large, now) and sat beside Rekhmire'.

'Zheng He will replenish his ship at Carthage,' Ty-ameny said. 'And while there, he will let it be thought that Alexandria has himself and his ship as an ally.'

Rekhmire' smiled: I supposed at my expression.

'For this, the Queen is prepared to lend her best pilot,' he observed cheerfully. 'And Carthage is not to know a pilot is guiding the Admiral *out* of the Middle Sea. For all the King-Caliph knows, the war-junk will be roaming the sea on our behalf indefinitely.'

He exchanged a smile with Ty-ameny.

'A theoretical Zheng He may be a great deal more useful as an ally than a material one, given that he can never change his mind and seek other alliances!'

The Pharaoh-Queen lifted her bare shoulders in a shrug, tracing routes on the blue- and gold-inked map. 'I understand from Admiral Zheng He that his country has contact along the Silk Road with the Rus, the Turk, and the Persians; Carthage is not an important ally for them. He's willing to show himself under our banner.'

She sat back on her heels, glossy hair sliding away to show her face.

'And then there is your home, Ilario.'

Head tight with effort, I strained to keep up with her thought. 'Aldro, you think Zheng He should sail to Taraconensis?'

Her thin finger traced a course. 'Taraconensis, before Carthage. I see it thus: it is imperative Carthage has no excuse to send legions into Taraconensis this year. War will begin if that happens, and it will draw all of us in. As the Franks cannot be allowed to think they can invade your northern frontier, so Carthage cannot be allowed to provoke them into an invasion, by putting a Carthaginian Governor into Taraco.'

Her words were only my thoughts spoken aloud, and no more than a natural consequence of the discussion with Rekhmire' – but I felt it all suddenly made more real.

Onorata stirred in her sling; I tried by force of will to quiet my pounding heartbeat.

'Will the Admiral agree to this, Aldro?'

'He sees the desirability of having an Alexandrine pilot.' Her grin was almost brutal. 'And he understands the necessity for trade. There must be some degree of trust – there's little to prevent him from kidnapping my pilot and attempting to leave the Middle Sea on his own. But I think he desires to leave a good name with us, as a civilised man in a world of barbarians.'

Worlds have turned on stranger things. I felt myself dizzy, not only from the humid heat.

Ty-ameny made fists of her hands, like bunches of knucklebones, and stretched; breaking the position to reach out and touch Rekhmire''s arm.

'Admiral Zheng He will also be carrying a humble book-buyer, along with my pilot – which, naturally, will have nothing to do with what impression the Carthaginians gain of relations between Alexandria and Chin.'

Naturally not. I would have answered in the same manner, but I couldn't speak.

'If you agree,' Ty-ameny concluded, looking at me, 'you will go to Taraco with them.'

The unexpected constriction in my throat kept me silent for an embarrassing minute.

I managed, finally, to croak, 'My family owes you a debt.'

Ty-ameny rose in one graceful movement, not putting her hand to the floor. 'Pay me by doing what you would in any case do – have your King Rodrigo Sanguerra summon Pirro Videric back as his first minister.'

The small woman looked at me, and at Rekhmire', in turn.

'This *must* happen. By any means possible.'

Part Five
Herm and Jethou

1

"'*Cào nî zûxian shi bâ dai*.'" I pronounced the sounds as closely to Jian's as I could manage, ignoring the plainly undisguised amusement on his face. Tracing ink deftly onto my paper, I continued in the haphazard mixture of bad North African Latin which Zheng He's crew appeared to have picked up on the West African coast, and scattered words from Alexandrine Egyptian. 'And this means . . . '

"'I am honoured beyond measure to meet you.'"

The small boat rocked, despite a calm that had been absolute enough to becalm the war-junk. I slitted my eyes against morning sunlight and the ship laying a hundred paces off. Easier to trace the marks Jian had made for me to copy.

A dozen or more ink studies lay discarded on the thwarts of the dinghy, careless of sea-water; each a less successful attempt to capture the war-junk with her immensely tall thin sails spread to catch every fraction of breeze.

So far, she did not travel so fast that Commander Jian's men couldn't row us back to her. In fact I thought she might not be moving at all.

'*Cào nî zûxian shi bâ dai* . . . ' I thought I heard a noise from one or other of the Chin men on the rowers' benches, but my suspicions were centred on Jian's far too innocent expression.

Twenty days have given me insight enough into him to read at least the broader emotions. And this game is called 'get the foreign devil into amusing trouble'.

"'Honoured to meet you,'" I mused, and looked at him brightly. 'So this is what I should say to the Admiral when we get back on board? Then I can ask him to reward *you* for teaching me so well.'

Jian's square frame went utterly still for a heartbeat.

He lifted his hand, slapped it down on his thigh, and burst into high-pitched laughter.

Out of the corner of my eye, I caught the rowers slapping each other on the back and wiping their eyes, which I thought was just as well; they showed every sign of rupturing themselves if they'd had to keep quiet much longer.

I smiled at Jian with deliberate innocence, and traced the lines that made up the drawn picture-words of Chin. 'So what does this mean?'

The Chin officer spluttered, waving his hand in plain refusal.

I brandished the paper. 'If I show this around the ship, someone will tell me . . . '

Jian was in the habit of treating me as a court eunuch, but I knew the man smart enough to know it not entirely true. *Yin yang ren!* got whispered sometimes when I passed: an impolite version of 'hermaphrodite'.

I watched Jian tripping himself up on what might be expected behaviour towards a man, or towards a woman, and let him squirm for a minute or two before copying him with a thigh-slap and a laugh.

The noise from our boat would frighten sea-birds away for miles, I thought. When every man aboard found himself permitted to laugh – and for once to laugh at his commanding officer – it was loud.

Jian solved his disciplinary problem by pointing to the youngest of the rowers, and firing off a rapid rattle of words that I knew must translate as '*You* tell her!'

If he'd been Iberian, the boy would have been blushing; he ducked his head and rattled off apologies non-stop.

'Is it rude?' I asked helpfully.

'Yes, Lord Barbarian!'

Ruder than 'barbarian'? I wondered. But none of them seem to think that word is anything more than purely descriptive.

'Is it *very* rude?'

The rest of the crew assured me, over the boy's squirming, that it was extremely rude, not meant for any man except the vilest of enemies, and that the great Lord Admiral would flay my skin off and tan it for a rug if I used it towards him, barbarian ignorance notwithstanding. I'd seen enough casual brutality aboard to not be completely convinced he was joking.

Jian seized my paper, and – with the tip of his tongue sticking out of the corner of his mouth – drew three or four lines that, as I stared hard, resolved themselves into an image. This—

I turned the page a quarter round, attempting to make out what I was seeing. 'Are they doing what I think they're doing?'

'Is rude. It means—' Jian's hand gesture was fairly universal.

'"Fuck"?' I prompted, in several of the languages they might have heard in Constantinople's harbour, and there was an outbreak of nodding and applause.

'Means, "fuck eighteen generations of your ancestors",' Jian exclaimed, and gave me a smile that made a square and ugly face beautiful. 'Not to say to the Admiral, no!'

I smiled and agreed that no, that probably wasn't wise, and the joke was repeated backwards and forwards in the boat until I got them to row me further south simply to put an end to it.

They shipped oars, having turned us into what would have been the direction of the wind, had it not been dead calm. Jian gave an order, which was evidently to stand down. I smoothed a fresh sheet of paper on my drawing board, set it firmly on my knees, and went back to attempting to draw the war-junk well enough that I could paint her at some time in the future. Who could miss the chance to see this ship, from a distance, with nothing else around her?

And somewhere on the ship, I thought, narrowing my eyes against the sunlight off the waves, Rekhmire' is negotiating exactly how long Zheng He will anchor off the shore of Taraco.

Because we can't tell how long it will take to solve this – and I can't blame Zheng He that he wants to be gone. Our wars aren't his concern; he comes from too far away.

And every man I spoke to seemed to take their 'lost fleet' for granted . . .

The wide-bottomed boat rocked. Jian's men ran up a slatted small sail without being ordered, steadying us where we stood, forty leagues out of sight of the North African coast.

There might be enough of a breeze to move our small boat; the war-junk, I saw – even with tier upon tier of slatted sails raised up on its seven main masts, and three smaller masts – remained stationary.

Commander Jian leaned over my shoulder, just as the shift of the boat sent my chalk skidding across the paper. 'That's not very good.'

'*Cào nî zûxian shi bâ dai!*'

Even as it came out of my mouth, I was appalled. He'll truly take offence—

Jian burst into deep, choking laughter.

His crew decided it was worth applause, too; banging their fists on the gunnels. I suspected they had not expected their commander to be told that. Or not by any man who'd get to keep his head afterwards.

'Perhaps I'm not a very good artist,' I said apologetically, and had the idea then of offering Jian paper and chalk of his own.

We passed an hour or two exchanging what we could of technique, hampered by lack of language. Jian's war-junk was mostly a matter of lines, but it was recognisably a war-junk; the fact that he put in islands we had passed above and below the ship, so that he seemed to be drawing everything on one long ribbon, I couldn't talk him out of. Pulling a small version of Leon Battista's perspective frame out of the snapsack, I attempted to show him how it related to what I was drawing on my paper – but I think neither of us understood my explanation.

With the sun descending into my eyes, I settled for adding in a quick sketch of a European cog to give me the scale of the war-junk. There was not, in truth, so much difference between the high poop of a Frankish ship and the curves of the junk's flat stern.

Only in sheer size.

As for how many ship-lengths the war-junk was long . . .

'If it's an inch less than four hundred feet, I'll boil my sandals and eat them!'

Jian looked bemused at my mutter. I was saved from explanation. A faint whooshing noise and a *pop!* was succeeded by a light falling down the sky – one of Zheng He's signal rockets, barely bright enough to show in daylight, but clear enough that Jian gave a grunting sigh and ordered his rowers to their oars.

I had seen much larger rockets in the war-junk's hold. I guessed them launched from some of the arbalest-like machines and tubes on the foredecks. How effective they might be in a sea battle, Ty-ameny's pilot Sebekhotep said he could have no professional opinion on.

But I saw he took note of them all the same.

Jian's crew brought the boat towards what seemed a vast wooden wall, when we got up close, rather than the side of a sea-going ship. I spent time in several languages making it known that if a stupid barbarian used insulting words, it would only be out of ignorance, and no reflection on the officer in question. Jian finally gave me a slap on the shoulder and a sip at his flask of tepid sour wine, taught me the proper pronunciation of 'foreign devil' in his own language, and I thought matters settled reasonably well. It helped that he could be amused by my attempts to scale the ladder to the entry-port of the war-junk.

The scent of salt and deep water faded, replaced by the spices and sandalwood of the junk, always underlying its permanent odour of sweat and cooking. I swung myself inboard.

A hand caught my elbow, steadying me enough that I didn't drop the leather sack of drawings.

Rekhmire', I found; looking up into his sun-flushed face. He glared down with unexpected disapproval.

I thought it best to ask plain and direct. 'What's the matter?'

The Egyptian snorted, with a sour look at the boat on its davits. 'I saw you scrambling down into that, earlier . . . '

Between the steps on the hull's slope, and a rope and wood ladder, 'scramble' is not an inappropriate term, both down and back up.

Rekhmire''s sun-darkened finger indicated the main one of the seven masts, and the platform high in the cross-trees. 'And you've climbed up there.'

The crow's-nest made me dizzy in a more than physical sense.

Gripping hard enough that my nails dug into the wood, I had found myself surrounded at dawn by a vast and chilly circle of sea, green as Venetian glass, with the sun laying stripes across the waves of a crimson so startling I would not have dared to paint it so. The sea turned innocent milky-blue as the sun rose, and I had heard the lookout's cry of a sail, and squinted into the light at the horizon.

The sails of a dhow appeared, blistering white, but not the ship itself –

I saw the tops of the lateen sails first, and then the mid parts, and only as it advanced to us up the slope of the world did the hull become visible.

It was that knowledge that we stand all the time at the crest of an invisible hill that dizzied me. I welcomed the return to the deck, and the illusion that the world is flat.

'Yes.' I drew a sharp, deep breath. 'I have. And?'

'Are you *trying* to leave your child an orphan!'

Silenced thoroughly, it was a moment before I could gather enough wit to say, 'Her grandfather Honorius would care for her, likely better than I could – and she would at least grow up without being watched to see if she turns into a monster!'

Rekhmire''s complexion darkened and reddened. He turned his back on me, knuckles white, swinging his crutch to shift himself down the deck towards the stern cabins.

I am a fool.

Sails towered above me as I ran to catch him up on the tar-spotted deck. Sails themselves taller than palace walls, creaking and swaying, but picking up no breeze. I scrambled after his unexpectedly brisk passage, past mast after mast, slatted shadows falling across the wood underfoot. The deck was hot despite my sandals.

'Rekhmire' – I know you'd climb if you could: you don't desire me to stop because of that?'

He glared at me. 'Of course not.'

Make that 'tactless fool'.

Heat-melted tar dropped from the rigging in hot black roundels. Rekhmire' strode on down the deck without being touched. I dodged one – only to catch another, streaking down the front of my linen tunic with a sharp sting.

Grins came at me from crewmen hauling on ropes or descending from the three main crow's-nests. I did not need to translate their remarks as I followed Rekhmire' into the welcome shade of the cabin.

'I'm sorry!' I blurted.

'"Stupid barbarian"!' Rekhmire' shot a smile over his shoulder, lifted one pointing finger to indicate the crew outside, and assumed an innocence as of one merely translating the words of others.

I stripped the tar-marked tunic off. Grinning in relief, I muttered, 'Fuck eighteen generations of your ancestors, book-buyer!'

I was careful enough to practise my Chin out of earshot of the crew, however much the tar stung.

'I *am* sorry,' I added. 'Where are we? Other than becalmed in Hell?'

Rekhmire' gave me an amused look. 'What have you got against the last eighteen generations of my ancestors in particular? And, becalmed in the Gulf of Sirte, Sebekhotep tells me.'

Passing into the first of the airy and spacious inner cabins we had been allocated – and certainly I had never known of such a thing on a

European ship of any kind – I threw myself flat on the low bed, letting the snapsack fall where it might, and rubbed at the reddened mark the tar left. 'You're not joking, are you? You do know the last eighteen generations of your family!'

'I share my ancestors with Queen Ty-ameny. That helps.' The large Egyptian smiled a little. 'I can trace my ancestors back to the first Cleopatra.'

'I can trace mine back to my father . . . '

He held his hand out: I realised it held an impossibly translucent porcelain cup. I beamed, took it, and drank. The herbal drink was bearable, cold, in this hot weather.

Trace my ancestry back to my father – and to my mother.

My smile died, the thought of Rosamunda still enough to make me cold in my belly.

A further door opened and shut, and cut off the sound of a crying baby.

'Carrasco . . . ' I lifted my head. 'How long?'

He shrugged. 'Not very long.'

I scrambled up, moving through the open door into the next room, and dropped into a crouch by Onorata's cradle. Fed an hour ago, not wet – I checked – and Carrasco had evidently been sitting by the fan that cooled her. I straightened up.

'She's bored,' I guessed. 'Take her to see the goats again.'

We travelled accompanied by two nanny-goats from the *Sekhmet*, their offspring, and a sire, in case we should need more. Onorata appeared to thrive on the warm fresh milk that I fed her, along with Carrasco's gruel. She was, I thought, passably fond of the goats, or at least she pushed herself up on her front with her round arms when I laid her in the straw, and laughed in what sounded like delight, staring at Carrasco or I milking them.

I went back through, to search out a clean tunic, and found Carrasco with his head down and shoulders hunched, as if he could avoid Rekhmire' looking at him. The book-buyer had sat on the wide ledge of the cabin window.

'Carrasco—' I pulled the new tunic on, and realised only in retrospect that I had not been in the least self-conscious exposing my small breasts.

I coloured, despite them now being covered.

'When you were spying,' I said bluntly. 'Did you send word back telling Videric—' *Rosamunda!* '—about being a grandparent?'

'That you were with child, yes.'

He did not say, *After she was born, I was in jail,* but I could read it in the flush that reddened his neck.

Rekhmire' swallowed his own cup of liquid, and spoke as if Carrasco did not exist. 'I've been looking at charts with Sebekhotep.'

Sebekhotep, with the face of a Pharaoh, a lean and wolfish body, and an appetite that could feed four men, had served on Queen Ty-ameny's naval fire-ships as well as commercial cargo ships; I suspected he might not actually need the many portolans and charts he'd come aboard with, to find his way around the Middle Sea. But he behaved as if he did, and I might have, in his place – too spectacularly good a navigator, and Zheng He might just decide he needed to keep this particular barbarian.

I accepted the change of subject. 'How long to Taraco?'

'Once we get a wind? A few days.' Rekhmire' frowned. 'We need to have our plans definitely made . . . '

The deck barely moved beneath me, although I heard the constant creak and slow shift of a becalmed vessel. Above the stern, on the deck that was our roof, I heard one of the bosuns yelling the omnipresent '*Mâshàng!*', 'Jump to it!', and a thunder of hurrying feet.

Onorata's yelling shifted up to an irritated scream.

'Take her along to the animal pens,' I directed Carrasco.

He ducked his head in an awkward gesture of respect. I watched him go in and pick her up from the cradle, together with the sail-awning we habitually tied up to shade her. Tottola and Attila sat visible in the far corner, playing at dice. For all the unlikelihood of an attack here, the brothers still slept watch and watch about, except for an hour or so of overlap.

Attila pocketed a string of the odd bronze coins, pierced through with a square hole, that the Chin men used as gambling chips, and stood to buckle on his sword. Approaching Carrasco's shoulder, Attila ignored the man, but hummed in a low bass at my daughter where she stared at him.

A lullaby, I realised after a moment. I couldn't help but smile.

Rekhmire''s gaze followed mine. 'Ah. They're fond of the little one . . . Of course, *they* don't have to wake to feed her three hours before dawn.'

If his expression seemed neutral, I could hear amusement in his voice.

'Remind me never to hire an Alexandrine nurse,' I remarked. 'The Iberians are much superior . . . '

Rekhmire' huffled a suppressed laugh.

Except that *I* can hire nobody.

If not for my father, I would be trying to keep the child on what I could earn as a painter: that thought still wakes me up in the long hours before dawn, in a cold sweat.

Breeding itself out of selfishness, I thought.

Because not only are there sufficient painters of funeral portraits and chapel frescoes in this world that I would be hard put to keep us – it would also mean I must work at that hard enough that I would never have a chance to stop, and learn to improve.

If I had a true mother's instinct, I would not at times hate my child.

Surprisingly enough, the only relief from that fear had come in Alexandria, when in a fit of sleepless volubility I voiced it to Ty-ameny.

'Great Sekhmet's claws!' She had shown her white teeth in a grin. 'I hated all of my three! Asenath wouldn't feed; Esemkhebe wouldn't stop, and Peshet was always bawling her head off for me when I needed urgently to sit in council. And then my breasts would leak milk all through the diplomatic meetings.'

Ty-ameny had shaken her head.

'Some mothers only like infants. Perhaps that's why they have more. I didn't *begin* to love mine until they were old enough to move about and talk.'

It made me feel a little less guilty.

I felt a touch on my arm, and returned to myself to find Rekhmire' frowning slightly.

'I had meant to broach this before,' he remarked, apparently idly. 'As an assistant to one of the Royal Library's buyers, you're entitled to a finder's fee, and a small remittance when your work is otherwise satisfactory.'

He indicated other drawings spilling across the low bed. The war-junk, from every angle that I could contrive; including the upper crow's-nests.

'You intend these as studies for a painting, but I doubt you ignorant of the fact that copies will be well-received by Ty-ameny and her philosophers.'

The philosophers having taken thorough advantage of my presence before we left Alexandria, I thought I could speak reasonably well as to their infinite curiosity.

I forced a smile. 'If I copy scrolls you want, yes; pay me a fee. You can have copies of these drawings in any case. It's not like I'm Ty-ameny's cousin . . . '

'Do you despise spies so much then?'

It came as a lightly-voiced question, Rekhmire''s gaze not on me, but directed at Carrasco and Attila's preparations in the far cabin, and Tottola's quiet amusement at the sheer number of things they took with them. The Egyptian spoke as if the answer would mean nothing of any significance.

I said, 'You were born to it. Alexandria's your home. It's not *my* country.'

He seemed unsatisfied.

I got up to hold the main door open, while Carrasco and baby and parasol and escort left the cabins. Not that I mistrust Attila or Tottola, but I knew how little Rekhmire' cared to discuss any business in front of Ramiro Carrasco.

The cabin's floor had been padded in places with some cloth very like a tapestry; it was soft under my feet when I kicked my sandals off. Padding back towards Rekhmire', I observed, 'You want to know if I despise you, for being a spy.'

The Egyptian rapidly smoothed down the folds of his linen kilt. That action was automatic by now: it hid his scars.

Apparently studying the ink-scroll hanging down from one ceiling-beam, he remarked, 'That would be one of the reasons I have never forced you to see what my business is.'

'*Chun zi!*'

His eyebrows climbed up towards his shaven scalp. 'And that would mean?'

'"Moron"!'

'Fascinating.' He took his tablets out of the bag at his belt, and incised a quick note in the wax. If he had been another man, I would have said he was suppressing a grin. 'Why is it you can be impolite in thirteen languages, painter?'

'Probably the people I travel around with, book-buyer!'

The Egyptian snorted.

'Of course,' I added, 'I may not be saying it right. My ear still isn't adjusted to Chin voices.'

'Perhaps,' Rekhmire' agreed. 'But the tone was unmistakable – at least to a foreign barbarian . . . '

He glanced away from me, at the dark wooden beams, and the intricately inlaid chests we had been loaned for our belongings. If he was pleased not to be despised, he was also embarrassed, although it would have been necessary to know him well to be aware of that.

'Listen—' He held up his hand.

For a long moment I heard nothing, only the natural creaking and shifting of a ship, even one this size.

Creaking in rhythm.

I shot to the cabin door and looked up.

Against the hazy sky, all of the sails were belling out, one by one, to catch the wind.

2

On the morning that we passed the Balearic Islands, Onorata taught herself to roll.

I had her on the floor-tapestry that the Chin-men used instead of fur rugs, laying on my belly so I might look her in the eye. She went from staring vaguely in the direction of the ceiling to thrusting with one still-small arm at the floor, and was abruptly over on her front.

We surveyed each other in equal surprise.

She broke out into a crow of laughter.

'Clever!' I wondered if she had wit enough yet to imitate, and if she copied the position of her mother-father. I sat up, thinking to encourage her to roll back the other way.

A fist rapped against the slatted wooden door, the knocking done in a Frankish fashion.

'In!'

A dark-haired figure slunk in from the deck: Ramiro Carrasco de Luis. He shot a wary look over at Tottola, apparently asleep in one corner with his arms and ankles crossed.

'May I speak to you, madonna? Mistress?'

Three months of seeing me in skirts in Venice evidently established me as a woman so firmly in his mind I will not shift it.

I sighed, and reached over to nudge Tottola's boot.

The large man's eyes were already open.

'Will you take her for a while?' I nodded towards the inner room. 'I won't be long. It's probably those *chou ba guai* goats again!'

Tottola's dark expression changed to a grin at that. He scooped an indignant Onorata up and made for the door.

Clearly he thinks Ramiro Carrasco will one day try again to assassinate me.

Well, I was hardly joking when I told Carrasco that, as a slave, I would take care to be trusted for a long time before I killed my master. And then the judges might blame someone else.

The German man-at-arms snorted, ducking under the door lintel to the inner room. Ramiro Carrasco kept quiet, in a manner that told me, if he wasn't yet used to being a slave, he had some idea of what behaviour was expected of him.

I stood, tugging my tunic straight, picking up my leather sack. The tiny inlaid drawers of the Chin furniture ideally suit painting tools. Remembering to clean and put them away is essential, however, and my hellion child had distracted me.

'You can get me a bucket of hot water when you're done . . . '

Ramiro Carrasco stood awkwardly in the middle of the cabin; a life study would show tension in his shoulders and spine.

'What?' I demanded.

'I need to talk to you.' He glanced at the door to the back cabin, that stood ajar, not by accident. I saw him take a breath, expanding his sternum; he scowled to himself.

His feet were bare, dirty, and callused, now. He wore a bleached and dirty tunic, pulled down over a Frankish shirt that hung to his mid-thigh, and his hose were rolled down to his knees in the heat. I saw his sleek black hair had grown down to touch his ears, and was no longer sleek, but breaking out into curled ends. Someone must have given him orders to shave: dark stubble patched his jaw.

His hand came up, fingers hooking under the smooth iron of his collar. In the clear light from the cabin window it was possible to read *::I am owned by Ilario::* engraved in Venetian script.

'Ramiro?'

'I have to . . . ' His head came up.

For a stark heartbeat I wondered, *Should I call Honorius's men?*

Ramiro Carrasco bent down, awkwardly, on one knee and then the next, until he was kneeling in front of me.

'Get up!' I must sound shrill, I realised.

'*Please.*' The Iberian hunched into himself. His face showed a shining pink where the stubble did not grow. His fingers locked into each other. 'Please, I'm begging you – slaves beg, don't they? Please. Ilario - mistress—'

I shot a glance at the inner door; Tottola was not visible. He would be alertly listening. Judging whether to guard Onorata or myself first.

Flushing as red as Carrasco, fully as embarrassed, I hissed, 'Stand up! *What* is this about?'

His head lifted.

I saw a vestige of Ramiro Carrasco de Luis in Venice in the jut of his jaw. His hands shook where he clenched them together. All of his body where he knelt down on the war-junk's deck had a faint shiver to it.

I grabbed him by the shoulders of his tunic and hauled, not caring that I heard fabric tear. All but throwing him up off the deck and onto his feet, I spat out, 'You don't kneel to me!'

He stared wildly.

Too used to thinking of 'Ilaria', with a woman's strength.

I stepped forward and he automatically stepped back, stopping only as his spine came into hard contact with the ship's hull beside the outer door.

He blurted out, 'You have to kill me!'

'*What?*'

Attila's voice sounded from the deck outside. 'Need any help?'

I stretched across Carrasco to open the outer door.

The German man-at-arms leaned up against the door-frame, apparently casual. I had seen him draw his blade in a heartbeat from just such a stance.

'What a way to live a life!' I muttered, saw him grin with feral teeth, and nodded politely. 'I'll shout if I need anything.'

Attila returned the nod. I believed he chose to view me a male at such moments: a man, who of course would need little assistance with Carrasco.

I pushed the door closed as Attila placed his back to it.

'Now.' I stared at Ramiro Carrasco without moving away from him. 'What is this?'

He stood as if the hull held him up. 'You have to kill me.'

'*Kill* you?'

In the port's clear light, his skin had an unhealthy shine. Ochre and green, if I had to choose pigments. Lines cut deeply into his face, and could have been dehydration, or pain, or fear, or all those things.

I shook my head, and pointed at a low stool. 'Sit.'

Ramiro Carrasco looked uncertain. I recognised that. The slave does not sit before the master.

I am doing you no favours, if you ever pass to another master, I reflected.

The unlikelihood of that circumstance made me feel a little better. I indicated the stool again. 'Do as I say.'

He collapsed onto the lacquered and padded stool as if his legs folded up under him. His eyes did not leave my face.

'Why would I *kill* you?' Exasperation sharpened my voice to high tenor; I dragged it downward. 'Carrasco. If I *wanted* you dead, I wouldn't have bought you in Venice!'

He began slowly to rub his hands over his arms. For all the heat, I could see the fine black hairs at his wrists standing up on gooseflesh.

'This ship is going to Taraconensis.'

No question in his tone. Keeping any rumour from a ship's crew is a lost cause, but Carrasco in any case might know the Balearic coasts by sight.

He raised his head. Luminous eyes showed rawly accessible pain, hatred, fear. 'You *have* to kill me. Because otherwise I'll betray you.'

I could not doubt the shaking honesty in his tone.

'Why would you tell me about it?'

'So that you can order your men – if I'm within Lord Videric's reach—' Ramiro Carrasco stuttered over the Aldra's name. 'He'll *find out* that I'm here. Once we sail into Taraco . . . He'll threaten my family. He'll offer me what he can give me, but he'll threaten them, and he owns them!'

He spoke in Iberian, clearly forgetting in his desperation that Attila and Tottola were both the other side of thin doors. He made fists of his hands, clenching them so hard that his nails must break the skin in a minute.

'What can Videric *offer* you?' I hesitated. 'You wouldn't trust him to offer you freedom?'

Ramiro's mouth curved a little, only at one side. I recall that ironic smile from Venice, when this dishevelled man was Federico's sleek secretary.

I do not expect to feel empathy for the man who would have killed me—

'Freedom after a fashion.' Carrasco shrugged. 'He'll offer me a quick death.'

I stared.

'He'll offer to keep my family safe,' he said, 'and he'll offer to give me what *I'd* promise, if I were him – a quick execution, to spare me the judicial torture of a slave, or being left to die after some ambush with my guts hanging out.'

He bit at his lip, and rose awkwardly to his feet as if he could not bear to be sitting while I stood. We were much of a height.

Slaves on their own – as, among foreigners like these Chin-men – have no acquaintance to confide in. Only too much time to think.

This is what Ramiro Carrasco has been thinking, over the cradle of my child.

'You want *me* to order your death, instead?'

His face crumpled in a way an adult man's should not.

'I want you to save my family! If I'm dead, then there's no reason for him to harm them!'

I cut him short with a cruel truth. 'Videric may make an example of them. To convince the men he uses as spies *after* you.'

Ramiro Carrasco wiped a hand over his face. He sweated now, but not from the humid heat. Bitterness and desperation sounded in his voice. 'I'm already your slave. One day you'll punish me for assaulting you in Venice. Why not make it now? I'll *beg* for punishment. But you have to keep me away from Taraco—'

'Christus! No. Stop embarrassing yourself!'

I wanted to shake him. I dared not touch him.

Because he is my slave, and no man can stop me if I whip the skin off his back.

Or if I kill him.

Ramiro Carrasco looked at me with sheer desperation. 'I *accept* I am your slave. In God's name, do something, because I can't!'

A man cannot be watched all day, every day.

If Ramiro Carrasco de Luis feels driven enough by this to kill himself, what will drive him is the contrast between the free man of Venice and the slave. There is no action he can take against the situation he is in. I have cause to know how fear is strongest then.

Carrasco let out a sound that was both sigh and groan. With one ragged swift movement, he drove his fist against the wooden wall: a loud crack echoed around the cabin.

'*No*—' I waved Attila away as the blond man-at-arms swung the door open again. 'Leave us!'

The door clicked shut.

I held my hand out. 'Let me see that.'

Carrasco's fingers felt cold in mine. Blood welled out of the scrapes on his knuckles.

Manipulating the joints with my thumbs got a suppressed grunt out of him, but I felt no unusual movement of bone under my pressure.

I wish I might get the flayed image of the Royal Mathematicians' autopsy from my mind to paper. I do not desire to know what the living flesh is like under the skin. Or how easily a man may be flayed alive, rather than dead.

But the truth is, my charcoal drawings of hands have been better since then.

Ramiro Carrasco muttered, 'What can a slave say to a master that's honest? You're right. Send me off to be beaten; have done with it!'

'So you can jump over the ship's rail?'

'No!'

He trod on my words far too quickly.

I pushed his hand back towards him. He flexed it, looking down; unkempt black hair falling into his eyes.

He did not look at me. 'Perhaps I *wish* you to believe I would do that.'

Men take their most stupid actions in such undecided passionate states.

'Sit.' I pointed at the low stool.

Returning to my sack for paper and a stub of charcoal, I saw in peripheral vision how he sank slowly down onto the stool again, never taking his eyes off me.

Long experience as a slave has me used to judging men, sometimes even accurately. But I read neither souls nor minds; I doubted I could read in him whether he was honest or not, with me or with himself.

I may know better after this.

I pulled up a second stool, sat down, and began sketching, with paper and board across my knee.

Sitting for me was calming him, I realised.

It's a familiar routine.

'Videric can threaten you again.'

'Yes.' The light didn't alter on his luminous brown eyes.

'He may have imprisoned your family as hostages by now.'

516

Eyes moving from his face to the paper, I knew him aware of that. I need not say Videric may also have sent in his soldiers to fire and burn the villages. A man can drive his serfs off his own estates, if he wishes. Or kill them. No one speaks for them; in law they're property.

'I know so little.' Ramiro shifted, meeting my eyes. 'And I was of the same kind as your Alexandrine – in possession of every fact and rumour.'

My chalk discovered the lines of frustration, anger, passion.

'I could have *killed* you in Venice! If.' He stopped dead.

I finished. 'If you could have brought yourself to do it.'

He glared as if I had deeply insulted him. 'You think I couldn't kill you?'

'I think you're the first man in your family to have a choice at anything except digging dirt – and you chose the university of Barcelona and training as a lawyer, not going for a soldier, like most farmer's sons.'

I watched the pupils of his eyes widen.

'I think Videric saw a man who could be blackmailed, and made a bad error of judgement about what he could be blackmailed into. A man who studies the law isn't necessarily the best choice for a casual murderer.' I sketched the slackened flesh around his jaw. 'Which leaves you caught with nowhere to go. Not the best situation.'

He visibly struggled, and at last managed, 'You're not as rash as you seem, are you?'

'Possibly you mean "not as stupid as I look"? I don't have to tell you – a slave studies people. When anyone can do anything to you, you learn to look.'

Ramiro Carrasco shot *me* a look, that I thought for the first time was not solely directed at 'Madonna Ilaria'.

I remarked, 'Only you would blush because I *don't* think you're a murderer.'

Having reduced him to silenced confusion, I used the charcoal to darken in the masses of his hair.

'You will have heard—' Because it could not be otherwise, travelling with us. '—that we intend Videric to return to court, in his old rank and position. If we succeed, that makes us safe.' I caught his eye. 'All of us.'

Abruptly his face creased. He gave me a look of sardonic scorn.

'You think if Lord Videric's back in power, he won't make damn sure to clear up every loose end? That he'll let you run around loose, knowing what you know?'

Ramiro Carrasco did not need to add, *And I, with what I know?*

This dread slicing coldly through me is not new. This wakes me at nights – suppose what we plan is not enough?

As calmly as I might, I said, 'You truly don't believe this will succeed.'

Carrasco snorted as if he were a freeman. 'I will not be responsible for the deaths of my family!'

The war-junk slowly tacking, the shift of sunlight altered all the tone and values of his face.

He will have thought what Rekhmire' and I have thought, because Ramiro Carrasco is not stupid. Only at the frayed end of his rope.

'Suppose I strike the rivets out, and take your collar off, and let you run?'

His eyes widened. My fingers rummaged in the sack for a white chalk to make highlights. Only a fool doesn't use what tool there is to hand.

'No!' He got the word out with difficulty. 'The sole reason he hasn't had me killed yet is that it's more difficult to kill both you and I at once!'

'Then we'll continue to make it difficult for him . . . '

Carrasco sat as if stunned.

To have refused your own freedom commits you – as I once discovered – to much.

'Two things,' I said.

I put in the curls of his hair, tumbling over his forehead, and found my skill not great enough to reproduce the confusion in his expression.

'First, Ramiro Carrasco, if I come out of this conversation even *thinking* you might kill yourself, you'll leave this cabin in chains, and you'll stay that way.'

Carrasco sat perfectly still, moving only with the minor movements of the ship. I smudged in the values of his stubble in the sunlight, botched it, and set the board and paper down at my feet.

'Secondly, Onorata will need feeding soon. You do it.'

His face turned so rawly open that it was painful to watch.

He spoke barely above a whisper. 'I don't understand.'

'I made use of you before,' I said, 'on the *Sekhmet*. I trust you, now, not to hurt a child.'

Ramiro Carrasco stared.

I said, 'Yes, there's no honesty between master and slave – but I can't free you yet; as you say, I need to have that threat over Videric. So if you have to trust me, then I have to trust you.'

He sat motionless – and all in a rush put his elbows on his knees and his hands over his face.

I would let you have that privacy. But I need to see.

I reached forward and took his wrists, pulling his hands down.

Ramiro Carrasco stared away, sounding stifled. 'You can't do this! If he demands of me—'

'If I choose to have trust in you—'

Water shone in the creases of skin about his eyes. He wrenched it out word by word: 'If it was a choice – my father – my brothers – I would choose them over your child. You must know that!'

'Then I'll see you won't be put where you have that choice to make.'

He made as if he would say something, struggled, and no word came out.

Rekhmire"'s tenor voice abruptly cracked through the silence in the cabin. 'Are you completely mad?'

The Egyptian stood in the cabin doorway.

Ramiro Carrasco sprang to his feet with the quickness of a man who has been whipped for not doing so. His hands tore out of my grip.

I stood, slowly, heart hammering in my chest. 'You were listening?'

The Egyptian snorted. 'And Attila, too!'

Rekhmire"'s expression was one I did not recognise. Scorn, I realised finally.

I have never seen him without his self-control—

Rekhmire' limped into the cabin, to the window-port, gazing out as if he did not see the masts and sails. Before I could speak, he swung clumsily around on his heel.

'What is it with you and your waifs and strays, Ilario? First Sulva. Then this . . . spy.'

It would have hurt less, been less surprising, had he walked up and slapped me in the face.

I raised my voice. 'Attila!'

The German put his head around the door.

'Take Ramiro down to the animal pens. He'll milk the goat for the baby.'

I stayed aware of them out of peripheral vision, my gaze locked with Rekhmire"'s.

Some of Honorius's authority evidently belonged to me by proxy; Attila did not hesitate, but stepped in, jerking his thumb expressively at Ramiro Carrasco. The slave-secretary moved as if his legs were made of wet paper, stumbling out of the cabin in front of the soldier.

I kicked the door closed behind them. 'Rekhmire'—'

'I apologise.' Rekhmire' wiped his hand over his shaven scalp. 'I know Sulva – is not mine to discuss.'

Sitting abruptly down on the low chair behind me, I caught a brush under my sandal and heard it crack.

I no longer look at the badly executed paintings I made of Sulva Paziathe. The shape of her face is marked out by my guilt.

Rekhmire' slid off his reed and linen headband, running the woven length of it through his fingers. He snorted. '*Carrasco*, on the other hand—'

'We need to trust him.'

'*Trust?*' Rekhmire' limped across the cabin and stood before me. The short stick let him walk only with a swivelling limp.

This close, he smelled of the Alexandrine spices kept in his clothes chest, and that different male sweat I had become used to in Constantinople.

'You can't trust a slave. You should know this.'

I glared. 'We need him on our side, or Videric will have him back, one way or another!'

It was not necessary to add that, spending months in our company, Carrasco will have learned too much of what we plan to do.

Exasperated, Rekhmire' snapped, 'You know there's no trust between slave and master!'

'No.' I pushed the stool back squarely onto all its legs, and found myself reaching out to the Egyptian's large hands. 'But sometimes it begins there.'

A dark ruddy colour showed on his neck, growing to stain him at cheek and brow.

It took me a moment to realise that I saw Rekhmire' blushing.

'I – that is – well—' He opened his hands to me as if we had done it a hundred times before.

His grip felt warm and strong.

'*Some* slaves,' he muttered, remarkably apologetically.

I couldn't help a cheerful barb in return. 'I might rescue Ramiro Carrasco de Luis; you needn't act as if I'm about to marry him!'

'Just as well, I think.' Rekhmire' stared at our hands. 'Marrying three times in the same year *might* be considered excessive.'

'This must be why Ty-ameny values your opinion so much, book-buyer – how keenly you see into a matter!'

He snorted.

I released Rekhmire''s hands, stooping to rescue board and tinted paper.

'I'll draw you, too,' I added, 'if you're jealous of that.'

The Egyptian stilled for a moment. He shot me a look. 'I'm transparent to you, evidently.'

Rekhmire' did not smile, but somehow warmth suffused his expression.

'I confess I would be curious to see the results of a sketch. But we should speak with Zheng He first, and settle how long he's prepared to give us at Taraco.'

'Long enough, I hope.' I swept my hair back, tied it with a leather thong, and re-buckled the thin leather belt (all I currently wore of my Iberian clothing) over an Alexandrine tunic.

The ship is surely large enough to cause panic. Is large enough, certainly, that I have felt no fear of the sea while aboard – as if I were not on a ship at all, but a wooden island.

Rekhmire''s head tilted, speculatively. 'I estimate the crew of this ship at between four and a half and five thousand Chin-men.'

'And there are the weapons.'

It was necessary to look up, given the inches of difference in our heights. Three parts of a year together: I read him so much more easily than I do Carrasco.

And now I see we have been thinking on parallel lines these last few days.
'I'm concerned,' I said.

He nodded.

I voiced it, nonetheless. 'However long we're here – how much of a panic there is, when we appear off the coast of Taraco – we need King Rodrigo to recall Videric. And . . . is this going to be enough?'

3

A sound like ripping paper tensed all the muscles of my shoulders and spine.

The rockets of Chin soared up from the launcher into the night sky. Lights exploded.

'*Kek and Keket!*'

'Amen!'

Rekhmire' put his hand up between his face and the luminous sky and squinted. I rubbed the after-impressions of brilliance out of my eyes; night vision entirely gone. I could make out nothing of the deck, the rigging, the creaking sails, the crawling waves so far beneath the rail.

Seven bright lights sank down towards the blackness that was the coast close to Taraco.

So near and I can see nothing of it!

I left home – for want of a better word – in August, in the sign of Leo, Now the Twins rule the night sky. Two months short of a year. And it feels at the same time no time, and an age. I might have stepped out of the palace yesterday, or in the days of the Caesars and Barcas.

Rekhmire''s arm brushed against mine, his skin warm. 'I can only imagine what the Royal Mathematicians would have done if the Admiral had demonstrated these at Alexandria.'

I grinned. 'Swarmed the ship, I think. If they had to swim to it!'

Anonymous figures jostled me in the dark, the crew moving around to reload the launcher and send another shower of fire into the sky.

'I see no explosion where they land. But there may be some part of the weapon not yet used, if they only signal. I wonder . . . '

The dark shapes of Attila and Tottola were at my shoulder. I could all but feel them speculating if Zheng He would sell the secrets of such weapons.

Not even to the Lion of Castile, I thought.

What I could see now of Admiral Zheng He, stroking his beard in the lightning-coloured illumination, showed a man with the expression of a civilised commander sending out a warning to barbarians.

I turned blindly in the direction of the cabins. 'I imagine King Rodrigo knows we're here by now.'

There had been fishing boats in view since we sighted the Balearic

Islands. If their captains hadn't raised every sail to race to the mainland and be paid for their information, I would be astounded.

King Rodrigo Sanguerra would first hold his few warships in reserve – and now this monstrous vessel cleared the horizon, he would send them up the coast or down it, but certainly out of our way.

I added, 'We should make final plans, as much as we can.'

Rekhmire''s hand gaining support from my shoulder, we steered a way to the war-junk's stern. The cabin held a welcome familiarity in the golden lantern-light, that put gleams of gilding on cabinets and low tables, and soft dark shadows in corners. Scattered Egyptian cushions surrounded one of the tables, on which there were plates of food.

I helped Rekhmire' sit; he swore under his breath – and aloud, as Ramiro Carrasco came out of the inner cabin, Onorata rocking in his arms.

I padded across to touch her warm, dozing face. 'Did the noise wake her?'

'For a while.' His tone was low. 'But she sleeps again, mistress. Master. Ah – shall I take her back to her cradle?'

I stroked Onorata's fine hair, that had grown a wispy matt black. Her eyelids screwed shut; her small sleeping mouth opened in a yawn, and she made contented noises.

Not desiring to miss this moment of her being angelic – since I had quite enough of her other moods – I reached to take her solid small body into my arms. 'I'll settle her. You wait here.'

In the inner room, I put her down infinitely carefully; on her back in the cradle as Ty-ameny's nurses had advised me. I nodded to Tottola and Attila, as Tottola settled himself on his palliasse, and Attila took up his sword to guard the outer doors.

I did not begin my life under armed guard.

And I desire to make certain that she doesn't need to – as soon as ever I can.

Walking back into the main cabin, I encountered raised voices, and snarled, 'Quiet!' in an intense whisper. 'Don't wake her!'

The two men fell silent as I sat by the low table. Ramiro Carrasco looked at me from under his shaggy hair, and knelt down beside and behind me.

'You will have him present?' Rekhmire' spoke with the utmost polite mildness.

I would sooner he shouted.

'He was Aldra Videric's man. We need to ask him questions.' I reached for a plate, unsure of what was before me. Stodgy clumps of white stuff, like maggots, nevertheless tasted reasonably bland. I poked among it with my fingers, removing sharp pickles. 'I know you don't trust Ramiro Carrasco—'

Rekhmire' arched a brow, all Alexandrine civility.

I wish I might slap him!

'Very well.' I passed a dirty plate back to Carrasco. 'I'll call you when I need you.'

As the door closed behind Carrasco, Rekhmire' took up a small translucent bowl, eating with a quick-fingered hunger that surprised me. Between bites, he said, 'Tell me reasons why – this ship may not be enough?'

My hunger vanished.

I counted factors off on my fingers.

'The opposition faction at Rodrigo's court are right, in fact. Even if for the wrong reason. Videric *did* endanger the country. He has robbed it of stability. They see that as stemming from the scandal—' I didn't look up at the Egyptian. '—which caused Carthage to be able to slap the King's wrist, and demand that Videric should be set aside as First Minister. I know the nobles of Taraco. Even with the threat of something the size of this war-junk, there'll be some hot-heads who think it's one ship, they can capture it or destroy it.'

Rekhmire' smiled his familiar hidden amusement. It failed to amuse me.

I crossed my legs in the fashion of Carthage, and reached for the wine. 'On the other hand . . . We go ashore, we explain this to Rodrigo, and I promise you the King will find every way possible to make it work! Because *he* will want Aldra Videric back.'

If I could have kept bitterness from my voice, I would have added, *Whether or not Videric tried to kill his freak offspring.*

He remains the man that Rodrigo needs to see standing beside his throne.

'Is this—' I gestured around at the cabin walls, and by implication the vast ship itself. '—enough to make men forget last year's scandal?'

Rekhmire' tipped his bowl towards me in acknowledgement. 'I've asked the Admiral to permit no contact with the land. He'll anchor here offshore. We go in and speak to your King. That way the ship remains an unknown threat, and more persuasive.'

'Zheng He is determined to let no man aboard?'

Attila's voice interrupted, from the shadows by the door. 'Boats will come out; they'll sell fruit, wine, whores if they can. The captain and officers can't watch all their men all the time.'

I put my cup down. 'Then I guarantee that within forty-eight hours, Videric and half the counts and dukes of Rodrigo's court will know about the ship's weapons, and anything else here on board.'

'Don't worry,' Attila reassured. 'Lord Honorius warned us you'd be in danger; we'll see you safe.'

There was a silence, in which I heard Carrasco's movements in the inner cabins, and the wind blew one of the shutters open. Standing and crossing the deck to latch it shut, I caught a face full of the wind off the land.

Instantly, the scents brought back the colonnades of Rodrigo's court. As if I stood there, in the palace that has been home to me from the age of fifteen.

But now I have travelled.

My fingers fumbled the latch; I swore and finally got the shutter fastened.

'Bear this in mind,' I warned. 'It's as likely to be an assassin looking for Carrasco, as one looking for me. We need Carrasco alive.'

In the shadows, I could not see if Attila disapproved, but he nodded obedience.

'Let's not forget the most important weapon in any soldier's arsenal, sir – ma'am.'

It seemed unfair to deprive him of something he'd evidently practised with company after company of armed men. 'And what would that be?'

'Dumb luck!'

I snorted. Even Rekhmire' smiled.

'So. The first move.' I sent a prompting look at the Egyptian.

'Our first move,' Rekhmire' said ponderously, 'is that you do not go ashore.'

I opened my mouth and Rekhmire' snatched two porcelain bowls and a cup off the low table close to me.

I stared at him.

Wine and pickle splashed his fingers.

'Just making sure.' There wasn't a smile on his face, but his eyes were bright.

I glared at the Egyptian – and nearly cracked when Attila, large and impressive as he was, looked frankly bewildered.

'Let's discuss this—' I reached over and recovered my cup from Rekhmire''s hand. '—like sensible and responsible adults.'

He lifted his own bowl, looking at me over the rim.

Catching a deep warmth in his gaze, I could not do otherwise than smile back at him.

'You can distract me as much as you like.' I leaned back on cushions embroidered with Sekhmet's sigils. 'But you need me ashore. King Rodrigo must speak to me. With all possible respect—'

'With complete *dis*respect,' Rekhmire' echoed in a muttered aside that made Attila's grin flash out of the shadows.

'—the King won't trust an Alexandrine spy as far as he could throw you. I don't think you can play the humble book-buyer this time.'

Rekhmire' reached into his robes and pulled out a leather scroll-case. He held it out. I put my bowl down, uncapped the case, unrolled the scroll, and found myself looking at the seal of the Pharaoh-Queen.

'I can play the diplomatic envoy of Ty-ameny of the Five Great

Names.' Rekhmire''s brows lifted towards his shaved scalp. 'I thought you'd assume something of the sort.'

The ancient pictorial script of Alexandria might have declared him envoy from the Moon, but there was a Latin copy also in the scroll case.

'Perhaps,' I said. 'I may have been gone from Taraco some time. But I know how much the east isn't trusted. Unless you outright plan to tell King Rodrigo that your Queen is using Admiral Zheng He to scare the shite out of Carthage—'

'That would be one option.' Rekhmire' took the scroll-case back. 'I do admit, the first approach might be better made by one of King Rodrigo's own subjects. But, Ilario, you're in too much danger. What use is all of this if a hired gang of thugs kills you at Taraco docks?'

'Unless you plan on locking me up with Ramiro, I'm going ashore. I want to see Honorius!'

The Egyptian slowly nodded. 'I understand. Again, it would be safer if the Admiral made an exception, and permitted the Captain-General to come here.'

I wavered. *Onorata is in the next cabin. And I cannot take her ashore with me.* 'Would Zheng He allow that?'

We talked, after one of Jian's officers took a message. I stood at the port for a time, and then paced. Ramiro Carrasco answered Onorata's sleepy cries, and I let him feed her again. I watched candle-light shift and change on men's faces; stretched my spine, and caught a glimmer of grey out in the open air.

'Attila, if I can borrow one of your mail-shirts,' I suggested – Attila being slightly less large around his chest than his brother. 'And wear a helmet. If I carry a sword as the Alexandrine's escort, no one will look at me; you *know* that. No man looks in obvious places.'

Rekhmire' opened his mouth to protest.

And clearly thought better of it.

'Then we must hope there's a way to get a message to Lord Honorius, once we're ashore.'

The cabin door opened. Commander Jian himself came in, meeting my gaze and nodding his head sharply.

'No man to come here,' he managed, in Mediterranean Latin. 'You go ashore now?'

A glimmer of white showed at the oared boat's prow.

Sebekhotep's robes.

The Egyptian pilot must be there for reassurance or curiosity's sake. From what I recall, a six-year-old child could steer a boat to the quay at Taraco.

We docked, and the ground was painfully hard beneath my boots.

How could I have forgotten the air and the light!

Even before dawn, with the east bright but unscarred by the sun, every dew-wet breeze brings the scent and reality of home to me. No brush will capture this.

I raised my head and looked around the quay as Rekhmire' disembarked with appropriate dignity. I might wish to be a guard in more than my clothing, but I was overwhelmed, as if I had not seen the city since childhood. And, at the same time, the ghost-white buildings, and the feather-silhouettes of the fronds of the trees, were as familiar to me as my own skin.

Dawn turned the sea-spray yellow, peach, scarlet; the Alexandrine banner unrolled in yards of blue silk down the offshore wind. I smelled salt, the old Roman drains of Taraco, and the scent of outdoor food-booths already beginning to cook for early workers. Fruit-sellers' cries echoed down the dusty streets.

I turned my head, looking thirty yards in the other direction.

There, where a coastal ship is tied up to the bollard, first catch of fish already unloaded – that's where I walked up the gang-plank of a galley sailing south down the coast to Carthage. Two hours beforehand, my mother attempted to stick a dagger into my stomach.

I thought of the blade, black with poison.

Most poisons that you can daub on metal do less harm than rust. There's always talk in court of such weapons; of poisoned cups, of scent that can poison a pair of gloves . . . In all honesty, more men die of the fever turning their guts out. And more women in childbed.

Tottola's elbow caught me ungently in the kidney.

I shouldered the pennant of Alexandria, becoming an anonymous soldier and banner-bearer. Tottola and Attila were in blue doublets of one shade or another, and scarlet hose. They had not yet replaced their household badges.

If we meet Aldra Videric at the top of this hill with a gang of hired criminals, I thought – or Rodrigo and the royal guard out to arrest us – these men could die around me now.

In which case, I'll step out in front of them, because in either case it's me they want. And wasting a life because of that would be stupid.

I resolved not to mention it to Rekhmire'. *The Egyptian will expect something more sensible from me.*

The same feeling of familiarity and strangeness suffused me on the winding road to the palace. Mountains shone on the horizon, blue glass; but would be yellow rough scrub under the noon sun. Every peak and trough, I remember. Plodding under the shade of palm-feathered branches, bare-footed children shinning up the trunks out of our way; a pavement shoe-maker looking up from his last as we passed him. And the dark eyes of men stopping their work at tavern or shop or household, momentarily and silently taking in the sight of soldiers as we trudged up the steep slope.

The intricacies of the Sanguerra fortress-palace begin with a crenellated gate-house at the bend of the road.

It had been dark when we left the ship. By the time we passed men at guard-house, courtyards, outer and inner baileys, and were allowed into the palace proper, the sun had risen over the sea high enough to make me sweat.

'How much *more* of this!' Tottola fingered under the unfamiliar woollen collar of his winter doublet. (Neither man-at-arms had summer gear with them.) Attila echoed his muttering.

'It's an old palace—'

'Rabbit warren!' Tottola interrupted me, under his breath.

'—and you wouldn't begrudge the King a chance to impress us, would you?'

The tall armoured brothers grinned, instantly, and as instantly looked as unimpressed as it is possible for a man to be.

The King's guards were leading us towards one of the eastern courtyards, I realised. This older part of the palace has Carthaginian influence, from ancient days before they were driven out to Africa. Two altars burned at the foot of a wide flight of steps, servants keeping the flames high, although invisible as the sun reached down to them. Above the steps, a wall of niches and crumbling urns enclosed an open square.

Beyond the wall, poplar trees screened masonry pyramids. My hand recalled painting the desert beyond Carthage. I shivered.

That chill, and the dusty green feathers of the poplars, took me suddenly to Venice's lazaretto islands; I turned my head to look at the walls as we were marched past them – *Before this was a courtyard . . . it was a necropolis.*

I have not ever noticed this before.

Would I notice, if I had not travelled?

Around the crumbled end of the wall, the character changed. We walked over cracked sandstone slabs, with ahead of us the walls of the castle's east wing – a million featureless pale bricks running up to corbels, and battlements, and the terracotta tiles roofing the machicolations. Guards' heads showed as small as grape-pips. The walls towered high enough to block out most of the sky: certainly enough to humble petitioners to a king.

King Rodrigo Sanguerra had his chair of state outdoors, under a striped awning, beside a flight of palace steps with stylised faces carved on their balustrades.

I could not see the King himself over the heads of the surrounding crowd. Most were guards or servants – only a few courtiers would attend an audience beginning this early; Rodrigo held it for common tradesmen and workers, so they might not lose too much of the working day. The guards shepherded us under the far end of the awning. Somewhat shaded by the sun, I lowered the Alexandrine banner so it would not catch on the billows of cloth, and shifted up on my toes, to see if I might see King Rodrigo.

Rekhmire' caught my eye. 'We shall doubtless wait the usual long time; no need to waste it . . . '

I nodded, and set myself to watching inferior courtiers as they came and went, and men and women from the kitchens, in case there might be a face I knew.

Heat bounced back off the stone, and the balustrade's ancient faces changelessly stared.

There!

'Hold this!' I hissed, and shoved my banner into Attila's hand. He caught it, much startled.

I stepped to intercept the path of a man whose broad face had often sat across from me in the royal scriptorium, on those occasions when Rodrigo Sanguerra had employed me for my actual talents.

'Galindus!' Seizing his upper arm, I shifted us into the partial concealment of the flight of steps, where the wall cast a shadow.

I smiled. He frowned, briefly. I saw him abruptly recognise me – more by voice than clothes, as many do.

'Ilario! You're back!'

'Yes and no.' I kept the smile with an effort, threw everything of our acquaintance into my expression, and got my demand out. 'You still hear all the gossip, don't you? Listen, Galindus, tell me this. Lord Licinus Honorius – is he here?'

'What?'

'Licinus Honorius. *Il leone di Castiglia.* Is he at court!'

Seconds dripped past like cold honey. Galindus shot an unmistakably prurient look at the crowd around Rodrigo's chair of state.

'Well . . . ' His voice held the avidity of a man with a piece of choice gossip. My heart thudded until I thought it would tear.

Galindus spoke.

'Well, yes. He's here. Licinus Honorius.'

Honorius is alive.

I had not known how much I feared otherwise, until warmth entered into every frozen blood-vessel in my body.

'Honorius is at court? In the palace?'

Galindus looked left and right, his long dark hair whipping with the jerky movement. He glanced above us, at the steps, for secrecy's sake.

'He's here,' Galindus whispered. 'He's in prison.'

4

Attila gripped me about the elbow, hauled me two steps back without so much as an acknowledgement to Galindus, and shoved the pennant's pole into my hands.

'What—'

'*Quiet!*'

One of the court officers, whose face I didn't know, scowled at the both of us, regarding us as men-at-arms who do not know a courtly discipline.

The officer rapped his ivory staff on the stone of the courtyard.

I stepped briskly in beside Rekhmire' as he moved forward, just catching the end of the herald's full-voiced cry:

'—of the city of New Alexandria, known commonly as Constantinople!'

A flutter of women-in-waiting and courtiers stepped back as we approached. Lesser men, according to some: mayors of distant hill-towns, and the captains of Rodrigo Sanguerra's frontier towers. Certainly leaner men. I could see none of the kingdom's more influential and powerful lords.

Is the King hiding us by making us seem unimportant?

A flare of hope seemed almost distant. Numb, I could only think, *But – Honorius!*

Rekhmire' paused before the rank of guards to either side, and for all the chair of state was on a stone dais, he looked down at my King.

With immense dignity, Rekhmire' began to kneel.

I saw the spasm of pain he suppressed.

Immediately I knelt, still clasping the banner pole. That put my shoulder where he could reach it. Large fingers bit deep into my muscles, hard enough that I thought he would still lose balance and sprawl.

The Egyptian thumped down on one knee beside me.

'*Rekhmire'!*' I bowed my head low enough that no man would see my mouth. 'My *father*! He's alive!'

Rekhmire' shot me a startled look – at why I sounded angry, I realised – and had time to do no more than raise his head as King Rodrigo, fifth of that name, looked up from his gilded chair, and leaned forward to speak graciously.

Blood thundering in my ears cut off the formalities.

Have you put my father in prison? Who *else* could be responsible!

The linen of the awning softened the sun's light. More white than dark showed now in Rodrigo's wiry short-cut beard. His eyes, under thick brows, might be bloodshot in the corners, but I could still feel the force of his personality, blazing from them.

It occurred to me, belatedly. The King will be frighteningly angry that no man apparently trusts him to hold his kingdom without Aldra Videric at his side.

But even King Rodrigo Sanguerra knows there's no fighting men's opinions. Whether they're right or wrong.

Rekhmire' rose, with equal effort, his weight almost pushing me down onto the sandstone paving.

King Rodrigo signalled his guards to step back, and his servants to pour wine; let his gaze imperceptibly stray while he continued to speak with the representative of New Alexandria, and stopped midway through a sentence.

'Master Envoy . . . '

Rekhmire' bowed his head. 'Ah. We thought this safer, Exalted One.'

Rodrigo Sanguerra Coverrubias stared at me.

A year ago, I thought, I could not have held your gaze so long.

'I freed you, hermaphrodite.'

I passed Rekhmire''s banner to Tottola and knelt down as one does before kings. 'Yes, Your Majesty.'

'And then you repay me as you did. Not well.'

Biting down on rage allowed me to control my voice. 'Is it well, Majesty, to have put the Lion of Castile into your prison?'

At my elbow, Rekhmire' twitched.

He would have advised me against that, I thought, and momentarily regretted my anger.

No more than a moment. The world is still carmine about me.

Rodrigo Sanguerra leaned back in his gilt chair, steepling his fingers. He gave the impression of choosing his words very carefully.

'Tell me, Ilario, what I *should* have done with Licinus Honorius?'

He did not say 'your father'. I had not the slightest doubt he knew.

Before I could stop choking and get out an answer, King Rodrigo lifted the full force of his gaze to me.

'Here is a lord of my kingdom,' he said, measuredly, 'Aldra Licinus Honorius, whose presence I require at court. I send to inform him. He does not come. I send to *order* him. He delays, says he will come . . . but does not. Meantime, all my other lords – less rich than Licinus Honorius, perhaps, and not "the Lion of Castile", but still noble lords – watch this behaviour . . . and judge how weak I've grown.'

No proper words of objection would form in my dry mouth.

'Therefore,' Rodrigo concluded, leaning back, 'when Aldra Honorius finally *does* deign to obey his King's summons, what do I do? Thank him kindly for his arrival? Ask him how I should have worded my summons, to be better obeyed?'

'Your Majesty—'

'*Yes!*' His hand slapped loudly down on the carved chair's arm. '"Majesty." "King." But only so long as men call me so! Licinus Honorius is a subject of mine. He defied me. He is therefore now serving me – by being an object lesson to any man who might think of doing likewise!'

Rekhmire' stirred, beside me.

It was the pain of his leg, I saw. Nothing in the Egyptian's expression signified dissent.

'It's not justice to put him in prison, Majesty!' I spoke fiercely. 'It's my fault he didn't come. He was helping me. If you put anybody in the dungeon, it should be me.'

Rodrigo Sanguerra briefly smiled.

'I know.' He rested his chin on his fist. The hooded lids of his eyes dipped down – in a way that had always, in the past, signalled covert amusement. 'But my hermaphrodite Fool in prison is hardly an object lesson to the men who covet my throne. Of which there are always some.'

'Sire . . . '

Rodrigo Sanguerra waved his free hand dismissively. 'Aldra Honorius can stay in my dungeons until I'm satisfied every man has realised he's there. *And* that he submits to his King. And then, on payment of a sufficiently large fine, he can find himself at liberty.'

He frowned, his pause unstudied.

'What, did you suppose I was going to execute the Lion of Castile?'

Dizziness made me unable to answer properly.

'You may see him,' King Rodrigo remarked, 'when we're done here. The more visitors, the more mouths to carry the story, after all.'

He smiled at me.

'Are you still free, hermaphrodite?'

What a question. Curtailing a long story, I said, 'Yes, Your Majesty.'

He would be in his late fifties or early sixties, this King of Taraconensis. If I tried to look at him as a stranger would – as Rekhmire' might be doing now – I saw the unforgiving and unwelcoming face of a country mostly composed of mountain, infertile plain, and rocky coast.

Growing up with the land, I know there are valleys that flower at the foothills of the mountains, and rich seas and forests, if a man can find the way to them. Rodrigo had been rumoured a less grave man before his Queen, Cixila, died in giving birth to their dead fourth child.

'Come here.' Rodrigo beckoned, and held out his hand. I moved to kneel on the dais steps, and kissed the cabochon-cut emerald he wore in his massive ouroboros-ring.

For a moment, he rested his hand on my head.

'You come back bringing trouble, Ilario.'

A flood of emotion would have had me in tears like a girl. I waited until it passed. And saw King Rodrigo had, as ever, read everything visible in a man's face.

'We'll break our fast and talk,' he said, glancing around absently for servants – and, on a sudden, looked back at me.

He gestured with his lined hand. 'Rise, Ilario.'

Stiffly, slowly, I stood up.

It is still instinctive in me – not to rise until he gives me direct permission.

'The envoy of Alexandria is best qualified to speak with you, Your Majesty.' I prayed he did not read how rigid I stood, and how much it was out of determination. 'No man knows I'm here, yet; no man will recognise me, dressed like this. May I be excused to visit Lord Honorius in prison?'

I did not suppose Honorius would be in a prison elsewhere than in Taraco. And not in the civil jail down in the city, reserved for men who are not noble. Somewhere in this palace's oubliettes and rat-infested dungeons, thick with the stench of ancient shit and despair . . . *Because if King Rodrigo desires to make an object lesson out of Honorius, he will keep him under his hand.*

Rekhmire''s fingers closed around my biceps. Without seeming to care that he broke protocol in speaking before the King did, he snapped, 'We need you here!'

The flash of Rekhmire''s gaze prompted *Videric!* very plainly.

'You were previously of the opinion I could stay on the ship, Master Rekhmire'. You can bring the introductory matters to my Lord King's attention. I'll continue after I've seen Lord Honorius—'

I bit back the words *my father.*

'—with His Majesty's permission.'

Rekhmire' glared at me, clearly divided between exasperation and a fear that I might throw something.

Observing us, King Rodrigo shifted his chin to his other hand, all the time watching me as closely as a painter does. He allowed silence to return.

Rekhmire' murmured, 'I apologise, Exalted One.'

I echoed him. 'I apologise, sire.'

Underlining that with silence, King Rodrigo did nothing more than observe me from under lowered lids.

'Very well!' He sat up, briskly. 'Master Egyptian, we will have a private audience. Ilario – one hour. And you will not afterwards whine to me that this is too brief!'

Without waiting for an answer, the King beckoned one of his men forward; a lugubrious-faced knight in a forest-green surcoat over Milanese armour.

'The prison, first; then bring Ilario to me in the east tower, when the hour of Terce has struck.'

5

The knight's lugubriosity appeared to be a function merely of his long features. He introduced himself as Safrac de Aguilar, and smiled amiably enough as I halted midway up a flight of sandstone spiral steps.

Four sets of steps serve the floors of the prison tower of the Sanguerra castle. One at each corner of the building. Any one of them enough to leave men breathless.

It was not the constriction of my ribs that made me stop, but a sudden thought.

'Aldra Aguilar, I have no money for a bribe!'

That we were going up, not down, the stairs, told me I was being taken to the governor or overseer – whatever knight King Rodrigo had placed in charge of prisoners, and who therefore kept his chambers at the top of this high square tower. And whose income depends on what prisoners' relatives will pay him for good treatment of a prisoner.

Appalled, I thought, *Nor do I have money to pay a jailer for food, or candles, or clean water, or anything my father will need!*

Safrac de Aguilar gave me a wry smile. 'Your money isn't needed.'

And *that* means?

He gave me no chance to question him, turning his back. I followed the muffled clack of plate armour up the ever-turning stairs. His was not a face I recalled from court life, but the King must think him honest and not prone to gossip.

Or else he wouldn't let the man see Honorius and I together, with kinship written on our faces.

Unless Honorius is not recognisable—

The steps ceased, and I all but fell over de Aguilar's heels. He opened the door set counter-wise into the tower's wall, and gestured for me to pass through.

'Could you lend me money, Aldra?' I persisted.

Safrac de Aguilar sighed, his face giving it the force of extreme misery. 'Just go inside!'

An arrow-slit window opened into the antechamber, spilling bright sunlight onto terracotta tiles. De Aguilar nodded to the guards in royal livery, beckoning them aside and speaking in an undertone. I caught a glimpse of the sea through the narrow slit, far out on the horizon, and wondered, *If I had my babe in my arms, would I be more likely to move a prison governor to sympathy?*

Sharp knocking brought me back to myself. De Aguilar was just lowering his hand from the nail-sprinkled oak door of the inner rooms.

The door opened. A young and curly-haired man put his head out. I stared. '*Saverico?*'

Safrac de Aguilar said something that did not penetrate the shock of seeing Ensign Saverico in clean green doublet and red hose, with a pewter lion badge sewn to his sleeve.

'Donna Ilario!' He grinned. 'I have your dress, still!'

The door was pushed further open from the inside: a shorter and skinnier man demanded, 'What is it *this* time?', and I recognised his voice before I saw his face – Honorius's Armenian sergeant, Orazi.

The door opened into a wide, well-furnished chamber. On the far side of the room, opposite the door, a window showed the sky to the north. Beneath the window stood a table. The chair on its left had been pushed back – by either Saverico or Orazi, when they came to open the door.

A chess-board stood on the table itself, and in the right-hand chair, Licinus Honorius, *il leone di Castiglia*, lifted his chin from his hand and contemplation of the board, and called without looking towards the door:

'By my calculation, Sergeant, you now owe me Carthage, Alexandria, and a year's dye-trade in Bruges ... Would you rather play me at dice?'

Orazi carries a sword at his side.

The sergeant stepped quickly back across the room, fast enough that I saw why Honorius might keep him as a bodyguard, and moved a bishop. 'Check!' He finished with a jerk of his chin towards us at the door.

Honorius looked. His eyes met mine.

I felt it in a blow to my stomach.

It was as if it took an age for him to rise from the chair.

Safrac de Aguilar murmured something behind me, stepping back with the royal guards; I was dimly aware that the solid oak door closed with them outside.

Honorius opened his mouth, and said nothing.

His cheeks were not sunken in or unshaven, his tunic looked clean; he carried a dagger scabbarded at his right hip.

'*I thought you were in some rat-infested piss-hole!*'

Words ripped out of my throat with the force of a winter storm.

'The King told me you were in *prison*! You're all right! *Why didn't you tell me?*'

Honorius stepped forward, his expression shifting from shock to wonder and solemnity.

I could do nothing but stare.

'Ilario . . . '

Honorius broke into a great wide grin, covered the remaining distance

536

in a moment, and threw his arms about me hard enough that I felt my ribs crunch.

'Ilario!'

'*Oof!*' It would have been more than a whisper, if I could have got the breath. And had I not been embracing him equally hard.

Without letting go, Honorius briefly turned his head. 'Saverico, get another goblet out! And the good wine. Tell Berenguer to put the kettle on the fire!'

He stepped back, hands gripping my shoulders, looking me up and down.

'Berenguer won't let me eat prison food,' he added absently, with a nod towards a door I had not noted; this was not one room, but a set of chambers, evidently. 'You're looking well. Have you eaten?'

'Have *I* eaten?'

'There's some beef left from last night, and chicken. And maybe a bit of mutton—'

'*Honorius!*'

I swore in Italian, Alexandrine Latin, and a little of the vocabulary of Chin.

Honorius beamed at me.

'*Mutton?* But you're in prison!' I protested.

My father put his fists on his hips and grinned. 'Yes, I am, aren't I?'

There was a long oak settle beside this room's hearth, a length of red velvet thrown over the back to prevent draughts. I collapsed down onto the wooden seat. 'I don't understand!'

Honorius signalled, without looking, and sat down on the settle beside me. A moment or two later another man-at-arms – I recognised Berenguer's angular features – entered wearing an apron over his doublet, and carrying a tray with wine and bread and cold mutton. He gave me a nod of greeting.

I looked around at the soldiers, as well as my father. 'You could walk right out of here! *Why* are you here?'

Honorius leaned his elbow on the back of the low settle. His hand, holding his wine goblet, just visibly shook. His face glowed, looking at me.

I tried again. '*Why are you in prison?*'

'Because I want to be.'

One should not regard one's own father as if he were stark mad. Except under this kind of provocation. 'Father—'

'Because it's necessary.' Honorius smiled. 'I may be a soldier, but I do understand *some* things about politics. I'm on display.'

Saverico and Orazi both nodded at that. Honorius waved a hand to dismiss them from their attentive stances – which meant they retired to the chess table five feet away, to watch us from there.

'On display,' Honorius repeated, 'and contrite. An object lesson. Soon to be impoverished. Well – comparatively, and for a while. Then all will be well between me and the King—'

'But you're in prison!' I couldn't conquer the enormity of it, even if the rats and dung were absent. 'You've vanished; Rodrigo could have you quietly killed! Why—'

'To keep the stupid from rebelling against their King.' Honorius rubbed his chin. 'Who, come to think of it, is *my* King. I don't like serving under a weak king.'

I saw the truth of it as if someone had flung shutters open to sunlight. I tried not to sound accusatory – and failed. 'Honorius, you *agreed* to this!'

'It's necessary,' he said simply.

Orazi, at the window table, prodded his bishop and grinned.

Words choked themselves in my throat. I put my goblet down before I should spill it.

'And you *didn't let me know!*'

Honorius cocked a brow.

He said nothing of the distance of Constantinople, or the likelihood that I would have been somewhere else by the time letters or messengers arrived. Which saved my pride, if nothing else.

'I wasn't certain this would happen until I got here.' He shrugged. 'One of the possibilities was execution, but you tell me your Rodrigo Sanguerra's a reasonable king, so that didn't seem likely. This didn't surprise me when he ordered it.'

He paused, putting his hand on my shoulder again as if reassuring himself of my solidity.

'Letters can be intercepted. What could I safely say to you?'

'I had the same difficulty in Alexandria . . . ' I watched Orazi passing the castle-piece back and forth between his fingers.

Honorius's grip tightened. 'Why are you here and not in Alexandria? What happened? And how did you get here?'

'Ah.' I craned my chin up to see what was beyond the window, but I had been correct before: it was the mountains and the north. No visible sea. 'Have you heard any gossip about a "devil-ship"?'

Honorius's lips pursed surprisingly delicately; he might have been a disapproving duenna in the Court of Ladies. 'I think you'd better explain.'

I explained.

He sat for a minute or more, after I had done.

Quietly, he asked, 'Is Onorata still with us?'

Relief and chagrin hit me in equal measures. *I should have told him that at once!*

'Oh, she is – in *loud* health.'

Awkward although it might be on the hard wooden seat, I leaned over and embraced my father again.

The lines around his eyes tightened as if he looked into sunlight. 'I didn't realise you'd miss my company, Ilario.'

Since it seemed appropriate to a soldier, and since I might otherwise weep, I said, 'Fucking idiot!'

He wrapped his arm about my shoulder and shook me, as if I were a much younger boy.

It left me sitting forward on the settle; I ran my fingers through my hair, and lifted my head to look into his face. 'If you agreed to prison . . . How long do you stay here?'

'Long enough, I suppose. I dare say I'll hear from the King.'

A frown dented his brows.

'Ilario – I sent no word for you to come home! Whether on a "devil ship" or not! What are you doing here? It can't be safe—'

I summarised it as briskly as I might.

'King Rodrigo will call Aldra Videric back as First Minister,' I concluded, 'now that Admiral Zheng He's ship is here causing panic. Then Videric's back in power, and we need not—'

'Wait, wait.' Honorius sliced the edge of his hand through the air. 'How is this one single ship to cause enough danger to Taraco that the King can justify that? If it had been a *fleet*, now . . . What use are a few hundred men?'

It was a reasonable supposition, given the crews of galleys. A man can hear 'giant ship' without any real conception at the reality of the matter.

'Five thousand men,' I corrected.

'Five – *thousand*.'

I had brought no sketchbook, there being no way of doing that. I called to Berenguer to rescue me a charred stick from the edge of the hearth-fire and, under all their eyes, sketched on the wooden table the lines of a Venetian galley, and the size, beside it, of Zheng He's war-junk.

'Bugger me!' Honorius said.

I left him staring at it and ate the remainder of the mutton, suddenly very hungry; and chewed on fresh bread while Honorius and Orazi had a long and technical argument about the probable effectiveness of a ship with a crew of five thousand men.

After that, Honorius picked scraps off my plate, and kept breaking off from his own words to look at me. I did not know whether to feel embarrassed, or valued, or both.

' . . . sent the rest of my men on with orders to my steward, at the estates,' he finished, licking grease and crumbs off his fingers. 'Get the damn place back in order now the King's promised to withdraw his garrison. I kept young Saverico because he's supposedly intelligent.'

The Ensign grinned.

'And at any rate, young and quick enough to get up and down these stairs when he's ordered. And Berenguer because he cooks. And Sergeant Orazi stayed because I needed a man who could hold a conversation and play chess, or I knew I was like to run mad in the first week. Doing nothing doesn't come easily to me.'

'I can believe that . . . '

Judging by Venice, I thought Orazi's idea of intelligent conversation was likely to be, *Do you remember when we got all of the foot-reserve into the battle-line that time in Navarra?*, but my father is a military man.

'And the Egyptian's here?' Honorius added. 'All's well with you and Rekhmire'?'

'Certainly.'

He looked a little blank at that, but I couldn't identify his reasons.

'And that weasel-assassin you had on a chain: what happened to Carrasco?'

'Actually – he's on the ship, looking after your granddaughter.'

It caught Honorius sufficiently off-balance that he inhaled wine, dropped his wooden goblet, and sprang up to dash the wine-lees off his hose, all the while spluttering in outrage and panic. Orazi gave me a reproachful look.

'Carrasco makes an excellent nurse.' It was more than I could do to restrain a grin, but I stifled it at the realisation that Honorius's panic was genuine. 'It's safe. I wouldn't put Onorata in danger.'

Grumbling, Honorius resumed his seat on the settle.

I looked around at the other three, as well as my father.

'I only landed at dawn today. Has there been gossip or news of Videric or Rosamunda? Oh—' The Rialto came vividly back to me. '—and Federico? Did he chicken out? Has he turned up back here in Taraco?'

Orazi shook his head. 'Nah, not him. Nor his lady wife nor family, neither. I reckon they've gone north like they said.'

Honorius said, 'I confess I think better of him for that.'

'I . . . think I may do, too.'

'As for Videric and Rosamunda—' Honorius gave the men-at-arms a questioning look, and spoke again when none of them did. 'There are no *credible* rumours. They're still on his estates.'

Now I am close enough to be in the same kingdom with Videric, I wonder if the idea is as splendid as it seemed in Venice.

A sideways look at Honorius confirmed the man a mind-reader, at least of his son-daughter.

'No rumours about Carthage, either.' Honorius signalled for more wine. 'But I had reason to be concerned about you, son-daughter, I thought. We heard stories of some "demon" attack on Queen Ty-amenhotep. Was that while you were in her city?'

I steadied my goblet with my other hand as Saverico poured.

'It was the golem.'

Honorius snapped his fingers in irritation. 'I should have guessed *that*. "Demon", indeed. What happened?'

'An envoy from Carthage tried to use the golem to kill the Pharaoh-

Queen.' I found it comforting to lean my shoulder against Honorius's. 'But we stopped it.'

Honorius ran his free hand through his cropped hair, looking queasy. 'Damned if I would have gone near it! Wait – *you* stopped it? Not the Queen's soldiers? You—'

I couldn't help but look innocent in the face of his bluster. 'I had the book-buyer's help . . . '

Honorius narrowed his eyes at me. 'How could you fight a monstrous thing like that?'

I took another swallow, feeling a relaxation that was partly drinking wine on top of too little food, and mostly the relief of Honorius's company.

'Who'd *fight* the thing? We disabled it beforehand. So when the envoy tried, nothing happened.'

'Disabled—'

Four pairs of eyes watched me. Saverico and Berenguer in wonder, Orazi both sceptical and bemused, and my father looking as if he suspected some trick was being played on the Lion of Castile.

'We used . . . A secret weapon.' I bit down on my lower lip and managed not to smile.

'Secret weapon,' Honorius echoed.

'You blew it up!' Saverico yelped excitedly.

Gravely, I said, 'No, I think they would have noticed that.'

Orazi snickered.

'And where did this "secret weapon" come from?' Honorius inquired.

'Out of Masaccio's workshop. Or – the recipe did.'

'"Recipe."' My father's eyes began to narrow. His lip twitched. 'They'd notice Greek Fire, too!'

Berenguer interrupted scornfully. 'What kind of weapon comes out of a painter's workshop?'

Over Saverico's and Orazi's raucous comments, I managed to make myself heard. 'It had lime in it . . . '

Honorius grinned and pounced. 'You burned the damn stone man!'

'No, no burning; not even with quicklime.'

A considerable hubbub arose from the men-at-arms, speculating what weapon might destroy a stone man without leaving signs of this. I paid no attention, watching the creasing of lines about Honorius's eyes.

'A secret weapon,' he speculated aloud, holding back a smile. 'Made out of what you may find in a painter's workshop. Which *you* had knowledge of. Beginning with lime—'

The room's outer door opened. Safrac de Aguilar stood with the royal guard, a regretful expression making his long face even longer.

'My apologies, but it's near on the hour of Terce. We must go.'

I rose from the settle, conscious that Honorius stood up beside me.

'It's not a time to annoy Rodrigo Sanguerra.' I looked up at my father. 'I'll be back later. As soon as I can.'

Honorius nodded soberly, and wrung my hands in a parting grip.

Halfway to the door, he called, 'Quicklime and what else? Give me a clue! What other secret ingredient is there?'

Safrac de Aguilar stepped aside to let me pass. I glanced back over my shoulder, and left the Lion of Castile with a single word.

'Cheese!'

6

By the time we reached the royal appartments, Terce had rung out from the chapel bells. De Aguilar looked apprehensive as he led me into King Rodrigo's council chamber.

King Rodrigo Sanguerra and the envoy of Alexandria both stood, chairs shoved rudely back from the inlaid wood table, shouting at each other in contesting bass and tenor.

I crossed my arms over my chest, and glanced at Aldra Safrac. 'No need to be concerned. If I got up on the table and took all my clothes off, I doubt either one of them would notice.'

Safrac de Aguilar proved to have a thoroughly pleasant laugh.

Neither of the quarrelling men reacted to it.

King Rodrigo Sanguerra sat decisively down in his chair.

'No,' he said. '*No.*'

It was Aldra Safrac's suggestion that the King might wish to break his fast which moved us all into one of the lesser chambers. Smaller, more comfortable, I felt it take the edge off Rodrigo's temper.

If I recall correctly, he was never even-tempered if ill-fed.

It would have been impolite to refuse food myself, so I ate in the King's company again. Rekhmire' copied me for the manners of Taraco. When we were done, King Rodrigo took off his overrobe and stretched out his arms, gazing down from the high window at the inland mountains. The late morning sun cut lined crevasses into his features.

'Your pardon, Majesty,' Rekhmire' said, with an inoffensiveness I envied. 'But will you tell me what does not please you about this?'

Rodrigo turned his back to the sculpted window. To my surprise, he gazed at me.

'I'm glad to see you not murdered,' he observed, 'despite all the trouble you've caused me. So much I can say. For the rest, and this "war-junk" . . . My high council is due to meet at Sext. If I tell them I intend to recall Aldra Videric – on what they will see as a pretext – we shall still be talking this time next month, and still nothing will get done!'

Rekhmire''s brandy-coloured eyes met mine, for the briefest of moments. I read *Not enough* perfectly clearly.

The Egyptian spoke deferentially; only someone who knew him well would have detected the acid quality to his speech.

'Would it speed matters if the foreign ship were to fire on that headland?' He indicated the chamber's other window, which faced south east. 'Just by way of a demonstration?'

Through the stone frame carved with oak leaves and acorns, I saw a coastal view long familiar to me. Roman ruins on a headland, a mile or so away from the city itself; broken-off stout pillars rounded by centuries of rain and frost. I remember taking stolen bottles of wine up there with other slaves, resting on the sun-heated rock, watching lizards dart into crevices.

'Even if it would, I do not permit the suggestion.' King Rodrigo seated himself in the oak chair at the table's head, taking his weight on his wrists like an old man. Even with the little time I had been gone, he seemed older to me.

Or perhaps, until now, I have never entirely stopped seeing the man I saw at fifteen. When he bought and paid for me.

Rodrigo Sanguerra studied me with an intent gaze.

Cao!

It sounded better in Chin.

I realised a little late that the light from the windows clearly illuminated my face. The King nodded as if his suspicions were confirmed.

'I think ... yes. Ilario, if there is anything to be done here, the representative of New Alexandria and I will do it. You should return to the monstrous ship as soon as you can. If anything's to be made out of this, we need not confuse people over who truly sired you!'

I spoke before Rekhmire' could interject.

'Does it matter, sire? My father's in prison, so no man will see us together. And no one will hear it from me if you desire me to say nothing.'

The King shot a look at me, clearly assessing.

'Rosamunda was your dam, I don't doubt it. But the Lion of Castile has left his imprint all over your face. If that story got out, every man would be calling Lord Videric a cuckold!'

Rodrigo shook his head.

'Bad enough that my boy-girl Court Fool should turn out to be First Minister Videric's child! That was scandal enough! If word gets out that all Pirro Videric is to you is your mother's husband ... '

He eased back in his chair, chin on fist again, watching me. *I know this of old*, I thought, relaxing a little. He doesn't trust an Alexandrine, but me – me he desires to convince him.

Rodrigo scowled. 'After the accusations made by Carthage, Videric's enemies here in my court can despise him for fathering a freak. With your true parentage known – they would laugh at my lord Videric because his wife had another man's child. Nothing is harder to recover from than laughter.'

Captain-General Honorius might resent being accused of fathering a freak, I thought. But the King would have spoken to my father, and would know that by now.

He's seeing if I can be goaded into unwise speech.

'I need Aldra Pirro Videric back.' Rodrigo's voice was a bass growl. He switched his glare to Rekhmire'. 'I don't believe I need Queen Ty-ameny to tell me this!'

Rekhmire' bowed his head, where he sat on a less-decorated chair; much in the manner that I'd seen him do when being book-buyer to a difficult client. 'It's in the interests of New Alexandria to offer what assistance we can, Majesty. No one wants a war.'

The King's gaze shifted to that window which allowed a view south. '*Carthage* wants war. And I dare say Constantinople and Carthage will at some date contest the future of the Middle Sea – although I take it, from what you say, that this is not yet?'

'The Great Queen fights to ensure it is not.'

The late morning haze had burned off the sea. At the window's edge, it was just possible to see Zheng He's impossibly large ship.

The King looked back towards me.

'You bring me *a* cause. Not a sufficient one to carry it through.'

My stomach plummeted.

Rodrigo Sanguerra shifted his gaze rapidly to Rekhmire'. 'So. What else have you to suggest?'

Refreshments were brought in from time to time, and I noted how certain faces appeared again and again among the servants. Like Safrac de Aguilar, who kept the door, men that King Rodrigo could trust not to spread rumours. When I excused myself to the necessary-room, I investigated long enough to find Attila and Tottola in an antechamber, boasting to the King's household guards.

I stopped long enough to arrange food and drink for them, and to comprehend that – however outrageous their stories – they were not touching on the truth.

'I hope you're getting somewhere in there,' Tottola grumbled. 'St Gaius himself would be bored with this!'

Somewhat out of temper myself, I shook my head. 'They might just as well have sent us back to the ship. If things don't change, I'll put a dress on and have a fit of female hysterics!'

That left the German brothers chuckling.

When Rekhmire' and the King began to circle the discussion of royal and clerical legalities for the third time, I gave in to temptation and pulled a folded sheet of paper out of my leather purse. Smoothing it out on my thigh, I began partial studies with a nub of chalk. The woollen hose were warm for summer, and the mail – where the links sucked on to my torso – breath-snatchingly hot. My knight's training is long enough ago that I had forgotten the breathlessness of wearing any armour in hot weather.

The interwoven strands of linen and reed that made up Rekhmire''s headband provided an interesting challenge to draw. I added the curve of his brow-ridge under it, the kohl-marked line of upper and lower eyelid; sketched the shape of his mouth . . .

Is Rekhmire' waiting until the King has talked himself dry before he introduces some idea of his own? Or have they already talked that through, and is he at a loss?

Talk dragged on for another quarter-hour by the King's water clock. I switched to drawing Rodrigo's hands.

The King's voice broke in on my thoughts. 'Well, it is a curious idea . . . '

Glancing up, I found myself the focus of looks from King Rodrigo and the Egyptian.

My hands were out of sight under the table. Or I hoped so. No matter how well-drawn, a study of a man's hands is unlikely to be well received as the reason why I have no idea what has been suggested.

King Rodrigo lifted his chin from his fist and eased back in the oak chair. He looked at me speculatively. 'Would you consider it?'

I shot a glance which the book-buyer seemed accurately to read as *Help!* The envoy of the Pharaoh-Queen stretched his leg out under the oak table, flinching barely perceptibly. 'Perhaps I could explain to you in more detail, Ilario?'

There was an odd glint in his dark eyes. *Yes: I know: I should have drawn less, and paid more attention!* But between the crucial decisions here, which may affect all my life, and Honorius in prison in another part of the palace, is it any wonder I desire only to lose myself in contour and value?

Rekhmire's large hand gestured towards the window. 'Let us agree that Admiral Zheng He's appearance at Taraco *begins* to be a cause for the recall of Lord Videric, but is not sufficient cause.'

The Egyptian switched his gaze to me.

'Last year's scandal that deposed Videric from his position of first minister was an accusation of attempted murder. That he sent his wife, in fact, to murder you – you until then not known to be Videric and Rosamunda's child. And Carthage took this attempted killing badly.'

Rekhmire' kept a perfectly even expression during his last words.

Had I been closer, I would have kicked his ankle under the table, injured knee or not.

'*And?*' I prompted, robbed of anxiety by minor irritation. Which, I realised, is likely his design.

'And . . . ' Rekhmire' glanced at Rodrigo. 'His Majesty agrees that if the scandal was between Videric and you – then any cure for that scandal must also be between Videric and you.'

Did this arise out of your discussion? I wondered. *Some moment I was lost in drawing? Or is this something you concocted aboard ship, and failed to tell me?*

I found myself chilled, despite the sun in the room.

'It must be assumed that you and Aldra Videric are father and child.' Rekhmire' directed his dark gaze at me, like a shock of cold water. 'Obviously this would involve some degree of untruth.'

'You mean I have to lie.'

I had not expected to hear myself sound so bitter. *This can't be unexpected, after all.*

Rekhmire' spoke with the greatest apparent innocence. 'Call it diplomacy.'

The humour – which I doubted any man might read there except for me – faded from the Egyptian's eyes as I failed to respond.

'Continue,' King Rodrigo murmured.

'If it were publicly supposed that there had been a *mistake*.' Rekhmire' emphasised the final word softly.

'If it were discovered that Carthage had been in error, and Lord Videric is *not* responsible for attempted murder. Then that discovery – in addition to negotiating friendly relations with Zheng He – might suffice as a pretext for reappointing him as Taraco's First Minister.'

King Rodrigo grunted. *I know that rumble of old.* 'Don't try my patience.' I slid the paper in my lap well out of sight.

I asked, 'How would this happen?'

Rekhmire''s eyes sought the King's, with a brief look at me that might have been apology. 'I had thought – some kind of public ceremony of reconciliation?'

I tasted the word in my mind. *Reconciliation.*

Reconciliation between me and Aldra Videric.

Pah!

The book-buyer continued. 'If Lord Videric and Aldro Rosamunda are greeted, on their return to Taraco, with every mark of friendship from their son-daughter Ilario . . . Majesty, might not your court assume the King-Caliph and Carthage's Lord-Amirs *must* be in error?'

Rodrigo Sanguerra blinked like one of the lizards that haunt ancient stone ruins. 'It would need to appear more than friendship.'

Rekhmire' rested his hands on the table before him, fingertips pressed together. I recognised his stance when closing a deal with some scroll-owner. *Yes, he thought this through on Zheng He's ship—*

Delicately, the Alexandrine spy suggested, 'Some formal ceremony, perhaps?'

The King nodded, thoughtfully. 'Some ceremony. Some formal reconciliation . . . In the cathedral, perhaps? Archbishop Cunigast could oversee it. Enough pageantry, enough piety, and a show of pardon . . . Yes!' Energised, Rodrigo Sanguerra sat upright in his chair. 'Yes: if only because my people greatly *desire* a reason to think that the King-Caliph was mistaken, and should therefore have kept his nose out of our business!'

I saw the shape of it in my mind. Lie and pretend. I braced myself and spoke. 'Your Majesty, yes. Provisionally, I would agree to that.'

Rodrigo snapped his fingers.

Servants entered the room, pouring wine and water again for the three of us. The glasses they brought were delicate blue, with double helixes of red and yellow glass in the stem.

Kek and Keket and Rekhmire''s Holy Eight! Put my father in prison, and then confiscate his export glass!

Light glimmered from my Venetian glass to the tabletop, casting twisted ellipses of light. I lifted it, tilting it in an ironic toast to King Rodrigo. He returned the gesture, his expression closed.

The empty spaces of the cathedral in Taraco have always impressed me. Any noise louder than a whisper echoes from the inside of the vast dome, ivory in colour, featureless as an egg; stark in contrast to the gold, ruby, emerald, and sapphire work encrusting the altars and chapels below. Full of the court and citizens of Taraco, a stunning spectacle; the midday sun falling clear down onto the main altar below.

I thought of standing there. Of Videric's face. Of Rosamunda.

'Wait—'

Rekhmire' and the King were talking: I broke into their relaxed speech more harshly than I meant.

'Your Majesty, I'm sorry. I apologise, but I've just thought – "a show of pardon", you said? Would you formally *forgive* Aldra Videric? How can you, if it's Carthage that's supposed to have made the error? What would you be forgiving him for—'

I broke off. King Rodrigo's stolid dark gaze transfixed me.

The shaking of my hand sent reflections of light across the inlaid geometric wood patterns.

Further down the table, Rekhmire' spoke in a smooth apologetic. tenor. 'Ilario, you haven't thought through the implications.'

It was difficult to get words out. 'I haven't?'

'His Majesty is suggesting a family reconciliation, to lead to a political reconciliation. But, yes, you're right: Lord Videric can't be pardoned if he's not the one at fault.'

The glass was hard as stone under my fingertips.

Rekhmire''s voice came again. 'Ilario, it won't be Lord Videric who must publicly apologise.'

Bright concentric circles rippled on the surface of my wine. 'Apologise?'

Rodrigo Sanguerra waved a hand at Rekhmire', his velvet sleeve pulling back to show white linen, and curling black hairs at his wrist. 'Listen to the Alexandrine envoy, Ilario.'

You freed me!
Both of you.
I shifted my gaze from the King to Rekhmire'.

The Egyptian interlaced his fingers, where his hands rested on the table. 'His Majesty needs to make the reputation of Lord Videric spotless. Lord Videric can't appear to have anything to do with a murder. Not if he's to return as First Minister.'

Rodrigo's gaze weighed me. 'Therefore, Ilario, it was not an attempted murder.'

I remember, less than a year ago, taking my first manumission papers from that creased hand. He unlocked the collar from my neck with his own fingers.

And this is the man who has worked twenty-five years in harness, if not in collar, with Videric. And whose own reputation, at the moment, is therefore suspect.

Rekhmire' spoke again. 'Ilario, it would be you. If the attempted murder is redefined as a mistake, then you would have to speak publicly. You would need to apologise to Lord Videric, because you allowed the Lord-Amir in Carthage to reach a wrong conclusion. And it won't be difficult to have it credited – men are usefully prone to believing slaves are foolish.'

I will not disgrace myself by throwing this wine in the Egyptian's face.

Rekhmire''s wide shoulders lifted in a minute shrug. 'You might say, for example, that you were attacked by criminals in Carthage. You were rescued by the Lady Rosamunda. Judge Hanno Agastes wrongly mistook her rescue for an attack. And you . . . were too afraid of punishment, when Carthage mistook her actions, to speak up and tell the truth. But now—'

Sharp pain shot through my hand.

Fine curved splinters of glass stood out of my skin.

I opened my palm, not yet wincing at the hot fire of the cuts. Only the stem of the glass was whole. Wine puddled on the table, spattered surprisingly far.

The King silently signalled for his servants to clear the mess.

I felt as if my neck creaked stiffly as I looked up at Rekhmire'. 'You've thought this through.'

And said no word to me.

Rekhmire''s fingers slid apart from each other: his large hands made fists. He met my gaze fearlessly. 'Yes, I've thought! You need to apologise, Ilario—'

'*I* did nothing wrong!'

'Apologise for not speaking up when Carthage drew an erroneous conclusion, thus causing the downfall of your father Lord Videric.'

The Egyptian's gaze was implacable, and Rodrigo Sanguerra sat back, letting him speak.

'You would beg Lord Videric's pardon for being coward enough not to speak at the time. And for being timid enough to run from Carthage afterwards, and not come back to Taraco to set matters right until now.'

Rekhmire''s round chin came up: he stared at me challengingly.

I picked the larger of the glass splinters from my palm. None had gone deep enough to scar, but there was a surprising quantity of blood.

If Honorius hears of this, no possible concern about politics will stop him from protesting!

'Apologise.' I could barely get the word out without stuttering. 'Lie and beg pardon. From Videric.'

King Rodrigo Sanguerra nodded, speaking for the first time in long minutes. 'Yes.'

In the city's cathedral, in front of four, five, perhaps six thousand people.

People that I know.

I desired more than anything to walk out. One shake of my hand, to scatter loose and bloody fragments across the delicate wood patterns; then I might push my way past Safrac de Aguilar and out—

But if I run through the passages of this castle, I will only meet more people that I know.

'You want me to claim that I lied. That I ran away. That I was too afraid to come back and tell the truth. You want me to say this in front of every prominent citizen and nobleman of Taraconensis.'

I found a kerchief in my leather purse. When I wrapped it about my hand, it turned scarlet through the bleached cloth.

'You know that if I say this in public, it doesn't matter what the truth is – I can't rewrite it, after. *That's* the story that will spread out and be believed.'

'Yes,' King Rodrigo Sanguerra said.

I did not look at Rekhmire'. I looked at the king who had owned me. 'No.'

7

Since too many eyes were watching every boat on the way out and back to Zheng He's great floating wooden island, His Majesty Rodrigo Sanguerra Coverrubias changed his decree, and said that his guests should live ashore for the time being, quietly out of the way, in an obscure part of the palace's south wing.

Rekhmire''s hand clamped on my elbow the moment we passed through the doors and were alone.

'Ilario, listen to me!'

'*Now* you talk to me? You should have done that before!'

I threw him off with a vicious movement, caught from the corner of my eye how he stumbled, and swung around fast enough to catch hold of him, preventing him falling.

Not strong enough to hold up his weight, I found the two of us taking staggering round steps as if we danced; until the room's wall caught me squarely between the shoulder-blades, and both of us leaned up against the other, gasping and panting.

I felt the taut expansion of his shoulder and arm muscles; had a moment to think, *Walking with crutches has begun to alter the shape of his body*, and then his other hand got a grip on his staff, and he pushed himself back from me and the wall.

He swayed but stayed on his feet. '*What* should I have spoken to you about?'

These chambers were higher up than Honorius's prison, I registered, and less well-appointed. But airy and light: Onorata would be content here.

I ignored his question. 'I'm risking this disguise once more. Tottola and I will bring Onorata and Carrasco ashore this evening at dusk. Is this my chamber, or yours?'

'They have given me the choice of rooms opposite,' Rekhmire' got out, sounding as if he choked. '*What have I not told you?*'

The exertion had not sapped my explosive temper: I had all I could do to rein it in. I desired to throw anything that would break. Instead, I faced the Egyptian, stabbing a finger towards the open windows, where Taraco drowned in the afternoon's white heat.

'This is not Carthage!' I yanked at the leather laces tying closed the neck of Attila's mail-shirt, but it made me no less heated. 'This isn't

Rome! Or Venice! Or Alexandria! What happens to me here happens in front of people I *know!*'

There are few ways to be got out of a mail-shirt with dignity. A thousand riveted metal rings form a net that cling to the body. Pulling one's shirt off upwards only results in yanking at chin, ears, and capturing hanks of hair to pull out.

The Egyptian was tall enough that he might have held the mail-shirt's shoulders still while I eased myself down out of it, but I felt absolutely no inclination to ask his help.

I copied remembered instructions from my master-at-arms, bending over and putting my hands flat on the floor. I shook myself until the armour's own weight inverted it, and brought it sliding smoothly down over my torso, shoulders, arms and head.

The mail-shirt thudded to the floorboards at my wrists as a small bundle of metal.

I straightened up, gasping with relief, kicked at it, and all but fell over with dizziness.

In the voice of a man who has lost his breath again, Rekhmire' observed, 'A sight I wouldn't have missed for the world . . . '

'*I will not look like a liar and a coward in front of the court I grew up in!*'

The Egyptian's amusement vanished. 'I would not laugh at you—'

There was a joint-stool by the couch: I kicked it the length of the panelled chamber.

'I will not look like a liar and a coward in front of *Videric!*'

Tottola was engaged at the outer door in conversation; I thought it might be with members of the royal guard. I had no hope of understanding a word with rage deafening me.

'Ilario.' Rekhmire' put out his hand: I stepped back.

'Videric made my mother try to kill me. I'll stand in the same room with him, but – claim this never happened? That I've *lied?*'

Rekhmire' grabbed my upper arms, staring down the inch or two difference in our heights.

'And you didn't plan your story well enough,' I said bitterly. 'Videric allowed his *child* to be abandoned and sold! To live here at court as Rodrigo's tame freak. How will *that* reform him in men's eyes?'

Rekhmire''s intent gaze made my heart hammer; I felt a pulse beating in my throat. His mouth quirked, in something like amazement.

'Oh . . . I can devise an answer for that, too. Say that Videric, as your father, wanted you to have a good life at court – but he knew you would suffer prejudice as a hermaphrodite. As the King's possession, no man could ever harm you.'

Rekhmire''s expression was sardonic.

'And if you lived anonymously, court factions could never use you to discredit the King or your father . . . Suppose we say, on Videric's behalf, that coming to court as the King's Freak is the only way you could have lived here as yourself? Not having to pretend to be either wholly a man or wholly a woman.'

Rekhmire''s fingers gradually loosened their grip.

I would have bruises, I realised absently. 'And why was I a slave?'

'Oh, that was *your* idea.'

I blinked.

'When you thought of coming to court, you were afraid you'd hear too much in royal company. You wanted to keep it confidential. If you were King Rodrigo's property, no man could ever ask you to bear witness against the King or your father.'

The surface of my eyes felt dry: now I found I couldn't blink. 'Is there more?'

Rekhmire' snorted. 'What could be more clear? Lord Videric has always had Ilario's best interests at heart. He wanted you safe from gossip and conspiracy and harm – and to be able to live openly as the hermaphrodite you are. Which you did. Until you were foolish enough to run away from some quarrel in Carthage . . . '

Tearing my gaze from his caused me to shake. To have such an interpretation of the facts, and to have it be so far from the truth – and so plausible.

I walked numbly to the window, not seeing the brightness beyond the rippling folds of draped linen, or smelling the sea. 'How long did it take you to cook *this* up?'

There was an audible sigh behind me.

'Ilario . . . I considered all aspects of the matter, from when it was raised at home in the city, all through our journey. Men here are *ripe* for belief. Don't assume only soldiers and courtiers can see that Carthage wants to send the legions in.'

Rekhmire''s voice came closer.

'This is an excuse and a pretext. In other words, it's what we wanted, to allow Aldra Videric back. Ilario's falsely-accused and dutiful father comes back to Taraco as First Minister. What does it matter what you have to say?'

My breath came short. 'It matters because he tried to kill me.'

'This is just pride!'

I spun about, and nearly collided with Rekhmire' directly behind me.

I glared up at him. 'It is not *pride*. I was all but killed in childbed because of Videric. *Onorata* would have died. Videric is the man who sent my mother to kill me in Carthage, and because of him, she was willing to do it!'

Anger's heat stifled me more than wearing the mail-shirt. I wrenched the laces of my doublet undone, pulled at the neck of my shirt, and sank down on the room's bed. My scant baggage was there: I dug in it so that I might go barefoot and in my Alexandrine tunic again. At least until I must return to the ship for Onorata.

I stopped with the linen tunic in my hands. It still smelled of Zheng He's ship.

'Don't ask me to do this. Would you let them brand *you* a liar? This would become the truth, for the rest of my life. And Honorius's. And Onorata's.' I winced. *'They'll say Videric is her grandfather.'*

The Egyptian frowned, seeming to turn inward to where that clever mind devised infinite complicated stratagems.

'If Onorata stays in these chambers, there's little enough to connect her with Videric. You'll dress as a man, I assume? Who would think you connected with a baby?'

That obvious, and it never occurred to me. And Honorius's soldiers would act as our servants, so less gossip will spread.

Rekhmire' observed, 'That answers the problem in the short term.'

'You haven't some long-term plan involving her, too? You surprise me!'

Rekhmire' supported himself on his stick, and lowered himself to sit on the edge of the bed. 'What would you have had me do?'

'Tell me!'

'If I have considered this before . . . ' He pulled off his headband and rubbed at his temples. The long curve of his broad back formed a slump. 'It was never certain this would happen. Not certain your King would agree to it, if I suggested it. I said nothing because I would not worry you with the matter, in case it never arose.'

Sheer disgust silenced me.

I leaped up, went to the door, spoke to Attila, and asked him to wake me at dusk. And with that done, I cast myself down fully clothed on the bed as if Rekhmire' were not present, and fell unexpectedly hard into sleep.

He did not wake me before he left for his own rooms.

Ramiro Carrasco and I endured the crossing back from ship to shore, Onorata screaming her displeasure at the boat, the sea-spray, and the palace apartments.

'You owe me a debt of some sort,' I remarked as we entered our chambers. 'As recompense for trying to kill me. What about an honest answer to a question? Forget you're my property. Tell me what you think.'

The secretary-spy hesitated, seeming bewildered. His hand soothed Onorata's back. She made a little fist and rubbed it up and down the arm of his tunic, screaming fit fading down to gulping sobs and then silence.

He made as if to offer her to me and I shook my head. 'The way I feel now . . . '

She'll scream all night if I take her.

Ramiro Carrasco smoothed Onorata's hair back from her pink forehead, as if it helped him to think. There were milk-stains on the shoulder of his tunic. Low and even, he murmured, 'Would this get what you want? Aldra Videric back in the King's service? All of us safe?'

I had debated not telling Carrasco what Rekhmire' had planned. Until I thought, firstly, that he knew so much of my business, a little more would make no difference – and, secondly, that it affects him almost as much as it does me.

I said truthfully, 'I don't know. Suppose it was asked of you? Would you do it? If it meant you were disgraced, here, at home. And there was no changing it, after?'

The secretary-spy gave me as ironic a look as I have ever had from any man.

'Ilaria, mistress, I'm dirt *now*. You bought me because a court in Venice convicted me of attempted murder. I am disgraced.'

'And?'

'If it saved my family?' He looked straight into my face. 'If it even *helped* save my family, I'd crawl over broken glass. Lie. In public; I wouldn't care. I would do anything. You know that: that's why you're a fool to trust me!'

Oddly, that made me smile. 'But I'm the nearest thing to an ally you and your family have, so I *may* not be as stupid as you think.'

He chuckled, the first unmediated mirth I had heard from him since the Doge's prisons. Unexpectedly, his voice softened.

'I understand that this child will have to live with whatever people think of her mother. Father. *Parent*. I understand that.'

He tucked in one edge of Onorata's linen wrap, his finger still showing the remnants of the callus that comes with holding a pen. Over that, it was scarred with the casual brutality that living as a slave entails.

'*I would do anything.*'

Perhaps because I had slept so deeply that afternoon, I could not sleep in the night.

The door of the apartments abruptly opened.

Since I was cleaning the child after her breakfast, and dirty myself because of it, I looked up with a curse, and found myself staring at Rekhmire'.

Not looking at me, I found.

He stared at Ramiro Carrasco de Luis, where the man had just returned from disposing of soiled shit-rags and emptying chamber-pots.

Rekhmire' pointed to the door he had entered by. 'You. Out.'

'Rekhmire'—' I set the wriggling baby on my lap and wiped at its hands.

'You have a visitor, Ilario. One who requires privacy.' The Egyptian looked pointedly at Carrasco.

I indicated the inner door and spoke as evenly to the assassin-nurse as

I could manage. 'Take Onorata through and dress her. Not too warmly. We're taking her up to see Honorius after this.'

'Yes, madonna.'

The Iberian didn't look at Rekhmire' as he walked past within a foot of the larger man.

'And keep your ear away from the door!' Rekhmire' grunted.

I stood up from the bed. 'What in your eight hells do you think you're—'

'I'm leaving the city.' Rekhmire' crossed to a chest I hadn't noticed, and began to recover small items of his own, which he threw into a bag. 'I have an escort from the King. I'm travelling to Lord Videric's estate, to speak with him.'

The book-buyer had his belongings together by the time a man could count a hundred. Half-sentences came into my mind: I couldn't get any of them out.

Going to Videric.

'Are you going to . . . put this suggestion to him?'

The Egyptian only glanced at me.

I wondered how Videric would be now. And Rosamunda. After six or eight months stewing in the provinces, in the winter cold and spring mud and summer heat. Among peasants and serfs, and whatever minor nobility were their neighbours. If their neighbours haven't snubbed them.

Rosamunda will have hated being away from foreign merchants, and Rodrigo's court entertainments. Who's the leader of the Court of Ladies now?

'Rekhmire'.'

He slammed a tiny chest shut with great vehemence. 'No matter your decision – I must talk to the man.'

He turned around, pushed himself on his stick towards the oak inner doors and turned the key in its lock, locking Carrasco and Onorata in. He limped towards the outer door again.

'I will send in your visitor.'

The door closed behind him before I could get a word out.

The room was frighteningly silent without Onorata's noises, without Honorius's voice, or his soldiers', or the Egyptian's. Only Attila and Tottola's tribal dialect in the antechamber made this sound like a human habitation.

Out of nowhere, I thought, *This is the first time in eight months or more that I won't be in Rekhmire''s company.*

The door creaked. I realised I was studying the pattern of grain in the floorboards, and lifted my head.

King Rodrigo Sanguerra stood just inside the closed door.

I sprang to my feet as rapidly as long-inculcated instinct could move me, and dropped down on one knee.

The King smiled crookedly, gesturing for me to rise.

He crossed past me to stare out of the south-facing windows; ran a finger across the sculpted frame's vine leaves, and picked up one of the translucent porcelain dishes that I had brought back from Zheng He's ship.

There was no noise except the singing of laundry women, hundreds of feet below, beating sheets in tubs in a courtyard exposed to the sun. My chest hurt. I realised I was holding my breath.

'Majesty.' I let the breath out with a little gasp. 'Is it safe for you to visit us here?'

His hooded eyelids dropped down over his large eyes; I knew it for amusement. It faded. 'King Rodrigo Sanguerra isn't here. But the slave Ilario's old owner is.'

'I was freed again. In Rome.' My mouth was dry. 'I won't do what you ask.'

Rodrigo didn't sit down. His habitual slow pace carried him from the windows to the shuttered cupboards that lined the walls, and to the dais on which the bed stood with its hangings closed, and the middle of the bare floor.

Rodrigo Sanguerra said, 'I owe you an apology.'

I could not have imagined this as something he would ever say.

I bit back suspicion. 'Majesty?'

'I won't lie.'

He turned on his heel, looking at me with a glint in his dark eyes. Rodrigo's strong features took the window's light, and I ached to draw him.

He added, 'I owe you an apology for owning you – or, for not freeing you before I did. But I won't lie: I'm more sorry that my ownership of you has come back to bite me . . . '

He walked to stand in front of me. You did not commonly notice, until he was in the (admittedly rich) doublet and hose and cap of any courtier, rather than cloak and crown of the King, that he was not a particularly tall man. I doubted him a hand taller than I. But whatever his stature, he contrived to give the impression of looking down at a man.

'Ilario . . . I know an apology doesn't matter to you—'

'It does!'

The reply startled out of me.

I blushed.

I shook my head, as if I could clear from it the shock of seeing Rodrigo Sanguerra here in these shabby rooms. And the wrench of all the old affection between us. Because affection is possible between master and slave, no matter how distorted.

I stared at Rodrigo. 'But I still won't do what you're— what's being asked of me. I can't. I shouldn't. Not for my sake. Not for my daughter's sake.'

And not for my father's, though I have not yet spoken to Honorius.

Rodrigo Sanguerra slowly shook his head. His presence seemed to fill the room. He came to the throne before I was born; there was white in his beard now. I wondered if he had summoned the Crown Prince back, some time between last year and now, or whether Prince Thorismund was still in the north fighting against Franks.

'You have recognised old friends here,' King Rodrigo said mildly.

Familiar faces among the men on the quayside at the chandlers' shops, and in the long market between the docks and the palace, and in the livery of King Rodrigo at the palace gates . . .

'Yes, Majesty.'

He lifted a blunt-fingered hand, pointing at the window. 'And you know, because you must in the past have ridden over, every mile between here and the mountains.'

'Yes, I've loved this place,' I gritted. 'You want me to make it so that I and Onorata can't come back here without disgrace.'

There would be layer upon layer of thoughts beneath what he actually said; I knew him of old. When he first bought me as a cocky fifteen-year-old, I thought a king would have too many affairs of state to be concerned with what his slave got up to. He sent me to the cane often enough to disabuse me of that very quickly. A king must at least try to think of everything.

Rodrigo looked directly at me. 'Ilario. Will you go through with making a public apology, if Aldra Videric will consent to it?'

Consent!

I stared at Rodrigo Sanguerra. If he asks 'will you do this for me?', I'll spit in his face.

'No. I won't do it. And if you order me, because you're my King – I still won't do it.' I held his gaze. 'I'm not looking for an *excuse* to give consent.'

'No, I see that.'

Rodrigo Sanguerra moved restlessly, walking to the window again, and turning on his heel and walking back.

'A king is a steward of his country.'

I shrugged. 'Slaves don't have a country.'

Rodrigo gazed down at me without acknowledging that. 'Steward. Not a Dictator or Tyrant, as the ancient Greeks had it, to hold everything his private property. Do you understand, a steward? To keep the peace? And to leave that peace to the next generation?'

I thought of Onorata, behind the door with Ramiro Carrasco.

'I understand.' I bit my lip. 'No. The answer is no. I won't have her grow up regarded as dirt because of what I'm supposed to have done. I won't lie!'

The King of Taraconensis knelt down on the bare dusty floor.

I gaped; I must have looked like a gaffed fish.

Rodrigo Sanguerra had moved stiffly getting down on his knees, and he knelt as if the bare boards hurt his bones. His spine was ramrod-stiff; his chin jutted up. I could only stare.

'I can't give you this in public.' His voice sounded low but not particularly quiet. 'Not the way you would wish it. I'm a king: I can't shake my people's confidence in me that way. But I will give you all the humiliation you wish of me, here in private. I once owned you. Ilario, I beg you to do this thing.'

Ilario, close your mouth, I thought.

And did.

'I beg you, on my knees. If you desire an apology for anything that occurred while I owned you, you have only to speak. I kiss your hands and feet and I beg you to go before the people and lie.'

Blood rose up in my face, I could feel it. When Ramiro Carrasco had knelt, the embarrassment was painful enough. This – *Oh, this is only impossible!*

'You can't do this, Majesty!'

'I came here to you to do this.' Rodrigo's dark eyes unwaveringly held my gaze. 'My life's work is tottering. The peace will fail. Carthage will send in legions. If fighting won't serve me, I'll grovel at any man's feet if it stops that.'

'Why don't you put me in prison? There are still torturers here, aren't there? Why don't you force me?'

'Will you make it necessary?'

In another man it would have been an implied threat. With Rodrigo (as I have long had cause to know), it is merely honesty.

He shook his head, as if at an afterthought, red lips quirking in his dark beard. 'And besides, penitence is rarely convincing and true, brought about by those means!'

I stared down at him, starkly disbelieving. Amazed.

There is nothing you will not do to save your home, I thought.

Or to set me an example.

The room, heating in the early sun, held a mere breath of air passing through from the south windows. I stood in hose and shirt and unlaced doublet; I must be stinking of sweat and my child, in no condition to see polite company.

The older man, much my senior, knelt on the hard boards in front of me and waited.

I thought of the long-ago morning when Father Felix had brought me into King Rodrigo's breakfast chamber, to listen to courtiers discussing the hermaphrodite's wedding night with a woman.

Now the King's shoulders were tense under the mole-black velvet of his doublet, sewn everywhere with the flower and serpent of Taraconensis. If I sketched him, I realised, I would have to dig deep to uncover those emotions behind the forced calm.

But they are there.

Bitterly, I said, 'I couldn't teach you what humiliation is, Majesty.'

Looking into those darkest of brown eyes, I thought of Ramiro Carrasco – and realised, in that moment, that Rodrigo Sanguerra of Taraconensis has no more idea of what to expect as a slave than Ramiro Carrasco had. And that, as with Ramiro, this is not the key of the matter.

'You're on your knees to me, Majesty.'

'Yes.' He didn't flush, but the lines in his face altered.

'Begging me.'

'Yes.'

'Because . . . ' I took a deep breath. 'Because you want me to see what you'll do for Taraco. And then – you want me to do the same thing.'

His shoulders went back as if he were one of Honorius's soldiers on parade. It was only in the rigidity of his spine that I could see how much fury, how much outrage, he suppressed in himself.

'What you have to do will be humiliating, yes.' He lifted his gaze, for the first time coming within a hair's breadth of true appeal. 'And I beg, the King begs you: humiliate yourself, in front of your enemy, because I need you to. We need you to.'

I went to speak and he interrupted.

'This is the country in which you were born a bastard, raised and sold and treated as a slave: I understand this—'

'You don't, Majesty.'

He hesitated for the first time. 'No. But there are people here, all the same. Some you know. Most you never will. And I ask you: do it for them. I don't ask you to do it for me. I may be many things, but I am not quite such a fool as that.'

He permitted me to stand in silence, then, watching him. Looking at the King of Taraco, down on his knees to a slave, a freed slave.

It moves me that he'll do this for the people here.

It moved me still more that I could read, in the lines of his body and face, quite how much he feared being made to grovel by someone too young, too spiteful, too unwise not to break another human being.

'Majesty, do you think I'm risking making you into an enemy because I want some petty apology?'

The fear left him.

I read in his face that he knew that, whether I agreed or not, I would not make a king perform the same tricks as a King's Freak.

I fell on my knees in front of him, as I have so often in my life, but never when he himself was kneeling before me. He reached out to take my hands. His grip was strong, but I felt him shaking. Kings are not treated so; undefeated kings, off the field of battle, do not expect to find themselves on their knees.

'Forgive me, Majesty!'

'You ask me? When a slave must have so many justified grudges against his master?'

'You never did anything any other man wouldn't have done, sire.'

Rodrigo winced. 'That is the worst condemnation I have ever had, I think.'

'Sire—'

'Help me up, Ilario. My knees aren't what they were as a young man.'

By the amount of weight he rested on my arm and shoulder when he had to rely on his right knee, he was correct in that.

'I'm sorry I did not treat you better.' His expression was still a touch that of a man speaking to a child or a hound, but less so than I had ever known him. 'Ilario, if you wish, I will implore you every day now. Do this. Please.'

'Stop.' I was still holding his arm, I found. Bewildered, I didn't release it. There were still the muscles of a knight and warrior under the velvet. 'Majesty, please. Do you think I can't see what's at stake?'

'Well then—'

'I'm not only afraid for myself.'

Finally I brought myself to let go of his arm, and look at the face I knew so well.

'I have a child. I have a father. There are others . . . And I know this won't be enough. Not for Videric. Majesty, he sent men to Italy to kill me – I don't know any *fewer* of his secrets now than I did then! If I go through some ceremony of reconciliation, then in a few months, or a few years, Lord Videric will come after me, and kill me. And he'll kill or disgrace or otherwise destroy all of us who know what did happen at Carthage. He'll kill Onorata. He'll kill Captain-General Honorius.'

I did not mention to my King that Rekhmire' and Ramiro Carrasco, Attila and Tottola, and all of Honorius's household guard, would be Videric's targets too. I don't deceive myself that they're of high enough rank for him to care as more than a point of principle.

I held Rodrigo's gaze. 'Taking up his place as your First Minister won't make Lord Videric safe again, Majesty. Not in his eyes—'

'Wait.' Rodrigo held up his scarred hand.

The bushy dark brows came down in a frown.

'While I grant that panic might, in the past, have forced Videric into errors – I know the man! He's worked beside me for twenty-five years. If his King commands him to treat you with all respect and civility, then he will do it. There can be no doubt of that.'

I looked at Rodrigo's expression of certainty.

And one day, one day there'll be bandits, or thieves, or robbers on the road, or pirates who swoop down on a ship, and leave no one they find alive or recognisable.

But this man is Videric's friend. And quite naturally, he won't believe that.

Rodrigo Sanguerra gave me a curt nod.

'Ilario. I'll call on you again tomorrow.'

8

Honorius and Sergeant Orazi were deep in discussion when I arrived at their chambers, debating how the Chin ship's rocket-arbalests and pottery grenadoes might be used in an Iberian army, should Zheng He ever be persuaded to part with any, or part with the plans for them.

'Which I doubt,' Honorius concluded rapidly, a broad grin spreading over his face. He reached out for Onorata with prison-pale hands.

Orazi and Saverico and even Berenguer allowed themselves to be brought to admit the child had grown bigger, and more active; and Honorius's men-at-arms exchanged grins over his head as he put her on a wolf-skin rug at his feet.

My child cooed and laughed, and thwacked her grandfather's toes with her fists.

'She'll be a quick one when she's grown,' Honorius observed. He gave Ramiro Carrasco a thoughtful stare, and directed Berenguer to take the man into the kitchens and feed him.

'Then,' the Lion of Castile added, 'you might feel inclined to tell me what has you worse concerned than yesterday?'

'God preserve me from mercenary commanders with a keen nose!' I could make little amusement sound in my voice.

Orazi took himself to the door, to engage the King's guards in conversation; Saverico appeared no older than fourteen as he sat down on the wolf-skin to prevent a wide-eyed Onorata eating two bone dice and a chess-man; and I detailed the actions of King Rodrigo to my father.

It took me while the sun rose a finger's width up the morning sky. I turned my head fifty times in the hour expecting Rekhmire' to walk in through the door.

' . . . And the King says he will come to me again. Until I agree, evidently.'

Expectant, I tensed for Honorius's bellowing rage.

Honorius presented me with his lean profile as he gazed towards the window. He rubbed a hand through cropped hair in which the sun showed more grey than when we had stood in Venice.

In a level tone, he said, 'I see why King Rodrigo suggests this.'

I sat perfectly still.

I wish I might ask Rekhmire' his opinion of this.

I wish Rekhmire' were not absent from Taraco now with the last word between us an angry one.

'If you were Videric,' I demanded. 'If you went through with this *farce* for public consumption, would you leave Ilario, and Honorius, and Rekhmire', and Onorata, alive afterwards?'

'I'd think it would look suspicious for those people to *die*, son-daughter.'

'So perhaps he'd wait a while—'

Honorius bent over and picked Onorata up from the wolf-skin. She bubbled happily, and pulled at the laces on Honorius's doublet with all ten fingers splayed. He hoisted her, with a grin, as if he tested her weight.

'She's thriving.' The grin became a beam. Honorius stood and tucked her into the crook of his arm, tickled with a forefinger, and was rewarded with a gurgle.

'There might not be war here yet,' he added quietly, continuing to smile down at her. 'But Carthage will most certainly send in legions and a governor this year, if nothing happens to prevent it. The fourteenth Utica and the sixth Leptis Parva, with Hanno Anagastes or the current head of House Barbas, would be my guess.'

That he could put names and legionary insignia to these fears didn't surprise me, but added to the knot in my stomach.

'Under guise of protecting us against the Franks, you understand.' Honorius looked quickly away from Onorata, as if some other memory had filled his mind. He walked to the window. 'You don't want to see what happens in Aragon and Leon and Castile happening here.'

The window-ledge might be several feet wide, but I was relieved he did not sit Onorata down on it, there being no bars. I leaned my elbows on cool stone and stared down.

'You think I ought to do this.'

'Because I can think of nothing else!'

The diminishing perspective looking directly down the castle's wall made me dizzy. I resolved to draw it some day, and lifted my head. Just visible over the castle's outer walls, grassy slopes lay speckled yellow like lizards under the heat. All Taraco's white houses and colonnades were busy with men and traffic, before they would become deserted under the noon sun. Ochre earth and lapis-blue haze in the distance . . .

'You think I should lie and beg Videric's pardon in public!'

'If you or the Egyptian have a better idea, I'll hear it!'

Onorata began to grizzle.

I shushed her, gently, and Honorius jiggled her a very little, giving her one of the gloves from his belt to chew on. She gummed enthusiastically and wetly at the fingers of it.

'Revolting child,' my father observed besottedly.

I caught Carrasco's voice in the kitchens, evidently in conversation with Berenguer.

'Ask Videric's assassin,' I said. 'He's under threat, and his family too. He'd drown men like kittens in a bucket if it kept his mother and father and brothers safe and *I know how he feels!*'

With considerable asperity, Honorius snapped, 'I am fifty years old: I have fought in all the major fields of the last thirty years of the Crusades; I can take care of myself!'

'And Onorata? Can she?'

I let Onorata grip my thumb. She smiled at me, or I thought she did.

Honorius made a sound I couldn't identify, and when I looked at him, he merely hitched her in his arms again, and carried her back to the rug, and set her down on it.

He sounded exasperated, even in a whisper.

'We need Videric back as the King's minister! This is what we came here for! We came here to have that bastard Videric owe us his job.'

He didn't take his eyes from the baby, even as he growled at me.

'I won't tell you to risk Onorata, you know that! But this is a dangerous world, there are thieves and pirates out there who *aren't* Videric's hired killers. We need to be prepared to protect her in any case. As for me . . . Ilario, I won't allow you to make an excuse out of me.'

The prison appartments rang with the sudden silence.

I felt heat rising in my face.

Because my father, it seems, is undergoing a formal imprisonment by King Rodrigo Sanguerra that – despite its purely political nature – is at some level a profound humiliation for Licinus Honorius. And Honorius suffers it because he wants the country secure.

'Perhaps I need no excuse,' I said. 'You'll be able to live in Taraco. If I do this, I doubt Onorata and I will – because Videric will insist that I leave.'

'Would you not seek an apprenticeship with a master painter somewhere, in any case?' Honorius shrugged, with every appearance of being casual. 'A lot may change in seven years.'

Yes, and my father is a fifty-year-old man: at the end of seven years, he may not be alive.

The day passed: twenty-four hours going by in not much more than a century or two. True to his word, Rodrigo Sanguerra came to my rooms privately, hooded in a linen cloak against discovery; and true to his word, he got down on his knees on the floor.

If anything it was the more excruciatingly embarrassing this second time, when we both knew what would happen.

When I failed to persuade him to stand up – and only just managed to reject the idea of hauling him up bodily – I sat down on my arse beside my King, on the bare floorboards, and put my head in my hands.

'I've been round this trail over and over, sire. Yes: I'll look a fool. I'll be branded a coward and a weakling. And . . . I'll be putting my family at the mercy of a man who wants me dead. I no longer know which is the most essential matter; which might be an excuse for any other. I can't think it through! I just know there are too many reasons why I shouldn't do this.'

King Rodrigo rested his hands on his thighs, sitting back on his heels, and then reached out to take hold of my jaw and turn me to face him.

'King's Freak,' he said softly, and then: 'The King begs you. I beg you.'

'Don't!'

'Don't make me, then.' His crooked smile was the same one that had always signalled a paternal warmth between us, in those rare moments that we had left position and power out of the equation.

I said, 'You've seen my baby.'

His smile flashed in his beard. 'The miraculous child! Yes. Although I suppose they all are. Any miracle that common will tend to be discounted.'

If I gave him a jaundiced look, he took it well.

I said, 'You want me to think about the children in Taraconensis if war comes.'

He gave a shrug, with bulky shoulders; and winced at kneeling on the hard wood. 'Of course. I want you to think about anything that speaks to my side of the argument!'

I might prove my own case, of what truly happened – but that wouldn't help bring Aldra Videric back as your adviser . . .

I sat with my elbows on my knees, and thrust my fingers through my hair

It would begin to prove the true story if I used Ramiro Carrasco de Luis as a witness. The confused emotions of guilt, gratitude, hatred, and attraction that he felt towards his hermaphrodite rescuer would make him speak.

I might make King Rodrigo believe in the extent of Videric's guilt.

But I should not seek to do that. Since he needs to retain that shred of trust to work with the man.

'Do I have to swallow the "forgiveness" of a man who sent people after me to kill me?'

The King of Taraconensis gave me the quirk-lipped look that I have known as long as I have known him. 'Ilario, I assure you, abasement becomes quite natural after a while . . . '

'It does?'

'No.'

I couldn't have painted Rodrigo's expression; the gleam in his dark eyes that was amusement, grief, anger, and self-mockery; all together.

'No,' Rodrigo Sanguerra repeated. 'And you're not my enemy. In fact, you bear a surprisingly small grudge against your King. I don't envy you on your knees before a man who hates you. But . . . '

He put one hand down, to begin to rise; I leapt up and offered hand and arm.

'You're wrong about the grudge, sire.'

'Am I?'

'All that's in the past. I can't carry it now.'

'Ah.' He made fists of his hands as he stood there, stretched his arms out, and I heard tendons and ligaments crack. 'I think I'm wearing you down. If I come tomorrow, who knows what you'll say?'

If there was an hour during the night when I slept, I didn't know about it.

The water clock marked what would have been watches on Frankish and Iberian ships, and were hours of prayer here. After a while I got up and dressed, and, when the time came, fed Onorata with the warm goat's milk that Ramiro Carrasco deftly obtained.

If we had both been slaves, I would have teased him with how a lawyer felt about being skilled in milking goats. As it was, I left him to resume his sleep.

Onorata rarely woke more than once in the night, now. I almost regretted that, leaning at the window and watching moonlight mimic the earlier sun on distant crawling waves. I could have done with somewhat to keep me occupied.

In all honesty, had it been a night in Carthage or Rome or Venice, I would have contrived some accident to wake up Rekhmire', just so that I could talk to the Egyptian.

I squinted out at the black featureless immensity that was the land-mass of Taraco. Wondering how long the mules would take to Aldra Videric's estates, and how riding was treating his knee.

It's possible to become surprisingly accustomed to someone's company, I concluded, and went back to wrestle with Iberian wolf-skin bed-covers, and lay awake until dawn.

Honorius liking Onorata's company, and I not knowing how long I would be here for him to have it, I spent more time in the prison than in my own quarters.

I sat on the wide ledge, one leg hanging down inside the room. From this acute angle, I might just see the sea in the north-east. Sun flashed like hammered gold. From this high citadel I could watch Zheng He's ship tacking slowly up and down the coast – showing its sheer dimensions off to Taraconensis' smaller towns, and bringing their knights and mayors hot-foot to Taraco and the King's presence.

Rodrigo Sanguerra had abandoned kneeling, and that morning had sat with me in my rooms with an air of relaxation. As if, despite what he must attempt to persuade me into, this time was a pleasant relief from court politics.

Now I recall why he kept his hermaphrodite slave . . .

Where the sun fell on the sea, it was bright enough to make eyes sting and water.

King Rodrigo had said, *Panic is spreading very well.* Up here, it's too high to see what men and women do when the dragon-painted ship threatens them; too far off to hear screams, or shouts of anger, or see whether any man is hurt.

I pushed myself back into the room, off the sill, and leaned on the back of the settle, watching with Honorius as Onorata tugged at the wolf's pelt. She might have been wriggling forward on her belly, or only wriggling by accident.

'This plan of the King's,' I began.

The door of the prison opened; royal guards strode in, Rodrigo Sanguerra behind them. Honorius sprang to his feet. I crouched to pick up Onorata, and put her into Saverico's arms, the young ensign being nearest me.

Honorius nodded and Carrasco and the three men-at-arms retired to the kitchens. He bowed his head to his King. 'Majesty?'

Rodrigo Sanguerra waved a hand to dismiss his escort. They filed out. Absently, he seated himself on the oak settle, gesturing that we might sit too if we so chose.

'You have knowledge of the Alexandrine envoy,' he observed. 'I thought I might therefore ask you questions, confidentially.'

'What?' I managed intelligently.

The King ignored me, passing a sheet of parchment to Honorius. 'Is this in his own hand?'

'His scribe would know better.' Honorius held it out to me.

It was signed *Rekhmire'* and a Pharaonic pictogram, as he had signed letters he had had me write.

I read it out. '"I find it compelling to stay with the Aldra Videric at his estate for some time longer. Perhaps a week or a month. His hospitality is overwhelming, and he desires me to stay for the hunting."'

'Is it genuine?' Rodrigo demanded impatiently.

Compelling. Overwhelming.

'Yes. He wrote it, Majesty. But . . . ' I tried to catch Honorius's eye.

Noblemen die of hunting accidents, horses and beasts are dangerous pastimes. But they die also of conspiracy or ambush and are reported as 'hunting accidents'. I saw Honorius recognised my thought.

He frowned. 'It *could* be true. The damned book-buyer – sorry, Majesty; I mean Master Rekhmire'. He might have decided he needs time enough there to persuade Lord Videric into seeing things his way . . . '

The words trailed off into the heated air of the chamber.

The King raised a bushy eyebrow. 'Ilario?'

My hands clenched into fists. 'Yes, it's *possible* – but also possible it's a flat lie! I think – Videric has decided to hold the Alexandrine envoy as a hostage.'

The King looked very close to startled. 'No. No, I think not. The Videric that I know is not a fool! If Master Rekhmire' has conveyed what we do here, Pirro must think he has only to wait for me to recall him. He would also know that Taraconensis can't afford to harm the representative of Queen Ty-ameny.'

I took several steps, pacing about the room, arms wrapped around my body. For all the heat, I was cold.

'Alexandria would only hear it was a hunting accident. Impossible to prove it wasn't.'

'Ilario, really—' King Rodrigo sighed, as I have known him sigh before. 'You allow your fear and hatred to distort your judgement. My lord Videric is not fool enough to allow harm to come to the Egyptian.'

Insight hit me as if it were a bolt from a crossbow.

I all but bit my tongue as the realisation struck.

'No.' I stepped forward, putting my hand on Honorius's shoulder, willing him to understand. 'No, that's right. I am misjudging him. Videric's not that stupid.'

'Then—'

'*Rosamunda is.*'

9

The King scowled, but I ignored him; aware I was gripping Honorius's shoulder hard enough that my fingers must hurt. He would have bruises. I felt as if I needed to urge the clarity of this truth into his body and blood.

My father frowned.

Thinking of . . . his Rosamunda? The woman who would have run away from her husband, until she was offered a choice between material comfort and my father's love?

The woman who twice, in Taraco and in Carthage, came close to killing her son-daughter?

Honorius's frown deepened. 'It's not in Aldro Rosamunda's interests to harm the book-buyer. She'll want her husband made First Minister again.'

'She won't think that far!'

The house of Hanno Anagastes came back to me: Rosamunda's expression behind her frozen eyes.

'Rekhmire' *ruined* her. You didn't see her face in Carthage!'

The frown became a scowl. Honorius absently reached up and peeled my fingers from the ball of his shoulder, and gripped my hand in his. 'She'd end up the wife of an exile if she did this. Or Videric would divorce her!'

'Rosamunda has a queue of rich and powerful men who'd marry her on the spot if she were divorced by Videric—'

Abruptly, I was silenced by the look that flashed across his face.

No way to apologise in front of King Rodrigo without enabling him to guess why Honorius would need an apology.

King Rodrigo slowly nodded. 'The Queen of the Court of Ladies? Yes . . . There are always men willing to take beauty and ignore the reputation that comes with it. Can you think Aldro Rosamunda honestly possessed of such a hatred against the Alexandrine—'

I interrupted a king. 'Can you ask me to bet Rekhmire''s life on the chance that she's more greedy than she is vindictive?'

I let go of Honorius's hands and glared at Rodrigo Sanguerra.

'Majesty, how soon can you talk to the bishops?'

King Rodrigo blinked, caught for once wrong-footed. 'The bishops?'

'This ceremony – reconciliation – apology – "ceremony of peace" –

penitence. Whatever you call it! How soon can it be arranged? How long will it take to summon Aldra Videric and get the bishops into the cathedral? Let's get this started before that lunatic woman does something to harm Rekhmire'!'

The King of Taraco looked at blankly at the Captain-General of Leon and Castile. My father smiled.

I found my face heating. I rubbed my hands across my cheeks.

More cautiously, Honorius inquired, 'Ilario . . . You do know what this involves?'

'Yes. I'm happy to eat dirt as publicly as required! Satisfied?'

A broad grin spread over Honorius's face, despite his evident best efforts to suppress it.

Rodrigo looked self-possessed; I couldn't read what else might be hiding under that efficient expression. 'Very well. The King's household guard may accompany the return message to Aldra Videric – in what strength would you suggest, Ilario?'

'I want him protected. Well protected.'

'Wise.' King Rodrigo stood, dropped a curt nod at Honorius and strode towards the door, barely waiting for us to rise. 'I'll send a full company. The more of the King's Guard, the more honour, after all.'

He broke out into a smile just before the door shut on his heels.

Honorius looked at me.

He said nothing.

'What!' I protested.

The retired Captain-General of Castile and Leon glanced over his shoulder at Saverico, as the men-at-arms came back into the room, and gestured for the young ensign to bring him Onorata.

Hefting the child into his arms, Honorius murmured, 'Taken you long enough to realise . . . '

Orazi smirked.

I swore. 'I'm not – I don't – there isn't – *cao*!'

Honorius pulled me into an embrace gentle only because of the child he also held.

'Rosamunda won't cause his death – because the damn book-buyer isn't stupid. Don't worry for him. Do what you have to do, Ilario. And I'll stand with you, if I have to disguise myself with a sack over my head!'

I spluttered out an uncertain laugh.

'That's better.' Honorius put one hand on the nape of my neck and shook me gently. 'I swear, in all my years as a soldier, I've learned how to tell rash men and fools from the rest – and Rekhmire' is neither.'

He paused. Smiled.

'Your judgement isn't so bad, son-daughter.'

There was no sensible reply to make, I thought.

And Honorius's grip felt surprisingly reassuring, even if his conclusions were self-evidently mistaken.

'Let's get this over with,' I said.

The initial part of the ceremony took three days.

If something excruciatingly humiliating can be boring, I thought, this is.

On the first day I knelt outside the church door as one of the *flentes*, those who weep; dressed only in a shirt, and formally asking the men and woman who went in to Mass to pray for me, and to intercede with God on my behalf. On the second day I was allowed into the narthex of the cathedral as one of the *audientes*, the hearers, and knelt on the cold mosaic floor behind the catechumens until the end of the sermon – not listening very much to what Bishop Ermanaric said, in fact, but lost in the sensation of chill stone under my shins, and trying to work out (in the slanting light from the ogee windows) what were the differences between these pale stones and the glass mosaics of Venice and Constantinople.

On the third day a different bishop, Heldefredus, preached about pardoning those who had sinned, and I took my place as one of the *genuflectentes*, kneeling between the cathedral door and the ambo, dizzy because of a whole day's fast, and speaking only to implore the procession of priests as they walked past me:

'Pray for me, a sinner!'

Again, I was taken out before the Mass was celebrated.

Videric was not present. Nor Rekhmire'.

Honorius let me know himself forbidden to come, and offered his presence all the same. I sent Orazi back with strict instructions to keep the Lion of Castile caged.

Let this not cause any more trouble than it has to!

King Rodrigo sent his household guard to assist in bringing me the plain meats that the bishops had allowed in my penitential cell on the first and second days.

Sergeant Orazi, scowling, told me each day in bad Alexandrine – incomprehensible to the junior priests who oversaw us – that none of our expected visitors had ridden into Taraco yet. And in the language of Taraconensis added that Onorata was well, and possibly missing me. Not knowing young babies, the sergeant said, he found it difficult to tell.

On the night of the first fast I didn't see any of the guard, since no man was to bring me food, and the bishops' priests evidently thought themselves capable of providing fresh water.

There was no candle or lantern in the hermit's cell built outside, up against the cathedral walls. I took advantage of what daylight there was left coming through the door-grate to take the smuggled paper and chalk out from under the thin straw palliasse.

I drew faces. Odoin, who'd been a lieutenant in Rodrigo's royal guard when I left, and now had his promotion to captain. Hunulf, and Winguric; who had worked with me in the scriptorium, and Galindus, of course.

I appreciated that they didn't visit, since every other man or woman I might know from nine years in Rodrigo's palace crowded close to satisfy their urge to stare at me.

The sheet of paper was not large. I drew faces in miniature. Egica, who taught me Latin and letters at sixteen, when it became apparent that Federico's hired tutor had been cheap for a reason. Egica's face was more lined, his nose more covered in red broken veins, in this last year; I could smell spirits on him when he stumbled past me, one hand outstretched as if he would have ruffled my hair in passing.

More men greeted me with shuttered faces. Less than a year, and I am ignored by those I have diced with and trained with in arms, and women-gossips with whom I debated what colours one might put together in embroidered tapestries . . . even young children whose parents had been passing friendly to the King's Freak –

The light was definitely gone.

I crumpled the paper up into a compressed ball in my hand, and crammed it under the palliasse.

This is not the Empty Chair, or the Most Serene, or the city of the Pharaoh in exile. This is not Carthage – *Although I am under a penitence of sorts*, I found myself thinking, and smiled crookedly in the dark.

It was the kind of irony Ramiro Carrasco would have liked, when he was a sardonic lawyer and not a slave.

They ought at least to send Carrasco to me here, a time or two; it would cheer him up to see me in sackcloth and ashes . . .

A voice outside the studded oak door of the hermit's cell said, 'Ilario?'

Yellow light glinted through the iron grate set into the door. An oil-lamp or a candle; oil by the smell.

The voice was for one dumb-struck moment strange to me, and then—

'*Father Felix?*'

'May I come in? They've sent me to instruct you.'

'Yes.' I said it before I thought. 'Yes, of course, Father!'

He had to duck almost double to get under the low lintel. The builders had left a ledge against the far wall, where the masonry was set deep; Father Felix put his lantern on the earthen floor with a muttered prayer, swept his green robes around him, and seated himself. He gazed directly at me.

He looks no different, I thought.

It only seems a decade since I left Taraco; in reality it is only ten or eleven months.

Father Felix's copper-brown features showed as strong as ever, illuminated under his hood; his astonishing pale grey eyes looked through me as much as they ever used to.

'The bishop wishes me to prepare you for the fourth and fifth stations of the exomologesis.' He leaned forward, and his fingers felt warm against my forehead as he brushed my hair back. 'Ilario, are you all right?'

'I haven't practised fasting this year, so I'm unused to it.' I could only stare at him. 'Father ... '

No man had ever known Father Felix's name outside the church, or his origins; all he would tell me was that he had travelled from beyond the lands of the Turk, beyond the Caucasus mountains. Seeing him with new eyes, I suddenly wondered if he would know more of Zheng He's land than the rest of us.

When this is done, I will persuade him to take word to Honorius, and bring news back to me.

'Tertullian,' Father Felix said, in a measured tone.

The black pupils in his grey eyes expanded in the dim lantern light.

'Tertullian instructs us that exomologesis is the discipline which obliges a man to prostrate and humiliate himself, so as to draw down God's mercy. You've performed three of the stations. Tomorrow, you take your place as one of the *substrati*, as Gregory Thaumaturgus defines it; prostrating yourself where you were kneeling today. The bishop will lay his hand on you and bless you. The day after tomorrow, on the final day, you'll act as one of the *consistentes*, and be allowed to be present to hear Mass. Then you come forward to the altar, recite a psalm and litany, and beg forgiveness of the man you've wronged.'

My stomach rolled over.

Father Felix continued, 'The King and the bishops and this man you have offended will hold a *concilium*, there and then, to determine if you deserve re-admission and pardon. And if so, you will be led around the cathedral carrying a lighted candle, prayers will be said, and you will be given public absolution. And the kiss of peace, by Aldra Videric.'

His voice altered on the last word.

'Felix ... ' I sought desperately for words. For some reason Rekhmire''s prayer-box came into my mind's eye: I wondered if he was praying to Kek and Amunet and the rest of the Eight tonight, in Videric's provincial fortress. 'Should I do this?'

Felix's robes were coarse homespun wool, dyed the colour of hedge-weeds. I suspected they were the same robes he had worn when I left last year, faded through many washings. His dark hands were the hands of a workman, if you looked at them apart from the rest of him.

'If your desire for pardon is in any way not genuine, I would need to inform the bishops.' He held my gaze with more ease than most men. 'Tomorrow they'll smear wood-ash on your forehead, and dress you in

573

coarse yellow linen. If you're not truly penitent, that's no more than a play-actor's costume. You can't insult God that way.'

I read the implied *And I won't allow it* without difficulty, knowing Father Felix as long as I have.

It never occurred to me – that as well as begging pardon of my stepfather Videric, I might have to mean it!

I delayed directly answering. 'Aldra Videric will be there on the last day?'

'Lord Videric arrived tonight. He will be in the cathedral tomorrow, as well as on the last day.'

Did he have an Egyptian spy with him!

No way to ask that question.

I drew up my knees where I sat on the thin mattress. The chill of the earth permeated through the straw. Linking my arms around my shins, I was at least grateful that the penitential shirt came down far enough to cover me to the knees.

I said, 'I very much want to ask pardon of Videric.'

Since that was true, I hoped it would sound true. Even if the reason for it isn't what Felix would think of as the correct one.

I shifted as my empty belly rumbled, and watched Father Felix's expression. 'I have a child, Father.'

Slowly, he smiled. It altered his face beyond belief. 'God has blessed you, then.'

'I'm still what I was. A man's body and a woman's body. Will the church re-admit a hermaphrodite?'

I had been five or six when it occurred to me that the rags the peasants tied on bushes at sacred wells and springs didn't alter their lives in any perceptible way. Valdamerca kept me in the women's section of the church at our estate, and I paid attention after that, and concluded this was much the same business as well-fairies and forest ghosts. The two-year-long argument over whether I could be permitted to attend Mass with King Rodrigo's household, therefore, had both taken me by surprise and completely bewildered me.

I suspected Felix knew that. He had argued fiercely for me to take communion. If a God as kind as the one Felix believed in had existed in this world, I would have resented the debate about my soul considerably more.

He ignored my question. 'Is your desire for pardon genuine?'

'Yes, Father.'

'You have done wrong, you have caused great wrong, to the Aldra Videric, and you humbly wish him to pardon you?'

The night felt cool, after the heat of the day, but my cheeks were hot. Father Felix watched me blush, himself apparently unmoved.

'You have to let me do this!' I said.

'Perjure yourself in court if you wish, Ilario, but not before God's face. And not before the altar in this church.'

Reaching out for his long-fingered hand, I knelt up on the straw mattress.

'Father, you go back and tell the bishops that this is right. If you don't, my family are in danger, the King is in danger, Carthage will take control of this country, and I guarantee that we'll be in a war with the Franks within two years. If God doesn't want towns burned and men slaughtered and women raped, then God will let me lay at Videric's feet and beg his pardon!'

Father Felix's hand felt cool. His skin glowed a dark hue on the back, where I could see tendons shifting under the skin. A pale gold for the creased palm.

Slowly, he brought his other hand up to grip mine.

It had not occurred to me before I left Taraco that Father Felix stands a head shorter than I do, and is wiry rather than strong. If I had Honorius's grasp of military necessity, I might put my hand around Felix's throat until he choked into unconsciousness, and claim the old man had a fit.

But even Honorius knows I have no ability to do that.

'Do you want me to lie to God, Ilario?'

'No, just to His bishops!'

Father Felix's lips formed a firm line.

I knew he would be thinking, with that keen mind of his; what I couldn't predict was how differently he might value things, having the faith in his God that he did.

'Rodrigo knows of this,' he mused.

'Yes.'

'If His Majesty hasn't informed the bishops, he presumably trusts in your – quite genuine penitence – to convince them.' Felix's pale eyes flickered a gaze at me, and then he resumed staring at our interlocked hands. 'Well . . . pride is a sin. And I shouldn't be proud enough to think I know better than the men of God in *concilium*. If God objects to you, Ilario, I think He's quite capable of making that plain to them at the appropriate time.'

He squeezed my hand and let it go, his knuckles like a bagful of jack-stones.

'Have you done anything you're ashamed of while you've been away, Ilario?'

'Yes.' My face was hot again, I found.

'Then I suggest you use this as an opportunity to ask God to forgive you for those things. Do you wish to confess them to me?'

The secrecy of the confessional might have been broken in the past, but not by men such as Father Felix.

I knelt on the packed earth floor and let him take me through antiphons and responses.

He gave me a searching look, as if I were both taller and older than he had expected. 'And what is it you're ashamed of?'

Dutifully, I said, 'I gave way to the lusts of the flesh, Father.'

'And you are sorry?'

His pale gaze made me shift a little, then. I reached for a pat lie, and could only find honesty. 'It brought me my child. So . . . I don't regret it.'

'Then what is it you do feel shame over?'

Masaccio's death. Paying money to own Ramiro Carrasco de Luis, and enjoying the power that gave me over the man. Exulting in the talent that made Masaccio call me in to paint the golem – although that could not be directly mentioned. I spoke in general terms of pride.

'And I've taken too much money from my – family.' I changed the word from *father* at the last moment. 'I owe a debt there—'

'Families should support each other.' Felix looked a little puzzled, as well he might, supposing that I must be talking about the absent Federico and Valdamerca. 'You would do the same for them, wouldn't you?'

I thought of the unlikelihood of the retired Captain-General of Castile needing support from me, and smiled. 'Yes. Of course.'

'The man you own as a slave: he attempted to kill you?'

'Yes, Father.'

'And you have forgiven him.'

'I trust him not to do it again,' I said grimly, and caught a slight smile on Father Felix's face. The *perigrinati christus* never smiled often. I must have looked puzzled.

'Has this man atoned, in your eyes?' Father Felix asked.

'I . . . Yes.' It startled me to find that true.

'Then it was not wrong to have bought him. Although you should free him as soon as possible. No matter what the law and the Old Testament say, I cannot believe that owning a man is good and right.'

The situation that kept Ramiro Carrasco in his collar couldn't be explained, and I didn't try. I talked to Father Felix of minor sins, finding more comfort in his voice and presence than in anything he might be saying. It was not until the lantern had almost burned out of oil, and he asked me for the last time if I had sins unconfessed, that something burst out of me:

'Is it a sin to hate your father and mother?'

Father Felix steepled his fingers on his chest, looked me up and down, and slowly shook his head – not answering my question, I saw, but in a general negation.

'The scriptures would say so.'

'What would you say? Father Felix?'

'I'd say I don't have answers for you, Ilario. Much as you always wished to believe I might. Is it wrong?'

I thought of Videric, my mother's husband, whom I will have to see tomorrow. And keep silent about so much.

I thought of Rosamunda, my mother – whose presence or absence I haven't asked after, because how can I bear either? The thought that she could see me subjected to this, or the thought that she could stay away?

I looked up from the floor at Father Felix. Eyes adjusted to the almost-dark, I could see every line of his sixty-year-old face. I desired desperately to paint him in the style of the New Art: recognisably Felix, *perigrinati christus* of Taraconensis.

'It's wrong.' I shrugged, half desperate. 'It's corrosive. Like sublimates in an alchemist's workshop. I only feel contempt for him. I hate her so much that it'll burn me away.'

He didn't ask me for names. 'And are you guiltless towards these people, yourself?'

This time I shook my head in confusion. 'You know I can't be, Father.'

'Spend your time in the cathedral meditating on that, then. I believe, as I believe in God Himself, that this will be of more use to your soul than any amount of grovelling in ashes.'

Even qualified relief went through me and lightened me, as if my body could float. I answered his small smile with one of my own.

'I have to do the grovelling in any case. But I'll take your advice, Father. Will you be present?'

He looked up from preparing to give me blessing, if not absolution. 'That's as you prefer. My duties don't compel me to it, but they don't keep me from it, either.'

'Don't come.' I couldn't make myself say anything less honest. 'Neither day. It'll be easier for me if I don't have to speak knowing you're there – and I do have to do this.'

Father Felix nodded.

'I think I understand why. Bless you, Ilario. Here. Take these.'

He stooped and picked up the lantern, muttering a little as the streaming heat caught his fingers, and got it into a safe grip.

His other hand, in the dark, pushed at me half a dozen sheets of folded blank paper, that recognisably came from the scriptorium, and two broken ends of chalks.

Videric wasn't there on the fourth day.

Nor Rosamunda.

Nor Rekhmire'.

10

Slaves are used to being on their knees in the presence of other men. But this is different – is intended, primarily rather than secondarily, to be humiliating.

Humbling, I thought. Ashes are no dirtier than a woman gets cleaning out hearths all day. I've worn coarser shirts working with King Rodrigo's horses in the royal stables. And wearing a shift that only comes down to mid-thigh, when I know every eye in the cathedral watches me to see if they can see a cock and balls under the hem, or women's nipples and breasts through the weave . . . That's not so different from some days at court, here.

But it *is* different.

My face burned: half of it shame, and half rage at the sheer injustice. A decision must have been made that to keep me from my child for five nights was cruel. Attila and Tottola brought her to the hermit's cell beforehand for a very few minutes, in the hour when other men would break their fasts. She whimpered. I touched her warm skin, murmured in her ear, and found her unharmed and well cared for.

The two soldiers had four priests with them, solemn faced, not permitting any word to be spoken; not even a greeting and a farewell. Tottola smiled at me. Attila looked intense.

I put my hands inside Onorata's linen shirt and blanket to find out why she grizzled, and encountered the hard nub of folded paper.

There was enough light when they left with her for me to puzzle out the words – the scribe's hand of Ramiro Carrasco. But my father Honorius's unmistakable irascible tone:

'*The damn book-buyer's back. Persuaded me I can't be there tomorrow. He says, Chances are, anyway, you'll have more parents there than you know what to do with.*'

This is supposed to humble, I thought. *But how can it do anything except make a man proud?*

Being at the centre of all this attention, as the sinner is.

Polyphonic voices echoed out from the great heights of the cathedral roof; like bells, organs, great waterfalls of sound. The reverberations struck me under the breastbone. I trembled. If I had had to walk, I might have fallen down. But I was directed to crawl.

Five thousand people lined the road to the cathedral doors. I could see through the great arched opening that the cathedral was full. Keeping myself conscious of lines of legs, lines of bodies, tonal mass of heads, I might reduce all to their component parts, I need not see them as men and women of the court, who know, or know of, the King's hermaphrodite Ilario.

The mosaic floor was hard under my hands and knees. One drum, tapped by a royal page walking behind me, kept to a rhythm. I crawled under the shadow of the great receding arches of the door, passing from under the gazes of the stone saints in their round-arched niches.

Not out of sight of the crowds. Their voices rumbled behind me, loud enough for me to hear even over the thunder of the choirs.

Scent is the most familiar thing, and sound next. The great horns blazing out anthems, echoing down the long aisles of the cathedral – how many times have I stood at the back, near this door, watching the King in procession to the altar? How many times have I smelled the flowers and dust on these ancient tiles: stags, bulls, boar, star maps, ships, all shaped out of tiny squares of coloured stone?

The wind whisked dust through the open door behind me and I pressed my chin down, staring at the floor, and praying that my shirt wouldn't blow up over my arse.

Bad enough to be crawling up the centre aisle, under the eye of every man.

Bad enough to know the women are up above, behind pierced stone screens, staring down with their hands over their mouths, frantic with enjoyment of the scandal.

For a second I pictured this from their perspective: looking down the great open space of the ochre-walled cathedral, all the spaces between the striped red pillars crowded elbow-to-elbow with Rodrigo Sanguerra's courtiers. Lines of priests in their green robes keeping the centre aisle clear. And there, on that wide empty paving, the lone small figure on hands and knees, creeping slowly, so slowly, forward . . .

All I could see were priests' sandals and the hems of green robes embroidered with gold oak leaves. I didn't lift my head to look higher. It cannot possibly be further to the lectern and the altar—

A hand touched my hair.

'Here,' Bishop Heldefredus's voice said above me, and his fingers pushed me to the side.

Light fell down in green and blue and scarlet and gold, patching the floor, drowning out the colours of the mosaic. The great Briar Cross stood in front of the coloured glass window, all the red glass centred about it, so the light fell over the altar like the Unspilled Blood of Christus Imperator, and the birth-blood of His Mother.

I didn't look higher than the bare feet of the Emperor tied to the Tree. I couldn't lift my head; I shook.

'We are brought here to witness reconciliation,' Heldefredus's voice called out, above my bowed head. 'Which is a holy state, belonging to God, and we will first pray for God's guidance.'

The antiphonal response thundered back.

My eyes were running; I blinked furiously to be able to see. The bishop's hand pressed down on my shoulder. *Yes, I remember*—

The stone floor between the altar and the lectern felt bare and cold, no different from when Bishop Heldefredus had led me here this morning to instruct me. Except that then the cathedral had been empty, open doors letting in slanting sunlight, and silence, and the smell of the sea. Not packed with sweating men, all in court clothes, all with their eyes on me.

I stood up on legs like water, saw my knees had bled onto the hem of my shirt, and stumbled two steps. I fell on the stone floor and pitched forward, caught myself on my hands, and lowered myself down, my arms before me as the bishop had directed.

Prostration is moral and mental, as well as physical, but it is also practical. Laying face down while Heldefredus mounted the lectern and began to preach over my prone body, I could lean my forehead against the muscles of my arms, and ease a little of the pain from the cold floor. The shirt they'd given me was long enough to be decent, if I stayed still. But it was thin. I felt every line of the mosaic, every shiver of the cold marble and basalt.

I shut the congregation out of my thoughts. Telling myself: This is only the cathedral I have attended since the age of fifteen: there is no one here to watch me—

Quieter than the preaching bishop could hear, one of the royal guards standing over me murmured, 'Bet his cock's cold down there.'

The answer from his companion came in the tone of a man being self-congratulatorily clever. 'Bet her tits are!'

I knew if I looked up, I wouldn't see anything but impassive expressions. By the voices, these are men whom I have known by name, to speak to when we passed in palace corridors . . .

Heldefredus stopped speaking.

As the second bishop, Ermanaric, climbed up to the lectern, I followed my instructions and pushed myself up and back, so that I was on my knees.

Aldra Pirro Videric met my gaze.

The packed faces in the body of the church vanished.

I turned my head swiftly away from him. Looking up—

I caught a movement. A dark silhouette, behind the fragile fretwork of stone that hides the women's congregation from the sight of the men.

My mother, Rosamunda.

Without seeing her face, without seeing the colour of her gown, without more than the hint of an outline – I know her.

For a heart's beat I was back in Carthage, on the great dock below the

Bursa-hill, under the brown twilight of the Penitence. Following Rekhmire' onto a ship. Looking back past Honorius and his then-unknown household guard as they embarked with us. Hoping that, even then – even though I knew she had gone back to Taraco in disgrace weeks ago – even then she might still come after me to make her apology.

No, not an apology, I thought, peering up at the stone screen with my neck aching. Sadder than that. If she had only come to take me into her arms, I would have imagined the apology without her needing to speak it.

And imagination would have been all it would be.

'Ilario!'

Heldefredus's whisper brought my head jerking back down.

Aldra Videric stared at me, his face impassive. Knowing him, I could see in his eyes that my turning to Rosamunda first had angered him almost to the point of losing that perfect control.

The stiff embroidered robes of the archbishop swept between me and my stepfather. I found myself staring at viridian silk, fine white lawn, and the ends of a stole crusted with gold thread and embroidered with Eagle, Boar, Oak-leaf, and *gladius hispaniensis*. Because this was an archbishop, the sword blade was sewn in silver thread.

A sweaty hand lay heavily on my head and I heard the blessing ring out.

'Penitent,' he added, removing the hand. With an effort I looked up at Archbishop Cunigast. Thought of sermons slept through in short winter days when the King has coal-braziers brought into his chapel in this cathedral, and it is necessary to break the ice on the holy water in the font.

The heated June afternoon swept back over me. I blinked, hardly able to hold Cunigast's gaze.

'Penitent, do you truly desire to make restitution?'

'Yes, my lord.' My voice broke from alto to baritone and back. I heard a flutter of amusement behind me.

Scarlet, I kept my gaze fixed on the folds of the archbishop's robes. Folds in cloth: an elementary difficulty for the novice painter.

'You will be prepared,' Cunigast said, and stepped away in a swirl of bullion thread and silk.

In the order of service it read *Prepare him* or *Prepare her*. Neither fitted me.

Two priests in plain green robes stepped smartly up beside me; one pulled my hair up and snipped briskly away at it with scissors; the other lathered soap and warm water in a silver bowl, and followed his brother, shaving away the trimmed hair. I shut my eyes as soapy water trickled down my forehead, soaking the front of my shirt.

A cloth dabbed across my closed eyes.

'Thank you.' I acknowledged the priest, forgetting I wasn't to speak, and he bobbed his head awkwardly, eyes wide.

If he's a day over sixteen, I'm Videric's natural son!

Eyes clear of soap, I had no excuse not to look in the direction of the altar while a third bishop, whom I didn't know, blessed me, and flicked consecrated water over me.

Am I blessed or exorcised? I wondered, and gave up to focus on Videric.

He seems – no different.

I suppose I had expected him to look older, or tired. Or more impressive, perhaps. Either less frightening than the Videric of my mind who had sent Ramiro Carrasco and others to kill me, or else more so.

No . . .

Four chairs had been set up below the altar, on the widest step. Black polished oak, with pointed Gothic arches cut into the woodwork, and finials crowning their high backs. The seats were boxes; the sides fretwork open enough to make a pattern by showing the coloured robes of each man. The King, Rodrigo Sanguerra, with the gold Roman laurels of one of the Ancient Kingdoms winding around his brow. The archbishop, in forest green and silver. One chair empty – *Aldro Rosamunda will not be permitted to sit down here in the main body of the church next to her husband, even today.*

And, in the chair nearest me, Videric.

A burly, fair-haired man, blue eyes half closed against the light pouring down from the highest ogee windows. His legs were encased in mirror-bright steel: sabatons on his feet, greaves and chausses covering shin and thigh. Over that, a striped blue and white livery coat covered all of his breastplate; all of his armour but his gorget and haut-pieces; and above that he was bare-headed. He wore Rodrigo Sanguerra's badge on the breast of his livery coat over his heart, and he had had himself shaven and his beard clipped down to a fine gold shadow. Nobleman; knight; a man entirely fitted to be first minister to a king.

His chin rested on his hand. His eyes were fixed on me.

My skin crawled. I felt worse than naked.

I rubbed my palm nervously over my scalp, feeling the tufts of hair the boy priests had missed. One single layer of cloth kept my body from the prurient interest of the court behind me. Videric . . .

Looks clear through me.

One of the bishops began to repeat the Penitential Psalms, his voice echoing confidently through the vast spaces of the church.

I allowed myself one glance back into the body of the cathedral, as if I looked up at the lectern above me and eased an ache in my neck.

No man that I could take to be a tall shaven-headed Egyptian.

Is he here? Would Honorius try to reassure me with a lie?

As if I put my hand back onto hot metal, I looked in the direction that I was supposed to. At the chairs. At my King and the churchman Cunigast. The empty chair . . . If I look at that, I thought, perhaps I need not look at Videric until the end; until I have to.

582

I must look.

Aldro Pirro Videric, eyes still slitted against the light, continued to rest his chin on the heel of his hand. The bulk of his body and shoulders filled the space the chair allowed him. There was a smudge of pale dust on the boot sole under one sabaton. He would have ridden down from the palace with King Rodrigo this morning, not trudged here like the townsmen outside, or some of the poorer courtiers in the cathedral.

I let myself meet his gaze.

His attention struck me like a physical shock.

How in the name of the eight gods am I going to sound convincing!

Panic flooded me. Tension weakened the muscles of my knees, or I might have sprung up and turned to run out of the building. This man, this man with absolute control over himself—

Fountains flashing in the palace's enclosed courtyards, Videric's sandals rapping on the tiles as he strode down the corridor, and his concerned tone as he glanced at me: *She wants to speak to you. I don't know why. Be kind to her.*

I met his eyes, deliberately, and stared him down.

She wanted to see me because you ordered her to kill me.

You ordered *her* to make friends with me. Long ago. So that she could be there if it became necessary to kill me.

Videric's mouth moved, lip curving up a small amount. He gave me a measuring smile.

Every muscle in my body tensed. I saw it as clearly as if I lay anatomised on a slab in Alexandria's Royal Library: the pull of tendon, the contraction and swelling of muscle, the support of bone.

I am four yards away from his chair, and once again they have forgotten that the King's master-at-arms trained me as a knight.

I am swift enough to cover the distance, snatch Videric's dagger out of that tooled leather sheath, and have the blade down between his collar and his gorget into his heart before any man can stop me.

Videric, his gaze on me, gave a little shrug with his brows, as if disappointed that I had not responded to his smile.

Momentarily I shut my eyes.

Sharp anger flooded through me; washed me away like an undertow of the sea. I bit the inside of my lip until I tasted blood, and opened my eyes and looked at him again.

The ex-First Minister Videric stared amiably back at me.

He truly desires to be Rodrigo's First Minister again. Therefore, I think – he doesn't taunt me. Videric truly thinks that if he smiles, I will assume him a friend.

It took my breath.

The pale lines that being in the sun had put at the corners of his eyes creased. Videric's chin dipped infinitesimally, on his fist. I know him well enough to read what he intends to convey: *Courage!*

'Courage . . . ' I breathed out.

A silence swept through the hot cathedral.

No man moved.

Videric shifted and sat upright in the chair of state. He turned to speak to the King.

'Sire, it will not be justice if my wife is not here to witness Ilario's penitence. I realise where we are – but she is willing to come veiled.'

His words fell like stones into water, in the great crowded building.

Glancing back at the pierced stone screen, I wasn't surprised to see the silhouette gone. Videric would not ask such a question unless he knew the answer. I barely bothered listening to Archbishop Cunigast explain just why God would make a merciful exception in the interests of justice.

Rosamunda walked out from the narthex, behind the altar, and walked past me to sit in the empty chair.

Her scent caught in the back of my throat.

Gold wire made a miniature moon-horn of her head-dress, and the veil that hung down was of the finest flax, perfectly translucent. I gazed at her curling black hair, and full warm lips, and did not let myself look her in the eye.

If I face her, I will not be able to do this.

Heldefredus's narrow hand bit into my shoulder, fingertips curling to catch me under the edge of my collarbone. 'Now, Ilario.'

A tingle shot down my arm. Not pain. Enough sensation to remind me what I must now do.

I stood up, took three paces forward, dropped down on my knees as the bishop had rehearsed me, and looked directly up at Videric where he sat on the chair above me.

The position placed me equally carefully. The slanting beam of light from the altar window shone down, illuminating me so that every man, every woman, in this building can see the broad shoulders and wide hips of the one who is man *and* woman.

And therefore not a man, and not a woman.

I knelt, my spine stiff, my head up.

'I beg for your pardon.' Tension cracked my voice again: deep one moment and falsetto the next. 'Aldra Pirro Videric, I humbly beg your forgiveness.'

Videric stood up, both hands momentarily gripping the arms of his chair.

The sun shone off his armour and livery surcoat. Steel and blue and white . . . With the sun so bright on him, the thinning of his hair was hidden, and the incipient rounding of his jaw lost.

A shame, I thought. It made him more human to me. Something in him might touch me if I thought him just a man of Honorius's age, subject to piles and insomnia and stomach-ache when he ate spices that hadn't troubled him if he ate them at twenty.

Rosamunda stood up, resting her hand on her husband's arm, flax linen gloves showing the delicate rose-pink of her fingers against the steel of his vambrace.

Get away from me!

I forced myself not to shout it aloud.

The humiliation of this is that I am still, after a year, afraid of them both.

The stone was hard under my knees. Through Rosamunda's veil I saw the shape of spite and pleasure on her face. Only I was close enough to see.

I stumbled over the words Bishop Heldefredus had rehearsed me in.

'Aldra Videric, I beseech you humbly to intercede on my behalf. With God and with His Majesty, for their, for their forgiveness. I swear to do as I have done these past days: to prostrate and humiliate myself, to lie in sackcloth and ashes, to clothe my body in rags and plunge my soul in sorrow—'

Videric took a step forward.

I had not expected it.

A shiver went through me; I thought it must be visible at least to the closest row of men watching.

'And, and.' I found my place in the words again. 'To correct my soul by harsh treatment of myself. And by prayer, and fasting. And whole days and nights together to weep and seek your forgiveness. I cast myself at your feet, who I have wronged.'

I couldn't look up at Rosamunda, close as she was. I stared at Videric's face as if he were a rope thrown to a drowning man.

'I swear to atone, I for this reason fall on my knees before you.' I licked at dry lips, conscious that the words were absorbed by the air. They should echo back, and it was fear that softened what I spoke. 'And I beg you to lead me to absolution if you see fit.'

He smiled.

Confident, all his weight back on his heels, not even glancing behind at the archbishop and the king. They will have discussed this beforehand.

He held out his right hand.

'I acknowledge you,' he said. 'Child of my wife's body—'

The intake of breath was audible through the cathedral.

They hear it as formal poetics, I realised, staring up at him. *Not as the literal truth.*

Another hand extended itself into my vision. Pale, smooth, clothed in transparent linen.

Rosamunda's voice rang like a soprano bell. 'I acknowledge you and pardon you, Ilario. Rise now and come with me.'

Videric's hand was hot and dry; he gripped my wrist as if I had been a young man in the knights' training halls, and his effort would have brought me to my feet even without my own.

My mother's hand lay bonelessly in mine and I couldn't look at her.

They led me forward, one on either side, to the archbishop at the main altar.

Cunigast lit a candle, and at last my hands were free.

I reached out and took hold of the cool wax. *Rather that than Rosamunda's waxen skin.* The yellow flame danced, all but invisible in sunlight.

The archbishop raised his voice. 'The penitent will join us in the celebration of Mass, and then the public absolution will be given.'

Videric put his hands on my shoulders and kissed me on either cheek with the brusque efficiency of a courtier.

Rosamunda lifted her veil with both hands, looking at me with those green eyes that I see in the mirror.

She stood on her toes to press her lips softly against mine.

As Archbishop Cunigast proclaimed the kiss of peace I fell down on my knees in front of the altar and didn't move.

Celebration of Mass went on around me – Rosamunda being hustled off back up to the women's area of the cathedral – and I didn't stand up; could not stand up. The back of my throat filled with bile. It took every ounce of concentration not to spit it across the ancient mosaics.

King Rodrigo Sanguerra moved to stand at my right hand side when the Mass ended. Videric stayed on my left. I caught Rodrigo's eye, and he nodded, briefly.

I turned about, facing the congregation between the two men.

I knelt again and begged pardon of both, and both men helped me rise. The kiss of absolution from Pirro Videric burned my forehead as if it had been painted there with alchemists' acid.

Every yard of the walk around the nave of the cathedral sank into my memory: every curious or avid or disgusted face that I passed. The candle shook, and hot wax spilled over my fingers, the momentary pains anchoring me in myself.

If I'm pale, they'll take it for humiliation and grief and gladness.

It was four hours before it was over.

Rodrigo Sanguerra held a banquet in the castle, with Aldra Videric and I at the high table.

I slid away before the sun touched the horizon, on the excuse of changing into the clean shirt and hose and doublet that Father Felix brought for me – and slipped out of the palace with a nod to the guards.

I sprinted through Taraco's streets, boots thumping up squirts of dry dust. Assuming that Honorius my father does not lie; assuming that Rekhmire' *is* here—

A silk dragon-banner unrolled on the wind at the quay. I saw Commander Jian sitting in the stern of one of the Chin boats, among his oarsmen. He lifted his hand in a Frankish gesture of greeting he must have learned since their ship entered the Middle Sea.

A cloaked figure stood on the quay beside them.

Behind that cloaked man, another man; standing with bare chest and head, the reddening sun shining on his shaven scalp and white linen kilt.

I staggered up to them and caught Honorius's hand; he pulled me into a hard embrace, and released me, staring into my face, and pushing me at the Egyptian.

As if I had done it a hundred times before, I put my arms tightly around Rekhmire', felt him grip me and run his fingers over my cropped scalp, and fell down on my knees in the dust.

My father held my shoulders, and Rekhmire' leaned over and steadied my head, and I vomited up bitter bile, time after time, into the harbour, until I was shaking, sore-throated, and empty.

It took me a time to be willing to let go of either man. The quick setting of the sun had given way to blue dusk, I found; blackening into night.

Honorius wore his brigandine, I noted as I lifted my head from his shoulder; an anonymous armour that any guard might wear, or a poor knight.

'All's well,' my father reassured, as if he might read my thoughts. 'His Majesty told me to come down here and meet the book-buyer. I won't be arrested again if I keep to my curfew.'

Rodrigo asked him for his parole, I realised.

Little enough chance Honorius will ever break it.

I caught sight of Orazi and Tottola in the shadows of the nearer warehouses; the German lifted his hand in acknowledgement.

'Master Rekhmire' . . . ' I strove for formality, and finally persuaded myself to look up at the Egyptian. His arm still lay heavily about my shoulder.

Rekhmire' signalled with his other hand. One of Jian's men handed up a snapsack.

'Zheng He sailed south at the King's request, and picked me up further down the Via Augusta,' Rekhmire' observed, dark eyes hidden by shadow. Even so, I could see the corners crease. 'For some odd reason I didn't desire to ride to Taraco in the company of Aldro Rosamunda . . . '

Dryly, I said, 'I wonder why.'

My supposition was exactly right!

'Were you in the cathedral?' I added.

I felt the Egyptian shrug, rather than saw it.

'Forgive me: I didn't desire to see it. I would have throttled the insolent barbarian.'

It was unclear whether he meant Videric, King Rodrigo, or any other man; the true accent of Alexandria reminded me that we are all barbarians in that city's eyes.

A scent of pitch and a flare of light let me know that Orazi had fired a torch. Honorius glanced at the stars on the horizon.

'We should get back.' He glanced at me, and at the book-buyer, and I thought I saw him smile.

Rekhmire' kept his arm over my shoulder, using me as well as his stick to propel himself along at a reasonable rate. The torchlight showed irregularities in the ground; his concentration was on those.

'No hunting accidents?' I observed.

He smiled without looking at me, giving him a profile that might well have appeared in one of Ty-ameny's bas-reliefs.

'That depends on your definition of "accident".' He scowled, mood changing. 'And hunting. The wild boar on Aldra Videric's estate are tame enough that they come to a whistle. It's not sport.'

The rising white light brought Sulva clearly into my mind's eye, the massive wild boar attentive to her aulos flute. I thought suddenly, *I should have confessed to Father Felix that I regret how badly I treated Sulva Paziathe.*

'I had crossbow bolts sent too close to me for my liking,' Rekhmire' observed, shooting a glance up at the Sanguerra castle's black bulk. 'If I had thought of myself as a hunter rather than prey, I might have come back more battered even than I went.'

He means his knee, I realised.

Before I could say anything rational or comforting, I saw other torches approaching us down the dock steps.

Honorius and Orazi exchanged a wordless look.

Only two torches, and – I squinted, now the night had fully fallen; the moon was not yet bright – only three men visible. Two guards, and one man who dressed like a knight.

'I have a message for you!' the leading figure called.

Under the flickering yellow light, I recognised his lugubrious features.

'That's Safrac de Aguilar – King Rodrigo trusts him,' I muttered briskly to Honorius.

We were four or five men to three, in any case – and I wondered when it had become natural for me to think that way in my home city.

Aldra de Aguilar evidently recognised Honorius in the torchlight. His voice became much less loud. 'Greetings, my lord. The King desires to see you, urgently.'

Honorius nodded and fell in beside the Iberian knight. I registered Tottola bringing up the rear, eyes scanning the darkness of the town as we made our way through black streets.

There should be words to say to Rekhmire', but for the moment, I could find none of them; I merely enjoyed his presence, and the assistance I could lend him.

King Rodrigo Sanguerra sat in his private chambers, the night wind blowing the scent of the city through the rooms, along with a firefly or two. He sat with his head down over a clutch of maps, not lifting it when his page announced us, but only waving a hand to gesture that we should be allowed in.

Not having been given permission to sit, I spent my energies in being a prop to the book-buyer, whose injury clearly – to my eyes, at least – pained him.

The King pushed a map aside and leaned back. Hooded black eyes surveyed us all, settling at last on Licinus Honorius.

Rodrigo Sanguerra beamed.

'Aldra Honorius,' he said. 'I'm pleased to have released you from confinement. If you will, I have a task that you may do for your King.'

My father's expression said *You do?*, but his voice smoothly managed, 'Yes, Your Majesty?'

'Yes.' King Rodrigo looked at Rekhmire', and at me, and back at Honorius. 'You're going to Carthage.'

11

'I'm doing *what*?' Honorius didn't give his King the chance to do so much as draw breath. '*Carthage!* Sire! You suspected me of conspiring with Carthage! Wanting to take your place as Carthage's governor! And now you *want* me to go there?'

His incredulity could have burst eardrums. I opened my mouth, a suggestion forming in my mind. King Rodrigo signalled forcefully for us to sit down at the table.

I loaned Rekhmire' my arm. 'But you're going to Carthage, in any case? For Ty-ameny?'

Rodrigo Sanguerra caught my low-voiced comment.

'If I understand it correctly . . . ' He pushed maps back as his page brought wine, and took a glass of Falernian. 'The Pharaoh-Queen desires you to go to Carthage, Master Rekhmire', to instruct the King-Caliph that the devil-ship is now your ally, and they should be duly alarmed?'

Rekhmire' inclined his head in agreement.

The King sipped at his wine. 'I had occasion to speak with the foreign Admiral, over the rendezvous to bring you back to Taraco. A very amiable man in many ways.'

I bit my tongue, managing not to tactlessly ask what my King and Zheng He might have in common – or what they might have discussed.

'In any case,' Rodrigo Sanguerra turned to Honorius, 'I desire you to travel to Carthage on the devil-ship, and do precisely the same thing.'

Honorius's eyebrows went up.

'Claim to be the Chin's allies, as well?'

'Claim them to be *our* allies,' Rodrigo corrected.

His hooded eyes watched my father, with a combination of amusement and judgement.

'I desire you to travel as my kingdom's Captain-General,' he added.

Honorius pushed his hand across his face, wiping sweat out of his eyes, and downed his wine in one swallow. 'If I wanted to stay a captain, I'd have stayed in Castile!'

'If I wanted a war, I'd appoint a Captain-General who wanted to fight!'

Rekhmire' broke out in a light tenor laugh. My father and the King stared at him. He shook his head apologetically.

'Pardon me, Your Majesty. What else would you wish Aldra Honorius to convey, officially, to the King-Caliph? Perhaps the news that First Minister Videric has recovered from his illness and resumed his position at court?'

Rodrigo watched the book-buyer for a moment.

He smiled.

'An excellent idea.'

'Oh, I see where this is going . . . ' Honorius's moroseness was not particularly convincing.

I nodded agreement. 'So do I!'

King Rodrigo Sanguerra linked his fingers on the maps of the Hesperides, and showed me his teeth. 'You tell us then, Ilario.'

Rekhmire''s look informed me I might have kept my big mouth shut with more advantage; Honorius merely beamed proudly. *The King may as well know his Freak has a mind,* I thought.

'You want Lord Honorius as Captain-General because every Frankish kingdom will be afraid to fight him,' I said. 'Even if all he ever does is stay on his estate and breed war-horses! You want him to go to Carthage as your Captain-General because that would make it very difficult for him to ally himself with Carthage. Especially if he's the one who tells King-Caliph Ammianus that Aldra Videric is back – the King-Caliph won't be pleased with whoever brings him that message!'

I did not add, *It nails Licinus Honorius's colours to your mast,* because no man at the table appeared to need that confirmation.

Rodrigo grinned like a boy.

'I should have sent you away before, Ilario. You've learned much.'

I've learned to be wary of compliments from powerful rulers . . .

'You understand, Ilario,' King Rodrigo added, 'that I need to send you away again. For a year or two, until there's no scandal attached to the resemblance between you and Licinus Honorius.'

That might mean anything from two years to 'don't come back until Pirro Videric is dead', but I saw I had no current choice, and nodded.

'I have business in Carthage, too,' I added, 'if you won't think it suspicious, sire. It's personal and to do with being a painter.'

King Rodrigo nodded absently. Most of his attention was on Honorius, which I had counted on. *At least I have my place on Zheng He's ship.*

Rekhmire' gave me a sideways look, but had to abandon the query when Rodrigo Sanguerra beckoned the page to fill his wine glass and addressed the Egyptian again.

'As I understand it, your Queen desires you and Pilot Sebekhotep to return at some time to Constantinople?'

'The Admiral will put into Gades,' Rekhmire' volunteered. 'That would be the nearest friendly port from which we could return to Alexandria.'

Rodrigo thoughtfully nodded. I wondered if he perceived that Admiral Zheng He would leave the Middle Sea.

I know the man: certainly he's thinking of something!

'Captain-General Honorius, you may return via Gades, or otherwise, depending on how long your business takes in Carthage.' King Rodrigo saluted him lightly with the wine glass. 'But I'm ahead of myself. Licinus Honorius. Will you accept this position at my court?'

My father caught my eye, and I glimpsed a grin. Almost demurely, for such a battle-hardened man, he murmured, 'Yes, sire. Of course.'

'Very well.' Rodrigo thrust a map across the table at him. 'When the celebrations attendant on Ilario's penitence and Videric's return are over, you may leave.'

Admiral Zheng He appeared to have no objection to my presence continuing on board his ship.

'We leave here in a . . . week?' He glanced at Sebekhotep, who nodded. 'A week. You may come.'

The Admiral cut off my thanks with a sharp gesture. A glance passed between him and Commander Jian.

'The sailors say you're good luck,' Jian ventured. With another look at Zheng He, he added, 'They find a eunuch clerk comforting, and familiar. It's what they take you to be. But that is not quite correct, is it?'

The Admiral signalled for wine. At Zheng He's gesture, I sat down again. One of the Admiral's clerks dodged in, with paper, brush, and ink-block on his wooden case. Commander Jian looked at me questioningly.

I suppose an explanation is a reasonable price for a voyage.

I regarded the Chin Admiral, and managed not to smile. 'Not a eunuch, my lord, no . . . '

Silverpoint is delicate, but I needed to give what I drew more body. If I had little enough left in the way of pigments now, I could still use tinted paper as a mid tone, and the earths for dark values, and white lead for highlights.

I ground burnt sienna as fine as Masaccio had ever taught me, and prepared with charcoal studies done by observation at Rodrigo's court. Although the majority of my images came from that hour in the cathedral, when I would have sworn I noticed nothing around me.

I used egg tempera, on a lime board to which I had applied gesso, and painted more quickly and with more skill than I had since Rome.

No, I thought, looking at the monochrome shapes taking on mass and depth. *Better than I ever have before.*

Father Felix came to my quarters, far too casually and often, until he was happy that I had no inclination to throw myself in the harbour, or off the castle's highest tower.

'Lies are poison,' he remarked at one point. And followed that up, later the same day, with, 'You're not welcome at the King's court.'

I had taken a walk along the battlements with him, the air being cooler on the castle walls. I took my gaze from the mountains of the north, just visible in this morning's impossibly clear aerial perspective.

There was no spite in Father Felix's tone.

'No,' I agreed. 'Not welcome.'

'A year or two, perhaps. But not yet.'

'I'll miss you, Father.'

His smile was white in his dark face, and startlingly beautiful. 'And I you. Where are you going?'

'Firstly,' I said, 'if I can, to the King's banquet at the week's end. And after that, on board a ship.'

'The second is wise. The first . . . ' Father Felix shook his head.

'I've been absolved,' I said. 'I can go anywhere I please.'

It took a week longer than Zheng He's estimate for the war-junk to be fully provisioned and the holds loaded up. That didn't displease me. It took that long for the paint to properly dry

The last of the celebratory banquets was lit by pages in Classical costumes holding torches, in the great gardens of the Sanguerra palace.

The last of the sun's red faded swiftly over the western mountains. I walked down between the fountains and into the garden, a painted board wrapped in a cloth and carried under my arm.

Rekhmire' drifted out of the crowd, Orazi and Saverico behind him. Honorius, stuck now on board Zheng He's ship, appeared to have determined to send men who would pick up gossip.

I looked up to meet the Egyptian's black gaze. He turned to limp with me through the throng of courtiers. Someone played a mandolin, under the vines. With every man speaking, it was loud enough that we might have discussed any matter without danger of eavesdroppers.

The book-buyer appeared to have nothing he wanted to say.

Similarly at a loss, I asked, 'How many days will it take us to Carthage?' and cursed myself for trivial chatter.

'A handful.' Rekhmire' narrowed his eyes at the Taracon courtiers. His expression suddenly turned sour. 'Would your journey to Carthage have somewhat to do with needing to keep your "wet-nurse" out of Taraco at the moment?'

I shook my head. 'You really don't like Ramiro, do you?'

'I like your nursemaid well enough. I'd like him better if he were somewhere else.'

'I won't tempt Videric to tidy up what he might see as loose ends. So, yes, I'm taking the "nursemaid" with us. Honorius says Onorata would miss him.'

'She's not old enough to know faces!'

'She grizzled enough when *you* were gone.'

The shock on his face was enough to make me smile.

'I didn't think the Little Wise One liked me,' he muttered.

'She's a sad judge of character.' I grinned at him. 'And now, I regret to say, I must go and be polite to the rest of my family . . . '

Neither Pirro Videric nor Rosamunda appeared to be present.

That, or I could not find them in the crowds.

My place at the banqueting table was well below Rekhmire''s, but above the court musicians, at least. There were enough men I knew casually at the table that I passed a reasonably entertaining evening, although the fireflies and other mites and pismires gave me no better an opinion than I have ever had of dining out of doors.

The formal toasts finished. King Rodrigo Sanguerra caught my eye, and beckoned me. I left my seat and walked up to the high table.

Since I was in male clothing, I bowed. 'Sire. Lady Rosamunda. Aldra Videric.'

The torchlight glinted on Videric's fair hair, and on a face superficially friendly. He smiled up at me from where he sat at the King's right hand.

He will be good for Taraconensis.

That doesn't mean I have to like him.

No man will ever bring him to judgement for sending Ramiro Carrasco de Luis to kill me. And there'll never be justice for the Carrasco and de Luis families; for the threat that has hung over them all this time, and to some degree always will.

More honestly – no man will ever hurt him for hurting me.

'I have a gift, Aldra Videric,' I said, bringing out the cloth-covered board. 'It's not valuable, and I have little enough talent, but I grew to know some of the New Art in the Italies, and I've made you this.'

King Rodrigo Sanguerra watched me, eyes dark in the candle-light, sipping from his gold goblet. Not far down the high table, Rekhmire' gazed at me with the imbecilic amiability that diplomatic envoys are supposed to assume at social events. Knowing both men as I did, I could feel how keenly I was watched.

Rosamunda, on the King's left, sipped from a silver goblet studded with sapphires, that she had evidently chosen to go with her white sarcenet and sapphire velvet gown. Her hair had no grey, her face no wrinkles; she had the kind of beauty that is unnatural because so perfect. I found myself rubbing one hand across my doublet over my belly, thinking, *She must have the lines of childbirth there at least!*

But even so it will not be this disfiguring scar.

Videric's wide, capable-looking hands took the package from me and unwrapped the cloth with deft care.

He stared.

Rosamunda leaned a little back in her chair to see.

She flashed a smile at me.

'Why, that's very well painted, Ilario! And thank you for the compliment.'

I bowed as men do. 'It was the least I could do, Aldro.'

Videric gazed down at the board, tilting it to catch the light of the torches.

I made drawings, the night after I paid for my absolution at the cathedral. Searched my memory, sketched studies, and then reached for pigments to put things down as accurately and as truthfully as I could.

Looking now, I saw things I would change if I had it to do again. Technical imperfections abound.

But I have managed to paint irrevocably one aspect of the truth.

The monochrome images of Videric and Rosamunda, my once-father and my mother, gleamed in the soft torchlight. Painted as lord and lady, they were seated side by side in high-backed wooden chairs. Both wore the court clothing of this year of Our Lord 1429; and through the arched window behind them, the forts and rivers and mountains of Taraconensis shone in miniature.

The image of Rosamunda gazed out at the world, every aspect of her beauty on show, her hands clasped modestly in her lap. Videric's painted hands clasped the carved ends of the chair-arms. He looks, not at us, but at her. She, beauty; and he, power.

'This is wonderful.' Videric tilted the board further. 'Sire, will you excuse me if I take it closer to the light? Ilario, will you explain your technique to me here?'

It was done smoothly enough that Rosamunda noticed nothing.

Rodrigo must know that Videric could simply summon a torch-bearer closer to us!

The King waved dispassionate permission. He deliberately turned back to converse with Rekhmire'.

The Egyptian's gaze followed me as I walked over to Videric, where he held the portraits up to the torch's gilding illumination.

I stood beside Pirro Videric in silence.

Videric's tone was almost absent-minded. 'I've studied the New Art. It's an interesting concept: to draw what is. Heresy, perhaps. Only God can judge what truly *is*. But this is a . . . different kind of representation to those I've seen before.'

I'd wondered what Videric found to keep him interested in his exile. Did you think you could find me by studying this art?

In all likelihood, yes.

His gaze was riveted on the images.

I thought the distortions of perspective might confuse him. Or the individuality of the faces and lack of symbols remove all the meaning.

Evidently not.

Videric lifted his chin, looking me challengingly in the eye. 'You know I will hang this privately? Where no other man can see it?'

'Not all men will see the same thing in it, Aldra Videric.'

'Oh, I think they will.' He tilted the painted board the other way.

It had already lasted longer than I thought; I had imagined he might throw it in one of the bonfires.

He mused aloud. 'There she is . . . Discovered. Disclosed, for any man to see. Who she is. What she is.'

He looked up at me.

'Shallow. Cruel. Greedy.'

It felt sharp as a punch in the gut.

I had no expectation of him being so honest!

Pirro Videric reached a fingertip towards his own painted face, but did not touch the surface. 'You've painted me as an unhappy man.'

'You love her. Rosamunda. My mother.'

He gave me a small smile. 'Yes. I do.'

If I could paint that smile to keep it with me always, I would count myself lucky and need no other revenge.

Even the remants of the smile slipped from his face. 'I will do anything to keep her. One day, perhaps, you will understand why. It's curious – you spent five days with the Church lying yourself black in the face. But this painting is one of the most truthful things I've ever seen.'

Videric's hands gripped the wood tightly enough that I heard it creak. I watched him.

He lowered his gaze to the limewood again. This surface where I have used gesso and pigment, wood and egg-yolk, to paint this man who – over the course of twenty-five years and against all odds – has fought to keep this woman with him.

His figure faces her: you can see his passion for her.

And you can see the woman who could abandon the lover who fathered her child. Abandon her baby in the snow. All to stay with the man who is rich and powerful – *while* he is rich and powerful. She looks out at the world, and does not see him there.

I took up the cloth Videric had dropped, folded it, and handed it to him.

And took up the remaining weapon left to me.

I said, 'You know she'll never love you.'

Videric looked at me. 'I know.'

12

Dragon pennants rippled ahead of us, unrolling down the wind.

I couldn't count how many of them I saw on the seven masts – dozens, perhaps a hundred. Chin men scrambled up the yards to release the sails. Wind strengthening behind us bellied out the cloth.

Zheng He's massive ship tacked around in a final curve that let us see all the coast of Taraco submerged in morning mist. And all the distant mountain peaks, west and north.

And the host of tiny cogs and galleys that, at King Rodrigo Sanguerra's insistence, escorted the war-junk south down the coast, until the land borders of Taraconensis were left behind.

Squinting at the land, I could make out dust on the Via Augusta, that ancient road that runs from the Frankish lands down to the straits that open the Atlantic. Clouds of dust.

The King and his court riding out, as a compliment to such far-travelled men as Zheng He and his officers, to bid them farewell.

The rail almost imperceptibly shivered under my hand. Deep waters darkened under our prow.

Honorius stood beside me, his hands clasped behind his back. On my other side, Rekhmire' wore Onorata's sling, and held her cautiously, gazing with a puzzled look into her tiny and messy features – possibly trying to deduce if she indeed recognised him.

I whipped out a kerchief to wipe her nose, and spent some time pointing out to my child the chief landmarks of Taraconensis as we left them behind, and naming the different parts of the war-junk in Chin.

'Ilario . . . ' Rekhmire' removed his hand from under the sling, examined it, and put it back. 'She's five months old!'

'It's never too early to start . . . '

Honorius choked off a laugh, and stepped aside to confer with Orazi. I knew more than half of the men-at-arms he had chosen to accompany the Captain-General of Taraconensis to Carthage: acquainted with them from Venice and Rome. The others were veterans of having His Majesty's royal guard garrisoned on Honorius's estate; the evenings were rife with exaggerated tales, each trying to out-do the other.

'Ilario.' Rekhmire''s eyes slitted against the brilliance. He stepped out of the way of two of Jian's sailors sprinting past. 'Do you see something? There, ahead?'

I looked into the shining mist of the horizon, and rubbed my dazzled eyes. 'Not a damn thing!'

I had not yet got over the relief of seeing Rekhmire' returned safe from Videric's estates. I would have said this to him, if not for the fact that he hardly ever spoke to me now.

He says more to Onorata . . .

I checked the ties on her tiny hood, and she yawned in my face. 'Charming child!'

Rekhmire' gave me a look of the greatest apparent innocence. 'Should I risk saying I know how she feels?'

'Not unless you want your shins kicked! Except that I suppose I can't while you have her – is that why you volunteered to carry the baby sling?'

The Egyptian made an unsuccessful attempt at appearing wounded.

'I should be wary of complaining about boredom,' he added, seeing me failing to be moved. 'That usually serves to call up sea-serpents and comets and acts of the gods . . . '

'I can do without any of those!'

I found I must step back out of another running man's way— Jian himself.

'What . . . ?' Squinting after the Chin commander, I found myself looking south, into sun and brilliant mist – and dark protuberances that could not be the Balearic Islands. *Not unless we've sailed infinitely faster than I thought we could!*

Rekhmire' closed both his large hands protectively around Onorata. Honorius appeared at the rail again, beside me. 'What is it?'

'I don't know. There are no reefs—'

I saw Carrasco come up from below, talking quite companionably with Berenguer and Tottola. The German man-at-arms suddenly seized Ramiro Carrasco's shoulder and pointed forward.

I turned and leaned forward over the rail, as if straining those few inches further forward would let me see what Tottola saw. Honorius's fingers clenched over the back of my belt.

The dark protuberances resolved a very little more out of the haze. 'Not islands . . . ' I whispered.

Rekhmire' choked out an obscene oath.

Honorius said, 'Ships.'

My father's eyes narrowed as he stared into the bright south. I felt the harsh luminosity bring tears running out of my own eyes.

But I see masts, stacked masts, narrow and impossibly high . . .

Zheng He's war-junk actually *leaned*. Every sail set, I saw, craning back to look overhead.

Feet thundered; I heard orders screamed at high pitch; the bows slowly tacked across.

'Two. Five. Eight. Ten.' Rekhmire' clasped my daughter against him with one hand and shaded his eyes with the other. 'Captain-General. How is my count?'

Honorius gazed south with eyes that have been too long used to looking into hostile distance. He mouthed numbers. I blinked, and looked back.

I will never paint that fire and light! I thought. The delicacy of water-drops with light shattered through them into colour, white foam at the foot of the prows—They swelled into existence on the morning sea, appearing out of the haze, unmistakable in their silhouette.

More than ten. More than twenty. More than fifty.

A signal rocket soared up and broke apart with a piercing shriek.

'What,' Honorius said carefully, his gaze on the southern waters, 'are those?'

My neck felt cramped and cold in the stiff wind. I couldn't stop staring. 'I think – that's the Admiral's lost fleet.'

The nearest one was close enough that I could see a green dragon-face painted on the flat prow.

Raising his voice over the shouting, and banging of signal rockets, Honorius protested, 'There can't be two hundred of them!'

I reached out my arms as Rekhmire' slid the sling's straps around me, and I cuddled my screaming child into my shoulder, putting hands over her ears against the noise.

'Of course there can't be two hundred! Who has two hundred ships like this? Half of them must be a mirage!'

Two Chin crewmen all but knocked me flying; I let Rekhmire' use his solid large body, and his stick, to shelter me across to the companionway.

Ramiro Carrasco climbed down in front of me, sheltering me all the way to the cabins.

A quarter of an hour later, when the noise was very nearly as loud in the cabin as it was outside, Rekhmire' limped in through the door.

'Not two hundred.'

'I knew it!' I made the final fold of cloth and picked Onorata up, her clouts changed for fresh cloth. 'I knew there couldn't be two hundred. How many are there?'

Rekhmire' sat down hard on a carved chair.

'One hundred and eighty-three.'

13

An uncomfortable four hours passed.

From the main deck, I witnessed men, obviously the captains of their war-junks, rowed to Zheng He's flagship. The sound of celebratory drums and conches made my ears numb.

The Armenian sergeant, Orazi, gave voice to every man's fear. Shooting a suspicious glance at the Admiral's cabin, he demanded, 'Where's the bastard going to take this fleet *now*?'

At the end of several hours the captains were rowed back; the towering ships set their sails, and began the long process of tacking for a wind.

Rekhmire' yanked with fingers and teeth at a strip of leather, which I saw he had tied round and over the ferrule of one of his crutches, for a better grip on the deck. He moved his mouth, as if at the taste.

'I dare not calculate the number of men Zheng He has here,' he observed. 'I will, however, see what course we're on . . . '

He stayed absent long enough for Honorius to entertain himself in speculating which kingdoms of the Middle Sea the Chin Admiral might now invade and conquer, if he so desired.

When Rekhmire' returned, he merely shrugged at us.

'By the compass, our course is set *sirocco levante.*'

Even recalling Onorata's lullaby, I looked momentarily blank.

'East south-east,' Rekhmire' said. 'And since compasses don't lie, I judge us to be on the course that will take us past the Balearic Islands and Sardinia, to Carthage. It appears the Admiral is a man of his word.'

The Chin rockets appeared much brighter under the Penitence, in Carthage's harbour. Soaring up in arcs, bursting in showers and fountains, they dimmed the aurora's curtains of light.

Down in the lower stern cabins, with only the small window-ports unshuttered for air, I found the drums and gongs and cymbals muted. But not by much. Even small round drums, wider than they are tall, shake the air when thousands of men sling them at their waists and beat them with hands and sticks.

Onorata lay on her back asleep, but only because she had screamed herself into exhaustion.

Somewhat sourly, Rekhmire' muttered, 'Zheng He won't be talking to

King-Caliph Ammianus for some time yet – since the man's likely stone-deaf!'

Honorius stuck his head out of the small port, gazing down the hull – so much larger than any other vessel in Carthage's port. His voice came back muffled. 'If Zheng He was a normal man, he'd be dead drunk!'

I took my father's point. More of the Admiral's junior captains had flocked aboard the war-junk. Two in particular appeared his friends: they called him 'Ma' instead of 'Zheng He', and I saw much male back-thumping and extremely rapid speech going on, before the general noise forced me to retire below.

Rekhmire' rubbed at his knee-joint. 'Apparently their religion doesn't allow drunkenness.'

He glanced away as I caught his eye.

The Egyptian is nervous.

Perhaps Ty-ameny's briefing for what he must say to the King-Caliph Ammianus?

Honorius, pulling on his furred demi-gown, spoke a little apologetically. 'I'd take you with me to the King-Caliph's audience if I could, Ilario.'

Does he read my mind?

I couldn't help but smile.

'As far as I can tell,' I said, stroking at the soft curls sweat-stuck to Onorata's ear, 'there's you, Admiral Black-Eyes, and the book-buyer here, all going up the Bursa-hill to tell the King-Caliph the same thing. "Look at those ships down in the harbour – now keep your nose clean!"'

Honorius chuckled.

'I'd like to see your performance,' I said. 'But King Rodrigo would skin me if I don't keep my face away from your company in public.'

My father held his arms out while Saverico buttoned the pleated demi-gown and arranged his flower-and-serpent-stamped leather belt. Chin awkwardly up as his collar was straightened, Honorius spoke loud enough to be heard over the drums.

'If you go into Carthage, take my men. If you don't need to go, stay on board.'

The din of drums and conches did not die down. I thought it would not until Zheng He and his officers and captains had made their way up to the King-Caliph's palace. And perhaps not even then.

I caught Rekhmire' watching me.

I said, 'I intend to send Ramiro Carrasco out, to find a rooming-house.'

I saw illumination dawn on Honorius's face that was not from the Chin fireworks.

'Even if it's only the once,' I finished, 'I want Onorata to meet her father.'

*

Honorius and Rekhmire' accompanied the Admiral up to the Bursa-hill numerous times over the next few days.

I claimed I would wait until they had space in their political business to accompany me to Marcomir's house.

Truthfully, my guts crawled with chills.

Honorius spent thirty years wanting a child he couldn't have. He would have loved anything, I sometimes think. And if he had been shocked by the idea of having an hermaphrodite offspring, he did all his thinking about that between Taraco and Carthage, before he ever met me.

Marcomir, though . . .

Marcomir never struck me as wanting children.

Brief as our acquaintance was.

'Ready?' Rekhmire' questioned.

He wore a simple white tunic, for much the same reason that Honorius – with sighs of relief – was allowing Saverico to buckle him into a blue velvet-fronted brigandine. A book-buyer and a soldier would pass unnoticed in Carthage's streets.

Especially with the city full of Chin strangers, to be studied, and stolen from, and seduced.

I checked, for the fourth or fifth time, that nothing essential was being left in the ship's cabin. That Onorata's clothing was clean, and her sling buckled firmly over my shoulders.

To Honorius, but with an eye on Rekhmire', I said, 'We should bring Ramiro Carrasco.'

Carrasco's expression was unexpectedly optimistic. Before either man could rebuke him, he said, 'Because I'm a lawyer?'

It had not occurred to me.

But he's right: a man trained in the university might serve us well.

'Yes. But also,' I added, 'you're a slave.'

Ramiro Carrasco rubbed his hand through his hair, dishevelling it thoroughly. 'Why do you need a slave, madonna? Master?'

I surveyed Onorata's belongings again by eye. Honorius's experiences with a mercenary baggage train are nothing once one needs to take a young baby out.

'Apart from general baggage-carrying? I don't want Marcomir to think I'm asking for money. If I own a slave, I'm not poor.' I shot a wry look at Honorius. 'Even if the money's yours.'

'We're family, brat!'

It cheered me.

'And,' I said, 'Marcomir might also think this is for revenge. Ramiro, you need not tell him what you did. But if necessary, you can tell him I forgave you a crime.'

And Marcomir did nothing to me that I didn't desire.

Ramiro Carrasco stared at the cabin floor. 'Madonna, if you wish, I'll tell him I tried to kill you.'

Any man who didn't know him would not have seen what the honesty cost.

'You can be the judge of whether he needs to hear that.'

Carrasco looked down at his hands. The cabin was dimly lit by oil-lamps, but I thought his skin showed a flush. He stuttered, seeming acutely conscious of the presence of Rekhmire' and Honorius. 'I don't know why you would forgive me!'

'Because since we left Venice, you've been completely trustworthy.'

He looked startled. 'I—That could be a ruse!'

'There are a hundred ways a slave can get back at a master. I know. Believe me. You didn't try any of them.'

Carrasco ducked his head, almost flinching.

If a man ever did good by stealth, or tried to atone without any other man actually *noticing* . . . that would be Ramiro Carrasco de Luis.

Atonement brought the cathedral and Father Felix to mind. I thought suddenly, *I wish I had confessed myself sorry over Sulva Paziathe!*

I did worse to Sulva, and I will never find her to atone for it – when people like the Paziathe disappear, they do it effectively, because lives depend on it.

If I can't pay a debt where it belongs, I must pay it where I may.

Carrasco picked up the sack with Onorata's clothes, toys, and food. As the Alexandrine and my father put on their cloaks, he ventured, 'Onorata's going to be hungry when she wakes up. She wouldn't eat, with all the noise.'

I rested my fingers briefly against her brow, not merely to see if she was feverish, but because her warm skin is a touch like no other. 'I'll feed her when we get there; I doubt they'll mind.'

The baby opened pale blue eyes, coughed, cooed, and loudly choked out, '*Mee-roh!*'

Honorius stared at my baby.

Rekhmire' opened his mouth, as if he would say something, and firmly shut it again.

Carrasco and I stared at each other.

'Did she *say* something? No,' I corrected myself, 'it's too early, surely. Surely? *What* did she say?'

Carrasco brushed the back of his fingers against her cheek.

If she was cool, I saw, he was hot as fire, his skin flushed now from neck to hairline.

He muttered, 'She's said that once or twice before. I . . . think it's what she calls me.'

'Calls . . . '

Ramiro. 'Miro.

'The first word my baby says is *your name*?'

He flinched.

In an unexpectedly peace-making tone, my father observed, 'It might equally have been my name. Or the sergeant's. Or the book-buyer's. Or yours, Ilario.'

'This child has too damn many fathers!'

And not a mother among them.

I sighed, shook my head, and hefted my child in her sling.

'Let's go and find another of them . . . '

A hollow moan shuddered through the air.

Outside the immediate area of the port, Carthage's windowless houses and steep, narrow streets resounded to it as if they were the body of a drum.

Impossibly, the sound came from a shell – although larger than any shell should be. Earlier, Jian had given me the spiral conch to hold in my hands and draw.

He all but laughed himself into an apoplexy when I attempted to blow it. All I did was go red-faced and watery-eyed, failing to get the merest squeak or fart out of the thing.

The alien sound echoed out again under the black midday sky.

The street stood deserted.

Because every man and woman in Carthage who could reach the docks crowded down there, I admitted. The novelty has not yet worn off. I could see dark lines of heads silhouetted against the naphtha illuminations of the quayside. And crowds of the King-Caliph's subjects stood up on their flat roofs, and tried to count the number of huge sailed war-junks cruising in the vicinity of the city.

Zheng He quartered a number of ships further down the gulf, I learned from Rekhmire' and Jian. Partly for logistical reasons, and partly because Zheng He had smiled, in a very civil manner, and set about demonstrating Alexandria's apparent new allies to every North African city for fifty miles around.

Almost inaudibly under the conch's racket, a brass horn blared to mark the first hour of the afternoon.

That used to mark my break for a meal, here.

I shot a look at Honorius, his face made sombre in the naphtha street-lights' glare. Light glinted off Orazi and Berenguer's steel sallets where they flanked him.

The narrow streets, cut into steps more often than not, gave Rekhmire' the most trouble. He drove himself forward, cursing under his breath, and I guessed his knee-joint would be inflamed tomorrow.

'Here.' Ramiro Carrasco pointed.

He stopped by a heavy iron door, set deep into the granite wall of a four-storey house. The iron surface showed featureless except for one keyhole.

No way to knock. No windows opening onto the street. They would be on the inside walls, opening into a central courtyard.

'All looks the same to me!' Honorius grunted, squinting up at the brown and gold aurora as if the midday Penitence sky could give him directions.

No point in asking any Carthaginian, I reflected. In the current excitement, Carthaginian Visigoths weren't interested in talking to any stranger who wasn't a man of Chin.

Surveying the iron door, I remarked, 'I don't recognise it.' I added a swift gloss: 'Carthage was new to me!'

I have no desire to tell my father how I stumbled up these stepped narrow streets in Marcomir's company, in a blind haze of arousal.

Since I had stout leather sandals on, I fetched the door a hefty kick. It juddered in the frame.

I raised my voice in case we were overheard. 'We can come back if they're out now—'

I caught the faint grate of metal against stone.

The door swung in, opening into darkness. The street's naphtha-light was not bright enough to show me who stood there. Between that and the sunless day-sky of the Penitence above, I could barely make out that it was a man who stood there.

'Forget your key?' His voice cut off.

The dim figure turned into a black silhouette, as a lamp shone behind him.

Yellow light swelled and swung on the clay walls, and a silver-haired woman walked up behind the man in the doorway. She held up the lamp, her eyes squeezed into slits. I recognised the hawk-nose.

'Donata!'

Now I could see the man. Lean, muscled, dark-haired, middle height. He has left nothing of his face in Onorata.

Marcomir frowned. He might not remember me well, either, I realised. *It was once, and a year ago.*

And these Alexandrine robes might make him think me male or female, according to his assumptions.

'Marcomir?'

He stared at me, finally grunting an assent.

I took a firmer grip on Onorata, cradled in the crook of my right arm. 'Marcomir. This is your daughter. Her name is Onorata.'

Ramiro must have mentioned armed men to him. Marcomir showed no overt reaction to Honorius and his soldiers.

He has not changed so much, in a year. Dark hair curling only a little lower on his neck, and his off-duty tunic cut in a different fashion.

Marcomir met my eyes, and looked away. It was normal human embarrassment I saw on his face.

I said, 'May we come in?'

He thrust his hand through his hair, looked around at each of us, and finally back at the baby in her miniature linen shift and coif.

'Yes . . . '

Donata echoed him. 'Yes, come in.'

He led us through into the inner part of the house.

Donata's face seemed to have strain scored more deeply into her lined skin. But that might just be this present situation.

Above us, feet thundered up and down the narrow stairs. Other occupants, I speculated, listening to the echoing noise.

It's still a rooming-house.

Lamp-light guided us through to the back, into the kitchen that overlooked a central courtyard. Donata caught my gaze as she set the lamp down on the low basalt table. It was no more than a shaped stone block. I recognised the stove, the table crowded with Roman-style pots, hanging onions; even the silver water ladle . . .

In the hoarse dialect that I thought was from Leptis Magna, or one of the other Carthaginian settlements, Donata broke the silence.

'One-Eye said you got a good master out of it.' She nodded at Ramiro Carrasco. 'If you've got slaves of your own, I guess he was right.'

There are no good masters!

A window stood open, into the communal courtyard. The shutters were ajar. Scents of fish and junipers and sewage came in on the early afternoon wind. It vividly brought back to me One-Eye's cells, Rekhmire''s hired house, the tophet.

I sat down on one of the long benches built into the kitchen wall. Onorata woke and began squirming gently in my lap. 'How did you know One-Eye sold me?'

'Oh, my son spoke to him, in the tavern? Afterwards? We always wanted to know people went somewhere comfortable.'

Comfortable.

The choice was between screaming or saying nothing. I doubted I might truly explain to this mother and son what happened to their guests. I still wake in dreams, cold sweat down my spine, as Rekhmire' turns away and does not throw his purse to One-Eye.

'My lord! Sit down, sit down!' Donata flurried around Honorius, ignoring his soldiers in much the same way that she ignored my slave. She put a Samian jug full of wine on the kitchen table, along with pottery cups that seemed remarkably crude after Jian's porcelain.

I caught her eye.

She flushed, defiantly poured out wine, and drunk her cup down in one.

Marcomir ignored her, sitting down on the ledge beside me. He stared at Onorata. 'Is this the . . . How did you – how did we— She's tiny.'

Donata glanced over, hawk-swift and analytic.

606

'Premature.' She registered my surprise. 'Seven-month baby?'

'Yes. How do you . . . ?'

'I saw enough of them dead at that age.' She shrugged. 'Never could keep a babe in my womb long enough until Marcomir, here. And look how that turned out!'

Her humour was rough teasing, but in any case Marcomir was oblivious. He gently smoothed the curls of black hair that poked up from under Onorata's linen coif. She turned her head and appeared to stare at him.

Rekhmire' thumped down onto the bench, rubbing his knee. I was vaguely aware that Honorius put his hand under Donata's elbow, steering her to sit down. He began to speak quietly to her.

Orazi stationed Berenguer at the door, he himself leaning on the windowsill. A jerk of his head summoned Carrasco.

There is a choice between security and privacy. The Armenian sergeant will give as much of the latter as he safely can.

Marcomir put his finger next to Onorata's hand, and examined the nails. Hers were identical to his, but so very small.

'Got into trouble about selling you, Ilario,' he murmured, quietly enough that Onorata rummaged herself back into a light doze, leaning against me.

'You did?' I stroked her cheek. Fed and changed and allowed to sleep – but for not too long – would usually mean she woke now in a good temper.

'Spoke to One-Eye, like she said.'

He jerked his head, indicating Donata, who stood to pour more wine for Honorius.

'Few weeks later, my boss down at the Hall, he calls me in. He says it doesn't look good if merchants and visitors to Carthage vanish. Not a hard slap on the wrist, but . . . the customs job keeps us. So I said no, of course not, wouldn't happen again. Even if it meant things would be a bit tight.'

He does think I intend to ask him for money.

Onorata screwed up nose and eyes and yawned.

Marcomir shook his head in wonder. He grinned up at me suddenly, and sat back.

'I *said* we were doing people favours! Look at you. One-Eye said your owner was a hard son of a bitch when it came to a bargain, even if he was good-looking. But I guess you got away from him?'

I deliberately refused to look in Rekhmire''s direction. 'My master freed me.'

Marcomir thrust a hand through his hair again. 'What do you want from me?'

I registered Donata's quick frown.

Donata stayed alert to her son's reactions, even though she was deep in conversation with my father. I wondered briefly how much Onorata might take after her, in the future; this . . . grandmother.

As much as Rosamunda is, Donata is Onorata's grandmother.

I pictured the queen of the Court of Ladies and Donata in the same room – or rather, failed to picture it.

'I can't keep a child on my wages.' Marcomir opened a long-fingered hand in my direction. 'But you're dressed well enough, and so's the babe, and you're free, so I suppose that's not what you want anyway. Is she truly mine?'

'You don't remember?'

The light from the clay lamp gave everything a golden cast, transmuting his flush from something pink by sunlight into something bruise-coloured.

'I follow in the Roman tradition,' he said, standing on his dignity. 'A boy or an older man, for true companionship. And a woman for marriage one day, I suppose we must have . . . with what you are . . . ' He shrugged again. 'It's not like I intended to – to—'

'That's my father over there: spare me the detailed explanations!'

The Carthaginian customs officer looked over at the retired Captain-General of the House of Trastamara.

Marcomir turned quickly back to me, being unfamiliar with that particular poker-face that in Honorius indicates the holding back of a belly-laugh.

'If it's not money,' Marcomir persisted, 'then what is it you want? *Oh.* I understand. You want Carthaginian citizenship for her! Through her father.'

We have had this conversation before!

Perceiving Honorius about to fume and swear, I said, 'No citizenship. That's not the issue.'

Marcomir's black eyes glinted in the light from the lamps. Bent over, Onorata evidently had him fascinated. He shook his head.

'I'd never thought of being a father!' He suddenly sat up. 'You're a hermaphrodite: are you sure you didn't do it yourself?'

Berenguer's jaw dropped. Orazi muttered at him, under his breath: 'That one was worthy of you!'

It startled me that I liked Marcomir's appalling honesty.

At least he acknowledges openly what I am.

I snorted. 'I'm a hermaphrodite, not a contortionist!'

I was suddenly faced by the backs of three brigandines: Orazi's shoulders shaking, and Berenguer evidently not daring to look at his Captain-General.

Marcomir only looked bewildered. 'Why did you bring her, then? Can I – can I hold her?'

'Sit closer to me.'

His thigh was warm against mine; I could feel the tension of his muscles. I eased Onorata from my lap to his, keeping my hands curved around her hip and the back of her head until she was safely settled.

Catching his glance, I explained, 'Not all men know how to handle babies.'

I did not add what would have been true: *I learned most of what I know from a failed assassin and a squad of soldiers . . .*

Marcomir held the sleeping form of my child.

I remember his long fingers, and his cool hands.

I remember the conception of this child.

Outside this room, I had seen narrow steps. They would lead to an upstairs room: Marcomir's clothes tossed absently on the floor. Blankets of striped wool spread over a truckle bed too small for two, but possible when one sleeps intertwined, knee socketing home behind knee; buttocks tucked into crotch . . .

I miss the warmth of sleeping with someone else.

In Taraco, I had a bed to myself in the hermit's cell; that was different to sleeping in a bundle with Rodrigo Sanguerra's other slaves. Sleeping communally has its disadvantages – not least any other slaves attempting what Marcomir and I had engaged in while not properly awake. But it has its comforts too.

I flushed and looked away, seeking the window for light, but finding only the brown darkness of the Penitence.

Because when I imagine the warmth of a body next to my skin, I don't think of Marcomir now. Or Sulva. Or Leon Battista; or even Ty-ameny, beautiful as the small woman is.

After some considerable reflection, I don't think of Ramiro Carrasco, either.

Marcomir stroked Onorata's temple very lightly. I wondered how long before she would wake up, cry for the brightly-dyed wooden blocks that Tottola had carved as toys for her, demand feeding, and in general cease to look like a sculpted angel in a chapel.

I felt a little shy. 'I thought you would want to know about her.'

'I'm glad I know.'

More clumsily, but with a willingness to be gentle, Marcomir guided her sleep-limp body back into my lap.

'I can't take her. Even if she was a son, I couldn't.'

I winced.

Harsher than I otherwise would have been, I snapped, 'I don't want you to!'

Donata sprang up. She bustled over to where we sat, and peered down into Onorata's pink, creased face. 'Just as well you got free of that Egyptian who bought you – he would have drowned her for you like a kitten!'

Caught between wanting to cry with laughter, and merely wanting to cry, I only shook my head.

609

'Oh, he would. And men are always happy if a girl or a cripple goes to the tophet.' The shadow of some old bitterness crossed her face. She seated herself on the other side of her son, leaning in to look at Onorata. 'Is she all right?'

'As much as we can know.'

As much as the Alexandrine physicians can swear to.

Donata reached out to touch Onorata's cheek. 'I know we didn't treat you too well when you were here last. If there's anything we can do . . . '

Without looking at Honorius, I said, 'I think a father, a good father, is one of the best things a child can have. If she had his friendship, that would be all I would ask.'

I found myself looking at the top of Marcomir's head as he gazed down at Onorata's black lashes, and the fingers of her clenched fist. Hesitantly, he put his hand over her hand, hiding half her arm in the shadow of his fingers.

It came to me that a man who works for the city's customs is probably used to looking keenly at things. Marcomir's examination of her might show him resemblances that I couldn't see.

Honorius's deep voice said, 'There'll be a place you can send word to. You can see her if you want to.'

It was Donata who said, 'Thank you,' in a creakingly graceless voice that was moving in its honesty.

Marcomir's finger absently brushed Onorata's forehead, and she opened blue eyes.

He stopped.

I saw they were looking at each other.

He moved his finger, watched her gaze follow it, and smiled at her.

'If the worst happens,' I said abruptly. 'If I and all my family die and she's left alone, I want her to have a father.'

Marcomir's head came up. I saw in his eyes that expectation of poverty, disease, accident, and war that slaves and poor men have. Wealth protects. But even then, not wholly.

His smile slipped slowly away. 'I couldn't pay for her keep.'

'Could you let her die of hunger?'

'I – no; I could not.'

A knock sounded on the room door. Donata glared, and went to the door, opening it a crack, and beginning a long and rambling quarrel with a man clearly a tenant.

Marcomir spoke under their rapid argument. 'It wouldn't be any use sending her to me. Mother's old. In a few years I'll be keeping both of us. There isn't money or room for a child as well.'

'I don't doubt you.'

'Wait . . . ' The Carthaginian glanced around, momentarily frowning. He got up and went to a small tin chest, pushed back on the highest niche by the shelves.

He lifted something out of it and came back to me.

I thought for a moment it was a pair of wax tablets, the two wooden shutters clapped together. But it was small, no larger than the palm of my hand, and the wooden shutters opened out from the centre. I had both hands busy with Onorata. Marcomir folded the shutters back.

'Look.' He cupped it in his hands. 'This isn't much, but, I don't know, maybe you could sell it, buy her something nice with the money?'

The tiny portrait of a girl's head had been cut from a much larger work, clearly, and glued onto the wooden backing. Or it might have been an androgynous young man: the halo backing the head and the rich trappings on the clothes could indicate a saint or angel.

'Thought it was real gold, when I saw it – gold leaf?' Marcomir's forefinger traced the line of the halo, and the gold embroidery on the front of the robe. 'But someone's just painted it to look like gold.'

He sounded more than a little disgusted.

Donata slammed the door on the argument from outside, with a curt dismissal. She stomped back across the room, shot a glance at what was in Marcomir's hands, and folded her lips together severely.

'I'll take it!' I said hastily. 'I'll tell her it was her father's gift.'

Marcomir nodded, with a smile.

Onorata made a small querulous sound, swiping her open hand at him. I had no time to point out that she missed holding onto his finger. The signs of storm began to show: she screwed up her eyes, and began to square her mouth and grizzle.

'I should take her back to the ship.' I jiggled her on my knee, easier to do now that she could hold her head up, but she wasn't mollified. The grizzle turned into a full-throated bawl, and began to work up to a scream.

At these moments, I look around for someone to hand her back to. Honorius only smiled at me.

I freed one hand to take the tiny shuttered portrait, slipped it inside my robe, and mouthed emphatically to Marcomir over Onorata's open-mouthed yelling. 'Remember, she's your daughter! You can always see her, when it's possible—'

'I'm sorry we sold you!' he blurted out. 'Can you forgive me, like you have the assassin?'

Onorata chose that moment to hiccup and draw breath, producing as absolute a silence as could be wished.

Marcomir's face turned as hot as mine felt.

'Things could have turned out worse,' I muttered – caught Honorius's eye, and grinned. 'Much worse!'

Marcomir smiled openly.

His black pupils dilated in the lamp-light. I felt myself shiver, skin prickling. Not difficult at all to remember, now, how arousal sparked between us.

Donata, muttering, stopped in front of Honorius, and threw her hands up with a sharp exclamation.

'We'll send you something!' she announced.

Honorius bemusedly looked down at the poorly-dressed elderly woman. '"Send" . . . '

'Every month or so. We can scrape a few ducats together. I know—' She cut him off. 'That you don't need it. I know that.'

Orazi and Ramiro Carrasco exchanged an inaudible word. Honorius nodded.

I ignored the yammering in my mind that said, *They're too poor, she's too old, it's hardly fair – and it certainly won't be honest—*

There are times to keep silent.

Donata sniffed, looking pointedly at Honorius. 'The brat doesn't have just one grandparent.'

Marcomir's daughter began to scream in the way that I knew from experience she would be happy to keep up for hours.

Donata reached down, picked her off my lap with astonishing dexterity, and put Onorata face-down over her skinny hip.

The crying cut off. Onorata hiccuped in surprise.

Donata shifted her weight, just enough to keep a rhythm.

My child began to giggle.

After a few moments, the old woman brought Onorata upright again, her strong skinny hand at the back of the baby's head. Donata sat Onorata straddling the same hip. She pursed her lips.

'You need a nurse!'

I was too busy staring at my Judas of a child, along with the others in the room. 'What?'

Donata seemed entirely unconcerned to be asking awkward questions. 'How in Tanit's name will *you* raise her?'

The room fell silent.

I had not planned to open this subject with Honorius yet.

The Captain-General's gaze pinned me.

'My problem . . . ' I reached out for Onorata's hand. ' . . . Is that I'm in exile from Taraco. I don't want to bring her up like a gypsy.'

The hawk-faced woman nodded. 'Oh, you can take 'em anywhere when they're this size, if they're not weaklings. But when they walk and talk, that's different!'

Rekhmire' leaned forward, his tenor voice cutting through the noise.

'There is Alexandria. Constantinople. I know Queen Ty-ameny would stand as godmother to the child.'

Marcomir's eyes widened.

'And she might also,' Rekhmire' concluded, 'be able to offer you employment as a scribe.'

Donata interrupted before I could say a word, her hands clasping protectively around Onorata. 'If the child's in Constantinople, we'll never see it!'

Honorius growled, 'Neither will I!'

Marcomir's head turned as if he watched a tourney.

Nothing showed him concerned about the outcome. *He has no fatherly feeling for her*, I realised.

Donata thrust Onorata at me, her hands cutting sharp chopping gestures in the air as she harangued Honorius.

Donata has turned into a grandmother . . .

'I will be away for short times on diplomatic missions!' Honorius's battle-loud voice drowned her out. 'But otherwise on my estate, where Ilario has a home always – and *I* can raise Onorata!'

Marcomir shook beside me. He was laughing, I realised.

'The old guy's men-at-arms can have bets about whether she'll grow up girl or boy!' he snickered.

Donata made a long arm and thwacked her son's ear; Berenguer (it surprised me to note) ambled across the room and loomed threateningly over Marcomir.

I met Honorius's gaze.

'I would have suggested this later,' I said, 'but it might be better for Onorata if you formally adopted her.'

The room went quiet. Honorius seemed to be waiting.

I said, 'All the while my name is attached to her, people will be waiting for her to grow up a monster.'

Honorius looked thoughtful.

'If I do,' he said after a moment, 'no one in our family will ever lie to her about her mother-father. She's my grandchild: she'll need in any case to know what political secrets are. But within the boundaries of my estate, she would be your child, and my grandchild.'

I could not speak.

'In any case,' Honorius's face took on an intent look, 'this all depends on what you intend to do when you leave Carthage, Ilario.'

Rekhmire' glanced at me; so did the Carthaginian mother and son; Carrasco and Berenguer and Orazi stared with varying degrees of curiosity and concern.

'Yes,' I said. 'And – I don't know.'

14

In the end there is no choice, I thought.

Even if she believes I abandon her.

Sunlight slid across the cabin floor as the war-junk tacked across the Gulf of Gades. I sat with neither charcoal nor paper, imprinting Onorata's face onto my memory.

Honorius will travel up the Via Augusta to Taraco, after he has completed the King's business in Gades, and take Onorata with him. She'll be as safe as life allows on his estates. And I will visit, secretly, even before King Rodrigo lifts what is, to all intents, my exile.

But Honorius will see her take her first step. And she will call for 'Miro before she calls for me.

The salt wind and bright sun made my reddened eyes sore.

Rekhmire' glanced up from where he was seated on one of the great hatch-covers. The shadows of sails and masts fell across his face. 'Are you well?'

The polished wood felt hot under my bare legs as I sat down beside the Egyptian.

'If it was the wrong decision, I wouldn't be able to weep for an hour and get it out of my system.'

He gave me a dubious look.

'Taking a baby on roads and ships and who-knows-where.' I shrugged, squinting up at the web of ropes against the sky. 'She's been so *lucky*. Not to die.'

In peripheral vision, I saw him nod.

I followed the lines of taut rope up to a clear sky, seeing blue shadows in the hollow of white sails, and the tapering lines of masts.

Bare feet pounded past, Zheng He's crew leaping for the rigging and swarming up. I tilted my head back, watching them jump, climb; agile and sure; taking in sails and letting others spring free . . .

The hatch-cover hit me squarely between the shoulder -blades.

I looked up at Rekhmire'.

'Perspective. Sometimes it's no man's friend.'

Rekhmire' wordlessly held out a hand, I interlocked fingers, and the world swooped around me as I came swiftly upright.

The Egyptian went back to massaging at his knee, where he had it in the sun.

The sun glittered a trail of fire and sparks off the long rolling waves. Zheng He's ship cut aloof through a swell that would have sunk a smaller ship. *We will make Gades itself before Sext.*

I took Marcomir's fragment of painted wood out of my belt-purse. 'Look at this.'

The Egyptian sat back, taking it carefully into his hands. 'That is not done by the encaustic wax technique?'

'No, but it must be close to it. It's not egg tempera.'

Chin's ink-drawing fascinated me, in the way that Alexandria's architecture did. *But they are both a dead end, in the face of this.* I pointed. Where the scrap of canvas had been glued onto the wooden background, much of the paintwork was spoiled. What was left was still enough to take my breath away, as unbelievable as the first time I saw it in Marcomir's hands.

'I think it's done by pigment and *oil* . . . '

The white face of a girl, or perhaps a male saint, the eyelids modelled subtly to make the downward gaze natural. Most of the hair and neck were gone. There was still a fraction of green cloth at the shoulder, the depths of the folds apple-coloured.

The highlights were the colour of new spring leaves.

And the graduation of colour between them . . .

I didn't dare touch a finger to it, ruined as it was. 'It's blended. See how seamlessly that's done? Those shadows aren't muddy; they're not coloured pigments mixed with black! It's . . . transparent colour. Done on a prepared white canvas, and with so *many* glazes . . . I've seen linseed oils used with pigments before, but not to give effects like this!'

Rekhmire' tilted the wooden shutters. 'It resembles gold more than gold leaf does!'

'One of the things Leon wrote – gold leaf will shine back dark and flat. A skilled paint should be able to *mimic* all the effects of light. Better painted gold than gold leaf painted on.'

The Egyptian slowly nodded. 'Where did Master Marcomir acquire it?'

It had been an awkward conversation, as it always is when one accuses a man of theft.

'As far as I can make out, they had a court painter staying over from Duke Philip's lands in Burgundy – the Duke sent him out to paint possible brides, but he sailed to Carthage to see the light under the Penitence. As for what part of the Burgundian lands . . . ' I shrugged.

'Ty-ameny would be happy to get reports from Bruges,' Rekhmire' observed, as if the matter were of no great interest to him.

He added, 'Burgundy is becoming one of the richest kingdoms of the Franks, and therefore likely to have a greater influence as times goes on.'

I found myself in a mood for taking no prisoners. 'Rekhmire' – can you still spy with your knee permanently injured?'

He did not look at me, but gazed down at the backs of his hands, spreading the fingers as wide as tendons will allow. 'You know the strangest thing? It makes me feel less than a man. Which, from a eunuch . . . '

His snort of amusement sounded bitter.

I persisted. 'But you can still work for Ty-ameny?'

He looked puzzled. 'Oh yes.'

I turned the wooden fragment about in my hands. 'The idea of staying seven years in one place, even in a workshop . . . Do you know, I think I begin to understand why you like travelling around? But could I paint something like this without masters teaching me their secrets? Which they won't, if I'm *not* an apprentice.'

Rekhmire' took my wrist and turned the painted surface to the light. 'There might be treatises like Leon Battista's. You learned from that.'

'That's true. But . . . '

Feet scurried on the deck. I glanced up to see Ramiro Carrasco duck past in something between fear and respect on his way to the cabins.

He barely looked at me. All his wariness was for Rekhmire'.

I don't believe the book-buyer would take up beating him!

In a tone of controlled sarcasm, Rekhmire' remarked, 'Suppose you travel as one of the Queen's book-buyers, while Captain Honorius brings up Onorata – you won't be able to take your pet slave with you if he's back in Taraco changing nappies.'

The Egyptian added something under his breath that a creak of masts and sails prevented me hearing clearly.

I thought it was, *Or do you think* he'll *give you brats as well?*

I covered the image carefully, closing the wooden flap down, and put it back into my purse.

'Rekhmire'—'

Tread carefully, I reminded myself.

No man is at his best in pain, and Carthage's Bursa-hill had not been kind to the Egyptian's body.

'If I do take Carrasco, it will be to keep him safe from Videric. But I do think it would be better if he could live on Honorius's estate – assuming he wants to. Onorata could still see him, then.'

Rekhmire' snorted. 'Don't know why you don't *marry* the damn prick!'

My temper went wherever tempers go.

'Because, like *so many people,* it never appears to have occurred to him to *ask me!*'

Some of Jian's crewmen jumped back, making a wide berth around the hatch-cover. Rekhmire' sat upright, fingers motionless on his knee, staring at me with a wide-eyed shock.

He dropped his gaze and muttered sullenly, 'It was the first thing I asked you – if you wanted a slave-contract to include bed.'

I would have said something, *anything!*, had I control of my wits or my mouth.

Evidently I had neither.

I stared at him.

Rekhmire' returned to gazing at the backs of his hands. 'You weren't interested. As you told me.'

'Not then. I thought it would be two freaks together because they had no other choice—'

He interrupted, his voice a squeak. '"Not then"?'

'Ah—'

My turn to look away. I stared over the rail at the approaching coast of Gades.

'Then again, I've been married twice this year . . . '

'"*Not then*"?' Rekhmire' all but bellowed. 'What do you mean, "not then"? When did it change? Did it change? Why didn't you tell me!'

He glared at me, surprisingly ruffled and breathless for such a large man.

I said, 'If I can put up with you when you're sick in bed in Venice, I've probably seen all your worse qualities . . . '

Rekhmire' looked thoroughly overthrown. 'That discouraged you.'

'I wasn't even *thinking*, at that time—!' I shook my head. 'I'm just saying. You with a bad temper because you're in pain. Nothing of it's a surprise.'

Rekhmire' lurched up, manhandling himself off the hatch-cover and striding to the port rail. He stared out at white spray. I watched the line of his back.

Without turning round, Rekhmire' said, 'The difference is that now I have to *prove* to Ty-ameny that I can do my job.'

I was appalled. 'She'd *dismiss* you over this?'

He laughed, turning to face me, showing me a broad smile. 'Sacred Eight, no! But if she thinks I'm having problems, she'll have me back in Alexandria at a bureaucrat's desk, before you can say "Royal Library"! She wants me *safe*. She'd make everything as comfortable for me as she could. But I . . . '

'Want to be here, doing this,' I completed.

I sat up, cross-legged; shifted again; and got up to walk to the rail beside him. For all the distraction, I couldn't bite back the remaining words in my mind.

'Yes, I'd noticed how close you and Ty-ameny are! She does *know* what you're like after a month in one place?'

His eyes slitted. A little defensively, he said, 'She's like a sister. And furthermore, I would be *perfectly capable* of working at home in the city!'

'Hope she doesn't mind her crockery thrown at people's heads . . . '

The Egyptian narrowed his eyes still further at me. 'Pot. Kettle. Black!'

I would not have laughed if I could have prevented it. Unfortunately, that and his expression reduced me to breathlessness.

'In any case,' he said, a while after my recovery, 'when I say I can offer you Ty-ameny's patronage as a cousin – you may not be aware, precisely, of what it would involve for you.'

He put a stress on the last word that stopped me telling him, *Yes, I understood the book-buyers' trade thank you very much.*

'I mean it would be offered in respect of your particular talents. As with the Admiral's ship at Alexandria harbour.'

Slowly, I said, 'You mean Queen Ty-ameny is offering me the chance to . . . go somewhere and *draw* things?'

'And paint them.' Rekhmire' raised a brow. 'Many places.'

'And be paid for this.'

'It is a very modest amount of money—'

'*Sign me up!*' I bounced on the deck, feeling all of fourteen. 'That's just what I want to do!'

The Egyptian smiled. Not as brightly as I had expected. I caught a glimpse of something bitter-sweet in his expression.

I paused.

'I suppose,' I said, 'before I go wandering around on my own, I'd need some training?'

Rekhmire' looked at me.

'A mentor?' I said. 'Someone more experienced? Someone who, for example, has been doing this for a long—'

'YES! I'll do it!'

I grinned up at the panting book-buyer.

'Did I say I was going to ask you? Maybe I should ask Ty-ameny to decide who she'd recommend—'

He had been reduced to speechlessness, I saw.

'—since she threatened to pull my intestines out of my body,' I added, 'if I ever did anything to hurt you.'

Rekhmire' stared at me.

'What?'

'When we were in the Library one time—'

'The – *interfering little brat!*'

He was too far away, I decided. I took the few steps that crossed the distance between us, on uncertain legs, and stood at the rail by his side.

'Actually . . . ' I surveyed the Gulf of Gades. 'It was Ty-ameny who made me realise that I'd miss you, if you went off somewhere else.'

'You would?'

Frightened as I was, I heard myself sound very definite. 'Yes, I would.'

'Oh.' He sat back. 'Good.'

'Rekhmire'—'

'Good. I suppose that in that case I can stop worrying that you're going to notice I've been *following you around for a year now*!'

All the crew for fifteen feet around briefly turned to stare at the mad barbarian. Rekhmire' gasped in a breath.

I watched his broad chest move.

'Really?' I said. 'All year?'

'I don't know *what* gave Ty-ameny the idea that you're in any way intelligent!'

'No, nor do I.'

I gave way to a temptation of long standing, and leaned my shoulder up against his. His skin felt heated, soft. *Prickling, like silk rubbed over amber*.

He didn't move away.

I shifted, pushing my way into the gap between his arm and his ribs.

Rekhmire' beamed and put his arm around me.

'Ilario!'

The voice spoke behind me without giving me any warning so I might move. I turned my head, looked down the deck, and found myself staring directly at Honorius.

Rekhmire' did not so much as twitch beside me – because, I realised from peripheral vision, he appeared to be in a blind panic.

Honorius let out an explosive sigh.

'Oh, thank *God*! It's about damn time!'

I managed to turn my head back and look up at Rekhmire'.

He gazed down at me, lips moving a little, as if he would have formed words if he could.

The Captain-General of Taraconensis snorted and turned his back, stalking away down the deck of the war-junk.

His mutter was perfectly audible.

' . . . Been expecting this since *Rome* . . . !'

We looked at each other.

Rekhmire' gave me his gravest expression. 'I suppose we'd better not disappoint him.'

I was too weak for laughter. I leaned against the warmth of his bare chest. He was not so much taller than I, and he smelled wonderful. 'Only if it's what you want. You know what I am.'

'You know what *I* am. Some things are less – urgent for me than for other men.' He moved his other arm, to enclose me, and I felt the weight as he leaned his smooth cheek against my temple. 'I can't give you children, either. But I can cherish the one you have.'

As long as we have her, I thought, melancholy in the midst of this happiness. What is valuable is always fragile.

The sea rocked us as we sat together on the hatch-cover, playing the game that lovers play of 'when did you first notice?', 'when did you first feel . . . ?'.

It was a long time before I moved, and then it was to get up and go to the ship's rail. I shaded my eyes as the war-junk opened the harbour of Gades.

'Something isn't right.'

Rekhmire' shoved himself to his feet and thumped across the deck to stand beside me.

The myriad other war-junks of Zheng He's fleet kept station astern across the Gulf of Gades – impossibly large under the brilliant sun; impossibly and spikily graceful.

At least a dozen European and North African ships out of Carthage were, out of apparent sheer curiosity, attempting to keep up with us. Frankish cogs, Venetian galleys . . . The wooden rail jammed hard under my ribs as I leaned out, looking toward our stern.

A cog flying the colours of Genoa tacked across the war-junk's wake, bowsprit jutting high out of the blue-grey waves – just as high as the top of our rudder. Their deck was a cliff's depth below me.

Sounding unusually confused, Rekhmire' murmured, 'What ought I to see?'

I pointed at the departing Genoese ship – and the other vessels sailing towards us from the entrance to the harbour.

'*That* isn't right,' I protested. 'It doesn't matter if they've heard rumours. This is Zheng He's giant devil-ship in the flesh – *and* his fleet! Why isn't Gades in a panic?'

15

'There's the answer.' I balanced uneasily, a knee on the boat's prow, and studied the quay of Gades ahead.

Under the banners, a group of men stood, evidently waiting to greet the Captain-General of Taraconensis. The tall man in Carthaginian robes would be the Governor. Beside him . . .

'That's Safrac de Aguilar.' I sat back beside Honorius, avoiding falling by a fraction. 'The man beside *him* is Videric.'

A muscle clenched at the hinge of Honorius's jaw.

'Is it so?'

He spent a moment adjusting his heavy sea-cloak over his demi-gown. With his temper bridled, he added, 'The King told me to return by way of Gades, and as a courtesy inform the Governor that the Admiral's ships have no ill intentions towards him – being our allies.'

The same method of wiping one's enemy's face in it as Rodrigo Sanguerra had ordered for Carthage, evidently.

'Therefore,' Honorius gritted, 'I should very much like to know what Pirro Videric is doing here!'

Wind caught the banners, rolling them out on the wind. I recognised the Sanguerra colours, as well as Videric's personal banner.

'The King trusts de Aguilar, for what *that's* worth.'

Honorius set his jaw and didn't speak.

I clung to the boat's side, wishing I might talk to Rekhmire' – who travelled with the other men in the second boat. Neither Honorius nor Orazi were willing to speculate. I concentrated, impatiently, on reaching the quay, and on not being sick.

Videric stepped forward out of the crowd as soon as Honorius finished his formal greetings to the Governor of Gades.

'King Rodrigo was uncertain when you'd complete your business in Carthage. Whether it would be done before the Pharaoh-Queen's subjects would be put ashore at Gades.' Videric smiled, his fair hair and open expression making him appear very guileless. 'The King sent me here in case you should miss the day.'

Of all the odd things I have seen in the last twelve months, my stepfather Videric walking amiably beside my natural father Honorius, towards the Governor of Gades' palace, must be the most remarkable of all.

'I see where you get your glass-throwing habits from,' the book-buyer remarked.

I winced at a crash from the opulent chambers the Governor had provided for Captain-General Honorius.

Tottola, idly leaning up against the archway, grinned and pulled the curtain aside for me to pass through.

Honorius halted, halfway through pulling off the fur-trimmed demi-gown, and fixed me with a glare. '*Your* stepfather!'

He threw his boot at my head.

I caught it neatly, since there had been no real force behind it, and returned it to him with a grin. 'I've had masters who threw so much harder and better than that . . . '

It evidently defused the remains of his bad temper. He ruffled my hair, reducing it to a haystack.

'I wish you'd gone through none of that.' He perked up. 'But are you sure you wouldn't like to see your stepfather challenged to a duel? I'm sure Rodrigo-damned-Sanguerra doesn't need his First Minister *that* badly . . . '

'Court politics.' I shrugged. 'Videric gets the glory of telling the Lord-Amir here in charge of Gades that no, he needn't worry, the devil-ships are just passing allies of Taraconensis . . . '

'I had Carthage. I suppose I can forgive him stealing Gades out from under me!'

Honorius's buoyant mood returned too readily for a man who would play court politics seriously. *But then*, I thought, *he'd likely rather be back on his estate, waiting for his mares to foal.*

'And another damn banquet tonight,' Honorius added, yanking at the strings of his shirt. 'I imagine I'll stay several days. Ilario, have you decided where you'll go from here?'

My face may have been a little hot as I glanced at the Egyptian. 'We haven't had time to discuss it, really . . . '

My father has very eloquent eyebrows, when he chooses.

I sighed. 'I suppose I ought to stay out of the way of the banquet, since you're there. How I suffer . . . '

'How *I* suffer,' Honorius snorted.

Voices at the arched doorway interrupted him. I turned, as he did, to find the German man-at-arms escorting a well-dressed Iberian into the Captain-General's room.

The Lord Pirro Videric gave me a tight smile.

'Lord Honorius. Ilario – I saw you at the dock. This may be unwise. I know you are only exiled from Taraconensis. But would it not be wiser if you left Iberia altogether?'

I was close enough to tread heavily on Honorius's foot.

'The First Minister is only looking out for King Rodrigo's interests.' I held Videric's pale gaze. 'And of course, he's correct. Aldra Videric, Gades *is* a seaport. I'll be gone by tomorrow.'

Rekhmire' made his excuses to leave the banquet early, and joined me in my room while I ate what I had managed to talk the kitchen staff out of.

'You eat better than *I* do.' He picked an olive off my plate. 'And your temper has certainly improved.'

I ignored that provoking compliment. 'I would have preferred to leave Gades by land ... The Via Augusta starts here. Or ends here. Depending on your perspective.'

I doubted I could rely on Zheng He's fleet to transport me, now Sebekhotep and Rekhmire' had come ashore. An attempt to bribe Commander Jian with two charcoal studies, one of him in profile and one full-face, had only resulted in him cheerfully remarking, 'Keeps the demons away!' as he brandished the papers.

Or at least, I think he said that. My acquaintance with the languages of Chin is still spotty.

Rekhmire' took a seat at the window, gazing out over the city of Gades. 'The Via Augusta? You'd need no ship at all. You could walk all the way back across Iberia to Taraco, to Marseilles, to Genoa, to Italy ... '

I saved him a last olive on my dish. 'What, am I not even allowed a mule to ride?'

'You have enough donkeys with you as it is.'

I couldn't help a smile. 'Oh, cruel!'

'Perhaps I'm wrong.' The Egyptian mimicked thought. 'Lord Honorius's men are quick-witted, for soldiers. Perhaps it's only the lawyer—'

The small weight of the olive made it very satisfactory to lob.

The Egyptian picked it up off the tiles, showing no inclination to eat it.

'But truly,' he said, as if it had been what we discussed. 'You'll let Pirro Videric force your hand, and leave tomorrow?'

When I would have succumbed to temper, now I might cross the room and press my fingers and palms against the large muscles of the Egyptian's neck. I found the touch of silk-warm skin both calmed and aroused.

'If I have to leave Honorius and Onorata, a quick farewell is at least quick, and not long drawn out and painful.'

'Then you need only decide where we are to go.'

'I will. Not now.' I looked up at the window, and the velvet moon. 'I think, since it seems I'll see so little of Gades, I should take this opportunity.'

Going out by way of the elegant marble entrance, we met up with Honorius's men, mingling with the governor's off-duty guards, and with Aldra Safrac de Aguilar.

The dark man's long face metamorphosed to a smile. And since he claimed he knew Gades well, having been here before, I thought it wise enough to let him show us its society.

I heard none of Aldra Videric's secrets, nor anything useful to Honorius, but I did discover the potency of the local wine.

The times when I have trusted any court far enough to get drunk are remarkably few. My previous experience of hangovers in Taraco was due to wine being forced on the King's Freak for the amusement of others.

Still, the buttery-hatch to the Governor's kitchens stood open, and the feeling of sitting in company in the Great Hall and dulling my morning headache with small beer and oatmeal porridge was not unpleasant. I found myself with elbows on the stained yellow linen of the trestle tables, talking casually with those of Honorius's men I knew less well.

Gades seems provincial, after Rome, Venice, Alexandria . . .

That evidence of my own snobbery made me chuckle out loud, and bury myself in my mug of nettle beer while conversations went on around me.

A hand fell on my shoulder. 'Ilario!'

Momentarily lost in studying the walls – considering how much more modern tapestries or even frescoes would look than the red-and-ochre chevrons painted on the stonework – I almost overturned the trestle table and bench as I pushed myself up and away.

'Ilario, no!' A man held up his hands. He wore a green demi-gown, and had only a dagger at his belt. 'No harm intended!'

'Safrac.' My grip on the leather and metal of my dagger's hilt pressed hard enough to turn skin white. It took me three tries to get the point back into the mouth of the scabbard, and sheathe the blade.

Safrac de Aguilar's dark eyes smiled, the rest of his face returning to customary melancholy. 'I was warned how unwise it is to disturb you. Forgive me: you don't always look like a knight. But you're late! Your mother's already left for the meeting.'

'My mother?'

I would be shocked, were I not bewildered.

Rosamunda is here with Videric?

Picking up the leather mug of nettle beer and draining it covered how a nervous shiver went through me, just at the mention of that woman. I tried not to sound as bewildered as I felt. 'What "meeting"? I don't know about any meeting!'

Safrac de Aguilar frowned. 'A few moments ago? I met Aldra Videric, and heard him bidding Aldro Rosamunda hurry, because "Ilario is there already".'

As a slave, I would continue to listen. Or ask apparently innocent leading questions, until I knew what was happening. But I have my freedom.

624

I took hold of Safrac de Aguilar's arm through the fine green velvet. Rodrigo thinks this man honest and incorruptible. *I hope he's correct.*

I lowered my voice below the level of general conversation in the hall. 'Were you *supposed* to overhear this, Safrac? Or was it an accident?'

He gave me the thoughtful look of a man who's been at court many years.

'I think, accidental. To be deliberate . . . It would have needed too much luck. They could hardly know I'd hear that and then encounter you now. You think he intends – what?'

'If I could tell you that, I would.' I found myself frowning. 'Videric never does anything without it being aimed at somebody.'

I see only two options here. And if it isn't me—

'*I* certainly don't know of any meeting,' I said. 'Did Aldro Rosamunda seem to know? Or was it a surprise to her?'

Safrac de Aguilar's brows dipped in concentration, a maze of lines creasing his forehead.

'She knew,' he said finally, giving me a shrewd look. 'Or I believe she did. But . . . You could, perhaps, have been told of this last night, and . . . forgotten during the celebrations?'

Drunk as a fiddler's bitch, they call it. My head did feel as if I'd been drinking the beer they put down in pans for his mastiff, all the night the fiddler plays. Truthfully, it was no large amount unless to an unseasoned drinker. And my head was clear enough last night.

I forget nothing concerning my mother.

I bit at my lip. The small pain helped me focus. 'There's no "meeting". If Rosamunda thinks there is . . . But she's not a fool, she knows there may be agents of Carthage here! Why would she go – Safrac, did either of them say where I was to meet her?'

My thoughts were a tumble of fears: Videric sending Ramiro Carrasco on a murderer's errand to Venice; the Carthaginian agent whose name I never knew dying on Torcello Island; Hanno Anagastes' armed guards surrounding Aldro Rosamunda, putting her under arrest.

Frustrated, I protested, 'There are too many rooms in this palace to search!'

'There's a hall with a fountain,' Safrac de Aguilar emerged from his reverie and interrupted. '*That* was where Aldra Videric said you were waiting for the lady Rosamunda, now.'

The breath went out of my chest, leaving ice and heat. A solid knot of cramped muscle and lung.

The fall of silver water; the ringing fall of steel.

Clear in my mind as that day twelve months ago.

If she expected to meet me – yes, she would go to such a place.

'You know the Egyptian, Rekhmire'?' I barely waited for de Aguilar's assent. 'Go and tell him what you heard. If not him, then Lord Honorius. Tell them – to be cautious.'

Safrac de Aguilar looked alarmed. 'Where will you be, Ilario?'

'Finding this hall with a fountain!'

For all his choked protests, he gave me brisk directions; and strode away from me towards the palace's guest-chambers.

I walked, because running attracts attention. If I ran out of the hall, there are those who would follow. Noblemen's sons, out of curiosity. Guardsmen, wondering what the fuss is about. The women servants who clean, who see everything and everybody.

But a preoccupied fast walk attracts little attention.

I should be thinking – planning—

I don't even know what I expect him to do!

Videric has lied to her.

I don't know *why*.

Breath hissed hot in my lungs. The gangways and stairs of Zheng He's ship had kept me fit. But I'd guessed wrong about the time: it was well past noon. Gades' heat as the sun burns around to the second half of the day is nothing to be sprinting in.

Fifteen minutes at a pounding run, once out of the public eye up corridors and down stairs, wondering if I had mistaken Aguilar's directions – and a stone colonnade opened up in welcome cool.

I slowed to a painful half-trot.

Think. *Think* what you can do—

Twelve months ago I walked another marble-floored corridor, with Aldra Videric; his blue and white linen robe swirling at his heels as he strode.

The sound of a fountain reached me from an open hall ahead.

The sound of a slap, and the flat clatter of a second-rate dagger skittering across the marble floor—

What will he do? Sell her to Carthage's highest bidder, because they think they can make use of her? Then have one of Carrasco's brothers assassinate her on board the ship?

Ridiculous speculations made me feel as if my head would burst.

I could understand if he attacked me. What does he want with her? And why is it *I* still think I should protect her?

Pain more agonising than the cramp in my ribs came from the immediate realisation.

She wants me to forgive her.

But not for my sake. For hers.

Now that the cathedral penitence means no gossip will ever forget I came out of her womb, she wants to appear magnanimously accepting of her monstrous child.

But she would meet me secretly because, no matter what she pretends in public, she is ashamed of me.

I slowed.

Heat bounced down the white walls from the clerestory windows, high above; a breeze barely penetrated. That was not the only reason I was sweating.

How rash will Rekhmire' say I'm being?

I thought it so clever to show Videric in pigment: 'You love her but she never loved you; never will.' So clever—!

A coldness went through my body and made my hands heavy. My fingers prickled. I thought desperately: No, Videric isn't a stupid man, he will have realised the truth before now. Years ago!

And you were the one who thought it so clever to push his face into it. What might *that* provoke a man to do?

Sound caught my attention.

Movement?

This doorway was a round Roman arch, the keystones white, outlined with gold paint. A beaded curtain hung down across the opening. Kicking off my scandals, I padded over the cool tiles, silencing my breathing.

The beads made an impenetrable barrier until I stood with my nose all but touching them. Vision altered: I saw clearly through their blur into the hall.

The fountains arced silver into the afternoon light, water spilling out of a jug held by a marble nude.

Terracotta pots held plants. The scent of the place was subtle: moist soil, green leaves . . . choked pipes.

I could see the textures of leaves, the patterns of edges; all things for which – before now – I would have reached for my drawing-book. 'Learn to see,' Masaccio said to me, one night in the taverna, his hand sketching flawlessly by candle-light. 'You see too much detail, Ilario. You draw it all. And you give it all the same importance. Look to see what parts of a thing are necessary: show only that.'

Now all I could do was stare through the blurry green and shimmering silver at Videric.

He knelt beside Rosamunda, where she lay supine on the floor.

His hands moved, busy at her mouth. Tying something.

A gag.

Light through the fretwork stone ceiling shone down on pillars and fountain-basins. And glistened off her eyes as she blinked.

Christus Imperator, she's still alive!

Three or four other men stood behind Videric where he knelt. They wore the livery of guards. There were no household badges on arm or cap. Evidently they waited for orders.

Rekhmire' will be behind me, sooner or later.

I swept the bead curtain clattering aside, and strode into the hall.

16

There's no blood.

It was the first thing I noted. No blood; no broken bones protruding through stretched-white skin. A slave learns how to see the crucial things in the first instant.

An absent part of my mind wondered, *Is that what Masaccio meant about an artist's vision?*

Her wrists and ankles were already bound; she squirmed and whimpered in an attempt to get free of Videric's hands. Two red bruises marked the sides of her jaw, where a thumb and forefinger might have gripped her. Nothing more. Her silk robes were rucked up about her knees, but clearly from struggling against being subdued, rather than rape. Sweat beaded across her unlined forehead. She strained against her arms, tied before her; Videric looked up from binding her kerchief into her mouth with silk rope.

Looked directly at me.

One of the other men started forward.

'Wait.' Videric spoke with a quiet intensity that froze the man where he stood.

I stared squarely down at Videric. 'I didn't know how vindictive you could be. But you can let her go now, since you've got me here.'

His face altered. If his control had not been perfect, it would have been a smile. He murmured, 'Nor did *I* know that you thought the world centred upon you.'

'Don't be naive.' I thought it the surest way to shake him. '*Everybody* thinks that.'

Videric turned his head as if I didn't exist. His attention focused on Rosamunda, on the floor. The small choked sound he made would not have carried as far as the guards wearing his livery.

The men were all much similar: Iberian, rather than Visigoth Carthaginian; middle-aged soldiers in doublet and hose, with riding-boots fastened up to their belts, and no surcoat over their mail hauberks. No crest, no coat of arms, no insignia. Nothing to link them to Videric's estates.

The glances between them told me they were his. I have seen similar looks between Honorius and Orazi.

'What's the matter? Do you need four men here to kill me? Can't you do your own murders?'

Videric's expression didn't change. I didn't expect it; he's too good a politician to allow that. But I caught the glance one of the men-at-arms shot at his captain. It wasn't, 'Damn, Ilario knows!' It was, 'You didn't say you were asking *that* of us.'

If he really doesn't want revenge on me, when it's freely offered— I must have made him desire *her* death.

If he's off-balance, I may find out more. I nodded at the soldiers, speaking with a hope of keeping Videric unsettled. 'Men in a jealous rage don't usually bring four witnesses. If you're not killing my mother, what are you doing to her?'

The Aldra Videric smiled appreciatively. He glanced up and back, at his captain. 'A shame there's not room for two . . . '

The man-at-arms smiled as one does at a lord's joke.

'Whatever you're doing to her—' I kept moving, coming closer to him, and Rosamunda, every moment. '—why *aren't* you doing it to me? I don't believe the – the man who told me about this "meeting" I'm supposedly having with my mother is one of your pawns. But since I'm here . . . why not kill me instead?'

The sun falling through the lattice-patterned ceiling made Videric's fair hair and beard glint. He came lightly up onto his feet, as if he were my age, and shrugged. 'Why *not* you? Honorius. And Alexandria, to a degree. You have powerful friends that make killing you unwise. Even an accident would be suspect.'

'But not for her?' I didn't look down as I reached Rosamunda. The toes of my studded sandals touched the shoulder of her robe. I looked at him across my mother's body. 'She has no powerful friends herself that aren't also your friends. So there's nothing to stop you.'

Videric laughed.

It caught halfway through, as if it snagged on something in his throat. 'I'm not killing her.' The Aldra Videric rubbed the cuff of his robe across his red lips. For the first time in years, he seemed to see me – to see Ilario, rather than the King's slave, or his wife's secret bastard. 'And now you're here, I suppose not you either . . . Not everything is about murder, Ilario.'

He looked at me with sardonic humour, as if he couldn't understand why I didn't smile in return.

The time will come when I don't hear the word 'murder' and see Masaccio's face in front of me, throat crushed in front of my eyes. But not today.

'Is it my fault? Did what I painted make you do this?'

The hall was silent except for the strained, muffled breathing of Rosamunda. And the noises she made in her throat.

I did not need to hear words to know she intended '*Yes: your fault: free me!*'

Videric's captain was a new face since I'd left Taraco; I didn't recognise him, but he had in-country features, and he was a little younger than the other soldiers. Recently promoted, I guessed. He would be a man loyal to Videric, who had been taught to blame me for his lord's initial forced resignation as First Minister.

The captain turned his head towards Aldra Videric, plainly requesting orders. *Kill the intruder? Subdue it?*

For three heartbeats, I was dizzy with the realisation that, had I been a slave still, stepping into this room would have been immediate suicide.

I flinched, momentarily. Two of the men-at-arms exchanged glances, cheered by that. *The hermaphrodite isn't the knight it was trained to be* was plain in their thoughts.

Videric made a gesture with his hand.

The clink and spatter of fountain-water did not drown out boots on the tiles. The men-at-arms went to take up stations at the remaining archways. I might escape if I spun around and dived back the way I came. But I wouldn't bet money.

And I'm not leaving.

Holding Videric's gaze, I sank down on one knee by Rosamunda. Peripheral vision gave me the ability to pull at the knots of her silk gag.

Videric quite deliberately made no move from where he stood. He turned the palms of his hands to me, to emphasise that he held no weapons. I wondered if he knew that it seemed to make him appear defenceless in other ways.

'I wouldn't do that,' he said, 'Wait.'

'"Wait."' I sounded like every speculative, unbelieving courtier I ever met in Rodrigo's court.

'Hear me out, first. Then ... ' He sighed and shrugged. Not quite 'your folly be on your own head', but something with more sorrow and resignation in than I was used to hearing from my *step*-father.

He'll tell you what you want to hear.

This man who lied, a year ago, about Rosamunda desiring to see me. When it was his own orders that she wait and kill me.

He looks different.

I'd paid attention to him physically, painting him in the new style. Masaccio taught me ratios: the placing of the eye according to the position of ears, jaw, nose. Given Masaccio's emphasis that first a painter needs to see – and wanting to understand him – I had studied my stepfather as lines, planes, shades, edges ...

As a man, Videric looks older than when I left Taraco, and tired enough that he might not have slept for days.

I said abruptly, 'You painted your face for the cathedral!'

Videric rubbed at his lower lip again. 'It was necessary to look as a man should. Women are not the only ones to mimic health with cosmetic aid.'

I knelt down on the tiles, lifting Rosamunda's head and resting it against my thighs, so that I could support her shoulders with my knees. She stirred, moaning; and looked frantically at me. It felt appalling, unbearable, to see the silk biting into the corners of her lips.

I stroked her soft, braided black hair. The weight of her head was heavy in my lap, and I wondered for a dazed moment if the embroidery on my Alexandrine tunic would leave its pattern embossed in her fine skin.

'Tell me what this is about.' I couldn't keep urgency out of my tone. *If Rekhmire' is following, I need to have heard this first.* 'And – let me untie her wrists. Please. She's hurting, and she can't escape, can she?'

Videric smoothed down the folds of his striped linen robe, his features composed in the look of a thoughtful statesman. I recognised it as a mask he often wore in council. Eventually, after my breath congealed and burned in my chest, he gave a casual nod.

Reaching down, I picked at the bindings where I could reach them while supporting her. She made a pained noise through the gag.

Videric seemed in no hurry.

The Ilario who left Taraco a year ago *would* have run to this meeting without a pause to tell anyone where I'd gone. The same way I left Taraco; the same way I sought out Rosamunda in Carthage.

The silk rope settled into tight, impenetrable knots under my fingertips.

Videric seated himself on the broad marble rim of the fountain beside me. His hand dipped in. He flicked sour water over his neck, cooling himself.

I craned my neck, from where I knelt by his feet.

Videric looked down at me. 'The problem . . . is Carthage.'

17

I stared. And spoke into a silence broken only by the spatter of water on marble:

'Carthage?'

Videric's captain stepped forward from the archway. I had not seen any order pass between him and Videric. The soldier bent over behind me, reaching around to unbuckle the belt from which I hung my dagger. Still holding Videric's gaze, I didn't move. Leather pulled against the fabric of my tunic; I felt the weight of the weapon go missing.

Over the noise of the captain's boots as he stepped back to the door, I repeated, '*Carthage?*'

'I realised, with your painted gift.' Videric tapped his fingers together. 'What it told me' . . . is perhaps not as important as what I've told Carthage.'

'I didn't know you were in contact with Carthage—' I stopped.

His smile had the air of sadness that meant I'd missed his point.

'Informed by my *actions*. Last year, you perceive, I had a choice. A scandal comes from Carthage. The First Minister's wife has tried to kill a slave. As my wife, her crimes reflect on me. I might repudiate this woman, put her aside, call her a barren wife, and stay with the King as his First Minister. But . . . that is not what I did.'

My fingers carded the loose hair at the back of my mother's neck, where a braid had come undone. Videric didn't look down at Rosamunda where she lay stiff and recalcitrant against me, the knot of her bindings irretrievably tight.

I wished I had cut her free before I was disarmed. No matter what it might have precipitated.

Videric gazed, his restless pupils following the fall of fountain-jets.

'What did I tell Carthage, by what I *did* do? I told them . . . that this woman is a gate by which any enemy can enter Taraco and break it. Because any enemy who has control of her has control of me. They have only to threaten her.'

'You resigned, left Rodrigo Sanguerra, left us to be at Carthage's mercy if the King-Caliph could manufacture the slightest excuse for sending in the legions . . . '

Videric's blue eyes glimmered in the light reflected up from the fountain basin. The water shone all the shadows on his face into the wrong places. 'And it will be assumed that I will do it again. That whatever threatens my wife, controls *me*. Whether it's to make me abandon my post again, or to guide the King in the way that Carthage wishes him to act.'

I thought of Hanno Anagastes, the King-Caliph, the Amirs for whom Rekhmire' had had me copying scrolls. All of whom assume their sacred right to Iberia.

'But you can't – King Rodrigo could – when they see he trusts you—'

'I've returned to court.' Videric marked off each point on a raised finger. 'My wife is once again Queen of the Court of Ladies. I'm Rodrigo Sanguerra's First Minister, reinstated as if I'd never been away. All despite the rumours that my wife tried to kill my . . . offspring . . . in Carthage.'

Something flinched, in his expression.

I know he hates being thought the father of a monster.

I had not appreciated, until now, quite how humiliating he would find it to make public the other alternative – to have everyone know that his wife had a child by another man, and that it's not she who is barren in this marriage.

Videric continued, 'If she's such a burden, and I *still* keep her, refuse to put her aside and marry again—'

His voice caught in his throat.

I stroked the soft hot skin behind Rosamunda's ear, in apology for speaking as if she weren't present. 'They must know the King will protect her as well as you.'

'Carthage now knows that she *needs* protecting. That is the fatal weakness I showed.'

He narrowed his eyes as if he looked into sunlit distance, rather than the green shadows of the hall.

'The Turks, too . . . Ilario, if any other lord had had his wife threatened, he'd keep her securely behind his own castle walls – and if she died by ambush or assassins, shrug and marry again.'

I wanted to protest it and didn't. If married couples wish it, all of a woman's life can take place in the Court of Ladies, and all of a man's life in the outside world, and their only meeting need be for the begetting of heirs. Few enough men get to see into the women's court, and see how their women's friendships, daughters, their politicking for marriages on behalf of their family name, can become their fulfilling life. And a man who rides, hunts, goes to war, and competes for rank and places of power at court with other noblemen; he doesn't *need* to know his wife, except carnally. Not if he doesn't have some leaning towards companionship that priests and lords never taught him. Men alone together talk as if women are children; women alone together speak as if men are not-very-intelligent animals. For nine years I saw it every day, from both sides.

Videric sighed, finally glancing down at where she lay with her cheek against my thigh. 'If I gave up everything for her once . . . Men will assume that I can be manipulated by any threat to her. And will assume it correctly. That makes me useless to the state. And I can't risk Taraconensis coming as close to disaster as we have this last year.'

It made a perfect and clear shape in my mind.

'I painted the truth. My mother doesn't love you.' I ignored her stir of protest. 'So why, now that you know that—'

'You painted the truth,' he repeated, not looking down at Rosamunda. 'It makes no difference. It never has.'

Because we lie to ourselves, and say it will be different one day.

'It ought to make a difference.'

Lightly, as if he welcomed a distraction from pain, Videric asked, 'Which one of them is it?'

'"Which"?'

'My spy? Or Queen Ty-ameny's spy?' His twist of the lips was very wry, under his moustaches. 'You desire one of them. Tell me which, so that I can make suitable use of the fact.'

For the first time in many years, I felt inclined to smile grimly at my stepfather.

'Perhaps not,' I suggested. 'But are you telling me, even now, with all she's done – Rosamunda—'

'*I* am not the one attempting to comfort the woman who twice tried to kill me.' Videric paused, a frown indenting his forehead. 'Three times.'

The dagger in the hall so like this one. The attempt in Carthage. And the baby left out on stone steps, exposed to the snow of a winter's night. Three times.

Now it was I who could not look down; could only memorise the fine texture of her braids with my fingertips. I felt her warmth, her heartbeat. The skin of her neck had – if only to the touch – the slight slackness of an older woman.

'Lord Barbas, Caliph Ammianus, Lord Hanno.' Videric stirred the moving fountain-water with a fingertip. 'None of them are stupid men. I've watched you observe the Governor's nobles here. I doubt your judgement would be at fault over Carthage – if possibly a little premature. Did you, in honesty, see anything to suggest I'm wrong when I say they will use Rosamunda against me?'

There was no need for me to voice an answer.

'You said you didn't trick her into coming here to kill her?'

'That's correct.' Videric wiped his wet fingers across his forehead. A lizard scuttled past Rosamunda's sandals, skidded, and flicked off behind one of the Roman fern pots.

'Then what *is* this?'

Videric spoke as if I hadn't asked the question.

'I can't put her aside as barren or unfaithful. Or rather, I *can*, but it would not be believed. Some agent of Carthage would kidnap her from her father's estate, or any other noble's castle at which she might be a guest. And then it would be plain how much of a fool I am. Perhaps you paid close attention only to half of what you painted? There is more here than her lack of – affection.'

He shook his head, continuing briskly.

'Rodrigo knows I can't be forced to choose between my country and this woman. The next time I should merely take poisoned wine. So she cannot be abandoned or divorced.'

'That doesn't leave any choices!' A pain went through my chest and stomach at a sudden thought. 'Unless – you've brought her here so she can *watch* you drinking poisoned wine now?'

The Aldra Videric's gaze sharpened enough to let me know I had given myself away. That I have thought of this man as my father for a decade, no matter how distant from me he might have been.

Since perception travels both ways, I could make a good guess that he had at least *considered* dying here. On those nights when a man can't sleep, or properly wake, and can only endlessly measure the walls of his trap.

What tilts the balance too much in his favour is that, as ever, it is the men in this world that I understand. I love my mother, but all the women I know seem to have grown up in cages. I find myself avoiding their company, unless, like Ty-ameny, they are powers in their own right. There's much of me mirrored and reversed in Neferet, that I didn't like to see. I understand how it is that Videric can love Rosamunda and not *know* her.

It is not what I want to be – since half of me *is* woman – but it's what I am.

Videric said quietly, 'No, I haven't come here to kill myself. Despite what men say of it being a coward's act, I think it would be harder than living and enduring the pain.' He hesitated. 'What do you say? You've endured enough, King's Fool. You never hanged yourself or drank poison.'

'I don't have Father Felix's faith.'

Videric nodded. Any other man would have asked if a lack of faith didn't make self-murder easy, since there would be no punishment for it. Videric's ready agreement, I thought, meant he looked at it the same way I do – that this sole and only world is very difficult to leave, no matter what; and that the desire to be dead usually passes into shame-faced appreciation of being alive.

'What will you do? You've left yourself nowhere to go, if anyone who can threaten her can control you. And through you, the King.'

His blue gaze stayed on Rosamunda. 'Do you want her to hear, now? Do you want her to know, while you're present?'

I already knew enough to be a danger to him the minute I stepped through that archway.

'Give me back my knife. She shouldn't be gagged.' I couldn't help my disgust showing.

'Wait until you hear her scream for help. And she may not be permitted that.'

Part of me agreed with him. The part that was half book-buyer by now, I thought, appalled. But the Ilario that lived at Taraco, that knew this woman as a mother – no matter how distant a mother—

'Take it *off*,' I muttered, picking at the knots again and wishing my fingernails were longer. 'It isn't . . . You can't.'

Even I can't bring myself to say 'it isn't fair'.

Fairness and justice can have nothing to do with what I feel for Rosamunda. Or I might be a greater danger to her than Videric is.

The captain of the men-at-arms knelt down beside me and cut the irrevocably knotted silk bonds of her gag. Something he would not do without Videric's orders; none of Videric's soldiers ever would. I looked up to thank my stepfather.

Rosamunda lifted her head from my thigh and rolled away from me, still bound hand and foot, sitting up on the white marble tiles, shaking out her dishevelled hair.

She screamed.

Shatteringly loud, raw-edged, ragged; panicked enough to send ice down my spine. The men-at-arms came to instant readiness, staring around, expecting the King's guardsmen to come running in—

I pushed myself across the cold, smooth stone, grabbed at her shoulder, and pulled her back up against my chest. I clapped my palm over her mouth, pinching her delicate nostrils between my thumb and finger.

Rosamunda's scream choked off into a gasp. Into coughs.

I loosened my grip as she tossed her head, as if she could clear her nose and throat that way – and she screamed again.

My hand felt slick with fluids as I clamped it over her nose and mouth again.

I loosed my grip by stages, cutting her off each time I felt the breath of a sound begin. She strained against me, as if she had forgotten how much stronger than an adult woman I am.

At last she slumped back against me, her chest shaking. I felt the hot tears running over my wrist before I realised she was weeping.

None of the men-at-arms had left their posts at the archways.

I held Videric's gaze. 'You shouldn't make me do this. *I* shouldn't make me do this.'

Videric spoke quietly. 'You might feel that you're a hermaphrodite monster. You grew up in Taraconensis, and you care for it, nonetheless. You wouldn't have humiliated yourself in the cathedral if that wasn't true.'

'I thought it was necessary!'

To my annoyance, I could feel myself hot behind the ears, and in my face; hot and cold with a sick shame at the memory of it.

'I thought it was *all* that was necessary! Now you tell me there's this!'

Videric interlaced his broad fingers and looked down at them. 'I know these things. I know, also, that she's . . . not the only one of us who has tried to murder you. I ask. In this. Will you give me a hearing?'

It's the portrait, I realised.

He wants to talk to me for many reasons, but one is that I'm the only other person who sees the truth of him and her. Who can he talk to about it? Not even King Rodrigo Sanguerra. And . . . Not Rosamunda.

'Mother – Aldro Rosamunda – you'll have to be quiet.' The way I held her was oddly like a mother holding its child. Releasing her, I wiped my hand down my tunic. 'Videric . . . You tell me how you solve the unsolvable.'

There was a look on his face of amusement and gratitude.

I saw the moment when Rosamunda realised it.

'You can't do what he tells you!' Her voice sounded wet and thick; not its usual melodious contralto. 'Ilario! *You can't*—'

I cut her off before her tone could rise. 'I'll hear what he has to say.'

She looked at me as if I were mad enough to be dragged away in sacks and chains and tethered in the lower dungeons, to amuse the courtiers when they visited the moon-touched. 'Videric tried to have you *killed*.'

I shrugged. 'Yes. But it seems to me – men spend their time hurting one another. I feel a woman should be different. A mother. *My* mother—'

Rosamunda smiled with complete spite. 'How long is it since you saw your child, Ilario? Have you seen her today?'

I reckoned the time by the sunlight burning down into the room. Well past Terce.

'I haven't seen Onorata since yesterday.'

Because she's safer with her grandfather. But that has the sound of an excuse. Had I wanted to see her, I need not have slept late.

'Carrasco will be looking after her,' I said briskly. 'He won't expect me. I have no *idea* how to be a mother. If I were inclined to thank Christus Imperator for anything, it's that Honorius knows how to be a father.'

I put out my hand, brushing Rosamunda's cheek.

She leaned into the touch unwillingly; her expression was spite and triumph mixed. And no guilt. Will she never ask herself *why* I need to learn how to mother my child?

The truth came up as inexorable as tidewater; not a surprise to me, but this time inescapable. *No, she'll never ask; it would never occur to her even to wonder.*

I helped Rosamunda to her feet, as young men are trained to do. And seated her on the marble surround of the fountain, arranging the folds of her skirt as ladies-in-waiting are taught. I dipped my kerchief in the cool water and cleaned her face, which she accepted with the air of accepting something usual from a servant.

I found a second clean kerchief and made a damp pad of it, holding it to her forehead. 'You should want to hear this too.'

She closed her eyes, without answering.

Videric's voice broke into my thoughts. I realised I had been standing in front of Rosamunda for several moments, lost in studying her.

'Wait as long as you like,' he said, 'but you won't hear an apology from her.'

'An *apology*? For *screaming*?'

'No.' He looked at me as if I were a fool.

I seated myself slowly beside the spread of her blackthorn-berry-coloured silken skirts. She didn't look at me. One protest about the situation in which she found herself, then – nothing.

With any other woman, I would have guessed that she ignored me out of embarrassment, or even shame. Watching her gaze intent on Videric, I knew Rosamunda saw no one here except the man who she thought had power over her.

Certainly I will never hear, *I'm sorry I tried to kill you in Carthage.* For her, that's forgotten; gone.

'*You* could shout as loudly as she,' Videric observed. 'This palace is infested with servants: someone would hear you and raise an alarm. So I see no reason not to disclose to you what I'm about to do. Then, if you wish to scream for your friends . . . ' He shrugged. 'Captain.'

The captain directing them, the men-at-arms went out through the archways; nominally out of earshot. If I concentrated, I could hear their boots shifting on the marble tiles.

'He's a trustworthy man,' Videric said, a nod of his head to the departing captain's back, deliberately not mentioning the man's name. 'Like Ramiro Carrasco. But I never like to give a man more information than he ought to hear.'

Trustworthy for the same reason as Carrasco?

I'd trust Orazi or any of Honorius's men. But if I explain why to Videric, he'll regard me as even more of a fool.

'My mother,' I said. 'Your wife. She's an Achilles' heel to you. You can't keep her at court. She won't be safe back on your estates.'

I would have touched Rosamunda's hand to comfort her, if I didn't know from her expression that she would jerk them away.

'You won't murder her.' I brought the word out coolly, ashamed a moment later when Rosamunda's eyes snapped open and she gazed about the hall, rumpled and clearly terrified.

Where is Rekhmire'? Where is my father?

I managed to say, 'This doesn't leave much, Aldra Videric.' I wiped at my sweaty forehead. 'In fact, I don't see that it leaves anything. If you send her away to any branch of her family—'

Like most of the nobles of the Iberian courts, she has relatives in Aragon, Castile, Granada, Catalonia, and the Frankish lands beyond.

'—Carthage *will* track her down. So. Tell me what you have planned.'

Videric nodded slowly. 'Rodrigo is the only other man to know. I don't suppose the King will be in the least surprised to hear that you've found your way into this.'

His smile was oddly poised between sympathy and malice.

'I'm half inclined to tell you all and let *you* decide, Ilario. Unfortunately, since it seems to need both Rodrigo Sanguerra and myself to keep the Carthaginian legions at home, I can't do that.'

'You're not so necessary,' I said coldly. 'If you died, Rodrigo would have another man in your place, performing perfectly well, inside three days.'

Videric smiled. 'But as you, especially, will have discovered – it doesn't matter what the truth is. It matters what people *think* the truth is. Because that's what they act on. In fact, my death may well bring the legions marching up the Via Augusta. So I must hope to be as long-lived as my grandfather . . . '

He got abruptly to his feet, pacing, gazing up at the arcing droplets of water. Stopping in front of both of us, he looked only at Rosamunda.

'I couldn't do anything to harm you. You've always known that.'

She brought her head up with that artificial arch of the neck that allows a woman to look up at a man through her lashes. It was familiar enough that I suspected the court deportment tutor, Dolores, had taught both of us. *Mother and . . . son-daughter.*

She fixed an intense gaze on him. 'Don't do this. Even when I was with Honorius, it was foolishness, infatuation—'

She cut her gaze across to me.

'—and I've been punished.'

I didn't hear what she said next; couldn't decipher the low, intense conviction in her words. It may have been some effort to recall their sexual connection to his mind.

'*I've been punished.*' After all this, this is what I am to you?

A piece on the board to be moved, to convince Videric how remorseful you are towards him.

Why did I imagine anything else? I should know, by now.

Videric's voice interrupted my dazed state. 'Hope dies last.'

He might have been referring to himself, or to me. Or to us both, I thought.

'Perhaps unfortunately,' he added, looking down at Rosamunda, 'this doesn't depend on Honorius, or on Ilario's parentage, or on your infidelity. If it did, I think I might eventually teach myself to hate you.'

Her huge dark eyes brimmed.

I could have told him, even at thirty or forty years younger than he, that hate is no different to love. Not in the intensity. Not in how much it occupies your mind, and wastes your time.

Videric shook his head. 'You're a weapon, Rosamunda. I've been fool enough to show myself besotted with my wife. That makes you a sword at my throat. And whatever the story is here, in Carthage the Lords-Amir *know* that you attempted murder—'

'Because you told me to!'

I winced at the shrill note in Rosamunda's voice. Shrill as when she claimed the same thing about my infant exposure: *He made me.*

'No one ever made you do anything,' I interrupted. 'You just chose whichever was easiest at the time and didn't think of what would happen after.'

Her eye caught the light as she turned to me. She had the blank-eyed gaze of a marble medusa.

'You be quiet, you monster! If it wasn't for you, *none* of this would have happened to me!'

I drew as much of my hard-earned court composure about me as I could, and looked at her without shaking, or weeping. I found voice enough to say, 'If I were in your position, I'd be trying to make an ally of *both* of us – Videric, me. But I don't know if you're too stupid to think of that, or if you just hate me too much.'

She narrowed her eyes, so that the smudge of kohl at the corner of one bled out into the incipient wrinkles there. 'All your fault!'

'You're mistaken,' Videric said gently.

Her face shifted; showed ingratiation and confusion.

He went on: 'You think I have the power here today, and you can sacrifice Ilario to that. But the truth is, *I* have no choice either. I did all I could in coming up with an alternative that Rodrigo preferred to your quiet and immediate execution.'

Rosamunda's eyes and mouth rounded.

She seemed to fall into herself, staring around the hall as if she searched out any way she could run.

'I doubt that's wholly correct.' I didn't trust myself to do more than sit, my hands shook so hard. 'If King Rodrigo knows she can be used to get at you, and knows that without you the legions sail for Taraco . . . He'd have killed Aldro Rosamunda long before now. Except for one thing.'

Videric cocked his head invitingly. Odd, how I had always wished to have him take what I said seriously. *Beware what you wish for.*

'It's truly hard to make a death look like an accident if it isn't,' I said. 'That only happens in bards' tales. And if anybody kills Rosamunda under those circumstances, you'd *know* the King was responsible. And I don't think you two could work together after that, not like you have done. So he loses you anyway.'

I shook my head, trailing fingers in the cold green endlessly disturbed water.

'As usual, you've got things so that you can do exactly as you want. Except . . . that I don't see how you can have what you want. Even if you hide – her – away as well as you can, someone would follow you to her, eventually.'

'I must personally congratulate Queen Ty-ameny, the next time I go on a diplomatic mission to Constantinople.' Videric's smile was wry, and genuine. 'You appear to have had a considerable education in the last twelve months.'

'Some of it in things I never wanted to know.'

It was not something I imagined saying to this man, my father, my stepfather. I saw how he looked at me when he turned. He may even have been a little impressed. I wished I were still the Ilario who could appreciate that.

I said, 'Even if you formally put her aside, nullify the marriage to a barren wife, no one would believe it. Not after you gave up your position at court for her.'

The position second only to the King's.

Not death, not divorce . . . what?

Rosamunda, her chin lifting defiantly, snapped, 'I am *not* barren! Remember the cathedral, lord husband? It may be a monster of a child, but I conceived and bore Ilario! And never anything from you, monster or not!'

She must see how she's affecting him—

I stopped breathing for a second, and caught it again in a rush.

Is it possible she's behaving this way, angering him, so that he doesn't feel so guilty over what it is he has to do? Is she sparing him anguish?

I looked at the lines that anger was starting to pinch permanently into the corners of her mouth. Nothing visible except anger, resentment – and the resentment seemed to be that all this should happen to *her*.

Hope dies last.

She snorted under her breath. 'If it's your doting that's the problem, then . . . I made you love me, Videric. I could make you stop loving me.'

Her sneering grated on me. If I could have got words out at that moment, they would have been, *I am ashamed to be your son-daughter!* Christ the Emperor knows, Videric is a bad enough man, but Rosamunda came close to making me pity him.

'Let me show myself at the Court of Ladies here tomorrow and take a lover,' she said coolly. 'Two or three, perhaps. Gossip will get around quickly enough. Carthage is ruled by *men*. They won't believe you could love me and let me fornicate with soldiers and stable-hands.'

She took my breath away.

More, I thought: 'soldiers and stable-hands' fell too easily off her tongue.

If she hasn't already practised what she advises, she certainly has her eye on particular men she'd like to seduce.

Videric stood with the arc of the fountains behind him, utterly motionless. In ten years I'd never seen him at a loss for words. He stared at Rosamunda in a dazed way, as if he looked into a bright light, and didn't speak.

My hatred for Videric is almost impersonal. What he'd tried to do to me, he would have done to anyone in my position; it didn't matter to him that I was Ilario.

It made it just that much easier to throw a rope to him, as I would have thrown a rope to a drowning enemy.

'That wouldn't succeed,' I said quietly. 'Rosamunda, *look* at him. I know he's a courtier. But no one is going to believe he's unaffected if you take a lover. Do you really think even he can hide that?'

Over Videric's mumbled protest, Rosamunda repeated with casual cruelty, 'I can make him stop loving me.'

'No.' Videric's burly shoulders were back, and his usually bland face tightened from the emotion in him. 'No. You didn't make me love you. You won't make me stop. If it were possible for me to stop . . . I would have done so by now.'

No sound but Videric's sandals on the marble floor as he began to pace again; Rosamunda utterly silent as her head turned back and forth, following him.

'Then tell me how you can make me safe.'

I heard the echo of other demands in that one. Thirty years since he married his child-bride of fifteen; thirty years of *Videric, make it right for me*, and him finding his satisfaction in pleasing this woman.

I should have thrown the portrait in the sea before I let Videric look at it. That, or only showed it to Rosamunda, so she'd know I understood her game. But no, I have to be so damn *clever* . . .

Videric's pale gaze met mine as if he could follow every thought and feeling in me.

Fifty years of experience. *He may as well read minds! What's the difference?* How did I ever imagine I was going to out-plan someone who's been at court longer than I've been alive?

'I'm not putting Rosamunda aside.' Videric spoke to me, but his gaze continued to slide sideways to her. 'The reverse, in fact. What will happen is that Rosamunda is going to apply to me, formally, to end the carnal part of our marriage—'

A choked sound from her bore no resemblance to a word.

'—and permit her to retire to a place of religious contemplation. To a nunnery, or a convent. So that she can purify her soul for the next world, and glorify the Emperor-Messiah with prayer.'

Rosamunda stood, her fists clenched before her straining against her bands. '*How long?*'

It is not unusual for widows, or wives who are known not to be able to bear their husband's rapes and beatings, to apply to the King for permission to retire to a convent. Whether it's an order of educated women, writing scrolls of theology, or whether it requires digging turnips to feed the other sisters and novices, evidently it seems preferable to what they can expect of life in the world.

I asked Rodrigo Sanguerra myself, once; when I was worse than desperate to escape the humiliations of being Court Fool. He made a public theological debate of it, with bishops arguing whether I could be allowed to join a monastery – where I would contaminate the men with the parts of me that were sinful woman – or a nunnery. It collapsed in riot when one of the male courtiers offered the opinion that I would be far too popular in a convent as a nun with a prick.

These days the thought makes me smile, if with an edge. Trust a man to think I would be popular for what so many of those women are escaping from.

'How *long*?' Rosamunda's voice echoed back from the marble walls, over the noise of the fountains.

Videric spoke as if he talked only to me. 'The Aldro Rosamunda will stay at several different convents, to flush out and elude pursuit. These will all be nunneries used to taking court ladies. The civilised establishments where the Mother Superior is often a rich noblewoman in her own right, and music and literature is practised as well as the worship and glorification of God.'

I found myself nodding as if entranced.

'Truthfully,' Videric said, 'I expect the agents of Carthage to have found and investigated every rich convent of that nature within three months of the announcement being made. Before Yule, certainly. There aren't more than twenty establishments that a woman of Rosamunda's rank would find appropriate.'

The water splashed in my palm where I intercepted a fountain-jet. If it smelled of metal pipes, it was nonetheless ice-cold. I dabbed it on my forehead, feeling it run down inside my tunic, over my small breasts, as it dried in my body's heat.

'However.' Videric's spine stiffened, seemingly without his volition. He didn't look in Rosamunda's direction. 'There are hundreds, perhaps thousands, of *ordinary* religious households in Taraco and Aragon and Granada. Small convents, closed to the world; poor nunneries that rely on local charity and the land to support ten or twenty praying Brides of Christ the Emperor. And a woman takes a new name when she enters religious life as a novice. Who's to know one "Sister Maria Regina" in a thousand convents where there are hundreds of Maria Reginas every year?'

Rosamunda repeated in the numb way that Brides tell their Green beads: 'How. Long?'

'They'll search Taraconensis, and Aragon,' Videric observed, 'and likely the smaller kingdoms if they get desperate. But no matter how hard the King-Caliph drives them . . .'

He blinked, as if he saw something far off.

' . . . For all their Crusades, the Franks haven't yet taken the Northern Islands from us. Jersey, Guernsey, Sark; they all have thriving Iberian populations and fishing ports. If you look at the royal maps, you'll see them clearly marked as part of the kingdoms of Aragon and Navarre.'

He paused.

'What you *won't* see, because they're too small, are the other islands of the archipelago. Some are mere rocks.'

Videric finally turned his head to look at Rosamunda.

'Midway between Sark and Guernsey, with twelve leagues of sea between them and the mainland, lies Herm. Herm is a mile and a half long, half a mile wide. It has a fort on it, and a small fishing village, and enough grass to graze milch-cows . . . And a stone's throw away from Herm, across a channel of sea, is the island of Jethou. Jethou is perhaps a third of a mile long; a little less across. It has grass, a few trees. It's no more than a rock. But on Jethou – there is a convent-house. It is a silent order.'

18

I couldn't have interpreted the look in Videric's eyes to save my own life, never mind Rosamunda's.

He said, 'In all honesty, I think Carthage will assume you're dead long before they think to send agents to a sea-swept and forgotten nunnery on the island of Jethou.'

You'll give out publicly that's she dead, I understood.

Rosamunda's blank expression told me she hadn't thought that far. But it would be an obvious next step.

I could paint her at work in the meagre fields, picking stones out of furrows with her bare hands; her nails broken, her skin cracked. Can paint the bare, plain building that will be the nunnery. A master's brush could paint well enough to make you smell sour vegetables and sour bodies; rancid feelings not able to break out in gossip. Silence, isolation, labour. If Videric does ride out to Jethou in five years' time, they will have pushed her well across the line from beauty to middle age.

If Videric's lucky, he'll find he was in love with a clear complexion and lustrous black hair.

And if Rosamunda's lucky, she'll find that, too; and he can declare her dead and marry again, while she returns to the material world under a different name, at least free of the nunnery.

I tried very hard not to enjoy the thought of her future: to hope that Videric does continue to love her, and so she'll stay there for as many years as it's possible to see ahead. Part of me still scrabbled frantically for some way to save her.

'I don't know how long it will last.' Videric's voice was a whisper. 'I think, for as long as Carthage is under King-Caliph Ammianus's rule—'

Rosamunda shouted, 'No!'

'Or until their conflicts with the Turks break into open war; that could be as soon as five years from now—'

For the first time, I saw them look at each other. Stare, as if each could read secrets in the other's so-familiar face.

A little desperately, Videric protested, 'I'll try to visit. To see you, when it's safe. When I can be sure I won't be followed—'

'*No!*' It was no more than a wheeze of breath.

Videric shrugged hopelessly. 'Five years from now is not so long. But even then, your face can't be seen at court again, it would be too dangerous—'

Rosamunda's body shook; I held her up.

Videric took a step forward, eyes all but glowing with his intensity.

'—but you'll be *safe*. Who'd look for the Queen of the Court of Ladies among poor sisters digging their own turnips, and milking goats? Who could recognise you in homespun black, when every other woman is in the same robes? You won't look the same – you'll have a different name – if no one from this court contacts you, Carthage will never stumble across you; you're too far out of the way—'

She stood – and fell forward off the fountain's marble rim, out of my support, her tied ankles tripping her. Her bound hands reached out, seizing Videric's robes.

The striped linen's stitching broke under her weight, and he caught her by the wrists, dragging her upright. She leaned her body against his from belly to chest and brought her mouth up for a kiss.

I saw it as clearly as if I had it at my brush's end: Videric looking into her face.

And if he could have seen anything in her kiss but desperation, neither King nor Carthage could make him send her away.

He didn't slump, but he withdrew into himself, his hand gently easing her cheek away from contact with his chest. He seated her implacably back on the fountain's marble surround.

She glared and twisted around, facing me.

'You bitch, you monster, you – eunuch! This is all your fault!'

I didn't know I would do it until it was done. My hand cracked across her face and my palm was stinging.

She lurched back where she sat, Videric catching her elbow. I forget that I hit so much harder than most women; almost as hard as the man I'm dressed as.

The mark was carmine on her cheek, turning the blue of sloe-berries already, over the bone.

I noticed coldly that I was shaking, as if I stood out in a damp winter gale.

'Tell me again you should have suffocated me at birth!'

'I should have! I tried!'

She flung out the last words like a child throwing any lie out, in the hopes that it will hurt.

'*You're* the child!' The irony would have made me laugh, under other circumstances.

I see it a lot in the Court of Ladies – women never allowed to deal with money, or property, or the decisions of who they'll marry and be with child by. Without experience, and with only rivalries, friendships, cliques, and lovers to occupy themselves, it's no wonder many of them are still twelve years old at the age of forty-five.

And if I were a man, I wouldn't know what goes on in the Ladies' Court, and if I were a woman, I wouldn't have any different experiences to make the comparisons.

This is what I knew, when I carried Onorata and it tried to make me something I'm not – that I may not be a man, but I have no idea how to be a woman.

She lifted her hands and Videric casually took hold of her bound wrist. It was evident she couldn't free herself, from the silk ropes or her husband.

'You were my punishment, Ilario.' The last word was a painful grunt. She momentarily caught her bottom lip between her teeth. 'I've suffered enough, haven't I? You can't take any *more* away from me!'

Paint would put two catch-lights in her eye, at the edge of the pupil and in the body of the white, to show how lustrous and large her eyes are. Paint could make every fold of her silk dress into rich soft fabric, so fine a rough edge of skin could snag it . . .

And if I painted, I thought, I could paint her life on Jethou, too. No longer Queen of the Court of Ladies. Men say all faces look alike in a Bride's wimple and hood. And even though that's not true – Rosamunda will always have the stunning bones that support her flesh and delicate skin – working outdoors on an island, summer and winter, will bring freckles, broken capillaries, the dryness and paper skin that comes with cold.

Rosamunda stared at me as if she had no consciousness that twelve months ago she tried to stab me in the stomach. Which is a slow and painful death, but she knew too little to know that. She struck at the body because, like most not trained as knights, she couldn't bear to strike at the face.

I saw recognition in her, as if the thought passed from my mind directly to hers.

'I couldn't do it,' she said, all the attention of those dark eyes fixed on me. 'You know that. I told you to run. Ilario . . . Videric's not your father; don't side with him. I'm your mother.'

Turning away, I scooped up a double handful of cool water and doused my face. The dazzles left my vision.

'How will you leave Gades?'

I had a sudden absurd vision of Aldra Videric sneaking out through the kitchen in his finest gown, and every servant staring at him.

'As we came.' Videric's eyes looked weary. 'This is a seaport, Ilario, as you told me. My wife will go aboard a ship for Jethou this evening. And tomorrow, I and my men, and one of the waiting-women in Rosamunda's clothing, will ride out of Gades on the Via Augusta for Taraco. As far as any man here is concerned, Aldro Rosamunda visited Gades and returned with me.'

Who would I tell, to prevent this?

Do I desire to prevent this?

Before I could say anything, I heard raised voices outside; Videric stepped to the archway – and stepped back again, as Rekhmire' strode through.

19

Rekhmire', striding in, took it all in an instant; I could see him do it. Lord Videric, armed men, the Lady Rosamunda with her wrists and ankles tied. And I, who was not apparently restrained in any way, nor had any weapons pointed at me.

A sweep of his glance at Videric and I saw he had it. Carthage. Other enemies of the kingdom. And the danger that Rosamunda will be. He looked as if he wanted to smack himself in the forehead.

'Tell me,' I said steadily. 'I will have missed something. Videric will have fooled me somehow, or told me half-truths that don't look like lies. Tell me this doesn't have to happen this way.'

Strain carved lines from Rekhmire''s nose to the corners of his mouth. With his bald head illuminated by the sun from the lattice roof, he looked even more like one of the statues shining in the Alexandrine palaces at Constantinople, for all he had a linen gown swathing him to the ankles to keep off what he referred to as 'this northern cold'.

'I should have seen this!' he murmured, looking from me to Videric.

He stood a head taller than my stepfather, was broader across the chest, and it wasn't until I saw them standing together that I realised Videric was bordering on late middle age.

But he was a decade older than Rosamunda when he married her for her dowry and for love . . .

'I didn't imagine you would involve *Ilario* in this.' Rekhmire' sounded almost uninterested, his expression bland. 'Is this wise?'

For a moment even I thought, *He knew this was going to happen!* And then read him well enough to see how he picked up cues from the people present, and how we were placed.

Videric wiped his hand over his forehead, taking away the beads of sweat that glistened in the sun. 'I didn't "involve" Ilario. Ilario, as you probably know very well by now, has a gift for finding out where he shouldn't be – and then she goes there!'

The last thing I wanted was a sympathetic look between these two men, even if it had been in Rekhmire''s mind to do it.

'He's – exiling her,' I cut in, choosing the best word I could find in that instant.

Rekhmire' looked down at Rosamunda, and gave her a polite nod.

She appeared to have no ability to conceal her emotion in the slightest.

She scowled, recovered the poise that the Queen of the Court of Ladies should have, and looked at him with slit-eyed hatred. 'I should have had my husband's men see to *you* in Carthage.'

I interrupted. 'Did Ramaz's arm heal up?'

Videric's twisted smile was as much an appreciation of that, in his own way, as the straight look of dislike that Rosamunda gave me. Videric waved a hand at the captain of his men-at-arms.

'Well enough,' the captain said grudgingly. He retained a strong western accent; it confirmed my thought that Videric hadn't brought the man to court before now. These will be all recently promoted men, still with everything to show about their devotion to their liege-lord.

I wasn't surprised, therefore, when the commander did no more than answer Videric's implied question; although the man looked at me with a wary respect, combined with that fear of the unnatural, that I tend to get in skirts when men learn I've done man's work. And an Alexandrine tunic is close enough to a women's robe – as Rekhmire' had been kindly informed by the fisher-children running about in the lower town . . .

'This is no business of Alexandria's,' Videric said. His glance made insinuations between Rekhmire' and myself. 'Nor any business of yours, Master Rekhmire'. I shall have to ask you to leave, now.'

A clatter of footsteps sounded outside the stone archways; I glimpsed mail and the flash of light from sword-pommels, and Videric's men-at-arms stepped back inside the hall, looking to their captain.

Perhaps twenty other men in mail and breastplates crowded in after them. I recognised Orazi first – Rekhmire' signalled an acknowledgement to him – and then another man pushed his way through.

Honorius.

Like his men, he didn't have his sword drawn. The fountain-jets reflected in the mirror of his breastplate. Nothing marked him out from his men, off-duty as they were, bar the lion's head badge on his left sleeve. He scratched slowly through his cropped salt-and-pepper hair.

'You're her husband,' he said, voice harsh in the echoing hall.

Videric's soldiers were red-faced at being so outnumbered and so easily, but I saw one elbow the other, and I guessed the story of their lord and their lord's wife had gone the rounds after last year in Carthage. Although in what detail, and how accurately, I couldn't guess.

You couldn't tell from Orazi's face, or the others, that anything out of the ordinary was taking place. I thought, *They all know*. But they won't embarrass the Lion of Castile.

Rekhmire' stood as impassive as any carved sandstone, and I thought him thinking furiously.

The lean, soldierly man my father squinted at Rosamunda as if he squinted into a desert wind, abrasive with particles of sand. She didn't take her eyes off him.

I recognised the split-second hesitation, and that look Honorius wore.

This is something I would have two or three times a week, when I was Rodrigo Sanguerra's Freak. The look that at first goes straight through you, not recognising you at all. And a moment later seems to ask, *Why does that person seem to know me?*, and *No, surely, it can't be*; before they greet me with a rush of relief at the recognition – '*Ilario! I didn't know you, dressed as a—*' man or woman, whichever the case might be.

Honorius's hesitation lasted barely longer than it took to draw breath. With a rush of relief, he exclaimed, 'Rosamunda!'

She went as red as if she'd been slapped.

Queen of the Court of Ladies, yes. Beautiful, poised, glorious: yes. But forty-five isn't twenty.

Is *so* different from twenty, it seems, that an old lover might not recognise that Rosamunda in this woman standing before him.

And two of us knew her well enough to know it had cut her like knives.

Slowly, Honorius said, 'I wouldn't have known you.'

Rosamunda made a little noise, and attempted to hide her bound hands in the silk folds of her skirt. Her fingers were shaking.

'I'm no different,' she whispered.

Honorius made a face, half-smile and half-grimace. 'That might be true.'

She turned her head and looked at Videric.

Not as a wife looks at the husband she's wronged; not as a sophisticated woman of the court looks at her husband in the socially embarrassing presence of an ex-lover. But plainly and simply for reassurance.

Videric stepped up to her and put his hand on her shoulder. Too quietly to be heard but by her and me, he said, 'You look the same as the day you turned twenty. Don't expect anything but malice from this man.'

She half-turned her head, in a gesture that was triply graceful because unstudied, and rested her forehead against the lower part of Videric's chest.

He looked down at her in the same way that a man looks at a wild animal that, for whatever reason, and for however long, trusts him far enough to touch her.

'I ought to horsewhip you,' Honorius ignored my stepfather and growled, taking a step forward. His only attention was for Rosamunda. 'You tried to kill that baby—'

I stepped forward, interposing myself between them, just as Rosamunda cried out in outrage behind me:

'*You* left me with the child!'

'I would have taken you. I would have taken Ilario.' His pain was bewildering to him, you could see it. After so long, he didn't expect to hurt like this.

And if this wasn't the first time in twenty-five years, perhaps he wouldn't.

Honorius shook his head. 'I remember your eyes as brown. They're . . . not.'

'It doesn't matter how many brown-eyed wenches you tumbled,' she snapped. '*You'd* never be the one with a big belly!'

My father looked frankly bewildered, and a little cross. 'Women have been having babies since the world was made. You can manage as well as the others, can't you?'

I raised my voice.

'Father, you didn't call me a whore for having got Onorata. I suppose I'm the only one here who *can* lay down as a man, and then get up with a child in my belly.'

That stopped the shouting.

What am I doing defending Rosamunda?

I saw how it defused something of the tension between them. There were still lines of force in the hall of the fountains, where desperate looks pinned people together: Honorius staring at Rosamunda, Rosamunda pressing her bound hands against Videric's thigh, Rekhmire' crossing the tiled floor and putting his hand on my shoulder.

His flesh was warm, heavy; and at once greeting and warning.

'I never thought I'd see my mother and father together in the same room,' I said.

Rosamunda stirred, a swathe of black hair coiled across her forehead and cheek where it fell down from her crown of braids. Her eyes flicked quickly from side to side. 'Saints and Sacred Beasts! I was *right*. You have only to stand in the same room together, you two. My lord—'

The sudden appeal, turning her head and looking up at Videric, brought home to me as nothing else could that these two have worked together to plot their rise at court.

That for all the people see Videric as necessary to Rodrigo Sanguerra, Rosamunda has performed Christ knows how much of the unattributed work and support. *And now we're sending her away.*

Rekhmire' was my best choice. I touched his arm, drawing his attention. His skin was hot and a little sweaty. I said, 'Find me a way that she doesn't have to go into exile.'

All three of them looked at me: Honorius, Videric, and my mother. Honorius with the long-suffering bad temper that he evidently only just controlled, not leaping in to say, *She birthed you, but that's all; you owe her nothing!* Rosamunda with the same puzzled bad temper with which she'd regarded me in Hanno Anagastes' court.

Only Videric worried me. What he hid under that bland exterior was enough experience to guess more than *I* could about my impulse not to let my sometime-mother be imprisoned on Jethou.

'Why am I to find an answer?' Rekhmire' sounded disgruntled, as well as still out of breath. 'If you're saying what I think, it seems a perfectly reasonable solution. It's not as if an innocent woman is being condemned to captivity.'

Rosamunda interrupted without appearing to notice that the Egyptian spoke. Her eyes were fixed on Honorius. 'You married, didn't you?'

I caught Videric's stifled surprise. I wondered if he was thinking what I was: *I didn't know she'd kept track of Licinus Honorius* . . .

'Who told you that?' Honorius sounded more interested than annoyed.

'After you came back and started to renovate the estate. There was a lot of gossip in the women's court. One of my friends has a cousin who was married to – well, it doesn't matter. But with the property, and their suspicion that you must have brought money back from Castile with you, there were enough of them with available daughters that they needed to know.'

She blinked, as if what took place in the women's court had happened centuries ago, although it couldn't have been more than twelve months.

'Licinus, what did she die of?'

It sounded odd to me to hear him called that. Shifting uncomfortably on the hard floor, I thought, *Why did he never invite me to call him by his personal name?* Or did he think I was more comfortable with 'Honorius'?

Honorius spoke with the reserve I associated with the man. You would not have known he and Rosamunda had been lovers – but then, I doubted they had, in more than the carnal sense.

'Her name was Ximena. You've obviously heard,' he added. 'She died bearing our second child. Our first had died before it could be baptised. This one . . . '

'Took her with it,' Rosamunda completed. She lifted her tied wrists, smoothing her hair out of her pale face with the backs of her hands. 'That would have been me. If I'd left with you. They say you had another wife before this Ximena. Did you kill her too?'

As dryly as a desert wind, Licinus Honorius observed, 'You *are* well informed. I used to know better than to underestimate the Ladies' Tower in any castle . . . No, Sandrine died of low-land sickness. She never carried a child long enough for it to distress her when it passed.'

Rosamunda's expression held a great deal of doubt on that point; I supposed mine might, also. And, to my surprise, Rekhmire' looked as if he would have spoken, under other circumstances.

'Ilario is my only living son or daughter.' Honorius raised a brow, still with his gaze on Rosamunda. 'In fact, both son *and* daughter—'

'And like all men, you wanted an heir. A true son.' Rosamunda looked dissatisfied.

'Not all men,' I said. 'And you of all people should know that! Since you're standing between two men who prove different to that.'

Rosamunda sighed.

For the first time, she looked at me without dislike; only with a tired melancholy that made me truly believe her a handful of years past forty.

'Perhaps,' she said. 'But it doesn't help. Two of you . . . It means nothing, not when everybody else is different. Ilario, *don't let them do this to me.*'

I caught Rekhmire''s glance. With an acknowledging look to my father and my stepfather, I touched Rekhmire''s arm, and drew him closer to the fountain, where the noise of the falling water would obscure what we said if we spoke quietly.

'It's what every man wants,' he said. 'Your enemy, dependent on *your* actions. Ilario . . . don't let it prove too intoxicating. And remember how very much people dislike being done a good turn.'

'I remember helping you with your knee,' I said acidly. 'You *still* owe me for my patience, book-buyer.'

Rekhmire' grinned at me.

I stopped smiling. 'Be honest with me. What is it I'm not seeing? And – is there any alternative, for her? It must have happened before; she can't be the *only* wife any man has ever been vulnerable through.'

'My lord Videric moves in the same circles as royalty, now, since he's as necessary to Taraconensis as people think he is. We're not discussing a minor nobleman and Carthage wheedling out occasional secrets. If she can be adequately threatened, the Fourteenth Augusta and Third Leptis Parva sail for Gades, and come marching up the Via Augusta to Taraco. The King-Caliph's talking of a *reconquista*, now; of taking Iberia back into the Carthaginian Empire . . . Taraconensis wouldn't be their ideal foothold, but it *would* give Carthage a land-border with the Franks. Somewhere to mass their legions, before they send them against Europe. King-Caliph Ammianus and Hanno Anagastes will take advantage of anything to get them through that gate. They won't kill Aldro Rosamunda – she's too valuable as blackmail – but they will take her and hurt her, if they can find her. And then set her free to come back to Aldra Videric, with the knowledge that they'll maim her worse the next time. It's easier to think of someone dying than it is to think of caring for them when they come home with their eyes gouged out, or half their skin flayed away . . . '

The shimmering cold water of the fountain was all that held me from vomiting. Cold, clear, clean. The sick sweat left my forehead after a while. I rested the palms of my hands against the cold marble.

'And we can't guard her?'

'You should know the answer to that, Ilario.'

Any guard that's strong enough to keep her safe is strong enough to make a prisoner out of her. And even if she were in Rodrigo Sanguerra's deepest dungeon, a servant or a slave would know where she was, and could be bribed into telling. Often for what would seem like a ridiculously small sum, if you're not the slave or servant.

Faith is a better barrier. Faith will keep Sister Maria Regina shut off from the mundane world, in communities where bribery means nothing. Because anyone who will live willingly on Jethou doesn't want anything the world can offer.

I stepped away from the arch.

Videric bent, cut her bands, and half-lifted his wife to her feet, urging her forward.

Rosamunda looked over her shoulder at me, on her way to the door.

'You don't understand.' She spoke quietly, frowning; I felt for the first time that she was straining to make me understand, rather than justify herself. She said, 'If no one buys you – if you're a slave and you're manumitted – then you're free.'

I was confused. 'Well, yes.'

She smiled. It was sad. 'Odd, that you should have given birth to a child, and still think like a man. Ilario, you're not legally a woman. Your father can't marry you to a man against your will and desires.' She glanced at Honorius. 'For a good match, *or* because he thinks it would be better for you. And if you take a man as a lover, he can't legally put you aside for not having babies as and when he wants them. I know you have none of the legal protections of being a man. You were made a slave as soon as that Valdamerca woman took you off the chapel steps. But if you'd been *all* girl, you would have been a slave as soon as you left my womb. Do you understand that?'

'Not truly.' I couldn't do anything else but be honest. 'Legally, I suppose I'm not a woman.'

'No,' Videric said. 'According to the Kingdom's best lawyers, you are, in fact, a eunuch.'

'*What*—' I began.

'I know.' Videric cut me off. 'It's the nearest definition they *do* have. Ilario . . . I know you don't wish to hear advice from me. I can't say I blame you. But the last thing you want is any legal taint of womanhood about you – trust me, Ilario.'

The look I gave him must have pierced even his hide. He appeared to wince. Or perhaps it was indigestion.

'It would alter your relationship with your father.' His nod at Honorius was civil, if not warm. His gaze travelled to Rekhmire'. 'And your husband, should you marry a man. That knowledge that you have absolute legal power over your wife . . . it follows you everywhere, do you understand me? Everywhere. If she can't say no, her yes is worth very little.'

Caught between sympathy and distaste – for both of them – I countered Videric with a stare very like his own. 'I understand you. All I need do is imagine being a slave whom no man can free.'

'Precisely.' He nodded agreement, as if unaware of any ironies.

Rekhmire' demanded coldly, 'Why were you making such inquiries?'

Videric inclined his head to me.

'You're not female.' He smiled. 'I had the lawyers look into it . . . If I could have you declared female, you would – as my publicly acknowledged child – belong to me.'

Before I could get a word out, Honorius cut in, in a tone like a stonemason sawing marble. 'Ilario is of *my* begetting, and would belong to me.'

Rekhmire', as urbanely as ever, put one monumental hand up. 'My claim pre-dates the court of Taraco – I bought and owned Ilario; Ilario would therefore be mine.'

The only true woman in the room, Rosamunda, looked up and caught my eye. 'I gave birth to you, but there's no way you'd belong to *me*!'

'Christus and St Gaius and Kek and Keket . . . !' I shook my head, even if it did make me feel cold inside. I eyed Videric warily. 'When you say I would belong to you—'

'Your money or property would be mine, if Master Honorius or any other client—' He stressed the word. '—paid for a painting. It would go into my treasury; you couldn't touch it. You would need my permission to travel, if you wished to study under another master. I could order you in what you wear, where you go, what you eat or drink, who you may speak to.' He shrugged. 'And beat you if you disobeyed, despite your being past the age of majority. It's arguable that, as a woman, the male age of majority wouldn't apply to you.'

The silence was one in which I could hear my heartbeat in my ears, deafening me.

Videric gave another shrug. 'But they seem to feel that a *membrum virile*, however small, qualifies you as a male. There's also the rumour that you fathered a child – that bastard that Carrasco acts as nursemaid to. I believe that carried weight with the justices.'

Fathered a child.

I didn't blink.

My mother looked at me. At Rekhmire'. Back at me.

She smiled sadly.

'There are men who don't want the law to apply. But that really doesn't matter, does it? It's the ones who *do* want it that matter, and then it's there for them, in all their dusty old scrolls, and there's no fighting it. Of the girls I went to school with, all but five are dead now. And ten of them died in childbed. The men are on their third wives.'

She studied me with finality.

'I suppose that it doesn't matter if you have the breasts to give suck, and the womb to carry a child – you have a penis. And no matter how small it may be, it may not make you a man, but it makes you *not* a woman.'

'Sadly, that avenue is closed to us.' Videric took Rosamunda's arm. 'And it remains to see what we may do, now.'

20

Rosamunda looked down intently at his hand, not moving forward as directed.

She spread the fingers of both her tethered hands, directing a searching glance at the skin there. Some thought tugged at the corner of her mouth. I could not tell what she felt.

'When I was a girl . . .' She made fists of her hands, regarding them as if their acts entirely surprised her. '. . . I used to keep a knife and cut my skin.'

She turned her head without raising it, and the light caught the surface of her eyes, obliterating iris and pupil, glimmering white in the sun. She was looking at me.

'I always wanted to cut my face,' Rosamunda said plainly. 'Ever since a man put my hand on his belly when I was twelve, and showed me how it made his male organ stand up. But I saw that plain and ugly women had worse marriages, and worse lives. I thought I'd grow up to marry a rich man, and then take lovers as it pleased me.'

She made a kind of snort, as if of amusement, but there was something wrong in the note of it. 'Then I *did* take a lover, and I found out what happened when a man's potent. The birth nearly killed me. The pain . . . And I came so close to child-bed fever. I could have died at the age of twenty. There is a reason I never left with your father, Ilario, although it's not the one he thinks. I realised that if I left and married Honorius, I could expect to conceive every year – perhaps only every two or three years, if I put the child to my own breast. The women's court *talk* about ways to stop conceiving a child, but most of them become big-bellied all the same. And then it's as dangerous to be rid of it as it is to carry and bear it. The brothers and sisters you never had, Ilario; they would have killed me . . .'

Her head came up: she addressed Videric without any pretence or seduction.

'If I'd already been married to you for five years, and it had taken another man to get me pregnant, I thought I'd be safe with you – so I stayed. If Ilario had been an heir, that would have been perfect. You couldn't have asked anything more of me. While there were no children . . . I wanted you to love me. There was nothing else to keep you from putting me aside. Then my father would have married me off to some other, much poorer, man; because *he* at least knows the bull is sometimes as much at fault as the cow. A garden can't grow if the seed is rotten.'

Videric's face was patched carmine and a colour like spoiled milk.

Rosamunda said quietly, 'I never did take another lover, after Honorius, despite what the Court of Ladies may say. It isn't difficult to flirt and seduce and then be uncomprehending at just the right time . . . And I had you, for the marriage bed, and I wasn't afraid of starting a child, and so I . . . began to enjoy it. I *liked* my life. It was perfect. When I saw what my child had grown up to be, I knew I could never have raised Ilario. I did the right thing, staying with you, my lord. If you asked me to do anything, I would have done it – but it's so difficult, knowing he, she, he was my own flesh . . . I *tried*.'

I thought of her voice, muffled among the green leaves whose water supply could keep hundreds of poor men in Taraco from thirst. '*Run!*' And she had let me run.

'I tried,' Rosamunda repeated. Her bound restless hands crept down, pressing against her belly. 'This last year or two, I've bribed the servants to lie when they did the washing and say I still had my regular courses. My mother, she was free of the moon's curse early; she wasn't forty. And my grandmother too. But if you knew there was never a chance of a child, now – I didn't know how you'd act. If you'd change towards me.'

She didn't look at me. Only at Videric.

'It would have been easier to obey you and kill Ilario if I hadn't known I could never give birth again.' She sighed. 'It feels as if I've spent all of my life avoiding pregnancy! But . . . I *did* have a child. Even grown to a man . . . a woman . . . Ilario's still mine. Even if I never fed her, him, at my breast, he's still my son, my daughter. But I . . . did try.'

Videric took in a deep breath through his nostrils. He looked at her, merely looked at her, entirely in silence, until I felt the stone walls might burst apart from the force of that silence.

He spoke, finally.

Gently, he said, 'I wish you'd told me. We might have worked out some other way it could be done. I assumed yours was the only hand I could trust to it, but – it might have been arranged differently.'

'How could I tell you? What man wants to be told he's loved because he's barren?'

Videric nodded thoughtfully. 'Still, we might have done it some other way.'

The stillness broken, I cut in on his words, a cold shiver prickling the hairs at the nape of my neck. 'I don't know what bothers me more – that you can discuss it this calmly, or that you can discuss my *murder* in front of *me*.'

Aldra Videric's smile turned very ironic indeed. 'We're family, Ilario. We need have no secrets from each other.'

Rosamunda ignored his macabre humour. Her gaze on me was

brilliant, and I wished I had my drawing-paper. It would take me a year to uncover the emotions in how she looked at me.

Her mouth twisted. 'At least you can *pass* as a man, Ilario. That's your escape. There's no life for a woman here; it's worse than being a slave.'

As cruelly as I could, I said, 'You would blame it all on something else, Aldro Rosamunda, wouldn't you? It's because you were born a woman; it's because women have no rights in law . . . If you felt that badly about it, what was to stop you running away to Alexandria, say? You might have been raped a couple of times on the way, but Alexandrine women can enter their government and needn't marry.'

I smiled at her, making sure she saw teeth.

'But, thinking about it – this should please you, then: what's to happen. Everybody's equal under the Mother Superior, in a convent-house. And you'll hardly be in danger of conceiving a child on Jethou. It's a shame you didn't think of running away to the Church when you were twelve . . . '

Her complexion blanched. Instinct hadn't led me wrong, I thought; nine years in the court as Rodrigo's Freak gives you an edge for protecting yourself by attacking people in their keenest fears.

I saw that she had wanted to run, but hadn't found the courage.

Or the court sparkled too brightly, and it drew her too strongly. But somewhere in her heart, she still reproaches that girl who has first had her courses, and then marked her arms with blood.

I said, 'You think if I hadn't been born, things would have been different? You think if I hadn't been born a hermaphrodite, none of this would have happened? I think you were set on this course long before *I* was born.'

My voice went up and down the scale, out of control from anger and pain.

'I'll tell you what would have made it *different*.' I stepped right up close, staring down at Rosamunda, and over her shoulder at Videric. 'I'll tell you. If, when I was born – no matter who fathered me – both of you had *acknowledged* me. Yes, I would have grown up a man-woman, but gossip only lasts so long. If you'd acknowledged me as your child, no one could have blackmailed you later. That fear wouldn't have made you think you should kill me. What could anybody have done to you if there hadn't *been* a secret?'

I couldn't speak for a moment.

'I wouldn't have been a slave, or a King's Fool,' I said quietly, 'but those are things that only caused hurt to me. When you think about where you are, *why* things are as they are – think what would have happened if you'd kept me in the family and raised me openly as what I am.'

I walked past Rosamunda and Videric, past Honorius and Rekhmire', my knees shaking. At the arch, I stopped and looked back.

My father and Rekhmire' looked at each other, and walked to join me.

I turned to go, and could not.

I looked back at Rosamunda.

This tie will not be undone or cut, not without death, and perhaps not even then. The past informs the present. And all I can do is speak as honestly as I have learned to be.

I said, 'The truth of it is – if I could find any way at all to get you free of this, I would do it. Still. But if I did find a way . . . I wouldn't hope for anything else. Not now. That's gone.'

I stepped back from the archway.

Videric grasped her bound wrists and led Rosamunda past me, and away into the palace.

The fountain rang clearly and bright on the stone, and my mother stumbled, but she never looked back.

Epilogue: Twenty-Four Years After

Rekhmire' spent time in Alexandria afterwards, but never lived there again, and he did not live to see the final fall of that great city in the year 1453, dying a few months before it.

Frankish Europe mourned Alexandrine Constantinople as the last of the Egyptians gone; Carthage was jealous; Mehmet II gloated; I mourned for the men and women I knew there, and for the aged Ty-ameny going out to fire cannon on the walls of Alexandria itself, before the Turkish bombards reduced all to flying splinters of rock. Fragile flesh vaporised, no trace ever found.

Frankish Europe mourned until the tide of manuscripts and books flooded to its shore; then it gobbled up science, medicine, and art in equal greed. Carthage fumed, no trace being found of how Alexandria's mathematicians had disabled their golem. But, since the Turks appeared to build none themselves, Carthage concluded that at least Alexandria had not learned to build what it could break.

Neferet, visiting me after Rekhmire''s funeral, announced herself an importer of books – products of the Royal Library's *machina*, which she sold the length of Italy and France.

When she asked how I would live without Rekhmire', I inquired as to how long it was since she had seen that cardinal's secretary and man of letters, Leon Battista, and we parted with a quarrel that more than twenty years had made familiar.

In the same year, Ramiro Carrasco and I travelled back to Iberia, reaching Taraco a few weeks before Licinus Honorius died falling from an untrained stallion, at the age of seventy-five. He lived long enough to require me to escort Onorata to Italy, and to look at me with boundless love.

Onorata apprenticed herself to a painter in the Empty Chair, and introduced me to men as her brother. I dressed as a male, as I had done with Rekhmire', for one kind of freedom – though dressing as a female gave me the right to kiss Rekhmire' publicly.

Six months after a rumour followed us from Taraco, it became known that I was a hermaphrodite, and Onorata took the Italian name of Rodiani, and asked me not to contact her for a time. I had no need to worry: her friendship with Honorius's soldiers had lasted all through her own childhood – which was at least hermaphrodite in its education and training – so I might always ask Orazi for news of her.

Ramiro Carrasco sought her out before we left the Empty Chair, and never told me what he said, but Onorata came out to say farewell in the public street, and gave me the kiss of kinship within the sight of all men.

North, south, hill, valley: I could wander where I liked, and draw what I might, but the absence of Rekhmire' was an unbearable pain to me.

Carrasco, having studied me for six weeks, chose to remark that eunuchs lived no great long lifetimes, like as not – certainly not while they were employed as book-buyers – and it was possible hermaphrodites need not live too long either, based on that principle.

It should not have eased pain, to hear Carrasco suggest it; it did, however. He knew me, also, after so many years.

'We might go to Carthage again,' he said, one day, out of a sky containing no warning cloud.

I declined. Instead we went north, to Jethou.

I found Rosamunda a keenly sharp abbess, hair white with age, but all six establishments of the Order of St Gaius under her skilled control. She did not manage men – or women, in this case – with the ease of one born to it, but what she had learned with pains and study, she had learned well.

I met her in a cold room, the casement window open to the grey sea, and her black Bride's clothing covered in addition with a fur-lined cloak, where she stood gazing at the implacable, endless sea.

'How did you manage,' I asked, 'when Videric was assassinated, and I answered none of your letters?'

If I hope to see pain made less raw by time, I did not see it on her austere face.

'Find yourself an occupation,' she said harshly.

I found the truth of it as I spoke. 'There is nothing left to do.'

'Then do what you will.' Rosamunda shrugged, under the heavy wool and wolf's fur. 'And remember.'

When I reached Carthage, to speak to Marcomir (Donata long since buried in the Fields of Baal and Tanitta), I found Onorata had been there before me, and I was not welcome.

I ended as I had begun, in Burgundy, in Bruges, in the house in which Rekhmire' had cursed the cold of all northern lands, suffered a week of coughing and wheezing, turned surprised eyes on me as he woke one morning, and died.

'Go back to your family,' I instructed Carrasco.

'Give me my collar again,' he grumbled, 'if you don't believe I'm already *with* my family, here.'

We slept back to back, for comfort in the northern cold, since I did not believe Rekhmire' would begrudge it.

When spring came, I walked the length of Burgundy to Dijon, in the south, and we lived within sight of the Good Philip's castle, and worked on painting panels by open windows, to the thundering of Dijon's water-mills.

And in the Duke's library, while my sight remained keen enough, I ornamented frontispieces for those books of his that were translations of the flood of knowledge to come to Europa after Alexandria fell, while the effect of those printed volumes began to change the world.